KU-317-192

Robert Crais

THREE GREAT NOVELS
The Bestsellers

Robert Crais is the bestselling author of the Elvis Cole novels. He has also written for such acclaimed television shows as *L.A. Law* and *Hill Street Blues*. He lives with his family in L.A. Visit his website at *www.robertcrais.com.*

Also by Robert Crais

The Monkey's Raincoat
Stalking the Angel
Lullaby Town
Free Fall
Voodoo River
Sunset Express
Indigo Slam
The Last Detective
The Forgotten Man

Robert Crais

Three Great Novels: The Bestsellers

L.A. Requiem
Demolition Angel
Hostage

ORION

L.A. Requiem Copyright © 1999 Robert Crais
Demolition Angel Copyright © 2000 Robert Crais
Hostage Copyright © 2001 Robert Crais

All rights reserved

The right of Robert Crais to be identified as the author
of this work has been asserted by him in accordance
with the Copyright, Designs and Patents Act 1988.

First published in Great Britain in 2005 by
Orion
An imprint of Orion Books Ltd
Orion House, 5 Upper St Martin's Lane,
London WC2H 9EA

A CIP catalogue record for this book is
available from the British Library

Typeset by Deltatype Ltd,
Birkenhead, Merseyside

Printed and bound in Great Britain by
Clays Ltd, St Ives plc

Contents

L.A. Requiem

An Elvis Cole Novel

Acknowledgements

Many people contributed to the writing of this novel, and to its moment of publication. They include: Detective-Three John Petievich, LAPD (Fugitive Section); Detective-Three Paul Bishop, LAPD (West Los Angeles Sex Crimes); Bruce Kelton JD, CFE (Director, Forensic Investigative Services, Deloitte & Touche); Patricia Crais; Lauren Crais; Carol Topping (for nights out with the girls); Wayne Topping (for putting up with it); William Gleason, Ph.D.; Andrea Malcolm; Jeffrey Gleason; April Smith; Robert Miller; Brian DeFiore; Lisa Kitei; Samantha Miller; Kim Dower; Gerald Petievich; Judy Chavez (for the language lessons); Dr Halina Alter (for keeping me in the game); Steve Volpe; and Norman Kurland.

Special contributions were made by the following, without whom this book would not exist in its present form: Aaron Priest, Steve Rubin, Linda Grey, Shawn Coyne, and George Lucas. Thank you.

Help, encouragement, and inspiration were given by many who requested anonymity. These secret creatures include TC, MG, TD, LC, and Cookie. Good to go on night patrol whenever, wherever.

This book is not solely mine; it also belongs to Leslie Wells.

For Ed Waters and Sid Ellis,
who taught more than words.

'And dat's da' name o' dat tune.'

Do you know what love is?
(I would bleed out for you.)

– Tattooed Beach Sluts

I've got the whole town under my thumb
and all I've gotta do is keep acting dumb.

We say goodbye so very politely
Now say hello to the killer inside me.

– MC 900 Ft Jesus

Mama, Mama, can't you see
What the Marine Corps has done to me?
Made me lean and made me strong
Made me where I can do no wrong.

– USMC marching cadence

The Islander Palms Motel

Uniformed LAPD Officer Joe Pike could hear the banda music even with the engine idling, the a.c. jacked to meat locker, and the two-way crackling callout codes to other units.

The covey of Latina street kids clumped outside the arcade giggled at him, whispering things to each other that made them flush. Squat brown men come up through the fence from Zacatecas milled on the sidewalk, shielding their eyes from the sun as veteranos told them about Sawtelle over on the Westside where they could find day labor jobs, thirty dollars cash, no papers required. Here in Rampart Division south of Sunset, Guatemalans and Nicaraguans simmered with Salvadorans and Mexican nationals in a sidewalk machaca that left the air flavored with epizoté, even here within the sour cage of the radio car.

Pike watched the street kids part like water when his partner hurried out of the arcade. Abel Wozniak was a thick man with a square head and cloudy, slate eyes. Wozniak was twenty years older than Pike and had been on the street twenty years longer. Once the best cop that Pike had then met, Wozniak's eyes were now strained. They'd been riding together for two years, and the eyes hadn't always been that way. Pike regretted that, but there wasn't anything he could do about it.

Especially now when they were looking for Ramona Ann Escobar.

Wozniak lurched in behind the wheel, adjusting his gun for the seat, anxious to roll even with the tension between them as thick as clotted blood. His informant had come through.

'DeVille's staying at the Islander Palms Motel.'

'Does DeVille have the girl?'

'My guy eyeballed a little girl, but he can't say if she's still with him.'

Wozniak snapped the car into gear and rocked away from the curb. They didn't roll Code Three. No lights, no siren. The Islander Palms was less than five blocks away, here on Alvarado Boulevard just south of Sunset. Why send an announcement?

1

'Woz? Would DeVille hurt her?'

'I told you, a fuckin' perv like this would be better off with a bullet in his head.'

It was eleven-forty on a Tuesday morning. At nine-twenty, a five-year-old girl named Ramona Ann Escobar had been playing near the paddle-boat concession in Echo Park when her mother, a legal émigré from Guatemala, had turned away to chat with friends. Witnesses last saw Ramona in the company of a man believed to be one Leonard DeVille, a known pedophile who'd been sighted working both Echo and MacArthur parks for the past three months. When the dispatch call had come about the missing girl, Wozniak had begun working his street informants. Wozniak, having been on the street forever, knew everyone and how to find them. He was a treasure trove of information that Pike valued and respected, and didn't want to lose. But Pike couldn't do anything about that, either.

Pike stared at Wozniak until Wozniak couldn't handle the weight any longer and glanced over. They were forty seconds away from the Islander Palms. 'Oh, for Christ's sake, what?'

'It isn't too late, Woz.'

Wozniak's eyes went back to the street, and his face tightened. 'I'm telling you, Joe. Back off with this. I'm not going to talk about it anymore.'

'I meant what I said.'

Wozniak wet his lips.

'You've got Paulette and Evelyn to think about.'

Wozniak's wife and daughter.

The cloudy eyes flicked to Pike, as bottomless and as dangerous as a thunderhead.

'I've been thinking about them, Pike. You bet your ass.'

For just an instant, Pike thought Wozniak's eyes filled. Then Wozniak gave a shudder as if he were shaking out his feelings, and pointed.

'There it is. Now shut the fuck up and play like a cop.'

The Islander Palms was a white stucco dump: two stories of frayed carpets, stained beds, and neon palms that looked tacky even in Los Angeles, all of it shaped into an L around a narrow parking lot. The typical customers were whores renting by the hour, wannabe pornographers shooting 'amateur' videos, and rent jumpers needing a place to stay while they found a new landlord to stiff.

Pike followed Wozniak into the manager's office, a skinny Hindu with watery eyes. First thing he said was, 'I do not wan' trouble, please.'

Wozniak had the lead.

'We're looking for a man with a little girl. His name is Leonard DeVille, but he might've used another name.'

The Hindu didn't know the name, or about a little girl, but he told them that a man matching the description Woz provided could be found on the second floor in the third room from the top of the L.

Pike said, 'You want me to call it in?'

Wozniak went out the door and up the stairs without answering. Pike thought then that he should go back to the car and call, but you don't let your partner go up alone. Pike followed.

They found the third door, listened, but heard nothing. The drapes were pulled. Standing on the exposed balcony, Pike felt as if they were being watched.

Wozniak took the knob side of the door, Pike the hinges. Wozniak rapped on the door, identifying himself as a Los Angeles police officer. Everything about Joe made him want to be the first one inside, but they had settled that two years ago. Wozniak drove, Wozniak went in first, Wozniak called how they made the play. Twenty-two years on the job against Pike's three bought you that. They had done it this way two hundred times.

When DeVille opened the door, they pushed him backward, Wozniak going first and pushing hard.

DeVille said, 'Hey, what is this?' Like he'd never been rousted before.

The room was tattered and cheesy, with a closet and bath off the rear. A rumpled double bed rested against the wall like some kind of ugly altar, its dark red bedspread stained and threadbare, one of the stains looking like Mickey Mouse. The room's only other piece of furniture was a cheap dresser edged with cigarette burns and notches cut by a sharp knife. Wozniak held DeVille as Pike cleared the bathroom and the closet, looking for Ramona.

'She's not here.'

'Anything else? Clothes, suitcase, toothbrush?'

'Nothing.' Indicating that DeVille hadn't been living here, and didn't intend to. He had other uses for the room.

Wozniak, who had busted DeVille twice in the past, said, 'Where is she, Lennie?'

'Who? Hey, I don't do that anymore. C'mon, Officer.'

'Where's the camera?'

DeVille spread his hands, flashing a nervous smile. 'I got no camera. I'm telling you, I'm off that.'

Leonard DeVille was five-eight, with a fleshy body, dyed blond hair, and skin like a pineapple. The hair was slicked straight back, and held with a rubber band. Pike knew that DeVille was lying, but waited to see how Woz would play it. Even with only three years on the job, Pike knew that pedophiles were always pedophiles. You could bust them, treat them, counsel them, whatever, but when you released them back into the world, they were still child molesters and it was only a matter of time.

Wozniak hooked a hand under the foot of the bed and heaved the bed over. DeVille jumped back and stumbled into Pike, who caught and held him. A rumpled overnight bag was nesting in about a million dust bunnies where the bed had been.

Wozniak said, 'Lennie, you are about as dumb as they get.'

'Hey, that ain't mine. I got nothing to do with that bag.' DeVille was so scared that he sprouted sweat like a rainstorm.

Wozniak opened the bag and dumped out a Polaroid camera, better than a dozen film packs, and at least a hundred pictures of children in various stages of undress. That's how a guy like DeVille made his living, snapping pictures and selling them to other perverts.

Wozniak toed through the pictures, his face growing darker and more contained. Pike couldn't see the pictures from where he stood, but he could see the vein pulsing in Wozniak's temple. He thought that Wozniak must be thinking about his own daughter, but maybe not. Maybe Wozniak was still thinking about the other thing.

Pike squeezed DeVille's arm. 'Where's the little girl? Where's Ramona Escobar?'

DeVille's voice went higher. 'That stuff isn't mine. I never saw it before.'

Wozniak squatted, fingering through the pictures without expression. He lifted one, and held it to his nose.

'I can still smell the developing chemicals. You didn't take this more than an hour ago.'

'They're not mine!'

Wozniak stared at the picture. Pike still couldn't see it.

'She looks about five. She matches the physical description they gave us. Pretty little girl. Innocent. Now she's not innocent anymore.'

Abel Wozniak stood and drew his gun. It was the new Beretta 9-millimeter that LAPD had just mandated.

'If you hurt that child, I'll fucking kill you.'

Joe said, 'Woz, we've got to call in. Put your gun away.'

Wozniak stepped past Pike and snapped the Beretta backhand, slamming DeVille in the side of the head and dropping him like a bag of garbage.

Pike jumped between them, grabbing Wozniak by the arms and pushing him back. 'That doesn't help get the girl.'

Then Wozniak's eyes came to Pike; hard, ugly little rivets with something behind the clouds.

When the two police officers went up the stairs, Fahreed Abouti, the manager, watched until they pushed the blond man back into his room. The police often came to his motel to bust the prostitutes and johns and drug dealers, and Fahreed never passed up a chance to watch. Once, he had seen a prostitute servicing the officers who had come to arrest her, and another time he watched as three officers beat a rapist until all the man's teeth were gone. There was always something wonderful to see. It was better than Wheel of Fortune.

You had to be careful, though.

As soon as the upstairs door closed, Fahreed crept up the stairs. If you got too close, or if they caught you, the police grew angry. Once, a SWAT officer in the armor and the helmet and with the big gun had grown so angry that he'd knocked Fahreed's turban into a puddle of transmission fluid. The cleaning cost had been horrendous.

The shouting started when Fahreed was still on the stairs. He couldn't understand what was being said, only that the words were angry. He eased along the second-floor balcony, trying to get closer, but just as he reached the room, the shouting stopped. He cursed the fates, thinking he'd missed all the fun, when suddenly there was a single loud shout from inside, then a thunderous, deafening explosion.

People on the street stopped in their tracks and looked. A woman pointed, and a man across the parking lot ran.

Fahreed's heart pounded, because even a Hindu knew a gunshot. He thought the blond man might be dead. Or perhaps he had killed the officers.

Fahreed heard nothing within the room.

'Hallu?'

Nothing.

'Is everyone all right?'

Nothing.

Perhaps they had jumped from the bathroom window into the alley behind.

Fahreed's palms were damp, and all his swirling fears demanded that he race back to his office and pretend to have heard nothing, but instead he threw open the door.

The younger officer, the tall one with the dark glasses and the empty face, spun toward him and aimed an enormous revolver. Fahreed thought in that instant that he would surely die.

'Please. No!'

The older officer was without a face, his remains covered in blood. The blond man was dead, too, his face a mask of crimson. The floor and walls and ceiling were sprayed red.

'No!'

The tall officer's gun never wavered. Fahreed stared into his dark bottomless glasses, and saw that they were misted with blood.

'Please!'

The tall officer dropped to his fallen partner, and began CPR.

Without looking up, the tall officer said, 'Call 911.'

Fahreed Abouti ran for the phone.

Part One

1

That Sunday, the sun floated bright and hot over the Los Angeles basin, pushing people to the beaches and the parks and into backyard pools to escape the heat. The air buzzed with the nervous palsy it gets when the wind freight-trains in from the deserts, dry as bone, and cooking the hillsides into tar-filled kindling that can snap into flames hot enough to melt an auto body.

The Verdugo Mountains above Glendale were burning. A column of brown smoke rose off the ridgeline there where it was caught by the Santa Anas and spread south across the city, painting the sky with the color of dried blood. If you were in Burbank, say, or up along the Mulholland Snake over the Sunset Strip, you could see the big multi-engine fire bombers diving in with their cargoes of bright red fire retardant as news choppers crisscrossed the scene. Or you could just watch the whole thing on television. In L.A., next to riots and earthquakes, fires are our largest spectator sport.

We couldn't see the smoke column from Lucy Chenier's second-floor apartment in Beverly Hills, but the sky had an orange tint that made Lucy stop in her door long enough to frown. We were bringing cardboard moving boxes up from her car.

'Is that the fire?'

'The Santa Anas are bringing the smoke south. Couple of hours, the ash will begin to fall. It'll look like gray snow.' The fire was forty miles away. We were in no danger.

Lucy shifted the frown to her Lexus, parked below us at the curb. 'Will it hurt the paint?'

'By the time it settles it'll be cool, just like powder. We'll wash it off with the hose.' Elvis Cole, Professional Angeleno, educating the recent transplant, who also happens to be his girlfriend. Wait'll we get a big temblor.

Lucy didn't seem convinced, but then she stepped inside, and called her son. 'Ben!'

Less than a week before, Lucille Chenier and her nine-year-old son had left Louisiana and settled into the apartment that they had taken in Beverly Hills, just south of Wilshire Boulevard. Lucy had been a practicing attorney in Baton Rouge, but was beginning a new career as a legal analyst for a local television station (a nouveau occupational fruit growing from the ugly tree that was the Simpson trial). Trading Baton Rouge for Los Angeles, she gained a larger salary, more free time to spend with her son, and closer proximity to *moi*. I had spent all of Friday, Saturday, and most of Sunday morning arranging and re-arranging the living room. That's love for you.

The television was tuned to the station she now worked for, KROK-8 ('Real News for Real People!'), which, like every other station in town, had interrupted regular programming with live coverage of the fire. Twenty-eight homes were threatened and had been evacuated.

Lucy handed Ben the box. 'Too heavy?'

'No way.'

'Your room. Your closet. *Neatly*.'

When he was gone I slipped my hand around her waist, and whispered, 'Your room. Your bed. Messy.'

She stepped away and considered the couch. 'First we have to get this house in order. Would you please move the couch again?'

I stared at the couch. I had moved it maybe eight hundred times in the last two days.

'Which wall?'

She chewed at her thumb, thinking. 'Over there.'

'That's where it was two moves ago.' It was a big couch. It probably weighed three thousand pounds.

'Yes, but that was when the entertainment center was by the fireplace. Now that we've put the entertainment center by the entry, the look will be completely different.'

'*We?*'

'*Yes. We.*'

I bent into the couch and dragged it to the opposite wall. Four thousand pounds.

I was squaring the couch when the phone rang. Lucy spoke for a minute, then held out the phone.

'Joe.'

Joe Pike and I are partners in the detective agency that bears my name. He could have his name on it if he wanted, but he doesn't. He's like that.

I took the phone. 'Hernias R Us.' Lucy rolled her eyes and turned away, already contemplating new sofa arrangements.

Pike said, 'How's the move going?'

I walked the phone out onto the balcony. 'It's a big change. I think she's finally realizing how big. What's up?'

'You heard of Frank Garcia?'

'The tortilla guy. Regular, large, and Monsterito sizes. I prefer the Monsterito myself.' You could walk into any food store in Los Angeles and see Frank Garcia smiling at you from the packages of his tortillas, eyes bright, bushy black mustache, big smile.

Pike said, 'Frank's a friend of mine and he's got a problem. I'm on my way there now. Can you meet me?'

Pike and I have owned a detective agency for twelve years, and I have known him even longer since his days as a Los Angeles police officer. He had never once asked a favor, or asked for my help on a personal problem in all of that time.

'I'm helping Lucy set up her house. I'm wearing shorts, and I've spent the morning wrestling a ten-thousand-pound couch.'

Pike didn't answer.

'Joe?'

'Frank's daughter is missing, Elvis. She's a friend of mine, too. I hope you can make it.' He gave an address in Hancock Park, then hung up without another word. Pike is like that, too.

I stayed out on the balcony and watched Lucy. She was moving from box to box as if she could no more decide what to unpack next than where to put the couch. She had been like that since she arrived from Louisiana, and it wasn't like her. We had had a long-distance relationship for two years, but now we had made a very real move to further that relationship, and she had carried the weight of it. She's the one who had left her friends. She's the one who had left her home. She was the one taking the risk.

I turned off the phone, went back inside, and waited for her to look at me.

'Hey.'

She smiled, but seemed troubled.

I stroked her upper arms and smiled back. She has beautiful amber-green eyes.

'You okay?'

She looked embarrassed. 'I'm fine.'

'It's a big move. Big changes for both of us.'

She glanced back at the boxes as if something might be hiding in them.

'It's going to work out, Luce.'

She snuggled against me, and I could feel her smile. I didn't want to leave.

She said, 'What did Joe want?'

'The daughter of a friend of his is missing. He wants me to help check it out.'

Lucy looked up at me, her face now serious. 'A child?'

'He didn't say. You mind if I go?'

She glanced at the couch again. 'You'll do anything to avoid this couch, won't you?'

'Yeah. I hate that damned couch.'

Lucy laughed, then looked into my eyes again.

'I'd mind if you didn't go. Take a shower and go save the world.'

Hancock Park is an older area south of the Wilshire Country Club, lesser known to outsiders than Beverly Hills or Bel Air, but every bit as rich. Frank Garcia lived in an adobe-walled Spanish villa set behind a wrought-iron fence just west of the country club. It was a big place, hidden by lush green tree ferns and bird-of-paradise plants as big as dinosaurs and leafy calla lilies that were wilting from the heat.

Forty minutes after Pike gave me Garcia's address, I followed an older Latina with a thick waist and nervous hands through Garcia's rambling home and out to where Frank Garcia and Joe Pike waited beside a tile-lined pool.

As I approached, Pike said, 'Frank, this is Elvis Cole. We own the agency together.'

'Mr Garcia.'

Frank Garcia wasn't the smiling man with the bushy mustache you see on his tortillas. This Frank Garcia looked small and worried, and it had nothing to do with him being in a wheelchair. 'You don't look like a private investigator.'

I was wearing one of those terrific Jam's World print shirts over the shorts. Orange, yellow, pink, and green. 'Gee, did I wear this on a Sunday?'

Garcia looked embarrassed, then raised his hands in apology. 'I'm sorry, Mr Cole. I'm so worked up about this thing with Karen, I'm not thinking. I don't care how you dress. I just want to find my daughter.' He touched Joe's arm. It was a loving gesture, and surprised me. 'That's why I called Joe. Joe says if anyone can find Karen, it's you. He says you're the best there is at finding people.'

Here's the scene: The three of us are by the Olympic-sized pool. The Latina with the thick waist is hovering in the shade of the veranda up by the house, her eyes on Frank in case he might want something, but so far he doesn't and he hasn't offered anything to me. If he did, I would ask for sunblock because standing here next to his pool is like standing on the sun side of Mercury. Gotta be ninety-six and climbing. Behind us is a pool house larger than my home, and through the sliding glass doors I can see a pool table, wet bar, and paintings of *vaqueros* in the Mexican highlands. It is air-conditioned in there, but apparently Frank would rather sit out here in the nuclear heat. Statues of lions dot the landscape, as motionless as Joe Pike, who has not moved once in the three minutes that I have been there. Pike is wearing a gray sweatshirt with the sleeves cut off, faded Levi's, and flat black pilot's glasses, which is the way he dresses every day of his life. His dark brown hair is cut short, and bright red arrows were tattooed on the outside of his deltoids long before tattoos were *au courant*. Watching Joe stand there, he reminds me of the world's largest two-legged pit bull.

I said, 'We'll do what we can, Mr Garcia. How long has Karen been missing?'

'Since yesterday. Yesterday morning at ten o'clock. I called the police,

but those bastards wouldn't do anything, so I called Joe. I knew he'd help.'
He patted Joe's arm again.

'The police refused to help?'

'Yeah. Those pricks.'

'How old is Karen, Mr Garcia?'

'Thirty-two.'

I glanced at Pike. Together, we had worked hundreds of missing persons
cases, and we both knew why the police had brushed off Frank Garcia.

I said, 'A thirty-two-year-old woman has only been missing since
yesterday?'

'Yes.' Pike's voice was soft.

Frank Garcia twisted in his chair, knowing what I was saying and angry
about it.

'What's your point, asking that? You think just because she's a grown
woman she'd meet some man and run off without letting anyone know?'

'Adult people do that, Mr Garcia.'

He shoved a piece of yellow legal paper into my hands, and now the
nervous eyes were rimmed with frustration, like I was his last best hope
and I wasn't going for it, either. 'Karen would've called. She would've told
me if she had to change her plans. She was gonna go run, then bring me a
bowl of *machaca*, but she never came back. You ask Mrs Acuna in her
building. Mrs Acuna knows.' He said it as though if he could only get it out
fast enough, it would become as important to me as it was to him. But
then Frank wheeled toward Joe, and now his voice held anger as well as
fear. 'He's like the goddamned police. He don't want to do anything.' He
spun back at me, and now you could see the man he had been before he
was in the chair, a teenaged gang-banger out of East L.A. with the White
Fence gang who had turned his life around and made a fortune. 'Sorry I
pulled you away from your donuts.'

From a million miles away behind the dark glasses, Joe said, 'Frank.
We're going to help you.'

I tried not to look embarrassed, which is hard to do when your face is
red. 'We'll look for your daughter, Mr Garcia. I just want you to know that
the police have their policy for a reason. Most people we think are missing
aren't. Eventually they call or show up, and they're embarrassed that
everyone went to so much trouble. You see?'

He didn't look happy about it.

'You know where she was going to run?'

'Somewhere around Hollywood up by the hills. Mrs Acuna said she was
going to this Jungle Juice, one of those little juice places? Mrs Acuna said
she always got one of those things, a smoothie. She offered to bring one
back.'

'Jungle Juice. Okay, that gives us a place to start.' How many Jungle
Juices could there be?

Frank was looking more relieved by the second. Like he could breathe again. 'I appreciate this, Mr Cole. I want you to know that I don't care how much this costs. You tell me how much you want, it's yours.'

Joe said, 'Nothing.'

Garcia waved his hands. 'No, Joe, c'mon.'

'Nothing, Frank.'

I stared at the pool. I would've liked some of Frank Garcia's money just fine.

Garcia took Joe's arm again. 'You're a good boy, Joe. You always were.' He hung on to Joe's arm as he looked at me. 'We know each other since Joe was a policeman. Joe and my Karen, they used to see each other. I was hoping maybe one day this boy might be part of the family.'

Joe said, 'That was a long time ago.' He said it so softly that I could barely hear him.

I smiled. 'Joe. You never told me about this.'

Joe turned my way, the flat black lenses reflecting sun. 'Stop.'

I smiled wider and shook my head. That Joe. You learn something every day.

The old man looked up at the sky as the first flecks of ash swirled around us, the flecks catching on his hands and legs. 'Look at this mess. The goddamned sky is melting.'

The woman with the thick waist showed us out through the cool of Frank Garcia's home. Joe's red Jeep Cherokee was parked beneath an elm tree at the curb. My car was parked behind it. Pike and I walked down the drive without speaking until we came to the street, and then Joe said, 'Thanks for coming.'

'I guess there are worse ways to spend a Sunday. I could be wrestling that damned couch.'

Pike canted the glasses my way. 'We finish this, I'll move the couch for you.'

Friends.

We left my car where it was, climbed into Pike's Jeep, and went to find Karen Garcia.

2

Frank Garcia had written his daughter's name, address, and phone number on the yellow sheet, along with a description of Karen's car (a red Mazda RX-7) and her license number (4KBL772). He'd attached a snapshot of Karen laughing about something as she sat at what was probably his dining-room table. She had a brilliant white smile, offset nicely against golden skin and rich black hair. She looked happy.

Joe stared at the photograph as if he were peering through a window at something far away.

I said, 'Pretty.'

'Yes. She is.'

'You had to be seeing her, when, before you knew me?'

His eyes never left the picture. 'I knew you, but I was still on the job.'

I remember Joe dating back then, but the relationships seemed as they were now, none more important than any other. 'I guess you were tight with this girl.'

Joe nodded.

'So what happened?'

Pike handed back the picture. 'I broke her heart.'

'Oh.' Sometimes prying is a lousy idea.

'A few years later she married and moved East to New York. It didn't work out, and now she's back here.'

I nodded, still feeling small for prying.

I used Pike's cell phone to call Karen Garcia's number. She didn't answer, but I identified myself to her machine, and asked her to call her father if she got this message. Frank had provided Mrs Acuna's phone, also, so I called her next, asking if she knew where Karen had gone to run. The dry winds were amping the air with so much static electricity that her voice sounded like bubbling fat, but I understood enough to get that the answer was no. 'Is it possible, Mrs Acuna, that Karen came home, then left again without your seeing her? You know, like maybe she came home long enough to get cleaned up, then went out with friends?'

'You mean yesterday?'

'Yes, ma'am. Yesterday after her run.'

'Oh, no. My husband and I live right here by the stairs. Karen lives right above us. When she didn't come back for the *machaca*, I was so worried. Her father loves my *machaca*. She always brings him a bowl. I just been up there again, and she still isn't back.'

I glanced at Joe. 'You see Karen much, Mrs Acuna? You two chat about things?'

'Oh, yes. She's such a sweet girl. I've known her family since before she was born.'

'She say anything to you about maybe getting back together with her ex-husband?'

Pike glanced over.

'No. Oh, no, she doesn't say anything like that. She calls him "the creep". He's still back in that place.' That place. New York.

Still looking at Pike, I shook my head. Pike turned to the window.

'What about other boyfriends?'

'She sees young men. Not a lot, you know, but she's very pretty.'

'Okay. Thanks, Mrs Acuna. I'll probably drop around later on. If Karen happens to come home, would you ask her to phone her father?'

'I'll call him myself.'

I ended the call, then looked over at Pike. 'You know she's probably with her friends. Probably went to Vegas, or maybe spent all night swing dancing and she's crashing at some guy's.'

'Could be. But Frank's worried, and he needs someone to help carry the load.'

'You really were close with these people.'

Pike went back to staring out the window. Getting him to talk is like pulling your own teeth with pliers.

The information operator told me that there were two Jungle Juice outlets, the original in West Hollywood on Melrose, the second on Barham in Universal City. West Hollywood was closer, so we went there first. Detective work defined by the process of least effort.

The first Jungle Juice was manned by a skinny kid with blue hair and Irish tattoos on his arms, a short girl with a bleach-blond buzz cut, and a guy in his early thirties who looked like he might be president of the local Young Republicans chapter. All three of them had worked yesterday when Karen would've been in, but none of them recognized her picture. The bleach blond worked every weekend and said she would know her if Karen were a regular. I believed her.

The Santa Anas continued to pick up as we drove north to the second Jungle Juice. Palm trees, tall and vulnerable like the necks of giant dinosaurs, took the worst of it. The wind stripped the dead fronds that bunched beneath the crowns and tossed them into streets and yards and onto cars.

It was a few minutes before noon when we reached the second Jungle Juice, just south of Universal Studios. It was set in a narrow strip mall that ran along Barham at the base of the mountains, and was crowded with Sunday shoppers and tourists trying to find the Universal City Walk, even with the wind.

Pike and I stood in line until we reached the counter and showed them the picture of Karen. The girl behind the register, all of eighteen with a clean bright smile and chocolate tan, recognized Karen at once. 'Oh, sure, she comes in all the time. She always gets a smoothie after her run.'

Pike said, 'Was she in yesterday?'

The girl didn't know, and called over a tall African-American kid named Ronnie. Ronnie was a good-looking kid a couple of inches over six feet whose claim to fame was six seconds in a Charmin commercial. 'Oh, yeah, she comes in here after her run. That's Karen.'

'Did she come in yesterday?'

Now Ronnie squinted at me. 'Is she okay?'

'I just want to know if she came in yesterday.'

The squint turned into a frown, went to Pike, then grew suspicious. 'What is this?'

I showed him the license. He squinted at that, too.

'Your name really Elvis?'

Pike stepped past me until his hips pressed against the counter. Ronnie was maybe an inch taller than Joe, but Ronnie took a fast step back. Joe said, 'Did she come in here or not?' Voice so soft you could barely hear him.

Ronnie shook his head, eyes bugging. 'Not yesterday. I worked from opening to six, and she didn't come in. I would've known because we always talk about her run. I jog, too.'

'You know where she runs?'

'Sure. She parks down here and runs up the hill there to the reservoir.' He gestured across Barham to the hill. Lake Hollywood Drive meandered up through a residential area to the reservoir.

The girl said, 'I'm pretty sure I saw her drive past yesterday. Well, it was a little red car. I didn't see her or anything. Just the car.'

Ronnie said, 'No way. Karen always comes in after the run, and she didn't come in.' Like he was disappointed that maybe she had come for the run and not stopped in to see him. 'No way.'

We thanked them, then went out to the parking lot.

I said, 'Well, that's something. She shows up for the run, but she doesn't go in for the smoothie, which is her habit.'

Pike walked to the street, then looked back at the parking lot. It was small, and empty of red Mazdas.

He said, 'She runs, but maybe she remembers something and doesn't have time to get the smoothie, or she meets someone and they decide to do something else.'

'Yeah. Like go to his place for a different kind of smoothie.'

Pike looked at me.

17

'Sorry.'

He stared up the hill. 'You're probably right. If she runs to the reservoir, she probably follows Lake Hollywood up. Let's drive it.'

We followed Lake Hollywood Drive past upscale houses that were built in the thirties and forties, then remodeled heavily in the seventies and eighties into everything from homey ranch-styles to contemporary aeries to post-modern nightmares. Like most older Los Angeles neighborhoods (until the land boom went bust), the homes held the energy of change, as if what was here today might evolve into something else tomorrow. Often, that something else was worse, but just as often it was better. There is great audacity in the willingness to change, more than a little optimism, and a serious dose of courage. It was the courage that I admired most, even though the results often made me cringe. After all, the people who come to Los Angeles are looking for change. Everyone else just stays home.

The road switchbacked up the hillside, meandering past houses and mature oaks that shuddered and swayed with the wind. The streets were littered with leaves and branches and old Gelson's Market bags. We crested the ridge, then drove down to the reservoir. It was choppy and muddy from the wind. We saw no red Mazdas, and no one who looked like Karen Garcia, but we didn't expect to. The hill was there, so you climbed it, and so far I wasn't too worried about things. Karen was probably just waking up at wherever she'd spent the night, and pretty soon she'd go home or collect her messages, and call her father to calm down the old man. The burden of being an only child.

We were halfway down the mountain and thinking about what to do next when a homeless guy with a backpack and bedroll strolled out of a side street and started down the mountain. He was in his mid-thirties, and burned dark by the sun.

I said, 'Pull over.'

When Pike slowed, the man stopped and considered us. His eyes were red, and you could smell the body odor even with the wind. He said, 'I am a master carpenter looking for work, but no job is too small. I will work for cash, or books.' He managed a little pride when he said it, but he probably wasn't a master carpenter and he probably wasn't looking for work.

Pike held out Karen's photograph. 'Have you seen this woman?'

'No. I am sorry.' Every word like that. Without contractions.

'She jogged through the neighborhood yesterday morning. Blue top. Gray shorts.'

He leaned forward and examined the picture more closely. 'Black ponytail.'

Pike said, 'Could be.'

'She was running uphill, struggling mightily against the forces that would drag her down. A truck slowed beside her, then sped away. I was listening to Mr Dave Matthews at the time.' He had a Sony Discman suspended from his belt, the earphones hanging loose at his neck.

I said, 'What kind of truck?'

He stepped back and looked over Pike's Cherokee.

'This truck.'

'A red Jeep like this?'

He shrugged. 'I think it was this one, but it might've been another.'

The corner of Pike's mouth twitched. In all the years I had known him, I have never seen Pike smile, but sometimes you'll get the twitch. For Pike, that's him busting a gut.

I said, 'You see the driver?'

He pointed at Pike. 'Him.'

Pike looked away, and sighed.

The homeless man peered at us hopefully. 'Would you have a small job that needs a careful craftsman? I am available, don't you know?'

I gave him ten bucks. 'What's your name?'

'Edward Deege, Master Carpenter.'

'Okay, Edward. Thanks.'

'No job too small.'

'Hey, Edward. We want to talk to you again, you around?'

'I am but a Dixie cup on the stream of life, but, yes, I enjoy the reservoir. I can often be found there.'

'Okay, Edward. Thanks.'

Edward Deege peered at Pike some more, then stepped back, as if troubled. 'Release your rage, my friend. Rage kills.'

Pike pulled away.

I said, 'You think he saw anything, or he was just scamming us?'

'He was right about the ponytail. Maybe he saw a four-wheel-drive.'

We followed Lake Hollywood Drive down to Barham, and when we turned left toward the freeway, Pike said, 'Elvis.'

Karen Garcia's red Mazda RX-7 was parked behind a flower shop on this side of Barham, opposite the Jungle Juice. We hadn't seen it when we were at the Jungle Juice because it was behind a building across the street. We couldn't see it until we were coming down, and I wished then that it wasn't there to see.

Pike turned into the parking lot, and we got out. The Mazda's engine was cool, as if it had been parked here a very long time.

'Been here all night.'

Pike nodded.

'If she went up to run, that means she never came down.' I looked back up the hill.

Pike said, 'Or she didn't leave by herself.'

'She's running, she meets some guy, and they use his car. She's probably on her way back to pick up the Mazda now.' I said it, but neither of us believed it.

We asked the people at the flower shop if they had seen anything, but they hadn't. We asked every shopkeeper in the strip mall and most of the employees, but they all said no. I hoped they had seen something to indicate that Karen was safe, but deep down, where your blood runs cold, I knew they hadn't.

3

With her father's money, Karen Garcia could've lived anywhere, yet she chose a modest apartment in a Latin-hip part of Silver Lake favored by families. The Gipsy Kings played on someone's stereo; the smells of chili and cilantro were fresh and strong. Children played on the lawns, and couples laughed about the heat storm. Around us, great palms and jacarandas slashed like the tails of nervous cats, but the area wasn't littered with fronds and limbs. I guess if you cared about your neighborhood you cleaned up the mess without waiting for the city to do it for you.

We left Pike's Jeep by a fire hydrant and walked into a courtyard burgeoning with hand-painted clay pots that overflowed with gladiolas. Apartment number 3 belonged to Marisol Acuna, but Pike didn't come with me to the door. We knew from Mrs Acuna that Karen's apartment was on the second floor.

A heavy woman in her late fifties stepped out of a ground-floor apartment. 'Are you Mr Cole?'

'Yes, ma'am. Mrs Acuna?'

She glanced at Pike. He was already climbing the stairs. 'She hasn't come home. Let me get the key, and I'll let you inside.'

'Frank gave us a key, ma'am. You should wait down here.'

A line appeared between her brows, and she glanced at Pike again. 'Why don't you want me up there? You think something bad is up there?'

'No, ma'am. But if Karen comes home I'd hate to have her walk in on a couple of strange men. You keep an eye out. If she comes while we're up there you can tell her what's going on and bring her up.' What a fine and wonderful lie.

Pike wasn't waiting for me. Karen's door opened.

I gave Mrs Acuna a final smile, then took the stairs three at a time, slipping into Karen's apartment behind Joe. He stood in the center of the living room, holding up a finger to stop me, his gun hanging loose in his right hand. Pike carries the Colt Python .357 magnum with a four-inch barrel. Firing a heavy bullet, it will generate over fifteen hundred foot-pounds of energy and can punch its way through an engine block. Pike uses the heavy bullet.

He went through a short hall into the apartment's only bedroom, then reappeared almost instantly, the Python now gone.

'Clear.'

Sometimes you just have to shake your head.

I said, 'Can we spell "paranoid"?'

Karen Garcia's apartment was furnished well beyond the rent she paid. An overstuffed leather couch with two matching chairs dominated the living room. A modern desk was positioned under two casement windows so that she had a view of the street; psychology texts were shelved on the desk, along with three Tami Hoag novels, a Nunzilla, and an AT&T telephone/answering machine combo. The red message light was blinking. A framed snapshot of Karen wearing a silly crown and holding a glass of wine was tacked beside the window. She was barefoot, and smiling.

I said, 'You want the messages or the rest of the place?'

'Rest of the place.'

All of Karen's messages were from her father except the one from me and one from a man named Martin, asking if she wanted to go to a *quebradita*. Martin had a Spanish accent, and a mellow voice. After the messages, I went through the drawers, and found a Rolodex. We would bring it to Frank to see whom he knew, and, if we had to, we would phone every name to see if we could find someone who knew where Karen was.

Pike reappeared from the bedroom. 'Jeans on the bed, sandals on the floor. Her toothbrush is still in the bathroom. Wherever she went, she wasn't planning on staying.' You take your toothbrush, you're thinking you'll stay the night. You leave it, you're coming home.

'Okay. She changed into her running things and left the other stuff, figuring to change back later.'

'That's my call.'

'You see any notes, maybe a calendar that says her plans?'

I thought he was about to answer when Pike held up his finger again, then took three fast steps toward the door. 'Someone's coming.'

'Mrs Acuna.'

'Someone bigger.'

Pike and I set up on either side of the door as a large, ruddy-faced man in a gray suit made the landing and looked in at us. Two uniformed LAPD officers appeared behind him. The man's eyes widened when he saw us, and he pawed under his jacket. 'Police officers! Step away from the door and move to the center of the room. Now!'

The suit clawed out a standard LAPD-issue Beretta 9 as the uniformed cops drew their own weapons. Mrs Acuna shouted something down in the courtyard, but no one listened to her.

I said, 'Take it easy. We're working for her father, Frank Garcia.'

The detective had the gun on us now, and the two uniformed cops were aiming past his head. One of them was young, and looked like his eyes were about to do the Pekinese pop-out. If I was the detective, I would've been more scared of them than me.

The detective shouted, '*Step back from the door and move to the center. Hands from your bodies.*'

We did what he said. He toed open the door and stepped through, the two uniforms spreading to cover us from the sides.

'My name's Cole. We're private investigators working for her father.'

'Shut up.'

'My license is in the wallet. Her father hired us a couple of hours ago. Call him. Ask the woman who lives downstairs.'

'Shut the fuck up and keep those hands where I can see them!'

The detective told one of the uniforms to see the woman, then edged forward, slipped out my wallet, and glanced at the license. He was more tense than he should've been, and I wondered why. Maybe he didn't like my shirt, either.

He brought my wallet to the phone, punched in a number without taking his eyes off me, then mumbled something I couldn't understand.

'We entered the apartment with a key the father provided and at his request. Would you lighten up?'

The uniform reappeared. 'Hey, Holstein, they're cool. She says the father called her and told her to expect'm.'

Holstein nodded, but the tension stayed.

'Can we put our hands down, or you like the view of our pits?'

'Sure, smart guy. Might as well relax. We're gonna be here a while.'

Pike and I dropped our hands. I guess Frank had raised so much hell that Hollywood Division had finally rolled out.

'I'm surprised you guys are on this. She's only been missing since yesterday.'

Holstein painted me with empty cop eyes, then took a seat on the edge of Karen Garcia's desk.

'Not anymore. Karen Garcia's body was found up at Lake Hollywood about an hour ago.'

I felt my breath catch. Joe Pike might've stiffened. He might've leaned forward just a hair, but if he did I could not tell.

I said, 'Holstein? Are you *sure?*'

More voices filled the courtyard, speaking with the distinct cadence of police officers. Down below, Mrs Acuna wailed.

I sat on Karen Garcia's leather couch and stared at the picture of her in the paper crown.

'Joe?'

He did not answer.

'Joe?'

April, three months prior to the Islander Palms Motel

Karen Garcia said, 'I'm a freshman at UCLA. I study child development there, and work with the day care part-time.' She was almost a foot shorter than Pike, and he had to remind himself to step back. He had been warned that he tended to stand too close to people, and it made them uncomfortable. He stepped away. She said to one of the little boys, 'Daniel, stay with the others, please. I have to speak with this police officer.'

Daniel blurped his tongue like an airplane engine and flew back to the group. LAPD patrol officer Joe Pike had already jotted in his notebook that there were eleven children, ages three through five, in the care of Ms Garcia and her children's group co-teacher, a slim young man with round spectacles and curly hair named Joshua. Joshua appeared nervous, but Officer Pike had learned that people often tensed when dealing with the police. It usually meant nothing.

They were surrounded by children in MacArthur Park, south of Wilshire by the lake in LAPD's Rampart Division. The day was warm and the sky overhead almost white from the smog. Pike's navy-blue uniform soaked up the heat and made the sun seem hotter than it was. The park was filled with women pushing carriages or playing with their preschoolers on the swings and slides. Homeless men were asleep on the grass, and some younger guys who were probably harmless but out of work had drifted away when the radio car had turned into the parking lot, responding to a see-the-woman call regarding a possible child molester. The woman was Karen Garcia, who had phoned 911 with the complaint.

Pike said, 'Do you see the man now?'

'No, not now.' She pointed to the brick rest rooms at the edge of the parking lot. 'He saw us watching him and went behind the rest rooms over there before you got here. I haven't seen him since. He had a camera with a long lens, and I'm sure he was taking pictures of the children. Not just mine, but other kids, too.'

Pike took notes. If the suspect saw her go to the phone, he'd be long gone. Pike would look, but the man was gone.

'Joshua asked him what he was doing, and he walked away the first time, but he came back. That's when I called you.'

Pike glanced at Joshua, who nodded.

Pike said, 'Description?'

'Pardon me?'

'What did the man look like?'

Karen said. 'Oh. He was shorter than you. How tall are you?'

'Six-one.'

'A lot shorter. I'd say five-eight or nine, but very wide and heavy. Fat, but he didn't look fat, just fleshy, with stubby fingers.'

Pike wrote. 'Hair, eyes, clothes, distinguishing characteristics.'

'Blond hair, but dyed. I mean, a real do-it-yourself job.'

Joshua said, 'Long and slicked back. Like, how many human beings still use Brylcreem?' Joshua grinned when he said it, maybe trying to feel out Pike's sense of humor or maybe just trying to dispel his own nervousness. He looked disappointed when Pike did not respond.

Ms Garcia said, 'He was wearing dark slacks and a white shirt with a kind of vest, a brown pattern of some kind, and he was carrying the camera.' She waited for Joshua to chime in. 'I didn't get close enough to see anything else.'

Joshua said, 'Zit scars.'

Ms Garcia stepped closer to Pike and touched his arm. 'Are you going to find him?'

Pike closed the notebook, and stepped away from her. 'We'll radio a dispatch to other cars in the area. If we spot him, we'll question him.'

Ms Garcia wasn't happy with that. 'That's all?'

'No. We'll also beat him to death.'

Joshua stared, uncertain, but Karen Garcia laughed, showing even white teeth and a strong laugh which Pike liked a very great deal. 'To protect and to serve.'

'Yes, ma'am.'

Karen Garcia said, 'You don't have to say ma'am, for God's sake.'

The little boy with the blurping sound raced away again, and Joshua chased him.

Pike said, 'We'll do what we can, but if you see him again, call right away.' Pike handed her a card. 'Tell them you spoke to car two-adam-six.'

Ms Garcia looked up at him with the dark brown eyes, as if she was trying to see through his sunglasses. Calm eyes that Pike also liked. 'I thought I was speaking to a man, not a car.'

Pike said, 'Two-adam-six. You have a good day, ma'am.'

Pike went back to two-adam-six, where his partner sat behind the wheel, idling with the air conditioning on. Pike slipped into the shotgun side, putting his nightstick in its holder. Woz didn't look at him, smoking a cigarillo as he watched a group of Honduran girls in halter tops. Gang bait. Pike said, 'Suspected pedophile with a camera. Got a description.'

His partner shrugged. 'So fuckin' what.'

'We're on it.'

'Maybe you.' Hard, with an edge to it.

'You going to retire?'

Wozniak's jaw clenched. He shook his head once.

'Then we're going to work this.'

Wozniak glared at Pike another moment, then sighed and seemed to relax. Accepting it. 'The guy a weenie wagger?'

'Shutterbug.'

Pike recited the description and related what Ms Garcia had said. Halfway through, Wozniak waved him quiet. 'Yeah, yeah, I know the guy.

Lennie DeVille. Another fuckin' perv, be better off with a bullet in his head.'

'Got a last-known?'

Wozniak was staring out the window again, watching the paddleboats on the lake. 'Creep like this moves around, livin' in motels and weeklies and jumping the rent when he can.' Wozniak drew deep on the cigarillo, then rolled down his window far enough to drop it outside. 'I'll ask around.' Wozniak looked past Pike, and scowled. 'Now fuckin' what?'

Pike turned, and saw Ms Garcia walking toward them.

Karen Garcia watched the officer walk back to his car, unable to take her eyes off the way his ass worked beneath the tight uniform pants, and the way the heavy John Brown belt rode his trim waist. His arms were tanned and muscular without being bulky, his hair short and thick, his face lean and handsome.

Joshua said, 'Better reel in your tongue before you trip.'

She felt herself flush. 'Is it that obvious?'

'Mm-hm. Maria, let me help with that, honey.' Joshua bent to tend to one of the children whose shoe had come untied. It was almost time for the van from the day care, so they needed to start back across the park.

Karen couldn't help but look back at the young officer. She liked the way he carried himself, and her stomach did a little flip when he'd stood next to her. She had called the police with serious concerns, but when he arrived it had been tough to keep her mind on what she wanted to say. He was older, but he couldn't have been any more than in his late twenties. She wondered if he thought she was a child. She'd said she was in college, hadn't she? The thoughts swirled in her head, and she smiled even wider.

Joshua rolled his eyes. 'Karen, please, not in front of the children!'

She laughed and shoved Joshua.

Watching Officer Pike slide into his car, she was suddenly overwhelmed with a fierce urge to see what was behind his dark glasses. She had tried to see his eyes and could not, but now she had to have a look.

Karen's pulse hammered all the harder as she fought the urge to do something she had never done before. In a moment the two officers would drive away and she would never see him again. The next thing she knew, she was walking hard toward their car, taking long crazy steps as if some secret creature had taken possession of her. The two officers within were watching her approach. Pike's window came down and he looked out at her. 'Yes, ma'am?'

Karen Garcia leaned forward with her hands on the window. 'I have a request.'

He stared at her, and her mouth went dry. She absolutely knew that she was making a fool of herself. 'Would you take off your glasses, please? I'd like to see your eyes.'

The older officer made a face like he wanted to spit; irritated, as if she had interrupted something. 'Oh, for Christ's sake.'

Officer Pike took off his dark glasses, and looked at her.

She felt her breath catch. His eyes were the most liquid blue, the blue of the sky over the high deserts of Sonora, the blue of the ocean where it has no bottom and is infinitely clean. But it wasn't the blue that stopped her breath. For just a moment when the glasses were first pulled away, she could have sworn that those eyes were filled with the most terrible and long-endured pain. Then the pain was gone and there was only the blue.

Karen Garcia said, 'Would you like to go to a movie with me this Friday night?'

Pike stared at her for so many heartbeats that she wondered if she'd really spoken the words aloud. But then, slowly, he fitted the dark glasses over the incredible eyes again and put out his hand for her to take. 'My name is Joe. May I have your phone number?'

When he touched her, she quivered.

4

Pretty soon the entire apartment building knew, and word spread through the block. I wanted to ask Pike how he felt, but not in front of these other men.

'How did she die, Holstein?'

'I don't know.'

'Was she murdered?'

'I don't know, Cole. I get a call out telling me to come here and secure the vic's apartment until the leads show up. That's what I'm doing.'

'You must know something. You got a fast ID.'

'Whoever found the body pulled an ID off her before they called it in. Looks like she's been there since yesterday.'

Pike said, 'Has her father been notified?'

Holstein glanced at Pike's shoulder tats, then his face. 'Sonofabitch. You're Joe Pike.'

When Pike left the job it hadn't gone well. A lot of cops didn't like him. More than a few hated him.

'Has her father been notified?' Voice softer now.

I went over, stepping in front of Joe. 'Her father hired us to find her, and now that's done. We should let him know.'

Holstein went to the couch and dropped his weight on it. The leather sighed. 'We're gonna wait here for the leads. They're going to want to know what you know.'

Pike touched my shoulder. 'They can ask us later. Let's go.'

Holstein reached under his jacket. 'I don't think so.'

'What're you going to do, Holstein? Shoot it out? C'mon, does Lou Poitras have the table today?'

'Yeah.' Lou Poitras has been one of my closest friends for years, and had recently moved from North Hollywood Division to the Hollywood Homicide table.

'Then call him. Poitras and I are tight. The leads can catch up to us at the father's. They're going to want to see him anyway.'

We were still arguing about it when the phone rang. Holstein answered, trying to make his voice anonymous. He listened, then held the phone

28

toward me, looking impressed. 'For you, hotshot. I don't know how you rate, but it's the watch commander.'

I took the phone and identified myself. A man whose voice I didn't recognize said, 'Hold on.'

Another man, this one with a slight Spanish accent, came on. He identified himself as Frank's lawyer, Abbot Montoya. 'Mr Cole, I'm here with the Hollywood Division watch commander at Mr Garcia's request, along with a representative of City Councilman Maldenado's office. You're aware that Mr Garcia and Councilman Maldenado are personally close, aren't you?'

'No.' He wasn't saying it for me. He was saying it for the people in the room with him at Hollywood Division.

'Frank would like you and Mr Pike to visit the murder site. He wants you to witness his daughter's situation.' Situation. There's a word for you. 'After, Frank would like you to go to his home and describe Karen's ... this is awkward for me, too, Mr Cole. I'm Karen's godfather.'

'I understand.'

'He would like you to tell him whatever you've found out about what happened. I know you're not being compensated, but we'll take care of that.'

'There's nothing to take care of.'

'Yes, well, we'll discuss that later. You and Mr Pike will do this?'

'Yes, sir. If the police let us.'

'They'll let you. And after, you'll see Mr Garcia?'

'Yes.'

'The watch commander would like to speak with Detective Holstein now, please.'

Holstein listened for another minute, then said, 'Yes, sir,' and hung up. When he put down the phone, his eyes were thoughtful.

Without a word he went to the door, held it open, and said, 'She's on the west side of the reservoir. They're sealing the lake, but Lieutenant Poitras will be expecting you.'

We left, and Holstein slammed the door.

It was early afternoon by the time we once more wound our way up Lake Hollywood Drive. Uniformed officers were still clearing the park. We passed runners and walkers on their way out, but pretty soon we came to half a dozen radio cars parked in the middle of the road with four unmarked sedans. An Asian-American man was fishing a large tackle box out of the rear of a white station wagon with L.A. COUNTY MEDICAL EXAMINER stenciled on the side. He would be the coroner investigator. As he went through the gate and down along the trail to the water, a cop who looked like a miniature King Kong came up to stand just off the road, waiting for us with his arms crossed. He was so big from a lifetime of pumping weights that his jacket fit him like a sausage skin about to split.

I said, 'Hey, Lou.'

Lou Poitras put out his hand and we shook. He didn't offer to shake with Pike. 'Understand you were trying to find her.'

'That's right. You got a suspect yet?'

'Take it easy. I've been here less than an hour.' Poitras glanced at Pike. 'I hear you knew the girl. I'm sorry.'

Pike nodded.

'You sure you want to go down there, Pike? You could stay up here at the car.'

Pike walked past him and through the gate.

Poitras grunted. 'Same old talkative Pike.'

We followed a narrow, winding trail through the trees. The leaf canopy above us rustled from the wind, but down on the floor the air was still. Ash from the fires to the north filtered through the canopy, floating in the still air. Poitras swatted at it as if the ash was insects he could drive away.

I said, 'What about the cause of death?'

'Coroner investigator just went down.'

'We saw him. What's your take?'

Poitras tipped his head toward Pike, clearly uncomfortable, and slowed his pace to let Pike pull ahead. 'Unofficial, it's one shot to the head. Looks like a .22, but it could've been a .25. She was popped up here on the trail, then fell down into a little ravine. No sign of assault or a sexual attack, but that's just my eyeball. They'll have to take smears back at the coroner's.' Smears. Looking for semen.

'Any wits?'

'I've got people making a house-to-house up along the ridge trying to get names, but you know how it is.'

The trail ran along a ledge about fifteen feet up from the water, sometimes in dense trees, sometimes not. When we reached a barrier of yellow crime scene tape, we followed a freshly broken path down to the lake, then traced the shoreline around a small finger. That's where we found the crime scene.

'The vic is right over here.'

Pike took two steps up the slope and stopped.

Karen Garcia lay head down at the bottom of a narrow ravine, wild purple sage obscuring her body. Her right arm was twisted behind her, her left extended straight from her torso. Her left leg was bent at the knee, left foot under her right leg. What I could see of her face was discolored with lividity, and the ugly smell of decay gases hung at the waterline like a pall. Giant black bottle flies and yellow jackets swarmed around the body. The CI swatted at them with his clipboard, as a Hispanic detective said, 'Fuckin' meat eaters.'

If Pike felt anything I could not tell.

The CI, now wearing latex gloves, leaned over her to look at something that the Hispanic detective was pointing out. Her exposed hand had already been taped into a plastic bag to preserve evidence that might be under her fingernails. They would check later when she was at the morgue.

'Who discovered the body?'

'Couple of hikers. They found her down here, and called it in on a cell phone. You guys know Kurt Asana?'

The CI made a little wave. Asana.

Pike said, 'How'd you get an ID so fast?'

'Doofs who found her. She had her driver's license in her shorts.' Officers arriving on the scene wouldn't touch the body. No one was allowed to touch the victim before the coroner investigator had his shot. That way, when a suspect was brought to trial, the defense attorney couldn't argue that ham-handed cops had contaminated the evidence. If the hikers hadn't done their search, the police would still be wondering who she was until Asana emptied her pockets.

Poitras said, 'Hey, Kurt. Can you give me a ballpark on the time?'

Asana tried to bend her shoulder joint, and found it stiff, but yielding. 'Rigor's starting to let go. I'd say about twenty-four hours.'

'She came up here to run between nine-thirty and ten in the morning.'

'Well, I'm just guessing right now, but that fits. When I get the BT, I'll be able to calc it out pretty close.'

Asana took a scalpel and a long metal thermometer from the box and moved back into the weeds. Pike and I both turned away. Asana would be going for a liver temperature. When he had the liver temp he would chart it against the outside air temperature and be able to tell how long the body had been cooling.

We were waiting for Asana to finish when three men in good-looking suits came around the finger like they owned the lake. Lou Poitras stepped forward to block the trail. 'Can I help you?'

Behind me, Joe Pike said, 'Krantz.'

The one called Krantz held up a gold detective's shield about two inches from Poitras's nose. He was a tall, leathery man with a high forehead and lantern jaw. He looked like the kind of guy who liked to jut the jaw at people to show them he meant business. He jutted it now.

'Harvey Krantz, Robbery-Homicide. Detective Stan Watts. Detective Jerome Williams.' Watts was an older white guy with beefy shoulders and a round head. Williams was black, and younger. 'Are you Lieutenant Poitras?'

'That's right.'

'Hollywood Division is off this case as of now. RHD is taking over.' Robbery-Homicide Division is LAPD's elite homicide division. Based out of Parker Center downtown, they could and did handle high-profile homicides all over the city.

Poitras didn't move. 'You're kidding.'

This was probably the biggest case Poitras had on his table, and he wouldn't like giving it up.

'Pull your men off, Lieutenant. We have the scene.' Krantz tucked his badge away and jutted his jaw some more. I made him for his mid-forties, but he could've been older.

'Just like that?'

'Like that.'

Poitras opened his mouth as if he wanted to say something, then took a single step back and turned toward the crime scene. His face was as flat as an empty plate. 'Two Gun. Chick. We're off.'

The Hispanic detective with Asana looked over. 'Say what?'

'We're off. Robbery-Homicide has the scene.'

The Hispanic detective and another detective who'd been poking around in the weeds stepped away as Watts and Williams went over. Neither of the RHD guys seemed to mind the flies.

Krantz was moving past Poitras to join them when his eyes widened, and he said, 'Joe Pike.'

Pike said, 'When did they start hiring chickenshits like you on Robbery-Homicide, Krantz?'

Krantz's face went bright red. He glared at Poitras and shouted so loud that Asana looked over. 'Do you know who this man is? Why is he at this scene?'

Poitras looked bored. 'I know who he is. The other guy is Elvis Cole. They're working for the vic's father.'

'I don't give a rat's ass if they're working for Jesus Christ! They don't belong here, and your ass is gonna be in a sling for opening this crime scene to unauthorized personnel!'

A faint smile flickered on Poitras's lips. Poitras and Krantz were about the same height, but while Krantz was bony, Poitras weighed two hundred sixty pounds. I had once seen Lou Poitras lift the front end of a '68 Volkswagen Beetle and turn the car all the way around. He spoke quietly. 'The watch commander ordered me to give them full access, Krantz. That's what I've done. The vic's father has juice with the City Council, and Pike here personally knew the vic.'

Krantz wasn't listening. He stepped past Poitras and stormed up to Joe. Maybe he had a death wish.

'I can't believe that *you* have the balls to come to a crime scene, Pike. I can't believe you have the gall.'

Joe said, 'Step back.' The voice soft again.

Krantz stepped right up into Pike's face then. Right on the edge of the cliff. 'Or what, you sonofabitch? You going to shoot me, too?'

Poitras pushed Krantz back and stepped between them. 'What's with you, Krantz? Get a grip on yourself.'

Krantz's mouth split into a reptilian smile, and I wondered what was playing out here. He said, 'I want this man questioned, Lieutenant. If Pike here knows the vic, maybe he knows how she got like this.'

Pike said, 'It won't happen, Pants.'

Krantz's face went deep red, and an ugly web of veins pulsed in his forehead.

I moved close to Pike. 'Is there something happening here that I should know about?'

Pike shrugged. 'Nothing much. I'm about to put Krantz down.'

Krantz's face got darker. 'You're going in, Pike. We'll talk to you at the Division.'

Behind us, Poitras's Handie-Talkie made a popping sound. Poitras mumbled things that we couldn't hear, then held it toward Krantz. 'It's Assistant Chief Mills.'

Krantz snatched the radio. 'This is Harvey Krantz.'

Poitras led us back toward the trail without waiting. 'Forget Krantz. The only place you guys are going is back to Mr Garcia's. The A-chief is down there now, and the old man is asking for you.'

Pike and I followed the trail back up the slope and through the trees. When we were away from the cops, and there was only the sound of the leaves crunching beneath our feet, I said, 'I'm sorry about Karen, Joe.'

Pike nodded.

'You going to tell me what all that was about?'

'No.'

The drive back to Hancock Park took forever.

5

An LAPD radio car was parked outside Frank Garcia's home, along with two anonymous detective sedans, a black Town Car, and three other vehicles. The older Latina opened the door again, but before we entered, a Hispanic man about Frank's age stepped past her, and offered a firm hand. Ancient pockmarks and steel-gray hair gave him a hard appearance, but his voice was gentle. 'Mr Cole, Mr Pike, I'm Abbot Montoya. Thank you for coming.'

Joe said, 'How's Frank?'

'Not well. His doctor's on the way.'

Somewhere behind him, Frank Garcia shouted, 'You cocksuckers as good as killed my little girl and I want you out of my house!'

He wasn't shouting at us.

We followed Montoya into a huge, arched living room that I hadn't seen before. Two command-level uniforms, a man in a suit, and an older man in a charming Nike tennis outfit were clumped together like a gospel quartet as Frank shouted at them. Frank's eyes were hollow red blurs, and every crease and line in his face seemed cut deep by something incomprehensibly sharp and painful. So much pain was in his eyes that it hurt to look at him.

City Councilman Henry Maldenado was standing as far from the cops as possible, but Frank shouted at him, too. 'I oughta throw your ass out with them, Henry, all the help I get from you! Maybe I should give my money to that bastard Ruiz next time!' Melvin Ruiz had run against Maldenado in the primary.

Montoya hurried to Frank, his voice soothing. 'Please calm yourself, Frank. We're going to handle this. Mr Cole and Mr Pike are here.'

Frank searched past Montoya with a desperate hope that was as hard to look at as his pain, as if Joe had the power to say that this horrible nightmare was not real, that these men had made a terrible mistake, and his only child had not been murdered.

'Joe?'

Joe knelt beside the chair, but I could not hear what he said.

While they spoke, Abbot Montoya led me across the room and

34

introduced me. 'Mr Maldenado, this is Mr Cole. The gentleman with Frank is Mr Pike. We'd like them to represent Mr Garcia during the investigation.'

That surprised me. 'What do you mean, represent?'

The man in the suit ignored me. 'Letting in an outsider would be a terrible mistake, Councilman. If he were privy to our investigation, we would have no security control.'

The tennis outfit agreed. 'We're more than happy to work with families to keep them informed, Henry, but if someone like this were to interfere, it could hamper the investigation or even jeopardize the case.'

The man in the suit was Captain Greg Bishop, boss of the Robbery-Homicide Division. The tennis outfit belonged to Assistant Chief Walter Mills. I guess he'd been called off his Sunday morning tennis game, and wasn't happy about it.

I cleared my throat. 'I don't mean to be obtuse, but am I the outsider in question?'

Montoya glanced at Frank, then lowered his voice. 'Rightly or wrongly, Frank blames the police for his daughter's death. He believes they were unresponsive, and would prefer his own representatives to monitor the investigation and keep him informed. He told me that Mr Pike and yourself would do that.'

'He did?'

Montoya looked surprised. 'You wouldn't?'

Bishop and Mills were watching me now; the two uniforms sizing me up like a couple of peregrines eyeing a chicken.

I said, 'If the police are involved, Mr Montoya, I'm not sure what it is I can do for you.'

'I think that's clear.'

'No, sir, it's not. We're talking about a homicide investigation. Joe and I can't do anything that LAPD can't do more of. They have the manpower and the technology, and they're good at it.' The uniforms stood a little taller and the assistant chief looked relieved. Like he had just dodged a runaway pit bull.

Bishop said, 'Mr Montoya, I will personally stay in touch with you and Mr Garcia to keep you apprised of the investigation. I'll give you my home number. We can have a daily chat.'

Maldenado nodded, encouraging. 'That seems reasonable to me, Abbot.' As he said it, the Latina showed in Krantz, who looked neither relieved nor encouraging. He eased up behind Bishop.

Montoya touched the councilman's arm, as if neither of them understood. 'The issue isn't the department's willingness to keep Mr Garcia informed, Henry. The issue is trust.'

Behind us, Frank Garcia said, 'When my little girl went missing yesterday, I called these people, but they didn't do a goddamned thing. I knew where she was going. I told'm where to look, but no, they said they couldn't do anything. Now I'm supposed to trust these same people to find who killed her? No. That will never happen.'

Maldenado spread his hands, and there was a plea in his voice. 'Frank, if you gave them a chance.'

'They're with Karen right now, probably messin' things up like with O.J., and I'm stuck in this goddamned chair. I can't be there to watch out for her, and that means someone else has to do it for me.' He twisted around to look at Joe. 'My friend Joe. His friend Mr Cole.' He twisted back to Councilman Henry Maldenado. 'That's the way it's going to be, Henry.'

Montoya said, 'We'd like Mr Cole and Mr Pike to have full access to all levels of the investigation. We wouldn't expect them to function as part of an official LAPD investigation, or to interfere, but if you allow them access, they can keep Frank informed in a way that lends comfort to a man who needs it right now. That's all we're asking.' Montoya turned back to me. 'You'd be willing to do that, wouldn't you? Just observe, and let Frank know what's going on.'

I glanced at Joe again. Joe nodded.

'Yes.'

Montoya turned back to Maldenado, and smiled like a priest explaining why you had to empty your pockets if you wanted to get to heaven. 'Frank will appreciate it, Henry. He'll remember this kindness come election time.'

Maldenado stared at the assistant chief, who stared back. They were looking at each other like a couple of mind readers, Maldenado thinking about campaign funding, and the assistant chief thinking that if he ever wanted to be chief, he'd need as many friends on the City Council as possible.

Finally, Councilman Maldenado nodded. 'That seems a reasonable position to me, Walt. I think that we can show Mr Garcia this small courtesy, don't you?'

Assistant Chief Mills offered his hand to Maldenado as if he were already being sworn in as chief. 'Councilman, we understand what Mr Garcia's going through, and we'll find a way to make this work.'

Montoya put his hand on my shoulder, and the soft voice was satisfied. 'It's settled, then. We'll work out the details and give you a call later this evening. Would that be all right?'

'That would be fine.'

Behind us, Frank said, 'Karen's still up there. I want somebody with her.'

Everyone looked at him.

Frank Garcia took my arm as he'd taken Joe's. He had a grip like pliers. 'You see that they take care of her. You go up there and watch these guys and make sure.'

Bishop looked as if someone had just suggested surgery. Krantz stared at Joe, but it was thoughtful and vague, not hard.

Montoya looked questioningly at the A-chief, who nodded, giving his permission.

I said, 'I will, sir.'

'I won't forget this.'

'I know. I'm sorry about Karen.'

Frank Garcia nodded, but I don't think he was seeing me. His eyes filled, and I think he was seeing Karen.

Krantz left before me. Pike wanted to stay with Frank, and told me that he would call later.

Montoya walked me back through the big house. 'Mr Cole, I know this isn't the kind of job that you normally take. I personally want to thank you for doing this.'

'It's a favor for a friend, Mr Montoya. Thank Joe.'

'I will, but I wanted to thank you, too. Frank and I have been friends for as long as I can remember. Brothers. Do you know White Fence?'

'Yes, sir. I know that Mr Garcia was a member when he was young.' The White Fence gang.

'As was I. We ran on Whittier Boulevard and Camulos Street. We fought the Hazard gang and the Garrity Lomas gang on Oregon Street, and we paid respect to the *veteranos*. It's a long way from the barrio to UCLA Law.'

'I imagine it is, Mr Montoya.'

'I'm telling you these things because I want you to know the depth of my loyalty to Frank, and my love for him, and Karen. If the police aren't cooperative, call me and I will take care of it.'

'Yes, sir. I'll call.'

'You are helping my brother, Mr Cole. If you need us, we will be there.'

'Sure.'

He put out his hand. We shook.

Latins.

I let myself out into the heat, and went down the drive to the street, ash from the fires still sifting down from the sky. Krantz and Stan Watts were standing by a clunky LAPD detective ride, smoking.

Krantz said, 'Where's your asshole friend?'

I kept walking. I wasn't happy about going back to the lake, and I wasn't happy about spending the rest of the day with a dead girl.

'Stop it, Krantz. It'll go someplace you won't like.'

Krantz flipped his cigarette into the street and followed me. 'See where it gets you. You'll go to Men's County and I'll own your license.'

I got into my car. Krantz stood on the street in front of me, ash collecting on his shoulders like dandruff.

'That old man might have the juice to jam you down my throat, but if you interfere with my investigation, I'll snap your license.'

'That old man just lost his daughter, you turd. Try being human.'

Krantz stared at me for about five centuries, then went back to Stan Watts.

I drove away.

I imagined that I could still hear Frank Garcia crying, even as I climbed the mountain to the lake.

6

Robbery-Homicide worked at the Karen Garcia crime scene for the next six hours. Everyone appeared professional and competent, as I knew they would. Even Krantz. A young criminalist named Chen, consulting with the detectives, photographed the area around her body in minute detail. I knew enough about homicide investigations to know that they would map the area for physical evidence, then map her life for suspects to fit that evidence. Every investigation is the same that way because most homicide victims are murdered by people they know.

I tried making conversation with the detectives, but no one answered me. I swatted at the bottle flies, all too aware of where they had been. I didn't want to be there, didn't like it, and would rather have been wrestling Lucy Chenier's couch. When the shadows down in the crook of the mountains made it hard to see, Krantz finally released the body.

The medical examiner's people zipped Karen Garcia into a blue plastic body bag, strapped the bag onto a stretcher, then worked their way up the slope. When the body was gone, Krantz called out to me. 'That's all you're here for. Beat it.'

He turned away without another word. An asshole to the end.

I watched them load the body into the coroner's van, then drove down to the little strip mall at the bottom of Lake Hollywood, where I phoned Lucy.

She said, 'I moved the couch without you.' First thing out of her mouth.

'The woman we were looking for was found murdered. Her father wanted me to be there while the crime scene people did their jobs. That's where I've been. She was thirty-two years old, and going to school so that she could work with children. Somebody shot her in the head while she was jogging at Lake Hollywood.' Lucy didn't say anything, and neither did I until I realized I had dumped it out on her. Then I said, 'Sorry.'

'Would you like to be with us tonight?'

'Yeah. Yeah, I'd like that very much. Would you guys come for dinner?'

'Tell me what to bring.'

'I'll shop. Shopping is good for the soul.'

At the Lucky Market, I bought shrimp, celery, green onions, and bell peppers. I also bought one bottle of Bombay Sapphire gin, two limes, and a case of Falstaff beer. I drank a can of the Falstaff while I was waiting in line, and got disapproving looks from the other shoppers. I pretended not to notice. They probably hadn't spent the day with a young woman with a hole in her head.

The cashier said, 'Are we having a nice day, sir?'

'Couldn't be better.' I tried not to blow beer in her face.

Twenty minutes later I pulled into the carport of the little A-frame house I have perched on the side of a mountain just off Woodrow Wilson Drive in Laurel Canyon. A fine layer of ash had blown into the carport, showing a single set of cat prints going from the side of the house to the cat hatch built into my door. People in Minnesota see things like this with snow.

The cat was waiting by his water bowl. It was empty. I put the groceries on the counter, filled the cat's bowl, then sat on the floor and listened to him drink. He's large and black, the black shot through with gray that grows from the lacework of scars on his head and shoulders. When he first came to me, he would watch me when he drank, but now he ignored me, and when I touched him, he purred. We had become a family.

When the groceries were away, I made a drink, drank most of it, then went up to my loft and took a shower. I showered twice, letting the hot run until the water was cold, but the smell of the crime scene stayed with me, and even the rush of water wasn't as loud as the buzz of the bottle flies. I pulled on a pair of loose cotton pants and went downstairs, barefoot and shirtless.

Lucy was in the kitchen, looking over the vegetables I had left in the sink.

I said, 'Hey.'

'Hey, yourself.' She eyed my empty glass without expression. 'What are we drinking?'

'Sapphire and tonic.'

'Pour. What are we making?'

'I was hoping you'd teach me how to make shrimp étouffée.'

She smiled then, softly and to herself. 'That would be nice.'

'Where's Ben?'

'Outside on the deck. We rented a tape for him to watch while you and I cook.'

'Back in five.'

'You take your time.'

Her smile pushed the bottle flies farther away.

Ben was on the deck that juts from the back of my house, hanging over the rail to look for the blacktail deer that browse in the wild grass between the olive trees below me. Here in the middle of fourteen million people we've got deer and coyote and quail and red-tailed hawks. Once, I even saw a bobcat on my deck.

I went out, leaned over the rail beside him, and looked down the slope. I saw only shadows.

'Mom said the woman you were trying to find was murdered.'

'That's right.'

'I'm sorry.'

His face was concerned and sorrowful. Nine years old.

'Me, too, buddy.' Then I smiled at him, because nine-year-olds shouldn't have such sorrow. 'Hey, when are you heading off to tennis camp?' Lucy and Ben were serious tennis players.

Ben leaned farther over the rail. 'Couple of days.'

'You don't look happy about it.'

'They make you ride horses. It's gonna smell like poop.'

Life is tough when the world smells like poop.

Inside, I got him set up with the VCR, then went back into the kitchen with Lucy. 'He says tennis camp is going to smell like poop.'

'Yes,' she said. 'It will. But it gives him the chance to meet three boys who go to his new school.'

'Is there anything you haven't thought of?'

'No. I'm a mom.'

I nodded.

'Also, it gives us two weeks alone.'

'Moms know everything.'

It took about an hour to make the étouffée. We peeled the shrimp, then wilted the vegetables in canola oil, and added tomatoes and garlic. I found peace in the small motor activity, and in telling Lucy about Frank and Joe and Karen Garcia. To cook is to heal.

Lucy said, 'Here's the important part. Pay close attention.'

'Okay.'

She pulled my face down, brushed her lips against mine, then let them linger.

'Feel better?'

I held up my hand. She laced her fingers through mine, and I kissed them.

'Better.'

We were waiting for rice to cook when Joe Pike let himself in. I hadn't expected him, but he'll drop by like that. Lucy put down her drink, and gave him a warm hug. 'I understand you knew her, Joe. I'm sorry.'

Joe seemed gigantic next to her, like some huge golem masked in shadow even in my bright kitchen.

Ben yelled, 'Hey, Joe! I've got *Men in Black*! You wanna watch?'

'Not tonight, little man.' He looked at me. 'Montoya worked out a deal with Bishop. We can report to Robbery-Homicide at Parker Center tomorrow morning. They'll assign a contact officer, and we'll be briefed.'

'All right.'

'They'll give us copies of all reports, transcripts, and witness statements.'

He was giving me the information, but I wondered why he had come. He could have phoned it over.

I said, 'What?'

'Can I talk to you about this?'

'Sure.'

Lucy and I followed Joe out onto the deck. Outside, the cat appeared, moving between Joe's legs. Joe Pike is the only other human being I've known who can touch this cat.

'How's Frank?'

'Drunk.'

Pike didn't say anything more. He picked up the cat, and stroked it. Lucy slipped her arm through mine and settled herself against me, watching him. She watches him often, and I always wonder what she's thinking when she does.

Finally, he said, 'The Garcias are my friends, not yours, but now you're going to have to carry the weight with the police.'

'You talking about Krantz?'

'Not just Krantz. You're going to have to deal with Parker Center. I can't do that.' He was talking about the entire Los Angeles police force.

'I figured that, Joe. It's not a problem.'

Lucy said, 'What do you mean, deal with Parker Center?'

Pike said, 'I won't take money from Frank, but I can't expect you not to.'

'Forget that.'

He looked at the cat, and I realized he was embarrassed. 'I don't want to forget it. I want to pay you for your time.'

'Jesus, Joe. How could you even ask that?' Now I was embarrassed, too.

Lucy said, 'Let's pretend I asked a question.'

I answered her just to change the subject. 'Parker Center is the LAPD headquarters. These cops we're dealing with, the Robbery-Homicide Division, they have their offices there. I'll have to go down tomorrow to get briefed on their investigation. It's no big deal.'

Lucy said, 'But why wouldn't they cooperate with Joe?' She wasn't making a point of it. She was just curious, but I suddenly wished she wasn't out here with us.

'Joe and LAPD don't get along. They'd freeze him out.'

Lucy smiled at me, still not understanding. 'But why on earth would they do that?'

Joe put down the cat and looked at her. 'I killed my partner.'

'Oh.'

The black lenses stayed on Lucy for a time, and then Joe left. The winds had died and the smoke hung over the canyon like a curtain, blurring the lights that glittered below us.

Lucy wet her lips, then had more of the drink. 'I shouldn't have pried.'

We went inside and had the étouffée, but nobody said very much.

Nothing stops a conversation like death.

Predation

Edward Deege, Master Carpenter, citizen of the free world and Dave Matthews fan, waited among the wild acacias that covered the ridge above Lake Hollywood until the twilight sky deepened and the bowl of the lake was dim and purple. The shadows would hide him from the police.

He had watched them work the murder site for most of the day, until the fading light had forced them to stop. Two patrol officers, one man, one woman, had been left to preserve the scene, but they seemed more interested in each other than in walking the yellow tape.

Edward had no knowledge of the murdered girl, no interest in the crime scene, and no wish to be questioned by the police. His interest was simpler: dinner. Restaurants dotted the strip malls at the foot of the mountain, where well-fed people could be depended upon to part with a dollar or two. An hour's panhandling, and Edward could purchase fresh double-A batteries for his Discman, then stroll to the food stands along Ventura Boulevard, where he might choose between a Black Angus hamburger, perhaps, or a *carne asada* burrito, or Vietnamese spring rolls. The choices were limitless.

Later, having fed, he would enjoy the climb back up to the shack he'd fashioned for himself above the lake. There, his interests would shift to partaking of a bit of the evil weed, jotting thoughts on the world eco-balance in his journal, and a satisfying bowel movement.

Now, however, Edward stayed among the trees until he was past the radio car, then worked his way down the spiderweb of roads through the neighborhoods that spilled down the mountain. He knew these neighborhoods well, walking them several times each day on his way to panhandle the traffic lights and freeway exits during the cooler parts of the day, returning to the lake at night, and when the day grew warmer.

Edward, behind his evening schedule because of the saturation of police at the lake, was anxious not to miss the prime panhandling hour. Lost time meant lost wages. He took the fast route down, headphones in place, matching his pace to Mr Dave Matthews's frenetic, multiworld beat. Edward slipped between two houses, skidded downhill along a water-course, and emerged behind a gutted house that was being remodeled. He had come this way a hundred times, and thought nothing of it. The house sat on a cul-de-sac, most of the houses there hidden by shrubs or walls. Eyeless houses. Edward often wondered if anyone really lived in them, or if they were movie facades that could be struck and moved at will. Such thoughts creeped out Edward, and he tried to avoid them. Life was uncertain enough, as is.

He was hurrying around a great blue Dumpster, expecting to see absolutely nothing, the same empty dark street that he'd seen a hundred times before, and was surprised when he saw the four-wheel-drive truck idling in the lightless street. He stopped, his first thought to run, but the hour was late, and his hunger gave him pause.

The truck was familiar. It took a moment for Edward to realize that this was the same vehicle he had earlier described to the two men looking for the jogging girl.

Run, or not run?

Hunger got the better of him. So did base greed.

Edward averted his face and plowed forward, hoping to slip past the truck and vanish between the houses before whoever was within could interfere. He was doing a good job of it, too, until the man with the sunglasses stepped out from behind the wheel. Here it was night, but he still wore the dark glasses.

'Edward?'

Edward quickened his pace. He did not like this man, whose muscular arms glowed blue in the moonlight.

'Edward?'

Edward walked faster, but the man was suddenly beside him, and jerked him roughly behind the Dumpster. Edward's headphones were pulled askew, and Dave Matthews's voice became tinny and faraway.

'Are you Edward Deege?'

'No!'

Edward raised his hands, refusing to look into the bottomless black glasses. Fear burned brightly in his stomach, and blossomed through his veins.

The man's voice softened, and grew calm. 'I think you are. Edward Deege, Master Carpenter, no job too small.'

'Leave me alone!'

The man stepped closer then, and Edward knew in that crazy, insane, heat-stroked moment that he was going to die. This man glowed with hostility. This stranger was awash in rage.

One moment, on his way to earn an honest wage; the next, at the precipice of destruction.

Life was odd.

Edward stumbled back, and the man came for him.

Powered by a triple shot of adrenaline, Edward gripped the Sony Discman and swung it at the man's head as hard as he could, but the man caught his arm, twisted, and Edward felt the pain before he heard the snap.

Edward Deege, Master Carpenter, threw himself backward and tried to scream –

– but by then the man had his throat –

– and crushed it.

7

John Chen on the case

The next morning, when John Chen ducked under the yellow police crime scene tape that sealed the trail leading down to Lake Hollywood, the pencil caddy in his shirt pocket fell into the weeds, scattering pens and pencils everywhere.

'Shit.'

Chen glanced back up the road at the two uniformed cops leaning against the front of their radio car, but they were looking the other way and hadn't seen him. Good. There was a guy cop and a girl cop, and the girl cop was pretty good-looking, so John Chen didn't want her to think he was a dork.

John gathered up the Paper-Mate Sharpwriter pencils that he collected like a dust magnet, then jammed the caddy back into his pocket. He thought better of it, and put the caddy into his evidence kit. He'd be bending over a lot today and the damned caddy would keep falling, making him look like a world-class geek. It didn't matter that once he was down at the crime scene no one would be around to see. He'd feel like a geek all the same, and John had a theory that he tried to live by: If you practiced being not-a-geek when you were alone, it would eventually rub off and you would become not-a-geek when you were around good-looking babes.

John Chen was the junior criminalist in the LAPD's Scientific Investigation Division, this being only the third case to which he'd been assigned without a supervisor. Chen was not a police officer. Like everyone else in SID, he was a civilian employee, and to be just a little on the nose about it (as John was), he couldn't have passed the LAPD's physical aptitude requirements to win a blow job from the Bunny of the Month. At six feet two, one hundred twenty-seven pounds, and with an Adam's apple that bobbed around with a life of its own, John Chen was, by his own merciless description, a geek (and this did not even include the horrendously thick glasses he was doomed to wear). His plan to overcome this handicap included working harder than anyone else in SID, rapid advancement to a senior management position (with the attendant raise in salary), and the immediate acquisition of a Porsche Boxster, with which Chen was convinced he could score major poontang.

As the criminalist assigned to the case, Chen's responsibility was any and all physical evidence that would help the detectives identify and convict the perpetrator of the crime. Chen could have rushed through his inspection of the Garcia crime scene yesterday, tagging and bagging everything in sight and leaving it to the detectives to sort out, but, in the failing twilight after Karen Garcia's body had been removed, he had decided to return today and had ordered the site sealed. The detectives in charge had closed the lake, and the two uniformed officers had spent the night guarding the site. As the male uniform had a hickey on his neck that was not in evidence yesterday, Chen suspected that they had also spent the night making out, that suspicion confirming what he believed to be an undeniable fact: Everybody was getting some but him.

Chen grimly put the good fortune of others out of his thoughts and continued along the trail until he came to the little clearing where the vic had been murdered. The wind had died sometime during the night, so the trees were straight and still, and the reservoir was a great pool of glass. It was as quiet as the proverbial tomb.

John put down his evidence kit (which looked like a large tackle box, but weighed more) and leaned over the lip of the bluff to see where the body had been. He had photographed the site yesterday before the body was moved, and had taken a sample from where the vic's blood had dripped onto a bed of olive leaves. A little metal wire with a white flag now stood at that spot. He had also tried to isolate and identify the various footprints around the body, and he believed he had done a pretty good job of separating the prints of the two men who discovered the vic (both were wearing cleat-soled hiking boots; one probably Nautica, the other probably Red Wing) and of the cops and the coroner investigator who had walked around the area like they were on a grade school field trip. The goddamned coroner investigator was supposed to be cognizant of the scene, but, in fact, didn't give a damn about anything but the stiff. Chen, however, had dutifully marked and measured each shoe print, then located it on a crime scene diagram, as he had located (and oriented) the body, the blood evidence, a Reese's Pieces wrapper and three cigarette butts (which he was certain were irrelevant), and all necessary topographical features. All the measuring and diagramming had taken a long time, and by the time he had moved up here to the clearing at the top of the draw – where the shooting occurred – he had only had time to note the scuff marks and broken vegetation where the vic had fallen. It was at this point that he had dropped a flag on the play and suggested to the detectives that he come back today. If nothing else, his coming back might score points when promotions rolled around, putting him that much closer to the 'tang-mobile.

Standing at the top of the bluff, John Chen imagined the vic at the water's edge where he had first seen her, then turned his attention to the trail. The lip of the bluff had crumbled where the vic had fallen, and, if Chen backed up a step, he could see a bright scuff at the edge of the trail. The vic had probably taken the bullet there, her left toe dragging as she collapsed, the lip giving way as she tumbled down toward the lake. He noticed something white at the edge of the trail by the scuff, and saw that it was a triangular bit of white plastic, maybe a quarter inch on a side, and soiled by what appeared to be a gray, gummy substance. It was probably nothing – most of what you found at a crime scene was nothing – but he took a marking wire from the evidence kit, marked the plastic, and noted it on his evidence diagram.

That done, he considered the trail again. He knew where the victim had been, but where was the shooter? From the wound, Chen knew that the shooter had been directly in front of her, on the trail. He squatted in the trail to try to pick out where the shooter had been standing, but couldn't. By the time the vic was discovered, by the time the police sealed the area and Chen arrived, an unknown number of walkers and runners had come by and damn near obliterated everything. Chen sighed as he stared at the trail, then shook his head in defeat. He had hoped for a shoe print, but there was nothing. So much for coming back the next day. So much for fast advancement and a poontang Porsche. His supervisor would probably raise hell about wasting overtime.

John Chen was listening to the wind and wondering what to do next when a soft voice behind him said, 'To the side.'

Chen jumped up, stumbling over his own feet as the diagram fell into the weeds.

The man said, 'We don't want extra prints on the trail.'

The man himself was standing off the trail in the weeds, and Chen wondered how he'd gotten here without Chen having heard. The man was almost as tall as Chen, but roped with lean muscle. He wore dark glasses and short military hair, and Chen was scared to death of him. For all John knew, this guy was the shooter, come back to pop another vic. He looked like a shooter. He looked like a psychopath who liked to pull the trigger, and those two damned uniforms were probably still making out, the girl slurping hickies the size of Virginia all over her partner's neck.

Chen said, 'This is a police crime scene. You're not supposed to be here.'

The man said, 'Let me see.'

He held out his hand and Chen knew he meant the diagram. Chen passed it over. It didn't occur to him not to.

First thing the man said was, 'Where's the shooter?'

Chen felt himself darken. 'I can't place him. There's too much obscuration.' He sounded whiny when he said it, and that made him even more embarrassed. 'The police are up on the road. They'll be down any minute.'

The man stayed with the diagram and seemed not to hear him. Chen wondered if he should make a run for it.

The man handed back the diagram. 'Step off the trail, John.'

'How'd you know my name?'

'It's on the document form.'

'Oh.' Chen felt five years old and ashamed of himself. He was certain he would never get that Porsche. 'Do you have any business being here? Who are you?'

The man bent close to the trail, looking at it from a sharp angle. The man stared at the scuff mark for a time, then moved up the trail a few feet where he went down into a push-up position. He held himself like that without effort, and Chen thought that he must be very strong. Worse, Chen decided that this guy probably got all the poon he could handle. Chen was just beginning to think that maybe he should join a gym (this guy obviously lived in one) when the man stepped to the side of the trail, and looked in the brush and weeds.

John said, 'What are you looking for?'

The man didn't answer, just patiently turned up leaves and twigs, and lifted the ivy.

John took one step closer and the man raised a finger, the finger saying: Don't.

John froze.

The man continued looking, his search area growing, and John never moved. He stood frozen there, wondering if maybe he should shout for help, sourly thinking that those two up in the radio car were so busy huffing and puffing that they'd never hear his cries.

The man said, 'Your evidence kit.'

John picked up his evidence kit and started forward.

The man raised the finger again, then pointed out a long half-moon route off the trail. 'That way.'

John crashed through the low brush where the man told him, ripping his pants in two places and picking up a ton of little scratches that pissed him off, but when he arrived, the man said, 'Here.'

A brass .22 casing was resting under an olive leaf.

John said, 'Holy jumpin' Jesus.' He stared at the man, who seemed to be staring back, though John couldn't tell for sure because of the dark glasses. 'How'd you find this?'

'Mark it.'

The man went back to the trail, this time squatting. John jammed a wire into the ground by the casing, then hurried to join him. The man pointed. 'Look. Here to the side.'

John looked, but saw nothing. 'What?'

'Shoe.' The man pointed closer. 'Here.'

John saw little bits and pieces of many prints, but couldn't imagine what this guy was talking about. 'I don't see anything.'

The man didn't say anything for a moment.

'Lean close, John. Use the sun. Let the light catch it, and you'll see the depression. A three-quarter print.' His voice was infinitely patient, and John was thankful for that.

John rested with his belly in the brush alongside the trail, and looked for the longest time where the man pointed. He was just about to admit that he couldn't see a goddamned thing when he finally saw it: Three-quarters of a print, partially obscured by a runner's shoe print, and so shallow on the hard edge of the trail that it couldn't have been more than three grains of dust deep. It appeared to have been made by a casual dress shoe of some kind, like that worn by a cop, but maybe not.

John said, 'The shooter?'

'It's pointing in the right direction. It's where the shooter had to be.'

John glanced back toward the shell casing. 'So you figured an automatic? That's why you looked over there?' An automatic would eject to the right, and would toss a .22 casing about four feet. Then John thought of something and squinted at the man. 'But what if the guy had used a revolver? A revolver wouldn't leave anything behind.'

'Then I wouldn't have found anything.' The man cocked his head almost as if he was amused. 'All the people around, and no one heard it. Can't silence a revolver, John.'

John felt a blush creeping up his face again. 'I know that.'

The man moved along the trail, dropping into his push-up position every few feet before rising and moving on. John thought that now would be an ideal time to run for the two uniforms, but instead jammed a wire into the ground to mark the print, and followed the man to a stand of leafy scrub sumac at the edge of the little clearing just up the trail. The man circled the trees, first one way, then another, twice bending low to the ground.

'He waited here until he saw her.'

John moved closer, careful to stay behind the man, and, sure enough, there were three perfect prints in the hard dirt that appeared to match the partial by the shell casing. As before, the prints were slight, and damn near invisible even after the man pointed them out, but John was getting better at this.

By the time John had taken it all in, the man was moving again. John hurried to wire the site before hustling to catch up.

They came to the chain-link fence that paralleled the road, and stopped at the gate. John guessed that the paved road would be as far as they could go, but the man stared across the road as if the slope on the other side was speaking to him. The radio car was to their left at the curve, but judging by the way the two cops were wrestling around in the back seat, they wouldn't notice an atom bomb going off behind them. Sluts.

The man looked up at the ridge. Off to their left were houses; to their right, nothing. The man's gaze went to a little stand of jacaranda trees at the edge of the road to their right, and then he was crossing and John was following.

John said, 'You think he crossed there?'

The man didn't answer. Okay. He wasn't talkative. John could live with that.

The man searched the slope in front of the jacarandas and found something that made his mouth twitch.

John said, 'What? C'mon?'

The man pointed to a small fan of loose dirt that had tumbled onto the shoulder of the road. 'Hid behind the trees until people passed, then went through the gate.'

'Cool.' John Chen was liking this. Big time.

They climbed the slope, the shooter's prints now pronounced in the loose soil of the side hill. They worked their way to the ridgeline, then went over the top to a fire road. John hadn't even known that a fire road was up here.

He said, 'I'll be damned.'

The man followed the fire road about thirty yards before he stopped and stared at nothing again. John waited, biting the inside of his mouth rather than again asking what the man was looking at.

But finally he couldn't stand it and said, 'What, for chrissake?'

'Car.' The man pointed. 'Parked here.' Pointed again. 'Coolant or oil drips here. Tire tread there.'

John was already marking the spots with wire.

The man said, 'Off-road tread. Long wheelbase.'

'Off-road? Like a Jeep?'

'Like that.'

John wrote notes as fast as he could, thinking that he'd have to call his office for the things he'd need to take a tire impression.

'He parked here because he's been here before. He knew where he was going.'

'You think he knew her?'

The man looked at John Chen then, and Chen reflexively stepped back. He didn't know why.

'Looked to be about a size-ten shoe, didn't it, John?'

'Uh-huh.'

'Pretty deep on the hard pack, which makes him heavier than he should be.' Pretty deep. Three grains of dust. 'You can use the shoe size and his weight to build a body type. An impression of the shoe print will give you the brand of shoe.'

'I know.' John was annoyed. Maybe John wouldn't have found any of this evidence on his own, but he wasn't an idiot.

'Take an impression of the tires. Identify the size and brand. From that, you get a list of makes.'

'I *know*.'

The man stared down at the lake now, and John wondered what could be going on behind those dark glasses.

'You one of the detectives from downtown?'

The man didn't answer.

'Well, you gotta tell me your name and badge number for the report.'

The man angled the glasses back at him. 'If you tell them this came from me, they'll discount it.'

John Chen blinked at him. 'But . . . what do I tell them about all this?'

'I was never here, John. What does that leave?'

'*I* turned the evidence?'

'If you'll play it that way.'

'Yeah. Well, sure. You bet.' His palms were damp with excitement. He felt his heart speed.

'Get the make of the tires and the list of cars. I'm going to call you. There won't be a problem with that, will there, John?'

'No, sir.' Automatic.

The man stared at him for a time, and then said something that John Chen would recall from time to time for the rest of his life, and wonder what the man had meant, and why he had said it. 'Never turn your back on love, John.'

The man slipped downhill through the brush, gone almost before Chen knew he was leaving.

John Chen slowly broke into a huge white smile, and then he was running, crashing down through the brush, tripping, stumbling, rolling once, then coming to his feet as he ran past the radio car to his SID van as fast as he could, yelling for those horny fuckers to knock off the lip lock.

Suddenly, advancement seemed a lot closer.

Suddenly, the 'tang-mobile was already parked in his garage.

Coming out a second day had paid off after all.

8

Parker Center is an eight-story white building in downtown L.A., just a few blocks from the *Los Angeles Times* and two dozen bars. The bars are small, and see most of the cop business after the shift changes; their reporter business is steady throughout the day. Letters on the side of Parker Center say POLICE DEPARTMENT – CITY OF LOS ANGELES, but the letters are small, and the sign is obscured by three skinny palm trees like maybe they're embarrassed.

The lobby guard gave me a visitor pass to clip to my lapel, phoned up to Robbery-Homicide, and four minutes later the elevator doors opened. Stan Watts peered out at me like I was eye boogers.

'Hey, Stan. How's it going?'

Watts ignored me.

'Look, no reason for us to get off on the wrong foot.'

He pushed the button for the fifth floor.

When we got up there, he led me to a large, brightly lit room, centered on a long rectangle of cubicles occupied by men with at least fifteen years behind a gold shield. Most were on phones, some were typing, and damned near everyone looked at home in the job. Krantz was talking with an overweight guy by the Mr Coffee. Williams was leaning against a desk, laughing about something. You'd never think that twelve hours ago they were swatting blowflies off a dead girl.

Krantz frowned when he saw me, and yelled, 'Dolan! Your boy is here.'

The only woman at the table was sitting by herself at the corner desk, scribbling on a yellow legal pad. She slid the pad into her desk when Krantz called, locked the drawer, and stood. She was tall, and looked strong, the way a woman who rowed crew or worked with horses might be strong. Other women worked the room, but you could tell from how they carried themselves that they weren't detectives. She was it. Guess if I were her, I'd lock my desk, too.

Dolan glared at Krantz as if he were a walking Pap smear, and glared at me even harder.

When she came over, Krantz said, 'Dolan, this is Cole. Cole, this is Samantha Dolan. You're with her.'

Samantha Dolan was wearing a stylish gray pants suit with a cameo brooch and dark blond hair that was cut short without being mannish. I made her for her early forties, but she might've been younger. When Krantz said the name, I recognized her at once from the stories and interviews and dozens of times that I'd seen her on TV.

I said, 'Pleased to meet you, Dolan. I enjoyed your series.'

Six years ago, CBS had made a television series about her based on a case in which she'd almost been killed apprehending a serial rapist. The series had lasted half a season and wasn't very good, but for a short period of time it had made her the most famous Los Angeles police officer since Joe Wambaugh. An article about her in the *Times* had focused on her case clearance rate, which was the highest ever by a woman, and the third highest in department history. I remembered being impressed. But then it dawned on me that I hadn't heard of her since.

Samantha Dolan's frown turned into a scowl. 'You liked that TV series they made about me?'

I gave her the friendly smile. 'Yeah.'

'It sucked.'

I can always tell when they like me.

Krantz checked his watch. 'We'll brief you in the conference room so this doesn't waste anybody else's time. Think about that, Cole. Right now the murderer could be getting away because one of our detectives is thinking about you instead of following up a lead.'

'You're a pip, Krantz.'

'Yeah. Get him down there, Dolan. I'll be along in a minute.'

Dolan led me to a small conference room where Watts and Williams were waiting, along with a tall thin detective named Bruly and a Hispanic detective named Salerno. Bruly whispered something to Salerno when we walked in, and Salerno smiled. Dolan took a seat without introducing me, or saying anything to the others. Maybe she didn't like them, either.

Williams said, 'This is Elvis Cole. He represents the family. He gets to keep an eye on us in case we fuck up.'

'I've already told'm about you, Williams.' I thought I might win them over with clever repartee.

Salerno grinned. 'You catch a lot of grief with that name?'

'What, Cole?'

Salerno laughed. You see about the repartee?

Krantz steamed in with a mug of coffee and a clipboard. 'You people want to keep wasting time, or you want to knock off the bullshit?'

Salerno stopped smiling.

Krantz had some of the coffee as he read over the clipboard, then said, 'Here's what we have: Karen Garcia was murdered at approximately ten A.M. Saturday morning by an unknown assailant or assailants at the Lake Hollywood Reservoir. We have recovered and impounded her car, which was located in a parking lot on Barham Boulevard. We believe the perpetrator fired one shot from a small-bore pistol at close range. Her body was discovered by two hikers the following day. We have their initial interviews in hand. We are also questioning other people known to have been at the lake on Saturday, or who live nearby, as well as people associated with the victim. Detectives from Rampart, Hollywood, West L.A., and Wilshire divisions are assisting in this effort. We have no suspects at this time.' Krantz sounded like Jack Webb.

'Is that it?'

Krantz flexed his jaw, pissed. 'The investigation's only twenty hours old. How much do you want?'

'I wasn't criticizing.'

I took out two sheets that I had typed, and slid them across the table. Krantz didn't touch them.

'This is everything that Frank Garcia told me about his daughter's activities on that Saturday, as well as everything I learned when I was trying to find her. I thought it might help. Pike and I spoke to some kids at a Jungle Juice stand who knew Karen's pattern. Their names are here, too.'

'We've already talked to them, Cole. We're mobilized. Tell that to the vic's father.' Like he couldn't be any more annoyed.

'We found a homeless man named Edward Deege below the lake. Deege claims he saw a female runner approached by a red or brown SUV. He's flaky, but you might want to question him.'

Krantz glanced irritably at his watch, like we were wasting more time than he'd allowed. Three minutes. 'Pike told us about this stuff last night, Cole. We're on it. Now, is there anything else?'

'Yeah. I need to attend the autopsy.'

Krantz and Watts traded raised eyebrows, then Krantz smiled at me. 'You're kidding me, right? Does her father want pictures?'

'It's like me going up to the lake. He just wants someone there.'

'My God.'

Watts had never stopped looking at Krantz. He cleared his throat. 'County's got a backlog down there. They got bodies stacked up, waiting two, three weeks. We're trying to get a rush, but I don't know.'

Krantz and Watts stared at each other some more, and then Krantz shrugged. 'I don't know when the autopsy's going to happen. I don't know if you can be there. I have to find out.'

'Okay. I want to see copies of any witness statements and the criminalist's report.'

'The criminalist's report isn't in yet. He's still working the scene. So far there aren't any witness statements except for the two guys who found the body.'

'If you have transcripts, I'd like to have copies.'

Krantz crossed his arms, and tipped back in the chair. 'You want to read the stuff, you can read it, but you're not making copies and you're not taking anything out of this building.'

'I'm supposed to be copied. If you've got a problem with that, we're going to have to call the A-chief, and ask him.'

Krantz sighed. 'Then we'll have to ask him. I hear you want the reports, Cole, but we don't have any reports to show you yet. As for getting copies, I'm going to have to talk that over with Bishop. If he says fine, then okay.'

I could live with that. 'Who's keeping the book, you or Watts?'

Watts said, 'Me. Why?'

'I'd like to see it.'

'No way.'

'What's the big deal? It'll save everybody time.' The murder book was a chronological record of all the facts of the investigation. It would include notes from participating officers, witness lists, forensic evidence, everything. It would also be the easiest way for me to stay up to date with their casework.

Watts said, 'Forget it. We get to trial, we'll have to explain to a defense attorney why a civilian was screwing around with our notes. We can't find something, he'll argue that you screwed with our evidence and we're so incompetent that we didn't know any better.'

'C'mon, Watts. I'm not going to take it home. You can even turn the pages, if you want. It'll be easier on everybody.'

Krantz checked his watch again and pushed up out of the chair.

'No book. We got a couple hundred people to interview, so this briefing is officially over. Here are the rules, Cole. As long as you're in this building, you're with Dolan. Anything you want, ask her. Any questions, ask her. If you gotta take a leak, she waits outside the door. You do anything without her, it violates the agreement we have with Montoya and you're history. You got it?'

'I still want to read the transcripts.'

Krantz waved at Dolan. 'Dolan will take care of that.'

Dolan glanced at Watts. 'I'm supposed to talk to the two uniforms who rolled out when her body was found.'

Krantz said, 'Salerno can talk to the uniforms. You stay with Cole. You can handle that, can't you?'

'I'd rather work the case, Harvey.' She said his name like it was another word for 'turd'.

'Your *job* is to do what I say.'

I cleared my throat. 'What about the autopsy?'

'I said I'd find out about it, and I will. Jesus Christ, we're trying to catch a killer and I've got to babysit you.'

Krantz walked out without another word. Except for Dolan, his detectives went with him. Dolan stayed in her seat, looking angry and sullen.

I said, 'Who'd you piss off to get stuck with me?'

Dolan walked away, leaving the door open for me to follow or not.

Krantz didn't want me wandering around on my own, but I guess she didn't mind.

No one had touched the two typed pages with the information I'd brought, or even looked at them. I gathered them together, and caught up with her in the hall. 'It won't be so bad, Dolan. This could be the start of a beautiful friendship.'

'Don't be an asshole.'

I spread my hands and followed, trying not to be an asshole.

When Dolan and I got back to the squad room, Krantz and Watts were talking with three men who looked like Cadillac salesmen after a bad month. One of the men was older, with a snow-white crew cut and sun-scorched skin. The other two gave me eye burn, then turned away, but the Buzz Cut stared like a worm was in my nose.

Dolan said, 'Take this chair and put it over there.'

She shoved a little secretarial chair at me and pointed at the wall near her desk. Sitting against the wall, I would look like the class dunce.

'Can't I use a desk?'

'People work at their desks. You don't want to sit there, go home.'

She stalked the length of the squad room, taking hard fast strides saying that if you didn't get out of her way, she'd knock you on your ass. She stalked back with two files, and slapped them down onto the little chair. 'The guys who found the vic are named Eugene Dersh and Riley Ward. We interviewed them last night. You want to read them, sit here and read them. Don't write on the pages.'

Dolan dropped into the seat behind her desk, unlocked the drawer, and took out her yellow pad. She was putting on quite a show.

Inside the envelopes were the transcribed interviews with Dersh and Ward, each being about ten pages long. I read the opening statements, then glanced at Dolan. She was still with the pad, her face gray with anger.

'Dolan?'

Her eyes came to me, but nothing else moved.

'As long as we're going to work together, we might as well be pleasant, don't you think?'

'We're not working together. You're here like one of the roaches that live under the coffee machine. The sooner you're gone, the faster I can go back to being a cop. We clear on that?'

'Come on, Dolan. I'm a nice guy. Want to hear my Boris Badenov impression?'

'Save it for someone who cares.'

I leaned toward her and lowered my voice. 'We can make faces at Krantz.'

'You don't want to read those things, you're wasting my time.'

She went back to the pad.

'Dolan?'

She looked up.

'You ever smile?'

Back to the pad.

'Guess not.'

A female Joe Pike.

I read both interviews twice. Eugene Dersh was a self-employed graphic designer who sometimes worked for Riley Ward. Ward owned a small advertising agency in West Los Angeles, and the two had met three years ago when Ward hired Dersh as a designer. They were also good friends, hiking or jogging together three times a week, usually in Griffith Park. Dersh was a regular at Lake Hollywood, had been up there the Saturday that Karen Garcia was killed, and had convinced Ward to join him Sunday, the day they discovered her body. As Dersh told it, they were following the trail just above the lake when they decided to venture down to the shoreline. Ward didn't like it much, and found the going hard. They were just about to climb back to the trail when they found the body. Neither man had seen anyone suspicious. Both men realized that they had disturbed the crime scene when they had searched Karen Garcia for identification, and both men agreed that Ward had told Dersh not to, but that Dersh had searched her anyway. After Dersh found her driver's license, they located a jogger with a cell phone, and called the police.

I said, 'You guys ask Dersh about Saturday?'

'He went for his walk on the opposite side of the lake at a different time of the day. He didn't see anything.'

I didn't remember that in his interview, and flipped back through the pages. 'None of that's in here. Just the part about him being up on Saturday.'

I held out the transcript for her to see, but she didn't take it.

'Watts covered it after we took over from Hollywood. You finished with those yet?' She held out her hand.

'No.'

I read the Dersh interview again, thinking that if Watts questioned Dersh about Saturday, he had probably written up notes. If Watts was keeping the murder book, he had probably put his notes there.

I looked around for Watts, but Watts had left. Krantz wasn't back yet, either.

'How long can it take to find out about the autopsy?'

'Krantz is lucky to find his ass. Relax.'

'Tell me something, Dolan. Can Krantz hack it?'

She didn't look up.

'I made a few calls, Dolan. I know you're a top cop. I know Watts is good. Krantz looks more like a politician, and he's nervous. Can he hack running the investigation, or is he in over his head?'

'He's the lead, Cole. Not me.'

'Is he going to follow up on Deege? Is he smart enough to ask Dersh about Saturday?'

She didn't say anything for a moment, but then she leaned toward me over the pad and pointed her pen at me.

'Don't worry about how we work this investigation. You wanna make conversation, make it to yourself. I'm not interested. We clear on that?'

She went back to the pad without waiting for me to answer.

'Clear.'

She nodded.

A muscular young guy in a bright yellow bowling shirt pushed a mail cart through the double doors and went to the Mr Coffee. A clip-on security badge dangled from his belt, marking him as a civilian employee. Like most police departments, LAPD used civilians whenever they could to cut costs. Most of the slots were filled by young men who hoped the experience would help them get on the job. This guy probably spent his days answering phones, delivering interoffice memos, or, if he was lucky, helping out on door-to-door searches for missing children, which was probably as close as he would ever come to being a real cop.

I glanced over at Dolan. She was staring at me.

'Okay if I get a cup of coffee?'

'Help yourself.'

'You want one?'

'No. Leave the transcripts on the chair. Stay where I can see you.' *Sieg heil!*

I strolled over to the Mr Coffee and smiled at the civilian. 'How is it?'

'The shits.'

I poured a cup anyway and tasted it. The shits.

His ID tag said that his name was Curtis Wood. Since Curtis was around all day, going from office to office and floor to floor, he probably knew which desk belonged to Stan Watts. Might even know where Watts kept the book. 'That Dolan is something, isn't she?' The professional detective goes into full-blown intelligence-gathering mode, furtively establishing rapport with the unsuspecting civilian wannabe. I was thinking I could work my way around to Watts and the murder book.

'They made a television series about her, you know?'

'Yeah, I know. I liked it.'

'I wouldn't mention it. She gets kinda weird if you bring it up.'

I gave Curtis one of my friendliest smiles and put out my hand. 'Already made that mistake. Elvis Cole.'

'Curtis Wood.' His grip said he spent a lot of time in the gym, probably trying to get in shape for the physical. He glanced at my pass.

'I'm helping Dolan and Stan Watts with the Garcia investigation. You know Watts?' The trained professional smoothly introduces Watts to the conversation.

Curtis nodded. 'Are you the guy who works for the family?'

These guys hear everything. 'That's right.' Note the relaxed technique. Note how the subject has proven receptive to the ploy.

Curtis finished his coffee and squared around to look me in the eye. 'Robbery-Homicide has the smartest detectives in the business. How's some dickhead like you come off thinking you can do better?'

He pushed the cart away without waiting for an answer.

So much for furtive intelligence gathering.

I was still standing there when Krantz steamed through the double doors, saw me, and marched over. 'What are you doing?'

'Waiting for you, Krantz. It's been an hour.'

He glowered at Dolan, who was leaning back in her chair. 'You letting him just walk around like this?'

'For Christ's sake, Harvey, I'm right here. I can shoot him if I have to.'

I said, 'I had a cup of coffee.' Like it was a federal case.

Krantz calmed down and turned back to me. 'Okay, here's the deal. We're still not sure about the autopsy, but I'll let you know this afternoon.'

'I had to wait here an hour for that?'

'You don't have to be here at all. Bishop says you can have the reports, so when they come in tomorrow we'll copy you on them. That's it.'

Stan Watts appeared in the hall, the Buzz Cut with him, but not the other two guys. Stan said, 'Harve. We're ready.' The Buzz Cut was still staring at me like I owed him money and he was trying to figure a way to get it.

Krantz nodded at them. 'Okay, Cole, that's it for today. You're out of here.'

'If I can have the reports, can I take copies of Dersh's and Ward's interviews?'

Krantz looked around for Dolan. 'Run off the copies for him.'

'You want me to suck his dick, too?'

Krantz turned red. Embarrassed.

'She's something, Krantz.'

'Get him the goddamned copies, then get him out of here.' Krantz started away, then stopped and came back to me. 'By the way, Cole. I'm not surprised you're here by yourself. I knew Pike didn't have the balls to come down here.'

'You didn't look so tough up at the lake when he stood in your face.'

Krantz stepped closer. 'You guys are in on a pass. Remember that. This is still my shop, and I'm still the man. Remember that, too.'

'Why'd Pike call you Pants?'

When I said it, Krantz flushed hard, then stalked away. I glanced over at Dolan. She was smiling, but when she saw that I was looking at her, the smile fell away. She said, 'Hang on and I'll make those copies.'

'I can make'm. Just show me where.'

'You have to enter a code. They don't want us running off union flyers or screenplays.'

Cops.

A few minutes later Dolan gave me copies of the two interviews.

'Thanks, Dolan. I guess that's it.'

'I've got to walk you out.'

'Fine.'

She brought me out to the elevators, pushed the button, and stared at the doors while we waited.

I said, 'I gotcha, didn't I?'

She looked at me.

'There at the end, with Krantz. I made you smile.'

The elevator doors opened. I got in.

'See you tomorrow, Dolan.'

She answered as the doors closed.

'Not if I see you first.'

In the Matter of Officer Joe Pike

Detective-Three Mike McConnell of the Internal Affairs Group was certain that he'd gotten a bad clam. He'd had lunch at the Police Academy's cafe some two hours ago where the special of the day was New England clam chowder, and ever since he could feel it rumbling through his intestines like the LAPD's battering ram. He'd been terrified that the Unmentionable would occur crossing the always crowded lobby here in Parker Center, where the Internal Affairs Group had their offices, or, worse still, riding up that damned elevator which had been jammed with the entire LAPD top command, not to mention most of the goddamned mayor's staff.

But so far so good, and Mike McConnell, at fifty-four years of age and two years away from a thirty-year retirement, had made it to his office for the case file, and now to the interview room, where, as senior administrative IAG officer, he could hurry that officious prick Harvey Krantz through the interview before he crapped his Jockeys.

When he walked in, Detective-Two Louise Barshop was already seated at the table, and inwardly McConnell frowned. The lead investigator on this case was that putz Harvey Krantz, whom McConnell hated, but he'd forgotten that the third IAG was a woman. He liked Louise fine, and she was a top officer, but he was having the Lord's Own rotten gas with the clam. He didn't feel comfortable farting in front of a woman. 'Hi, Louise. How's the family?'

'Fine, Mike. Yours?'

'Oh, just fine. Fine.' He tried to decide whether or not to warn her of his flatulence or just take things a step at a time and see what passed, so to speak. If he had a problem, maybe he could act like Krantz was responsible.

McConnell took his seat and had decided on the latter strategy when Krantz entered, carrying a thick stack of case files. Krantz was tall and bony, with close-set eyes and a long nose that made him look like a parrot. He had joined IAG less than a year ago after a pretty good run in West Valley burglary, and would be the junior detective present. Because it was his case, he would also handle the bulk of the questioning. Krantz made no secret that he was here to use IAG as a stepping-stone to LAPD's upper command. He had left the uniform as fast as he could (McConnell suspected the street scared him), and had sniveled his way into every stepping-stone job he could, invariably seeking out the right ass to kiss so that he could get ahead. The sniveling little prick never passed up an opportunity to let you know that he'd graduated from USC with honors, and was working on his master's. McConnell, whose personal experience with college was pulling riot duty during the late sixties, had joined the Marines right out of high school, and took great pride in how far he had risen without the benefit of a college diploma. McConnell hated Harvey Krantz, not only for his supercilious and superior manner but also because he'd found out that the little cocksucker had gone over his head two months ago and told McConnell's boss, the IAG captain-supervisor, that McConnell was mishandling three cases on which Krantz was working. The prick. McConnell had vowed on the spot that he would shaft the skinny bastard and fuck his career if it was the last thing he did. This, even though Mike McConnell only had to sweat out two more years before retiring to his beachside trailer in Mexico. Jesus, even looking at the little skeeze made McConnell's skin crawl. A human parrot.

Krantz nodded briskly. 'Hello, Louise. Mr McConnell.' Always with the 'Mr', like he was trying to underline the difference in their ages.

Louise Barshop said, 'Hi, Harvey. You ready to go?'

Krantz inspected the empty witness chair with his parrot eyes. 'Where's the subject?'

McConnell said, 'You talking about the officer we're going to question?' You see how he did? The subject, like they were in some kind of snooty laboratory!

Louise Barshop fought back a smile. 'He's in the waiting area, Harvey. Are we ready to begin?'

'I'd like to go over a few things before we start.'

McConnell leaned forward to cut him off. Something loose was shifting in his lower abdomen and he was getting a cramp. 'I'm telling you right now that I don't want to waste a lot of time with this.' He riffled through his case file. 'This kid is Wozniak's partner, right?'

Krantz looked down his parrot nose and McConnell could tell he was pissed. Good. Let him run back and bellyache to the boss. Get a rep as a whiner. 'That's right, Wozniak. I've developed this investigation myself, Mr McConnell, and I believe there's something to this.' He was investigating a uniformed patrol officer named Abel Wozniak for possible involvement in the theft and fencing of stolen goods. 'As Wozniak's partner, this guy must certainly know what Wozniak's up to, even if he himself isn't involved, and I'd like your permission to press him. Hard, if necessary.'

'Fine, fine, whatever. Just don't take too long. It's Friday afternoon, and I *want to get out of here. If something presents itself, follow it, but if this guy's in the dark, I don't wanna waste time with it.'*

Harvey made a little oomping sound to let them know he wasn't happy, then hurried out to the waiting room.

Louise said, 'Harvey's quite a go-getter, isn't he?'

'He's a prick. People like him is why they call us the Rat Squad.'

Louise Barshop looked away without responding. Probably exactly what she'd been thinking, but she didn't have the cushion of twenty-eight years on the job to say it. In IAG, the walls grew ears, and you had to be careful whose ass you kicked today because they'd be waiting their turn on you tomorrow.

The interviewee was a young officer named Joseph Pike. McConnell had read the officer's file that morning, and was impressed. The kid had been on the job for three years, and had graduated number four in his Academy class. Every fitness report he had received since then had rated Pike as outstanding. McConnell was experienced enough to know that this, in and of itself, was no guarantee against corruption; many a smart and courageous young man would rob you blind if you let him. But, even after twenty-eight years on the job, Mike McConnell still believed that the men and women who formed the police of his city were, almost to a person, the finest young men and women that the city had to offer. Over the years he had grown to feel that it was his duty – his obligation – to protect their reputation from those few who would besmirch the others. After reading Officer Pike's file, he was looking forward to meeting him. Like McConnell, Pike had gone through Camp Pendleton, but unlike McConnell, who had been a straight infantry Marine, Pike had graduated from the Marine's elite Force Recon training, then served in Vietnam, where he had been awarded two Bronze Stars and two Purple Hearts. McConnell smiled as he looked at the file, and thought that a smug turd like Krantz (who had managed to avoid military service) didn't deserve to be in the same room with a kid like this.

The door opened, and Krantz pointed to the chair where he wanted Pike to sit. The three IAG detectives were seated together behind a long table; the interviewee would sit opposite them in a chair well back from the table so as to increase his feelings of isolation and vulnerability. Standard IAG procedure.

First thing McConnell noticed was that this young officer was strac. His uniform spotless, the creases in his pants and shirt sharp, the black leather gear and shoes shined to a mirror finish. Pike was a tall man, as tall as Krantz, but where Krantz was thin and bony, Pike was filled out and hard, his shirt across his back and shoulders and upper arms pulled taut. McConnell said, 'Officer Pike.'

'Yes, sir.'

'I'm Detective McConnell, and this is Detective Barshop. Those glasses gotta go.'

Pike doffed his sunglasses, revealing brilliant blue eyes. Louise Barshop shifted in her seat.

Pike said, 'Do I need an attorney present?'

McConnell turned on the big Nagra tape recorder before answering. 'You can request consultation with an attorney, but if you do not answer our questions at this time, which we are hereby ordering you to do – and we ain't waitin' for some FOP mouthpiece to mosey over – you will be relieved of your duties and brought up on charges of refusing the administrative orders of a superior officer. Do you understand that?'

'Yes, sir.' Pike held McConnell's gaze, and McConnell thought that the boy looked empty. If he was scared, or nervous, he hid it well.

'Do you wish an attorney?'

'No, sir.'

Louise Barshop said, 'Has Detective Krantz explained why you're here?'

'No, ma'am.'

'We are investigating allegations that your radio car partner, Abel Wozniak, has been or is involved in a string of warehouse burglaries that have occurred this past year.'

McConnell watched for a reaction, but the boy's face was as flat as piss on a plate. 'How about that, son? How you feel, hearin' that?'

Pike stared at him for a moment, then shrugged so small it was tough to see.

Krantz barked, 'How long have you been partnered with Officer Wozniak?'

'Two years.'

'And you expect us to believe you don't know what he's doing?'

The blue eyes went to the parrot, and McConnell wondered what on earth could be behind those eyes. Pike didn't answer.

Krantz stood. He was given to pacing, which annoyed McConnell, but McConnell let him do it because it also annoyed the person they were questioning. 'Have you ever accepted graft or committed any act which you know to be in violation of the law?'

'No, sir.'

'Have you ever witnessed Officer Wozniak commit an act which you know to be in violation of the law?'

'No, sir.'

Louise Barshop said, 'Has Officer Wozniak ever mentioned committing such acts to you, or done or said anything that would lead you to conclude that he had?'

'No, ma'am.'

Krantz said, 'Do you know Carlos Reena or Jesus Uribe, also known as the Chihuahua Brothers?' Reena and Uribe were fences operating out of a junkyard near Whiteman Airport in Pacoima.

'I know who they are, but I don't know them.'

'Have you ever seen Officer Wozniak with either of these men?'

'No, sir.'

'Has Officer Wozniak ever mentioned them to you?'

'No, sir.'

Krantz fired off the questions as fast as Pike answered, and grew increasingly irritated because Pike would pause before answering, and each pause was a little longer or shorter than the one before it, which prevented Krantz from working up a rhythm. McConnell realized that Pike was doing this on purpose, and liked him for it. He could tell that Krantz was getting irritated because he began to shift his weight from one foot to the other. McConnell didn't like fidgeters. His first wife had been a fidgeter, and he'd gotten rid of her. McConnell said, 'Officer Pike, let me at this time inform you that you are under orders not to reveal that this interview has taken place, and not to reveal to anyone what we have questioned you about. If you do, you will be brought up on charges of failing to obey a lawful administrative order, and fired. Do you understand that?'

'Yes, sir. May I ask a question?'

'Fire away.' McConnell glanced at his watch and felt a cold sweat sprout over his skin. They had been at this only eight minutes, and the pressure in his lower gut was building. He wondered if anyone else could hear the rumble going on down there.

'Do you suspect that I'm involved?'

'Not at this time.'

Krantz glared at McConnell. 'That's still to be determined, Officer.' Krantz actually stalked around the table and leaned over so the three of them could have a little huddle, Krantz whispering, 'Please let me drive the questions, Mr McConnell. I'm trying to create a certain mood with this man. I have to make him fear me.' Saying it like McConnell was just some incompetent old fuck standing in the way of Harvey Krantz driving in the game-winning run so he could be elected Chief of Police of the Lord Jesus Christ Amen!

McConnell whispered back, 'I don't think it's workin', Harvey. He don't look scared, and I wanna finish up.' McConnell was certain that if he didn't find a way to pass some gas soon, he was gonna have a major explosion back there.

Krantz turned back to Pike and paced the length of the table. 'You don't expect us to believe this, do you?'

The blue eyes followed Krantz, but Pike said nothing.

'We're all police officers here. We've all ridden in a car.' Krantz fingered through his stack of files. 'The smart way to play this is to cooperate. If you cooperate, we can help you.'

McConnell said, 'Son, why did you become a police officer?'

Krantz snapped an ugly scowl his way, and McConnell would've given anything to slap it off his face.

Pike said, 'I wanted to do good.'

Well, there it is, McConnell thought. He was liking this boy. Liking him just fine.

Krantz made a hissing sound to let everybody know he was pissed, then snatched a yellow legal pad from the table and started barking off names. 'Tell us whether or not you know anything about the following places of business. Baker Metalworks.'

'No, sir.'

'Chanceros Electronics.'

'No, sir.'

One by one he named fourteen different warehouses scattered around the Ramparts Division area that had been burglarized, and after every location, Pike answered, 'No, sir.'

As Krantz snapped off the names, he paced in an ever-tightening circle around Pike, and McConnell would've sworn that Pike was following Krantz with his ears, not even bothering to use his eyes. McConnell reached under the table and rubbed his belly. Christ.

'Thomas Brothers Auto Parts.'

'No, sir.'

'Wordley Aircraft Supply.'

'No, sir.'

Krantz slapped the tablet in frustration. 'Are you telling us you don't know about any of this?'

'Yes, sir.'

Krantz, red-faced and eyes bulging, leaned over Pike and shouted, 'You're lying! You're in on it with him, and you're going to jail!'

McConnell said, 'I think we've walked far enough down this road, Harvey. Officer Pike seems to be telling the truth.'

Harvey Krantz said, 'Bullshit, Mike! This sonofabitch knows something!' When he said it, Krantz jabbed Pike on the shoulder with his right index finger, and the rest happened almost too fast for McConnell to see.

McConnell would later say that, for a guy who looked so calm that he might've been falling asleep, Pike came out of the chair as fast as a striking snake. His left hand twisted Krantz's hand to the side, his right clutched Krantz's throat. Pike lifted Krantz up and backward, pinning him against the wall a good six inches off the floor. Harvey Krantz made a gurgling sound and his eyes bulged. Louise Barshop jumped backward, scrambling for her purse. McConnell jumped too, shouting, 'Step back! Officer, let go and step back!'

Pike didn't let go. Pike held Harvey Krantz against the wall, Krantz's face turning purple, his eyes staring at Pike the way deer will stare at oncoming headlights.

Louise Barshop shouted, 'Leave go, Pike. Leave go now!' She had her purse, and McConnell thought she was about to pull her Beretta and cut loose.

McConnell felt his stomach clench when Pike, who hadn't let go, whispered something to Krantz that no one else could hear. For years afterward, and well into his retirement, Detective-Three Mike McConnell wondered what Pike had said, because, in that moment, in that lull amid the shouting and the falling chairs, they heard the drip-drip-drip sound and everybody looked down to see the urine running from Krantz's pants. Then the most awful smell enveloped them, and Louise Barshop said, 'Oh, God.'

Harvey Krantz had shit his pants.

McConnell said, as sternly as he could muster, 'Put him down, now, son.'

Pike did, and Harvey hunched over, his eyes filling with rage and shame as the mess spread down his pants. He lurched knock-kneed out of the room.

Pike returned to his seat as if nothing had happened.

Louise Barshop looked embarrassed and said, 'Well, I don't know.'

Mike McConnell retook his seat, considered the young officer who had just committed a dismissible offense, then said, 'He shouldn't have laid hands on you, son. That's against the rules.'

'Yes, sir.'

'That's all. We'll contact you if we need to see you again.'

Pike stood without a word and left.

Louise said, 'Well, we can't just let him leave like that. He assaulted Harvey.'

'Think about it, Louise. If we file an action, Harvey will have to state for the record that he shit his pants. Do you think he'd want to do that?' McConnell turned off the Nagra. They'd have to erase that part of the tape to protect the boy.

Louise glanced away. 'Well, no. I guess not. But we'd better ask him when he returns.'

'That's right. We'll ask him.'

Harvey Krantz would choose to let the matter drop, but Mike McConnell wouldn't. As he and Louise waited awkwardly for Krantz's return, it occurred to McConnell just how he could fuck the arrogant, supercilious little prick for going over his head the way he had. In less than six hours, McConnell would be playing cards with Detective Lieutenant Oscar Munoz and Assistant Chief Paul Winnaeker, and everyone knew that Winnaeker was the biggest loudmouth in Parker Center. McConnell was already planning how he would let the story slip, and he was already enjoying how the word of Harvey's 'accident' would spread through the department like, well, like shit through a goose. In the macho world of the Los Angeles Police Department, the only thing hated worse than a fink was a coward. McConnell had already chosen the name he would dub the little prick: Shits-his-pants Krantz. Wait'll Paul Winnaeker got hold of that!

Then McConnell felt his own guts knot and he knew that the goddamned clam had finally gotten the best of him. He rocked to his feet, told Louise he was going to check on Harvey, then hurried to the men's room with his cheeks crimped together tighter than a virgin's in a whorehouse, barely making it into the first available stall before that goddamned clam and all of its mischief came out in a roar.

As the first wave passed, he heard Harvey Krantz in the next stall, sobbing with shame. 'It's okay, boy. We'll keep the lid on. I don't think this will hurt your career too badly.'

The sobbing grew louder, and Mike McConnell smiled.

9

I spent the afternoon at my office, waiting for Krantz to call about the autopsy, then went home and waited some more. He still hadn't called by the time I went to bed, and I was getting irritated about it. At nine-forty the next morning, I still hadn't heard anything, so I called Parker Center and asked for Krantz.

Stan Watts said, 'He's not available.'

'What does that mean, Watts? He said he would call.'

'You want to know every time we wipe our asses?'

'I want to know about the autopsy. It's going on three days since she was murdered, and I'm supposed to be there. Did you get it moved up or not?' Giving back some of the irritation.

'Hang on.'

He put me on hold. LAPD had installed one of those music-while-you-wait systems. It played the theme from *Dragnet*.

I was on hold for almost ten minutes before Watts came back. 'They're making the cut this afternoon. Come on over, and I'll have someone bring you down.'

'Good thing I asked about it.'

At ten forty-five, I once more parked in the sun at Parker Center, presented myself to the lobby guard, and claimed a visitor's pass. This time when the guard phoned RHD, they let me ride up on my own. Maybe they were starting to trust me.

Stan Watts was waiting when the doors opened.

'You my guide today, Stan?'

Watts made a snort. 'Sure. You're all I got to do with my time.'

The RHD squad room was quieter than yesterday. The only face I recognized was Dolan's. She was talking on the phone at her desk with her arms crossed, and she was staring at me, almost as if she had been waiting for me to come through the doors.

I stopped, and Watts stopped with me. 'Dolan again?'

'Dolan.'

'I don't think she likes me.'

'She doesn't like anyone. Don't take it personally.'

Watts brought me over. 'I'll leave you two lovebirds alone.'

Dolan cupped her receiver. 'C'mon, Stan. How about I follow up on these calls I got? Can't someone else take him?'

Watts was already walking away. 'Krantz says you.'

Her mouth pruned and she cupped the receiver. 'Fuckin' Pants.'

Watts laughed, but he didn't turn around.

I said, 'Hi, Dolan. Long time no see.'

She pointed at the little secretarial chair, but I didn't sit.

Dolan thanked whoever she was talking to for their cooperation, asked them to call her if they remembered anything else, then hung up. She hung up hard.

I said, 'Looks like today's going to be another good day, doesn't it?'

'Speak for yourself.'

The drive from Parker Center to the L.A. County coroner's office takes about fifteen minutes, but the way Dolan launched out of the parking garage I thought we might make it in five, even in the busted-out detective ride she drew out of the motor pool. Dolan turned off the unit's mobile two-way with an angry snap as soon as she was behind the wheel, and tuned to an alternative rock station that was blaring out L7's 'Shove'. L7 is an L.A. chick band known for their aggressive, in-your-face lyrics.

I said, 'Kind of hard to talk with the radio that loud, don't you think?'

We careened out of the parking lot, leaving a smoking rubber trail. Guess she didn't agree.

L7's singer screamed that some guy just pinched her ass. The words were angry; the music was even angrier. So was Samantha Dolan. Everything in her manner said so, and said she wanted me to know it.

I cinched the seat belt, settled back, and closed my eyes. 'Too on the nose, Dolan. The music should be counter to your character, and then the statement would be more dramatic. Try Shawn Colvin.'

Dolan jerked the sedan around a produce delivery truck and blasted through an intersection that had already gone red. Horns blew. She flipped them off.

I made a big deal out of yawning. Just another day at the demolition derby.

We roared past a crowd of short, stocky people trying to cross the street to catch a bus. We missed them by at least two inches. Room to spare.

'Dolan, throttle back before you kill someone.'

She pressed the pedal harder and we rocketed up the freeway on-ramp.

I reached over, turned off the ignition, and the car went silent.

Dolan screamed, 'Are you out of your mind?!'

She hit the brakes, wrestling the dead power steering as she horsed the car to the side of the ramp. She got the car stopped and stared at me, breathing hard.

'I'm sorry you've got to eat shit from a hack brownnoser like Krantz, but it's not my fault.'

The horns started to go behind us. Something that might've been hurt flickered in Dolan's eyes, and she took a breath.

'I guess maybe you should be the lead on this case. I guess it's hard accepting the fact that you aren't.'

'You don't know me well enough to say something like that.'

'I know Krantz is scared of you, Dolan. He's scared of anyone who threatens him, so you get stuck doing the work that no one else wants to do. Like babysitting me, and running off copies, and having to sit in the back seat. I know you don't like it, and you shouldn't have to, because you're better than that.' I shrugged. 'Also, you're the woman.'

She stared at me, but now she wasn't glaring. She had lovely hands with long slender fingers, and no wedding band. She wore a Piaget watch, and the nails were so well done that I doubted she'd done them herself. I guess the television series had been good for her even if it sucked.

Dolan wet her lips, and shook her head. Like she was wondering how I could possibly know these things.

I spread my hands. 'The finest in professional detection, Dolan. I see all, I hear all.'

She gazed out the window, then nodded.

'You want to get along, we can get along.'

Grudging. Not confirming anything I'd said. Not even putting it on Krantz. She was some tough cookie, all right.

Dolan started the car, and ten minutes later we pulled down into the long curving drive that led to the rear parking lot of the L.A. County medical examiner's office behind County-USC Medical Center.

Dolan said, 'You been here before?'

'Twice.'

'I've been here two hundred times. Don't try to be tough. If you think you're going to barf, walk out and get some air.'

'Sure.'

The rear entrance opened to a yellow tile hall where the smell hit us like a sharp spike. It wasn't terrible, like bad chicken, but you knew you were smelling something here that you wouldn't smell any other place. A combination of disinfectant and meat. You knew, on some primitive level deep in the cells, that this meat was close to your own, and that you were smelling your own death.

Dolan badged an older man behind a counter, who gave us two little paper masks. Dolan said, 'We've gotta wear these. Hepatitis.'

Great.

After we put on the masks, Dolan led me along the hall through a set of double doors into a long tile cavern with eight steel tables. Each table was surrounded by lights and work trays and instruments, not unlike those you see in a dentist's office. Green-clad medical examiners were working on bodies at each table. Knowing that they were working on human beings made me try to pretend that they weren't. Denial is important.

Krantz and Williams were clustered at the last table with the Buzz Cut and his two buddies. The five of them were talking with an older, overweight woman wearing lab greenies, surgical gloves, and a Los Angeles Dodgers baseball cap. She would be the medical examiner.

Karen Garcia was on the table, and even from across the big room I could see that the autopsy was complete. The medical examiner said something to two lab techs, one of whom was washing off Karen Garcia's body with a small hose. Blood and body fluids streamed along a trough in the table and swirled down a pipe. Her body had been opened, and a blue cloth fixed to cover the top of her head. The autopsy had happened without me.

The Buzz Cut saw us first, and tipped his head. Krantz turned as we approached. 'Where the hell were you, Cole? The cut was at nine. Everybody knew that.'

'You were supposed to call me. You knew her father wanted me here.'

'I left word for you to be notified. No one called you?'

I knew he was lying. I wasn't sure why, or why he didn't want me at the autopsy, but I was as sure of it as I've ever been sure of anything. 'What am I supposed to tell her family?'

'Tell'm we fucked up. Is that what you want to hear? I'll explain it to her father myself, if that's what you want.' He waved at the body. 'Let's get out of here. This stink is ruining my clothes.'

We went back into the tile hall, where we pulled off the masks. Williams gathered the masks from everybody and tossed them in a special can.

I stepped up to the Buzz Cut. 'We haven't met. I'm Elvis Cole, employed by the family. Who are you?'

The Buzz Cut smiled at Krantz. 'We'll wait in the car, Harvey.'

The Buzz Cut and his two friends walked away.

I turned back to Krantz. 'What's going on with you, Krantz? Who are those guys? Why didn't you want me here?'

'Our lines got crossed, Cole. That's all there is to it. Look, you wanna go back in there and inspect the body, help yourself. You wanna talk to the ME, talk to her. The girl died of a .22 just like we thought. We recovered the bullet, but it's probably too deformed to give a rifle pattern. I don't know yet.'

Williams shook his head. 'No way. There won't be a pattern. Trust me.'

Krantz shrugged. 'Okay, the expert says no way. What else you want to know? There was no sign of a struggle or of any kind of sexual assault. We lasered the body for prints and fibers, but it was a wash. Look, Cole, I know you were supposed to be here, but you weren't, and what were we supposed to do? We lose our turn, it might be another three, four days before we can work into the schedule again. You wanna go see the bodies they got stacked in the cooler?'

'I want the autopsy report.'

'Sure. You want the report, fine. Might be tomorrow or the next day.'

'I want the crime scene report, too.'

'I already said you could have that, didn't I? We'll print out a copy for you when we get the autopsy report. That way you'll have everything. I'm really sorry about this, Cole. If it's a problem for the old man, I'll tell him I'm sorry, too.'

'Everybody's sorry, that it?'

Krantz grew red in the face. 'I don't need lip from some freelance like you. All you are is a peeper. If you'd been a cop, you'd know we're busting our asses. Bruly and Salerno are knocking on every door up at the lake. No one saw anything. We've interviewed two dozen people so far, and no one knows anything. Everybody loved this girl, and no one had a motive to kill her. We're not just sitting around.'

'Did you ask Dersh about the SUV?'

'C'mon, Cole. Get off of that.'

'What about the homeless guy? Anyone question him?'

'Fuck you. I don't need you telling me how to do my job.'

Krantz and Williams walked away.

'This is bullshit, Dolan, and you know it.'

Dolan's lips parted as if to say something, then closed. She didn't seem angry now. She looked embarrassed, and I thought if they were keeping secrets, she was part of it.

We drove back to Parker Center at the same furious pace, but this time I didn't bother asking her to slow down. When she let me off in the parking garage, I walked up to my car, where it had spent the noon hour parked in the sun. It was hot, but at least nobody had slashed the interior. Even parked at the police station, that can happen, and does.

I pulled out of the lot and drove exactly one block, then pulled to the curb in front of a taco shop, and used the pay phone there to call a friend of mine at the Department of Motor Vehicles. Five minutes later I had Eugene Dersh's home and work addresses, and his phone number. The addresses were the same.

I called him, and said, 'Mr Dersh, my name is Elvis Cole, calling from Parker Center. Be all right if I dropped by and asked you a couple of follow-up questions about Lake Hollywood? It won't take long.'

'Oh, sure. Are you working with Stan Watts?' Watts had been the one who interviewed him.

'Stan's down here at Parker Center, too. I was just talking with him.'

'You know how to get here?'

'I can find it.'

'Okay. See you soon.'

If Krantz wouldn't ask him about the SUV, I would.

Dersh lived in a small California bungalow in an old part of Los Feliz just south of Griffith Park. Most of the homes were Spanish stucco with faded tile roofs, and most of the people in the neighborhood appeared to be older, but as they died off, younger people like Dersh would buy their homes and renovate them. Dersh's house was neatly painted in bright Sante Fe earth colors, and, from the looks of the place, he had put a lot of work into it.

I left my car at the curb, went up the walk, and pressed the buzzer. Some of the yards still showed ash from the fire, but Dersh's was clean. He must've come out and swept. A welcome mat at the front door read *Welcome Aboard.*

A short, stocky guy in his late thirties opened the door and smiled out at me. 'Are you Detective Cole?'

'I'm the detective.'

He put out his hand. 'Gene Dersh.'

Dersh led me into an attractive room with bleached oak floors and brightly colored modern paintings over white walls. 'I'm having coffee. Would you like a cup? It's Kenyan.'

'No, thanks.'

The room opened into another at the back of the house. It was fixed with a large art table, jars of brushes and colored markers, and a high-end PowerMac. Classical music came from the back, and the house smelled of Marks-a-lots and coffee. His home felt comfortable. Dersh was wearing pressed chinos and a loose knit shirt that showed a lot of chest hair, some of it gone gray. Ink smudges tattooed his fingers. He'd been working.

'This won't take long, Mr Dersh. I only have a couple of questions.'

'Call me Gene. Please.'

'Thanks, Gene.' We sat on an overstuffed taupe couch.

'Don't feel you have to rush. I mean, what a horror for that poor girl, murdered like that. If there's any way I can help, I'm happy to do it.' He'd been like that in the interview with Watts, anxious to cooperate. Some people are like that; thrilled to be a part of a criminal investigation. Riley Ward had been more tentative and clearly uncomfortable. Some people are like that, too.

He said, 'You aren't the first today. When you called, I thought you were more of the TV people.'

'The TV people called you?'

He had some of the coffee, then put his mug on the table. His eyes were bright. 'A reporter from Channel 4 was here this morning. Channel 7 called, too. They want to know what it was like, finding her body.' He tried to make himself sound disapproving, but you could see that he was thrilled that newspeople with cameras and lights had come to talk with him. He would dine out on these stories for years.

'I'll check it out this evening. See if I can catch you.'

He nodded, smiling. 'I'm going to tape it.'

'You were up at the lake on Saturday as well, weren't you, Gene?'

'That's right.'

'You recall seeing a red or brown SUV up there, like a Range Rover or a

Four-Runner or one of those things? Might've been parked. Might've been coming in or going out?'

Dersh closed his eyes, thinking about it, then shook his head, looking disappointed. 'Gee, no, I don't think so. I mean, so many people drive those things.'

I described Edward Deege. 'You see a guy like that up there?'

He frowned, thinking. 'On Saturday?'

'Saturday or Sunday.'

The frown turned into a squint, but then he shook his head again. 'Sorry. I just don't remember.'

'I knew it was a long shot, Gene, but I was just wondering.'

'Did that man or the car have anything to do with what happened?'

'Don't know, Gene. You hear things, you have to follow up, you know?'

'Oh, sure. I just wish I could help you.'

'You know anyone else who might've been up there on Saturday?'

'Uh-uh.'

'Mr Ward wasn't with you on Saturday, was he?' If Ward was there, I could ask him, too.

'No. Riley came with me on Sunday. He'd never been up to the lake before. Can you believe that? Here's Riley, a native for chrissake. He lives, what, two miles from the lake, and he's never been there.'

'I know people who've never been to Disneyland.'

Dersh nodded. 'Amazing.'

I stood, and thanked him for his time.

'That's all you wanted?'

'Told you it wouldn't take long.'

'Don't forget. Channel 4.'

'I'll watch.'

Dersh brought his mug of Kenyan coffee to the door. 'Detective Cole? Are you going to be, ah, seeing the girl's family?'

'I will be. Yes.'

'Would you tell them how sorry I am? And give them my condolences?'

'Sure.'

'I thought I might drop around sometime, since I was the one who discovered her body. Me and Riley.'

'I'll tell her father.'

Dersh sipped at his coffee, frowning. 'If I remember anything else, I'll be sure to call. I want to help you. I really want to help catch the person who did this.'

'If you remember anything, give Stan Watts a call. Okay?'

'Stan, and not you?'

'It'd be better if you called Stan.'

I thanked him again, then went out to my car. I hadn't really expected that Dersh would have seen the SUV, but, like I told him, you hear something, you have to run it down. Especially when the cops won't.

I said, 'What was so hard about that, Krantz? It took fifteen minutes.' The detective, talking to himself.

I worked my way out of the foothills south to Franklin, then east toward Hollywood. Traffic was terrible, but I was feeling better about things, even though I hadn't learned much. Doing is better than watching, and now I felt like a doer, even though I wasn't supposed to be. I thought that I might phone Dolan and tell her that Krantz needn't go back to Dersh about the car. I could probably sound pretty smug when I said it, but Dolan probably wouldn't be impressed. Also, they would find out I'd gone to see Dersh sooner or later. I thought my telling them would make Krantz a little less apoplectic, but you never know. I was hoping it would make him worse.

I left Franklin trying to get away from the traffic, but the roads stayed bad. Another sinkhole had appeared in Hollywood like an acne crater brought on by the subway construction, and Cal Trans had several streets blocked. I turned down Western to pick up Hollywood Boulevard, found the traffic even worse, then cut onto one of the little side streets there, hoping to work my way around the worst of it. That's when the same dark blue sedan that I'd been seeing in my rearview since I'd left the hills turned in behind me.

At first I thought it was nothing. Other cars were turning to get away from the traffic, too, but those cars hadn't been floating behind me since Franklin.

Cars were moving a little better on Hollywood. I passed under the freeway, then turned north and pulled to the curb in front of a flower kiosk with huge signs printed in Spanish. *Rosas $2.99.*

The sedan pulled past, two men in the front, both with sunglasses and both yucking it up and doing their best to pretend that they weren't interested in me. Of course, maybe they weren't. Maybe all of this was a coincidence.

I copied their tag number, then bought a dozen red roses for Lucy. Serendipity should not be ignored.

I waited for a short Salvadoran man to finish with the pay phone outside the flower stand, then called my friend at the Department of Motor Vehicles. I asked her to run the tag, and waited some more.

She came back in a few seconds. 'You sure about this?'

'Yeah. Why?'

'It came back "No ID". You want me to run it again?'

'No, thanks. That's fine.'

I hung up, took the roses to my car, and sat there.

'No ID' is what you get when the car is registered to the Los Angeles Police Department.

10

The sun was settling over the city like a deflated balloon when I got to Lucy's apartment. I had stopped for groceries after the flower stand, and then a liquor store, all the while watching my rearview. The blue sedan didn't return, and if anyone else was following me, I didn't spot them. Just the kind of paranoid experience you want before a romantic evening.

When Lucy saw the roses, she said, 'Oh, they're lovely.'

'Do you see their tears?'

She smiled, but looked confused. 'What tears?'

'They're sad. Now that they've seen you, they know they're not the prettiest things on earth.'

She touched the flowers, then sighed playfully. 'They'll just have to get used to it, I guess.'

Lucy brought a small overnight bag as we went down to my car.

'Ben get off to camp okay?'

'Once he met a couple of the other kids he was fine. I set my call-forwarding to ring at your place. I hope you don't mind.'

'Of course not. You sure you don't want to take your own car?'

'This is more romantic. My lover is spiriting me away for a night of passion at his love nest in the mountains. I can come back for my car tomorrow.'

I had never thought of my house as a love nest, but there you go.

'What's in the bag?'

She smiled at me from the corner of her eye. 'Something you'll like. A surprise.'

Maybe having a love nest wasn't so bad.

It felt good to be with her, and good to be with her alone. We had been together a lot since Lucy moved to L.A., but always with Ben or other people, and usually with the major part of our time spent in the necessary tasks of moving them into their new apartment. Tonight was just for us. I wanted that, and knowing that she wanted it, too, made it all the more special. We drove in silence, rarely speaking, though smiling at each other in that way lovers do. She held the roses in her lap, occasionally lifting one to touch her nose.

When we got to the love nest, Joe's Jeep was parked in front.

Lucy smiled at me. Prettily. 'Is Joe staying over, too?'

Ha-ha. That Lucy. What a kidder, huh?

We brought the groceries and the roses in through the kitchen. Pike was standing in my living room. Anyone else would've been sitting, but there he was, holding the cat. When the cat saw Lucy, it squirmed out of Joe's arms, ran to the stairs and growled.

Lucy said, 'How nice. Always the warm welcome.'

Joe looked at the roses, and the grocery bags. 'Sorry. I should've called.'

'It couldn't hurt.'

Lucy went over and kissed his cheek. 'Don't be silly. Just don't plan on staying too long.'

The corner of Pike's mouth twitched.

Pike said, 'Got a copy of the criminalist's report. I thought you'd want to see it.'

I stopped with the bags.

'Krantz told me it wouldn't be ready until tomorrow.'

Pike nodded toward the dining-room table.

I left the bags on the kitchen counter, then went to the table and found a copy of a Scientific Investigation Division criminalist's report signed by a guy named John Chen. I flipped through a couple of pages, and saw that the report detailed the evidence found at Karen Garcia's murder site. I looked at Joe, then back at the report. 'Where'd you get this?'

'The man who wrote it. Got that copy this morning.'

'Something odd is going on here, Joe.'

Lucy said, 'Something odd is always going on here. It's Los Angeles.' She took a bottle of Dom Pérignon from one of the bags. Eighty-nine ninety-five, on sale. 'Very nice, Mr Cole. I think I may purr.'

I waved my hand like it was nothing. 'Standard fare at the love nest.'

Pike said, 'Love nest?'

I frowned at him. 'Try not to spoil the fantasy.'

Pike went to the fridge, took out a bottle of Abita beer, and tipped it toward me.

'Sure.'

He tipped the bottle at Lucy.

'No, sweetie, but thank you.' Joe Pike being called sweetie. Amazing.

Joe took out a second bottle, and brought it to me. Abita beer is this terrific beer they make in south Louisiana. Lucy brought five cases when she moved.

I said, 'Luce, you mind if I read this?'

'Not at all. I'll put away the food and pretend we're doing it together. I'll pretend some nice romantic music is on the stereo, and you're reading poetry to me. That way I can pretend I'm about to swoon.'

I looked at Joe. He shrugged.

The report was direct and easy to read because of its clarity. Two detailed drawings noted body position, bloodstains, and the location of physical evidence. The first drawing was the lower site, where Garcia's body had been found, the second was of the trail area at the top of the bluff, where the shooting had occurred. Chen noted that he had discovered several Beeman's gum wrappers, an as yet unidentified triangular bit of white plastic, a Federal Arms .22 caliber Long Rifle shell casing, and several partial and complete shoe prints. Tests were being run on the wrappers, the plastic, and the shell casing, but from the size of the shoe print Chen had estimated the shooter's body weight. I read this part aloud. 'Shooter wears a size eleven shoe with an estimated body weight of two hundred pounds. Photographs of the sole imprint have been forwarded to the FBI in Washington for identification of brand.'

Lucy said, 'My, that's romantic.' She came out and sat next to me, her foot touching mine beneath the table.

Chen had followed the tracks to tread marks left by a parked vehicle on a fire road above the lake. He had made castings of the tread marks, and had taken soil samples containing what appeared to be oil drips. All of this he had also sent along to the FBI for brand identification. He determined the tire type as F205 radials, matching any number of American and foreign SUVs. These particular F205s showed uneven wear on the front tires, indicating that the front-end camber was out of alignment.

I put down the report and looked at Joe. 'Tell you the truth, I thought Deege was making it up, him saying the car looked like yours and you were the driver.'

Pike shrugged.

'So he saw something, then had fun with it.' I glanced at the report again. 'Wow. This guy Chen does good work.'

Pike's mouth twitched.

'What?'

'Nothing.'

I tapped the pages. 'Krantz didn't lie to me only about this.' I told them how Krantz had given me the runaround about the autopsy. 'I'm sure Krantz knew when it was scheduled the whole time. Five people were at the table when we arrived, and Williams was grousing about how long the cut had taken.'

Lucy said, 'That isn't necessarily odd. You said he doesn't like you. Maybe he kept you out of the autopsy just to annoy you.'

'After the autopsy I went to see Dersh. When I left Dersh, two guys in a blue sedan were on me. It was an LAPD license.'

Pike thought about it. 'You sure they didn't follow you from Parker Center?'

'Nobody knew I was going to see Dersh, so that means they were already there. Only why would they be sitting on Dersh?'

Pike nodded. 'Now we're talking odd.'

'Yeah.'

Lucy touched my arm and traced her fingers to my hand. She tangled her feet with mine and smiled.

Joe stood. 'Guess I'll be going.'

Lucy realized what had happened and took back her hand, blushing. 'I was teasing before, Joe, really. You're welcome to stay for dinner.'

Joe's mouth twitched again, then he left.

Lucy groaned and covered her face. 'God. He must think I'm a slut.'

'He thinks you're in love.'

'Oh, sure. I'm pawing at you like I'm in heat.' I had never seen Lucy that red.

'He's happy for us.'

'Mr Stoneface? How can anyone tell what he's thinking? God, I'm so embarrassed.'

We stared at each other then, not speaking. The depth and movement that glimmered in her eyes held me until I said, 'Wait.'

The Dom wasn't as cold as I wanted, but that was okay. I filled two flute glasses, and brought them out. I put Natalie Merchant on the CD player, singing 'One Fine Day', and then I opened the big glass doors. The canyon was still. The early evening air was cooling, and the smell of summer honeysuckle was sweet. I offered Lucy my hand, and she stood. I offered a glass of the champagne. She took it.

Lucy glanced at her overnight bag, still on the floor in the kitchen, and her voice came out husky. 'I want to change. I've got a surprise for you.'

I touched her lips. 'You're my surprise, Lucille.'

Her eyes closed as she rested her head on my chest.

I thought for a moment of dead girls, heartbroken old men, and things that I did not understand, but then those thoughts were gone.

Natalie sang sweetly about a love that was meant to be. We danced, slowly, our bodies together, floating on an unseen tide that carried us out to the deck, and finally up to my bed.

Forged

The boy sat in a green world. The broad, furry elm leaves that sheltered him caught the afternoon light like floating prisms, coloring him with a warm emerald glow. Hidden there, staring between the mask of leaves at the small frame house that was his, the boy felt safe. Three black ants crawled on his bare feet, but he did not feel them.

Joe Pike, age nine. Tall for his age, but thin. An only child. Wearing shorts cut off just above the knee, and a striped tee shirt long since grimed to a murky gray. Known as a thoughtful, quiet boy at school. A bright child who kept to himself and, some teachers thought, seemed moody. In the third grade now. His first-grade teacher had asked to test the boy to see if he was retarded. The teacher then was a young man fresh from an out-of-state teachers college.

Joe's father had threatened to beat him to death and cursed him as a faggot. Joe didn't know what a faggot was, but the teacher had paled and left the school midway through the year.

Joe sat cross-legged beneath the young trees at the edge of the woods, low branches cutting his line like breaks in a jigsaw puzzle as he watched his father turn into the yard and felt the same rush of fear he felt every day at this time.

The blue Kingswood station wagon stopped by the front porch, gleaming as if he had just driven it off the showroom floor. Joe watched a short, powerfully built man get out of the wagon, climb the three wooden steps to the front porch, and disappear into the house.

Daddy.

Joe's father built the house himself, three years before Joe was born, on a plot of land at the edge of the small town in which they lived, only two miles from where Mr Pike worked as a shift foreman at the sawmill. Not much out here except some woods and a creek and some deer. It was a modest clapboard design of small unimaginative rooms sitting on a raised foundation. The house was painted a bright clean yellow with white trim, and, like the car, gleamed spotlessly in the bright sunlight. It looked like such a happy home. Every Wednesday afternoon, when Joe's father got home from work, he washed the house. Three times every week, he washed the Kingswood. Joe's father worked hard for his paycheck, and believed in taking care of the things that he had. You took care of things by keeping them clean.

Five minutes later, Joe's mother came out onto the porch and called him to supper. She was a tall woman with heavy hips, dark hair, and anxious eyes. She was almost as tall as her husband. She would have supper on the table at four o'clock on the dot because that's when Joe's father wanted it. He went to work early, came home after a long day of busting his ass, and wanted to eat when he wanted to eat. They ate at four. He would drink himself to sleep by seven.

Mrs Pike walked to the lip of the porch and called-without direction because she did not know that her son was watching her. 'You come in now, Joseph! We'll be having supper soon.'

Joe didn't answer.

'Suppertime, Joe! You'd better get home!'

Even as she said it, Joe could feel his heart quicken as the fear spread through his arms and legs. Maybe tonight would be different and nothing would happen, but he couldn't count on that. He just never knew, and so Joe waited silently until she went back into the house. He never went when she first called. He got home from school at three, but got gone fast, and stayed out of the house until the last possible minute. In the woods was better. Safe from the fear was better.

But ten minutes later his mother reappeared, and now her face was pinched and anxious. 'Goddamnit, boy, I'm warning you! Don't you make your father wait! You get your butt in here!'

She stalked back into the house and slammed the door, and only then did Joe slip between the branches.

Joe could smell the booze in the air as soon as he opened the door, and the smell of it and what it meant made his stomach knot.

His father was sitting at the kitchen table, feet up, reading the paper, and drinking straight Old Crow whiskey on the rocks from a Jiffy peanut butter jar. The table was set for dinner, but Mr Pike had pushed the plates to the side so he could put his feet up. His father watched him come in, finished what was in the glass, then jiggled the ice in the glass to draw Joe's eye. 'Fill 'er up, sport.'

Joe's big job. Filling his father's glass with Old Crow.

Joe got the bottle from the cabinet under the kitchen sink, pulled out the cork, and poured a little bit into the glass. His father scowled. 'That ain't even a swallow, boy. Give a man a fit highball and people won't think you're cheap.'

Joe filled the glass until his father grunted.

His mother said, 'You ready to eat?'

Mr Pike's answer was to take down his feet and pull his plate closer. Joe and his father didn't look anything alike. Where Joe was tall and thin for his age with a lean, bony face, his father was shorter than average, with heavy forearms and a round face. Mr Pike said, 'Christ, can't you say hello to your old man? A man comes home, he wants his family to give a damn.'

'Hi, Daddy.'

Mrs Pike said, 'Get the milk.'

Joe washed his hands at the kitchen sink, then got the milk from the refrigerator and took his seat. His mother was working on a highball of her own, and smoking a Salem cigarette. His mother told Joe that she drank just to keep some of the booze from his father. Joe also knew that she poured out some of the whiskey and refilled it with water, because he'd seen her do it. His mother had told him, 'Joe, your father's a damned mean drunk.'

And Joe guessed that his father was.

Mr Pike rose at four every morning, knocked back a couple of short ones to 'get his feet under him', then went to the mill. His father didn't drink in bars, and almost always came straight home unless he'd picked up a second job doing carpentry, which he sometimes did. If there wasn't the second job, the old man was home by three-thirty, pouring his first one even before he'd opened the paper, knocking back two or three before supper. After supper, he'd turn on the television, settle back in his EZ Boy to watch the news, and drink until he fell asleep.

Unless something set him off.

If something set him off, there would be hell to pay.

Joe knew the signs. His father's eyes would shrink into hard, tiny pits, and his face would glow bright red. His voice would get louder, letting everyone know he was about to let go, but Joe's mother would shout back at him curse for curse. That was the scariest part to Joe, the way his mother did that. It was like his father was giving them fair warning, letting them know he was losing control of himself, that there was still time to settle him down, only Mrs Pike just couldn't seem to see it. Joe was only nine, but he could see it coming as fearfully as you could see a hundred-car freight train bearing down on you if you were strapped to the tracks. Joe would see the signs, and watch with horror as his mother ignored them, just kept digging at the old man in that way she had as if she wanted to set him off, when all Joe wanted was for her to stop, was to say and do the things that would calm the old man, was just get the hell out of there and run into the woods where he could hide and be safe.

But no.

His mother was blind to it, and Joe would watch as she pushed harder and harder, Joe getting so scared that sometimes he cried, begging her to leave Daddy alone, none of it doing any good until the old man finally had had enough and jumped up, shouting, 'There's gonna be hell to pay.'

His father said it every time.

That's when he started to hit.

Mrs Pike brought a roast beef to the table for her husband to carve, then went back to the stove for mashed potatoes and string beans. His mother and father weren't looking at each other, and barely spoke, and that had Joe worried. Things had been tense between them since Saturday, when his father was watching the Game of the Week with Pee Wee Reese and Dizzy Dean. His mother was vacuuming the floor around the television, which had the old man pissed off enough, but then she'd run over the antenna wire with the vacuum and screwed up the reception at the bottom of the eighth inning in a three-two game. It had been building every day since then, with both of them retreating into silence and hostility until the air in the house seemed charged with fire.

Nine-year-old Joe Pike, the only child in this house, could feel their building anger, and he knew with terrified certainty what was coming as surely as the coming of the full moon.

Mr Pike took another slurp of his whiskey, then set about slicing the roast. He cut two pieces, then frowned. 'What kind of cheap meat is this you bought? There's a goddamned vein right through the middle.'

Here we go.

Joe's mother brought potatoes and string beans to the table without answering.

His father put down the carving knife and fork. 'You forget how to speak American? How you expect me to eat something that looks like this? They sold you a piece of bad meat.'

She still didn't look at him. 'Why don't you just calm down and eat your supper? I didn't know there was a vein. They don't put a label, this meat has a vein.'

Joe knew his mother was scared, but she didn't act scared. She looked angry and sullen.

His father said, 'I'm just saying is all. Look at this. You're not looking.'

'I'll eat the goddamned vein. Put it on my plate.'

Mr Pike's face began its slow, inexorable crawl to red. He stared at his wife. 'What kind of comment is that? What's that tone in your voice?'

Joe said, 'I'll eat it, Daddy. I like the veins.'

His father's eyes flashed, and they were as small as steel shot. 'Nobody's eating the goddamned veins.'

Mrs Pike took the roast. 'Oh, for Christ's sake, this is a helluva thing to argue about. I'll cut out the vein and then you don't have to see it.'

Mr Pike grabbed the plate from her and slammed it on the table. 'I've already seen it. It's garbage. You wanna see what I do with garbage?'

'Oh, for Christ's sake, stop.'

Her husband jumped to his feet, scooped up the roast, kicked open the kitchen door, and threw it into the backyard. 'There's what I gotta eat. Garbage. Like a dog in the yard.'

Joe seemed to grow smaller in the chair, and wished that he was. That he would shrink smaller and smaller and finally disappear. The freight train was caving in the sides of the house, coming for them now, and no one could stop it.

His mother was on her feet, too, face red, screaming, 'I'm not cleaning it up!'

'You'll goddamned clean it up, else there'll be hell to pay.'

The magic words. There'll be hell to pay.

Joe whimpered, 'I'll clean it up. I'll get it, Daddy.'

His father grabbed his arm and jerked him back into his seat. 'My ass you will. Your goddamned mother's gonna do it.'

Mrs Pike was shouting now, her own face livid. She was shaking, and Joe didn't know if it was because she was scared or angry or both. 'YOU threw the boy's supper out the door! YOU clean it up. I'll let it stay there for everybody to see.'

'I'm telling you, there's gonna be hell to pay.'

'You hate it here so damned much, maybe you oughta leave. Go live somewhere they don't have veins!'

His father's eyes shrank to wrinkled dots. Arteries bulged in his red face. He charged across the kitchen and punched his wife in the face with his fist even as Joe shrieked, knocking her into the kitchen table. The Old Crow bottle fell, shattering in a splash of glass and cheap whiskey.

His mother spit blood. 'You see what kind of man your father is? You see?'

His father punched her again, knocking her to her knees. His father didn't slap. He never slapped. He used his fists.

Joe felt liquid fire in his arms and legs, as if all the strength and control drained from them and he couldn't make himself move. His breath came in deep gasps, tears and snot blowing out of his nose. 'Daddy, don't! Please stop!'

His father punched her in the back of the head then, and she went down onto her stomach. When his mother looked up again, her left eye was closing, and blood dripped from her nose. She didn't look at her husband, she looked at her son.

Mr Pike kicked her then, knocking her onto her side, and Joe saw the fear flash raw and terrible in her eyes. She cried, 'Joe, you call the police. Have them arrest this bastard.'

Nine-year-old Joe Pike, crying, his pants suddenly warm with urine, ran forward and pushed his father as hard as he could. 'Don't hurt Mama!'

Mr Pike swung hard at the boy, clipping the side of the boy's head and knocking him sideways. Then he kicked, the heavy, steel-toed work boots catching Joe on the thigh and upending him with an explosion of nerve-shot pain.

His father kicked him again, and then the old man was over him, pulling off his belt. The old man didn't say anything, just doubled the thick leather belt and beat the boy as his mother coughed up blood. Joe knew that his father couldn't see him now. His father's tiny red eyes were lifeless and empty, clouded by a rage that Joe did not understand.

The thick belt rose and fell again and again, Joe screaming and begging his father to stop, until finally Joe found his feet and bolted through the door, running hard for the safety of the trees.

Nine-year-old Joe Pike ran as hard as he could, crashing through the low sharp branches, his legs no longer a part of him. He tried to stop running, but his legs were beyond his control, carrying him farther from the house until he tripped over a root and fell to the earth.

He lay there for what seemed like hours, his back and arms burning, his throat and nose clogged with mucus, and then he crept back to the edge of the woods. Shouts and cries still came from the house. His father kicked open the door again and threw a pot of mashed potatoes into the yard before going back into the house to curse some more.

Joe Pike sat hidden in the leaves, watching, his body slowly calming, his tears drying, feeling the slow burn of shame that came every time he ran from the house and left his mother alone with his father. He felt weak before his father's strength, fearful before his rage.

After a time, the shouting stopped and the forest grew quiet. A mockingbird chittered, and tiny flying bugs spiraled through shafts of dimming sunlight.

Joe Pike stared at his house, and seemed to float free of time and place, simply being, existing invisible and unseen here at the edge of the woods, hidden.

Here, he felt safe.

The sky grew red and the forest darkened, and still Joe Pike did not move.

He took the hurt and the fear and the shame and imagined himself folding them into small boxes, and placing those boxes away in a heavy oak trunk at the bottom of a deep stair.

He locked the trunk. He threw away the key. He made three promises:

It won't always be this way.

I will make myself strong.

I will not hurt.

As the sun set, his father emerged from the house, got into the Kingswood, and drove away.

Joe waited until the Kingswood disappeared, and then he went back to his house to see about his mother.

I will make myself strong.

I will not hurt.

It won't always be this way.

11

Light from the morning sun shone through the glass steeple that is the back of my house and filled the loft. Lucy was naked, sleeping on her belly, her hair tangled from the hours before. I snuggled against her, fitting myself to the line of her hip, enjoying her warmth.

I touched her hair. Soft. I kissed her shoulder. The salty warmth good on my lips. I looked at her, and thought how lucky I was to have this view.

Her skin was a dark gold, the line of her legs and back strong even in sleep. Lucy had attended LSU on a tennis scholarship, and worked hard to maintain her game. She carried herself with the easy grace of a natural athlete, and made love the way she played tennis, with aggression and passion, yet with moments of shyness that moved me.

The cat was perched on the guardrail at the edge of the loft, staring at her. She was in his spot, but he didn't look upset. Just curious. Maybe he also liked the view.

Lucy murmured, 'Go back to sleep.'

Her eyes half opened, drowsy with sleep.

Hearing her, the cat bolted down the stairs and growled from the living room. You just have to ignore him.

'We never got to your surprise.'

She snuggled closer. 'You can look forward to it tonight.'

I touched my tongue to her back. 'I'm looking forward to it right now.'

· She giggled. 'You're insatiable.'

'For you.'

'I've got to go to work.'

'I'll call and tell'm you're busy making love to the World's Greatest Detective. They'll understand. They always do.'

She pushed herself up on her elbows. 'Always?'

'A slip of the tongue. Sorry.'

'Not half as sorry as you're going to be.'

She jumped on top of me, but I wasn't sorry at all.

Later that morning, I took Lucy back to her car, then drove down to Parker Center without letting Krantz know I was coming. I thought he would raise nine kinds of hell because I'd gone to see Dersh, but when I pushed through the double doors, he said, 'Hope you didn't get in trouble about the autopsy screw-up.'

'No, but the family wants the report.'

'We'll have it for you in a few minutes. You ready for the brief?' Like we were buddies, and he was only too happy to include me on the team.

'Sure. By the way, you get the criminalist's report yet?'

'Should be soon. Get you both at the same time.'

Then he smiled and disappeared down the hall.

Maybe someone had slipped him Prozac. Maybe his good humor was a ploy to get me into the briefing where he and Watts and Williams would beat me to death for having seen Dersh. Whatever the case, he was still lying to me about the report.

We assembled in the conference room where Stan Watts gave the brief, telling me that they had checked out the ex-husband (playing softball in Central Park at the time of Karen's murder), finished canvassing the homes surrounding Lake Hollywood (no one had seen or heard anything), and were in the process of questioning those people with whom Karen worked and attended school. I asked Watts if they had developed a theory about the shooter, but Krantz answered, saying they were still working on it. Krantz nodded at every point Watts ticked off, more relaxed than at any other time I'd seen him, and still none of them mentioned my visit to Dersh. They had to know, and I found that even more odd than Krantz's behavior.

I said, 'When can I expect the reports? I'd like to get out of here.'

Krantz stood, reasonable, but all business. 'Dolan, see if you can chase down that paper. Get Mr Cole on his way.'

Dolan flipped him off behind his back as she left.

After the briefing, I went back to the squad room looking for her, but she wasn't at her desk. Krantz wasn't the only one in a good mood. Bruly and Salerno high-fived each other at the Mr Coffee and walked away laughing. Williams and the Buzz Cut came through the double doors, Krantz offering his hand and the Buzz Cut taking it. The Buzz Cut was smiling, too.

When I was here before, the fabric of the room had been stiff with tension, as if the place and the people were caught in the kind of electrified field that made their hair stand on end. But now something had happened to cut the juice. A sea change had occurred that had freed them from electric hair, and let them overlook the fact that I had interfered with their investigation by visiting Dersh. That is no small thing to overlook.

I got a cup of coffee, sat in the dunce chair to wait for Dolan, and wondered about it until the kid with the mail cart pushed his way in through the doors. Bruly slapped the kid a high five, the two of them laughing about something I couldn't overhear. Salerno joined the conversation, and the three of them talked for a few minutes before the kid moved on. When he moved on, he was smiling, too, and I wondered if he was smiling about the same thing as everyone else.

When he pushed the cart past, I said, 'Hey, Curtis. Can I ask you a question?'

He eyed me suspiciously. The last time I tried to milk Curtis Wood for information it hadn't gone so well.

'First, you were right when you told me that these guys are the best in the business. I've got a whole new respect for them. They really get results.'

'Uh-huh.'

'I was wondering if you hear what they say about me.'

Now he wasn't looking so much suspicious as confused.

'What do you mean?'

'I guess it's just a professional consideration, you know? I've really grown to respect these guys. I want them to respect me, too.'

I watched him hopefully, and when he understood what I was driving at, he shrugged. 'They think you're okay, Cole. They don't like it that you're around, but they've checked up on you. I heard Dolan say that if you were half as good as people say, your dick would be a foot long.'

'That Dolan is a class act, isn't she?'

'She's the best.'

This time it was going better. I had established rapport, and put our conversation on an intimate basis. Soon, I would have him eating out of my hand.

'It's good you're telling me these things, Curtis. With all the whispering today, I thought they were cracking jokes about me.'

'Nah.'

I gave a big sigh as if I were relieved, then made a show of looking around at Bruly and Salerno and the others. 'With all the grinning around here, they must've made a breakthrough in the case.'

Curtis Wood turned back to his cart. 'I don't know anything, Cole.'

'Anything about what?' Mr Innocent.

'You're so obvious, Cole. You're trying to pump me for information I don't have. If you think something's going on, have the balls to ask someone instead of just sneaking around.'

He shook his head like he was disappointed, then pushed the mail cart away, muttering.

'Foot long, my ass.'

Shown up once again by the civilian wannabe. Maybe next time he'd just shoot me.

Dolan came out of the copy room a few minutes later and handed me a large manila envelope without meeting my eyes. 'These are the reports Krantz wants me to give you.'

'What's going on around here, Dolan?'

'Nothing.'

'Then why do I get the feeling I'm being kept out of something?'

'You're paranoid.'

So much for the direct approach.

I went down to my car, raised the top for the sun, and waited. Forty minutes later, the Buzz Cut nosed out of the parking garage behind the wheel of a tan Ford Taurus. He made his way to the Harbor Freeway, then drove west through the center of Los Angeles, then north on the 405 into Westwood. He didn't hurry, and he was easy to follow. He was relaxed, too. And smiling. I copied his tag number to run his registration, but I needn't have bothered. I knew what he was as soon as he turned onto the long, straight drive of the United States Federal Building on Wilshire Boulevard.

The Buzz Cut was FBI.

I cruised past the Federal Building to a little Vietnamese place I know for squid with mint leaves. They make it hot there, the way I like it, and as I ate, I wondered why the FBI would be involved in Karen Garcia's homicide. Local police often call in the Feebs to use their information systems and expertise, but the Buzz Cut had been around at almost every step in the dance. I thought that odd. Then, when I introduced myself at the autopsy, he'd refused to identify himself. I thought that odd, too. And now the Feeb was smiling, and they don't smile for very much. You make one of those guys smile, you'd need something pretty big.

I was pondering this when the woman who owns the restaurant said, 'We make squid you like?'

'Yes. It's very nice.' The woman was small and delicate, with a graceful beauty.

'I see you in here very much.'

'I like the food.' The conversation I could do without.

The woman leaned close to me. 'Oldest daughter make this food you like. She think you very handsome.'

I followed the woman's eyes to the back of the restaurant. A younger imitation of the woman was peeking at me from the kitchen door. She smiled shyly.

I looked at her mother. Mom smiled wider and nodded. I looked back at the daughter, and she nodded, too.

I said, 'I'm married. I've got nine children.'

The mother frowned. 'You no wear ring.'

I looked at my hand. 'I'm allergic to gold.'

The mother's eyes narrowed. 'You married?'

'I'm sorry. Nine children.'

'With no ring?'

'Allergies.'

The woman went to the daughter and said something in Vietnamese. The daughter stomped back into the kitchen.

I finished the squid, then drove home to read the reports. Some days you should just eat drive-thru.

The autopsy protocol held no surprises, concluding that Karen Garcia had been killed by a single .22 caliber bullet fired at close range, striking her 3.5 centimeters above the right orbital cavity. Light to moderate powder stippling was observed at the wound entry, indicating that the bullet had been fired at a distance of between two and four feet. A cut-and-dried case of homicide by gunshot, with no other evidence having been noted.

I reread the criminalist's report, thinking that I would call Montoya to discuss these things, but as I thought about what I would say to him, I realized that the white plastic was missing.

When I read the report that Pike brought last night, I recalled that Chen had recovered a triangular piece of white plastic on the trail at the top of the bluff. He had noted that the plastic was smudged with some sort of gray matter and would have to be tested.

In this new report, that piece of plastic was not listed.

I checked the page numbers to make sure all the pages were there, then found Pike's copy and compared them. White triangle in Pike's report. No white triangle in Krantz's report.

I called Joe. 'You get the report you brought over directly from John Chen?'

'Yes.'

'He gave it to you himself?'

'Yes.'

I told him about the missing plastic.

'That sonofabitch Krantz doctored this report. That's why he delayed giving it to me.'

'If he left something out of Chen's report, I wonder what he left out of the autopsy.'

I was wondering that, too.

Pike said, 'Rusty Swetaggen might be able to help.'

'Yeah.'

I hung up and called a guy I know named Rusty Swetaggen at his restaurant in Venice. Rusty drove an LAPD radio car for most of his adult life, until his wife's father died and left them the restaurant. He retired from the cops the same day that the will was read, and never looked back. Dishing out fried cheese and tap beer was more fun than humping a radio car, and paid better. Rusty said, 'Man, it's been forever, Elvis. Emma thought you'd died.' Emma was his wife.

'Your cousin still work for the coroner?' I'd heard him talk about it, time to time.

'That's Jerry. Sure. He's still down there.'

'A woman named Karen Garcia was cut two days ago.'

'The one belongs to the tortilla guy? The Monsterito?'

'His daughter. I'm on the case with Robbery-Homicide, and I think they're keeping something from me.'

Rusty made a little whistling sound. 'Why does Robbery-Homicide have it?'

'They say it's because the tortilla guy owns a city councilman.'

'But you don't think so?'

'I think everybody's keeping secrets, and I want to know what. An ME named Evangeline Lewis did the autopsy. Another report these cops gave me was doctored, so I'm thinking maybe the autopsy protocol was altered, too. Could your cousin find out about that?'

'He doesn't work down in the labs, Elvis. He's strictly front office.'

'I know.'

I waited, letting Rusty think about it. Six years ago he had asked me to find his daughter after she'd run away with a crack dealer who'd wanted to bankroll his business by putting Rusty's little girl in the gang-bang sex business. Without telling her. I had found his daughter and destroyed the tapes, and now his daughter was safe, and married to a nice young guy she'd met in her recovery group. They had a baby. Rusty never let me pay for a drink, never let me pay for food, and after I stopped going to his place because I was embarrassed by all the free stuff, I'd had to beg him to stop sending it to my home and office. If there was a way to help me, Rusty Swetaggen would do it.

'Jerry would have to get into the case files, maybe. Or the ME's personal files.' He was thinking out loud.

'Would he do that and talk to me?'

'Who's the ME again?'

'Evangeline Lewis.'

'He'll talk to you or I'll beat him to death.' Rusty said that with an absolute lack of humor. 'I'll give him a call, but I can't say when I'll get through to him.'

'Thanks, Rusty. Call me at home.'

'Elvis?'

'Yeah, Rusty.'

'I still owe you.'

'You don't owe me anything, Rusty. You say hi to Emma. Give my love to the kids.'

'Jerry will do this for you if I have to strangle him.'

'It won't go that far, Rusty. But thanks.' You see what I mean?

I spent the next hour cleaning the house, then went out onto the deck to work my way through two *asanas* and two *katas*. As I worked, I thought about Rusty's need to repay something that didn't need to be repaid. Psychologists would speculate that Rusty wanted to vicariously participate in his daughter's salvation, as if he were somehow struggling to recapture the manhood he had lost by the violation of his daughter. I thought not. I knew Rusty Swetaggen, and I knew men like him. I believed that he was filled with such a terrible and powerful love for his daughter, and for me, that the great pressure of that welling love had to be relieved or it would kill him. People often die from love, and this is a secret we all keep, even from ourselves.

When I went back inside there was a message waiting. It was Rusty, telling me to meet his cousin before the day shift began at five the next morning at a place called Tara's Coffee Bar. He had left the address, and he had given directions.

I knew it would be like that.

12

I left the house at fifteen minutes after four the next morning, leaving Lucy warm in my bed.

Earlier that night, when she had come to me after work, we decided that she would live with me for the two weeks that Ben was away. We had gone down the mountain to her apartment, and brought back clothes and the personal items she would need. I watched Lucy place her clothes in my closet, and her toiletries in my bath, letting myself toy with a fantasy of permanence. I had lived alone for a long time, but sharing my house with her seemed natural and unforced, as right as if I had shared myself with her my entire life. If that's not love, it's close enough.

We ate take-out from an Italian place in Laurel Canyon, drank red wine, and listened to the swing sounds of Big Bad Voodoo Daddy on the stereo.

We made love on the living-room couch, and after that, as she traced the scars on my body in the bronze glow of candlelight, I felt a wetness on my back. When I looked, she was crying.

'Luce?' As gentle as a butterfly's kiss.

'If I lost you, I'd die.'

I touched her face. 'You won't lose me. Am I not the World's Greatest Detective?'

'Of course you are.' I could barely hear her.

'You won't lose me, Lucille. You won't even be able to get rid of me.'

She kissed me then, and we snuggled close and fell asleep.

I worked my way down the dark mountain curves under a sky that was clear and bright and empty of stars. No fire now. No heat now. The heat was waiting for later.

When I first came to Los Angeles, I was fresh out of the Army and accustomed to using the constellations to chart my passing. The L.A. skies are so bright with light that only the most brilliant stars are visible, and those are faint and murky. I used to joke that it was this absence of stars that caused so many people to lose their bearings, but back then, I thought answers were easy. Now I know better. Some of us find our way with a single light to guide us; others lose themselves even when the star field is as sharp as a neon ceiling. Ethics may not be situational, but feelings are. We learn to adjust, and, over time, the stars we use to guide ourselves come to reside within rather than without.

Man. I'm something at four A.M.

At four-forty I left the freeway for empty downtown streets and a pool of yellow light called Tara's Coffee Bar. Two uniformed cops sat at the counter, along with a dozen overweight, tired men who looked like they worked in the printing plant for the *Times.* Everyone was scarfing eggs and bacon and buttered toast, and no one seemed worried about cholesterol or calories.

The only man there wearing a suit said, 'You're Cole, right?' Soft, so that no one else could hear.

'That's right. Thanks for meeting me.'

Jerry Swetaggen hunched over his coffee as if it were a small fire, keeping him warm. He was a big guy like Rusty, with a pink face and ash-blond hair. He looked younger than he probably was, sort of like a bloated fourteen-year-old who'd been dressed in a hand-me-down suit. The suit looked as if it hadn't been pressed in weeks, but maybe he'd been up most of the night.

'Did you get the Garcia file?'

He glanced at the two cops. Nervous. 'I could lose my ass for this. You tell Rusty. You guys owe me big for this.'

'Sure. Coffee's on me.' You'd think I was asking for government secrets.

'You got no idea. Oh, man, you don't even come *close* to having an idea.'

'So far, the only idea I'm getting is that I could've slept in. You get me a copy of the Garcia file?'

'I couldn't get the file, but I got what you want, all right.' Jerry's hand floated to his lapel as if something lived up under the rumpled jacket and he wanted to let it out. He glanced at the cops again. Their backs were made broader by the Kevlar vests they wore under their shirts. 'Not in here. Get the coffee, and let's walk.'

'What's the big deal? What's up with Karen Garcia that has everybody so weird?'

'Get the coffee.'

I put two dollars on the table and followed him out. A warm breeze had come up, pinging us with tiny bits of grit.

'I didn't get a copy for you, but I read it.'

'Reading it won't help. I wanted to compare it with another copy I have.'

'You already got a copy? Then why'd I have to risk my ass?'

'The copy I got might have been doctored. Maybe something was left out, and I want to know what. Might just be a little thing, but I don't like it that somebody's jerking me around.'

Now he was disappointed. 'Well, Jesus. You want numbers? You want charts and graphs? I can't remember all the shit in Lewis's report.'

'What I want is to know if there was anything about her murder that the cops would want to hide.'

Jerry Swetaggen's eyebrows arched in surprise. 'You don't know?'

'Know what?'

'I figured you were already on to this, coming after Garcia. Rusty owes me, man. You owe me, too.'

'You've said that. What do we owe you for?'

'The skin section identified fourteen separate particulates at the entry wound. They're running a spec analysis now – it takes forty-eight hours to cook through the process – so Dr Lewis won't have the results until tomorrow. But everybody already knows they're gonna find the bleach.'

'The bleach?' Like I was supposed to know what that meant.

'The plastic gives them that. It's always on the plastic.'

I stared at him. 'White plastic.'

'Yeah.'

'They found white plastic in her wound.' There was no mention of plastic particulates in the autopsy report I'd read. No mention of bleach.

'The plastic comes from a bleach bottle that the shooter used as a makeshift silencer. They'll probably find adhesive from duct tape on it, too.'

'How do you know what they're going to find?'

Jerry started for the lapel again, but the two uniformed cops came out. He pretended to brush at something, turning away.

'They don't even know we're alive, Jerry.'

'Hey, it's not your ass on the line.'

The shorter cop shook himself to settle his gear, then the two of them walked up the street away from us. Off to fight crime.

When the cops were well down the street, Jerry brought out a sheet of paper that had been folded in thirds. 'You want to know what they're hiding, Cole? You want to know why it's so big?'

He shook open the page and held it out like he was about to blow my socks off. He did.

'Karen Garcia is the fifth vic murdered this way in the past nineteen months.'

I looked at the paper. Five names had been typed there, along with a brief description of each. The fifth was Karen Garcia. Five names, five dates.

I said, 'Five?'

'That's right. All done with a .22 in the head, all showing the white plastic and bleach and sometimes little bits of duct tape. These dates here are the dates of death.' Jerry smacked his hands together as if we were back East someplace where the temperature was in the thirties, instead of here in the eighties. 'I couldn't sneak out the report because they're kept together in the Special Files section, but I copied the names and this other stuff. I thought that's what you'd want.'

'What's the Special Files section?'

'Whenever the cops want the MEs to keep the lid on something, that's where they seal the files. You can only get in there by special order.'

I stared at the names. Five murders, not one murder. Julio Munoz, Walter Semple, Vivian Trainor, Davis Keech, and Karen Garcia.

'You're sure about this, Jerry? This isn't bogus?'

'Fuckin' A, I'm sure.'

'That's why Robbery-Homicide has the case. That's why they came down so fast.'

'Sure. They've had a Task Force on this thing for over a year.'

'Is there any way I can get a copy of the file?'

'Hell, no. I just told you.'

'Can I get in to read the reports?'

He showed me his palms and backed away. 'No way, man. And I don't care how much Rusty threatens. Anybody finds out I've said this much, it's my ass. I'm out of it.'

I watched him walking away, and called to stop him.

'Jerry.'

'What?'

Something with hundreds of sticky feet crawled along my spine.

'Are the five vics connected?'

Jerry Swetaggen smiled, and now his smile was scared. The smirk was gone, replaced by something fearful. 'No, man. The cops say they're random. Totally unconnected.'

I nodded.

Jerry Swetaggen disappeared into the murky light that precedes dawn. I put the sheet in my pocket, then took it out and looked at the names again.

'The cops were keeping secrets, all right.'

I guess I just needed to hear a human voice, and even my own would do.

I put away the sheet, then tried to figure out what to do. The sheer size of it was as impossible to grasp as it is to put your arms around the Goodyear blimp. This explained why the FBI were involved, and why the police didn't want me around. If the cops were keeping their Task Force secret, they probably had good reasons, but Frank Garcia would still ask what the police were doing about his daughter's murder, and I would still have to answer. I didn't want to tell him that everything was fine if it wasn't. If I told him what Jerry Swetaggen had just told me, nothing would be secret anymore, and that might hurt the police efforts to nail the shooter. On the other hand, Krantz had kept the truth from me, so I didn't know what they had, or where they were in the investigation. I could take their efforts on faith, but Frank Garcia wasn't looking for faith.

And it was his daughter who had been killed.

I went back into the diner, found a pay phone at the rear by the bathrooms, and called Samantha Dolan's office number. Sometimes the day-shift people come on early, but you never know.

On the fourth ring a guy with a smoker's voice said, 'Robbery-Homicide. Taylor.'

'Is Samantha Dolan in yet?'

'Nah. You wanna leave a message?'

'I'll call back. Thanks.'

I bought a cup of coffee to go, then drove over to Parker Center, where I parked across from the entrance in the coral light of the approaching dawn.

I tried again to figure out what I could do and how I would do it, but my thoughts were jumbled and uneasy, and left little room for solutions.

Someone had been stalking people in the streets of Los Angeles for almost two years. If the vics are connected, you call the shooter a hit man. If they're random, there's another name.

Serial killer.

13

Little by little, the night shift drifted away, and the day shift arrived. Samantha Dolan turned in driving a dark blue Beemer. Her license plate frame read I WANNA BE BARBIE, THAT BITCH HAS EVERYTHING. Most of the other cops were driving American sedans or pickup trucks, and almost all of their vehicles had a trailer hitch because cops like boats. It's genetic. Dolan didn't have a trailer hitch, but none of the other cops had Beemers. Maybe that made them even.

I followed her down, and parked next to her. She saw me as I parked, and raised her eyebrows, watching me as I got out of my car, then climbed into hers. The Black Forest leather went nicely with her Piaget watch. 'Guess the TV series wasn't so bad, Dolan. Nice car.'

'What are you doing here this early, for chrissake? I thought you private guys slept in.'

'I wanted to talk to you without Krantz around.'

She smiled, and suddenly looked very pretty. Like the bad girl next door. 'You're not going to talk dirty to me, are you? I might blush.'

'Not this time. I read through those reports you gave me and saw that some facts are missing, like the little bit of plastic the criminalist found and the white particulates that the ME IDed in Karen Garcia's wound. I was hoping maybe you could help get me the real reports.'

Dolan stopped smiling. A maroon leather daybook was in her lap, along with a briefcase and a Sig Sauer 9-millimeter. The Sig was in a clip holster, and had probably been under her front seat. Most cops carry Berettas, but the Sig is an easy gun to shoot, and very accurate. Hers had glow-in-the-dark sights.

I said, 'Do us both a favor and don't say you don't know what I'm talking about. It would make you look ordinary.'

Dolan abruptly took a cell phone from the center console and put it in her purse. 'I gave you the reports Krantz gave me. If you've got a problem with that, you should talk to him. You may not remember this, but I work for him.'

'And who does Krantz work for, the FBI?'

She continued gathering things.

'I followed the guy with the white crew cut, Dolan. I know he's FBI. I know why they're on the case, and I know what you're covering up.'

'You've been watching too much of *The X-Files*. Get out. I've got to get in to work.'

I took out the sheet of paper with the five names and gave it to her. 'If I'm Mulder, are you Scully?'

Dolan stared at the five names, then searched my face. 'Where did you get this?'

'I'm the world's greatest detective, Dolan. This isn't early for me. I never sleep.'

Dolan handed back the sheet as if she didn't believe this was happening, and by handing it back could pretend she hadn't seen it.

'Why did you come to me with this? Krantz is the lead.'

'I figure you and I can do this off the record.'

'Do what?'

'You guys have been feeding me bullshit. I want to know what's really going on with this investigation.'

Dolan was shaking her head before I finished, raising her hands. 'Absolutely not. I won't have anything to do with this.'

'I already know who the victims are, how they were murdered, and when. By the end of the day I'll have their life histories. I know you're sitting on Dersh, though I don't know why. I know Robbery-Homicide has been running a Task Force, that the FBI is involved, and that you've got the lid clamped.'

Dolan watched me as I said it, and something like a smile played on her lips. Not the bad-girl smile; more like she appreciated what I was saying.

When I finished she said, 'Jesus.'

'No. But almost.'

'I guess you're a pretty good investigator, Cole. I guess you're pretty good.'

I spread my hands and tried to look modest. No easy task. 'The world's –'

'– greatest. Yeah, I know.' She took a breath, and suddenly I liked her smile a great deal. 'Maybe you are. You've been a busy boy.'

'So talk to me, Dolan. Tell me what's going on.'

'You know what kind of spot you're putting me in?'

'I know. I don't want to come on like an adversary, Dolan, but Frank Garcia is going to ask me what's happening, and I have to decide whether or not to lie to him. You don't know me, and you probably think nothing of me, but let me tell you, I don't view that lightly. I don't like lying, I like lying to a client even less, and I will not do so unless there's a compelling reason. Understand this, Dolan, my obligation here isn't to you or Krantz or the sanctity of your investigation. It's to Frank Garcia, and later today he's going to ask. I'm sitting here right now so you can tell me why I shouldn't give this to him.'

'What if you don't like what I tell you?'

'We'll take it a step at a time.'

A sharp vertical line appeared between her eyebrows in a kind of scowl as she thought about what to tell me. I hadn't seen many women who looked good scowling, but she did.

'Remember David Berkowitz, the Son of Sam?'

'Sure. Shot people in parked cars back in New York.'

'Berkowitz just walked up to cars, shot whoever was inside – male, female, it didn't matter – then walked away. He got off on shooting people, and it didn't matter who. The Feebs call guys like that "random assassin killers", and they're the hardest type of killer to catch. You see why?'

'No connection to the victims. No way to predict who he might go for next.'

'Right.'

'Most killers kill people they know, and that's how they're caught. Husband kills wife. Junkie kills dealer. Like that. Most murders aren't solved by clues like you see on *Murder, She Wrote*, or forensics like you read about in a Patricia Cornwell novel. The easy truth of it is that almost all murders are solved when somebody rats out somebody else, when some guy says, "Elmo said he was gonna shoot him", and the cops go to Elmo's place and find the murder weapon hidden under Elmo's bed. It's that cut-and-dried. And when there isn't anyone to point the finger at Elmo, Elmo gets away.

'That's what we've got here, Cole. Julio Munoz was the only one of the vics with a sheet. He was a former prostitute who'd cleaned up his act and was working as a counselor in a halfway house in Bellflower. Semple was a roofing contractor who lived in Altadena. Totally unlike Munoz. No record, deacon in his church, the wife, the kids, the whole nine yards. Vivian Trainor was a nurse, a real straight arrow like Semple. Keech, a retired City Parks custodian, lived in a retirement home in Hacienda Heights. Now Karen Garcia. So we're talking about a street hustler, a Sunday-school teacher, a nurse, a retired custodian, and a wealthy college student. Two Hispanics, two Anglos, and a black, all from different parts of the city. We've gone to each of the families and floated the names of the other vics, but we haven't been able to link them. We're trying to tie in Garcia, but we're coming up empty there, too. Maybe you can help with that.'

'How?'

'Krantz is scared to press the girl's father, but we need to talk to him. Krantz keeps saying to let him cool down, but I don't think we can afford to wait. I want to run the names past him. I want to look through the girl's things.'

'You go through her apartment yet?'

'Of course. We didn't need his permission for that. But she might've left things at her father's house. I did, when I moved out.'

'What do you want to find?'

'Something that puts her with one of the other vics. Anything like that, and we're not talking random anymore. That makes this asshole a lot easier to catch.'

'I'll talk to Pike. We can make that happen.'

'This guy's smart. Five head shots, all with a .22, and none of the bullets match. That means he's using a different gun each time. He probably chucks them, so we won't find the murder weapons in his possession. Each shooting takes place in an isolated location, three of the five at night, so we have no wits. We've recovered two .22 caliber shell casings. No prints, both fired from different semiautomatics, and different brands. We've found shoe prints at three of the murder scenes, but, get this, three different shoe sizes, ten, ten and a half, and eleven. He's playing mix and match with us.'

'So he probably dumps the shoes, too.'

The scowl deepened, but now it wasn't because of me.

'Probably, but who knows. A nut like this, he might videotape his goddamned murders. Jesus, I wanna bust this scumbag.'

We sat there a while, neither of us saying anything until Dolan glanced at her watch.

'You've given me a lot of background, Dolan, but so far you haven't told me why I shouldn't level with Frank.'

'A lot of times, these guys will initiate contact, like Son of Sam with his letters, you see?'

'I'm listening.'

'Here was Berkowitz, getting away with murder, and he felt powerful because of it. He wanted to flaunt the fact that the cops couldn't catch him, so he started sending notes to the newspapers.'

'Okay.'

'Well, our guy hasn't done that. The Feebs say our guy doesn't want publicity, and may even be scared of it. That's one of the reasons we decided to keep this thing boxed. If we go public, maybe this guy changes his MO, or maybe he even moves to another town and starts all over again. You see what I'm saying?'

'But maybe if you go public, somebody feeds you a tip that lets you nail this guy.'

Her eyes hardened, irritated. She had nice eyes. Hazel.

'Well, shit, World's Greatest, that's the problem here, isn't it? There's no goddamned rule book on how to catch a shooter like this. You make it up as you go along, and hope you're doing the right thing. Don't you think we've talked about this?'

'Yeah, I guess you've talked about it.'

I thought about the change I'd seen up in Robbery-Homicide, how everyone was suddenly more relaxed, about the smiles and high fives, and even the grinning Feebs, and suddenly I knew there was more.

'Who's your suspect, Dolan?'

She stared at me as if she was deciding something, then wet her lips. 'Dersh.'

'*Eugene* Dersh?' That's why the cops were on him.

'Nuts like this, they can't stand not knowing what you know. They like to get up close and find out what you're saying about them. One of the ways they do it is to claim some connection to the crime. They pretend to be a witness or they say they overheard something in a bar, like that. The feds said we might get a break that way, and Krantz thinks Dersh is our break.'

'Because Dersh found this body.'

'It isn't just that. Krantz and a couple of Feebs flew back to Quantico to talk with one of their behavioral science people. They built a profile based on the evidence we had, and Dersh pretty much matches up with it.'

I frowned. 'You're talking the talk, Dolan, but you don't seem all that convinced to me.'

She didn't say anything.

'Okay, if it's Dersh, how does Riley Ward fit in?'

'If the Feebs are right, he was just Dersh's cover for finding the body. You read their statements. Ward suggested that Dersh was directive in finding the body. When Dersh tells the story, he puts a different spin on how they went down to the lake. It makes everybody wonder which story is correct and why there are two stories.'

'In other words, you've got nothing. There's no physical evidence, and you guys are trying to hang it on Dersh because of an FBI profile.'

The hazel eyes stayed with me, but she shrugged. 'No, we're trying to hang it on Dersh because Krantz is feeling heat from upstairs. Bishop gave him the Task Force a year ago, but he doesn't have anything to show for it. The brass are screaming a shitstorm, and that means Bishop can't carry Krantz forever. If another body drops, and Krantz doesn't have a suspect, he'll be out of the job.'

'Maybe they'll give it to you, Dolan.'

'Yeah. Right.' She looked away.

I thought about Dersh and his Kenyan coffee. Dersh, with the bright paintings and his house smelling of Marks-a-lots. 'What about you? Do you think it's Dersh?'

'Krantz thinks Dersh is the shooter. I think Dersh is a legitimate suspect. There's a difference.'

I took a breath and nodded, still trying to figure out what to do. 'The criminalist's report suggests the shooter was driving an off-road vehicle or an SUV. Remember the homeless guy I told you about?'

'Krantz may be a dud, Cole, but not all of us got into Robbery-Homicide on a pass. I took a ride up there yesterday, but couldn't find Mr Deege. Hollywood Division uniforms have been told to keep an eye out.'

I suddenly felt better about Frank Garcia and what I would tell him.

'Well, okay, Dolan. I'm going to sit on it.'

'You're not going to tell Garcia?'

'No. The only person I'll tell is my partner.'

'Pike.' Her eyes suddenly sparkled, and the bad girl was back. 'Christ, wouldn't Krantz love that. Joe Pike knows his big secret.'

I held out my hand. 'Nice doing business with you, Dolan. I'll give you a call later about talking to Frank.'

Her hand was cool and dry and strong. I liked the way it felt, and felt a faraway stab of guilt that I liked it a little too much.

She squeezed once, and then I opened the door to get out.

'Hey, Cole.'

I stopped.

'I didn't like passing you those bum reports.'

'I know. I could tell.'

'That's good work you did, putting all this together. You would've made a good cop.'

I let myself out of her Beemer. She watched as I walked away.

14

I reached my office just after seven, but I did not stay there. I gathered the interviews with Dersh and Ward, then walked across the street to a bagel place I like. I ordered Nova lox on a cinnamon-raisin bagel, then took a seat at a window table. An older woman at the next table smiled a good morning. I wished her a good morning back. The older man with her was reading a paper, and didn't bother with either of us. He looked snotty.

It was an ideal place in which to consider multiple homicide.

I went to the pay phone by the rest rooms, and called Joe Pike. He answered on the second ring.

'I'm at the bagel place across from the office. Karen Garcia was the fifth victim in a string of homicides going back nineteen months. The police know that, and they have a suspect.' If you're going to say it, you just have to say it.

Pike didn't respond.

'Joe?'

'I'll be there in twenty minutes.'

I reread Dersh's and Ward's interviews while I waited, all the while thinking about Eugene Dersh. Dersh didn't seem like a homicidal maniac to me, but maybe they said that about Ted Bundy and Andrew Cunanan, too.

Both Dersh's and Ward's versions of events agreed that it was Dersh who had suggested the hike at Lake Hollywood, but differed importantly about why they had left the trail to hike along the shoreline. Ward stated that it was Dersh's idea to walk along the shore, and that Dersh picked the spot where they left the trail. The police called this being 'directive', as if Dersh was directing the course of events that led to their finding the body. But where Dersh was clear and decisive in describing their actions, Ward seemed inconsistent and uncertain, and I wondered why.

The elderly woman was watching me. We traded another smile. The elderly man was still lost in the paper, neither of them having shared a word in the entire time I had been there. Maybe they had said everything they had to say to each other years ago. But maybe not. Maybe their silence wasn't two people each living separate lives, but two people who fit so perfectly that love and communication could be derived by simple proximity. In a world where people kill other people for no reason at all, you want to believe in things like that.

When Joe Pike walked in, the old man glanced up from his paper and frowned. There goes the neighborhood.

I said, 'Let's walk. I don't want to talk about it here.'

We walked along the south side of Santa Monica Boulevard, heading east into the sun. I gave Pike the sheet with the five names.

'You recognize any of these names?'

'Only Karen. These the other vics?'

'Yeah. Munoz was first.' I went through the others, giving him everything that I'd learned from both Samantha Dolan and Jerry Swetaggen. 'The cops've been trying to connect these people together, but they haven't been able to do it. Now they're thinking the guy picks his victims at random.'

'You said there's a suspect.'

'Krantz thinks it's Dersh.'

Pike stopped walking, and looked at me with all the expression of a dinner plate. The morning rush-hour traffic was heavy, and I wondered how many thousands of people passed us in just those few minutes of walking.

'The man who discovered the body?'

'Krantz is under the gun to make a collar. He wants to think that it's Dersh, but they don't have any physical evidence putting Dersh to the killings. All they have is some kind of FBI profile, so Krantz has a twenty-four-hour watch on the guy. That's how they picked me up when I went over there.'

'Mm.'

The passing traffic was reflected in Pike's glasses.

'This thing has been top secret since the beginning, Joe, and the cops want to keep it that way. The deal I made with Dolan is that we'll respect that. We can't tell Frank.'

Pike's chest expanded as he watched the traffic. His only movement. 'Big thing not to tell, Elvis.'

'Krantz may be a turd, but Dolan is a top cop, and so is Watts. Hell, most of those guys are aces. That's why they're in Robbery-Homicide. So even if Krantz is half-cocked, the rest of them are still going to work a righteous case. I think we have to give them time to work it, and that means keeping quiet about what's going on.'

Pike made a quiet snort. 'Me, helping Krantz.'

'Dolan needs to ask Frank about the four other vics and look through Karen's things. Will you talk to him?'

Pike nodded, but I'm not sure the nod was meant for me.

We walked again, neither of us speaking, and pretty soon we came to Pike's Jeep. He opened the door, but didn't get in.

'Elvis?'

'Yeah?'

'Could I see those?' He wanted the interview transcripts.

'Sure.' I gave them to him.

'You think it was Dersh?' Like if it was, you wouldn't want to be Dersh.

'I don't know, Joe. The always reliable but overworked hunch says no, but I just don't know.'

Pike's jaw flexed once, then that, too, was gone.

'I'll talk to Frank and let you know.'

Joe Pike climbed into his Jeep, pulled the door shut, and in that moment I would've given anything to see into his heart.

Pike wanted to see Eugene Dersh.

He wanted to witness him in his own environment, and see if he thought Dersh had murdered Karen Garcia. If it was possible that Dersh was the killer, then Pike would ponder what to do with that.

Pike knew from the police interview transcripts that Dersh worked at home. All LAPD interviews started that way. State your name and address for the record, please. State your occupation. Pike's instructor at the academy said that you started this way because it put the subject in the mood to answer your questions. Later, Pike had been amazed to learn how often it put the subject in the mood to lie. Even innocent people would lie. Make up a name and address that, when you tried to contact them weeks later, you would find to be an auto parts store, or an apartment building packed with illegals, none of whom spoke English.

Pike pulled into a Chevron station and looked up Dersh's address in his Thomas Brothers map. Dersh lived in an older residential area in Los Feliz where the streets twisted and wound with the contours of the low foothills. Seeing the street layout was important because Krantz's people were watching Dersh's place, and Pike wanted to know where they were.

When Pike had the names of the streets bracketing Dersh's home, he used his cell phone to call a realtor he knew, and asked her if any properties were for sale or lease on those streets. The police would establish a surveillance base in a mobile van if they had to, but they preferred to use a house. After a brief search of the multiple listing service, Pike's friend reported that there were three homes for sale in that area, two of which were vacant. She gave Pike the addresses. Comparing the addresses with Dersh's on the map, Pike saw that one of the homes was located on the street immediately north of Dersh's, and kitty-corner across an alley. That's where the police would be.

Pike worked his way across Hollywood, then wound his way into the quiet of an older neighborhood until he came to Dersh's small, neat home. Pike noted the two-story dwelling just off the alley that would be the police surveillance site. In the flicker of time as he drove past the mouth of the alley, Pike saw the glint of something shiny in the open second-floor window. The officers roosting there would have binoculars, a spotting scope, and probably a videocamera, but if Pike kept Dersh's house between them and himself, they wouldn't see him. In a combat situation, those guys would fast be a memory.

The neighborhood was easy. Small houses set back from the street, lushly planted with trees and shrubs, showing little clear ground between the houses. No one was clipping flowers in their front yards, no housekeepers were peering from their living-room windows, no strollers were passing, no yapping little dogs.

Pike parked at the curb two houses west of Dersh, then disappeared between the shrubs of the nearest house, one moment there, the next gone. In that instant when he allowed himself to be enveloped by leaves and twigs and green, he felt an absolute calm.

He moved along the near house, staying beneath the windows, then crossed between the trees into the prickly shrubs that surrounded Dersh's house. He neither touched nor disturbed the plants, but instead moved around and between them, the way he had done since he was a boy.

Pike eased to the corner of the living-room window, snuck a fast glance into a bright room, caught movement deeper within the house, and heard music. Yves Montand, singing in French.

Pike followed the west wall of the house through a small stand of rubber trees planted with ferns and pickle lilies, passing beneath the high window of a bathroom to the casement windows of Dersh's studio, where he saw two men. Dersh, the shorter of the two, wearing jeans and a Hawaiian shirt. Had to be Dersh, because the other man, younger, was wearing a suit. Dersh moved as if this place were his home; the other moved as a visitor. Pike listened. The two men were at a computer, Dersh sitting, the other man pointing over Dersh's shoulder at the screen. Pike could hear Yves Montand, and catch occasional words. They were discussing the layout of a magazine ad.

Pike watched Dersh and tried to get a sense of the man. Dersh did not appear to be capable of the things that the police suspected, but Pike knew you could not tell by appearances. He had known many men who looked and acted strong, but had cores of weakness, and he had known men who seemed timid who had shown themselves capable of great strength and of accomplishing terrible things.

Pike drew even, steady breaths, listening to the birds in the trees, and remembering the Karen Garcia with whom he had spent so much time, and how she had died. Joe considered Dersh, noting his finger strokes on the keyboard, the way he held himself, the way he laughed at something the other man said. He thought that if Dersh had killed Karen Garcia, he might end the man. He would lay open the fabric of justice, and let it be Dersh's shroud. He could do such a thing now, even here in the daylight as the police watched.

But after a time Pike eased away from the window. Eugene Dersh did not seem like a killer, but Pike would wait to see what evidence the police produced. Seeing the evidence, he would then decide.

There was always plenty of time in which to deliver justice.

School

'We did eight hundred push-ups every goddamned day, some days over two hundred chins, and they ran us. Christ, we ran ten miles every morning and another five at night, and sometimes even more than that. We weren't big guys, like badass football linemen or any of that, you know, Rambo with all those pansy protein-shake muscles bulging. We were skinny kids, mostly, all stripped down and hungry, but, hell, we could carry hundred-pound packs, four hundred rounds, and a poodle-popper uphill at a run all goddamned day. You know what we were? We were wolves. Lean and mean, and you definitely did not want us on your ass. We were fuckin' dangerous, man. That's what they wanted. Recon. That's what we wanted, too.'

– excerpt from *Young Men at War: A Case by Case Study of Post Traumatic Stress Disorder,* by Patricia Barber, Ph.D. M.F.C.C. Duke University Press, 1986

Gunnery Sergeant Leon Aimes stood on the low ridge overlooking the parched hills at Camp Pendleton Marine Training Depot just south of Oceanside, California, scanning the range with a pair of Zeiss binoculars that had been a gift from his wife. He'd been pissed as hell when he'd opened the box at his forty-fourth birthday and seen what they were because the Zeiss had set back the family three months' pay. But they were the best viewing glass in the world, none finer, and he'd gone to her later feeling like a dog to apologize for carrying on. These Zeiss were the best, all right. He would use them hunting blacktail deer this fall, and, a year from now, after his posting as a Force Recon company instructor, when he returned to Vietnam for his fourth combat tour, he would use them to hunt Charlie.

Aimes sat in a jeep with his best drinking buddy, Gunnery Sergeant Frank Horse, the two of them wearing black tee shirts, field utilities, and Alice harnesses, both of them smoking the shitty cigars they'd bought down in TJ two months before. Horse was a full-blood Mescalero Apache, and Aimes believed him to be the finest Advanced Infantry Instructor at Camp Pendleton, as well as an outstanding warrior. Aimes, though African-American, had once been told by his grandmother that he had Apache blood (which he believed) and was the descendant of great warriors (which he absolutely knew to be true), so he and Horse often joked about being in the same tribe when they'd had a little too much tequila.

107

Horse grinned at him around the cigar. 'Can't see'm, can you?'

Aimes rolled his own cigar around in his mouth. Three hundred acres of coastal desert rolled out below them, dipping down into a little creek bed before rising again to another finger ridge half a mile away. Somewhere out in those three hundred acres was a young Marine that Horse thought had the warrior spirit. 'Not yet, but I'm lookin'.'

Horse smiled wider and nodded at nothing in particular. 'He's right under your goddamned nose, Leon. Hell.'

'Bullshit he is. If he's out there, I'll find him.' Leon Aimes scowled harder and imagined a huge checkerboard laid upon the land. He carefully searched each block on the board, noting clumps of manzanita and puppy grass as he ran a mental comparison to see if anything had moved in the minutes since he'd last scanned the terrain. He could find no trace of movement, yet he knew that somewhere out there a young Marine was slowly creeping toward him.

Horse drew deep on the stogy, making an exaggerated deal out of it, and blew a great plume of smoke into the breeze. 'Been here damn near two hours, pard.' Really rubbing it in. Really digging at Leon. 'You know he's good, else you woulda found him by now. We gonna keep the boy out there all day, or has this turned into something about you instead've something about him?'

Finally, Gunnery Sergeant Leon Aimes sighed and lowered the glasses. His friend Frank Horse was a wise man as well as a warrior. 'Okay, goddamnit, where is he?'

Horse's eyes crinkled, like he'd won some kinda goddamned bet with himself, and Aimes could tell from the smile that Horse liked this boy, all right. Horse pointed off to their left and ahead of them with his cigar. 'Heading three-four-zero. See that little depression about three hundred meters out?'

Aimes saw it at once without even lifting the glasses. The barest of shadows. 'Yeah.'

Horse reached behind them for the bullhorn. 'He came up through that little cut in the creek bank out there off to the right and has been working his way up.'

Aimes spit a load of brown cigar juice, pissed. 'How in hell did you see'm?'

'Didn't see shit.' Horse spit his own load, then looked over at his friend. 'That's the way I told him to come.'

Their eyes met and Aimes smiled. 'Get the boy in here, an' let's talk to him, then.'

Horse keyed the horn and called out across the range. 'This program is terminated, Private. Come to your feet.'

The little depression three hundred meters out on heading three-four-zero did not move. Instead, a loose collection of twigs and burlap and dirt slowly rose from the earth off to their right and less than two hundred meters away. Horse's cigar nearly fell out of his jaw, and Aimes burst out laughing. Aimes clapped his old friend on the back. 'Three-four-zero, all right.'

'I coulda sworn . . .'

'Lucky that boy wasn't gonna shoot our old asses.'

Then the two combat veterans were beyond the laughing, and Aimes nodded. Horse keyed the mike again. 'Get in here, Private. Triple time.'

Running up to them across the broken ground, Aimes thought that the ghillie suit made the private look like some kind of matted Pekinese dog, all its mats bouncing up and down. Aimes said, 'He in good shape?'

'Came here in good shape.'

'Farm boy?'

'Lived in the country, but I don't think they farmed.' Aimes liked boys who grew up on the land and knew its ways.

'What kind of name is that, Pike? English? Irish?'

'Dunno. He don't talk about his people. He don't talk much at all.'

Aimes nodded. Nothing wrong with that. 'Maybe he's got nothing to say.'

Now Horse was looking a little nervous, like they had come upon something in the road that didn't sit well with him and that maybe he was hoping that they wouldn't come upon. 'Yeah, well, just so you know, he don't say much. I don't think he's stupid.'

Aimes glanced sharply at his friend. 'You know better than to waste my time with an idiot.' He glanced back at the running Marine. 'Boy ain't stupid who scores as high on his tests as this one.' This boy had tested higher than most of the college boys who came through, and he stood first in every class he was required to take.

'Well, some of the DIs find him a little odd, and some of the platoon do, too. Keeps to himself, mostly, and reads. Doesn't grabass during free time, none of that. Don't think I ever seen the boy smile once since he come to me.'

That concerned Aimes. 'You can tell a lot by a man's laugh.'

'Yeah, well.'

They watched him come closer, and finally Aimes sighed. 'Got no use for a man ain't a team player.'

Horse spit. 'We wouldn't be standing here if he wasn't. Got a lot of fast twitch in that boy, but out on the course, he'll throttle back to help his mates. Did it without having to be told, either.'

Aimes nodded, liking that one just fine. 'Then what's all this business about being odd? You say he's the best young man in your training platoon, you show me a file on this boy saying he stands top of his class, then you bring me out here and we both get snaked by a boy seventeen years old same as he had three years as a Scout/Sniper.'

Horse made a little shrug. 'Just wanted you to know, is all. He ain't your standard recruit.'

'Force Recon isn't interested in standard recruits, and you and I both know that better'n anyone. I want moral young men I can turn into professional killers. End of story.'

Horse raised his hands. 'Just wanted you to know.'

'Well, all right.' Aimes chomped on the nasty cigar and watched the young Marine. 'What is it he reads?'

'Just reads, is all. Anything he can get his hands on. Novels, history. Caught him with some Nietzsche once. Found some Basho in his locker.'

'Do tell.'

'Knew you'd like that, too.'

'Yes, sir. Yes, I do.'

Leon Aimes pondered the private with renewed interest, as he believed that all the best warriors were poets. Those old Japanese Samurai proved that, and Aimes had his own theory as to why. Aimes knew that you could fill a young man's head with all the notions of duty, honor, and country you wanted, but when the shit hit the fan and the bullets started flying, even your bravest young man didn't stand there and die for little Sally back home or even for the Stars and Stripes. If he stood at all, he stood for his buddies beside him. His love for them, and his fear of shame in their eyes, is what kept him fighting even after his sphincter let loose, and even when his world turned to hell. It took a special man to stand there all alone, without the weight of his buddies to anchor him in place, and Aimes was looking for young warriors that he could train to move and fight and win alone. Die alone, too, if that's what it took, and not just any man was up to that. But poets were different. You could take a poet and fill his heart with the notions of duty and honor, and sometimes, if you were very lucky, that was enough. Aimes had learned long ago, perhaps even in an earlier life, that a poet would die for a rose.

Horse gestured with the cigar as the private came pounding up and fell in at attention before them, the monstrous ghillie suit making the boy look like a tall, skinny haystack.

Horse said, 'Belay that ghillie suit and stand at ease, Private. This here is Gunnery Sergeant Aimes, who is just about the best Marine in this man's Corps outside of Chesty Puller and myself. You will listen up to him. Is that clear?'

'Yes, Gunnery Sergeant!' the young Marine shouted.

Private Pike peeled out of the ghillie suit, stowed it in the back of the jeep, and returned to his position. Neither Aimes nor Horse spoke while he was doing this, and, after he was done, Aimes let him stand there a minute, thinking about things. Aimes recalled from the file he had read that the young man's name was Pike, Joseph, no middle initial. He was tall, maybe about six one, all lean and corded and burned tan by the Southern California sun. His face and hands were covered in cammie greasepaint, but he had the damnedest blue eyes Aimes had ever seen, real white-boy ice-people eyes, like maybe his people came from Norway or Sweden or some damn place, which was also okay by Aimes. He had enormous respect for Vikings, and considered them almost as fine a group of warriors as his African ancestors. Aimes looked into the blue eyes and thought that they were calm, holding neither guile nor remorse. Aimes said, 'How old are you, son?' Aimes, of course, knew how old the private was, but he wanted to question the boy, get a sense of him.

'Seventeen, Gunnery Sergeant!'

Aimes crossed his arms, and the large muscles there pulled the fabric of his black Marine Corps tee shirt tight. 'Your mother sign the papers to get you in early, or you fake'm yourself?'

The boy did not answer. Beads of sweat dripped down from his scalp and etched tracks along his gaunt face. Nothing else about the boy moved.

'I didn't hear you, Marine.'

The boy floated there with no response, and Horse drifted around behind his back so the boy couldn't see him smile.

Gunnery Sergeant Leon Aimes stepped very close to the private and whispered into his ear. 'I don't like talking to myself, young man. I suggest you answer me.'

The young Marine answered. 'Don't know it's any of your business, Gunnery Sergeant.'

Horse jumped into the young Marine's face faster than an M16 chambering a fresh round, screaming so loud that his face turned purple. 'Everything in this world is the sergeant's business, Marine! Are you stupid enough to embarrass me in front of a Marine I know to be a hero in two wars, and who is a finer man than you could ever hope to be on your very best day?'

Aimes waited. The boy didn't look scared, which was good, and he didn't look arrogant, which was also good. He looked thoughtful.

Then the boy said, 'My father.'

'You in some kinda trouble, that why your old man put you in my Corps? You a car thief or a troublemaker or something like that?'

'No, Gunnery Sergeant.' The blue eyes met Leon Aimes. 'I told him that if he didn't sign the papers I would murder him.' There was no humor in the boy when he said it. None of that smart-ass attitude Aimes hated so much. The young Marine said it as simply as you say anything, but in that moment Aimes knew it to be true. And Aimes wondered about that, but it did not put him off. Violent young men often came into the Corps, and the Corps taught them how to channel that violence, else it got rid of them. So far, this young man was more than making the grade.

Gunnery Sergeant Aimes said, 'You know what Force Recon is, son?'

'Small-unit reconnaissance, Gunnery Sergeant.'

'That's right. Small units of men who go into the Valley of Death all by their lonesome little asses to gather up intelligence and/or hunt down and kill the enemy. I myself am a Force Recon warrior, which is the loftiest species of human life yet devised by God, none finer.'

Horse said, 'Fuckin'-A, bubba. None finer.'

'Recon takes a special man, and it ain't for everybody. Force Recon warriors are the finest warriors on this earth, and I don't give a rat's ass what those squid SEALs and green beanies over in the Army's Special Forces got to say about it.'

The private simply stood there, maybe seeing Aimes, maybe not, and Aimes was disappointed. Usually the spiel he just pitched got a smile out of them, but this one just stood there.

'Force Recon training is the hardest training in this man's Corps, or any *other. We run twenty miles a day in full packs. We do more push-ups than Hercules. We learn how to see in the dark like a buncha muthuhfuckin' ninjas and how to kill the enemy with the power of our minds alone and I wanna know how come you ain't smilin', Private, 'cause this is the funniest shit anybody ever laid on your ass!'*

Still no reaction.

Horse was behind the private, shaking his head and grinning again. Told you so, the grin was saying.

Aimes sighed, then uncrossed his big arms and stepped behind Pike so that he could roll his eyes. Horse was damn near busting a gut back there, trying not to laugh. 'All right, young man. I may not be Flip fuckin' Wilson, but Gunnery Sergeant Horse, who is as fine a warrior as I know, none finer, thinks you just might have what it takes to be one of my young men, and I think he might be right.' Aimes came around the other side of Pike and stopped in front of him, only now Aimes had taken anything even remotely humorous from his eyes and carefully folded it away. 'The gunnery sergeant says you're good at hand-to-hand.'

Nothing again, and Aimes wondered why this boy said so little. Maybe he just came from people who didn't say much.

Aimes unsnapped his fighting knife from its Alice sheath. He held it out handle first to the boy. 'You know what this is?'

The blue eyes never even went to the knife. 'It isn't a K-Bar.'

Aimes considered his knife. 'The standard Corps issue K-Bar fighting knife is a fine weapon, none finer, but not to a warrior such as myself.' He twirled the knife across the backs of his fingers. 'This is a handmade fighting dagger, custom-made to my specifications by a master blade maker. This edge is so goddamned sharp that if you cut yourself the asshole standing next to you starts to bleed.'

Horse nodded, pursing his lips knowingly as if truer words had never been spoken.

Aimes flipped the knife, caught its tip, then handed it to the boy, who held it in his right hand.

Aimes spread his hands. 'Try to put it in my chest.'

Pike moved without the moment's hesitation that Aimes expected, and he moved so damned blurringly fast that Aimes didn't even have time to think before he trapped the boy's arm, rolled the wrist back, and heard the awful crack as the wrist gave and the boy went down on his back.

The boy did not grimace, and he did not say a word.

Aimes and Horse both made a big deal, helping the kid to his feet, Aimes feeling just horrible, feeling like a real horseshit donut for pulling a bush stunt like that when the private put those blue eyes on him and said, 'What did you do?' Not to accuse or blame, but because he wanted to know the fact of it.

Aimes helped the young Marine into the back of the jeep, telling him, 'That was an arm trap. It's something they do in a fighting art called Wing Chun. A Chinese woman invented it eight hundred years ago.'

'Woman.' The boy almost seemed to nod, not quite but almost, thinking it through. He didn't seem bothered at all that Aimes had just broken his wrist. He said, 'You used me against me. A woman, smaller, would have to do that.'

Aimes blinked at him. 'That's right. You were driving forward. I trapped that energy and used your own momentum to roll your hand over and toward you.'

The boy looked down at his hand as if seeing it now for the first time, and cradled it.

Aimes said, 'Christ, you're fast, boy. You're so damned fast it got a little away from me. I'm sorry.'

The boy looked back up at Aimes. 'You teach stuff like that in Recon training?'

'It's not part of our normal syllabus, but I teach it to some of the men. Mostly we learn ground navigation, escape and evasion tactics, ambush techniques. The art of war.'

'Will you teach it to me?'

Aimes glanced at Horse, and Horse nodded, his job now done. He got behind the jeep's wheel and waited.

Aimes said, 'Yes, Marine. You come over and become one of my young men, I'll make you the most dangerous man alive.'

The young Marine didn't speak again until they were at the infirmary, where, in filling out the accident report, Aimes took full and complete responsibility for the injury. What the boy said to him then was, 'It's okay you hurt me.'

That evening, still feeling nauseated from guilt, Aimes and Horse practiced the art of unarmed war in the Pendleton gym with an ugly ferocity that left both men bloody as they desperately tried to burn away their shame. Later, they drank, and later still Leon Aimes confessed all to his wife, as he always did whenever one of his young men was injured and he felt responsible, and she held him until the very small hours of the dawn.

As a warrior and a man, Leon Aimes was above reproach, none finer.

Eight days later, PFC Pike, Joseph, no middle initial, completed Advanced Infantry Training even with the broken wrist, graduated with his class, and was reassigned to the Force Recon Company for additional schooling. He was rotated to the Republic of Vietnam in the waning years of the United States' involvement in that war. Leon Aimes followed the young Marine's progress, as he did with all of his young men, and noted with pride that Private Pike served with distinction.

There were none finer, just as Leon Aimes always said.

15

Pike phoned to tell me that Frank would see us at three that afternoon. I passed the word to Dolan, who said, 'I'm impressed, World's Greatest. I guess you're kinda useful.'

'Are you going to call me that, Dolan?'

'Beats some other things that come to mind.'

These cops think they're such a riot.

When I arrived, Frank Garcia's home was as still as a sleeping pit bull and just as inviting. No cop brass now, no city councilman; just a mourning old man and his housekeeper. I wondered if Frank would see the lie in my eyes, and thought that maybe I should borrow Pike's sunglasses.

I parked in the shade cast by one of the big maples to wait for Pike and Dolan. The tree and the neighborhood were so silent that if one of the fat green leaves fell you would hear it hit the street. The devil wind was gone, but I could not escape the feeling that it was only resting, hiding in the dry, hard canyons to the north to gather its strength before clawing back through the city from a surprising and unexpected direction.

Pike arrived a few minutes later, and got into my car. 'I saw Dersh.'

Anyone else would be joking, but Pike doesn't joke. 'You saw Dersh. You *spoke* with him?'

'No. I just saw him.'

'You went over there just to *look* at him.'

'Mm.'

'Why on earth did you go see him?'

'Needed to.'

'Well, that explains it.'

You see what I have to deal with?

Dolan parked her Beemer across the street. She was smoking, and dropped her butt on the street after she got out of her car. We climbed out to meet her.

'What does he know?'

'He knows what I know.' He. Like Pike wasn't there.

Dolan considered Joe for a moment, then wet her lips. 'Can you keep your mouth shut?'

Joe didn't respond.

Dolan frowned. 'Well?'

I said, 'You got your answer, Dolan.'

Dolan grinned at Pike. 'Yeah. I heard you don't say much. Keep it that way.'

Dolan walked on ahead of us toward the house. Pike and I looked at each other.

'She's on the tough side.'

Pike said, 'Mm.'

The housekeeper let us in, and led us to the living room. She glanced nervously at Dolan as we went, almost as if she could sense that Dolan was a cop and that there might be trouble.

In the living room, Frank was staring out the French doors at the pool and the fruit trees where the stone lions prowled. It had been only three days since I'd seen him, but his skin was pasty with a drunk's sweat, his hair was greasy, and the air was sharp with BO. A short glass, now empty, rested in his lap. Maybe it had to be that way when you lost your only child.

Pike said, 'Frank.'

Frank gazed at Dolan without comprehension, then looked at Joe. 'Is Karen all right?'

'How much have you had to drink?'

'Don't you start that with me, Joe. Don't you start that.'

Joe went over and took the glass. 'This is Detective Dolan, the one I told you about. She needs to ask questions.'

'Hello, Mr Garcia. I'm sorry for your loss.' Dolan held up her gold detective's shield.

Frank squinted at the badge, then considered Dolan almost as if he was afraid to ask the thing he most wanted to know. 'Who killed my daughter?'

'That's why I'm here, sir. We're trying to find out.'

'You people been on this for a week. Don't you have any idea who did this?'

It couldn't have been more pointed than that.

Dolan smiled gently, telling him that she understood his pain, and perhaps even shared it. 'I need to ask you about some people that you or Karen might've known.'

Frank Garcia shook his head, but when he spoke we could barely hear him. 'Who?'

'Did Karen know somebody named Julio Munoz?'

'Is that the bastard who killed her?'

'No, sir. We're contacting everyone in Karen's Rolodex, but four names have outdated numbers. We want to ask about their last contact with

Karen, what she might've said, things like that.' Dolan was good. She told her lie smoothly and without hesitation as if it were an absolute fact.

Frank seemed annoyed that this small reason was all there was to it. 'I don't know any Julio Munoz.'

'How about Walter Semple or Vivian Trainor or Davis Keech? Karen might've known them in school, or maybe they worked for you.'

'No.' You could see he was trying to remember, and was disappointed that he couldn't.

'Karen never mentioned them to you?'

'No.'

Dolan said, 'Mr Garcia, when I moved out of my parents' house, I left boxes of things behind. Old school things. Old pictures. If Karen left anything like that here, could I look at them?'

He wheeled just far enough around to see his housekeeper. 'Maria, take her back to Karen's room, *por favor*.'

I was following Dolan when Frank said, 'I want to see you guys for a minute.'

He waited until Dolan disappeared through the big doorway, then lowered his voice. 'She knows more than she's telling, and I'll bet my last tortilla those people she asked about aren't what she said. Keep an eye on her back there. See if you can't get her to let on what she's really after.'

I guess a man doesn't go from being a stonemason to a multimillionaire by being an idiot.

Joe stayed with Frank, but I followed the hall until I came to Maria, waiting for me outside a door.

'*Gracias*, Maria. We'll be fine.'

I stepped into what had been Karen's room, and in a way still was. A teenager's furniture froze the room in time. Books and stuffed animals and posters of bands that hadn't existed for a dozen years made the door a time portal taking me into the past. A Flock of Seagulls. Jesus.

Dolan was thorough. Except for old clothes and the knickknacks young women collect, there wasn't much left in the room, but we spent almost three hours going through high school and college notebooks, high school yearbooks, and the bits of a life that accumulate in the shadows of a child's room. Other than clothes, the closet was a floor-to-ceiling wall of board games. Parcheesi, Monopoly, Clue, Life. We opened every box.

Maria brought Mexican iced tea at one point, sweet with lime and mint. We found more boxes under the bed. Most of them held clothes, but one was filled with notes and letters from a pen pal named Vicki Quesada that Karen had had during her first two years at UCLA. We skimmed every letter, looking for the four names, but found none of them. I felt a kind of distance, reading the letters, until one of them mentioned Joe. The date put it about the time Karen was a sophomore. Vicki had written that Joe sounded really hot, and she wanted Karen to send a picture. I smiled. 'That Joe.'

'What's that?'

'Nothing.'

Dolan frowned and touched her waist. 'Oh, shit.'

'What?'

'I'm being paged. Goddamnit, it's Krantz. I'll be right back.'

Dolan took her purse and left the room.

I finished going through the letters, and found six more references to Joe, the next being that Joe was 'soooo cute' (she'd gotten the picture). The letters were organized by date, so were easy to follow, but most of the references were questions: *What's it like dating a policeman? Aren't your friends nervous around him? Does he take you for rides in the car?* The first two or three references made me smile, but the last references didn't. Vicki wrote that she was sorry things weren't working out with Joe, but that men were bastards and always wanted what they couldn't have. In the last letter that mentioned him, she wrote, 'Why do you think he loves someone else?'

I felt awkward and ashamed, as if I had peeped through a keyhole into a part of Joe's life that he had not shared with me. I put the letters back in the box, and the boxes under the bed.

Dolan came back, looking irritated. 'You find anything?'

'No.'

'I've got some good news for the old man. We're releasing the girl's body. He can have her buried, at least.'

'Yeah. He'll appreciate that.' I was still thinking about Joe.

'Here's the bad news: Krantz isn't going to stake the funeral.'

That stopped me. 'Come on, Dolan. Staking the funeral is a no-brainer.' Killers will sometimes attend their victims' burials. Sometimes they'll even give themselves away.

'I *know* that, Cole, but it isn't up to me. Krantz is scared of putting in for so much overtime when he's got a twenty-four/seven on Dersh. He says how can he justify the other when we already know who did it.'

'He doesn't have squat on Dersh. Barney Fife would stake that funeral.'

Her mouth hardened until white dots appeared at either corner. 'We'll deal with it, World's Greatest, okay? I'm going to attend. I can probably scare up a couple of the other guys to come in off the clock. I hate to ask this, considering, but you think you could help out?'

I told her that I would.

'What about Deege? Did anyone ever follow up on him, or is *that* too much overtime?'

'You're a real shit, you know that?'

'I know it's not you, Dolan. I'm sorry.'

She shook her head then, and raised her hands. Suddenly tired with it all.

'I told you the uniforms are keeping an eye out. He hasn't turned up yet, is all. Okay?'

'I know it's not you.'

'Yeah. Right.'

She frowned at the room like maybe we'd forgotten the one place to look that would give us what we need. Finally, she said, 'I guess we're done here, Cole. Hell, it's after six. You want to grab a drink or something?'

'I'm having dinner with my girlfriend.'

'Oh. Right.' She put her hands on her hips and frowned at the room again. 'Listen, thanks for the help. I appreciate you getting me in here.'

'No problemo.'

She walked out ahead of me. When Dolan was gone, Frank said, 'She didn't take anything, did she?'

'No, Frank.'

He hunched in his chair, scowling. 'You find out what she wanted?'

'Just what she said. She was looking for names.'

'That bitch was lying.'

Joe and I walked out of his house feeling like dogs.

When we got to the cars, I said, 'When we were going through her room we found some letters in a box under the bed. Some of them mentioned you. I had to read them.'

Pike took that in.

'I'm sorry it didn't work out, Joe. You and Karen. She seemed like a nice girl.'

Pike looked up into the elm trees. Their leaves were a light green canopy. As still as if they were a painting.

'What did the letters say?'

I told him some of it.

'That's all?' Like he knew what was there and wanted me to say it.

I told him about the one that said he loved someone else.

'They say who?'

'No. It's none of my business.'

Rampart Division Family Day . . . June, fourteen years earlier

The tail car was a brown Caprice, floating four cars behind in the light Sunday morning traffic, two white guys with Internal Affairs Group crew cuts and sunglasses. CIA wannabes.

They were pretty good, but Pike was better. He made them on his way to pick up Karen.

When Pike walked her out to the truck, he could not see them, but as he settled into a groove on the Hollywood Freeway, they were with him again. He wondered if they knew where he was going and thought they must. If they didn't, they were in for a surprise. Karen said, 'Do I look okay?'

'Better than okay.' He'd been watching the rearview.

Now she gave him the little look out the corner of her eye. 'How much better?'

He held up his thumb and forefinger, maybe a quarter inch apart.

She slapped his leg.

He spread his fingers as wide as they would go.

'Better.'

She slid across the Ford Ranger's bench seat and snuggled into him, oblivious to the car or the men in the car or what might happen because of that car. She was wearing a bright yellow sundress and sandals, the yellow going well with her golden skin and white smile. Her black hair glistened in the late morning sun and smelled of lavender. She was a lovely young woman, bright and funny, and Pike enjoyed her company.

When he took the Stadium Way exit off the Golden State Freeway, the tail car left him. That meant they knew where he was going, and either were content to break off the surveillance or had someone assigned to pick him up inside.

He followed Stadium Way through the manicured green lawns of Elysian Park to Academy Road, saw that cars were already parking along the road just up from the gate to Dodger Stadium, and pulled the Ranger to the curb. Karen said, 'Look at all these cars. How many people will be here?'

'Five or six hundred, I guess.' Wozniak would be here. Along with his wife and daughter. Pike wondered again if the IAG spooks would have a man out.

Pike walked around the front of the truck and helped her out. Wilt Deedle, a Rampart bunco detective who weighed almost three hundred pounds, pulled in behind the Ranger and nodded. Joe nodded back. They didn't really know each other, but they were familiar enough to nod. Deedle's wife and four kids were wedged into his car. Deedle, his wife, and three of the kids were wearing matching Hawaiian shirts. The fourth kid, a teenaged girl, was wearing a black tee shirt and looked sullen.

Families and couples were leaving their cars and walking up a little road into the canyon. Pike took Karen's hand, and the two of them followed. Karen said, 'It doesn't look anything like I expected. It almost looks like a resort.'

Pike let his mouth twitch, as much for the little girl's wonder in her eyes as the notion of the Los Angeles Police Academy as a resort. 'Not much of a resort when it's a hundred degrees and you're running the obstacle course. You never been here before?'

'I knew it was here, but the closest I've been is Dodger Stadium. It's pretty.'

The Academy was snuggled between two ridges in the foothills of Elysian Park, a point-blank pistol shot north of Dodger Stadium. The buildings were Spanish and laid out beneath mature red pines and eucalyptus trees. You could stand in the Academy parking lot and see across acres of stadium parking past the bleachers and into the first-base seats. That close. The Ramparts Division Events Officer had wisely made sure that the Dodgers were out of town before booking the Academy on this particular Sunday for the Family Day Picnic. They wouldn't have to worry about game traffic, but the police were making plenty of their own. A burglary detective named Warren Steiner and one of the senior Rampart uniforms, Captain Dennis O'Halloran, were trying to pick the lock to the Dodgers' gate so the arriving families could use the ball club's parking lot. They weren't having much luck with it.

Pike led Karen uphill past the guard shack and the armory, along a little tarmac road that ran between the pines to the target range and the Recruit Training Center. A couple of hundred people were already spread around the track field, some already having staked out positions with spread blankets, others tossing Frisbees or Nerf balls, most just standing around because they hadn't yet had enough beer to loosen up. Three long barbecue grills were set up at the far end of the field by the picnic tables, clouding the trees with smoke and the smell of burning chicken. Rampart Homicide had drawn chef duty this year, and wore matching tee shirts that said Don't ask where we got the meat.

Cop humor.

Karen said, 'Do you see anyone you know?'

'Know most of them.'

'Who are your friends?'

Joe didn't know what to say to that. He was looking for Wozniak and for faces he had seen downtown at Parker Center. He thought it possible that IAG might've worked through Rampart command for an officer to continue the surveillance, but he didn't think so. Wozniak had a lot of years on the job, and IAG wouldn't be certain where the Rampart commander's loyalties would lie.

Karen tugged at his arm and grinned at him. 'We can't just stand here. Come on!'

The Division had set up a soft-drink table in front of a cement wall painted with the Academy symbol and the LAPD's motto, To Protect and to Serve. When Pike was a recruit, his class had been doing physical training on the track field one hot winter afternoon as their PT instructor shouted that unless they got the lead out of their asses they wouldn't be fit to protect dog shit or serve hot beer. A black kid named Elihu Gimble cracked that he'd be happy to serve, but only after coffee and donuts, and the entire class had had to run an extra five miles. Five months later, when Gimble was a probationary officer on patrol in East L.A. he'd been shot in the back by an unknown assailant while responding to a see-the-woman call. The shooter was never identified.

Pike led Karen to the table, and together they stood in line for their drinks. Karen kept her arm looped in his, and before long she was chatting with everyone around them. Pike admired her. Whereas he rarely spoke, she spoke constantly. Whereas he felt obvious, and apart from others, she fit easily with an openness that was quickly returned. By the time they had their sodas, she had found another couple with whom to sit, a pale woman with twin boys whose husband was a uniformed officer named Casey. Casey worked the evening shift, and Pike had never met him.

They were spreading their blankets when Paulette Wozniak appeared behind them. 'Hello, Joe. Is this the young lady we've heard so much about?'

Karen flashed the wide, friendly smile and put out her hand. 'Karen Garcia. And I can't imagine Joe saying very much about anything, but if he's been talking about me, I'm glad. That's a good sign.'

The two women shook, Paulette returning her own smile, which was slow and real and pure in a way that made Pike think of a clean, deep pool. 'Paulette Wozniak. I'm married to Joe's partner, Abel. Everyone calls him Woz.' She pointed across the field to the trees beyond where Homicide was burning the mystery meat. Abel Wozniak and a little girl were just coming through the trees. Pike guessed that Woz had been showing his daughter the obstacle course. 'That's him with the bow legs and the girl.'

Paulette was eight years older than Joe, with short light brown hair and soft brown eyes and even teeth. Her fair skin was beginning to line around the eyes and the corners of her mouth. She didn't seem bothered by the lines, and Pike liked that. She rarely wore makeup, and Pike liked that, too. The lines made her face interesting and knowing.

Paulette touched Joe's arm. 'Could I borrow you for a minute, Joe?' She put the smile on Karen. 'I won't keep him long.'

Karen said, 'I'll finish spreading the blanket.'

Joe followed Paulette onto the track, and noticed that she stood so that she could see her husband. Her smile was gone, and her brow knitted into a tight line. Woz had stopped to speak with a black couple. She said, 'Joe, is something going on with Woz?'

Pike didn't answer.

'Why is he working so many extra shifts?'

Pike shook his head, and felt himself falling inward.

She frowned at him, and he thought that he might do anything to stop that frown, but he didn't know what to do. He didn't think it his place to tell her things that Woz should tell her. She said, 'Please don't play the voiceless man with me, Joe. I'm scared, and I'm worried about him.'

'I don't know what to tell you.' Not a lie. He didn't.

Her eyes went back to her husband, and she crossed her arms. 'I think he has a girlfriend.' She looked back at Joe again, and there was a lot of strength in her now. The strength made him want to hold her, but as soon as he realized that, he took a half-step away. She didn't notice. 'I want to know if he has someone.'

'I don't know anything about a girlfriend, Paulette.'

'Even when he doesn't work an extra shift, he leaves the house. When he's home, he's always pissed off. That isn't like him.'

Pike glanced over at Woz, and saw that he was looking at them. The black couple moved on, but Wozniak stood there. He wasn't smiling. Pike glanced over at the drink tables again, and saw two men he didn't recognize speaking with the Division commander. Behind them, another man was aiming a long-lens camera at them. The camera might've been pointing at the DC and the two strangers, but Pike knew it was pointing at him. Getting a shot of him speaking with Wozniak's wife. Even here at the Division picnic, they were watching.

Joe said, 'Would you like me to speak with him? I'll talk to him if you want.'

Paulette didn't say anything for a time, and then she shook her head. When she touched Joe's arm again, he felt something electrical tingle through his arms and legs, and he forced himself deeper into the pool. Even more calm. More still. She said, 'Thank you, Joe, but no. This is mine to deal with. Please don't tell him that I mentioned this to you.'

'I won't.'

'He's coming now. I'll tell him that I was inviting you and your girlfriend to the house. Is that all right?'

'Yes.'

'In fact, it's true. Because you are invited.'

Paulette Wozniak squeezed his arm, her hand lingering dry and warm, and then she walked across the field to meet her husband.

Joe Pike stood on the track, watching her walk away, and wished that the secrets they had weren't about this.

Karen smoothed the edges of the blanket, and listened to Marybeth Casey carry on about her twins (one of whom was a bed wetter), her husband, Walter (who didn't enjoy being an officer, but night school was just too much for them right now), and how these Division picnics were always such fun because you got to meet new people.

As Marybeth went on to describe the fibroid tumors in her left breast, Karen found that she was no longer listening. She was watching Joe and Paulette Wozniak, together on the running track. Karen told herself that she was being entirely too Latin at the flush of fear that surged through her when Paulette put her hand on Joe's arm. They were friends. She was married to Joe's partner, and she was so much older than Joe.

Karen stared at Joe so intently that her vision seemed to telescope, zooming close to his face, so that every pore seemed to stand out, every nuance exaggerated. Joe was the most difficult man to read she'd ever known. He was so enclosed that she thought he must've put himself in some small secret box that he kept deep within himself. That was part of why she was attracted to him, she knew. She'd read enough psychology texts to know that much. That she was drawn by the mystery, that some great and needing part of her wanted to open that box, to find his secret self.

She loved him. She'd even told her friends that she loved him, though she hadn't yet told Joe. He was so silent, she was afraid that he wouldn't respond in kind. He was so contained that she couldn't be sure.

Karen watched them talk, and felt the flush of jealousy when Paulette Wozniak touched him, but Joe was as unreadable with Paulette as he was with her. 'You're being silly,' she thought. 'He is like that with everyone.'

Paulette Wozniak touched Joe's arm again, then walked across the field toward her husband, and Karen knew then that she was wrong.

A sour wash of fear jolted through her as she watched Joe staring after Paulette Wozniak. Everything she saw in Joe's face and stance told her that his heart belonged to someone else.

16

On the morning that Karen Garcia was buried, I stood naked on my deck, stretching in the darkness. The sun had not yet risen, and, for a time, I watched the few stars brilliant enough to burn their way through the halo of light that floated above the City of Angels, wondering if, somewhere out there, a killer was watching them, too. I thought not. Psycho killers probably slept in.

Little by little, the stiffness of sleep faded as my body warmed, and I eased from the stillness of hatha yoga to the dynamic tension of tae kwon do *katas*, starting slowly at first, then moving faster until the movements became explosive and fierce. I finished the *katas* wet with sweat as the canyon below my house lightened with the first purple glimmers of sunrise. I let the sweat cool, then gathered my things and went inside. Once, I stayed out too long, and the woman who lives in the next house saw me and made a wolf whistle. Her husband came out onto their deck, and he made a wolf whistle, too. Life in L.A.

I was standing in my kitchen, drinking orange juice and watching eggs boil, when the phone rang. I grabbed it on the first ring so it wouldn't wake Lucy.

Samantha Dolan said, 'I've got two guys who'll be at Forest Lawn with me.'

'Two. Wow, Dolan. There won't be room for the mourners.' I was still pissed off about Krantz.

'Save the attitude and keep your eyes open. You and Pike make five of us.'

'Pike will be with Frank.'

'He can still see, can't he? We're looking for a white male between twenty and forty. He may linger after, and he may approach the grave. Sometimes they leave something, or they'll take a souvenir.'

'Krantz's buddy at the Feebs tell you that?' It was typical behavior for a serial killer.

'The burial's scheduled for ten. I'll be there at nine-thirty. And, Cole?'

'What?'

'Try not to be such an ass.'

Forest Lawn Memorial Park is four hundred acres of rolling green lawns at the foot of the Hollywood Hills in Glendale. With immaculate grounds, re-creations of famous churches, and burial areas with names like Slumber-land, Vale of Memory, and Whispering Pines, I have always thought of it as a kind of Disneyland of the Dead.

Since Dolan was going to get there at nine-thirty, I wanted to get there earlier. But when I turned into the grounds and found Karen Garcia's burial site, Dolan was already there, and so were a hundred other people. She was parked with an easy eyes-forward view of the crowd on the slope. A long-lens Konica camera rested in her lap. She would use it to take pictures of the crowd for later identification.

I slipped into the passenger side of her Beemer, and took a breath. 'Dolan, I know you're doing what you can. I was a jerk this morning. I apologize.'

'You were, but I accept. Forget it.'

'Just wanted to get that out. Makes me feel small.'

'That's your girlfriend's problem.'

I looked over at her, but she was staring out the window. Ouch.

'You know where Krantz is this morning?'

'On Dersh?'

'A surveillance team is on Dersh. Krantz and Bishop are going to the service. Mills is going, too. They want to sit where Councilman Maldenado can see them.'

I couldn't do what she did. I couldn't work with guys like Krantz and Bishop. Maybe that was why I'm on my own.

'I thought you said you were coming at nine-thirty.'

'I figured you'd try to beat me, so I came earlier.'

I looked over at her, and she was smiling.

'You're something, Samantha.'

'Guess we're cats of the same stripe, World's Greatest.'

I smiled back. 'Okay. So it's me, you, and two other guys. How do you want to play it?'

She glanced up the hill toward a marble mausoleum. 'Got a guy up at that mausoleum, and another guy down below. They see anyone who looks suspicious, they'll get the license numbers.' The high man was sitting on the grass outside the mausoleum above us. A little road ran in front of it, identical to the road where we were parked. If the killer wanted to come and watch, he could park up there. People were scattered throughout the slope below us, the low man invisible among them. 'I figure you can work in close with the crowd since you know some of these people. I'll stay here snapping shots of the procession, then I'll come up.'

'Okay.'

'Right now, why don't you walk the perimeter.'

It wasn't a question.

She looked at me. 'Well?'

'Yes, ma'am.' If you're on free time, I guess you can tell everyone what to do.

As I slid out of the Beemer, she said, 'By the way, that was the first time you called me Samantha.'

'I guess so.'

'Don't let it happen again.'

But she was smiling, and I grinned as I walked away.

I spent the next few minutes drifting along the perimeter of the crowd, counting sixteen Anglo men between twenty and forty. When I glanced down at Dolan, she was pointing the camera at me. I guess she was bored.

A blue Nissan Sentra came up the hill a few minutes before ten, parked where the other cars had parked, and Eugene Dersh climbed out.

I said, 'Oh, man.'

Dersh was conservatively dressed in a beige sport coat and slacks. He locked his car, and was walking up the hill when two unmarked detective rides turned in and idled by the front gate, unsure what to do. Williams was driving the second car. The first car was the same guys who had followed me.

The cop by the mausoleum stood and stared at them. He hadn't seen Dersh, but he recognized the RHD cars.

I trotted down to Dolan. 'Looks like the gang's all here.'

Dersh saw us looking at him, recognized me, and waved.

I waved back.

At a quarter after ten, four LAPD motorcycles escorted the hearse through the main gate. Three gleaming black limos followed, trailing a line of cars that had been waxed and buffed until they glittered with bits of the sun. Dersh watched them come, a kind of benign curiosity on his face.

When the line of cars reached us, a dozen people who looked like family members emerged from the limos. The driver of the lead car took Frank's wheelchair from the trunk as Joe and another man helped Frank out. Joe was dressed in a charcoal three-piece suit. The dark glasses made him look like a Secret Service agent, but since this was L.A., everyone was wearing sunglasses. Even the priest.

Councilman Maldenado and Abbot Montoya climbed out of the last limo. Bishop and Krantz and Assistant Chief Mills squeezed out of the sixth car, and hurried to fall in behind the councilman. Anxious to protect and to serve him, I guess.

Dolan and I were walking over when Krantz and Bishop saw us. 'What in hell are you doing here with Cole?'

Dolan pointed at Dersh.

Krantz and Bishop turned and saw Dersh looking back. Dersh smiled broadly and waved.

Krantz said, 'Holy shit!'

Bishop nudged Krantz. 'Wave back, goddamnit, before he suspects something.'

They waved back.

Bishop said, 'Smile!'

Krantz smiled.

Joe had pushed Frank most of the way up the hill when a news van from one of the local network affiliates tore through the gate. Vans from a second network affiliate and then Lucy's station barreled through ten seconds behind it, braking hard alongside the hearse. Their microwave dishes extended even as camera operators and on-air reporters jumped out.

Dolan said, 'This can't be good.'

Dolan and I walked faster, Krantz and Bishop after us.

The three reporters hurried toward Frank, two of them with radio mikes and one without.

I said, 'Wake up, Bishop. Have the uniforms keep those people away.'

Dolan and I put ourselves between Frank and the reporters as Krantz ran for the motorcycle cops. A good-looking red-haired woman leaned past me, reaching for Frank with her microphone. 'Mr Garcia, have the police made any progress in catching the serial killer?'

Bishop said, 'Oh, shit.'

A tall African-American reporter who had played professional football tried to press between me and one of the uniforms, but neither of us gave ground. 'Mr Garcia, do you believe a man named Eugene Dersh killed your daughter, and, if so, sir, why?'

Bishop jerked at Krantz's arm, his voice a panicked whisper. 'How in hell did these bastards find out?'

Behind us, Frank Garcia said, 'What is this? What are they talking about, serial killer? Who's this man, Dersh?'

Councilman Maldenado stepped forward, trying to turn the press away. 'Please. His child is about to be buried.'

Eugene Dersh had come to the edge of the growing crowd, too far away to hear, but curious like everyone else.

The redhead's camera operator saw Dersh and punched her in the back. He didn't tap her; he punched her. '*Sonofabitch! That's Dersh.*'

She shoved the black reporter out of the way and ran toward Dersh. The black reporter ran after her. Dersh looked as surprised and confused as everyone else.

Frank Garcia tried to see Dersh, but since he was in the chair, people blocked his view. 'Who is that?' He twisted around to Maldenado. 'Henry, do they know who killed Karen? *Did that man kill Karen?*'

Up the hill, Dersh was afraid and embarrassed as the two reporters barked questions. The mourners around the grave heard the reporters with Dersh, and began to murmur and stare.

The final reporter was an Asian-American woman who stayed with Frank. 'There were others, Mr Garcia. Haven't the police told you? Five people have been murdered. Karen was the fifth.' The reporter glanced from Frank to Maldenado, then back to Frank. 'Some maniac has been *hunting human beings* here in Los Angeles for the past nineteen months.' You could see she liked saying it because of how the words would play on the news. She pointed at Dersh. 'The police suspect that man. Eugene Dersh.'

Frank lurched higher in his chair, craning to see Dersh. 'That man killed Karen? That sonofabitch murdered my daughter?'

Maldenado shouldered in and forced the Asian-American reporter away. 'This isn't the time. I'll make a statement, but not now. Let this man bury his daughter.'

Above us, Eugene Dersh pushed past the two reporters, walking fast back down the hill to his car. They dogged him, peppering him with questions as their cameras recorded it. Dersh would be able to see himself on the news again, though he probably wouldn't be as happy about it this time.

Frank's face was the color of dried blood. He bobbed in his chair, wrestling the wheels to try to chase after Dersh. *'Is that him? Is that the sonofabitch?'*

Dersh climbed into his car, the reporters still shouting their questions. His voice carried in the still air, high and frightened. 'What are you talking about? I didn't kill anyone. I just found her body.'

Frank screamed, *'I'll kill you!'*

He twisted so hard that he pitched forward, falling out of the chair. His family gasped and two of the women made sharp sounds. Pike, Montoya, and several of the family clustered around him, Pike lifting the old man back into the chair as if he weighed nothing.

Dersh drove away, and when he sped through the gate, the two plainclothes cars quietly fell in behind him.

The priest told Frank's brothers to get the family seated as quickly as possible. Everyone was embarrassed and uncomfortable, and Frank's housekeeper cried loudly, but the crowd settled as the pallbearers gathered at the hearse. I tried to find Dolan, but she had joined Mills, Bishop, and Krantz in a frantic conversation at the edge of the crowd. Krantz saw me, and stormed over. 'You and your buddy, Pike, get your butts to Parker Center as soon as she's in the ground. We're fuckin'-A gonna figure out what happened here.' He walked away fast.

The climbing sun became a hot torch in the sky as the family took their seats, and the pallbearers delivered Karen's body to its grave. Heat soaked into my shoulders and face until I could feel the delicate tickle of sweat running out of my hair. Around me, a few people cried, but most simply stared, lost in a moment that was both sad and unsettling.

The three news cameras stood in a line below us, recording Karen Garcia's burial.

They looked like a firing squad.

17

News vans lined Los Angeles Street outside Parker Center. Reporters and technicians milled nervously on the sidewalk, clustering around every cop who came out to grab a cigarette like piranha on bad meat. The city didn't allow smoking in its buildings, so addicted officers had to sneak butts in the stairwells and bathrooms, or come outside. These guys didn't know anything more about Dersh or the murders than anyone else, but the reporters didn't believe it. Word had spread big, and someone had to feed the networks' hunger for news.

The three skinny palms outside Parker Center seemed bent and fragile as Joe and I turned into the drive, two cars behind Dolan. Frank's limo was already at the curb, Frank's driver and Abbot Montoya helping him into the chair.

We parked between a silver Porsche Boxster and a taupe Jaguar XK8. Lawyers, here to cut deals. We got out, and for a moment Pike stared up at the squat building. The midmorning sun bounced hard off the seven strips of blue glass and burned down on us, mirrored in Pike's glasses.

Pike surprised me by saying, 'It's been a long time since I was here.'

'You don't want to go in, you can wait out here.'

The last time Joe Pike was here was the day that Abel Wozniak died. Pike made his little non-smile. 'Won't be as bad as the Mekong.'

He pulled off the suit coat, unfastened the shoulder holster, and wound its straps around the .357 Python revolver. He put his jacket in the little storage bay behind the seats, then unbuttoned the vest, and put it with the jacket. He stripped off the tie and the shirt. He was wearing a white guinea tee beneath the shirt, and let it go with that. The guinea tee, the charcoal pants, the black leather shoes, countered by the cut muscles of his shoulders and chest and the brilliant red tattoos, made quite a fashion statement. A female detective coming out to her car stared.

We gave our names to the lobby guard, and Stan Watts came down a few minutes later.

I said, 'Frank Garcia go upstairs?'

'Yeah. You're the last.' Watts stood to the side of the elevator with his arms crossed, staring at Pike.

Pike stared back behind the dark glasses.

Watts said, 'I knew Abel Wozniak.'

Pike didn't respond.

'If I don't get another chance to say this, fuck you.'

Pike cocked his head. 'You want a piece, step up.'

I said, 'Hey, Watts. You really think Dersh is good for it?'

Watts didn't answer. Guess he was thinking about Joe.

We left the elevator on the fifth floor and followed Watts through the Robbery-Homicide squad room. Most of the detectives were working their phones, and more phones were ringing. They were busy because of the news coverage, but as we entered, a ripple of attention swept through the room. Eyes went to Joe, tracking him across the floor.

Behind us, a voice I didn't recognize spoke just loud enough to be heard. 'Cop killer.'

Pike didn't turn.

Watts led us to the conference room, where Frank Garcia was saying, 'I want to know why the sonofabitch is still walking around. If this man killed my daughter, how come he's not in jail?'

Councilman Maldenado stood on one side of him, arms crossed, and Abbot Montoya stood on the other, hands in his pockets. Dolan was seated as far from everybody else as she could get, just like in the briefings. Krantz and Bishop were with Frank, Krantz trying to explain. 'Dersh is the suspect, Mr Garcia, but we still have to build a case. The district attorney won't file without enough evidence to get a conviction. We don't want to leave any wiggle room here. We don't want another O.J.'

Frank rubbed at his face. 'Oh, Jesus Christ. Don't even joke about that.'

Bishop told us to take a seat. 'I know you're wondering what happened back there. We were just explaining to Mr Garcia that there's been more to this investigation than we've let on.'

Bishop was good. His voice was smooth and sure, and both Montoya and Maldenado looked a lot calmer than they had at the cemetery, though Frank was visibly shaking.

Maldenado wasn't happy. 'I only wish you had seen fit to tell us that there were things you needed to keep secret, Captain. It would've saved Mr Garcia the shock of what just happened. I mean, we're *all* shocked. *Five* people killed. A *serial* killer. And the man you say did it comes to the *funeral.*'

Krantz sat with half his ass on the table, and looked directly at Frank. 'I want the bastard who killed your daughter, Mr Garcia. I'm sorry you had to find out this way, but we made the right decision to keep this thing under wraps. Now that Dersh knows we suspect him, well, that takes away our advantage. I wish I knew how the goddamned press found out because I'd crimp his nuts but good.'

Frank said, 'Listen, I'm not pissed you didn't tell me, okay? I was pissed off at you guys at first, but maybe I was wrong. All I care about is getting the sonofabitch who killed Karen. That's all.'

Bishop said, 'Why don't you finish bringing them up to date, Harve.'

Krantz was making a good impression, and Bishop was pleased.

Krantz gave them everything, admitting that there were now a total of five murders, and that they had been running a Task Force for almost a year. Montoya asked about the first four victims and Krantz went through the names, starting with Julio Munoz.

When Krantz said their names, Frank straightened in his chair, looking at me, then Dolan. 'Those are the people you asked about.'

Krantz shook his head, certain that Frank was mistaken. 'No, sir. Cole couldn't've asked about them. He didn't know.'

Frank said, 'Not Cole. Her.'

Dolan cleared her throat, and shifted in her chair. She looked at her hands flat on the table for a moment, then met Krantz's eyes. 'Cole knew it all.'

The room stopped.

Krantz said, 'What are you talking about, Detective?'

'Cole came to me with the five vics. He knew the signature, and their identities, so I told him about the Task Force. He got me in to see Mr Garcia so I could ask about the first four.'

Krantz considered Pike, and seemed, in a way, pleased. 'If he knew, then Pike knew.'

Pike said, 'Yes.'

'I guess we know who shot off his mouth.'

Dolan said, 'That's bullshit, Harvey. They didn't say anything.'

Frank Garcia looked hurt. 'You knew this and you didn't tell me?'

Pike said, 'It was smart not to tell you. Krantz is right about that. It was better for the investigation.'

Dolan said, 'He was going to go to Mr Garcia with it, but I convinced him not to, Harvey. Why the hell would he leak it to the press? There's nothing in it for him.'

Bishop said, 'How'd you find out about the other victims, Cole?'

'I'm a detective. I detected.'

Krantz slid off the table, disgusted and showing his palms to Bishop. 'You see what happens when you let people in? We're on top of this for a year, and now we're fucked because of these guys. And Dolan.'

Dolan stood then, eyes hard as bullet casings. 'Fuck you, Pants. It was the only way to play it.'

When she said it, Krantz turned purple.

Bishop cleared his throat and moved closer to Maldenado. 'We're not fucked, Harvey. We're still going to make an arrest.' Saying that for the councilman. He turned toward Dolan. 'I can't believe you compromised our investigation like this, Detective. This is a serious breach. Serious.'

I said, 'I already had it, Bishop. I had the vics, the feds, and I knew that you guys were running a Task Force. I was just trying to find out why you were putting so much into Dersh.'

Krantz squared his jaw again. 'What in hell does that mean? We're putting it into Dersh because Dersh is the shooter.'

'You've got nothing for the shooter. You're pressing Dersh because you're desperate for a collar.'

Frank pushed his chair forward, accidentally hitting Montoya. 'Waitaminute. It's not Dersh?'

Krantz said, 'Yes. It's Dersh.'

'All they have is a profile that says the shooter is probably someone like Dersh. They don't have any evidence that it's really him. Nada.'

Williams leaned forward, the first of the others to say anything. 'You're off base, Cole. The Feebs said the perp would try to insert himself into the investigation, maybe by pretending to know something, and that's just what Dersh did. You've read the interviews. Dersh dragged Ward down that slope just so they could find the vic.' Williams realized what he was saying then, and looked embarrassed. 'Sorry. Ms Garcia.'

Frank was nodding. He wanted it to make sense because he wanted to know who killed his daughter.

'So, you say this Dersh is the man, but you can't prove it?'

Krantz spread his hands, reasonable. 'Not yet. We believe he did it, but, as Cole says, we don't at this time have any direct evidence linking him to these crimes.'

'Then what are you doing to get the bastard?'

Krantz and Bishop traded a look, and then Krantz shrugged. 'Well, now that we've lost the advantage, the only thing we can do is sweat him. We'll have to get aggressive, search his residence for evidence, and keep up the pressure until he either confesses or makes a mistake.'

I shook my head. 'You're out of your mind, Krantz.'

Krantz raised his eyebrows at me. 'Good thing you're not conducting this investigation.'

Bishop watched Maldenado for a reaction. 'How does that sound, Councilman?'

'Our only concern is that the killer be apprehended, Captain. Certainly for the murder of Karen Garcia, but also for the sake of our city and the other victims. We want justice.'

Krantz tipped his head toward me and Joe. 'Before we do anything, we'd better plug the leak.'

I said, 'It didn't come from us, Krantz. It could've been some uniform who overheard something or maybe just some sharp reporter who dug out the facts. Maybe it was you.'

Krantz smiled a reasonable smile. 'I heard that your girlfriend works for KROK. I wonder if that has something to do with it.'

Everyone in the room stared at me. Even Dolan.

'I didn't tell anybody, Krantz. Not my girlfriend. Not anyone.'

Krantz took his seat on the table again, gazing pointedly at Maldenado. 'Well, we're going to find out, but right now we've got a maniac to get off the street. We've had one major leak, we can't afford to have another. It could mean the difference whether we nail this guy, or not.'

Frank looked from me to Joe. Joe was watching Frank, and I wondered what he was thinking.

Frank said, 'I don't believe they said anything.'

Maldenado maintained the eye contact with Krantz, then spread his hands. 'Frank, I think the police have proven that we can trust their efforts. I certainly hope that Mr Pike and Mr Cole weren't behind this, ah, lapse in judgment, but as long as we have confidence in the police, there's no reason we can't work with them directly.'

Frank said, 'Get Dersh.'

Krantz said, 'That's right, Mr Garcia. We've got to get Dersh. We can't afford to be distracted.'

Frank nodded again, and reached a gesture toward Joe. 'Sure. That makes sense, doesn't it, Joe? I don't believe you told anyone. But as long as the police are doing such a good job, I don't need you to waste your time staying on them, right?'

Pike spoke so softly you couldn't hear it. 'Right, Frank.'

Krantz went to the door and opened it. No one said anything as we left.

We walked out through the squad room, and out to my car. When we got there, I said, 'Is it me, or were we just fired?'

'It's not you.'

Pike's Jeep was still at the church. I drove the wrong way up the parking lane to let Pike out, pulling in across the Jeep's stern. We hadn't spoken on the ride, and I was wondering, as I often do, what he was feeling behind the dark glasses and beneath the blank mask of his face.

He had to hurt. He had to be feeling loss, and anger, and shame.

'You want to come up to the house and talk about this?'

'Nothing to talk about. We're off, Krantz is on.'

Pike took his gun from the glove box and clothes from behind the seats, got out, and drove away.

I guess I would feel those things for both of us.

18

The woman who lives in the next house was standing on her slope, watering bright red ice plants. The Santa Anas were gone, but the stillness made me think that they would return. The air is never more still in Los Angeles than in those moments before the wind screams down on us again, once more torching the world into flame. Maybe the stillness is a warning.

The woman called, so far away I could barely hear her, 'How are you doing over there?'

'Hot. How're those boys?'

'They're boys. I saw you on TV.'

I didn't know what she was talking about.

'On the midday news. At that funeral. Oh, there's my phone.'

She turned off her hose and ran inside.

I let myself in through the kitchen and turned on the television, but it was soap operas. Guess my fifteen minutes had come and gone, and I had missed it.

I changed into jeans and a tee shirt, then made scrambled eggs. I ate at the sink, staring out the window while I drank milk from the carton. The floor in my kitchen is Mexican paver tiles, some of which were still loose from the '94 earthquake. When you're unemployed you have time to think about fixing things like that, only I didn't know how. I thought I could learn. It would give me something to do, and there might even be a measure of satisfaction in it. Unlike private detecting.

I stepped from tile to tile until I had stood on every tile, rocking a bit to see if the tiles were sound. Six of them were loose.

The cat came in and sat by his bowl, watching me. He was holding something in his mouth.

'What you got there?'

The something moved.

'I think I'm going to fix these tiles. You want to help?'

The cat took the something back out again. He'd seen me attempt repairs before.

By twenty minutes before five I had chipped up four of the tiles, covering the floor with little bits of cement. I turned on the TV again, figuring to let the news play while I worked on the tiles, but Eugene Dersh was standing outside his house while a dozen cops carried evidence boxes past the camera. He looked scared. I switched channels and found a taped report of Dersh being interviewed at his front door, peeking out through a two-inch crack, saying, 'I don't understand any of this. All I did was find that poor girl's body. I didn't kill anyone.' I switched channels again, and found Krantz surrounded by reporters. Every time a reporter asked a question, Krantz answered, 'No comment'.

I turned off the set. 'Krantz. You prick.'

At six-twenty, I was back to fixing the tiles when Lucy let herself in carrying a large white bag filled with Chinese food. 'I tried calling to warn you that the story was breaking.'

'I know. I was at Forest Lawn.'

She put the bag on the counter. 'What's all this on the floor?'

'I'm fixing the tiles.'

'Oh.'

She sounded as impressed as that cat.

'Elvis, do you think it's him?' Dersh was already 'him'.

'I don't know, Luce. I don't think so. Krantz wants to believe it's Dersh, and he thinks the way to prove it is to put on so much pressure that Dersh breaks. Everything we're seeing now is being fed by Krantz. He was already planning it when I left Parker Center. These reporters are saying just what Krantz wants them to say, that Dersh is guilty because it says so in the profile.'

'Waitaminute. They don't have anything specific that ties Dersh to these crimes?'

'Nothing.'

I sat in the cement dust on my floor and told her everything I knew, starting with Jerry Swetaggen but not naming him. I went through the forensics reports and the autopsy results, and every detail of the case that I remembered from Dolan's brief. As I talked, she took off her shoes and her jacket, and sat with me in the dust. Wearing a six-hundred-dollar pants suit, and she sat with me in the dust. Love.

When I finished, Lucy said, 'Did I wake up in Nazi Germany?'

'It gets better.'

'What?'

'Frank fired us.'

She gave me a look of infinite care, and touched my head. 'It's been a rotten day, hasn't it?'

'The pits.'

'Would you like a hug?'

'What are my other choices?'

'Whatever you want.'

Even when I'm feeling bad, she can make me smile.

After I vacuumed the kitchen, Lucy put Jim Brickman on the stereo as I made drinks, the two of us setting the containers of food in the oven to warm. We were doing that when the doorbell rang.

Samantha Dolan was standing there.

'Hope you don't mind my coming by like this.'

'Not at all.'

She was wearing jeans and a man's white shirt with the tail out. Her eyes glistened, but not from crying. She didn't look too steady.

When Dolan walked in, she saw Lucy, still in the kitchen, and plucked at my arm. 'I guess that's the girlfriend.'

She'd had a couple, all right.

Dolan followed me into the kitchen, where I introduced them. 'Lucy, this is Samantha Dolan. Dolan, this is Lucy Chenier.'

'You don't have to call me Dolan, for Christ's sake.' She put out her hand and Lucy took it.

Lucy said, 'Pleasure to meet you. I understand you're with the police.'

Dolan held on to her hand. 'So far.' Then Dolan saw our drinks. 'Oh, you're drinking. Don't mind if I do.'

She'd had more than a couple.

I said, 'Gin and tonic okay?'

'You got any tequila?' Call it three or four.

As I made Dolan a drink, she squinted at the tiles. 'What's up with the floor?'

'Home repairs.'

'First time, huh?'

Everyone has something to say.

Lucy said, 'We were just about to eat Chinese food. Would you like to stay?'

Dolan smiled at Lucy. 'That's some accent. Where you from?'

Lucy smiled back nicely. 'Louisiana. And you?'

'Bakersfield.'

'They raise cows there, don't they?'

I handed Dolan the tequila. 'So what's up, Dolan?'

'Krantz busted me off the Task Force.'

'I'm sorry.'

'Not your fault. I didn't have to play it the way I did, and I don't believe it was you who ratted to the press.' She tipped her drink toward Lucy. 'Not even with your friend here being one of them. Anyway, I don't blame you, and I wanted you to know.'

'So what're you going to do?'

She laughed, but it's the kind of laugh you give when your only other choice is to cry. 'Nothing I can do. Bishop put me back on the table, but he won't let it go. He says he's going to take a few days to cool off, then he's going to talk it over with the assistant chiefs and figure out the appropriate action. He's thinking about transferring me out.'

Lucy said, 'Just because you confirmed what Elvis already knew?'

'They're serious about their secrets downtown, Counselor. It's called compromising an investigation, and that's what they think I did. If I'm a good enough girl and kiss Bishop's ass, maybe he'll keep me around.'

Lucy frowned. 'If this becomes a gender-bias issue, you could have legal recourse.'

Dolan laughed. 'Honey, gender bias is the only reason I'm still there. Look, that's not why I came.' She glanced back at me. 'I agree with you about Dersh. That poor bastard is getting railroaded, but there isn't much I can do about it right now without tanking what little career I have left.'

'Okay.'

'Krantz is right about one thing in all this. Dersh and Ward are lying about something. I was behind the two-way glass when Watts interviewed them. You can see it a little bit in the transcript, but you could see it for sure in the room. That's why Krantz is so convinced.'

'I'm listening. What are they lying about?'

'I don't have a clue, but I'm sure Ward is scared. He knows something that he doesn't want to talk about. I'm not in a position to do anything about it, World's Greatest, but you could.'

I nodded. 'Yeah. Maybe I could.'

Dolan finished the drink, and put it down. It hadn't lasted long. 'I'd better go. Sorry to barge in.'

'Are you sure you wouldn't like to stay for dinner?'

Dolan went to the door, then gazed back at Lucy.

'Thanks, anyway, but there probably wouldn't be enough for both of us.'

Lucy smiled the nice smile again. 'No. There isn't.'

When I got back to the kitchen, Lucy had the containers out of the oven and was opening them.

'She likes you.'

'What are you talking about?'

'You don't think she came here just to talk about Eugene Dersh, do you? She likes you.'

I didn't say anything.

'Bitch.'

'Are you jealous?'

Lucy turned the sweet smile on me.

'If I were jealous, she'd be getting stitches.'

There isn't much you can say to that.

When Lucy spoke again, her voice was soft. 'So, are you going to do it?'

'What?'

'Try to help Dersh.'

I thought about it, and then I nodded. 'I don't think he's the shooter, Lucille. And if he isn't, then he's just some guy out there all alone with the weight of a city on him.'

Lucy came close and put her arms around me.

'I guess that's you, lover boy. The last white knight.'

That's me.

19

Lake Hollywood was quiet the next morning, the air cool in the early hour. I went up just after sunrise, hoping to get the jump on newspeople and the morbidly curious, and I had. Walkers and joggers once more looped the four-mile circumference of the lake, but none of them gawked at the murder site, or even seemed aware of it.

Having opened the crime scene, the police had taken down their yellow tape and withdrawn the guards. I left my car by the chain-link gate, and followed the trail down through the brush to the place where Karen Garcia's body had been found. The ripped footprints where the coroner's people had carried her out were still there, cut into the soil. Blood marks the color of dead roses flagged her resting place.

I stared at that spot for a moment, then went north along the shore, counting paces. Twice the bank dropped away so quickly, and was so overgrown with brush, that I had to take off my shoes and step in the water, but most of the shoreline was flat and bare enough to make good time.

Fifty-two paces from the blood marks, I found a six-inch piece of orange tape tied to a tree where Dersh and Riley reached the water. The slope was steep; their long, skidding footprints still visible, winding down through a clutter of small trees. I backtracked their footprints up, and pretty soon I was pushing my way through a dense overgrowth before popping out onto the trail. Another piece of the orange tape was tied here, too, marking where Dersh had told the investigator they had left the trail.

I walked up the trail a hundred yards, then turned back past the tape for about the same distance. I could see the lake from further up the trail, but not from the orange tape, and I wondered why they had picked this spot to find their way down. The brush was thick, the tree canopy dense, and the light poor. Any kid with a couple of years in the Scouts would know better, and so would just about anyone else. Of course, maybe neither Dersh nor Ward had been a Scout, or maybe they just had to take a leak. Maybe they just figured what the hell, here was as good a place as any, even though it wasn't.

I went back to my car, drove down the hill to the Jungle Juice, and used their phone book to look up Riley Ward & Associates. I copied the phone number and address, then drove to West Hollywood.

Ward had his offices in a converted Craftsman house on what was once a residential street south of Sunset Boulevard. The Craftsman house had a lovely front porch, and elaborate woodwork that had been painted in bright shades of peach and turquoise, neither of which went with the two television news vans that were parked out front.

I parked in a little lot belonging to a dentist's office, and waited. Two people went into Ward's building, one of them being an on-air reporter I recognized because he looked like a surfer dude. They were inside maybe three minutes, then came out and stood by their van, disappointed. Ward was still refusing interviews. Or maybe he wasn't there.

A third van arrived. Two young guys got out, one Asian-American with black horned-rim glasses and the other blond with very short hair. The Asian-American guy had white streaks in his hair, going for that Euro-trash look. The new guys joined the surfer and his friend, the four of them laughing about something as a young woman got out of the other van and went over. She was wearing a bright yellow spring dress and thick-soled shoes that had to be damned near impossible to walk in, and cat's-eye glasses. Fashion slaves.

I went over, grinning like we were all just journalists together. 'You guys here to get Ward?'

The surfer shook his head. 'He's not having it. We'll wait him out, though.'

'Maybe he's not in there.'

The young woman in the canary dress said, 'Oh, he's in there. I saw him go in this morning.'

'Ah.'

I headed across the street.

The girl said, 'Forget it, amigo. He won't talk to you.'

'We'll see.'

The little porch opened to what had once been the living room but was now a reception area. The smell of fresh coffee was strong in the little house, hanging over a sweeter smell, as if someone had brought Danish. A young woman in a black body suit and vest watched me suspiciously from behind a glass desk with a little name plate that read Holly Mira. 'May I help you?'

'Hi, Holly. Elvis Cole to see Mr Ward.' I gave her the card, and then I lowered my voice. 'About Karen Garcia.'

She put the card down without looking at it. 'I'm sorry. Mr Ward isn't giving interviews.'

'I'm not a reporter, Holly. I'm working for the dead girl's family. You can understand how they'd have questions.'

Her face softened, but she still didn't touch the card. 'You're working for the family.'

'The Garcia family. His attorney is a man named Abbot Montoya. You can call them if you like.' I took out the card Montoya had given me and put it next to mine. 'Please tell Mr Ward that the family would appreciate it. I promise that I won't take much of his time.'

Holly read both cards, then gave me a shy smile. 'Are you really a private investigator?'

I tried to look modest. 'Well, I'm what you might call the premier example.'

Holly smiled wider. 'I know he's got a conference call soon, but I'm sure he'll speak with you.'

'Thanks, Holly.'

Two minutes later Riley Ward followed Holly out to the reception room, and now Ward was holding the cards. He was wearing a burgundy shirt buttoned to the neck, gray triple-pleated slacks, and soft gray Italian loafers, but even the nice clothes couldn't cover his strain. 'Mr Cole?'

'That's right. I appreciate your seeing me, considering what's happened.'

He bent the cards back and forth, looking nervous and uneasy. 'You wouldn't believe. It's been a nightmare.'

'I'll bet.'

'I mean, all we did was find her, and now, well, Gene isn't a killer. He just isn't. Please tell her family that. I know they won't believe me, but he isn't.'

'Yes, sir. I'll tell them. I'm not here about Mr Dersh, though. I'm trying to put some of the family's concerns to rest, if you know what I mean. About the body.' I glanced at Holly and let it drop, implying that the family's concerns were better discussed privately.

Ward nodded. 'Well, okay. Ah, why don't you come into my office.'

His office was spacious, with a large plank desk, an overstuffed couch, and matching chairs. Pictures of Ward with an attractive woman and two bucktoothed children lined a narrow table behind the desk. Ward gestured to the couch. 'Can I get you a cup of coffee?'

'No, thanks.'

Riley peeked out the window at the news vans, then took the chair facing the pictures. 'They're driving me crazy. They came to my home. They were here when I arrived this morning. It's insane.'

'I'm sure.'

'Now I have to waste my day hiring an attorney, and it's so much worse for poor Gene.'

'Yes, sir. It is.' I took out a pad as if I were going to take notes, then leaned toward him, glancing at the windows like they might have ears. 'Mr Ward, what I'm going to say here, well, I'd appreciate it if you didn't repeat it, okay? The family would appreciate it. You let this out, and it might hurt the investigation.'

Ward peered at me, his eyes nervous and apprehensive. You could almost hear him think, *now* what?

I waited.

He realized I was waiting for him, and nodded. 'All right. Yes. Of course.'

'The family thinks that the police are off base about Mr Dersh. We're not confident that they have the right man.'

Hope flashed over his face, making me feel like a turd.

'Of *course* they don't. Gene couldn't do this.'

'I agree. So the family, well, we're conducting our own investigation, if you know what I mean.'

He nodded, seeing a way out for his friend Gene.

'So I have a few questions, you see?'

'You bet. I'll help any way I can.'

Anxious now. Raring to go.

'Okay. Great. It has to do with why you left the trail.'

He frowned, and didn't look so anxious anymore. 'We wanted to see the lake.'

I smiled. Mr Friendly.

'Well, I know, but after I read your statements I went up to the lake and walked through it with the police.'

Ward pursed his lips and glanced at his watch. 'Holly, hasn't that damned attorney called yet?'

She called back, 'Not yet, Riley.'

'I found the little tape they used to mark where you left the main trail. The underbrush was pretty dense right there.'

He crossed his arms and frowned harder, obviously uncomfortable. 'I don't understand. These are things the family wants to know?'

'I'm just curious about why you left the trail where you did. There were easier places to walk down.'

Riley Ward stared at me for a full thirty seconds without moving. He wet his lips once, thinking so hard that you could almost see the wheels and gears turning in his head. 'Well, we didn't discuss it. I mean, we didn't *research* what was the best way to get down. We just *went.*'

'Another ten yards the brush was a lot thinner.'

'We wanted to go down to the lake, we went down to the lake.' He suddenly stood, went to the door, and called to Holly again. 'Would you try him for me, please. I can't stand this waiting.' He put his hands in his pockets, then took them out and waved at me. 'Who cares why we left the trail right there? Can it *possibly* matter?'

'If you left because someone threatening scared you, then, yes, it could matter a great deal. That person could be the killer.'

Ward blinked at me, then suddenly relaxed. As if whatever was bothering him had receded to a far spot on the horizon. A smile flickered at the corners of his mouth. 'No, I'm sorry. No one scared us off the trail. We didn't see anyone.'

I pretended to write.

'So it was pretty much Gene saying let's go down to the lake right here, and you just went? That's all there was to it?'

'That's all. I wish I had seen someone up there, Mr Cole. Especially now. I'm sorry about the girl. I wish I could help you, but I can't. I wish I could help Gene.'

I stared at the notebook as if I knew there was something missing. I tapped it with my pen. 'Well, could there have been another reason?'

'I don't know what you mean.'

'A reason you had for leaving the trail at that certain spot.' I looked at him. 'Maybe to do something that you didn't want anyone else to see.'

Riley Ward turned white.

Holly appeared in the door. 'Riley. Mr Mikkleson is on.'

Ward lurched as if he'd been hit with a cattle prod. 'Thank God! That's the attorney, Mr Cole. I really do have to take this.' He went behind the plank desk and picked up the phone. Saved by the bell.

I put away my pad and joined Holly at the door.

'I appreciate your time, Mr Ward. Thank you.'

He hesitated, his palm covering the phone.

'Mr Cole. Please give the family my condolences. Gene did not harm that girl. He was only trying to help.'

'I'll tell them. Thanks.'

I followed Holly back out through the reception area to the front door. The reporters were still out there, clumped in the street. A fourth van had joined the others.

I said, 'He seems like a nice man.'

'Oh, Riley's a peach.'

'Can't blame him for being nervous, I guess.'

Holly held the door for me, fighting a tiny smile. 'Well, he's had to answer a lot of delicate questions.'

I looked at her. 'What do you mean, delicate?'

'Riley and Gene are very close friends.'

She looked at me.

'*Very* close.'

I stepped out onto the porch, but she stayed inside.

I said, 'Closer than hiking buddies?'

She nodded.

'We're talking *really* close?'

She stepped out with me, closing the door behind her. 'Riley doesn't think we know, but how can you hide it? Gene went head over heels for Riley the first time he came into the office, and chased him shamelessly.'

'How long has this been going on?'

'Not long. Riley takes these walks with Gene three times a week, but we know.' She raised her eyebrows when she said it, then leaned back inside and glanced over her shoulder to make sure that no one could hear. 'I wish some good-looking guy would chase me like that.'

I gave her my very best smile. 'I think some guy is going to knock himself out for you, Holly.'

She fluttered the big eyes at me. 'Do you think?'

'Got a girlfriend, Holly. Sorry.'

'Well, if you ever decide to trade up.' She let it hang, gave me her nicest smile yet, and started back inside.

'Holly?'

She smiled at me.

'Don't tell anyone else what you just told me, okay?'

'It's just between us.' Then she shut the door and was gone.

I stepped off the porch of the pretty little Craftsman house, and crossed the street to my car, the reporters and camera people watching me. The surfer guy looked pissed. He called, 'Hey, did Ward talk to you?'

'Nope. They let me use their bathroom.'

The reporters let out a collective sigh and relaxed. Feeling better about things.

I sat in my car, but did not start the engine. Working a case is like living a life. You could be going along with your head down, pulling the plow as best you can, but then something happens and the world isn't what you thought it was anymore. Suddenly, the way you see everything is different, as if the world has changed color, hiding things that were there before and revealing things you otherwise would not have seen.

I once was close to a man, a police officer with sixteen years on the job, who was and is a good and decent man, who had been married and faithful to his wife for all of those years, had three children with her and a cabin in Big Bear and a fine and happy life, until the day he left her and married another woman. When he told me the news, I said that I hadn't known he and his wife were having problems, and he said that he hadn't known, either. His wife was devastated, and my friend was horribly guilty. I asked him, the way friends will, what happened. His answer was both simple and terrible. He said, 'I fell in love.' He had met a woman while in line at their bank and in the course of a single conversation his world turned upside down and would never be the same. Blindsided by love.

I thought about Riley Ward, and the woman and two children in the pictures in his office. I thought that maybe he had been blindsided, too, and suddenly the inconsistencies in his and Dersh's version of events at the lake, and why Riley Ward seemed evasive and defensive in his interview, made all the sense in the world, and none of it mattered a damn with the theories of cops and private operators with too much time on their hands.

Dersh and Ward had left the trail in thick cover to be hidden from other hikers. They had not wanted to see; they had wanted to be unseen.

They went down to the water's edge *because* of its impassable nature, never guessing that Karen Garcia's body was waiting in a manner that would force them to cook up a story to explain how they had come to be in such an unlikely place. They had lied to protect the worlds each had built, but now a greater lie had come to feed on their fear.

I sat in my car, feeling bad for Riley Ward with his wife and two kids and secret gay lover, and then I left to call Samantha Dolan.

The office was filled with a golden light when Dolan returned my call. I didn't mind. I was on my second can of Falstaff, and already thinking about the third. I had spent most of the day answering mail, paying bills, and talking to the Pinocchio clock. It hadn't answered yet, but maybe with another few beers.

Dolan said, 'She sounds like Scarlett O'Hara, for Christ's sake. How can you stand it?'

'I went to see Ward this morning. You were right. They were lying.'

I finished the rest of the can and eyed the little fridge. Should've gotten the third before we started.

'I'm listening.'

'Ward and Dersh left the trail because they're lovers.'

Dolan didn't say anything.

'Dolan?'

'I'm here. Ward said that? He told you that's why they left the trail?'

'No, Dolan, Ward did not say that. Ward's got a wife and two kids, and I would think he'd do damned near anything to keep them from knowing.'

'Take it easy.'

'I picked it up from someone who works in his office. It's all the talk, Dolan, and it took me about twenty minutes to find out. I guess you people didn't exactly break your asses doing the background work.'

'Take it easy, I said.'

I listened to her breathe. I guess she listened to me.

She said, 'You okay?'

'I'm pissed off about Dersh. I'm pissed off that all of this is going to come out and hurt Ward's family.'

'You want to go have a drink?'

'Dolan, I'm doing okay on my own.'

She didn't say any more for a while. I thought about getting the next beer, but didn't. Pinocchio was watching me.

She said, 'I was going to call you.'

'Why?'

'We found Edward Deege.'

'He have anything?'

'If he had anything, we won't know it. He was dead.'

I leaned back and stared out the French doors. Sometimes the gulls will swing past, or hover on the wind, but now the sky was empty.

She said, 'Some construction guys found him in a Dumpster up by the lake. It looks like he was beaten to death.'

'You don't know what happened?'

'He probably got into a beef with another homeless guy. You know how that goes. Maybe he was robbed, or maybe he snatched somebody's stash. Hollywood Division is working on it. I'm sorry.'

'What are you going to do about Ward?'

'I'll tip Stan Watts and let him follow up. Stan's a good guy. He'll try to go easy.'

'Great.'

'It's the only chance Dersh has.'

'Great.'

'You sure about that drink?'

'I'm sure. Maybe some other time.'

When Dolan finally spoke again, her voice was quiet.

'You know something, World's Greatest?'

'What?'

'You're not just mad about Ward.'

She hung up, leaving me to wonder what she meant.

20

That Day

The pain burns through him the way his skin burned when he was beaten as a child, burns so hot that his nerves writhe beneath his skin like electric worms burrowing through his flesh. It can get so bad that he has to bite his own arms to keep from screaming.

It is all about control.

He knows that.

If you can control yourself, they cannot hurt you.

If you can command yourself, they will pay.

The killer fills the first syringe with Dianabol, a methandrostenolone steroid he bought in Mexico, and injects it into his right thigh. The next he fills with Somatropin, a synthetic growth hormone also from Mexico that was made for use with cattle. He injects this into his left thigh, and enjoys the burning sensation that always accompanies the injection. An hour ago, he swallowed two androstene tablets to increase his body's production of testosterone. He will wait a few more minutes, then settle onto the weight bench and work until his muscles scream and fail and only then will he rest. No pain, no gain, and he must gain strength and size and power, because there is still murder to be done.

He admires his naked body in the full-length mirror, and flexes. Rippling muscles. Cobblestone abs. Tattoos that desecrate his flesh. Pretty. He puts on the sunglasses. Better.

The killer lies back on the weight bench and waits for the chemicals to course through his veins. He is pleased that the police have finally found Edward Deege's body. That is part of his plan. Because of the body, they will question the neighbors. Evidence he has placed will be discovered, and that is part of the plan also; a plan that he has crafted as carefully as he crafts his body, and his vengeance.

He cautions himself to be patient.

The military manuals say that no plan of action ever survives first contact with the enemy. One must be adaptable. One must allow the plan to evolve.

His plan has already morphed several times – Edward Deege being one such morph – and will morph again. Take Dersh. All the attention on Dersh annoyed him until he realized that Dersh could become part of the plan, just like Deege. It was an epiphany. One sweet moment when, through Dersh, the plan changed from death to lifelong imprisonment. Humiliation. Shame.

Adaptability is everything.

He himself is morphing. Everyone thinks him so quiet. Everyone thinks him so contained.

He is what he needs to be.

The killer relaxes, letting his thoughts drift, but they do not drift to Dersh or the plan or his vengeance; they drift back to that horrible day. He should know better. He always goes back to that day as if to torture himself. Better to play the constant chess game of his plan than wallow in hurt, but for so many years hurt was all he had. His hurt defines him.

He feels the tears which he has never allowed anyone to see, and clenches shut his eyes. The wet creeps from beneath the sunglasses, leaving a trail of acid memories.

He feels the beating. The belt snaps against him until his skin is numb. Fists pound his shoulders and back. He screams and begs and cries, but the people who love him most are the ones who hate him most. *There's no place like home.* Running. Walking. A trip on a bus. He escapes from a place where kindness and cruelty are one and the same, and love and loathing are indistinguishable. He is outside a diner when a man approaches. A kindly man who recognizes his pain. The man's hand touches his shoulder. Words of consolation and friendship. The man cares. Comfort. The rest follows so easily. Love. Dependence. Betrayal. Revenge. Regret.

He remembers that day so vividly. He can see every image as if the movie of his life were broken frame by frame, each picture stark and clear, colors brilliant and sharp. The day the hated ones took the man from him. Took him, destroyed him, killed him. That day, after all these years and all these changes, burns so deeply that every cell is branded.

He was fucked up for years until he gained control over himself. Mastered his feelings, and life. Mastered himself, contained himself, prepared himself so that he can do this:

The tears stop and he opens his eyes. He wipes away the residue, and sits up.

Control.

He is in control.

His loss must be repaid, and he has the means for that now. No longer weak, no longer helpless.

He has a plan of vengeance against the one who hurt him the most, and a list of the conspirators.

He is killing them one by one because payback is a motherfucker, and he is the baddest motherfucker to ever walk with the angels through the streets of this city.

The military calls this 'mission commitment'.

His mission commitment is second to none.

They will pay.

He rolls off the bench and flexes his muscles in the mirror until the skin pulls tight, his veins bulge, and the bright red arrows glow hotly on his deltoids.

Dersh.

Pike's Dream

He ran without a trail because it was harder that way. Dead branches from fallen trees raked at his legs like claws reaching from the earth. The brown leaves that covered the forest floor made for slippery footing as he dodged and twisted around the trees and vines and sinkholes that made him work to maintain his balance. He couldn't fall into a runner's rhythm because he was climbing over deadfalls and jumping over downed limbs as much as he was running, but that was why he did it this way. The Marine Corps Fitness Manual that he bought from a secondhand bookstore called this type of running 'fartlek training', which was something the Swedish Alpine troops thought up, and was the grueling basis behind the Corps's legendary obstacle course. The Fitness Manual said tough training was necessary to build tough men.

Joe Pike, age fourteen.

He loved the smell of the winter woods, and the peace that came from being by himself. He spent as much time as he could here, reading and thinking and following the exercise dicta of the Manual, which had become his bible. There was joy in exhaustion, and a sense of accomplishment in sweat. Joe had decided to join the Marines on his seventeenth birthday. He thought about it every day, and dreamed about it at night. He saw himself standing tall in his dress uniform, or sneaking through the Asian jungles in the war that was waging half a world away (though he was only fourteen, and that war would probably end soon). He enjoyed a thousand different fantasies of himself as a Marine, but, in truth, he mostly saw himself getting on a bus that would take him away from his father. He had his own war right here at home. The one in Vietnam couldn't be any worse.

Joe was still tall for his age, and beginning to fill. He hoped that if he looked old enough when he was sixteen, he might be able to get his mother to fake the papers so that he could join the Corps even sooner. She might do that for him.

If she lived long enough.

Joe pushed himself harder as he neared the end of his run. His breath plumed in the cold air, but he was slick with sweat and didn't feel the cold even though all he wore were red gym shorts and high-top Keds and a sleeveless green tee shirt. He had followed the creek upstream for almost an hour, then turned around, and now he was almost back where he'd begun when he heard the laughter and stopped. The creek ran along the bottom of a slope beneath a gravel road, and, as Pike watched, two boys and a girl appeared at the top of the slope and made their way down a well-worn trail toward the creek.

Pike slipped between the trees.

They were older than Joe, the boys bigger, and Joe thought they might be seniors at the high school where he was a freshman. That would make them about seventeen.

The larger boy was a tall kid with a coarse red face and zits. He was leading the way, pushing low-hanging branches aside and carrying a feed sack with something in it. The other boy brought up the rear. He had long hair like a hippie, and a wispy mustache that looked silly, but his shoulders and thighs were thick. A cigarette dangled from his lips. The girl was built like a pear, with a wide butt. Her features were all jammed together in the center of a Pillsbury doughboy face, her eyes two narrow slits that looked mean. She carried a one-gallon gas can like Joe used to fill his lawn mower, and she was laughing. 'We don't have to walk all the way to Africa, Daryl. There ain't nobody around.'

When she said his name, Joe recognized the boy with the sack. Daryl Haines was a high school dropout who worked at the Shell station. For a while, he had worked at the Pac-a-Sac convenience store, selling cigarettes and Slurpees, but he'd been caught filching money from the cash register and been fired. He was eighteen, at least, and might even be older. Once, Daryl had gassed up the Kingswood, but Mr Pike discovered gas splattered on the paint. He'd gotten the red ass and raised nine kinds of hell. Now, when Mr Pike rolled into the Shell, he pumped his own gas and Daryl kept the fuck away from his car. He'd pointed out Daryl to Joe once, and said, 'That kid's a piece of shit.'

Now, Joe heard Daryl say, 'Just take it easy, baby. I know where I'm goin'.'

The girl laughed again, and her little slit eyes looked worse than mean, they looked evil. 'I ain't gonna wait all day for my fun, Daryl. Just so's you don't chicken out.'

The kid in the rear made a chicken sound. 'Bawk-bawk-bawk.' The cigarette bounced up and down when he made the sound.

Daryl hit the brakes and glared. 'You want me to hand you your ass, you dumb fuck?'

The other kid showed both palms. 'Hey, no, man. I didn't mean nothing.'

'Dumb fuck.'

Now the girl went, 'Bawk-bawk-bawk,' looking at the cigarette boy.

Daryl liked that, and they continued on the trail.

Joe let them get ahead, then followed. He moved carefully, taking his time to avoid twigs and branches, staying off leaves where possible, and, where not, working his toes under the crispy top layer to put his weight on the damp matter beneath. Pike spent so much time in the woods that he had learned its ways, easily tracking and stalking the whitetail deer that fed through the area. He found comfort in being so much a part of this place that he was invisible. Once, his father had chased him into the woods behind their house, but Joe had slipped away and his father couldn't find him. To be hidden was to be safe.

They didn't go far.

Daryl led them up the creek to a small clearing. It was a popular spot for drinking parties, the ground scarred with the remains of bonfires and beer cans. The girl said, 'Well, all right! Take it out of the bag and let's see the show!'

The kid with the cigarette said something Pike couldn't hear, and laughed. Yuk-yuk-yuk. Like Jughead.

Daryl put the sack on the ground and took out a small black cat. He held it by the scruff of the neck and the back legs, saying, 'You better not scratch me, you sonofabitch.'

Pike slipped down into the creek bed, and eased along the soft earth there to work closer. The cat was grown, but small, so Pike thought it was probably a female. It made itself smaller against Daryl, its yellow eyes wide with fear. Frightened by the bag, and these people, but by the woods, too. Cats didn't like unknown places, where something might hurt them. The little cat made a squeaking mew that Joe found sad. It only had one ear, and Pike wondered how it had lost the other.

The girl unscrewed the can, grinning as if she'd just won a prize. 'Splash it real good with this, Daryl!'

The cigarette boy said, 'Shoulda got gasoline.'

The girl snapped, 'Turpentine is better! Don't you know anything?'

She said it as if she'd done this a hundred times. Pike thought she probably had.

For the first time in two hours, Joe Pike felt the cold. They were going to burn this animal. Set it on fire. Listen to it scream. Watch it twist and writhe until it died.

Daryl said, 'Get the can. C'mon, quick, before the bastard bites me.'

Daryl held the cat to the ground as far from himself as he could, while the cigarette boy took the can and splashed turpentine on the cat. When the turpentine hit it, the cat hunched and tried to get away.

The girl said, 'I wanna light it.' Her eyes bright and ugly.

Daryl said, 'Well, Jesus, don't set me on fire.'

The cigarette kid fumbled some safety matches out of his shirt pocket, dropping most of them. The girl snatched one up, and tried to strike it on the zipper of her jeans.

Daryl said, 'Hurry up, goddamnit. I can't hold this sonofabitch forever!'

Joe Pike stared at the two larger boys and the ugly girl. His chest rose and fell as if he was still running.

The first match broke, and the girl said, 'Shit!'

She picked up a second, scratched it on her zipper, and it burst into flame.

The cigarette boy said, 'All right!'

Daryl said, 'Hurry.'

Joe pulled a deadfall limb from the mud. It was about three feet long and a couple of inches thick. The sucking sound it made coming out of the mud made them look, and then he stepped up out of the creek bed.

The cigarette boy jumped back, almost tripping over his own feet. 'Hey!'

The three of them stared at Joe, and then the moment of their surprise passed.

The match burned the girl's fingers, and she dropped it. 'Shit, it's just some kid.'

Daryl said, 'Get out of here, fuckface, before I kick your ass.'

The cat still squirmed. Joe smelled the turpentine.

'Let it go.'

The girl said, 'Fuck you, retard. You watch how this thing's gonna jump.' She bent to pick up another match.

Joe hoped they would just leave. Just set the cat free and go because they'd been caught. He stepped forward. 'Can't let you burn that cat.'

Daryl's eyes went to the stick, then Joe, and he smiled. 'Looks like you already had your ass kicked, shitball. You want, I can bust your other eye. I can kick your fuckin' guts out for you.'

The cigarette boy laughed.

Purple-and-green bruises were fading from Joe's left eye, the remains of the beating his father had given him six days ago. He thought that these big boys could probably beat him, too, but then it occurred to him that he'd been beaten so often, another beating wouldn't matter much. That struck Joe as funny, and he wanted to laugh, thought he might just roar with laughter, but all that came out was a twitch at the corner of his mouth.

The little cat's eyes found Joe, and Joe thought that his eyes might look like that when his father was beating him.

He stepped toward Daryl. 'Only an asshole picks on a helpless little cat.'

Daryl grinned wider, then glanced at the girl. 'Light it up, goddamnit. Then I'm gonna kick this turd's ass.'

The second match flared, and the girl hurried toward the cat.

The world as Joe Pike saw it receded as if he was looking through the wrong end of a looking glass. He felt calm, and absolutely at peace as he lifted the stick and ran at Daryl as hard as he could. Daryl shouted, surprised that Joe was really going to take him on, and rose to meet the charge. The cat, suddenly free, streaked between the trees and was gone.

The girl screamed, 'It's getting away!' Like her little show was over and she'd missed the best part.

Joe brought the stick down as hard as he could, but the stick was half rotten and broke across Daryl's forearms with a wet snap.

Daryl threw a wild windmill of punches, catching Joe in the forehead and the chest, and then the other boy was behind Joe, punching as hard as he could. Joe felt their blows hitting him, but oddly felt no pain. It was as if he were somewhere deep within himself, a small boy alone in a dark wood, watching the action without being a part of it.

The fat girl had gotten over her disappointment, and was now jumping up and down, pumping her fists like she was rooting for her football team to make the game-winning score. 'Kill him! Kill the motherfucker!'

Joe stood between the two older boys, punching wildly. The cigarette boy hit him hard behind the right ear, and when Joe turned to meet him, Daryl kicked him in the back of the leg, and Joe fell.

Daryl and the cigarette boy leaned over Joe, throwing a flurry of blows that rained on Joe's face and head and back and arms, but still he felt nothing.

They were big kids, but his father was bigger.

They were strong boys, but his father was stronger.

Joe rolled onto his knees, feeling their punches and kicks even as he lurched to his feet.

Daryl Haines hit him hard in the face again and again and again. Joe tried to hit the bigger boys, but more of his punches fell short or missed.

Then someone tripped him, and, again, he fell.

Daryl Haines kicked him, but his father kicked harder.

Joe climbed to his feet.

The girl was still screaming, but when Joe was once more erect, Daryl Haines had a strange look on his face. The cigarette boy was breathing hard, winded from throwing so many punches, arms leaden at his sides. Daryl was breathing hard, too, looking at Joe as if he didn't believe what he was seeing. His hands were covered in red.

The girl screamed, 'Beat him, Daryl! Beat him real good!'

Joe clawed at Daryl, trying to gouge his eyes, but missed and fell, landing on his side.

Daryl stood over him, blood dripping from his hands. 'Stay down, kid.'

'Beat him to death, Daryl! Don't stop!'

'Stay down.'

Joe pushed himself to his knees. He tried to focus on Daryl, but Daryl was hazy and red, and Joe realized his eyes were filled with blood.

'Are you fuckin' nuts? Stay down.'

Joe lurched to his feet and swung as hard as he could.

Daryl stepped outside of it, then jumped forward and hit Joe square on the end of the nose. Joe heard the crack and felt it, and knew that Daryl had broken his nose. He'd heard the sound before.

Joe fell, and immediately tried to get up again.

Daryl grabbed him by the shirt and shoved him down. 'You little shit! What's wrong with you?'

The cigarette kid was holding his side like he had a stitch. 'Let's get out of here, man. I don't wanna do this no more.'

Joe said, 'Gonna beat you.' His lips were split and it was hard to speak.

'It's over!'

Joe tried to hit Daryl from the ground, but the punch missed by a good foot.

'It's over, goddamnit. You're beat!'

Joe tried to hit Daryl again, but this time he missed by a yard.

'Not over . . . until I win.'

Daryl stepped back then, his face a raw mask of rage. 'Okay, you dumb shit. I warned you.'

Daryl reared back, kicked Joe as hard as he could, and Joe felt the world explode between his legs. Then there were stars and blackness.

Joe heard them leaving, or thought he did. It seemed like hours before he could move, and when he finally worked his way to his knees, the woods were still. His groin ached, and he felt nauseous. He touched his face. His hand came away red. His tee shirt was splattered with drying blood. More blood streaked his arms.

It was several minutes before he smelled the turpentine again, and then he saw the one-eared cat, staring at him from beneath the rotten branches of a fallen tree.

Joe Pike said, 'Hey, cat.'

The cat vanished.

'That's okay, girl. You're okay.'

He thought she was probably scared.

He wondered why he wasn't.

After a while he went home.

Three days later Daryl Haines scowled at the envelope and said, 'Fuck this shit.'

It was five minutes before 8 P.M. at the Shell station. Daryl was sitting on the hard chair he kept out front by the Coke machine, leaning back the way he did, snug in his down jacket, but pissed off about the letter. It was a notice from the goddamned Army to report for his induction physical.

Daryl Haines, eighteen years old and without the luxury of a college deferment, was 1-A infantry material. He had to take the bus down to the city this Saturday just to have his ass poked and prodded by some faggot Army doctor so they could ship him over to Vietnam.

Daryl said, 'This sucks.'

Maybe he should join the Air Force.

Daryl's older brother, Todd, was already over there. He had a cushy job working on trucks at an air base near Saigon and said it wasn't so bad. You got to screw around a lot, smoke all the pot you wanted, and fuck good-lookin' gook women for twenty-five cents a throw. His brother made it sound like goddamned Disneyland, but Daryl figured with his rotten luck he'd probably have to carry a gun and get shot.

'Fuck.'

At eight o'clock, Daryl shut the lights, turned off the pumps, locked the station, and headed down the street, wishing he could stop in a bar. Eighteen years old being old enough to kill gooks, but not old enough to down a beer when you were thinking about it.

Daryl was thinking that he could drown his sorrow between Candy Crowley's legs if the fat psycho bitch would ever come across. He was almost there last Sunday, when the nutty bitch got it in her head to burn a cat. You just had to shake your head sometimes, where she came up with stuff like that. But it seemed to get her righteously damp, and Daryl thought he'd finally get the old ball between the uprights, as it were, when that weird kid spoiled the deal. Another fuckin' nut. That kid had taken the best beating that Daryl Haines ever dished out, and he just wouldn't quit. Didn't cry, either, not even after Daryl scrambled his eggs for him. You'd think the goddamned cat belonged to the kid, the way he carried on, but Daryl had stolen it from Old Lady Wilbur, his next-door neighbor.

You just had to shake your head.

Daryl was still thinking about it when this voice said, 'Daryl.'

Daryl said, 'Yeah?'

The kid stepped out from behind this big azalea bush, his face swollen and lumpy with bruises. A big piece of tape covered his nose, and black stitches laced his lip and left eyebrow like railroad tracks.

Daryl, feeling righteously cranky because he'd been drafted, said, 'You want some more, you little fuck, you picked the right time. I'm goin' to Vietnam.'

But that didn't impress the kid, who suddenly had a Louisville Slugger baseball bat in his hands and hit Daryl on the outside of the left knee as if he was swinging away for the green wall at Fenway Park.

Daryl Haines screamed as he fell. It felt as if someone had sewn an M80 in his knee and touched the sucker off. Daryl clutched at his knee, still howling as the kid brought the bat down again. Daryl saw it coming and raised his hands, and then a second M80 went off in his right arm. Daryl screamed, 'Jesus Christ! Stop it! Stop! Don't hit me again!'

The kid tossed the bat aside and stared at him. The kid's face was empty, and that scared Daryl even more than all the gooks in Vietnam.

The kid kicked Daryl in the side of the head, kicked him again, then leaned over and punched Daryl three fast times in the face. Daryl's sky filled with a million little sparkly stars against a black field, and then Daryl puked.

'Daryl?'

'Uhn . . .'

'It's not over until I win.'

Daryl spit blood. 'You win. Jesus Christ, you win. I give up.'

The kid stepped back.

Daryl was crying so bad he felt like a baby. The kid had broken his leg and arm. Jesus, it hurt.

'Daryl.'

'Please, Christ, don't hit me again.' Scared the kid was gonna bash him some more.

'How could you want to hurt something so weak?'

'Jesus. Oh, Christ.'

'You ever do that, Daryl, I'll find you and kill you. That cat would kill you if it could, but it can't. I'll kill you for it.'

'I swear to Sweet Jesus I won't do that! I swear!'

The kid picked up his bat and walked away.

Twelve weeks later, after the casts were removed and the last of the stitches had come out, the Army doctors finally did their examination. Daryl Haines was determined to be 4-F due to a permanently disabled left knee. Unfit for military service.

He did not go to Vietnam.

He never tried to burn another cat.

21

His eyes opened, and Pike was as alert as if it were the middle of the afternoon, not two in the morning. Sleep would not come again after the dream, so he rose and pulled on briefs and shorts. He thought for a moment that he might read, but he usually exercised after the dreams. The exercise worked better for him.

He put on the blue Nike running shoes, then buckled on a small fanny pack, not bothering to turn on the lights. He was comfortable in the dark. Years ago, the Marine doctors told him that his excellent night vision was due to high levels of vitamin A and 'fast rhodopsin', which meant that the pigment in his retinas which responded to dim light was very sensitive. Cat eyes, they called it.

He let himself out into the cool night air, and stretched to loosen his hamstrings. Even though he often ran forty miles a week, his muscles were loose from the years of yoga and martial arts, and responded well. He settled the fanny pack on his hips, then jogged out across the complex grounds, through the security door, and into the street. The fanny pack held his keys, and a small black .25 caliber Beretta. You never know.

Much of his running was done early like this, and he found peace in it. The city was quiet. When he chose, he could run on the crown of the street, or through parks or across a golf course. He enjoyed the natural feel of grass and earth, and knew these feelings were resonances from his youth.

He ran west on Washington Boulevard toward the ocean, taking it easy for the first quarter mile to let his body warm, then picked up his pace. The air was cool, and a ground fog hazed the streets. The fog caught the light and hid the stars, which he didn't like. He enjoyed reading the constellations, and finding his way by them. There was a time as a young Marine when his life depended on it, and he found comfort in the certainty of celestial mechanics. Two or three times every year, he and his friend Elvis Cole would backpack or hunt in remote terrain, and, during those times, they would test themselves and each other by navigating via the sun and moon and stars. More times, Pike would venture out alone to remote and alien locales. He had learned long ago that a compass and GPS could fail. You had to look to yourself. You could only depend upon yourself.

Images came. Flashing snapshot pictures of his childhood, of women he had known, men he had seen die, and men he had killed. Of his friend and partner Elvis Cole, of the people he employed in his various businesses. Sometimes he would ponder these images, but other times he would fold them smaller and smaller until they vanished.

He followed Washington Boulevard as it curved north through Venice, then left Main for Ocean Avenue, where he could hear the waves crashing on the beach below the bluff.

Pike increased his kick past the Santa Monica Pier, past the shopping carts and homeless encampments, extending his stride as he worked his way to a six-minute-mile pace. He sprinted past the Ivy-by-the-Shore and the hotels, feeling himself peak, holding that peak, then throttled back to an easy jog before walking to the rail at the edge of the bluff, where he stopped to look at the sea.

He watched ships, stars on a black horizon. A breeze caressed his back, inland air drawn to the warmth of the sea. Above him, dried palm fronds rustled. A lone car slid past, lost in the night.

Here on the bluff overlooking the water, there were green lawns and bike paths and towering palms. A bush to his right rustled, and he knew it was a girl before he saw her.

'Are you Matt?'

She was tentative, but not afraid. Early twenties or late teens, with short hair bleached white, and wide brown eyes that looked at him expectantly. A faded green backpack hung from her shoulder.

'You're Matt?'

'No.'

She seemed disappointed, but was completely relaxed, as if the reality that she should be frightened of a strange man in so deserted a place had never occurred to her. 'I guess you wouldn't be. I'm Trudy.'

'Joe.'

He turned back to the lights on the horizon.

'Pleased to meet you, Joe. I'm running away, too.'

He considered her briefly again, wondering why she had chosen those words, then returned to the ships.

Trudy leaned against the rail, trying to see over the edge of the bluff to Palisades Beach Road. She gave no indication of leaving. Pike thought that he might start running again.

She said, 'Are you real?'

'No.'

'No kidding, now. I want to know.'

He held out his hand.

Trudy touched him with a finger, then gripped his wrist, as if she didn't trust her first touch.

'Well, you might've been a vision or something. I have them, you know. Sometimes I imagine things.'

When Pike didn't respond, she said, 'I've changed my mind. I don't think you're running away. I think you're running toward.'

'Is that a vision? Or something you imagined?'

She stared up at him as if she had to consider which it might be, then shook her head. 'An observation.'

'Look.'

Three coyotes had appeared at the edge of the light, having worked their way up the bluff from the Palisades. Two of them sniffed at one of the garbage cans that dotted the park, the third trotted across Ocean Avenue and disappeared in an alley. They looked like thin gray dogs. Scavengers.

Trudy said, 'It's so amazing that wild things can live here in the city, isn't it?'

'Wild things are everywhere.'

Trudy grinned at him again. 'Well. That's certainly deep.'

The two coyotes suddenly came alert, looking north toward the Palisades an instant before Pike heard the coyote pack's song. Their singing rode down on the breeze coming out of the hills, and Pike guessed their number at between eight and twelve. The two coyotes by the garbage cans looked at each other, then lifted their snouts to test the air. *You're safe enough*, Pike thought. The others were at least three miles away, well up in the canyons of the Palisades.

The girl said, 'That's such a terrible sound.'

'It means they have food.'

She hitched her backpack. 'They eat people's pets. They'll bait a dog away from its home, then surround it and rip it to pieces.'

Pike knew that to be true, but still. 'They have to live.'

The singing grew to a higher pitch. The two coyotes by the garbage can stood frozen.

The girl looked away from the sound. 'They have something now. They're killing it right now.'

The girl's eyes were vacant. Pike thought she didn't seem to be within herself, and wondered if she was with the pack.

'They'll pull it to pieces, and sometimes, if too much blood gets on one of their own, the others will mistake it for the prey and kill their own kind.'

Pike nodded. People could be like that, too.

The singing abruptly stopped, and the girl came back to herself. 'You don't say very much, do you?'

'You were saying enough for both of us.'

The girl laughed. 'Yeah, I guess I was. Hope I didn't weird you out, Joe. I do that to people sometimes.'

Joe shook his head. 'Not yet.'

A black minivan turned off Wilshire and came along Ocean Avenue, washing them with its headlights. It stopped in the middle of the street near where the coyote had crossed.

Trudy said, 'Gotta be Matt. It was nice talking with you, Running Man.'

She hitched the backpack, then trotted to the van. Trudy spoke to someone through the passenger's window, then the door opened, and Trudy climbed in. The van had no plates, and no dealer card, though it gleamed with the newness of a vehicle just driven off the lot. In seconds, it was gone.

Pike said, 'Goodbye, Running Girl.'

Pike glanced toward the garbage cans, but the coyotes were gone. Back to their own place in the hills. Wild things lost in the dark.

Pike leaned against the rail to stretch his calves, then ran inland up Wilshire.

He ran in the darkness, away from cars and people, enjoying the solitude.

Amanda Kimmel said, 'Good riddance!'

Seventy-eight years old, loosely wrapped in skin that made her look like a pale raisin, and with a left leg that tingled as if bugs were creeping in all the little wrinkle troughs, Amanda Kimmel watched the two detectives sneak out of the house they were using to spy on Eugene Dersh and drive away. She shook her head with disgust. 'Those two turds stand out like warts on a baby's ass, don't they, Jack?'

Jack didn't answer.

'Wouldn't cut the mustard in Five-O, I'll bet. You'd have their sorry asses back on the mainland faster than rats can fuck.'

Amanda Kimmel dragged the heavy M1 Garand rifle back to the TV and settled in her BarcaLounger. The TV was the only light she allowed herself these days, living like a mole in the goddamned darkness so she could keep an eye on all the cops and reporters and nutcase lookieloos who had been crashing around outside since they'd learned her neighbor, Mr Dersh, was a maniac. Just her goddamned luck, to live right behind the next fuckin' Son of Sam.

Amanda said, 'This is the shits, ain't it, Jack?'.

Jack didn't answer because she had the sound off.

Amanda Kimmel watched *Hawaii Five-O* reruns every night on Nick-at-Nite, feeling that Jack Lord was the finest police officer who ever lived, and *Hawaii Five-O* the finest cop show that had ever been made. You could have your Chuck Norris and Jimmy Smits. She'd take Jack Lord any day.

Amanda settled back, had a healthy sip of scotch, and patted the M1 lovingly. Her second husband had brought the M1 home from fighting the Japs a million years ago and stuck it under the bed. Or was it her first husband? The M1 was as big as a telephone pole, and Amanda could barely lift the damned thing, but what with all the strangers creeping around outside these days as well as her living next to a maniac, well, a girl had to do what a girl had to do.

'Right, Jack?'

Jack grinned, and she just knew that he'd agree.

The first few days, armies of people poured through her neighborhood. Cars filled with rubber neckers and mouth breathers. Numbskulls who wanted their picture taken standing in Dersh's yard. (Get a goddamned life!) Reporters with cameras and microphones, making God's own noise and not giving two hoots and a damn who they disturbed. She'd even caught one reporter, that horrible little man on Channel 2, tromping through her roses as he tried to get into Dersh's yard. She'd cursed him a blue streak, but he'd gone ahead anyway, so she turned on her sprinklers and hosed the weaselly sonofabitch down good.

After that first few days, the crush of reporters and numbskulls had slacked off because the cops ran out of places to search, so there wasn't much for the TV people to tape. The cops pretty much stayed on the street in front of Dersh's house, leaving when he left and coming when he came, except for the cops who sucked around the empty house next door at four-hour intervals. Amanda suspected that the reporters didn't know about the cops in the house, which was fine by her because the cops made enough noise by themselves, managing to wake her each time the shifts changed, because she slept so poorly what with the leg and all.

'Being old is hell, isn't it, Jack? Can't sleep, can't shit, and you don't get laid.'

Jack Lord punched a fat Hawaiian on the nose. Yeah, Jack knew that being old was hell.

Amanda drained the rest of her scotch and eyed the bottle, thinking maybe it was time for a little refill when a car door slammed, and she thought, 'Those goddamned cops with their noise again.' Probably forgot their cigarettes up in the house.

Amanda shut the TV, then dragged the big M1 back to the window, thinking that she just might scream holy hell at the bastards, keeping her up like this, only it wasn't the two cops.

Between the half-moon and the streetlamp, she could see the man pretty well, even with seventy-eight-year-old eyes and a belly full of scotch. He was walking from the street down along the alley toward Dersh's house, and he certainly wasn't a cop or a reporter. He was a large man, dressed in blue jeans and a sweatshirt without sleeves, and something stuck out about him right away. Here it was the middle of the night, dark as the inside of a cat's butt, and this asshole was wearing sunglasses.

Her first thought was that he must be a criminal of some kind – a burglar or a rapist – so she hefted up the M1 to draw a bead on the sonofabitch, but before she could get the gun steadied, he disappeared past the hedges and was gone.

'Goddamnit! C'mon back here, you sonofabitch!'

She waited.

Nothing.

'Damn!'

Amanda Kimmel propped the M1 against the window, then went back to her chair, poured a fresh slug of scotch, and took a taste. Maybe the guy was some friend of Dersh's (he had male friends visit at all hours, and she certainly knew what *that* meant), or maybe he was just an after-hours lookieloo (Lord knows, there'd been plenty, often dressed more oddly than this).

The short, sharp *bang* damned near knocked her out of her chair.

Amanda had never in her life heard that sound, but she knew without doubt what it was.

A gunshot.

'Holy shit, Jack! I guess that sonofabitch wasn't a lookieloo, after all!'

Amanda Kimmel scooped up her phone, called the police, and told them that Eugene Dersh had just been murdered by a man with red arrows tattooed on his arms.

Part Two

22

The morning heat brought the smell of wild sage up from the canyon. Something rumbled far away, a muffled thumping like the sound of heavy bombs beyond the horizon. I hadn't thought of the war in years, and pulled the sheet over my head.

Lucy snuggled into my back. 'Someone's at the door.'

'What?'

She burrowed her face into me, her hand sliding across my side. I liked the dry heat of her palm. 'At the door.'

Knocking.

'It's not even seven.'

She burrowed deeper. 'Take your gun.'

I pulled on gym shorts and a sweatshirt, and went down to see. The cat was squatting in the entry, ears down, growling. Who needs a Doberman when you've got a cat like this?

Stan Watts and Jerome Williams were on the other side of the door, looking like they'd been up a while. Watts was chewing a breath mint.

'What are you guys doing here?'

They stepped in without answering. When they did, the cat arched his back and hissed.

Williams said, 'Hey, that's some cat.'

'Better watch it. He bites.'

Williams went over to the cat. 'Hell, cats like me. You'll see.'

Williams put out his hand. The cat's fur stood up and the growl got as loud as a police siren. Williams stepped back fast.

'He got some kinda thing with black people?'

'He's got a thing with everybody. It's seven in the morning, Watts. Did Dersh confess? You guys ID the shooter?'

Watts sucked at the mint. 'Wondering where you were last night, is all. Got a few questions.'

'About what?'

'About where you were.'

I glanced at Williams again, and now Williams was watching me.

'I was here, Watts. What's going on?'

'Can you prove it?'

Lucy said, 'Yes, he can. But he doesn't have to.'

The three of us looked up. Lucy was standing at the loft's rail, wearing my big white terry-cloth robe.

I said, 'Lucille Chenier. Detectives Watts and Williams.'

Watts said, 'You here with him?'

Lucy smiled. Sweetly. 'I don't think I have to answer that.'

Watts held up his badge.

'Now I know I don't have to answer that.'

Williams said, 'Man. First this cat.'

Watts shrugged. 'We were hoping to be nice.'

Lucy's smile dropped away. 'You'll be nice whether you want to be or not, and unless you have a warrant, we can and will ask you to leave.'

Williams said, 'Well, for Christ's sake.'

'Lucy's an attorney, Watts, so don't get cute on us. I was here. Lucy and I went down to the Ralph's for some things, and made dinner. The receipt's probably in the trash. We rented a movie from Blockbuster. It's over there on the VCR.'

'How about your buddy Pike? When was the last time you saw him?'

Lucy had come down the stairs and was standing next to me with her arms crossed. She said, 'Don't answer him until he tells you why, and maybe not even then. Don't answer any more of his questions.' She faced me and her eyes were serious. 'This is the lawyer talking, do you understand?'

I spread my hands. 'You heard her, Watts. So either tell me what's going on or hit the road.'

'Eugene Dersh was shot to death last night. We picked up Joe Pike for it.'

I stared at him. I glanced at Williams.

'Are you guys joking?'

They weren't joking.

'Is Krantz running a number on Joe? Is that what this is?'

'Eyewitness saw him going into the house. We've got him downtown now to run a lineup.'

'That's bullshit. Pike didn't kill anyone.' I was getting excited. Lucy touched my back.

Watts spoke quietly. 'Are you saying he was here at the house with you two?'

Lucy stepped directly in front of me. 'Are you arresting Mr Cole?'

'No, ma'am.'

'Are you exercising any warrants at this time?' Her voice was all business.

'We just wanted to talk, is all.' He looked at me past her. 'We don't think you're good for it. We just wanted to see what you knew.'

Lucy shook her head. 'This interview is at an end. If you are not prepared to arrest him, or me, please leave.'

*

The phone rang even as I locked the door.

Lucy answered, scooping up the phone before I could get there. 'Who's calling, please?'

She was in full-blown protectress mode, still my girlfriend and the woman I loved, but now as focused as a female tiger protecting her mate; face down, concentrating on what was being said.

Finally, she held out the phone. 'It's someone named Charlie Bauman. He says he's a criminal attorney representing Joe.'

'Yeah.'

Charlie Bauman had been a United States attorney prosecuting federal cases until he decided to make five times the money defending the same guys he'd once tried to put behind bars. He had an office in Santa Monica, three ex-wives, and, at last count, eight children among them. He paid more in child support than I earned in a good year, and he'd represented Joe and me before.

He said, 'Who in hell is that woman?'

'Lucy Chenier. She's a friend of mine. She's also a lawyer.'

'Christ, what a ball-buster. You hear about Joe?'

'Two cops were just here. All I know is they said Dersh was murdered, and they've got an eyewitness who puts Joe at the scene. What in hell is going on?'

'You know anything about it?'

'No, I do not know anything about it.' Irritated that he would ask.

'Okay, okay. *Watch out, dickhead! Christ!*' Horns blew. Charlie was on his car phone. 'I'm on my way down to Parker Center now. They're waiting for the lineup to book him.'

'I want to be there.'

'Forget it. They'll never let you.'

'I'm coming down there, Charlie. I'm going to be there. I mean it.'

I hung up without another word. Lucy was watching me, her face grave. 'Elvis?'

I've been in war. I've faced men with guns, and dangerous stronger men who were doing their best to hurt me, but I could not recall a time when I was more afraid. My hands trembled.

Lucy said, 'Elvis? Is this man good?'

'Charlie's good.'

She still watched me, as if she was searching for something.

I said, 'Joe didn't do this.'

She nodded.

'Joe didn't do this. Dersh didn't kill Karen. Joe knows it. He wouldn't kill Dersh.'

Lucy kissed my cheek. There was a kindness in her eyes that bothered me. 'Call me when you know more. Give Joe my best.'

She went up the stairs, and I watched her go.

*

Parker Center uses the ground floor for booking and processing suspects. A few minutes after I checked in, Charlie hurried out a gray metal door.

'You just made it. Another five minutes, you'd've missed it.' Charlie Bauman is several inches shorter than me, with a lean pockmarked face and intense eyes. He smells like cigarettes.

'Can I see Joe?'

'Not till after. We get in the room, there's gonna be the witness. She's some little old lady. You let the cops do all the talking, doesn't matter what she says.'

'I know that, Charlie.'

'I'm just telling you. No matter what she says, you don't say anything. Me and you, we can't talk to her, we can't ask her any questions, we can't make any comments, okay?'

'I got it.' Charlie seemed nervous, and I didn't like that.

I followed him back along a tile hall as we spoke. The hall opened into a wide room that looked like any other corporate workplace, except this one had posters about drunk-driving fatalities.

'Have you had a chance to talk to him?'

'Enough to get the gist. We'll talk more, after.'

I stopped him. Behind us, two detectives I didn't know were positioning a black guy in front of a camera like they use to take driver's license pictures, only this guy wasn't up for renewal. His hands were cuffed, and his eyes were wide and afraid. He was saying, 'THIS IS BULLSHIT. THIS THREE STRIKE CRAP IS *BULLSHIT*.'

'Charlie, do these guys have anything?'

'If the witness makes a positive ID and they write the paper, then we'll see. She's old, and when they're old they get confused. If we're lucky, she'll pick the wrong guy and we can all go home early.'

He wasn't answering me.

'Do they have anything?'

'They've already got a prosecutor coming down. He'll lay it out for us when he gets here. I don't know what they have, but they wouldn't've called him down if they didn't think they have a case.'

Krantz and Stan Watts came out of an adjoining hall. Krantz was holding a cup of coffee, Watts was holding two.

Charlie said, 'Okay, Krantz. Whenever you're ready.'

I looked at Krantz. 'What are you pulling on Joe?'

Krantz appeared more calm than I'd ever seen him. As if he was at peace. 'I can show you Dersh's body, if you want.'

'I don't know what happened to Dersh. What I'm saying is that Joe didn't do it.'

Krantz raised his eyebrows and looked at Watts. 'Stan here told me that you were at home with a woman last night. Was he wrong about that?' He looked back at me. 'Were you with Pike?'

'You know what I'm saying.'

Krantz blew on his coffee, then sipped. 'No, Cole, I don't know that. But here's what I do know: At three-fifteen this morning a man matching Pike's description was seen entering Eugene Dersh's backyard. A few moments after that, Dersh was shot to death by one shot to the head with a .357 magnum. Could be a .38, but judging from the way the head blew apart, I'm betting .357. We've already recovered the bullet. We'll see what it tells us.'

'You got any fingerprints? You got any physical evidence that it was Joe, or is this another investigation like you ran with Dersh, you just working off an urge?'

'I'm going to let the prosecutor explain our case to Pike's lawyer. You're just here on a pass, Cole. Please remember that.'

Behind us, Williams appeared, saying that everything was good to go. Krantz nodded at me. Confident. 'Let's see what the witness says.'

They led us past six holding cells into a dim room where a uniformed cop and two detectives were waiting with a shrunken woman in her late seventies. Watts gave her the second cup of coffee. She sipped at it and made a face.

Charlie whispered. 'Amanda Kimmel. She's the wit.'

Krantz said, 'You okay, Mrs Kimmel? You want to sit?'

She frowned at him. 'I wanna get this done and get the hell outta here. I don't like to move my bowels in a strange place.'

The wall in front of us was a large glass double-paned window that looked into a narrow room lit so brightly that it glowed. Krantz picked up a phone, and thirty seconds later a door on the right side of the room opened. A black cop with bodybuilder muscles led in six men. Joe Pike was the third. Of the remaining five, three were white and two were Hispanic. Four of the men were Joe's height or shorter, and one was taller. Only one of the other men wore jeans and a sleeveless sweatshirt like Joe, and that was a short Hispanic guy with skinny arms. The other three wore a mix of chinos or dungarees or coveralls, and long-sleeved sweatshirts or short-sleeved tees, and all six were wearing sunglasses. Every man in the room except Joe was a cop.

I bent to Charlie's ear. 'I thought they had to be dressed like Joe.'

'Law says it only has to be similar, whatever the hell that means. Let's see. Maybe this works for us.'

When all six men were lined along the stage, Krantz said, 'Nobody on that side of the glass can see in here, Mrs Kimmel. Don't you worry about that. You're perfectly safe.'

'I don't give a rat's ass if they can see me or not.'

'Is one of the men in there the same man you saw going into Eugene Dersh's yard?'

Amanda Kimmel said, 'Him.'

'Which one, Mrs Kimmel?'

'The third one.'

She pointed at Joe Pike.

'You're sure, Mrs Kimmel? Take a careful look.'

'That's him right there. I know what I saw.'

Charlie whispered, 'Shit.'

Krantz glanced at Charlie now, but Charlie was watching Mrs Kimmel.

Krantz said, 'Okay, but I'm going to ask you again. You're saying you saw that man, number three, walk down the alley beside your house and go into Eugene Dersh's backyard?'

'Damned right. You can't miss a face like that. You can't miss those arms.'

'And when the officers took your statement, that is the man you described?'

'Hell, yes. I saw him real good. Look at those damned tattoos.'

'All right, Mrs Kimmel. Detective Watts is going to take you up to my office now. Thank you.'

Krantz didn't look at her when he said it; he was staring at Joe. He did not look at me or Charlie or Williams or anyone else in the room. He did not watch Mrs Kimmel leave. He kept his eyes on Pike, and picked up the phone.

'Cuff the suspect and bring him in, please.'

Suspect.

The big cop handcuffed Joe, then brought him into the observation room.

Krantz watched Pike being cuffed, watched as he was brought in. When Pike was finally with us, Krantz took off Joe's glasses, folded them, and dropped them into his own pocket. For Krantz, no one else was in that room except him and Joe. No one else was alive, or mattered, or even meant a damn. What was about to happen meant everything. Was the only thing.

He said, 'Joe Pike, you're under arrest for the murder of Eugene Dersh.'

23

Krantz handled the booking himself, taking Joe's fingerprints and snapping his booking photo and typing the forms. Hollywood Homicide raised a stink, trying to keep jurisdiction of Dersh's murder since it fell in their area, but Krantz sucked it into the Robbery-Homicide black hole. Related to the Dersh investigation, he said. Overlapping cases, he said. He wanted Pike.

I watched for a time, sitting with Stan Watts at an empty desk, wishing I could talk to Pike. One minute you're asleep in bed, the next you're watching your friend being booked for murder. You put your feelings away. You make yourself think. Amanda Kimmel had picked Joe out of a lineup, but what did that mean? It meant that she had seen someone who looked more like Joe than the other men in the lineup. I would learn more when I spoke with Joe. I would learn more when I heard the prosecutor's case. When I learned more, I could do something.

I kept telling myself that because I needed to either believe it or scream.

I said, 'This is bullshit, Watts. You know that.'

'Is it?'

'Pike wouldn't kill this guy. Pike didn't think Dersh was good for those killings.'

Watts just stared at me, as blank as a wall. He'd sat with a thousand people who had said they didn't do it when they had.

'What's next, Stan? The serial killer's dead, so you guys are going to declare victory and head for the donuts?'

Watts's expression never changed. 'I realize you're upset because of your friend, but don't mistake me for Krantz. I'll slap your fucking teeth down your throat.'

Finally, Watts took Charlie and me to an interview room where Joe was waiting. His jeans and sweatshirt had been replaced by blue LAPD JAIL coveralls. He sat with his fingers laced on the table, his eyes as calm as a mountain lake. It was odd to see him without his sunglasses. I could count on both hands the number of times I'd seen his eyes. Their blue is astonishing. He squinted, not used to the light.

I sighed. 'All the people in the world who need killing, and you've got to pick Dersh.'

Pike looked at me. 'Was that humor?'

Inappropriate is my middle name.

Charlie said, 'Before we get started, you want something to eat?'

'No.'

'Okay, here's what's going to happen. The ADA handling your case is a guy named Robby Branford. You know him?'

Pike and I both shook our heads.

'He's a square guy. A pit bull, but square. He'll be here soon, and we'll see what he's going to show the judge. The arraignment will be this afternoon over in Municipal Court. They'll keep you locked down here, then bring you over to the Criminal Court Building just before. Once we're there, it shouldn't take more than an hour or two. Branford will present the evidence, and the judge will decide if there's reasonable cause to believe you're the guy popped Dersh. Now, if the judge binds you over, it doesn't mean there's proof of your guilt, just that he believes there's enough reason to go to trial. If that's the way it breaks, we'll argue for bail. Okay?'

Pike nodded.

'Did you kill Dersh?'

'No.'

When he said it, I let out my breath. Pike must've heard, because he looked at me. The edge of his mouth flickered.

I said, 'Okay, Joe.'

Charlie didn't seem impressed, or moved. He'd heard it a million times, too. *I'm innocent.* 'Dersh's next-door neighbor just picked you out of the lineup. She says she saw you going into Dersh's yard this morning just before he was killed.'

'Wasn't me.'

'You go over there last night?'

'No.'

'Where were you?'

'Running.'

'You were running in the middle of the goddamned night?'

I said, 'He does that.'

Charlie frowned at me. 'Did I ask you?' He opened a yellow legal pad to take notes. 'Let's back up. Give me your whole evening, say from about seven on.'

'I went by the store at seven. Stayed until a quarter to eight. Then went home and made dinner. I was home by eight. Alone.'

Charlie wrote down the names of Joe's employees, and their home phone numbers. 'Okay. You went home and made dinner. What'd you do after dinner?'

'I went to bed at eleven-ten. I woke a little after two, and went for a run.'

Charlie was scribbling. 'Not so fast. What'd you do between eight and eleven-ten?'

'Nothing.'

'What do you mean, nothing? You watch TV? You rent a movie?'

'I showered.'

'You didn't shower for three goddamned hours. You read a book? Maybe call a friend, someone call you? Did your laundry?'

'No.'

'You had to be doing something besides the goddamned shower. Think about it.'

Pike thought.

'I was being.'

Charlie wrote on the pad. I could see his mouth move. BEING.

'Okay. So you ate, took your shower, then sat around "being" until you went to bed. Then you woke up a little after two and went for a run. Give us the route.'

Joe described the route he followed, and now I was writing, too. I was going to retrace his route during the day, then again at the same time he'd run it, looking for anyone who might've seen him.

Pike said, 'I stopped at the bluffs on Ocean Avenue between Wilshire and San Vicente, where you can see the water. I talked to a girl there. Her name was Trudy.'

Pike described her.

Charlie said, 'No last name?'

'I didn't ask. She was meeting someone named Matt. A black minivan arrived. New Dodge, no license or dealer tag that I could see. Custom teardrop windows in the back. She got in and they left. Whoever was inside would've seen me.'

I said, 'When was that?'

'Got to the bluffs about two-fifty. Started running again just at three.'

Charlie raised his eyebrows. 'You're sure about the time?'

'Yes.'

I said, 'That's only fifteen minutes or so before the old lady heard the shot. No way you could get from the ocean to Dersh's in fifteen minutes. Not even at three in the morning.'

Charlie nodded, thinking about it and liking it. 'Okay. That's something. We've got the girl, maybe. And all this running could give us plenty of potential witnesses.' He glanced at me. 'You're gonna get started on that?'

'Yes.'

Someone rapped at the door, and Charlie yelled for them to come in. Williams stuck his head in. 'DA's here.'

'Be right out.'

When Williams closed the door, Joe said, 'What about bail?'

'You've got your business. You've got a home. All of that is to the good when I'm trying to convince a judge you won't run. But when you're talking murder, it depends on the strength of their evidence. Branford will make a big deal about this old lady, but he knows – and so does the judge – that eyewitness testimony is the least dependable evidence you can admit. If all he has is the old lady, we're in good shape. You just sit tight, and don't worry, okay?'

Pike put the calm blue eyes on me, and I wished I knew what was behind them. He seemed peaceful, as if far worse things had happened to him, and nothing that could happen here would be as bad. Not even here. Not even charged with murder.

He said, 'Don't forget Karen.'

'I won't, but right now you have to come first. Edward Deege is dead. He was found murdered.'

Pike cocked his head. 'How?'

'Dolan says it looks like a street beef, but Hollywood has the case. They're investigating.'

Pike nodded.

'I'll see about finding Trudy.'

'I know.'

'Don't worry about it.'

'I'm not.'

I took my sunglasses from my shirt pocket and held them out. Pike's eyes flicked to the glasses.

'Krantz would just take them.'

Charlie Bauman said, 'Come on, for chrissake. We don't have all day.' I put the sunglasses back in my pocket and followed Charlie out.

Robert Branford was a tall man with large hands and bristling eyebrows. He met us in the hall, then walked us into a conference room where Krantz was sitting at the head of a long table. A TV and VCR were in the corner, and a short stack of files and legal pads were on the table. The TV was on, showing a blank blue screen. I wondered what they'd been watching.

Even before we were all the way in the room, Charlie said, 'Hey, Robby, you meet your eyewitness yet?'

'Mrs Kimmel? Not yet. Gonna see her after the arraignment.'

'Better see her before.'

'Why is that, Charlie? She got three heads?'

Charlie made a drinking motion. 'Booze hound. Jesus, Krantz, I'm surprised you could stand being so close to her at the lineup. Damn near knocked me out when she walked past.'

Branford had gone to his own briefcase and was taking papers from different manila folders. He raised his eyebrows toward Krantz.

To his credit, Krantz nodded. 'She's a drinker.'

Charlie took a seat at the table without bothering to open his briefcase. 'Did Krantz tell you about the M1? If you're going to her place, you'd better wave a white flag before you get out of your car.'

Krantz said, 'I told him, Bauman. What does that have to do with anything?'

Charlie spread his hands, Mr Innocent. 'Just want to make sure Robby knows what he's getting into. A seventy-eight-year-old lush gives a visual on a guy she's trying to plug with an M1 Garand rifle. That's going to look real good when you get to court.'

Branford laughed. 'Sure, Bauman. You're thinking about my best interests.' Branford took a slim stack of papers from his briefcase and handed them to Charlie. 'Here's Mrs Kimmel's statement, plus the reports written by the officers responding to her call. We don't have anything in from the CI or the criminalist yet, but I'll copy you as soon as we get anything.'

Charlie flipped through the pages absently. 'Thanks, Robby. Hope you got more to offer the court than Mrs Kimmel.'

Branford smiled tightly. 'We do, but let's start with her. We've got an eyewit who puts your man at the scene, and picked him out of a line. Second, the swabs came back positive, confirming that Pike recently fired a weapon.'

I said, 'Pike owns a gun shop. He shoots every day of his life.'

Krantz leaned back. 'Yeah. And today he took one shot too many.'

Charlie ignored him. 'SID match the slug and Pike's gun?'

'SID has the weapons at the shed now, running them.'

Krantz said, 'You know how many guns we found at his place? Twelve handguns, four shotguns, and eight rifles, two of which are fully automatic assault weapons. This guy's a friggin' poster boy for gun control.'

Charlie made a hurry-up gesture. 'Yeah, yeah, yeah, and every one of those weapons is legally registered. Here's a prediction, Robby. You're not going to get a match.'

Branford shrugged. 'Probably not, but it doesn't matter. He's an ex-cop. He knows enough to dump the murder weapon. Does he have an alibi?'

Now Charlie was looking annoyed. 'Pike was in Santa Monica. At the ocean.'

'Okay. I'm listening.'

'We're locating the wits now.'

Branford didn't quite manage a smile. 'And all I've got to do is believe you.' He took the chair near his briefcase and leaned back. Maybe he and Krantz had rehearsed it. 'For the motive, we've got Karen Garcia. Pike blamed Dersh for murdering his girlfriend. Here he was, inside the investigation, and it was killing him that everybody knew that Dersh was the one, but that the police couldn't put together a case.'

I said, 'Their relationship was over years ago. Talk to her father and check it out.'

'What does that matter? Men get weird when it comes to women.'

Branford brought another manila folder out of his briefcase and tossed it on the table.

'Besides that, we're not dealing with the most stable personality here, are we? Look at this guy's record. You see all the shootings he's been involved in? You see how many people he's killed? Here's a guy, he thinks nothing of using deadly force to solve his problems.'

I was watching Krantz. Krantz nodded every time Branford made a point, but so far the points didn't add up to much. Yet here was Krantz, looking assured and confident, and not at all bothered by the pissant nature of things like 'prior history'. Even Branford seemed amused, like he knew he was giving us nothing.

I said, 'I don't get how you put it on Joe.'

They looked at me.

Branford said, 'The old lady.'

'She knows Joe by sight? She called 911 and said she saw Joe Pike sneaking down the alley?'

Krantz uncrossed his arms and leaned forward. 'Figure it out, Sherlock. How many guys run around at night with the no sleeves and the tattoos and the sunglasses?'

'Somebody who was trying to look like Joe Pike, *Sherlock*.'

Krantz laughed. 'Oh, please, Cole. You don't have to be Einstein to figure this out.'

Charlie put the papers Branford had given him into his briefcase, then stood. 'You guys are light. Way light. Here I was, thinking you were going to lay out real evidence like Pike's fingerprints on Dersh's doorknob, and all I'm getting is that you don't like that he's in the NRA. This is lame, Robby. I'll have the old lady saying she saw Santa Claus, and the judge is going to laugh you out.'

Robby Branford suddenly looked smug. 'Well, there is another thing. You wanna see it now?'

He didn't wait for us to answer. He went to the VCR and pressed the play button.

The flat blue screen filled with a soundless color surveillance video of the back of a house. It took me a moment to realize that it was Dersh's house. I had only seen it from the front.

Krantz said, 'This is a surveillance tape of Dersh's house. See the date down here?'

The time and date were in the lower left corner of the screen. The date showed it to be three days before Karen Garcia's burial. That would be the day I had learned the truth about the five victims. It was the day Pike had gone to see Dersh.

We could see a large picture window off Dersh's studio, and inside, two blurred figures I took to be Eugene Dersh and another man.

I said, 'That's not Pike.'

'No, it's not. Watch here, past the edge of the house where you can see the street.'

Krantz tapped the upper left side of the screen. Part of Dersh's drive was visible, and, beyond it, the street.

Krantz hit a button, and the image slowed. A few seconds later, the nose of a red Jeep Cherokee eased into the frame. When the cab was visible, Krantz hit the freeze frame.

Krantz said, 'That's Pike.'

Charlie's face drained, and his mouth formed a thin, dark line.

The picture advanced frame by frame. Joe's head turned. Joe looked at the house. Joe disappeared.

'When a jury sees this, they're going to put it together with everything else we have and think just what we think. Pike was doing a drive-by to case the area, working up his nut to pull the trigger.'

Robby Branford put his hands in his pockets, pleased with himself and his evidence. 'Looks pretty good now, doesn't it, Charlie? I'd say your boy's going to jail.'

Charlie Bauman took my arm and said, 'Come on. Let's go outside and talk about this.'

Charlie kept hold of my arm until I shook him off in the booking area. 'It's not what it seems. That was three days before Karen Garcia's funeral. Pike only went over there to see Dersh.'

'Don't talk so loud. Why'd he go see Dersh?'

'I'd just found out about the other victims, and that Krantz suspected Dersh for the killer.'

'So Pike wanted to go check out the suspect?'

'Yeah. That's pretty much it.'

Charlie led me to the elevators, making sure no one was close enough to hear. 'He go over there to talk to Dersh? Ask him if he did it?'

'No. He just wanted to look at him.'

'He just *looked* at him?'

'He wanted to see if he thought Dersh could do it.'

Charlie sighed and shook his head. 'I can see me trying to explain that to a jury. "*You gotta understand, ladies and gentlemen, my client is a goddamned swami and he was just trying to vibe whether or not the victim was a killer.*" ' Charlie sighed again. 'This really, really is gonna look bad for us.'

'Will it come up in the arraignment?'

'Sure, it's gonna come up. Look, I can tell you right now that Joe is gonna get bound over for trial. He's going to stand for this one. Our problem isn't with the arraignment judge anymore, it'll be with the jury.'

'What about bail?'

'I don't know.' Charlie took a pack of cigarettes from his jacket, and stuck one in his mouth. Nervous.

A passing cop said, 'They don't want you smoking in here. City building.'

Charlie fired up the cigarette. 'So arrest me.'

The cop laughed and went on.

'Look, Elvis, I'm not going to tell a jury that Pike just wanted to see the guy. I'll make up a better story than that, but it still looks bad.' He checked his watch. 'They're gonna transfer him to the Criminal Court Building in a few minutes. I'll go over there to talk with him again before the arraignment.'

'I'll meet you there.'

'No, you won't. You're going to look for the girl Pike saw at the beach. There's nothing you can do sitting in a room with me.'

The elevator doors opened and we went in. Two women and an overweight man were inside. The shorter of the women sniffed at Charlie's cigarette. 'There's no smoking in here.'

Charlie blew out a cloud of smoke, and waved his hand. 'Sorry. I'll put it right out.'

He didn't.

'How bad is it, Charlie?'

Bauman drew deep on the cigarette, then blew a huge cloud of smoke toward the woman.

'Can you spell *plea bargain*?'

24

As I walked out through Parker Center, the voices of the people around me were distant and tinny. The world had changed. Karen Garcia, and Eugene Dersh were gone, and Frank Garcia had turned away from us. The police thought their assassin killer was gone, but even if he wasn't, it didn't matter.

There was only Joe in jail, and the need to save him.

I spent the afternoon retracing the six-mile route that Pike had run, listing every business along the way that might employ twenty-four-hour help. When I reached the part of Ocean Avenue where Pike had met the girl, I left my car and walked. Small groups of homeless people were dotted through the park, some sleeping on blankets in the hot sun, others clustered in small groups or busy searching through trash containers. I woke them if they were sleeping or interrupted them if they were talking to ask if anyone knew Trudy or Matt, or if, last night, they had seen a jogging man who wore sunglasses even after dark. Almost everyone said yes, and almost everyone lied. Trudy was tall and skinny, or short and fat, or had only one eye. The jogging man was a black guy looking to harvest the organs of unwilling donors, or a government operative bent on mind control. The schizophrenics were particularly cooperative. I didn't stop for lunch.

I worked my way through every Ocean Avenue hotel, asking for the names of nighttime staff, and when I finished I drove home hard to begin calling. Completing my first pass along Joe's route had taken almost five hours, and left me with a sense that I was falling behind.

Dersh's murder was the headline story on every four o'clock newscast in town. LAPD had released Joe's name as the suspect, and one station supered a picture of Joe with the legend VIGILANTE KILLER. Everyone reported that Dersh was the main suspect in the recent string of killings, with sources 'among the upper echelons of LAPD' saying that that investigation would remain open, though no other suspect was expected to be identified. The cat came in during the newscast, and watched with me.

At ten minutes before five, my phone rang, and Charlie Bauman said, 'The arraignment just ended. He's bound over.'

Charlie sounded hollow.

'What about bail?'

'No bail.'

I felt dull and weary, as if my frantic pace had taken its toll.

'We'll have another arraignment in Superior Court in about a month. I can argue for bail again there, and maybe that judge will swing in our favor. This one didn't.'

'So what happens now?'

'They'll let him sit in Parker for another couple of days, then transfer him to Men's Central. They'll keep him over in the safe wing because he used to be a cop, so we don't have to worry about that. All we have to worry about is building his defense. You find anyone who saw him?'

'Not yet.' I told him how I'd spent the day.

'Christ, how many names you got?'

'Between hotel people and businesses, two hundred fourteen.'

'Man. You work fast.'

It didn't seem like very much to me.

'Listen. Fax your list to my office. I'll have my secretary get on it tomorrow. That way you can keep pounding the pavement.'

'I'll make the calls.'

Charlie hesitated. When he spoke again his voice was calm. 'Don't freak out on me, Elvis.'

'What are you talking about?'

'It's after six. Businesses are closing, and the night shifts aren't on yet. Who're you going to call?'

I didn't know.

'Joe's okay for now. We've got time. Let's just do a good job, all right?' Like I was a little boy who'd lost his best friend, and he was my dad telling me everything would be okay if I just stayed calm.

'I'll fax the list, Charlie.'

'Good. We'll talk tomorrow.'

After we hung up, I sent the list, then got a beer and brought it out onto the deck. The air was hot, but the canyon was clear. Two red-tailed hawks floated in lazy circles overhead. They hung on nothing, patient, tiny heads cocking from side to side as they searched for field mice and gophers. I have seen them float like that for hours. Patient hunters are successful hunters. Charlie was right. When I was in Ranger School at Fort Benning, Georgia, they taught us that panic kills. Men who had lived through three wars taught us that if you panicked you would stop thinking, and if you stopped thinking you would die. A sergeant named Zim ran us for five miles every day carrying sixty-pound field packs, a full issue of ammunition, and our M16s. Between each cadence he made us shout, 'My mind is my deadliest weapon. Sergeant Zim says so, and Sergeant Zim is never wrong. Sergeant Zim is God. Thank you, God.'

When you're eighteen, that leaves an impression.

I said, 'Okay, moron. Think.'

If Amanda Kimmel had seen a man dressed like Joe, wearing sunglasses like Joe, and sporting tattoos like Joe, then someone was pretending to be Joe. Finding that person would be an even better way of clearing Joe than finding Trudy or Matt, but so far, all I had was something that no one else seemed to have: An absolute and complete belief that Joe Pike was telling the truth. I did not doubt him. I would not. They could have videotape of Joe walking into that house, and if Joe pointed at the television and said, 'That's not me', I would believe him.

You work with what you have, and all I had was faith. An awful lot of people have found that to be enough.

You look for connections.

Krantz came at this by looking for people with a motive to kill Dersh. He thought Pike's motive was Karen. Frank Garcia had the same motive, and had the money to have Dersh killed, but he wouldn't put it on Joe. That meant someone else, and I wondered if that someone had some true connection to Dersh, or had only used Dersh as a means to an end. Getting Pike. Maybe this wasn't about Dersh at all, but was about Pike.

I went inside for a yellow legal pad, came back out again, and made a timeline. From Karen's murder until the story broke that Dersh was the suspect took six days. From the story breaking about Dersh until his murder was only three days. I tried to imagine some guy with a grudge against Pike watching his TV. He's out there hating Pike, and he's never before in his life heard about Karen Garcia or Eugene Dersh, but he sees all this, and the world's biggest lightbulb blinks on over his head. *Hey, I can cap this guy Dersh to get Pike!* All in the span of three days.

Uh-uh.

That meant he knew of Dersh prior to the story breaking, and had time to think about it. Also, all of L.A. knew that the police had been surveilling Dersh around the clock. Yet this guy had picked a time after the surveillance had been scaled back. I wondered about that.

I brought my beer inside, poured it out, then went back onto the deck. The hawks were still up there. I had thought they were hunting, but maybe they were just enjoying the air. I had thought they were looking for prey, but maybe they were looking at each other instead, and finding joy in each other's company there above the earth. Love hawks.

Relationships are often different than they appear at first glance.

I decided that the killer was someone connected both to Joe and to Dersh. Joe was connected to Dersh the same way Frank was connected to Dersh: Through Karen. Maybe the killer was connected to Joe through Karen, also.

I went inside, dug around for Samantha Dolan's home number, and called her.

She said, 'Hey, it's the World's Greatest Everything. Callin' little ol' me.'

She sounded drunk.

'Are you okay, Dolan?'

'Jesus. Would you call me Samantha?'

'Samantha.'

'This has got to be about your buddy, right? I mean, you're not just calling to flirt?'

'It's Joe.'

'I'm out of that, remember? I'm off the Task Force, I don't know what Krantz is doing, and I don't care. Hey, from what I heard, Pike sounds good for it.'

'I know that Branford has a case against him, but I'm telling you that Pike didn't do this.'

'Oh, puh-lease. You weren't there, were you? You didn't see it.'

'I know him, is all. Pike wouldn't go into Dersh's house in the middle of the night and shoot him like that. It isn't Pike's style.'

'What style murder would he use, you know him so well?'

'The kind that can't be seen. Pike could do it and you would never know and would never even think that it might be him. They would disappear, one day here, the next day gone, and you'd be left wondering what happened, Dolan. That's the way Pike would do it, and, believe me, you would never find the body. Pike is the most dangerous man I know, and I've known more than a few. He is without peer.'

Dolan didn't say anything.

'Dolan? You still there?'

'Something tells me you could be pretty dangerous, too.'

I didn't answer. Let her think what she wanted.

Dolan sighed. 'Okay, World's Greatest. What do you want?'

'Whoever killed Dersh might be connected to Joe through Karen Garcia, and that goes back to the days Joe rode a black-and-white. Joe's partner was a guy named Abel Wozniak.'

'Sure. The cop Pike killed.'

'You don't have to say it like that, Dolan.'

'There's only one way to say it.'

'I want to find out who was around back then who might hate Pike enough to kill Dersh and frame Pike for it. I'm going to need files and records, and I can't get them without help.'

She didn't answer again.

'Dolan?'

'You got a fucking set on you, you know that? The trouble I'm in.'

She hung up.

I called her back, but she had the phone off the hook. Busy. I called every five minutes for the next half hour. Busy.

'Shit.'

Twenty minutes later I was sitting at the dining-room table and thinking about calling Dolan again when Lucy let herself in. She took off her suit coat and shoes, and went to the fridge without looking at me.

I said, 'I guess you heard about Joe.'

'I followed the story at work. We had people at the arraignment.'

'Uh-huh.'

She hadn't come out to give me a kiss, and she hadn't yet looked at me.

'Can I get you something to eat?'

She shook her head.

'Want a glass of wine?'

'Maybe in a minute.'

She was staring into the box.

'What's wrong?'

She stopped staring and closed the door.

'I never knew these things about Joe.'

The day's tension crept back into my shoulders with a dense tightness.

'I saw a tape of Branford arguing against bail. He talked about all the shootings Joe's been involved in, and the men he's killed.'

The tension turned into a stabbing ache.

'I thought of Joe as this strong, quiet man who was your friend, but now it feels like I never knew him. I don't like knowing these things. I don't like knowing a man who would do things like this.'

'You know he treats you well and with respect. You know he's good with Ben, and that he's my best friend.'

Something confused and fearful worked in her eyes. 'Branford said that he's killed fourteen men, for God's sake.'

I shrugged. 'If you can make it in L.A., you can make it anywhere.'

'This isn't funny to me.'

I tried to do something with the ache but there was nothing to be done. I wanted to call Dolan again, but I didn't. 'The men he's killed were trying to kill him, or me, or someone that Joe wanted to protect. He is not a hit man. He has never committed murder for hire, or killed someone simply to kill them. If he's killed, it's because he's put himself in situations that have required it. Just as I have. Maybe there's something wrong with both of us. Is that what you're getting at?'

Lucy came to the door but did not cross through. 'No, that isn't what I'm saying. There's just so much to assimilate here. I'm sorry. I don't mean to be like this.' She put on a smile, but it was strained. 'I haven't seen you all day and I miss you, and all of this about Joe made me miss you more. I just don't know what to think. I read the documents that Branford submitted to the court, and what was there scared me.'

'They were supposed to scare you, Lucy. That's why Branford used them to argue against bail. You know that.'

I wanted more than anything else to get up and go to her but I couldn't. I thought she might want me to, or that she wanted to come to me, but something was stopping her, too.

'Elvis?'

'What?'

'Did Joe kill that man?'

'No.'

'Are you sure of that?'

'Yes. Yes, I'm sure.'

She nodded, but then her voice came small and from far away.

'I don't think I am. I think that he could've. Maybe I even think that he did.'

We stood without speaking for a time, and then I went into the living room and put on the radio. I did not return to the kitchen.

I sat on the couch, staring out at the darkening sky, and realized that where Joe Pike sat this night, he could only see walls.

I wondered what the killer could see.

Number six

The hot breeze carries the stink of the public rest room to where the killer hides in a stand of red oleander. MacArthur Park is quiet this time of night, a perfect time for hunting.

The killer is flush with excitement at how well things are going. The Task Force still has not connected the five homicides, Hollywood Division detectives have begun turning evidence in Edward Deege's murder, and killing Dersh has proven to be inspired.

Joe Pike is in jail, and will stay there for the rest of his life, until some rat-house lifer pushes a shank between his ribs.

And won't that be fitting.

The killer smiles, just thinking about it. The killer doesn't smile often, learning that trait from Pike, from having studied Pike for so long now, Pike, whom he hates more than any other. But this is a special time, and there is plenty of hate to go around.

Pike, in perfect control.

Pike, in absolute command.

Pike, who took everything from him, and then gave him purpose.

Payback is a motherfucker.

The only possible fly in the ointment is this girl Trudy. The killer did what he could to protect himself from someone like her: He staked out Pike's home, making sure Pike was alone, waiting until the lights went out, then waiting longer still to be sure Pike was asleep before setting off to kill Dersh. The killer suspects that there is no Trudy, and that Pike is making it up, but he can't be sure, and thinks that he may have to find Trudy himself. He could run her name on the NCIC computers, and on VICAP through the FBI. And if someone beats him to her, well, he'll know as quickly as anyone. And deal with her then.

Still, the heavy lifting is done, and now all that remains is killing the rest of them, and ensuring with absolute certainty that Pike is convicted.

That means preparing for Pike's partner, Elvis Cole.

What a stupid name.

The killer is considering how he might deal with Cole when he hears Jesus Lorenzo approaching, and grips the .22 caliber pistol that he's taped into a plastic Clorox bottle. There is no mistaking Lorenzo. He is five feet ten, wearing red pumps with four-inch heels, a red satin micro-sheath, and a platinum wig. The killer has watched him cruise MacArthur Park on six separate nights at this time, waiting for this moment.

When Jesus Lorenzo disappears into the men's room, the killer steps out from the oleander and follows. No one else is around, no one is in the men's room. The killer knows this because he's been here for almost two hours.

The plan continues.

Payback, you motherfucker.

25

Lucy and I started the next day with a careful hesitancy that left me uncomfortable. Something new had been introduced to our relationship that neither of us knew how to approach. We had slept together, but we had not made love. Though she appeared to sleep, I think it was feigned. I wanted to speak with her about Joe. I wanted her to be all right with him, but didn't know if that was possible. By the time I decided to plunge in, she had to leave for work.

As she was walking out, she said, 'Are you going to see Joe today?'

'Yes. Probably later.'

'Would you give him my best?'

'Sure. You could come with me, see him yourself.'

'I have to get to work.'

'Okay. I know.'

'But maybe.'

'Luce?'

She looked at me.

'Whatever Joe is, that's what I am, too.'

She probably didn't want to hear that.

'I guess what bothers me is that you're not disturbed by these things. You accept them as ordinary, and things like this aren't ordinary.'

I didn't know what to say that wouldn't sound self-serving, so I didn't say anything.

Lucy pulled the door closed and went to work.

Another fine day in the City of Angels.

I wanted to call Charlie Bauman's secretary to tell her what I had already done, but she probably wasn't yet in the office. Charlie would tell her, but I wanted to tell her, too. I also wanted to contact both the FBI and the California State Sheriffs to access the data bank they keep on missing and runaway children. I wanted to see if I could get any hits on the first names, Trudy and Matt, and I also wanted to run the stolen vehicle reports for a black Dodge minivan. I decided to call Dolan first, and got Williams.

'Hey, Williams. Is Dolan there?'

'What's it to you?'

'I want to talk to her.'

'Haven't seen her. You wanna know what I heard Krantz say?'

'I'm not going to like this, am I?'

'Krantz says you were probably in on it with that bastard, Pike. He says if he can tie you into it, maybe you and Pike can do the IV tango together.' Williams chuckled when he said it.

'Hey, Williams.'

'What?'

'You're the whitest black man I ever met.'

'Fuck you, Cole.'

'You, too, Williams.'

I hung up, thinking that if the day got any better my cat would die.

I was on my way upstairs to take a shower when the doorbell rang. It was Samantha Dolan, looking hungover.

'I just called you.'

'Was I there?'

'You know what, Dolan? Today isn't a good day for humor.'

She walked in past me, again without being invited, and peeked into the kitchen. She was wearing a navy blazer over a plain white tee shirt and jeans, and oval Italian sunglasses. The shirt looked very white beneath the dark blazer. 'Yeah, well, I have days like that, too. You never fixed the tiles.'

'I don't want to be rude, but what are you doing here?'

'You worried the little woman's going to get jealous?'

'Do me a favor and don't call her the little woman. It's pissing me off.'

'Whatever. You think I could have some juice or water? I'm a little dry.'

I brought her into the kitchen and poured two glasses of mango juice. When I handed the glass to her, she took off her sunglasses. Her eyes were bloodshot, and I caught a whiff of tequila. 'Jesus, it's eight in the morning, Dolan. You hit it this early?'

The bloodshot eyes flashed angrily. 'Is it any of your business when I "hit it"?'

I raised my hands.

Dolan put the sunglasses back on.

'I was thinking about what you said last night. That maybe the killer is connected to Pike through Garcia. Maybe you've got something there, but I sure as hell couldn't call you from the office to talk about it.'

'That mean you'll help?'

'It means I want to talk about it.'

The cat nosed through his cat door. He got halfway inside, and stopped, staring at her.

Dolan scowled at him. 'What in hell are you looking at?'

The cat cocked his head, still staring.

'What's wrong with this cat?'

'I think he's confused. The only other person in the world he likes is Joe Pike. Maybe it's the glasses.'

Dolan scowled deeper. 'How nice for me. Mistaken for a two-hundred-pound bruiser with a butch cut and no tits.'

Dolan took off the glasses and bugged her eyes at him.

'Better?'

The cat cocked his head the other way.

'Why does he hold his head that way?'

'Someone shot him.'

Dolan squatted and held out her hand.

I said, 'Don't do that, Dolan. He bites.'

'Samantha.'

'Samantha.'

The cat sniffed. He eased toward her and sniffed again.

'He doesn't seem so mean to me.'

She scratched his head, then finished her juice.

'He's just a damned cat.'

I stared at him, then her. I had seen that cat claw a hundred people over the years, and I had *never* seen him let anyone other than me and Joe touch him.

'What?'

I shook my head again. 'Nothing.'

She took a hard pack of Marlboros from her pocket. 'You mind if I smoke?'

'Yeah, I do. If you gotta have one, we can go out on the deck.'

We went out. Yesterday's gray haze still hung in the air, but it had thinned. Dolan went to the rail and peered down into the canyon. 'This is nice. You got your chairs out here. You got your Weber.'

She fired up a Marlboro and blew a great fog of smoke to add to the haze. Inviting.

I said, 'So what were you thinking last night?'

'I wasn't on the job when that happened with Wozniak and Pike, but Stan Watts was. I asked him about it. Do you know what happened?'

'I know.'

A little girl named Ramona Ann Escobar had been seen leaving a park with a man the police believed to be a known pedophile and child pornographer named Leonard DeVille. Pike and Wozniak learned that DeVille had been sighted entering the Islander Palms Motel, and had driven there to investigate. When they entered the room, Ramona was not present. Pike had never spoken to me of these things, but I recalled from the newspaper coverage that Wozniak, the father of a young daughter, had apparently been fearful that DeVille had harmed the girl. He drew his weapon, and struck DeVille. Pike, feeling that Wozniak might endanger the suspect, intervened. A struggle followed, during which Wozniak's weapon discharged, killing Wozniak. Internal Affairs conducted an investigation, but brought no charges against Pike. What the articles I'd read didn't say is that even though IAG didn't bring charges, damn near every officer on the job at that time blamed Pike for Wozniak's death, hating him all the more because Pike had killed Wozniak defending an asshole like Leonard DeVille. A child molester.

Dolan said, 'So if you're looking for people with a grudge, you're gonna have to start with a couple of thousand cops.'

'I don't believe that.'

'I'm talking *hate*, buddy. They got cops still around who *hate* Pike for what happened to Wozniak.'

'Think about what you're saying, Dolan. You believe some random cop has been carrying a grudge so big he's willing to kill an innocent man like Dersh just to set up Pike?'

'*You* say innocent, and this is your theory, not mine. If one of these cowboys thinks Dersh is a serial killer, maybe he figures it's a no-brainer sacrifice. And if it isn't a cop, you're probably talking about one of the two or three hundred assholes that Pike arrested. That's still a pretty big suspect pool.'

I spread my hands. 'I can't go there, Dolan. There are so many variables here that if I try to deal with all of them I'll just sit home and wait for Krantz to crack the case.'

'Guess that wouldn't work for you.'

'Does it work for you?'

She smiled. 'No. Christ, that sun is hot.'

Dolan took off the blazer and draped it over one of the deck chairs. Her Sig was in a clip holster on the right hip of her jeans, and her tanned arms looked strong. The white shirt was so bright it made me squint.

I said, 'I've got to stay with what's in front of me, and that's Wozniak and Karen Garcia, and how they all came to meet. I need to find out everything I can about Wozniak and DeVille, and what happened in that room. I want the shooting team report, the incident report, and whatever Internal Affairs had.'

She was shaking her head before I finished. 'I can tell you right now you can forget the IAG documents. They're under seal. You'd need a court order.'

'I need Wozniak's personnel file and DeVille's case file. I'm going to talk to Joe and see what he says.'

'Man, you don't want too much, do you?'

'What else can I do?'

She took another deep pull on the cigarette. 'Nothing, I guess. I'll make some calls for you. It might take a while.'

'I appreciate your doing this for me, Samantha.'

She rested her elbows on the rail, looking out at the canyon. 'I've got nothing better to do. You know what Bishop has me doing? Due-diligence calls on last year's robbery cases. You know what that is?'

'No.'

'We gotta go through unsolved cases every three months just to keep the cases alive. You call the detective off record, ask if he's learned anything new, he says no, and you log it. A fucking clerk could do it. And every time I see Bishop, he shakes his head and walks away.'

I didn't know what to say.

She finished the cigarette and dropped it in the juice glass.

'I'm sorry, Samantha.'

She looked at me. 'You've got nothing to be sorry about.'

'I jammed you into coming across about the Task Force, just like I'm jamming you now. I apologize for doing that. I wouldn't've told Krantz that I knew about it, or that we'd had that conversation in your car that morning.'

'Everything always comes out, buddy. I'm on thin ice now, but if I'd lied that day and they'd found out, I'd be underwater for sure. Like I said, maybe if I kiss enough ass, Bishop will let me stick around.'

I nodded.

She glanced over. 'I feel like a damned lush.'

'Because you had a couple this morning?'

'Because I want one right now.'

She stared at me some more.

'I didn't take the drink because of this shit with the job, you dumb ass.'

I looked at her, thinking that she didn't need to come to my house, that she could've called. I thought how she'd rung the bell just a few minutes after Lucy had gone.

Dolan was leaning on the rail, her back stretched long and taut, the white tee shirt pulled tight. She looked good. She saw me looking and shifted her weight so that her ass swayed. I looked away, but it wasn't easy. I thought about Lucy.

'Elvis.'

I shook my head.

Dolan stepped close and put her arms around my neck and kissed me. I could taste the cigarettes and the tequila and the mangoes, and I wanted to kiss her back. Maybe, for a moment, I did.

Then I took her arms from around my neck.

'I can't, Samantha.'

Dolan took a fast step back. She went a very bright red, then turned and ran back through my house. A moment later, I heard the Beemer rev to life and pull away.

I touched my lips, and stood on the deck for a long time, thinking.

Then I went inside and phoned Charlie Bauman.

26

Charlie listened without comment as I told him why I wanted to speak with Pike.

When I was done, he said, 'Visiting starts at ten unless they're bringing him over to Men's Central this morning. Let me call over there to find out, then I'll get back to you.'

The cat came downstairs to the landing and looked at me while I waited. He went into the guest room, then came back into the living room, where he looked at me again.

I said, 'She's gone.'

He fell onto his side and licked his penis. Cats.

I couldn't get Dolan out of my head, and having her there made me feel a guilt unlike any I had known since the first time I killed a man. Dolan was leaning on the rail, and then she was pressed against me. I could still taste her cigarette. I went into the kitchen and drank a glass of water, but it didn't wash away the taste. The love I felt for Lucy flared into something white and fierce, and I wished she were here. I wanted to hold her, and tell her that I loved her, and hear her say the same back. I wanted her caress, and the comfort of her love. Most of all I wanted to stop wanting Samantha Dolan, but I didn't know how. It made me feel disloyal.

I stared out the kitchen window for a time, then washed the glass, put it away, and forced myself to think about what I had to do.

Charlie called back four minutes later, and told me to meet him in the Parker Center lobby at eleven.

I used the time until then to look for Trudy, calling the Department of Motor Vehicles for a transfer and registration check on all new minivans sold in the past two months, sorted by color. I told them I was only interested in black. We got twenty-eight hits. I asked if they could fax the information to me, but was told no, they'd have to mail it. The government in action. After that, I spent almost two hours on the phone talking to the FBI, the United States Marshals, and the L.A. County Sheriffs. Most of that time was spent on hold, but I learned that no current model year black minivans had been stolen in the past three months. I arranged to have the names Trudy and Matt run through the law

enforcement agencies' VICAP and NCIC computers, which show outstanding fugitive warrants from around the country, and also contain a
database of missing or abducted children. When they asked me why I
wanted this, I didn't tell them about Pike; I told them I was working for
the parents. Everyone was more cooperative that way, but everyone told
me the same thing: With no last name, the odds of getting any useful
information were slim.

I drove to Parker early, scanning the smokers out on the walk as I turned
in for Dolan. She wasn't among them, and I wondered if she was getting
the files I needed, or if she would. And then I thought that maybe I was
looking for another reason, and the guilt burned like bitter coffee.

Even though I was early, Charlie Bauman was already in the lobby,
waiting. He said, 'You look like hell. What's wrong?'

'Not a goddamned thing.'

'That's just what I need. Attitude.'

An overweight cop with a red face led us back along the corridor to the
interview room. Charlie and I sat without speaking for the five minutes it
took them to bring Joe. He was wearing the blue jumpsuit, but he'd rolled
the sleeves. The veins in his wrists and forearms bulged as if he'd been
exercising when they'd come for him.

The same black cop with weight-lifter arms who had brought Joe out of
the lineup now led him through the door. 'You gonna be good?'

'Yes.'

Pike was wearing the cuffs and shackles. The black cop unlatched the
handcuffs and pocketed them.

'Gotta leave the ankles.'

Pike nodded. 'Thanks for the hands.'

When the cop was gone, I smiled. Joe wasn't squinting anymore. He'd
grown used to the light.

Joe said, 'You find Trudy?'

'Not yet.'

'So how come you haven't broken me out?'

'Too easy. I'd rather do it the hard way and figure out who set you up.'

Charlie leaned forward like he was going to dive across the table. 'Cole
has an idea that maybe whoever popped Dersh is also connected to you
through Karen Garcia. Maybe it's even the same guy who killed her.'

Pike looked at me. I thought he might be curious, but you never know
with Pike.

I said, 'Whoever killed Dersh hates you so much that he made himself
up to look like you, and even used a .357 like you. That means he knows
you, or at least has made an effort to learn about you.'

Pike nodded.

'If he hates you that much, why wait until now, and why kill Dersh just
to frame you? Why not just take you head-on?'

Pike's mouth flickered. 'Because he can't.'

Charlie rolled his eyes. 'I shoulda brought my waders. The testosterone is getting pretty deep in here.'

I went through what I'd been thinking about the timeline, and the coincidence of it all. 'He's been thinking about this, Joe. Since before the story broke about Dersh. Maybe even since before Karen was killed. He doesn't want to kill you. He wants to punish you. This guy's been carrying a grudge for a long time, and now he's seen a way to work it out, and that makes me wonder if he isn't connected to Karen also.'

Pike canted his head, and now the calm blue water of his eyes held something deeper.

'He wouldn't have to be connected to Karen. I arrested two hundred men.'

'If it's just some guy, then why here and why now? Just some guy, then we're spiking the coincidence meter, and I can't buy it.'

Charlie smiled like a wolf, and nodded. He was getting into it. 'Goddamned right.'

Pike said, 'Leonard DeVille.'

The man Joe and Wozniak went to arrest the day Wozniak died.

Charlie said, 'Who?'

We told him.

Joe said, 'DeVille was there at the end, but he was also why Karen and I met. Woz and I responded to a report she called in about a suspected pedophile. Woz thought it might be DeVille.'

Charlie said, 'So maybe it's DeVille.'

Joe shook his head. 'DeVille died in prison. An Eighteenth Street gang-banger cut him two years into his term.' Child molesters didn't last long in prison.

I said, 'Okay. What about Wozniak? Maybe there's something through him.'

'No.'

'Think about it.'

'Woz is dead, too, Elvis. There's nothing to think about.'

Someone knocked hard twice on the door, and Charlie shouted for them to come in.

It was Krantz and Robby Branford.

Krantz frowned when he saw Charlie's cigarette. 'No smoking in here, Bauman.'

'Sorry, Detective. I'll put it right out.' Charlie took another drag and blew the smoke at Branford. 'You planning on talking to my client without me around, Robby?'

Branford fanned the air, annoyed.

'They knew you were here and called me. If you hadn't been here, I would've phoned. You're going to kill yourself with those things, Charlie.'

Charlie said, 'Yeah.'

I didn't like the expressions on their faces, and neither did Charlie.

He said, 'What? I'm in the middle of a conference with my client.'

Robby Branford took out a tiny leather notepad and glanced at it. 'At seven twenty-two this morning a transvestite named Jesus Lorenzo was found dead in a public bathroom in MacArthur Park. One shot with a .22, white plastic particulates have been identified in the wound. Initial time of death is about three this morning.'

He closed the pad, put it away, and looked at Pike.

'A full day after you killed Dersh.'

I leaned back and stared at Krantz. 'So Dersh didn't kill Karen Garcia or anyone else.'

Charlie Bauman said, 'What the hell does that have to do with us? You gonna charge Pike with that one, too?'

Branford shook his head. 'No, not that one. It's bad enough when somebody takes the law into his own hands to get revenge, but it's even worse when they fuck up and kill the wrong man.'

Charlie said, 'Pike didn't kill anyone.'

'We'll let the jury decide that. In the meantime I wanted to put you on notice.'

'What?'

'When we arraign in Superior Court next month, we're going for Special Circumstances. We'll ask for the death penalty.'

A tic started beneath Charlie's left eye. 'That's bullshit, Robby.'

Branford shrugged. 'Dersh's relatives might disagree. We're going to want to talk to your man after lunch. Why don't you and I get together and set a time when you're done here.'

I was still staring at Krantz, and Krantz was staring back.

'You going to charge Krantz with getting an innocent man killed?'

Branford walked out without answering, but Krantz paused in the door. He said, 'Yeah, Dersh was the wrong man, and I'll have to live with that. But I've still got Pike.'

He walked out and closed the door.

Sunday Afternoon with the Wozniaks

Pike said, 'Hold on tight.'

Evelyn Wozniak, age nine, grabbed his outstretched hands as tightly as she could.

'Bet you can't lift me! I'm too big!'

'Let's see.'

'Don't drop me!'

Joe lifted, holding the girl at arm's length, and slowly turned in a circle. Evelyn squealed.

Abel Wozniak called from the barbecue. 'Evie, tell your mother I need more water in the spray bottle. Hurry up before I burn the goddamned chicken.'

Pike returned Evelyn to the earth, where, flushed and breathless, she ran into the house. A few minutes ago, Joe and Abel had set a picnic table on the covered patio out of the sun, while Karen and Paulette had gone inside for the place settings and fresh drinks. Now, Joe sat in the lawn chair beneath the big sun umbrella and sipped his beer. Across the lawn, Abel prodded at the chicken and cursed the hot coals.

Joe had always admired the Wozniaks' backyard. Abel and Paulette kept it simple and neat. They lived in a modest home here in San Gabriel, where many officers and their families lived, and they both worked hard to keep the house and the yard looking nice. It showed, and Joe had always enjoyed coming to their home for a Sunday afternoon cookout.

Abel cursed the coals again, shouted that he needed the goddamned water, then covered the grill and came over to sit next to Joe. Abel had a beer of his own. He'd had several.

Joe said, 'You deal with it yet?'

'Fuck off. You don't know what you're talking about.' Abel stared at the smoke pouring out of the barbecue's vents.

'I followed you, Woz. I saw you with the Chihuahua Brothers. I saw you with that girl. I know what you're doing.'

Wozniak took a Salem from the pack on the ground next to his chair and lit up. Wozniak said, 'Why the hell are you doing this?'

'I can't let it go on.'

'I'm your goddamned partner, for chrissakes.'

Joe finished his beer and placed the empty bottle on the lawn. Paulette and Karen came out, Karen with a huge bowl of potato salad, and Paulette the spray bottle and a tray of forks and knives and napkins. Abel went over, used the water on his coals, then came back. The women stayed busy with the table.

Wozniak muttered, 'Fuckin' chicken looks like shit.'

'I mean it, Woz. I won't ride with this forever.'

Woz flicked at his cigarette. Nervous. 'I got responsibilities.'

'That's why I'm giving you the choice.'

Wozniak leaned toward him so far that the chair tipped. 'You think I like this? You think I want it to be this way? Man, I feel like I'm caught in a goddamned vise.'

Karen flashed a great brilliant smile at Joe, and Joe waved. Paulette smiled, and waved, too. They couldn't hear what the men were saying.

'I know it's a vise, Woz. I'm trying to help you with it.'

'Bullshit.'

'You don't have a choice.'

Wozniak watched the two women, then considered Joe. 'Don't think I don't know how you feel about her.'

Pike stared at him.

Wozniak nodded. 'I've seen you looking at Paulette. A great kid like Karen, and you're looking at my wife.'

Pike stood and looked down at his partner.

'You're going to resign, Woz. And it's going to be soon.'

'I'm warning you, you sonofabitch. If you don't back off, one of us is going to die.'

Paulette and Karen had gone to the grill and were frowning at the chicken. Paulette called, 'Abel! I think this chicken is dead!'

Abel Wozniak stared at Joe for a moment longer, and then he stalked back to the grill.

Pike watched Abel and Paulette and Karen, but soon he saw only Paulette. It was as if everything else had grown more and more faint until only she remained.

He had not felt such emptiness since he was a child.

27

When I left Parker Center even more smokers were outside, watching the news vans arrive. From the number of cops on the sidewalk, there probably weren't many left inside, but you never know. Samantha Dolan wasn't among them, and neither was Stan Watts. Half the dicks on the walk were probably from IAG, and most of them weren't smoking. They were probably taking names of those who were.

I walked down to the covered level looking for Dolan's Beemer, found it, then walked back to the lobby pay phone, and called her. She answered on the second ring.

'Dolan.'

'It's me.'

'Listen, I'm busy right now. I don't want to talk.'

'I'm downstairs, and I want to talk to you. I need those files.'

She lowered her voice. 'I'm feeling just a little bit humiliated right now, can you understand that? I don't usually . . . I don't do what I did this morning.'

'Yeah. I get that. I'm feeling pretty awkward myself.'

'You weren't the one rejected.'

'I'm with somebody else, Samantha. I told you that.' I felt defensive, like I had to justify myself.

'The little woman.'

'Don't call her that. Lucy's tough, too, and she might kick your ass.'

Dolan didn't say anything.

'That was a joke, Dolan.'

'I know. I didn't say anything because I'm smiling.'

'Oh.'

'Maybe I'll call her out and see who's left standing.'

'Did you find out about the files I wanted?'

'It's really hard to talk right now. You know about this new vic?'

'I was with Pike when Krantz and Branford came down. Will you come down to your car? I really need your help right now, but I don't want whatever it is you feel about me to get confused with that.'

When she answered, it was frosty and cool. 'I think I can manage not to get confused. Five minutes.'

'Samantha.'

But she'd already hung up.

Dolan was standing at the mouth of the garage, watching the news vans. She wasn't smoking, but a crushed butt was by her toe. Guess I'd caught her between puffs. She also wasn't carrying the files.

She said, 'They're going to go crazy with this.'

'Yeah. How are you doing?'

The cool eyes came to me. 'You mean, has my ego survived your rejection, or am I grieving the loss of my self-esteem?'

'They don't come any tougher than you, do they?'

She turned back into the garage, and I followed her to the Beemer.

'Okay. Here's what I found out: Wozniak died so long ago that Rampart won't have his file anymore. They would've sent it down to the file morgue by Union Station.'

'None of this is on computer?'

'This is the LAPD, World's Greatest. We got shit for computers.'

I nodded.

'Internal Affairs has their own separate storage facility, with their own procedures for getting into their records. Forget it. But the file morgue is different. We've got a shot at that.'

'Okay.'

'I talked to a detective I know over at Rampart. He said it's pretty much the same story with DeVille. Since he died in prison, the Rampart sex crimes detectives who worked that case would've boxed the file and sent it to storage. We could order it from the district attorney's case file morgue, but we won't have to do that.'

'You got a way to get at the files in storage?'

'I'm there almost every damned day with running the due diligence, but we can't just go in and sign the stuff out. You see?'

'So what do we do?'

'Steal it. You up for that?'

'Yes.'

'Glad you're up for something.'

The Los Angeles Police Department storage facility is an ancient, red brick building in an industrial area just south of the railroad yard. The bricks looked powdery, and I thought that there was probably no way the building could pass an earthquake inspection if it wasn't owned by the LAPD. It was the kind of place that, while you're in it, you're spending most of your time hoping we don't get a big temblor.

Dolan parked the Beemer well away from the other cars that were there, then led me through a plain gray door and along a short hall.

I said, 'Hot.'

'The frigging air must be out again. Listen, do us both a favor and don't say anything. I'll do all the talking.'

I didn't answer her.

'Well?'

'You said not to say anything.'

'Try not to act smart. You don't pull it off.'

An overweight civilian clerk named Sid Rogin was reading a magazine behind a low counter. He was in his sixties and balding, with thin, wispy hair, and a glass eye. He brightened when he saw Dolan and put down the magazine. He was also sweating, and had a little fan going. The fan was pathetic. He would've gotten more air from a chihuahua wagging its tail.

'Hey, Sammy, what it is? They still got you running down due diligence?' The middle-class white man does black.

Dolan gave him a sparkling grin. I would've guessed that if anyone called her Sammy she would gun them down on the spot. 'Yeah, same old same old. We've got to run down a deceased officer and a perp he was working named Leonard DeVille, also deceased.'

Rogin turned a sign-in log toward her. 'Names and badge numbers. What kind of time frame we talking here on the perp?'

She picked up his pen and glanced at me. 'I've got it. No sweat.' She told Rogin when DeVille had died.

'You taking out the files?'

'Not if we're lucky. Just gotta look up some dates.' She flashed the bright smile again. 'Figure my partner here could look up the officer while I get the perp, save everybody some time.'

'Okay. Step around behind.'

Dolan and I followed Rogin into a series of rooms lined with industrial shelving stacked with dusty cardboard boxes.

'What's the officer's name?'

'Stuart Vincent.' She spelled Vincent.

'Good enough. Officers on this floor. You and I will have to go up to the second for the perps.'

'No problemo.'

We followed Rogin along the aisles, me thinking that all the crummy cardboard boxes looked like little crypts.

We turned a corner into a section of aisle marked *T-Z*. Rogin said, 'Here ya go, *V* as in Vincent.' Six boxes were marked with *V*'s. He pulled down the one that would hold *Vi*. 'All you wanna do is look through the file?'

Dolan glanced at me, and nodded.

I said, 'That's right.'

Rogin had the lid off, pulling out a thick file that had been tied with a string. He frowned. 'It's awful thick, Sammy. You gotta read through the whole thing?'

'You look busy, Sid. Sorry to put you out this way.'

'Well, it's not that. They just don't like people back here.'

Dolan raised her eyebrows back at him and stiffened. 'Well, Sidney, I guess if you'd rather I go back to Parker and have them call down.' She let it drop, watching him.

'Oh, no, hell, you don't have to do that. It's just I gotta get back up and watch the front.'

I said, 'I'll be done by the time you guys get back from the second floor. No sweat.'

'You sure?'

'Absolutely.'

Dolan clapped Sid on the shoulder and grinned at him some more. 'Let's do it, Sid. Get outta this goddamned heat.'

I pretended to be interested in Vincent's file until their steps were gone, then I searched down the aisle for the *W*'s. Twelve boxes were marked with a *W*, the eighth and ninth file boxes holding *Wo*.

We could have asked for Wozniak's file and signed for it, but we didn't want a written record connecting Dolan to what we were doing. She was in enough trouble, and if things went wrong I didn't want her in more.

I pulled Wozniak's file, then pushed the boxes back in their rows.

Wozniak's personnel file was too thick to shove down my pants, but most of it didn't concern me. I pulled the sheet listing his partners prior to Pike and their badge numbers, then flipped back to the beginning of his career and pulled the sheet noting his training officers. Wozniak was a top cop: He'd been awarded the Medal of Valor twice, twelve certificates of commendation, and a half dozen public service commendations for working with schools and troubled youth. The list of his arrests went on for pages, listing the arrestee, date of arrest, and charge. I jerked those pages, folded them, and put them in my jacket. The next section in the file was devoted to disciplinary actions. I wasn't even thinking to look at it except that Abel Wozniak had been called to appear before the Internal Affairs Group on two occasions six weeks prior to his death. The requesting Internal Affairs officer being one Detective Harvey Krantz.

I said, 'Damn.'

No other information was given except the notation that the inquiry was terminated, along with the date of termination.

Krantz.

I jerked that page, too, and put it with the others.

Dolan's voice came along the aisle, Dolan saying, 'Hey, buddy, I hope you're ready to go. We're outta here.'

I stuffed the remains of the file together and pushed it between the boxes, then hurried back to the *V*'s. I picked up Vincent's file just as Dolan and Rogin came around the corner.

She said, 'You find what you need?'

'Yeah. You?'

She shook her head. Slow.

'DeVille's file isn't here.'

I raised my eyebrows. 'Where is it?'

Rogin waved his hand. 'Some other dick probably checked it out. You want me to look it up?'

I said, 'If you don't mind. Maybe I can call the guy and get what we need.'

We followed him back to the counter and waited while he fingered through a box of little index cards. He scratched his head, checked some numbers he'd written on a little pad, then frowned. 'Hell, it ain't here. If it was signed out, I woulda had the log-out card in here, but it ain't.'

'Any way to tell how long it's been gone?'

'Not without the card. Ain't this the shits?'

Dolan glanced at me again, then pulled at my arm.

'Maybe you just misfiled it, Sid. It's no big deal.'

When we were on our way out to her car, she said, 'I don't believe in coincidences.'

'You thinking someone ripped off that file?'

'I'm thinking I don't believe in coincidences. But we can still get a copy. The district attorney's office keeps a record of all their case files in their own storage facility. I can order up theirs.'

'How long will that take?'

'A couple of days. Don't be peevish, World's Greatest. What'd you get?'

'I got some names, and his collar jacket, but something else, too.' I told her about the disciplinary notation showing Wozniak had been the subject of an investigation, and that Krantz was the investigating officer.

Dolan made a hissing sound. 'That's IAG, man. You can't just ask Krantz.'

We got into her car. The leather was so hot it burned through my pants. Dolan lifted her butt off the seat.

'I never should've got black.'

She started the engine and turned on the air conditioner, but didn't put the car in gear.

I took out the pages and looked at them again. I skimmed over the arrest pages, but ended up back with the disciplinary sheet and the two meetings with Krantz. The dates were there. 'If I can't get the files, and I can't ask Krantz, maybe there's someone else I can ask.'

She held out her hand for the sheet. 'This doesn't say shit.'

'No. It doesn't.'

'It doesn't say if he was the subject, or if they wanted to question him about someone else.'

'Nope.'

She handed the sheet back, thinking, then took out her cell phone and punched a number.

'Hang on.'

She made three phone calls and spoke for almost twenty minutes, twice writing in a notepad. 'This guy might be able to help you. He was an IA supervisor when Krantz was there.'

'Who is he?'

She handed me the sheet. 'Mike McConnell. He's retired now, living out in Sierra Madre. That's his number. He owns a sod farm.'

'Sod.'

'He grows grass.'

'I know what it means.'

'I wasn't sure. Sometimes you're stupid.'

She floored the gas, spun her tires, and brought me back to my car.

28

Sierra Madre is a relaxed community in the foothills of the San Gabriel Mountains to the east of Los Angeles. Mature green trees line the streets and kids still ride bikes without worrying about getting shot in a drive-by. The town has a peaceful, rural feel that Los Angeles lost when the developers took over city hall. It is also where Don Siegel filmed the exterior locations of the original *Invasion of the Body Snatchers*. I haven't yet seen a pod person there, though I keep looking. Farther west, L.A. is filled with them.

Mike McConnell's sod farm was on a broad flat plain near the Eaton Canyon Reservoir. The reservoir has been dry for years, and the property beneath it has been leased to farmers and nurseries who've put it to good use. Model airplane builders come fly their tiny machines out of the unused land, which is scrubby and dead, but the irrigated parcels are brightly alive with acre after acre of flowers and yearling plants, and sod.

I turned off the paved street and followed a gravel road between flat green fields of buffalo grass, Bahia grass, St Augustine and Bermuda grasses, and others I didn't recognize. Rainbirds dotted the fields like Erector Set scarecrows, spraying water, and the air smelled of fertilizer. I was hoping to find a field of pulsating pods, but instead I came to a service area where a trailer and a large metal shed sat surrounded by spindly eucalyptus trees. Live in hope.

Three Hispanic guys were sitting in the bed of a Ford pickup, eating sandwiches and laughing. They were soiled from working in the sod fields, and burned deep umber by the sun. They smiled politely as I pulled up and got out of my car. A thin brown dog was lying beneath the pickup's gate. He looked at me, too.

I said, 'Señor McConnell?'

The youngest guy nodded toward the trailer. A late-model Cadillac Eldorado was parked next to it between the trees. 'He's inside. You want me to get him for you?'

'That's okay. Thanks.'

McConnell came out as I was crunching across the gravel. He was in his sixties, with a large gut hanging over khaki trousers and Danner work boots. An unbuttoned Hawaiian shirt let the gut show like he was proud of it. He held a Negro Modelo beer in the dark bottle, but he offered his free hand. 'Mike McConnell. You Mr Cole?'

'Yes, sir. Please, call me Elvis.'

He laughed. 'Don't know as I could do that with a straight face.'

What do you say to something like that?

'I'd invite you in, but it's hotter in there than out here. You want a beer? All I got is this Mexican shit. Fresh out of American.'

'No, sir. But thanks.'

A slim Chicana who couldn't have been more than twenty appeared in the trailer's door and frowned out at him. Somebody had sprayed a thin cotton print dress over her body, and she was barefoot. Hot in there, all right.

She said, '*No me hagas es perar. No me gusta estar sola.*'

McConnell looked scandalized. '*Quidado con lo que dices o te regreso a Sonora.*'

She stuck out her tongue and pouted back into the trailer. The guys on the truck nudged each other.

McConnell shrugged apologetically. 'She's young.'

He led me to a redwood table set in the shade between the eucalyptus trees, and had some of the Modelo. A USMC globe and anchor was so faded on his right forearm that it looked like an ink smudge. 'Got two thousand square yards of St Augustine goin' out this evening to a Chinaman in San Marino. If you're looking for St Augustine I might not be able to help you, but I got twelve other kinds of sod. What are you thinking about?'

I gave him one of my cards. 'I'm afraid I wasn't being straight with you, Mr McConnell. I apologize about that, but I need to ask you about an IA investigation that happened on your watch. I'm hoping you'll talk to me about it.'

He read over the card, then put it on the table. He reached around behind him like he was going for a handkerchief, but came out with a little black .380 automatic. He didn't aim it at me, he just held it.

The men on the truck stopped eating.

'Lying's a poor way to start, son. You carrying?'

I tried not to look at the gun. 'Yes, sir. Under my left arm.'

'Take it out with your left hand. Two fingers only. I see more than two fingers on metal, I'll pop you.'

I did what he said. Two fingers.

'You keep holding it like that, away from your body like it smells bad. Walk on back over there and drop it in your car, then come on back.'

The hired hands were poised on the bed like swimmers on their starting platforms, ready to dive if the shooting started. Imagine: Coming north all the way from Zacatecas to get shot in a sod field.

I dropped the gun into the front seat, then walked back to the table.

'I didn't come here to make trouble for you, Mr McConnell. I just need a few answers. It's been my experience that if I warn people I'm coming, they have a tendency to be gone when I get there. I couldn't afford that you'd be gone.'

McConnell nodded.

'You always carry that little gun out here?'

'I spent thirty years on the job, twenty-five in Internal Affairs. I prosecuted cops who were every bit as rotten as any thug on the street, and I made enemies doing it. More than one of'm has tried looking me up.'

I guess I'd carry the gun, too.

'I'm trying to learn about a deceased officer named Abel Wozniak. He was investigated when you were on the job as a supervisor, but I don't know why, or what came of it. You remember him?'

He gestured with the .380. 'Why don't you tell me what your interest is in this first.'

Retired Detective-Three Mike McConnell listened without expression as I told him about Dersh and Pike. If he knew anything of the headline news happening just a few miles to the west, he gave no indication. That's the way cops are. The first time I mentioned Joe's name, McConnell's eyes flickered, but he didn't react again until I told him that the investigating detective for Internal Affairs had been Harvey Krantz.

McConnell's weathered face split into a mean grin.

'Shits-his-pants Krantz! Hell, I was there the day that squiggly weasel let go!' He enjoyed the memory so much that the .380 drifted away from me. The guys in the truck relaxed then, and pretty soon they were balling up paper bags and climbing into the truck's cab. The show was over and it was time to get back to work.

McConnell said, 'So Pike's your partner now, is he?'

'That's right.'

'Pike's the one made Krantz shit his pants.'

'Yes, sir. I know.'

McConnell laughed. 'That boy damn near made me shit mine, too, the way he grabbed Krantz. Damn, that boy was fast. Lifted Pants right off the floor. I remember he was a Marine. So was I.'

I thought about that, and how humiliated Krantz must've felt. It had hurt his career, and he still carried the name.

'You remember why Krantz was investigating Wozniak?'

'Oh, sure. Wozniak was involved with a burglary ring.'

He said it like it was nothing, but when I heard it I stiffened as if he'd reached out and flipped my off switch.

McConnell nodded. 'Yeah, that's right. Krantz developed it off a couple of Mexican fences working out of Pacoima, up in the valley. Little bitty guys named Reena and Uribe. We called them the Chihuahua Brothers, they were so short. Near as we could figure, Wozniak tipped these Mexicans whenever a business's alarm was on the fritz, or when he found out the watchman had called in sick, or whatever, and they'd send a crew over to rob the place. Auto parts, stereos, that kind of thing.'

'You're saying that Wozniak was dirty.'

'That's right.'

'You're telling me that Joe Pike's partner was part of a burglary ring.' Like maybe I'd heard him wrong and wanted to be sure.

'Well, we weren't at a point in the investigation where we could make the case and charge him, but he was good for it. After he died we could've kept going, but I decided to let it drop. Here was this man's family, a wife and the children, why put them through that? Krantz was livid about it, though. He wanted to keep going and nail Pike.'

'Because Pike had embarrassed him?'

McConnell was about to take another sip of the beer when he paused, and considered me.

'Not that at all. Harvey believed that Pike was involved.'

Sometimes you hear things that you never want to hear, things so alien to your experience, so outlandish that it seems you've rolled out of bed into a Stephen King novel.

'I don't believe that.'

McConnell shrugged. 'Well, most people thought what you thought, that Krantz was just hot to get Pike because Pike's the one made him shit his pants. But Krantz told me he really did believe Pike was involved. He didn't have any proof, but his feeling was how could they not be, the two of them riding together every day. I told'm if he'd spent more time in the car being a real cop instead of trying to suck ass his way into fancier jobs, he'd know. It's like being married. You can spend your whole life with someone and never know them.' He glanced out toward the field. The truck had stopped by the control station of the rainbirds. The two older guys were working there, but the younger guy was out on the sod, jumping and waving his arms and splashing around in the water.

McConnell slid off the table. 'Now what do you suppose that fool is doing?'

McConnell shouted something in Spanish, but the men couldn't hear him. The girl reappeared in the door to see why he had shouted. She looked as mystified as McConnell.

McConnell fished around in his pants for keys to the Caddie. 'Sonofabitch. I'm going to have to go out there.'

'Mr McConnell, I only need a few more minutes. If there wasn't any proof, what made Krantz think Pike was involved? Just because they were in the same car?'

'Harvey didn't believe Pike's story about what happened in that motel room. He thought they'd had a falling-out with each other because of the investigation, and that maybe Pike was worried that Wozniak was going to give him up to cut a deal. Krantz had been trying to do that, you know.

Play them against each other. He was sure that Pike murdered Wozniak to keep him quiet.'

'Do you believe that?'

'Well, I never believed that we knew what really happened in that room. Wozniak lost it with DeVille and knocked him out. We know that much for sure because DeVille and Pike told the same story. But after DeVille was out, all we know is what Pike told us, and some of it didn't make sense. Here was Pike, young and strong and fresh out of the Marines, knowing all that karate stuff the way he did. It just doesn't make a lot of sense that he'd have that much trouble trying to cool out Wozniak. Krantz thought Pike was stonewalling us, and maybe he was, but what are you going to do? We couldn't make the case.'

I didn't like hearing any of this. I was getting irritated with it, and pissed off that McConnell was distracted by the guys in the field. Now the other two guys joined the younger guy in the artificial rain, jumping around with him.

McConnell said, 'Oh, this really is out of hand.'

'Do you think Krantz was right?'

McConnell shouted in Spanish again, but the men still didn't hear him.

I went around and stepped in front of him so he had to look at me instead of the men.

'Was Krantz right?'

'Krantz hadn't turned anything that we could make a case on. I figured one tragedy was enough, so I told Krantz to drop it. That's what we did. Look, I'm sorry I can't help you, but I gotta get out there. Those crazy bastards are costing me money.'

He started around me, and when he did I trapped his hand and twisted away the gun. He wasn't expecting it, and the move had taken maybe a tenth of a second.

McConnell's eyes widened, and he froze.

'What about these two fences? You think either of them might be trying to set up Joe Pike?'

'Wozniak was nothing to those two. Reena hauled ass back to Tijuana because he got into a beef with some meth-head. Uribe was shot to death at a gas station when he got into an argument.'

'Wozniak's file showed that he had received administrative punishments on five separate occasions, and twice been suspended for using excessive force. Seven complaints, and in five of those the complainant was either a pedophile or a pimp dealing in child prostitution. Do you know who the informant was who tipped Wozniak about DeVille?'

McConnell's eyes flicked to the gun, then came back to me.

'No. Wozniak probably had several. That's what made him such an effective patrol officer.'

'How could I find out?'

'The divisions keep a registered informant list. They have to do that to protect the officers. But I don't know if Rampart would still have one for Wozniak, all of that being so long ago.'

McConnell looked past me to the fields again, then shook his head. 'Goddamnit, you gonna shoot me, son, or you gonna let me go take care of my business? Look at the water they're wasting.'

I looked at the gun, then handed it back to him. I felt myself turn red. 'I'm sorry. I don't know why I did that.'

'Kiss my ass.'

He stalked toward the Cadillac. When he got to the door, he turned back to me, but he didn't look angry anymore. He looked sad.

'Look, I know how it is, your partner gets in trouble. Just so you know, I never believed that Pike had anything to do with that burglary ring. And I don't think he murdered Wozniak. If I'd thought he had, I would've stayed after him. But I didn't.'

'Thanks, Mr McConnell. I'm sorry.'

'Yeah. Right.'

McConnell climbed into his Caddie and roared away into his fields.

I went back to my car, put my own gun back in its holster, and sat there, thinking. The smell of the fertilizer was stronger now. Rainbows floated around the dancing men in the mist from the rainbirds. The Caddie skidded to a stop behind the truck and McConnell got out, pissed off and shouting. One by one the men stopped jumping and went back to work. McConnell turned off the water and the rainbirds died.

Sitting there, I reread the LAPD incident report and found the reference again: *Acting on information received from an unnamed informant, Officers Wozniak and Pike entered room #205 of the Islander Palms Motel.*

The more I sat there thinking, the more I thought about the unnamed informant, and what he might know. He or she probably didn't know anything, but when you've got nothing the way I had nothing, a long shot starts to look pretty good.

I went back through the rest of my notes and found Wozniak's widow. Paulette Renfro.

Maybe Wozniak talked about his work to his wife, and maybe she knew something about the informant. Maybe she knew something about Harvey Krantz, and how the Leonard DeVille file had come to be missing.

You look for connections.

I started my car, pulled in a wide circle, and drove back toward the highway.

Behind me, the sod had already begun to bake in the afternoon heat. Steam rose from the ground like a fog from hell.

29

You're getting close to Palm Springs when you see the dinosaurs.

Driving through the Banning Pass, a hundred miles east of L.A. where the San Bernardino and San Jacinto Mountains pinch together to form a gateway to the high deserts of the Coachella Valley, you emerge into the Morongo Indian Reservation. A towering apatosaur and tyrannosaurus rex stand just off the freeway, built there by some sun-stricken desert genius long before Michael Crichton created Jurassic Park. Years ago, they were the only thing out here, monstrous full-sized re-creations standing in the desert heat as if they were frozen in time and place. You could pay a dime and walk around them, and maybe have your picture taken to send to all the folks back home in Virginia. *Look, Ma, here we are in California.* The dinosaurs have been there for years, but drunks and hopheads still stumble into the bars down in Cabazon, swearing they've seen monsters in the desert.

A few miles past the dinosaurs, I left the freeway and followed the state highway along the foot of the San Jacintos into Palm Springs.

During the winter months, Palm Springs is alive with tourists and weekenders and snowbirds come down from Canada to escape the cold. But in the middle of June with temperatures hovering at one hundred twenty degrees the town is barely breathing, its pulse undetectable as it wilts in the heat like some run-over animal waiting on the side of the road to die. The tourists are gone, and only the suicidal venture out during the day.

I stopped in a tee-shirt shop to buy a map of the area, looked up Paulette Renfro's address, then made my way straight north across the desert, one moment with dinosaurs and Indians, the next passing the science-fiction weirdness of hundreds of sleek, computer-designed windmills, their great flimsy blades rotating in slow motion to steal energy from the wind.

Palm Springs itself is a town of resorts and vacation homes and poodle groomers for the affluent, but the men and women who keep the city running live in smaller communities like Cathedral City to the south or North Palm Springs on what's considered the wrong side of the freeway.

Paulette Renfro lived in a small, neat desert home in the foothills above the freeway with a view of the windmills. Her home was beige stucco with a red tile roof and an oversized air conditioner that I could hear running from the street. Down in Palm Springs the people can afford to irrigate for grass lawns, but up here the lawns were crushed rock and sand, with desert plantings that required little water. All their money goes into the air conditioner.

I parked off the street and walked up her drive past an enormous blooming century plant with leaves like green swords. A brand-new Volkswagen Beetle was parked behind a Toyota Camry, only the Camry was in a garage and the Beetle was out in the sun. Visitor.

A tall, attractive woman answered when I rang the bell. She was wearing a nice skirt and makeup, as if she planned to leave soon or had just returned.

I said, 'Ms Renfro?'

'Yes?' Nice teeth and a pretty smile. She was five or six years older than me, but that meant she must've been younger than Abel Wozniak.

'My name's Cole. I'm a private investigator from Los Angeles. I need to speak with you about Abel Wozniak.'

She glanced inside like she was nervous about something. 'Now isn't really a good time. Besides, Abel died years ago. I don't know how I could help you.'

'Yes, ma'am. I know. I'm hoping you can answer a few questions about a case he was working on at the time of his death. It's pretty important. I've come a long way.' Sometimes if you look pathetic enough it helps.

A younger woman appeared behind her, the younger woman saying, 'Who is it, Mom?'

Paulette Renfro told me that we were letting out all the cold and asked me to come in, though she didn't look happy about it. Most people don't. 'This is my daughter Evelyn. Evelyn, this is Mr Cole. From Los Angeles.'

'I have to finish moving.' Annoyed.

'Hi, Ms Renfro.' I offered my hand, but Evelyn didn't take it.

'My name's Wozniak. Renfro was *her* mistake.'

'Evie, please.'

I said, 'This shouldn't take any more than ten minutes. I promise.'

Paulette Renfro glanced at her watch, then her daughter. 'Well, I suppose I have a few minutes. But I have things to do, and I have an appointment to show a house in less than an hour. I'm in real estate.'

Evie said, 'I don't need your help. I just need to bring in the rest of my things.'

Evie Wozniak stalked out of the house and slammed the door. She looked like a twenty-something version of her mother in the face, but where Paulette Renfro was neat and well put together, her daughter was puffy and overweight, her features pinched with a set that said most things probably annoyed her.

I said, 'Looks like I interrupted something. Sorry about that.'

Ms Renfro seemed tired. 'There's always something to interrupt. She's having boyfriend problems. She's always having boyfriend problems.'

The house was neat and attractive, with an enormous picture window and comfortable Southwestern furniture. The living room flowed through to a family-room combination with the kitchen on one side and a hall that probably led to bedrooms on the other. Beyond the family room, a small blue pool glittered in the heat. From the picture window, you could look down across the freeway and see the windmills, slowly turning, and further south, Palm Springs.

'This is very nice, Ms Renfro. I'll bet Palm Springs looks beautiful at night.'

'Oh, it does. The windmills remind me of the ocean during the day, what with their gentle movement like that, and at night the Springs can look like one of those fairy-tale cities from *A Thousand and One Nights*.'

She led me to a comfortable couch that looked toward the view.

'Could I offer you something to drink? With our heat out here, you have to be careful to keep yourself hydrated.'

'Thanks. Water would be good.'

The living room was small, but the open floor plan and a spare arrangement of furniture made it feel larger. I hadn't expected Paulette Renfro to keep any fond memories of Joe Pike, but as I waited for the water, I noticed a small framed picture resting in a bookcase among a little forest of bowling trophies. Paulette Wozniak was standing with her husband and Pike in front of an LAPD radio car that was parked in the drive of a modest home. Paulette was wearing jeans and a man's white shirt with the sleeves rolled and the tails tied off in a kind of halter.

Joe Pike was smiling.

I went over to the bookcase, and stared at the picture.

I had never seen Pike smile. Not once in all the years that I'd known him. I had seen a thousand pictures of Joe in the Marines, of him hunting or fishing or camping, pictures of him with friends, and in none of them was he smiling.

Yet here was this picture of her former husband and the man who had killed him.

Smiling.

Paulette Renfro said, 'Here's your water.'

I took the glass. She'd brought water for herself, too.

'That's Abel on the left. We were living in the Simi Valley.'

I said, 'Ms Renfro, Joe Pike is a friend of mine.'

She stared at me for a moment, holding her glass with both hands, then went to the couch. She sat on the edge of it. Perching.

'I imagine you find it odd that I would keep that picture.'

'I don't find anything odd. People have their reasons.'

'I've been reading about all that mess down in Los Angeles. First Karen, now Joe being accused of murdering this man. I think it's a shame.'

'You knew Karen Garcia?'

'Joe was dating her in those days, you know. She was a pretty, sweet girl.' She glanced at her watch again, then decided something. 'You say you and Joe are friends?'

'Yes, ma'am. We own the agency together.'

'Were you a police officer, also?' Like she wanted to talk about Joe, but wasn't sure how to go about it.

'No, ma'am. Private only.'

She glanced at the picture again, almost as if she had to explain it. 'Well, what happened to Abel happened a long time ago, Mr Cole. It was a terrible, horrible accident, and I can't imagine that anyone feels worse about it than Joe.'

Evelyn Wozniak said, 'Your child feels worse about it, Mother. Since he killed my father.'

She had come through the kitchen carrying a large cardboard box. Paulette's face tightened. 'Do you need a hand with that?'

Evelyn continued on through the living room to disappear down a hall without answering.

Paulette said, 'It was hard on Evelyn. She's moving back home now. This boyfriend, the one who just left her, took their rent money and now she's lost her apartment. That's the kind of men she finds.'

'Was she close to her father?'

'Yes. Abel was a good father.'

I nodded. I wondered if she knew about Krantz's investigation. I wondered if she knew about Reena and Uribe and the burglaries.

'I really do have to be leaving soon. What is it that you want to know?'

'I want to know what happened that day.'

Paulette stiffened, not much, but I could see it.

'Why do you want to know about that?'

'Because I think someone is trying to frame Joe for Eugene Dersh's murder.'

She shook her head, but the stiffness remained.

'I couldn't even guess, Mr Cole. My husband didn't talk about his job with me.'

'On the day your husband died, he and Joe were tipped to the whereabouts of this man DeVille by one of your husband's informants. Would you know who?'

Paulette Renfro stood, and now she wasn't looking so much like she wanted to help. Now she was looking uncomfortable and suspicious.

'No, I'm sorry.'

'He didn't talk about that kind of thing with you, or you don't remember?'

'I don't like to talk about that day, Mr Cole. I don't know anything

212

about it, or about my husband's job, or any of that. He never told me anything.'

'Please take a moment and think, Ms Renfro. It would help if you could come up with a name.'

'I'm sure I never knew.'

Her daughter came back through the room then, carrying empty boxes and clothes hangers.

Paulette Renfro said, 'Do you have all your things?'

'I'm going back for the last of it.'

'Do you need money?'

'I'm fine.'

Evelyn Wozniak stalked on through the living room and slammed the door. Again.

Paulette Renfro's jaw knotted. 'Do you have children, Mr Cole?'

'No, ma'am.'

'You're lucky. I really do have to be going now. I'm sorry I couldn't be more help.'

'Could I call you again if I think of something to ask?'

'I don't think I'll be any more help then than now.'

She walked me to the door, and I went back out into the heat. She didn't come out with me.

Evelyn was waiting by her Beetle. She'd put on little sunglasses, but she was still squinting from the glare. Waiting for me in this insane heat. The boxes and hangers were in her car.

'She wouldn't talk about him, would she? My father.'

'Not very much.'

'She won't talk about that day. She never would, except to defend that guy.'

'Joe?'

Evie glanced toward the windmills, but shrugged without seeing them.

'Can you imagine? The bastard kills her husband, and she keeps that goddamned picture. I used to draw on it. I've broken that goddamned thing so many times I can't count.'

I didn't say anything, and she looked back at me.

'You're his friend, aren't you? You came out here trying to help him.'

'Yes.'

'Do you know that they were investigating my father? The Internal Affairs?'

'Yeah. I know.'

'She tried to keep it from me. And so did Daddy.' Daddy. Like she was still ten years old. 'Men came to the house and questioned her, and I heard. I heard her screaming at my father about it. Can you imagine what that's like when you're a child?'

I thought that I could, but I didn't say anything.

'She just won't talk about it. She'll talk about anything else, but not that, and that's the most important thing that's ever happened to me. It ruined my whole fucking life.'

Standing on the cement drive was like standing on a bright white beach. The heat baked up through my shoes. I wanted to move, but she seemed about to say something that wasn't easy for her to say, and I thought that if I moved it would break her resolve.

'I want to tell you something, you're his friend. That man killed my father. It was like my world ended, I loved my father so much, and there is nothing I would love more than to hurt the goddamned awful man who took him from me.'

Pike.

'But there's something I want more.'

I waited.

'She's got all Daddy's things in storage somewhere. You know, one of those rental places.'

'You know where?'

'I'll have to find out. I don't know if there's anything there that will help, but you're trying to find out what happened back then, right?'

I told her that I was, but that I also wanted other things. I said, 'I'm trying to help Joe Pike. I want you to know that, Evelyn.'

'I don't care about that. I just want to know the truth about my father.'

'What if it's bad?'

'I want to know. I guess I even expect that it is, but I just want to know why he died. I've spent my whole goddamned life wanting to know. Maybe that's why I'm so fucked up.'

I didn't know what to say.

'I don't think it was an accident. I think your friend murdered him.'

Exactly what Krantz had thought.

'If I help you, and you find out, will you tell me?'

'If you want to know, I'll tell you.'

'You'll tell me the truth? No matter what?'

'If that's what you want.'

She wiped at her nose. 'It's like if I just knew, then I could go on, you know?'

We stood there for a time, and then I held her. We had been in the sun for so long that when my hands touched her back it felt as if I'd gripped a hot coal.

I watched the windmills stretching across the plain of the desert, turning in the never-ending wind.

After a time, Evie Wozniak stepped back. She wiped her nose again. 'This is silly. I don't even know you, and here I am telling you my life's secrets.'

'It works like that sometimes, doesn't it?'

'Yeah. I guess you'd better give me your phone number.'

I gave her the card.

'I'll call you.'

'Okay.'

'You can't tell her, all right? If she knew, she wouldn't allow it.'

'I won't tell.'

'Our little secret.'

'That's right, Evie. Our little secret.'

I drove back down off the mountain, Palm Springs far in the distance, shimmering in the heat like a place that did not exist.

Man of Action

The cell was four feet wide by eight feet long by eight feet high. A seatless toilet and a basin stuck out from the cement wall like ceramic goiters, almost hidden behind the single bunk. Overhead, bright fluorescent lamps were secured behind steel grids so the suicidal couldn't electrocute themselves. The mattress was a special rayon material that could not be cut or torn, and the bed frame and mattress rack were spot-welded together. No screws, no bolts, no way to take anything apart. The single bunk made this cell the Presidential Suite of the Parker Center jail, reserved for Hollywood celebrities, members of the media, and former police officers who had found their way to the wrong side of the bars.

Joe Pike lay on the bunk, waiting to be transferred to the Men's Central Jail, a facility ten minutes away that housed twenty-two thousand inmates. His hair was still damp from the basin bath he'd given himself after exercising, but he was thinking that he wanted to run, to feel the sun on his face and the movement of air and the sweat race down his chest. He wanted the peace of the effort, and the certain knowledge that it was a good thing to be doing. Not all acts brought with them the certainty of goodness, but running did.

The security gate at the end of the hall opened, and Krantz appeared on the other side of the bars. He was holding something.

Krantz stared at Pike for a long time before saying, 'I'm not here to question you. Don't worry about your lawyer.'

Pike wasn't worried.

'I've waited a long time for this, Joe. I'm enjoying it.' Joe. Like they were friends.

'You look bad, being wrong about Dersh.'

Pike spoke softly, forcing Krantz to come closer.

'I know. I feel bad about Dersh, but I've got the Feebs to share the blame. You hear Dersh's family already filed suit? Two brothers, his mother, and some sister he hadn't seen in twenty years. Bellying up to the trough.'

Pike wondered what was with Krantz, coming here to gloat.

'They're suing the city, the department, everybody. Bishop and the chief can't fire me without it looking like an admission that the department did something wrong, so they're saying we just followed the FBI's lead.'

'They should win, Krantz. You're responsible.'

'Maybe so, but they're suing you, too. You pulled the trigger.'

Pike didn't answer that.

Krantz shrugged. 'But you're right. I look bad. A year from now when everything's calmed down, that's it for me. They'll ship me out to one of the divisions. That's okay. I've got the twenty-five in. I might even make thirty if I can't scare up something better.'

'Why are you here, Krantz? Because I humiliated you?'

Krantz turned red. Pike could tell that he was trying not to, but there it was.

'I didn't ruin you, Krantz. You took care of that yourself. People like you never understand that.'

Krantz seemed to think about that, then shrugged. 'For the humiliation, yes, but also because you deserve to be here. You murdered Wozniak and got away with it. But now you're here, and I like seeing it.'

Pike sat up. 'I didn't murder Woz.'

'You were right in with him on the burglaries. You knew I was going to nail him, and you knew I would get you, too. You were a chickenshit, Pike, and you decided to take out Wozniak because you're an amoral, homicidal lunatic who doesn't think twice about snuffing out a human life. Which is about as much thought as you gave to Dersh.'

'All the time you spent investigating, and that's what you came up with. You really think I murdered Woz in that room to keep him quiet?'

Krantz smiled. 'I don't think you killed him because you thought he'd give you up, Pike. I think you killed him because you wanted his wife.'

Pike stared.

'You had something going with her, didn't you?'

Pike swung his feet off the bunk. 'You don't know what you're talking about.'

Krantz smiled. 'Like your asshole friend says, I'm a detective. I detected. I was watching her, Pike. I saw you with her.'

'You're wrong about that, and you're wrong about Dersh, too. You're wrong about everything.'

Krantz nodded, agreeable. 'If you've got an alibi, bring it out. If you can prove to me that you didn't do Dersh, I'll personally ask Branford to drop the charges.'

'You know there's nothing.'

'There's nothing because you did it, Pike. We've got you on tape casing his house. We've got the old lady picking you out of the line. We've got the residue results and your relationship with the girl. We've got this.'

Krantz showed Pike what he was carrying. It was a revolver wrapped in plastic.

'This is a .357 magnum. SID matches it with the bullet that killed Dersh. It's the murder weapon, Pike.'

Joe didn't say anything.

'It's a clean gun. No prints, and all the numbers have been burned off, so we can't trace it. But we recovered it in the water off Santa Monica exactly where you said you talked with the girl. That puts you with this gun.'

Pike stared at the plastic bag, and then at Krantz, wondering at the coincidence of how the murder weapon turned up at the very place where he admitted to being.

'Think about it, Krantz. Why would I admit to being there if that's where I threw the gun?'

'Because someone saw you. I think you went there to ditch the gun, and did, but then someone saw you. I didn't believe you about the girl at first, but maybe you were telling the truth about that part. Maybe she saw you there, and you were worried we'd find her and catch you in a lie if you denied it, so you tried to cover yourself.'

Pike looked at the plastic bag again. He knew that cops often showed things to suspects and lied about what they were to try to elicit a confession.

'Is this bullshit?'

Krantz smiled again, calm and confident, and in an odd way Pike found it warm. 'No bullshit. You can ask Bauman. The DA's filling him in on it right now. I've got you, Joe. I couldn't make the case with Wozniak, but this time I've got you. Branford's making all this noise about Special Circumstance, but he's full of shit. I couldn't get that lucky, Pike, you getting the needle.'

'I didn't put the gun there, Krantz. That means somebody else did.'

'That's some coincidence, Joe, you and the gun just happening to be in the same place.'

'It means they knew my statement. Think about it.'

'What I think is that we've got plenty for a conviction. Charlie is going to tell you the same thing.'

'No.'

'Bauman's already floating plea arrangements. Bet he didn't tell you that, did he? I know you're telling Bauman no plea, and he's saying sure, like he's going along with it, but he's not an idiot. Charlie's smart. He'll let you sit in Men's Central for six months, hoping you're telling the truth about this girl you claim you saw, but when she doesn't turn up he'll deal you a straight hand about taking the plea. My guess is that Branford will let you cop to twenty with the possibility of parole. Saves everybody looking bad about how we fucked over Dersh. Twenty with time off means you serve twelve. That sound about right to you?'

'I'm not going to prison, Krantz. Not for something I didn't do.'

Krantz touched the bars. He slipped his fingers along the steel like it was his lover.

'You're inside now, and you're going to stay inside. And if you're dumb enough to go to trial, and I'm thinking you might do that because you're such a hardhead, you'll be in a cage like this for the rest of your life. And I did it, Pike. Me. You're mine, and I wanted to tell you that. That's why I came here, to tell you. You're mine.'

The black jailer with the big arms came down the cellblock and stopped next to Krantz. 'Time to take your ride, Pike. Step into the center of the floor.'

Krantz started away, then turned back. 'Oh, and one other thing. You heard we found the homeless guy dead, didn't you?'

'Deege.'

'Yeah, Deege. That was kind've goofy, wasn't it, Pike, him telling you guys that a truck like yours stopped Karen, and a guy who looked like you was driving?'

Pike waited.

'Someone crushed his throat and stuffed him in a Dumpster on one of those little cul-de-sac streets below the lake.'

Pike waited.

'A couple of teenagers saw a red Jeep Cherokee up there, Joe. Parked in the middle of the street and waiting on the very night that Deege was killed. They saw the driver, too. Guess who they saw behind the wheel?'

'Me.'

'This gets better and better.'

Krantz stared at Pike a little longer, then turned and walked away.

Earlier, there had been a prisoner who made monkey sounds – oo-oo-oo – that Pike had thought of as Monkeyboy, and another prisoner with loud flatulence who had thrown feces out of his cell while shouting, 'I'm the Gasman!'

They had been taken away, and Pike had dubbed the jail cop with the big arms the Ringmaster.

When Pike was standing, the Ringmaster waved down the hall. Jailers didn't use keys anymore. The cell locks were electronically controlled from the security station at the end of the cellblock, two female officers who sat behind a bulletproof glass partition. When the Ringmaster gave the sign, they pushed a button and Pike's door opened with a dull click. Pike thought that it sounded like a rifle bolt snapping home.

The Ringmaster stepped through, holding the handcuffs. 'We won't use the leg irons for the ride, but you gotta wear these.'

Pike put out his wrists.

As the Ringmaster fit the cuffs, he said, 'Been watching you work out in here. How many push-ups you do?'

'A thousand.'

'How many dips?'

'Two hundred.'

The Ringmaster grunted. He was a large man with overdeveloped arm and shoulder and chest muscles that stretched his uniform as tight as a second skin. Not many prisoners would stand up to him, and even fewer could hope to succeed if they tried.

The Ringmaster snugged the cuffs, checked to see they were secure, then stepped back.

'I don't know if you're getting a square shake with this Dersh thing or not. I guess you probably did it, but if some asshole popped my lady I'd forget about this badge, too. That's what being a man is.'

Pike didn't say anything.

'I know you're an ex-cop, and I heard about all that stuff went down when you were on the job. It don't matter to me. I just wanted to say I've had you here in my house for a couple of days, and I read you as a pretty square guy. Good luck to you.'

'Thanks.'

The two 'female cops buzzed them out of the cellblock into a gray, institutional corridor where the Ringmaster led Pike down a flight of stairs and into the sheriff's prisoner holding room. Five other prisoners were already there, cuffed to special plastic chairs that were bolted to the floor: three short Hispanic guys with gang tats, and two black guys, one old and weathered, the other younger, and missing his front teeth. Three sheriff's deputies armed with Tasers and nightsticks were talking by the door. Riot control.

When the Ringmaster led Pike into the room, the younger black prisoner stared at Pike, then nudged the older man, but the older man didn't respond. The younger guy was about Pike's size, with institutional tats that were almost impossible to see against his dark skin. A jagged knife scar ran along the side of his neck, as if someone had once cut his throat.

The Ringmaster hooked Pike to the bench, then took a clipboard from the deputies.

Pike sat without moving, staring straight ahead at nothing, thinking about Krantz, and what Krantz had said. Across the room, the younger guy with the knife scar kept glancing over. Pike heard the older man call him Rollins.

Fifteen minutes later, all six prisoners were unhooked from their chairs and formed up in a line. They were led out into the parking garage and aboard a gray L.A. County Jail van, climbing through a door in the van's rear while two deputies with Mossberg shotguns watched. A third dep, the driver, sat at the wheel with the engine running. They needed the engine for the air conditioner.

Inside the van, the driver's compartment was separated from the rear by the same heavy-gauge wire mesh that covered the windows. The rear compartment where the prisoners sat was fixed with a bench running along each wall so that the prisoners faced each other. The van was set up to hold twelve, but with only half that number everyone had plenty of room.

As they climbed in, a deputy named Montana touched each man on the shoulder and told him to sit on the left side or the right side. One of the Mexicans got it wrong and the deputy had to go inside and straighten him out, holding up the process.

Rollins sat directly across from Pike, now openly staring at him.

Pike stared back.

Rollins snarled up his lips to show Pike the double-wide hole where his teeth should be.

Pike said, 'Sweet.'

The trip to the Men's Central Jail would take about twelve minutes with the usual downtown traffic delays. When the last of the six was in and seated, Deputy Montana called back through the cage. 'Listen up. No talking, no moving around, no bullshit. It's a short trip, so nobody start any crap about having to pee.'

He said it a second time in Spanish, then the driver put the van in gear and pulled out of the parking garage and into traffic.

They had gone exactly two blocks when Rollins leaned toward Pike.

'You the one was a cop, aren't you, muthuhfuckuh?'

Pike just looked at him, seeing him, but not seeing him. Pike was still thinking about Krantz, and about the case that was slowly coming together against him. He was letting himself float and drift and be in places other than this van.

Rollins poked the older black guy, who looked like he'd rather be anyplace else on the planet. 'Yeah, this muthuhfuckuh the one. I got a nose for shit like that. I heard'm talkin' about him.'

Pike had arrested a hundred men like Clarence Rollins, and had fronted off five hundred more. Pike knew by looking at him that Rollins had been institutionalized for most of his life. Jail was home. The world was where you went between coming home.

'You a real Aryan muthuhfuckuh, ain't you, them fuckin' pale ass eyes o' yours. Lemme tell you somethin', muthuhfuckuh, it don't mean shit to me you killed some muthuhfuckuh. I killed so many muthuhfuckuhs you can't count, an' there ain't nuthin' I hate more'n a motherfuckin' cop like you. Lookie here –'

Rollins peeled back a sleeve to show Pike a tattoo of a heart with *LAPD 187* written inside it: 187 was the LAPD's code for homicide.

'You know what that means, muthuhfuckuh? LAPD one eighty-seven? Means I'm a cop-killin' muthuhfuckuh, that's what it means. You best fear my ass.'

Rollins was working himself up for something. It was as predictable as watching a freight train round a bend, but Pike didn't bother paying attention. Pike was seeing himself in the woods behind his boyhood home, smelling the fresh summer leaves and the wet creek mud. He was feeling the steambath heat of Song Be, Vietnam, when he was eighteen years old, and hearing his sergeant's voice shouting at him across the dry scrub hills of Camp Pendleton, a voice he so wished to be his father's. He was tasting the healthy clean sweat of the first woman he loved, a beautiful proud farm girl named Diane. She had been from a proper family who despised Joe, and had made her stop seeing him.

'How come you ain't sayin' nothin, muthuhfuckuh? You goddamned well better answer me when I talk to your muthuhfuckin' ass, you know what's good for you. Your ass is trapped in here with me.' When he said that, Rollins flashed the long slender blade hidden in his sock.

The other places and people melted away, leaving only the van and Pike and the man across from him. Pike felt as peaceful as the woods behind that childhood home.

'No,' Pike whispered. 'You're trapped with me.'

Clarence Rollins blinked once, clearly surprised, then launched off the bench, driving the blade square at Pike's chest and pushing with all the power of his legs.

Pike let the blade slip past his hands, then trapped and folded the wrist, channeling all the speed and power of Rollins's own attack in turning the knife. Gunnery Sergeant Aimes would be pleased.

Rollins was a large, strong man, and considerable force went back into his forearm. The radius and ulna bones snapped like green wood, slicing through muscles and veins and arteries as the bones exploded through his skin.

Clarence Rollins screamed.

Deputy Sheriffs Frank Montana and Lowell Carmody both jumped at the scream, bringing their Mossbergs to port arms. The three Hispanic prisoners were bunched together at the front screen, making it hard to see, but Rollins was thrashing around in the aisle like something was biting him.

The driver shouted, 'The fuck is going on back there?'

Carmody yelled, 'Knock it off! Get back in your seats!'

Pike was down in the aisle with Rollins, who kept turning over and flailing and spinning around. Rollins was screaming in a high, little girl's voice as a three-foot geyser of blood sprayed all over the back of the van.

Montana said, 'Holy fuck! Pike's killing him!'

Montana and Carmody both tried to sight past the Hispanics over their Mossbergs. Montana screamed, 'Get away from him, Pike! Get back in that seat, goddamnit!'

The Mexicans saw the shotguns and scrambled out of the way, still trying to avoid the blood. They were probably thinking about AIDS.

Pike lifted his hands away from Rollins and eased back onto the bench.

Clarence continued thrashing and rolling and screaming as if his whole body was on fire.

Montana shouted, 'Shut up, Rollins! What the hell is going on back there?'

The older black man said, 'He's hurt! Can't you see that?'

Montana shouted, '*Knock off that shit and get back in your seat, Rollins!*
What the hell are you doing?'

The older man said, 'He's bleeding to death, goddamnit it. That's blood.'

Rollins kept howling, the blood spraying everywhere. The older man was
squatting on his seat, trying to stay clear.

Pike said, 'I can help him. I can stop the bleeding.'

'Stay the fuck in your seat!'

Carmody peered through the mesh. 'Shit, he ain't faking it, man. He's
bleeding like a stuck goat. One of these bastards musta cut him.'

The older man said, 'He ain't been cut! That's his goddamned bones
stickin' out! His arm's broke. Can't you see that?'

Montana could see it even with the way Rollins was carrying on. The
bones looked like pink ivory.

The driver said that they were only another ten minutes from the jail,
but when he said it they were locked down in the thick traffic. The van
didn't have a flash bar or siren, so there was no way to get the cars to
move.

The old man yelled, 'Ten minutes in your butt! This man needs a
tourniquet. We ain't got no belts or nothing back here. You just gonna let
him bleed like that?'

Montana said, 'Fuck. We'd better do something.' He could see the
bastard bleeding out back there, and the three of them getting sued by the
ACLU.

Montana told the driver to radio their sit-rep and request a medical unit.
He left his shotgun and his sidearm with Carmody because he didn't want
to tempt any of these bastards with a weapon, then pulled on vinyl gloves.
He just knew that bastard had AIDS. Every one of these scumbags probably
had it.

'You cover my ass, goddamnit,' he told Carmody.

Carmody shouted at everyone to stay in their goddamned seats, trying to
make himself heard over Rollins's moaning and flopping. Every time the
blood squirted toward the Mexicans, they jumped in a little herd.

Montana trotted around to the rear, keyed open the door, and looked
inside. Christ, there was blood everygoddamnedplace.

'Settle down, Rollins. I'm gonna help you.'

Rollins spun around on his back like he was break-dancing, kicking his
feet and crying. Montana thought that Mr 187 was a big goddamned baby.

Pike was sitting to his left and the old guy was to his right and the
Mexicans were all bunched together in the front on the left side. Carmody
had the shotgun at port arms, and the driver had his handgun out.

Carmody said, 'Just drag his ass out of there and lock the fuckin' door.
We can take care of him outside.'

That's the plan.

Pike said, 'You want help?'

'Stay on that goddamned bench and don't move a fuckin' muscle.'

Montana climbed into the van, trying to watch the prisoners and get a handle on Rollins at the same time.

Rollins rolled end over end, squirting blood on Montana's pants, then flopped backward up the aisle toward the Mexicans. All three jumped up on the seats in front of Carmody.

'Goddamnit, Rollins. You got the AIDS I'm gonna beat you to death, you fucker. I swear to God I'll kill you myself.'

Montana scrambled up the aisle past Pike and the older guy to where the three Mexicans were trying to kick the hysterical Rollins away.

Montana gritted his teeth, cursed, then grabbed Rollins by the leg, standing to tow him back down the aisle, when both Carmody and the driver shouted, 'Getouttatheway getouttatheway! He's running!'

Both their Mossbergs were pointing right at Montana.

Frank Montana felt an icy rush in his stomach as he dropped to the floor, spun around, and saw that Joe Pike had escaped through the open door.

30

The mirrored towers of Los Angeles rose up out of the basin like an island from the sea. Reflections of the setting sun ricocheted between the buildings, making them glow hot and orange in the west, backdropped with a purple sky. The freeway was a lava flow of red lights chasing the sun. Twilight was beginning.

When you're coming to my house and reach Mulholland at the top of the mountain, you make a hard turn onto Woodrow Wilson Drive, then follow it along its winding path through the trees until you reach my little road. Wide shoulders flare off Mulholland there at the mouth of Woodrow Wilson, and are often used as parking by guests visiting the surrounding houses, so I don't usually pay attention. But tonight a boxy American sedan with a man and a woman in the front seat was the only car off the road. They looked away when I glanced at them. It was like having a neon sign that read COPS.

Five minutes later, I pulled into the cool shadows of my carport, let myself in, and knew why the cops were there.

Joe Pike was leaning against my kitchen counter in the dark, arms crossed, the cat sitting nearby, staring at him with abject worship.

Joe said, 'Surprise.'

It seemed normal and natural that he was here in my home, only there was no Jeep outside and he was supposed to be in jail. He wore a loose cotton beach shirt that showed little brown dolphins jumping free in the sea, the sleeves hiding his red tattoos, the shirt's tail out over his jeans. He was wearing the glasses again, even standing here in my dark house.

I flipped on the light.

'Don't.'

I flipped it off.

'Charlie didn't get you out, did he?'

'It was a do-it-yourself program.'

I went around the ground floor, pulling the drapes and drawing the shades.

'I'm home now. It would look odd if there weren't lights.'

He nodded, and we turned on the lights.

'There's a car on Mulholland at Woodrow Wilson. Anything else, or should you just start telling me why the hell you escaped?'

'There's another car at the top of Nichols Canyon. They probably have a third unit down below, coming up out of Hollywood. Two units are on my condo and another on the gun shop.'

'Sooner or later, the police are going to come here to question me.'

'I'll leave before then.'

'You have a place to stay? You've got wheels?'

The corner of his mouth twitched, like it was silly of me to ask.

'They're probably watching my house, too. Maybe they weren't when you got here, but they've had time to set up. Wait until it's full dark before you leave. Full dark, you can get all the way down to Hollywood and they won't see you.'

He nodded.

'Jesus, Joe. Why?'

'I'd rather be out, Elvis. Krantz has a case. Even though I didn't do it, they have a case, and they could win. Out here I can help clear myself. In there, I could only be their victim. I don't do victim.'

Pike told me what had happened, and how. As he spoke, he picked up the cat and held it, and I thought that there were times when even tough men needed to feel a beating heart.

When he told me that the murder weapon had been recovered off the point where he'd met the girl, I said, 'They planted it.'

'Someone did. Else we're back to coincidences again. You hear about Deege?'

'He's dead.'

'Murdered. A couple of kids saw a red Jeep where it happened. Saw a guy who looked like me behind the wheel.'

I stared at him. I wanted to say something, but I didn't know what to say. It just kept getting deeper.

'It fits together pretty well. I killed Dersh. I killed Deege. Pretty soon it's going to look like I killed all these people.'

'Except Lorenzo. You were in jail when Lorenzo was killed.'

Pike shrugged, like maybe he thought there might be a way to pin that one on him, too.

I said, 'Krantz hates you. It all comes back to Krantz.'

'It all comes back to me and Woz and DeVille. Krantz was part of that. So was Karen.'

I said, 'Maybe it isn't just Karen and Dersh. Maybe all six victims go back to that day. Before Dersh we've got a shooter who's murdered five people. He's sent no notes, left no messages, but he used the same method to murder all five. That means part of him wants the cops to know that he's responsible.'

'A power thing.'

'His way of sticking out his tongue. The vics are killed three months

225

apart, no one can find a connection, and everything points to a serial killer. But what if he's not a serial killer? What if he's just a murderer with a grudge, and a plan for his killings?'

Pike nodded.

'I tried pulling DeVille's file, but it was missing. I know you and Wozniak located DeVille through an informant, so I pulled Wozniak's file, too, but there was nothing in there. Do you know where he got the information?'

'No. Woz had people up and down the food chain.'

'I went to see his widow, but she didn't know, either.'

Pike stopped stroking the cat.

'You went to see Paulette?'

'Her name's Renfro now. She didn't want to talk about it, but her daughter is trying to help.'

Pike stared at me for a long time, then let the cat slip from his arms. He got two beers from the kitchen, handed one to me, then poured a little beer on the counter. The cat lapped at it.

'It's been a long time, Elvis. Leave Paulette alone.'

'She might be able to help.'

A car pulled up then, and Joe vanished into the living room, but I knew the car.

'It's Lucy.'

I opened the kitchen door, letting her in with a bag of groceries and two suits still in plastic laundry bags. I guess she'd gone by her apartment. Her face was ashen, and she moved with quick short steps, looking nervous. The cat hissed once, then sprinted through his cat door.

'Oh, shut up. Something's happened. Joe escaped custody.'

'I know. He's here.'

As I closed the door, Joe stepped out of the living room.

Lucy stopped in the center of the kitchen, looking at Joe. She was not happy to see him.

She said, 'What were you thinking?'

'Hello, Lucy.'

She put her purse and the grocery bag on the counter, but did not put down the two suits. Her face was hard; no longer nervous, but angry. 'Do you know what a bad move this is?'

Joe didn't answer.

'They've got him in a box, Luce. I don't know if this is the smart way to play it, but it's done.'

Lucy glared at me, and there was an anger in her face I did not like. 'Don't defend this. Let there be no doubt, I can assure you both that this is *not* the smart way to play it.' She turned back to Joe. 'Have you spoken to your attorney yet?'

'Not yet.'

'He's going to tell you to give yourself up. You should.'

'Won't happen.'

Lucy turned back to me. 'Did you have anything to do with this?'

It felt like Mama was angry at her two little boys, and I was liking it even less.

'No, I didn't have anything to do with it, and what's with you? Why are you so upset?'

She rolled her eyes as if I were an idiot, then draped the suits over the grocery bags. 'May I see you?'

She stalked across the living room.

When we were as far from Joe as we could get, I said, 'Do you think you could be a little less supportive?'

'I don't support this, and neither should you.'

'I don't support this, either. I'm dealing with it. What would you like me to do? Kick him out? Call the cops?'

Lucy closed her eyes, calming herself, then opened them. Her voice was measured and calm.

'I have spent the last three hours worried sick about him, and about you. I tried to reach you, and couldn't. For all I knew, you were part of this. You and the Sundance Kid over there, partners jumping off a cliff.'

I started to say something, but she held up a hand.

'Do you realize that his being here jeopardizes your license under California law? You're harboring a fugitive. That's a felony.'

'He's here because we have to work together if we're going to beat this thing. He did not murder Eugene Dersh.'

'Then let him prove that in court.'

'We've gotta have *proof* to prove it. So far, the state has a case and we don't have any way to dispute it. We're going to have to find the person who really killed Dersh, and right now I'm thinking that's the same person who killed Karen Garcia and those other five people.'

Lucy's mouth was tight, her face set in a hard mask because it wasn't what she wanted to hear.

'It's dangerous for him here, Lucy. He knows that, and I know it, too. He's not going to stay, but he can't leave until it's dark.'

'What if the police knock at your door right now? With a search warrant?'

'We'll deal with it if it happens.'

She stepped back from me.

'You're not the only one in jeopardy here.'

She steeled herself in a way that was visible. 'I am not Joe's attorney. As long as I'm living here with you, my license to practice law could be at risk. Worse, what is happening here now could call into question my fitness as Ben's mother if Richard sues for custody.'

I glanced at Joe, then back to Lucy.

Lucy kept the emotionless eyes on mine.

'If Joe stays, I have to leave.'

'He's going as soon as it's dark.'

She closed her eyes, then said it again, slowly and carefully.

'If Joe stays, I have to leave.'

'Don't ask me this, Lucy.'

She didn't move.

'I can't ask him to go.'

A long time ago in another place I was badly wounded and could not get immediate medical attention. Little bits of hot steel had ripped through my back, tearing the arteries and tissues inside me, and all I could do was wait to be saved. I tried to stop the bleeding, but the wounds were behind me. My pants and shirt grew wet with blood, and the ground beneath me turned to red mud. I lay there that day, wondering if I would bleed to death. The minutes turned to hours as the blood leaked out, and the passage of time slowed to a crawl in a way that made me think that I would always be trapped in that single horrible moment.

The time passed like that now.

Lucy and I stood by my fireplace, neither speaking, staring at each other with hurt eyes, or maybe eyes that didn't hurt enough.

I said, 'I love you.'

Lucy went back across the living room into the kitchen, snatched up her suits, and went out the door and drove away.

Joe said, 'You should go after her.'

I hadn't heard him approach, I hadn't felt him put his hand on my shoulder. He was in the kitchen, and now he was beside me.

'If it's about me, I would've gone.'

'Your chances are better when it's dark.'

'My chances are what I make them.'

He moved to the table, pulling the chair and sitting so quietly that I heard no sound. Maybe I was listening for other things. The cat reappeared and jumped onto the table to be with him.

I went back into the kitchen, and looked in the bag she'd brought. Salmon steaks, broccoli, and a package of new potatoes. Dinner for two.

Joe spoke from the dining room. 'Ever since I've known you, I've looked to you for wisdom.'

Pike was a shape in the shadows, my cat head bumping his hands.

'What in hell does that mean?'

'You're my family. I love you, but sometimes you're a dope.'

I put the food away, and went to the couch. 'If you want something, get it yourself.'

Two hours later it was fully dark. During that time, we decided what we would do, and then Joe let himself out the kitchen door, and slipped away into darkness.

Then I was truly alone.

31

I sat on the couch in my empty house, feeling a tight queasiness as if I'd lost something precious, and thinking that maybe I had. After a while, I called Lucy, and got her machine.

'It's me. Are you there?'

If she was there, she didn't pick up.

'Luce, we need to talk about this. Would you please pick up?'

When she still didn't pick up, I put down the phone and went back to the couch. I sat there some more, then opened the big glass doors to let in the night sounds. Somewhere outside the police were watching, but what did I care? They were the closest thing to company that I had.

I poached one of the salmon steaks in beer, made a sandwich with it, and ate standing in the kitchen near the phone.

Lucy Chenier had been out here for less than a month. She had changed her life to come here, and now everything had gone to hell. It scared me. We weren't mad because we liked different movies, or I had been rude to her friends. We were mad because she had given me a choice between herself and Joe, and she felt I'd chosen Joe. I guess she was right, but I didn't know what to do about that. If she gave me the same choice again, I would decide the same way, and I wasn't sure what that said about me, or us.

Someone pounded hard on the front door. I thought it was the cops, and in a way it was.

Samantha Dolan swayed in the doorway with her hands on her hips, four sheets to the wind.

'You got any of that tequila left?'

'Now isn't a good time, Samantha.'

She started to step in past me just like she'd done before, but this time I didn't move.

'What, you got a hot date with the little woman?'

I didn't move. I could smell the tequila on her. The smell was so heavy it could have been leaking from her pores.

Dolan stared at me in the hard way she has, but then her eyes softened. She shook her head, and all the arrogance was gone. 'It isn't a good time for me, either, World's Greatest. Bishop fired me. He's transferring me out of Robbery-Homicide.'

I stepped out of the door and let her in. I felt awkward and small, and guilty for what happened to her, which stacked nicely atop the guilt I felt about Lucy.

I took out the bottle of Cuervo 1800 and poured a couple of fingers into a glass.

'More.'

I gave her more.

'You're not going to have one with me?'

'I've got some beer.'

Dolan sipped the tequila, then took a deep breath and let it out. 'Christ, that's good.'

'How much have you had?'

'Not nearly enough.' She raised her eyebrows at me. 'Had a little tiff with your friend?'

'Who?'

'I'm not talking about your cat, stupid. The little woman.' Dolan tipped her glass toward the kitchen. 'A purse is sitting on your counter. You aren't the only detective in the house.' She realized what she'd said, and had more of the drink. 'Well. Maybe you are.'

Lucy's purse was by the refrigerator, put there when she'd set down the bags. She'd taken her clothes, but forgotten the purse.

Dolan had more of the tequila, then leaned against the counter. 'Pike wasn't smart, playing it this way. You talk to him, you should get him to turn himself in.'

'He won't do that.'

'This doesn't help him look innocent.'

'I guess he figures that if the police aren't going to try to clear him, he should do it himself.'

'Maybe we shouldn't talk about this.'

'Maybe not.'

'It just looks bad, is what I'm saying.'

'Let's not talk about it.'

The two of us stood there. It's always a laugh a minute at Chez Cole. I asked her if she wanted to sit, and she did, so we moved into the living room. The tequila followed us.

'I'm sorry about Bishop.'

Dolan shook her head, thoughtful.

She said, 'Pike would've been in uniform just before I came on. You know what areas he worked?'

'Did a year in Hollenbeck before moving to Rampart.'

'I started in West L.A. There weren't as many women on the force then as now, and what few of us there were got every shit job that came along.'

She seemed as if she wanted to talk, so I let her talk. I was happy with the beer.

'My first day on the job, right out of the Academy, we go to this house and find two feet sticking up out of the ground.'

'Human feet?'

'Yeah. These two human feet are sticking straight up out of the ground.'

'Bare feet?'

'Yeah, Cole, just lemme tell my story, okay? There's these two bare feet sticking up out of the ground behind this house. So we call it in, and our supervisor comes out, and says, "Yeah, that's a couple of feet, all right." Only we don't know if there's a body attached. I mean, maybe there's a body down there, but maybe it's just a couple of feet somebody planted.'

'Trying to grow corn.'

'Don't try to be funny. Funny is another in the long list of things you can't pull off.'

I nodded. I thought it was pretty funny, but I'd been drinking.

'So we're standing there with these feet, and we can't touch them until the coroner investigator does his thing, only the coroner investigator tells us he won't be able to get out until the next morning. The supervisor says that somebody's gotta guard the feet. I mean, we can't just leave'm there, right? So the supervisor tells me and my partner to watch the feet.'

'Okay.'

She killed the rest of her tequila, and helped herself to another glass as she went on with her story.

'But then we get this disturbance call, and the supervisor tells my partner he'd better respond. He says to leave the girl with the feet.'

'The girl.'

'Yeah, that's me.'

'I'm up with that part, Samantha.'

She took another blast of the tequila and took out her cigarettes.

'No smoking.'

She frowned, but put the cigarettes away.

'So they take off, and now I'm there alone with the feet in back of this abandoned house, and it's spooky as hell. An hour passes. Two hours. They don't come back. I'm calling on my radio, but no one answers, and I am pissed off. I am majorly pissed. Three hours. Then I hear the creepiest sound I ever heard in my life, this kind of ooo-ooo-ooo moaning.'

'What was it?'

'This ghost comes floating between the palm trees. This big white ghost, going "*ooo-ooo-ooo, I want my feet.*" Real creepy and eerie, see, just like that.'

'Don't tell me. Your partner in a sheet.'

'No, it was the supervisor. He was trying to scare the girl.'

'What did you do?'

'I whip out my Smith and shout, "Freeze, motherfucker, LAPD." And then I crack off all six rounds point-blank as fast as I can.'

'Dolan. You killed the guy?'

She smiled at me, and it was a lovely smile. 'No, you moron. I knew those assholes were going to try some shit like that sooner or later, so I always carried blanks.'

I laughed.

'The supervisor drops to the ground in a little ball, arms over his head, screaming for me not to shoot. I pop all six caps, and then I go over, and say, "Hey, Sarge, is this what they mean by foot patrol?" '

I laughed harder, but Dolan took a deep breath and shook her head. I stopped laughing.

'Sam?'

Her eyes turned red, but she shook back the tears. 'I put everything I had into this job. I never got married and I didn't have kids, and now it's gone.'

'Can you appeal it? Is there anything you can do?'

'I could request a trial board, but if I go to the board, those pricks could fire me. Bishop just wants me out of Robbery-Homicide. He says I'm not a team player anymore. He says he doesn't trust me.'

'I'm sorry, Samantha. I'm really, really sorry. What happens now?'

'Administrative transfer. I'm on leave until I'm reassigned. They'll put me in one of the divisions, I guess. South Bureau Homicide, maybe, down in South Central.' She looked down at her glass, and seemed surprised that it was empty.

'At least you're still on the job.'

A kindness came to her eyes, as if I was a slow child. 'Don't you get it, Cole? Wherever I go, it's downhill. Robbery-Homicide is the top. It's like being in the majors, then having to go down to the farm team in South Buttcrack. Your career's finished. All you're doing is killing time until they make you leave the game. You got any idea what that means to me?'

I didn't know what to say.

'My whole goddamned career has been forcing men like Bishop to let me be a starting player, and now I don't have a goddamned thing.' She looked over at me. 'God, I want you.'

I said, 'Sam.'

She raised a hand again and shook her head. 'I know. It's the tequila.'

She looked into the empty glass and sighed. She put the glass on the table, and crossed her arms as if she didn't know what to do with herself. She blinked because her eyes were filling again.

She said, 'Elvis?'

'What?'

'Will you hold me?'

I didn't move.

'I don't mean like that. I just need to be held, and I don't have anyone else to do it.'

I put down my beer and went over and held her.

Samantha Dolan buried her face in my chest, and after a while the wet of her tears soaked through my shirt. She pulled away and wiped her hands across her face. 'This is so pathetic.'

'It's not pathetic, Samantha.'

She sniffled, and rubbed at her eyes again. 'I'm here because I don't have anyone else. I gave everything I had to this goddamned job, and now all I have to show for myself is a guy who's in love with another woman. That's pretty fucking pathetic, if you ask me.'

'No one asked you, Samantha.'

'I want you, goddamnit. I want to sleep with you.'

'Shh.'

Her breast moved against my arm. 'I want you to love me.'

'Shh.'

'Don't shush me, goddamnit.'

She traced her fingers along my thigh, her eyes shining in the dim light. She gazed up at me, and she was so close that her breath felt like fireflies on my cheek. She was pretty and tough and funny, and I wanted her. I wanted to hold her, and I wanted her to hold me, and if I could fill her empty places maybe she could fill mine.

But I said, 'Dolan, I can't.'

The kitchen door opened then, an alien sound that had no part in this moment.

Lucy was in the kitchen, one hand still on the door, staring at us, a terrible pain cut into her eyes.

I stood.

'Lucy.'

Lucy Chenier snatched her purse from the counter, stalked back across the kitchen, and slammed out the door.

Outside, her car roared to life, the starter screaming on the gears.

Outside, her tires shrieked as she ripped away.

Dolan slumped back into the couch, and said, 'Oh, hell.'

The ache in my heart grew so deep that I felt hollow, as if I were only a shell and the weight of the air might crush me.

I went after her.

Lucy's Lexus was parked in front of her apartment, the engine still ticking when I got out of my car. Her apartment was lit, but the glow from the pulled drapes wasn't inviting. Or maybe I was just scared.

I stood in the street, gazing at her windows and listening to her car tick. I leaned against her fender, and put my hand on the hood, feeling its warmth. One flight of stairs up to the second floor, but they might as well have gone on forever.

I climbed, and knocked softly at her door.

'Luce?'

She opened the door, and looked at me without drama. She was crying, sad tears like little windows into a well of hurt.

'Dolan came over because she was fired. She's in love with me, or thinks she is, and she wanted to be with me.'

'You don't have to say this.'

'I told her that I couldn't be with her. I told her that I love you. I was telling her that when you walked in.'

Lucy stepped out of the door and told me to come in. Boxes had been put away. Furniture had been moved.

She said, 'You scared me.'

I nodded.

'I don't mean with Dolan. I mean from earlier. I'm angry with you, Elvis. I'm hurt with you.'

Joe.

'You changed your life to come here, Luce. You're worried about Richard, and what's going to happen with Ben. You don't need to worry about me. You don't need to doubt what we have, or how I feel, and what you mean to me. You mean everything to me.'

'I don't know that now.'

I felt as if the world had dropped away and I was hanging in space with no control of myself, as if the slightest breeze could make me turn end over end and there was nothing I could do but let the breeze push me.

'Because of Joe.'

'Because you were willing to put everything that's important to me at risk.'

'Did you want me to call the cops and turn him in?' More tension was in my voice than I wanted there to be.

She closed her eyes and raised a palm.

'I guess you're mad at me, too.'

'I don't like these choices, Luce. I don't like being caught between you and Joe. I don't like Dolan coming to my house because she doesn't have anywhere else to go. I don't like what's happening between us right now.'

She took a breath and let it out. 'Then I guess we're both disappointed.'

I nodded.

'I didn't come two thousand miles for this.'

I shook my head.

I said, 'Do you love me?'

'I love you, but I don't know how I feel about you right now. I'm not sure how I feel about anything.'

It sounded so final and so complete that I thought I must have missed something. I searched her face, trying to see if there was something in her eyes that I was missing in her voice, but if it was there I couldn't find it. I wanted an emotional catharsis; her measured consideration made my stomach knot.

'What are you saying here, Luce?'

'I'm saying I need to think about us.'

'We're having a problem right now. Is it such a big problem that you'd question everything we feel for each other?'

'Of course not.'

'That's what thinking about us means. One thing happens, you don't stop being an us.'

I looked around at the boxes. The stuff of her life. This wasn't going the way I had hoped. I wasn't hearing things that I wanted to hear. And I wasn't doing a good job of saying the things I had wanted to say.

Lucy took my hand in both of hers.

'You said I changed my life to come here, but my coming here changes your life, too. The change didn't end when I crossed the city line. The change is still happening.'

I put my arms around her. We held each other, but the uncertainty was like a membrane between us.

After a time, she eased away. She wasn't crying now; she seemed resolved.

'I love you, but you can't stay here tonight.'

'Is it that clear to you?'

'No. Nothing's clear. That's the problem.'

She took my hand again, gently kissed my fingers, and told me to leave.

Sacrifice

The killer presses the needle deep into his quadriceps and injects twice the usual amount of Dianabol. The pain makes him furious, his rage causing his skin to flush a deep red as his blood pressure spikes. He throws himself onto the bench, grips the bar, and pushes.

Three hundred pounds.

He lowers the weight to his chest, lifts, lowers, lifts. Eight reps of herculean inhuman effort that does nothing to appease his anger.

Three hundred motherfucking pounds.

He rolls off the bench and glares at himself in the mirror here in his shitty little rental. Muscles swollen, chest flushed, face murderous. *Calm yourself. Take control. Put away the rage and hide yourself from the world.*

His face empties.

Become Pike to defeat Pike.

The killer takes a calming breath, returns to the bench, sits.

Pike's escape has changed things, and so have Cole and that bitch Dolan. Knowing that he's been framed, Pike will try to figure out who, and will be coming for him. Cole and Dolan have already tried to get DeVille's file, and that's bad, but he also knows they didn't get it. Without DeVille's file they cannot follow the trail back to him, but they're getting closer, and the killer accepts that they are very close to identifying him.

He must act now. He decides to jump ahead to the final targets, and nothing must stop him. Pike is the wild card, but Cole he can account for. Cole must be distracted. Get his mind off saving Pike, and onto something else.

He believes that Dolan has always been overrated as an investigator, so the killer discounts her. But Cole is another matter. He has met Cole, and studied him. Cole is dangerous. An ex-Army guy who wears the Ranger tab, and an experienced investigator. Cole does not appear dangerous in an obvious way, but many officers respect him. He heard one senior detective say not to let the wisecracks and loud shirts fool you, that Cole can carry all the weight you put on him, and still kick your ass. The killer takes this opinion seriously.

When you are plotting against the enemy, you always look for an exploitable weakness.

Cole has a girlfriend.

And the girlfriend has a child.

32

I walked down the infinite flight of steps from Lucy's apartment to sit in my car. I thought about starting it, but that was beyond me. I tried to be angry with her, but wasn't. I tried to resent her, but that made me feel small. I sat there in my open car on her quiet street until her lights went out, and even then I did not move. I just wanted to be close to her, even if she was up in her apartment and I was down in my car, and for most of the night I tried to figure out how things could go so wrong so quickly. Maybe a better detective could've found answers.

The sky was pale violet when I finally pulled away. I was content to creep along in the morning traffic, the mindless monotony of driving the car familiar and comforting. By the time I reached home, Dolan was gone. She had left a note on the kitchen counter. What it said was, *I'll talk to her if you want.*

I cleaned our glasses from the night before, put away the tequila, and was heading upstairs for a shower when the phone rang.

My heart pounded as I stared at the phone, letting it ring a second time. I took a breath, and nodded to myself.

On the third ring I picked it up, trying not to sound like I'd just run ten miles.

'Lucy?'

Evelyn Wozniak said, 'Why didn't you call?'

'What are you talking about?'

'I left a message yesterday. I said you should call no matter what time you got in.'

I had checked my message machine when Pike was still in the house, but there had been no messages. I looked at it now, again finding nothing.

'Okay. You've got me now.'

Evelyn gave me directions to the storage facility that her mother used in North Palm Springs. She had had a duplicate key made for the lock, and had left it for me in an envelope with the on-site manager. I asked her if she wanted to be there when I went through her father's things, but she said that she was scared of what she might find. I could understand that. I was scared, too.

When she was done, I said, 'Evelyn, did you leave any of this on your message?'

'Some of it. I told you the name of the place. I know it was your machine and not somebody else's, if that's what you're thinking. Who else would have a message that says they're the world's greatest human being?'

I put down the phone, then went upstairs, changed clothes, and drove to Palm Springs, wondering if Pike had heard the message, and if he'd erased it.

And why.

When I was thinking about Pike, I didn't have to think about Lucy.

Two hours and ten minutes later, I left the freeway and again made my way through the wind farms. The desert was already hot, and smelled of burning earth.

The storage facility was clusters of white cinder-block sheds set in the middle of nowhere behind a chain-link fence with a big metal gate. A cinder-block building sat by the gate with a big sign saying LOWEST RATES AROUND. Since nothing else was around, it was an easy guarantee to keep.

An overweight woman with skin like dried parchment gave me the key. Her office was small, but a Westinghouse air conditioner big enough to cool a meat locker was built into the wall, running full blast and blowing straight at her. It was little enough.

She said, 'You gonna be in there long?'

'I don't know. Why?'

'Gonna be hot,' she said. 'Make sure you don't pass out. You pass out, don't you try to sue me.'

'I won't.'

'I'm warning you. I got some nice bottled water in here, only a dollar and a half.'

I bought a bottle to shut her up.

Paulette Renfro's storage unit was located at the rear of the facility. Each unit was a cinder-block shell that sprouted corrugated-metal storage spaces. There was no door on the shell, so you walked inside what amounted to a little cave to get to the individual storage spaces.

From the tarnish on the lock, it was clear that Paulette rarely if ever came here, but the key worked smoothly, and opened into a space the size of a closet. Boxes of various size were stacked along the walls, along with old electric fans and suitcases, and two lamps.

I emptied the closet, putting the unboxed things to the side, then carried out the boxes. When all the boxes were out, I went through the older boxes first, and that's where I found the notebooks that Evelyn Wozniak remembered. Her father had kept field notes much like a daybook, jotting notes about the young officers he trained, the perps he busted, and the kids he was trying to help, all dated, and crammed into seven small three-ring binders thick with pages. I was pretty sure that the most recent would be the most relevant.

I put the seven binders aside, then went through the rest of the boxes to see if anything else might be useful, but the only other things of Abel's were a patrol cap in a plastic bag, a presentation case with Wozniak's badge, and two framed commendations from when he was awarded the Medal of Valor. I wondered why the commendations were here in a box, but she had remarried. I guess over time she'd lost track of them.

I was repacking the boxes when a shadow framed itself in the door, and Joe Pike said, 'I wanted to get here before you.'

I glanced over at him, then went on with the packing.

'It's so easy to show you up.'

'Find anything?'

'Wozniak's daybooks.'

'You look through them yet?'

'Too hot to look through them here. I'll take them where it's cooler.'

'Want some help?'

'Sure.'

He put the boxes I had finished repacking back in the closet. I sealed the last two boxes, then handed them to him one by one.

'You erase Evelyn's message?'

He nodded.

'Why?'

'I wanted to make sure you didn't find anything here that would hurt Paulette.'

'I'm looking for something to help you.'

'I know. Maybe we'll get lucky.'

'But maybe there's something here that will hurt Paulette.'

Pike nodded.

I took that in, and it was like taking in volumes.

'How did you break Karen Garcia's heart, Joe?'

Pike stacked the boxes until the last box was in place, and then he went to the door and looked out toward the desert as if something might be there. All I could see past him were other cinder-block buildings with other people's memories.

I said, 'Karen loved you, but you loved Paulette.'

Pike nodded.

'You dated Karen, but you were in love with your partner's wife.'

He turned back to me then, the flat lenses empty.

'Paulette was married. I kept waiting for the feelings I had for her to go away, but they didn't. We didn't have an affair, Elvis. Nothing physical. Woz was my friend. But I felt what I felt. I tried dating other people to feel other things, but love doesn't just come and doesn't just go. It just is.'

I stared at him, thinking about Lucy.

'What?'

I shook my head.

'You already know that Krantz thought Wozniak was involved with a burglary ring.'

'Yes.'

'It was true.'

I watched him.

'Krantz thinks I murdered Woz for Paulette.'

'Did you?'

The corner of Pike's mouth twitched, and he tipped the glasses my way. 'You believe that?'

'You know better. Krantz also thinks you were involved with Woz in the ring. I don't believe that, either.'

Pike tipped his head the other way, and frowned. 'How do you know that?'

I spread my hands.

'Right.'

Pike drew a deep breath, then shook his head. 'I didn't have any idea. All that time in the car with Woz, and I never knew until Krantz talked to Paulette and scared her. She asked Woz about it, and he denied it, so she asked me. That's how I found out. I followed Woz and saw him with the Chihuahuas. He'd gotten some girl pregnant, and he'd set her up in an apartment in El Segundo. He was paying for it by tipping the Chihuahuas on easy places to rob. Krantz had it all. He just couldn't prove it.' Just what McConnell had said.

'You tell Paulette?'

'Some of it. Not all. He was her husband, Elvis. They had the child.'

'So what happened?'

'I told him he had to resign. I gave him the choice, and I gave him the time to think about it. That way it was between me and him. That's why he died.'

I thought that maybe Krantz had been right about many things.

'What happened in the motel, Joe?'

'He didn't want to resign, but I didn't give him any choice. I didn't want to give him to Krantz, but I couldn't let a bad officer stay on the job. If he didn't hang it up, I would've brought in Paulette, and I would've arrested the Chihuahuas.'

'The Chihuahuas would've rolled on him.'

'If he resigned I would've found another way at them, but it never got to that. We got the call about the missing girl and DeVille, and Woz got the location. When we got over there, Woz was already short, and that's when he lost it and hit DeVille with his gun. I think he was just working up his nut, because he already knew what he was going to do. It was about me, and the box he was in, and how he was going to get out of it.' Pike stopped for a time, then went on. 'He let DeVille have it, and when I pushed him away he pointed his gun at me.'

'You shot him in self-defense?'

'No. I wouldn't shoot him. I didn't draw my weapon.'

I stared at him.

'He knew I loved his wife, and he knew she loved me. His career was over, and if Krantz could make the case he would go to jail. Some men can't take the weight. Some men break, and will do anything to stop the pressure.'

'Abel Wozniak killed himself.'

Pike touched his chin. 'Pointed the gun here and pulled the trigger, up through his chin and out the top of his head.'

I asked, but I had already guessed. 'Why take the blame?'

'It had to be explained. If I tell the truth, Krantz would be able to make the case, and if Woz goes out a felon, his pension and benefits could be withheld. Paulette and the girls would've lost everything. Maybe Parker Center might've felt sorry, and cut them slack, but how could I know? If he goes out a suicide, there's no insurance. The insurance we had then wouldn't pay if you capped yourself.'

'So you took the weight.'

'DeVille was going to wake up and say that Woz hit him. I just went with it. I told them that we struggled, and that's how it happened. It would fit with what DeVille was going to say, and it would explain Woz being dead.'

'Only you get marked rotten for causing your partner's death to protect a pedophile.'

'You do the best you can with what you've got.'

'Did Paulette know the truth?'

Pike stared at the cement. 'If Paulette knew, she would've told the department. Even if it meant losing the benefits.'

'Wasn't that her decision to make?'

'I made the decision for all of us.'

'So she doesn't know that her husband killed himself.'

'No.'

Pike just stood there, and I thought that this was his single lonely way of protecting the woman he loved, even if it had cost him any chance at her love, forever and always.

Pike would take that weight.

And had.

I said, 'All this time, all these cops hating you for nothing.'

Pike cocked his head, and even in the dim light of the little building the glasses seemed to glow.

'Not for nothing. For everything.'

'Okay. So now what?'

'She still gets his survivor benefits. I want to make sure that whatever leaves here doesn't affect that.'

'Even if it's something that could help you?'

The corner of Pike's mouth twitched. 'I didn't come this far to quit now.'

'Then let's see what we find.'

We sat in a Denny's just off the freeway for the next two and a half hours, drinking tea and going through the day books. The Denny's people didn't mind. With the heat, they didn't have much business.

We started with the most recent book and worked backward. Eight pages were missing from that book, but the rest were there, and legible. Wozniak's entries were often cryptic, but pretty soon they made sense to me.

At one point I saw that Pike had stopped reading, and asked him, 'What?'

When he didn't answer, I leaned closer and found what had stopped him.

'*This Pike is a sharp kid. He'll make a good cop.*'

Pike pulled back the book, and kept reading.

Many of the entries were about arrests that Wozniak made, with notes on crimes and criminals and witnesses that he took for future reference, but much of what he'd written was about the street kids whom Wozniak had tried to help. Whatever he had become, Wozniak had been sincere in his efforts to help the people he was sworn to protect and to serve.

In all seven books, only three names were used in a context that suggested they might be informants, and only one of those seemed a possible, that being in an entry dated five months prior to Wozniak's death.

I read that entry to Pike.

'Listen to this. "*Popped a kid named Laurence Sobek, age fourteen, male hustler. Likes to talk, so he might be a good source. Turned out by the Coopster. ID? Fucked up kid. Gonna try to get him inside.*" ' I looked up. 'What's that mean, get him inside?'

'Get him into a halfway house or a program. Woz did that.'

'Who's the Coopster?'

Pike shook his head.

I stared at the page.

'Could it be DeVille?'

Pike considered it. 'Like a nickname. Coupe DeVille.'

'Yeah.'

'Thin.'

'You remember Laurence Sobek?'

'No.'

'Anything else in here look good?'

Pike shook his head again.

'Then this is what we go with.'

We paid the bill, then brought the books out to our cars. I took the notebook that mentioned Laurence Sobek with me.

'How can I reach you?'

'Call the shop and tell them you need me. I'll have a pager.'

'Okay.'

We stood in the heat and watched the trucks go by on the freeway. Behind us, the windmills churned for as far as we could see. Pike was driving a maroon Ford Taurus with an Oregon license plate. I wondered where he'd gotten it. When I finally looked over, he was watching me.

I said, 'What?'

'I'm going to beat this. Don't worry about me.'

I made like Alfred E. Neuman. 'What, me worry?'

'Something's eating you.'

I thought about telling him about Lucy, but I didn't.

'You take care of yourself, Joe.'

He shook my hand, and then he drove away.

33

It was late when I got home, but I called Dolan anyway. I called her house twice, leaving messages both times, but by the next morning she still hadn't gotten back to me. I thought that she might be at Parker Center, clearing her desk, but when I called her direct line there, Stan Watts answered.

'Hey, Stan. It's Elvis Cole.'

'So what?'

'Is Dolan there?'

'She's over, man. Thanks to you.'

Like I needed to hear that.

'I thought she might be there.'

'She's not.'

Watts hung up.

I called Dolan again at home, still got her machine, so this time I took Wozniak's notebook and drove over there.

Samantha Dolan lived in a bungalow on Sierra Bonita just a few blocks above Melrose, in an area more known for housing artists than police officers.

I parked behind her BMW, and heard music coming from the house even out in my car. Sneaker Pimps. Loud.

She didn't answer the bell, on my knock, and when I tried the door, it was locked. I pounded hard, thinking maybe she was dead and I should break in, when the door finally opened. Dolan was wearing a faded METALLICA tee shirt and jeans and was barefoot. Her eyes were nine shades of red, and she smelled like a fresh dose of tequila.

'Dolan, you've got a drinking problem.'

She sniffed like her nose was runny. 'That's what I need today, you giving me life advice.'

I walked in past her and turned off the music. The living room was large, with a nice fireplace and a hardwood floor, but it was sloppy. The sloppy surprised me. A big couch faced a couple of chairs, and a mostly empty bottle of Perfidio Anejo tequila sat on the floor by the couch. The cap was off. An LAPD Combat Shooting trophy sat on top of the television; the room smelled of cigarettes. I said, 'Why didn't you call me back?'

'I haven't checked my messages. Look, you want me to talk to your friend, I will. I'm sorry about what happened last night.'

'Forget it.'

I tossed Wozniak's binder to her.

'What's this?' She scooped a pack of cigarettes off the floor, and fired up, breathing out a cloud of smoke like a volcanic fog.

'A day book that Abel Wozniak kept.'

'Abel Wozniak as in Pike's partner?'

'Read the pages I marked.'

She frowned through another deep drag, reading. She flipped back several pages, then read forward past the point I had marked. When she was done, she looked at me. The cigarette forgotten.

'You're thinking this kid is talking about DeVille?'

'This kid had a relationship with Wozniak, that much we know. He was turned out by someone called the Coopster. If that's DeVille, then DeVille links Sobek to Karen Garcia, too.'

Dolan squinted at me. 'You're saying Sobek killed Dersh.'

'I'm saying maybe he killed everybody. Krantz and the Feds have been chasing a serial killer, but maybe this guy isn't, Dolan. At first I thought the connection was through Wozniak, but maybe these killings don't have anything to do with Wozniak. Maybe they're about DeVille.'

She shook her head, scowling and cranky. 'I was one of the cops trying to find a connection, remember? We didn't.'

'Did you check out DeVille?'

She waved her cigarette. 'Why in hell would we?'

'I don't know, Dolan. I don't know why you didn't find anything, but you ordered DeVille's file from the DA's Record Section, right? Let's check it out and see what's there.'

She took another pull on the cigarette, and stared into the cloud. I could almost see the wheels turning, weighing the odds and what all of this might mean. For her, it was a shot at getting in again. If she could turn something that advanced the case, it could keep her on Robbery-Homicide and save her career.

Dolan pushed off the couch, went to her phone, and called Stan Watts, asking him if she'd gotten anything from DA Records. When she hung up, she said, 'Give me five.'

She showered and dressed and took almost twenty.

When we went outside, she said, 'Move your car and we'll take mine.'

'No way, Dolan. You scare the hell out of me.'

'Move your goddamned car or I'll back into it.'

She powered up the Beemer as I moved my car.

We drove to Parker Center without saying very much, each of us keeping our thoughts to ourselves. She pulled into the red zone by the front door, told me not to touch anything, then hurried inside. Ten minutes later she came out with DeVille's file.

'You didn't fuck with the radio, did you?'

'No, I didn't fuck with anything.'

We parked a block away in a little parking lot. Dolan went through the file first, peeling away pages and dropping them on the floorboard.

'What's that?'

'Lawyer crap. This stuff won't tell us anything. We want the detective's case presentation.'

The lead detective in charge of the case was a Rampart Division sex crimes D-2 named Krakauer. Dolan told me that the case presentation was the sum total of the compiled evidence used in building the case, and would include witness statements, testimonial evidence, interviews; anything and everything that the detective accumulated along the way.

When Dolan had the lawyer crap separated, she took half of the detective's case presentation, gave me the other half, and said, 'Start reading. The case will be divided by subject and chronology.'

I was hoping for some indication that Sobek was connected to DeVille, and perhaps had been the informant that put Pike and Wozniak in that motel room on the day Wozniak died, but most of what I read concentrated on Ramona Ann Escobar. There were statements from her neighbors and the motel desk clerk and her parents, and a transcribed statement from Ramona describing how DeVille had paid her ten dollars to take off her clothes. Ramona Ann Escobar had been seven years old. It was uncomfortable to read, but I read in hopes of finding Sobek.

I was still searching when Dolan quietly said, 'Oh, holy shit.'

She was pale and stiff.

'What?'

She handed me a witness list that compiled the names of the people who had lodged complaints about DeVille. The list was long, and at first I didn't understand until Dolan pointed at a name midway down the list.

Karen Garcia.

Her face still ashen, Dolan said, 'Keep reading.'

They were all there, the first five victims, plus the newest, Jesus Lorenzo. Dersh wasn't there, but he was the exception.

Dolan stared at me. 'You were right, you sonofabitch. These people weren't random. They're linked. He's killing everyone who helped put away Leonard DeVille.'

All I could do was nod.

'Maybe you're the world's greatest fuckin' detective, after all.'

Only one of the six victims actually gave testimony against DeVille, that being Walter Semple, who had seen DeVille at the park from where the little girl disappeared. The others were part of what Dolan called the clutter, people who had been questioned by Krakauer because they had lodged sex crime complaints against a man Krakauer believed to be

DeVille, but not directly related to the case for which DeVille was finally prosecuted.

Dolan's breast rose and fell as we read through the rest of the file. A copy of DeVille's criminal arrest record was attached, listing several aliases, one of which was the Coopster.

I said, 'It's Sobek. It's got to be Sobek. We have to take this to Krantz. The other people on this list have to be notified.'

'Not yet. I want more.'

'What do you mean, more? This will break open the case. It's a showstopper.'

'It links Sobek with DeVille, but it doesn't prove he's the shooter. If I can bring them the shooter, Bishop's gotta let me on again.'

'You've already got something, Dolan. We've found a connection between these people, and we've got leads. You're going to turn this case around.'

'I want more. I want to put the whole thing right on the table. I want the headline, Cole. I want to push Krantz's face in it. I want it so tight that Bishop can't not take me back on the team.'

I stared at her, and thought that if I were her I would want it this badly, too. But maybe I wanted it more. If we got the shooter, then maybe that would clear Joe Pike.

'Okay, Samantha. Let's find this guy.'

We drove back to her place. It took Dolan almost two hours of phone calls, but we learned that Laurence Sobek wasn't in the adult system, and the system had no record of his present whereabouts. This meant one of two things: Either he'd straightened out and gotten his life together, or he'd moved away before the age of eighteen. Of course, he could always be dead, too. Boys who work the streets often end up that way.

While Dolan made the calls, I went into her kitchen for a glass of water. A couple of million photographs were stuck to her refrigerator with little magnets, including several of Dolan posing with the actress who'd played her in the series. Dolan looked like she could kick your ass and would enjoy doing it, but the actress looked like an anorexic heroin addict. Showbiz.

The picture that Dolan had taken of me at Forest Lawn was stuck near the handle with a little Wonder Woman magnet. Seeing it there made me smile.

I finished my water, then went back into the living room as she put down the phone.

Dolan said, 'We've got to go to Rampart.'

'Why?'

'Because that's where Sobek was busted as a juvenile. The Juvie Section there will know where to find his sheet. They might have it loaded on their system, but maybe somebody will have to dig through paper.'

'I thought you said we'd need a court order to get at the juvenile stuff.'
She frowned, annoyed. 'I'm Samantha Dolan, you idiot. Get up to speed.'
And this woman wanted to sleep with me.

The Rampart Division station house is a low-slung, brown brick
building facing Rampart Street a few blocks west of MacArthur Park, where
Joe Pike had first met Karen Garcia. We parked in a small lot they have
behind the place for officers, then entered the division through the back.
This time Dolan didn't tell me to keep my mouth shut and try to look
smart. Looking smart would be out of place in a station house anyway.

Dolan badged our way into the Juvenile Section, which was microscopic
in size, just four detectives attached to the robbery table in the corner of a
dingy room. Where Parker Center and the Robbery-Homicide offices were
modern and bright, the detective tables at Rampart seemed faded and
small, with outdated furniture that looked as tired as the detectives.
Rampart was a high crime area, and the detectives there busted their asses,
but the cases rarely made headlines, and no one was lounging around in
six-hundred-dollar sport coats waiting to be interviewed on *60 Minutes*.
Most of them just tried to survive their shift.

Dolan zeroed on the youngest detective in the room, badged him, and
introduced herself. 'Samantha Dolan. Robbery-Homicide.'

His name was Murray, and his eyebrows went up when she said that.
'I know you, don't I?'

She gave him the smile. 'Sorry, Murray. Don't think we've met. You
mean from the TV show?'

Murray couldn't have been more than twenty-six or twenty-seven. He
was clearly impressed. 'Yeah. You're the one they made the show about,
right?'

Dolan laughed. She hadn't laughed when I'd mentioned her show, but
there you go. 'These Hollywood people, they don't know what being a
detective really means. Not like we do.'

Murray smiled wider, and I thought if she told him to roll over and
bark, he wouldn't hesitate. 'Well, that was some case you put together. I
remember reading about it. Man, you were news.'

'Hey, it's just Robbery-Homicide, you know? We get the hot cases, and
the press tags along. No different than what you do here.'

Dolan didn't look good playing modest, but maybe that was just me.

Murray asked how he could help her, and Dolan said that she wanted to
look at an old juvie packet, but she didn't have a court order for it. When
Murray looked uneasy about that, she grew serious and leaned toward him.
'Something we got down at Parker Center. Headline case, man. The real
stuff.'

Murray nodded, thinking how cool it would be to work the real stuff.

Dolan leaned closer. 'You ever think about putting in for RHD, Murray?
We need sharp cops who know how to make the right call.'

Murray wet his lips. 'You think you could put in a word for me?'

Dolan winked at him. 'Well, we're trying to find this kid, you see? So while we're reading his file, maybe you could run a DMV check and call the phone company. See if you can't shag an address for us?'

Murray glanced at the older detectives. 'My supervisor might not like it.'

Dolan looked blank. 'Gee. I guess you shouldn't tell him.'

Murray stared at her a moment longer, then got busy.

I shook my head. 'You're something, all right.'

Dolan considered me, but now she wasn't smiling. 'Something, but not enough.'

'Let it go.'

She raised her hands.

Twenty minutes later we had the file and an interview room, and Murray was making the calls.

Laurence Sobek had been booked seven times from age twelve to age sixteen, twice for shoplifting and four times for pandering. The DOB indicated he would now be in his late twenties. Abel Wozniak was twice the arresting officer, first on the shoplifting charge, then later for the second pandering charge. Sobek's most recent booking photo, taken at age sixteen, showed a thin kid with a wispy mustache, stringy hair, and aggravated acne. He looked timid and cowed.

At the time of his arrests, he had lived with his mother, a Mrs Drusilla Sobek. The record noted that she was divorced, and had not come to pick up her son or meet with the officers any of the seven times.

Dolan scowled. 'Typical.'

Murray interrupted us, knocking once before opening the door. He looked crestfallen.

'Doesn't have a California driver's license and never had one. The phone company never heard of him, either. I'm really sorry about this, Samantha.' He was seeing his chance at the hot stuff fizzle and melt.

'Don't worry about it, bud. You've been a help.'

The booking sheets showed that his mother had lived in an area of South L.A. called Maywood.

I said, 'If she's still alive, maybe we can work through the mother. You think she's still at this address?'

'Easy to find out.'

Dolan made a copy of the booking photo, then used Murray's phone to call the telephone company.

As Dolan called, Murray sidled up to me. 'You really think I got a shot at Robbery-Homicide?'

'Murray, you've got the inside track.'

Three minutes later we knew that Laurence Sobek's mother was still down in Maywood.

We went to see Drusilla Sobek.

Detective Murray was disappointed that he could not tag along.

*

Drusilla Sobek was a sour woman who lived in a tiny stucco house in a part of Maywood that was mostly illegal aliens come up from Honduras and Ecuador. The illegals often lived eighteen or more to a house, hot-bedding their cots between sub-minimum-wage jobs, and Drusilla didn't like it that they'd taken over the goddamned neighborhood. She made no bones about it, and told us so.

She peered at us heavily from her door, her flat face wrinkled and scowling. She was a large woman who filled the door. 'I don't want to stand here all goddamned day. These Mexicans see me here with this door open, they might get ideas.'

I said, 'These folks are from Central America, Mrs Sobek.'

'Who gives a shit? If it looks like a Mexican and talks like a Mexican, it's a Mexican.'

Dolan said, 'We're trying to find your son, Mrs Sobek.'

'My son's a faggot whore.'

Just like that.

When she'd first come to the door, Dolan had badged her, but Mrs Sobek had said we couldn't come in. She said she didn't let in strangers, and I was just as glad. A sour smell came from within her house, and she reeked of body odor. Behind the hygiene curve.

I said, 'Can you give us an address or phone number, please?'

'No.'

'Do you know how we can find him?'

Her eyes narrowed, tiny and piglike in the broad face. 'There some kind of reward?'

Dolan cleared her throat. 'No, ma'am. No reward. We just need to ask him a few questions. It's very important.'

'Then you better look somewhere else, lady. My faggot whore son ain't never even been *close* to important.'

She tried to close the door, but Dolan put her foot in its base and jammed the sill. Dolan's left eye was ticking.

Drusilla said, 'Hey! What the hell you think you're doing?'

Dolan was a little bit taller than Drusilla Sobek, but a couple of hundred pounds lighter. She said, 'If you don't get the stick out your ass, you fat cow, I'm gonna beat you stupid.'

Drusilla Sobek's mouth made a little round O, and she stepped back. Surprised.

I started to say something, but Dolan raised a finger, telling me to shut up. I shut.

She said, 'Where can we find Laurence Sobek?'

'I don't know. I ain't seen him in three or four years.' Drusilla's voice was small now, and not nearly so blustery.

'Where was he living the last time you knew?'

'Up in San Francisco with all those other faggots.'

'Is that where he's living now?'

'I don't know. I really don't.' Her lower lip trembled and I thought she might cry.

Dolan took a breath, forcing herself to relax. 'Okay, Mrs Sobek, I believe you. But we still need to find your son, and we still need your help.'

Drusilla Sobek's lip trembled harder, her chin wrinkled, and a small tear leaked down her cheek. 'I don't like being spoken to in such a rude manner. It ain't right.'

'Did you ever have an address or phone number for your son?'

'Yeah. I think I did. A long time ago.'

'I need you to go look for it.'

Drusilla nodded, still crying.

'We have his booking photo from when he was sixteen, but I'd like a more recent picture, too. Would you have one of him as an adult?'

'Uh-huh.'

'You get those things. We'll wait here.'

'Uh-huh. Please don't let in the Mexicans.'

'No, ma'am. You go look.'

Drusilla shuffled away into her house, leaving the door open. A fog of the sour smell billowed out at us.

I said, 'Christ, Dolan, you're harsh.'

'Is it any wonder her kid turned out screwed up?'

We stood there in the sun for almost fifteen minutes until Drusilla Sobek finally shuffled back to the door, like a sensitive child who had disappointed her family.

'I got this old address up there with the faggots. I got this picture he gimme two years ago.'

'It's a San Francisco address?'

She nodded, her jowly chin quivering. 'Up with the faggots, yeah.'

She handed the address and the picture to Dolan, who stiffened as soon as she saw them. I guess I stiffened, too. We wouldn't need the address.

Bigger, stronger, filled out and grown, and with much shorter hair, we recognized the adult Laurence Sobek.

He worked at Parker Center.

Final Action

Laurence Sobek, his true name and not the name by which he is currently known, finishes stapling black plastic over his windows. He has already nailed shut every window but the small one in the bathroom, leaving only the front door as a point of egress. It is sweltering in the converted garage.

The plan was simple and obvious once Sobek lifted DeVille's case file from the records section. There in black and white he knew all the people who had helped the Sex Crimes detectives put the Coopster into prison where he died, all the people who had lodged complaints or made statements, and fed the Coopster to the prison population like a sacrifice. Sobek designed the sequence of homicides to take advantage of the weaknesses in LAPD's system: He started with the peripheral complainants it would be impossible for LAPD to connect, intent on working steadily up the food chain until it was too late to stop him even when the Task Force finally realized what was happening.

Now, thanks to Cole and that bitch Dolan, he must spare the remaining minor players, and kill the people he holds most responsible. The lead Sex Crimes detective, Krakauer, died of a heart attack two days after he retired. (All to the good, as Krakauer was the only person with even a remote chance of tying together the names of the early victims.) Pike had arrested the Coopster, then sat in the witness chair at his trial and hammered the nails into DeVille's coffin, but Pike is now a fugitive.

That leaves one other.

The apartment now sealed, Sobek pulls DeVille's case file from its hiding place in the closet, along with the brittle, yellowed newspaper articles about DeVille's arrest. He has read these a hundred thousand times, touching the grainy photographs of the Coopster being led from the motel in handcuffs. He touches them again now. He hates Wozniak, who spotted him at a Dunkin' Donut shop that day, and manipulated him into revealing what he knew. *This asshole is using you,* Wozniak had said. *What this guy is doing to you is wrong,* he said. *Help me help you.*

The Islander Palms Motel. Arrest. Prison. Dead.

Sobek closes his eyes, and puts away whatever is left of his feelings for DeVille. He has studied Pike, and learned well. Abandon humanity. Feel nothing. Control is everything. If you are in control, then you can re-create yourself. Become larger. Control everything.

Sobek closes his eyes, steadies his breathing, and feels an inner calm that only comes from certainty. He admires himself in the mirror: jeans, Nikes, gray sweatshirt with the sleeves cropped. He runs a hand over his quarter-inch hair, and imagines that he is not looking at Laurence Sobek, but is seeing Joe Pike. He flexes. The red arrows he had painted on his deltoids are gone, but he thinks that when this is over, he will have them tattooed there permanently. He rubs at his crotch, and enjoys the sensation.

Control.

He places the dark glasses over his eyes.

He has a cut-down double-barrel shotgun that he lifted from the Parker Center evidence room, and a box of twelve-gauge shells filled with #4 buckshot. He pulls the weight bench to the center of the floor, then fixes the shotgun to it with duct tape. He runs a cord from the knob to both triggers, rigged so that the gun will go off when the door opens, and pulls back the hammers.

He lays out the evidence that he wants Cole and the police to find, then lets himself out the back window. He will never return to this place.

Laurence Sobek drives away to do murder.

34

Dolan ripped away from Drusilla Sobek's house like the queen of the Demolition Derby. She was so excited she was shaking. 'We got the sonofabitch. Right under our own goddamned noses, but we got him.'

'No, Dolan, we don't have him yet. It's time to take it inside.'

She glanced at me, and I knew what she was thinking. That she'd like to snap the cuffs on him herself and cut Krantz and Bishop and their whole damned Task Force out of the bust.

'This is what you wanted, Samantha. This is going to get you back on the team, but not if you piss off Bishop even more than he already is.'

She didn't like it much, but she finally went along. 'This guy works the day shift, so he's probably at Parker Center right now. I'm putting this on Bishop's desk in person. We've got the files and Wozniak's book. I'm giving Bishop the whole load, and fuck Krantz.'

'Whatever. I've got to use a phone. Stop somewhere.'

'Use mine. It's in my purse.'

'I'd rather use a pay phone. It won't take long.'

She glanced at me like I was crazy. 'Sobek is there right now.'

'I need a phone, Dolan.'

'You're going to call Pike.'

I just looked at her.

'I fuckin' knew it.'

She jerked the Beemer into the nearest gas station, blasting past a crowd of people waiting to board a bus. She screeched up to the pay phones, and left the engine running.

'Don't take all goddamned day.'

I did the same thing I'd done before, calling Pike's man, giving him the pay phone's number, then hanging up. Pike called back in less than two minutes. From the static I could tell he was on a cell phone.

'We were right, Joe. It's Sobek.'

'Is he in custody?'

'Not yet. I wanted to tell you that we're bringing it to Bishop now. If we get lucky, Sobek will cop to Dersh. If not, maybe we'll find something that links him to it and clears you.'

'It's going to bring up Woz.'

'Yeah, it is. We've got to show Wozniak's notebook to tie Sobek to DeVille, and to Wozniak. Once the story breaks, they're going to dig into what happened between you in that room. I just wanted to warn you. After we're finished with Bishop, I'll call Charlie, then go see Paulette and Evelyn so they aren't caught flat.'

'You won't have to. I will.'

I didn't know what to say, but I smiled.

Dolan blew her horn.

Pike said, 'It's been a long time. I guess it's time we spoke.'

'Okay, but stay safe until this guy takes the weight for Dersh. You're still wanted, and we don't know what we'll get from him.'

When I was back in her car, Dolan swerved through the gas station, cut in front of the bus, and blasted toward the Los Angeles River.

'Dolan, have you ever killed anybody in this thing?'

'Cinch your belt tighter if you're scared. You'll be fine.'

I glanced at her and she was smiling. I guess I was smiling, too.

When we reached Parker Center, Dolan didn't bother going into the parking lot; she put it in the red zone out front. We trotted in, Dolan badging us past the desk guard. I looked at everyone we passed, wondering if Sobek would be standing there when the elevator doors opened, but he wasn't.

We pushed into Robbery-Homicide, Watts and Williams raising their eyebrows when they saw us. Dolan steamed straight into Bishop's office, surprising him on the phone.

Dolan said, 'We've got the shooter.'

He covered the phone, annoyed. 'Can't you see I'm on the phone?'

She put the photograph of Laurence Sobek on his desk. 'His real name is Laurence Sobek. Here's another picture when he was booked under his true name as a juvenile. He's our shooter, Greg. We got him.'

Bishop told whoever was on the phone that he'd get back in five and hung up. He leaned closer to the pictures. Sobek had gained muscle and changed his appearance, but when the pictures were side by side you could tell they were the same guy.

'This is Woody something.'

I said, 'You know him as Curtis Wood. He's a civilian employee here. He pushes the mail cart around.'

Krantz and Watts appeared in the door, Williams standing on his toes to see past them.

Krantz said, 'Is there a problem, Captain?'

Dolan laughed. 'Oh, please, Krantz. Like you could do something.'

'They say he's our shooter, Harvey.' Bishop squinted up from the pictures. 'Where'd you get this booking picture?'

I said, 'Sobek's juvenile record. We got the recent picture from Sobek's mother.'

I showed them the pages we'd copied from Abel Wozniak's notebook, pointing out the passages about Sobek and DeVille, and their relationship, then the copy of Sobek's juvenile record showing Wozniak as one of his arresting officers.

Even as I said it, Krantz made a sour face as if he'd bitten into a rotten carrot. 'All this proves is we've got someone working here under a false name. For all you know, he changed it legally because of the problems he had as a child.'

'No, Krantz, we've got more than that.'

Dolan said, 'You find a connection yet between the six vics, Harvey?'

Krantz stared at her, suspicious. You could tell he wanted to say they weren't connected, but he knew she wouldn't have asked if she weren't about to drop a bomb. Instead, he glanced at me. 'What's your connection in all of this?'

'If Sobek did the six vics, then he probably killed Dersh, too.'

Krantz scowled at Bishop. 'We're being scammed. This is just some bullshit Cole cooked up to save Pike.'

Bishop was looking dubious, but Stan Watts grew thoughtful. 'How are they connected?'

Dolan said, 'Leonard DeVille was the pedophile in the motel when Abel Wozniak was killed. Wozniak and Pike had gone in there on a tip, possibly from Sobek, looking for a little girl named Ramona Escobar.'

Watts nodded. 'I remember that.'

'Cole worked backward from Dersh, asking who'd have a motive and why would they put it on Pike.'

Krantz said, 'This is bullshit. Pike killed that man.'

Bishop raised his hand, thinking about it.

Watts looked at me. 'How'd you make the jump to DeVille?'

'I wasn't thinking the connection was through DeVille. I was thinking it had to be through Wozniak, but it turned out to be the other.'

Dolan went on. 'We tried to pull DeVille's case file out of stores, but it's missing. Sobek could've slipped in there and lifted it. I ordered this copy up from the DA's section. This is the witness list from that case file. All six vics are on this list.'

Bishop stared at the witness list without expression for almost thirty seconds. No one else in the room moved, and then Bishop quietly said, 'Fucking-A. Goddamned fucking-A. All six victims are right there.'

As Krantz read it, Watts and Williams looked over his shoulder, Williams making a whistling sound.

Bishop said, 'Okay, this is looking good. This is major, but what have you got that locks Sobek to the killings?'

'So far just what you see here. The relationships. You'll need to bring Sobek in and sweat him. You've got more than enough for warrants to search his home and automobile.'

Williams was still with the list, shaking his head. 'This fuckin' guy I see every day. We were just talkin' about the new Bruce Willis movie.'

Krantz jutted his jaw. He hated giving anything to Dolan or me, but he could read Bishop, and he knew Bishop wanted it. 'It's good, Captain. Let's find Sobek or Wood or whatever his name is and get him in here. I can get a phone order for the search, and get that done while we're talking to him.'

Bishop picked up his phone. No one said anything while he spoke, but Stan Watts caught Dolan's eye and winked. She smiled when he did. After a couple of minutes, Bishop wrote something, then put down the phone. 'Wood didn't come in today. He didn't come in yesterday or the day before, either.'

Krantz peered at Dolan. 'I hope you didn't do anything to make him bolt.'

'We didn't go near him, Harvey, and no one could've tipped him. We didn't see his mother until twenty minutes ago, and she doesn't know how to contact him.'

Bishop said, 'Now, Harve, let's not make accusations. I think Sam's done a good job here.'

Krantz smiled, smooth and friendly, and squarely in Bishop's butt.

'I wasn't accusing you, Samantha. This is good work. This really is.' He turned to Bishop. 'But we've got to take this a step at a time now. If this stands up, and I believe it will, Samantha, then this man is a civilian employee of the Los Angeles Police Department. He was murdering people while he worked here, and he was using our information sources to do it. If we're not careful, we could have another public relations nightmare on our hands. We need to match his prints. We've got to field some physical evidence, maybe correlate the daytime homicides with the days this guy had off or missed work, that kind of thing. Then hope for something physical when we raid his home.'

He looked at Dolan, then the others, like he was trying to drive home a point. In command and on top of things.

'If he's not here, we have to find him, and that might take time. I want to move fast, but I don't want to lose this guy because we didn't get all the signatures we should've, and I don't want him tipped because word leaked out.' Krantz looked at Dolan when he said that, and she turned red.

Bishop laced his fingers, nodding. 'Okay. How do you want to play it, Harvey?'

'Let's keep it small until we know what we're dealing with. Just us, and maybe two radio cars, but let's not make a big show with SWAT. If something goes wrong, the press will be all over us. Until he's in custody, I don't want him to know we're on him. If we miss the guy, the press will have it all over the air and he could slip through our fingers.'

'Okay, Harvey, that sounds good. Set it up the way you want, and roll on it.'

Krantz clapped Stan Watts on the shoulder, then turned for the door. He looked like Errol Flynn heading off with the Dawn Patrol.

Dolan said, 'I want a piece.'

Everyone stopped, and looked at her.

'Captain, I earned a place here. I want this. I want to be there when we get this fucker.'

Krantz's jaw tightened, and he made the little jut. He wanted to tell her no so badly that he had cramps, but he was watching Bishop.

Bishop tapped his desk for a moment, then leaned back and nodded. 'It's Harvey's Task Force, Samantha. I never force a commander to take someone he doesn't want.'

Krantz nodded, and jutted his jaw again.

'But I think you deserve a second chance. How about you, Harve? Think you could find room for Dolan?'

It was clear what Bishop wanted, and Krantz hated it. His jaw rippled with tension, but he nodded gamely. 'We'll meet you in the parking lot, Dolan. You're welcome to come along.'

Everyone filed out as the meeting broke, Stan Watts and even Williams slapping Dolan on the back or shaking her hand. She accepted their congratulations with a wide, bright smile, sparkling eyes, and a flush of excitement that was breathtaking. Samantha Dolan was beautiful.

I would never again see her as happy.

35

When we got down to her car, Dolan opened the trunk, and tossed me a bullet-resistant vest. 'Here. Gonna be small, but you can adjust the straps.'

I held it up to myself, then put it back in her trunk. 'Not my color.'

'Your call.'

Dolan stripped off her shirt right there in the parking lot until she was down to her bra, then put on her own vest. All the people out on Los Angeles Street could see her, and so could the cops coming out of Parker Center, but she didn't seem to mind.

Dolan caught me watching and grinned nastily. 'See anything you like, go for it.'

I waited in the car.

When Dolan was dressed, she got behind the wheel. 'I've been thinking about all this, hotshot, and I'm putting you on notice. I'm not giving up on you.'

I looked at her.

'I'm not calling it quits just because you've got your Southern Belle. I want you, and I always get what I want. Maybe I'll put Scarlett O'Hara on notice, too. I intend to take you away from her.'

I shook my head and stared out the window.

'Be the best you've ever had.'

'Dolan, let's just not go there, okay?'

Her voice and her eyes softened. 'I know you love her. I just gotta make you love me more.'

She looked away then, and I looked away, too.

We sat quietly after that with the air conditioner running until Krantz and Watts rolled out of the covered parking in their D-ride, Williams and Bruly behind them. Dolan keyed a small black radio. 'I'm on.'

Watts came back, 'Okay.'

Williams said, 'Up.'

We pulled into line behind them, and eased out of the lot.

I said, 'Hey, Dolan.'

'Mm?'

I stared at her until she glanced over.

'I like you a lot. I mean a lot, you know?'

She made a gentle smile that crinkled her eyes, but she didn't answer.

The plan was simple: We would proceed directly to Sobek's address, reconnoiter the area, then withdraw to decide what to do while waiting for two Rampart Division radio cars to come in as backup units.

Two blocks from Sobek's address, Krantz slowed as we passed an AM-PM Minimart, and called us over the radio. 'We'll meet back at this minimart after we make the pass.'

Everybody rogered that.

'Dolan. You go in from this side, and we'll follow in a couple of minutes. Williams, swing up and come down from the north. We don't want to look like a parade.'

Dolan double-clicked her radio to roger, then glanced at me. 'First smart thing that airhead has said.'

'Watts probably suggested it.'

Dolan laughed.

Williams swung up a side street as Dolan and I continued on by ourselves.

Laurence Sobek, also known as Curtis Wood, lived in a converted garage apartment in a depressed residential area less than one mile from Parker Center. An undersized house like a little square box cut into a duplex sat near the street, with a driveway running along its side to a smaller box at the back of the property, which was Sobek's conversion. A stocky Hispanic woman and three small children were in the front yard of the house next door, playing with a garden hose. The neighborhood wasn't unlike where his mother lived: Rows of small stucco boxes and older apartment buildings, mostly inhabited by immigrants from Mexico or Central America. Sobek's box was run-down and sad.

I said, 'I make two doors, one facing the main duplex and another on the side. Looks like something's on the windows.'

'You see anyone in the main house?'

'Couldn't tell, but it looks quiet.'

'I didn't see a car.'

'Me neither. But it could be one of these on the street.'

We passed Williams and Bruly coming in opposite us, then took two right turns and went back to the AM-PM. The two Rampart radio cars were waiting when we got there. We pulled in beside them and left the engine and air conditioner running. Williams pulled in thirty seconds after us, and Krantz followed almost a minute after. We joined him at his car.

Krantz said, 'We got the telephonic warrant, so we're good to go with entering the property. Stan, how do you want to play it?'

Dolan nudged me. There was Krantz, giving it over to Watts again.

Watts said, 'Secure the duplex first. I want to get that woman and her children out of there. Put one of the radio cars on the house directly behind Sobek's conversion in case he makes a run out the back. The rest of us cover the doors and windows. If he doesn't answer the door, I don't want to break it down, 'cause then he'll know we were here. Maybe see if we can slip the lock, and if not maybe we can crack one of the windows.'

I said, 'How do you want to approach the house?'

Krantz frowned at me. 'Let us worry about that.'

Watts answered anyway. 'I'd say two groups, one down the drive and the other from the side yard to the north. Again, we want to keep a low profile. If he's not home, it's best if he doesn't know we were here.'

Krantz gave the radio units their assignments, describing Sobek and giving them copies of the file shots the employment office had taken. He told them that if this guy came hauling ass through the yard they should consider him dangerous and act accordingly.

When the uniforms had gone back to their cars, Krantz turned back to the rest of us. 'Everybody got their vest?'

Dolan said, 'Cole doesn't.'

Krantz shrugged. 'Won't matter. He's going to wait here. So are you.'

'Excuse me?'

'This is as far as you go, Dolan. I was fine with letting you tag along, but this is it. This is a Task Force operation, and you're not part of the Task Force.'

Dolan charged up to Krantz so fast that he jumped back, and Williams lurched between them.

'Take it easy, Dolan!'

Dolan shouted, 'You can't do this, goddamnit! Cole and I *found* this guy!'

'I can do anything I want. It's my operation.'

I said, 'This is really chickenshit, Krantz. If you felt this way, you should've made the play in front of Bishop.'

Krantz jutted the jaw. 'I've inspected the scene and determined it's best for the operation if only Task Force members participate. We're going to look too much like an army back there as it is. If you and Dolan were there, we'd be crawling all over each other and the odds of someone getting hurt would increase.'

I smiled at Watts, but Watts was staring at the ground. 'Sure. It's a safety issue.'

Dolan's face grew as tight and hard as a ceramic mask, but her voice softened. 'Don't cut me out of this, Harvey. Bishop said I could go.'

'You did. You're here. But this is far enough. When the location is secure, you and your boyfriend can come in.'

He jutted his jaw at me, and I wondered how it'd feel to kick it. The 'boyfriend' would like kicking it just fine.

I said, 'Why are you doing this, Krantz? Are you scared she's going to get the credit for doing your job?'

Watts said, 'You're not helping.'

I spread my hands and stepped back. 'You want me out of it, fine, I'm out of it. But Dolan earned a piece of this.'

Krantz considered me, then shook his head. 'That's big of you, Cole, volunteering like that, but I don't give a shit what you want or not. I still think your partner killed Dersh, and I still think you had something to do with breaking him out. Bishop might be willing to overlook that, but I'm not.' He glanced back to Dolan. 'Here's the way it is: I run this Task Force. If you want any chance, and I mean *any*, of getting back on Robbery-Homicide, you'll sit your fanny back in that car and do exactly as I say. Are we clear on that?'

Dolan's face went white. 'You want me to be a good little girl, Harvey?'

Krantz drew himself up and tugged at his vest. It made him look bulky and misshapen, like a deformed scarecrow. 'That's exactly what I want. If you're a good girl, I'll even make sure you get some of the credit.'

Dolan stared at him.

Krantz told the rest of them they'd be going in one car – his – and then the four of them got into it and drove away.

I said, 'Jesus, Dolan, what a prick. I'm sorry.'

She looked at me as if I was confused, and then she smiled.

'You can sit here if you want, World's Greatest, but I'm going in through the back.'

I didn't think it was a smart idea, but that didn't do any good. She climbed into the Beemer without waiting for me, and it was either stand there like Krantz's toad or go with her.

Krantz had gone up the front street, so we drove up the back, straight to where the second radio car was waiting. The two uniforms were standing against the fender, smoking while they waited for Krantz's call.

Dolan said, 'You guys hear from Krantz yet?'

They hadn't.

'Okay. We're gonna move in. Wait for the call.'

I said, 'Dolan, this isn't smart. If we surprise one of these guys, they could blow our heads off.' I was thinking about Williams, looking so hinky he'd pop a cap if someone behind him sneezed.

'I told you to wear a vest.'

Great.

The property behind Sobek's was a single-family bungalow about the size of an ice chest. Nobody was home, except for a yellow dog in a narrow wire pen. I was worried the dog would bark, but all it did was wag its tail and watch us with hopeful eyes. Dolan and I moved up the drive, and into a backyard that was separated from Sobek's by a chain-link fence overgrown by morning glories that were brown and brittle from the heat. His converted garage was close to the fence and easy to see.

Dolan made a hissing sound to get my attention, then motioned for us to go over the fence.

When we were on Sobek's side, we separated and circled the building. I listened close at the windows, and tried to see inside, but couldn't because they'd been covered by what looked like plastic garbage bags. The bags meant he was hiding something, and I didn't like that.

Dolan and I met near Sobek's front door, then moved to the side.

I whispered, 'I couldn't see anything in there. Did you?'

'Every damned window is like this. I couldn't see anything and didn't hear anything. If he ain't our guy, he's a goddamned vampire. Let's try the door.'

Stan Watts and Harvey Krantz came down the drive, and froze when they saw us. Krantz made an angry wave for us to come over to him, but Dolan gave him the finger.

'You're cutting your own throat with that guy, Dolan.'

'He's fucked me long enough. You got your gun?'

'Yeah.'

'Let's try the door.'

Dolan went to the front door and knocked, just the way you'd knock if you wanted to ask your neighbor for a small favor. I stood three feet to her left, gun out, and ready to get on Sobek if he answered.

Stan Watts drew his gun and hurried over beside me. Krantz stayed out by the duplex. I could hear Williams and Bruly in the next yard.

Watts said, 'Goddamnit, Samantha.' But it was only loud enough for me.

Dolan knocked a second time, harder, and said, 'Gas company. We got a problem we've traced to your house.'

No answer.

She said it louder. *'We've got a gas company problem out here.'*

Still no one answered. Watts stood, and Krantz hurried over from the duplex. His face was red, and he looked like he wanted to bite someone in the neck.

'Goddamnit, Dolan, I'm going to have your ass for this.' He was whispering, but it was harsh and loud, and if anyone was inside they would've heard. 'This is *my* collar.'

I said, 'He's not here, Dolan. Pull back and let's figure out what to do.'

Krantz put away his gun and jabbed me with his finger. 'I'm going to have your ass for this, too. You, and her. Stan, you're a witness.'

The three of us were still off to the side when Dolan touched the knob. 'Hey, I think it's open.'

I said, 'Dolan. Don't.'

Samantha Dolan eased open the door just far enough to peek inside, but she probably couldn't see anything.

Dolan relaxed.

'We're clear, Krantz. Looks like I've done your job again.'

Then she pushed the door open and something kicked her backward with a sound like a thunderclap.

Stan Watts yelled, 'Gun!' and hit the ground, but I didn't hear him.

I pushed low through the door, firing at a smoking double-barrel shotgun even before I knew what it was. I think I was screaming.

I fired all six rounds before the hammer clicked on nothing, and then I was running back into the yard, where Watts was trying to stop the bleeding, but it was already too late.

The point-blank double load from the shotgun had blown through her vest like it wasn't there.

Samantha Dolan's beautiful hazel eyes stared sightlessly toward heaven. She was dead.

36

As Detective Samantha Dolan's blood seeps into Los Angeles' dry earth, Laurence Sobek parks his red Cherokee in the next victim's drive. He no longer carries the little .22 with his homemade Clorox suppressors; he carries a full-blown .357 magnum loaded with light, fast hollow points. When he shoots his victims now, they will blow apart like overripe avocados, with no chance for survival.

Sobek has the gun in his waist, his hand tight on its grip as he goes to the door. He knocks, but no one answers, and, after knocking again, walks around to the back, where he tries the sliding glass doors. He considers forcing the doors, but sees a Westec alarm light blinking from its control panel.

Sobek is ready to kill. He is ready to do murder, and wants to with such a ferocity that his palm is slick on the pistol's wood grip.

He goes back to the Jeep, and drives up the hill until he finds a parking place with an unobstructed view of the house.

He waits for the child.

Krantz said, 'Oh, holy Jesus. Oh, Christ.'

He dry-heaved, and turned to lean against an avocado tree. Williams and Bruly came around the corner, guns out and eyes wild, the four uniforms following with their shotguns. Someone shouted from one of the surrounding houses. The yellow dog howled.

Bruly yelled, '*Is she dead? Jesus, is she dead?*'

Watts's hands were red with Samantha Dolan's blood. 'Krantz, clear the house. Williams, clear the house, goddamnit.'

No one was paying any attention to the house. If Sobek had been in there, he could've shot the rest of us.

I said, 'It's clear.'

Watts was still shouting. 'Williams, secure the evidence. Wake up, goddamnit, and be careful in there. Do *not* contaminate the evidence.'

Williams crept to the door, gun out and ready. Watts went over to a garden spigot, washed his hands, then took out his radio and made a call.

I draped my jacket over Dolan's face, not knowing what else to do. My eyes filled with tears, but I shook my head and turned away. Williams had stopped outside the door and was staring at her. He was crying, too.

I felt her wrist, but it was silent. I rested the flat of my hand on her belly. She was warm. I blinked hard at the tears, then put Samantha Dolan and everything I was feeling out of my head to concentrate on Joe.

I went to Sobek's garage.

Krantz saw me from the tree and said, 'Stay out of there. It's a crime scene. Williams, stop him, goddamnit.'

'Fuck you, Krantz. He could be out there killing someone else right now.'

Williams went back to staring at Dolan. 'She's really dead.'

'She's dead.'

He cried harder.

Watts called, 'Cole, be careful. He could have the whole fucking thing booby-trapped.'

I went inside without stopping, and Krantz came in behind me. Bruly came to the door, but stopped there.

The air was layered with drifting gun smoke. It was intensely hot and dark, with the only light coming through the open door. I turned on the lights with my knuckle.

Sobek didn't have furniture; he had weights. A weight lifter's bench sat squat and ugly in the center of the room, black weight disks stacked on the floor around it like iron toadstools. No one walked in front of the shotgun even though smoke still drifted from both barrels. Residual fear. Articles from the *Times* about the killings and Dersh and Pike were pinned to the wall, along with a Marine Corps recruiting poster and another poster depicting LAPD SWAT snipers.

Bruly said, 'Jesus, look at this shit. You think he's coming back?'

I didn't look at him; I was looking for trip wires and pressure plates, and trying to smell gasoline, because I was scared that Sobek had rigged the garage to explode. 'You don't rig a booby trap the way he's rigged this place and expect to come back. He's abandoned it.'

Krantz said, 'We don't know that, Cole. If we can get Dolan cleaned up fast enough, we can secure the area and wait for him.'

Even Bruly shook his head.

I said, 'You're really something, Krantz.'

Bruly took a small book from a cardboard box, then a couple more. 'He's got the Marine Corps Sniper Manual in here. Check it out: The Force Recon Training Syllabus, Hand-to-Hand Combat. Man, this turd is the ultimate wannabe.'

Krantz opened the fridge and took out a glass vial. 'It's filled with drugs. Steroid products. The guy's a juicer.'

It wasn't much of an apartment, just one large room divided by a counter from a kitchenette, with a bath and closet. All I cared about and wanted was to find a slip with Dersh's address, or the clothes that Sobek used to dress as Pike – anything at all that would tie Sobek to Dersh and clear Joe.

'Over here, Lieutenant.'

Bruly found seven empty Clorox bottles in the closet, along with three .22 pistols and some ammunition. Two of the Clorox bottles had been reinforced with duct tape.

Krantz slammed Bruly on the back. 'We got the sonofabitch!'

I said, 'Dolan got him. You just came along for the ride.'

Krantz started to say something, then thought better of it, and went to the door. He spoke to Stan Watts. Outside, a siren approached.

Leonard DeVille's original case file was spread across the kitchen counter, along with yellowed clippings about Wozniak's death, the lead detective's witness complainant list, and notes and addresses on all six victims. Karen Garcia's address was there. Her habit of running at Lake Hollywood, and notes on her route were there, as were similar notes on Semple, Lorenzo, and the others. It was creepy; like getting a glimpse inside a cold and evil mind that was planning murder. He had watched some of these people and charted their lives for months.

Krantz said, 'I've got to hand it to you, Cole. You and Dolan made a right call. That was good work.'

'See if there's anything about Dersh.'

Krantz's jaw jutted, but he didn't say anything. Maybe, just then, he thought it was possible.

We were still shuffling through Sobek's planning notes when we came to my listing in the yellow pages, and a DMV printout showing my home address and phone numbers. Dolan's home address was listed, also.

Bruly whistled. 'He has you, dude. I don't know how, but he knew you and Dolan were on him.'

Krantz fingered through the papers. 'He was all over Parker Center every day. He could've heard anything. He could've asked damn near anyone anything, and no one would've thought anything of it.'

The way Krantz said it made me think that he and Sobek had had more than one conversation.

Bruly spread more loose pages, exposing a snapshot that was so wrong to this place and moment that I almost didn't recognize it. A snapshot of three boys talking to a teenaged girl holding a tennis racket. The girl's back was to the camera, but I could see the boys. The boy on the right was Ben Chenier. Two other snapshots of Ben were mixed with the papers, all three taken from a distance at his tennis camp in Verdugo. Lucy's apartment address was scratched on a corner of the DMV printout.

Krantz saw the pictures, or maybe he saw the expression on my face. 'Who's this boy?'

'My girlfriend's son. He's away at this tennis camp. Krantz, this address is my girlfriend's apartment, this one's my home. That's the television station where Lucy works.'

Krantz cut me off to yell outside for Watts. Somewhere out on the street, the siren died, but more were coming.

'Stan, we've got a problem here. It looks like Sobek was going to shut down Cole. He might be on the girlfriend, or the girlfriend's son, or on Cole's home.'

Something sharp and sour blossomed in the center of me, and spread through my arms and legs and across my skin. I felt myself shaking.

Watts looked through the papers and photographs as Krantz spoke, and turned away with his cell phone before Krantz finished. Watts read out the addresses into the phone, requesting patrol officers be dispatched code three. Code three meant fast. Sirens and lights. Watts cupped the phone to glance back at me. 'We got the camp's name?'

I told him. I was shaking when I borrowed Bruly's phone to call Lucy.

When Lucy came on, she was hesitant and contained, but I cut through that, telling her where I was, and that officers were on their way to her, and why.

Krantz said, 'Cole, do you need me to speak with her?'

When I told her that Laurence Sobek had snapped Ben's picture, her voice came back higher and strained.

'This man was watching Ben?'

'Yes. He took photographs. The police are on their way to the camp now. They've dispatched the Highway Patrol.'

Krantz said, 'Tell her we have officers on the way to her, too, Cole. She'll be safe.'

Lucy said, 'I'm going to Ben. I'm going to get him right now.'

'I know. I'll come get you.'

'There's no way I could wait. I'm leaving now.'

'Luce, I'll meet you there.'

'He's got to be safe, Elvis.'

'We'll keep him safe. Stan Watts is talking to the camp, now.'

When I said it, Watts looked over and gave me a thumbs-up.

I said, 'Ben's okay, Luce. The camp people have him. He's with them right now, and we're on the way.'

She hung up without another word.

I tossed the phone back to Bruly on my way out the door, trying to ignore the tinge of accusation I'd heard in her voice.

The Verdugo Tennis Camp was a good hour east of L.A. in the rural foothills of the Verdugo Mountains. Krantz used a bubble flasher, and knocked a hundred most of the way. He left Watts to coordinate the surveillance of my home and Lucy's apartment, and spent much of the drive on his cell phone talking to Bishop. Sobek's landlady provided a license number, and both the LAPD Traffic Division and the Highway Patrol were alerted. The make and model of Sobek's Jeep were identical to those of Pike's.

Williams sat ahead of me in the front seat, crying and muttering. 'A fuckin' shotgun. He about cut her in half with that goddamned thing. Motherfucker. I'm gonna cap that sonofabitch. I swear to Christ I'm gonna cap his ass.'

I said, 'We're taking this guy alive, Williams.'

'No one asked you, goddamnit.'

'Krantz, we're taking this guy alive. If he's alive, he'll cop to Dersh.'

Krantz patted Williams's leg. 'Worry about yourself, Cole. My people can handle themselves, and we're bringing this asshole to trial. Right, Jerome?'

Jerome Williams stared out the window, jaw flexing.

'We're bringing this man to trial, right, Jerome?'

Williams twisted around so he could see me. 'I ain't forgot what you said. When this is over, I'm gonna show you just how goddamned black I am.'

The sheriffs were already there when we arrived, four radio cars parked on the camp's dirt-and-gravel lot. The camp administrators were talking nervously with the sheriffs, as, behind them, horses snuffled in their stables. Ben had been right: It smelled of horse poop.

Krantz hoped to spot Sobek and capture him, so he had the sheriffs park their vehicles inside the camp's barn, then spoke with the senior sheriff about setting up surveillance positions. We did all this in the camp's dining hall, a screen-walled building with unfinished wood floors. The kids were being held together in the boy's dormitory.

Other parents arrived before Lucy, collecting their children and leaving as quickly as possible. Krantz was pissed that the camp administrator, a woman named Mrs Willoman, had called the families, but there wasn't anything he could do about it. If the cops tell you that a multiple-homicide killer might be dropping around, there aren't many responsible alternatives.

Lucy arrived ten minutes later, her face strained when I went out to meet her. She took my hand, but didn't answer when I spoke to her, and didn't look at me. When I told her that we were in the dining hall, she walked so quickly that we broke into a trot.

Inside, she went directly to Mrs Willoman, and said, 'I want my baby.'

A teenage camp counselor brought Ben from the bunk room. Ben looked excited, like this was a hell of a lot better than riding horses or even playing tennis.

Ben said, 'This is cool. What's going on?'

Lucy hugged him so tightly that he squirmed, but then her face flashed with anger. 'It isn't cool. Things like this aren't *cool*, and aren't *normal*.'

I knew she was saying it for me.

Krantz asked Lucy to stay until we received word that her apartment had been secured. After, we would follow them home to make sure they arrived safely. Krantz offered to provide twenty-four-hour protection, and Lucy accepted. She stared at Ben, rubbing his back, and said that maybe they should go back to Louisiana until this was over. When I told her I thought that might be a good idea, she went over to the screen wall and looked out.

I guess she just wanted to be someplace where she could feel safe.

We sat around a big table, sipping something red that the counselor called bug juice, Krantz and I explaining Sobek to Lucy and Ben. Lucy kept one hand on Ben, and held my hand with the other, but still did not look at me. She spoke only to Krantz, though she occasionally squeezed my hand as if sending a message she was not yet capable of saying aloud.

Finally, Krantz was paged, and checked the number. 'That's Stan.'

He called Watts, listened for a few seconds, then nodded at Lucy. 'We've secured your home. Manager let us in, and officers are on the site.'

The tension drained out of her like air from a balloon. 'Oh, thank God.'

'Let me just wrap up here, and we'll get you home. If you decide you want to leave town, let me know and we'll bring you to the airport. I'll call the Baton Rouge PD, if you'd like, and bring them up to speed.'

Lucy smiled at him like Krantz was human. 'Thank you, Lieutenant. If I decide to go home, I'll call you.'

Home.

She took my hand again, and smiled at me for the first time in a while. 'It's going to be all right.'

I smiled back, and everything seemed much better in the world.

While the counselors were getting Ben's things, I took my bug juice to the door and stared out at the tree line, searching it the way I had when I was eighteen, and in the Army. I thought about Sobek, and what we had found in his garage. His goal was to kill the people he blamed for putting DeVille in prison, and he had started with the people most removed from the prosecution, probably because it would be hardest for LAPD to connect them together. I wondered if that was the only reason. I wondered if maybe he also didn't blame them the least, which meant he was saving the people he blamed the most. Pike, for sure, but there was also Krakauer and Wozniak, though they were both dead. The more I thought about it, the more it bothered me, because he had had a personal relationship with Wozniak, and there was every possibility that it was Sobek who had been the one who had tipped Wozniak to DeVille's location that day. I stared at the stables and thought about the horses within; I couldn't see them, but I heard them and smelled them. They snorted and whinnied and talked to each other, I guess, and were real even though they were beyond my sight. Life is often like that, with realities layered over other realities, mostly hidden but always there. You can't always see them, but if you listen to their clues, you'll recognize them all the same.

Krantz was having two of the sheriffs load Ben's things when I said, 'He's not coming here, Krantz.'

Krantz nodded. 'Maybe not.'

'You don't get it. He's not coming here, or my place, or Lucy's. It's a diversion.'

Now Krantz frowned, and Lucy looked over, both hands draped on Ben's shoulders.

'Think about it, Krantz. He wants to kill the people he blames for DeVille, and he's doing that, but then he realized we're onto him. His game's over, and he knows it, right?'

Krantz was still frowning.

'He knows that it's only a matter of days before we link the vics, and when we do we'll have a suspect pool, and he's in the pool.'

Krantz said, 'Yeah, that's why he decides to take you out of the play.'

'But to what end? He can't go on working at Parker, killing another couple of dozen people. If he believes we're on to him, he's going to cut to the chase. If he's thinking that his play is over, then he's going to want to kill the people he blames the most. He can't get to Pike, Krakauer's dead, so that leaves Wozniak.'

'Wozniak's dead, too.'

'Krakauer was a bachelor. Wozniak had a wife and a child, and they're in Palm Springs. That's where I got Wozniak's daybook. That's where we should be.'

Lucy's hands tightened around Ben, as if her newfound security was falling away. 'But why would he take Ben's picture? Why would he have our address?'

'Maybe he put those things together to distract us. We're here with you now; we're not with Wozniak's widow, and that's where he's going.'

'But you're just guessing. Did you see her address there? Were there pictures of her and her daughter?'

'No.'

'We *know* he had our address. We *know* he's a killer.' She gripped my arm then, as hard as Frank Garcia had gripped me when he had begged me to find his child. 'I need you right now.'

I looked at Krantz. 'Krantz, he's going to Palm Springs.'

Krantz didn't like it, but he was seeing it. 'You got her name and address?'

'Her name is Paulette Renfro. I don't remember the address, but I can tell you how to get there.'

Krantz was already dialing his phone. 'The States can get the address. They can get a car there before us.'

Krantz frowned as he made the call, and I knew what he was seeing in his head, a couple of sheriff's deps snapping the cuffs on Sobek, the two deputies getting the headlines and being interviewed by Katie Couric.

I looked back at Lucy, and gave her my best reassuring smile, but she wasn't at home to receive it.

'That's where he's going, Luce. I can't go back with you now, but just stay here until I get back. I'll take you home when I get back.'

Lucy's eyes were distant and cold, and hurt.

'I don't need you to take me home.'

Krantz went for the door even as he worked the phone, calling to Williams. 'Jerry, let's mount up. We're going over there.'

When we left the cafeteria, I glanced back at Lucy, but she wasn't looking at me. I didn't need to see her to know what was in her eyes:

I had chosen someone else once again.

37

Sobek has not moved for the better part of an hour. The desert sun has driven the temperature inside his Jeep to almost 130 degrees, and his sweatshirt is soaked, but he imagines himself a predatory lizard, motionless in the brutal heat as he waits for prey. He is armored by muscle and resolve, and his mission commitment is without peer. He will wait for the rest of the day, if necessary, and the night, and for all the days to come.

It does not take that long.

A car eases up the residential streets below and pulls into the vic's drive. Sobek fingers the .357 when the car turns in, thinking it's her, but it isn't. A man gets out and stands looking at the house in the brilliant desert light, the man wearing jeans, an outrageous beachcomber shirt with the tail out, and sunglasses.

Sobek leans forward until his chest touches the steering wheel.

It is Joe Pike.

Pike goes to the front door, rings the bell, then goes around to the back of the house. Sobek can't see him back there, and thinks Pike must be sitting on the little veranda, or that he's found a way inside.

Sobek waits, but Pike does not return.

His heart pounds as he clutches the .357 with both hands. The gun is nestled between his legs where he can feel the weight of it on his penis. It feels good there.

He allows himself to smile, the first expression of emotion he's had in days. Pike has come to him.

Control.

Sobek settles back and waits for Paulette Wozniak and her daughter to return.

Paulette picked up her daughter Evelyn earlier that morning from Banning, where Evelyn had dropped her car for service. Evelyn's Volkswagen Beetle had gone kaput, and now Evelyn was without a car. First the boyfriend, then the apartment, now the car. Paulette had taken Evelyn to her job at Starbucks, then picked her up again, and was bringing her home to wait until her car was ready at the end of the day. Evelyn, of course, wasn't happy about it. Paulette never expected to find a strange car in her drive.

Evelyn was sulky and angry, and glowering in the passenger seat like she was fit to choke a dog. The only thing she'd said that morning was to ask if Paulette had heard from Mr Cole again. Paulette hadn't, and thought it odd that Evelyn would ask.

Paulette Renfro turned onto her street thinking the old cliché was true: When it rains, it pours. What could be next?

Evelyn glared at the strange car. 'Who's that?'

'I don't know.'

A neat, clean sedan was parked to the side of her drive, leaving her plenty of room to get into her garage. She did not recognize it, and wondered if one of her friends had gotten a new car without telling her. It was so hot out that they were probably in back, waiting under the veranda, though she couldn't imagine why anyone would be waiting for her unannounced.

Paulette pressed the garage opener, eased her car inside, then let Evelyn and herself into the house through the laundry room.

She went directly to the back glass doors in the family room, and that's where she saw him, standing tanned and lean and tall in the shade on the veranda. He was waiting for her to see him. He wore a flowered shirt that looked a size too big and dark glasses, and her first thought, the very first thought that came to her after all these years was, '*He hasn't aged a day and I must look like hell.*'

Evelyn said, 'There's a man outside.'

Joe raised a hand in greeting, and Paulette felt herself smile.

Evelyn said, 'You know that guy?'

Paulette opened the door, then stepped back to let him inside.

'Hello, Joe.'

'It's good to see you, Paulette.'

She had thought of this moment – of seeing him again – in her dreams and over morning coffee and during long quiet drives across the desert. She'd imagined what she would say and how she would say it in every possible way, but all she managed to get out was so lame.

'Would you like some water? It's so hot out.'

'That would be fine. Thank you.'

Evelyn got that ugly sulk on her face, the one that said she was unhappy and everyone was supposed to know it. You had to know it and do something about it, else she'd get even sulkier.

Evelyn said, 'You called him Joe.'

Paulette knew what was coming. 'Joe, this is Evelyn. Evie, you remember Joe Pike.'

Evelyn crossed her arms, then uncrossed them. Her face grew blotched. She said, 'Oh, fuck.'

Joe said, 'Paulette, I need to talk to you. About Woz, and about something that's going to happen.'

Before Paulette could say anything, Evelyn leaned toward Joe and shrieked, 'What could you *possibly* have to say? You killed him! Mother, he's wanted! He just murdered someone else!'

Paulette took her daughter by the arms, wanting to be gentle, but wanting to be firm, too.

'Evie. Go in the back. I'll talk to you later, but I want to talk with Joe now.'

Evelyn pulled away, livid and furious from a lifetime of mourning her father. 'Talk to him all you want! I'm gonna call the police!'

Paulette shook her daughter with a fierceness she hadn't felt in years. 'No! You won't!'

'He killed Daddy!'

'You *won't!*'

Joe spoke quietly. 'It's okay, Paulette. Let her call.'

Evelyn looked as surprised as Paulette felt, the two of them staring at Joe for a moment before Evie ran back toward the bedrooms.

Paulette said, 'Are you sure? I saw on the news.'

'I'll be gone before they get here. You look good, Paulette.'

He spoke with the absolute calm at which she had always marveled, and secretly envied. As if he were so certain of himself, so secure and confident that there was no room left for doubt. Whatever came, he could handle it; whatever the problem, he would solve it.

She felt herself blush. 'I've gotten older.'

'You've grown more beautiful.'

She blushed deeper, suddenly thinking how odd this was, to be here with this man after all this time, and to blush like a teenager because of him.

'Joe, take off those glasses. I can't see you.'

He took off the glasses.

My God, those eyes were incredible, so brilliantly blue that she could just stare. Instead, she got him the water.

'Joe, I've seen the news. A friend of yours was here. What happened?'

'We can talk about it later.' He glanced after Evelyn and shrugged. 'The police are coming.'

She nodded.

'I didn't kill that man. Someone else did. The same person who killed another six people.'

'That's what your friend said.'

'His name is Laurence Sobek. He was one of Woz's informants. When the story is out, you're going to have the press and the police bring up everything that happened on that day. They're going to dig into Woz again. Do you understand?'

'I don't care.'

'It could hurt you.'

'It can't.'

Behind them, Evelyn spoke in a voice so soft that Paulette hadn't heard it since Evie was a child.

'Why could it hurt her, and why do you care?'

Paulette turned and looked at her daughter. Evelyn was peeking around the corner like a five-year-old, her face distant and smooth.

'Did you call the police?'

Evie shook her head.

Pike said, 'Go call. Your mother and I have to talk.'

Evelyn went to the bookcase and took down the picture of her father and Paulette and Joe Pike.

'She keeps this out where anybody can see it.' She looked at Paulette. 'Why do you keep this goddamned picture? Why keep a picture of someone who killed the man you loved?'

Paulette Wozniak considered her adult daughter for a time, then said, 'The man I love is still alive.'

Evie stared at her.

Paulette said, 'Joe didn't kill your father. Your father killed himself. He took his own life.' She turned back to Joe and looked at the placid blue eyes, the eyes that made her smile. 'I'm not stupid, Joe. I figured it out years ago when I went through his notebooks.'

Joe said, 'The missing pages.'

'Yes. He wrote about the Chihuahua brothers, and that whole mess. And then, later, just days before it happened, he wrote how he felt trapped. He didn't say he was planning on it. He didn't say what he was going to do or how, but he wrote that there was always a way out, and that a lot of cops had gone that way before.'

Evie was pulling at her fingers now, pulling and twisting like she was trying to rip them off.

'What are you talking about? What are you saying?'

Paulette felt a horrible pain in her chest. 'I didn't know for sure until I went through his books after he was dead, and then, I don't know, I just didn't want you to know the truth about him. You loved him so. I took out those pages and destroyed them so you could never find them, but I know in my heart what he was saying there. Joe didn't kill your father. Your father took his own life, and Joe took the blame to protect you, and me.'

Evie shook her head, and said, 'I don't believe you.'

'It's true, honey.'

Paulette tried to put her arm around Evelyn, but Evelyn pushed her away. Paulette looked at Joe then, as if maybe he would know what to do in the sure certain way of his, but that's when a large, muscular man wearing sunglasses stepped out of the kitchen behind Joe, aimed a black pistol, and pulled the trigger.

Paulette screamed, 'Joe!'

Her shout was drowned by a deafening sound that hit her like a physical blow and made her ears ring.

Joe hunched forward, then spun so quickly that he seemed not to move at all, was just suddenly facing the man, a big gun in his own hand, firing three huge times so fast that the shots were one BAMBAMBAM.

The big man slammed backward, hitting the kitchen floor with a wheezing grunt, and then there was silence.

The moment was absolutely still until Joe hunched again, and that's when Paulette saw the blood spreading on Joe's back like some great red rose.

She said, 'OhmyLord! Joe!'

Joe winced when he tried to straighten, then looked at Paulette, and smiled. She hadn't seen that smile in so many years that her heart filled and she wanted to cry, though the smile was small and hurt.

He said, 'Gotta go now, Paulette. You take care of your baby.'

Joe Pike held her gaze for another moment, then turned away as the large man sat straight up on the kitchen floor as if rising from the dead and shot Joe again.

Joe Pike fell hard.

The two women finally arrive, and Sobek eases down the hill to Paulette's house. He knows from watching that none of the neighbors are home, so he strolls up the drive and into Paulette Wozniak's garage without fear of being seen.

He creeps through the garage past Paulette Wozniak's ticking car, and puts his ear to the utility door, but doesn't hear anything. He knows that doors like this usually open to a laundry room or a kitchen, and decides to take the chance that Pike and the others aren't poised on the other side. He turns the knob, then cracks the door, and sees a washer and dryer.

He can hear voices now, and then a woman shouts, 'What could you *possibly* have to say? You killed him! Mother, he's wanted! He just murdered someone else!'

Sobek grips the .357, pulls back the hammer, then eases into the laundry. He peeks into the kitchen. No one. He creeps through the kitchen, careful not to make any noise, getting closer and closer to the voices until they are just around the corner in the family room. Two women and the Pikester.

Sobek takes a deep breath, then another, then steps around the corner and shoots Joe Pike in the back.

Ka-Boom!

The .357 kicks harder than the little .22s, and before he can shoot again Pike has a gun in his hands and fires BAMBAMBAM. Three bricks hit Sobek in the chest all at the same time, knocking him flat on his ass, and making him see stars.

He thinks he is dead, then realizes that the Kevlar vest he's wearing under the sweatshirt has saved him. Most cops wear lightweight vests designed to stop common rounds like the 9mm or .45, but Sobek wears the heavier model, rated at stopping anything up to and including the .44 Magnum.

Control.

He hears voices. They're talking. Pike is still alive, but wounded.

Second chance.

Sobek sits up and shoots Joe Pike again even as the younger woman screams.

Pike drops like a bag of wet laundry, and Sobek says, '*Cool!*'

The older woman falls to her knees beside Pike and grabs for his gun, but Sobek runs forward and kicks her in the ribs. He is dizzy from the hits that he's taken, but his kick is solid and upends her.

A red pool spreads through Pike's shirt.

Sobek looks at Paulette Wozniak, then the younger woman. 'Are you Abel Wozniak's daughter?'

Neither of them answer.

Sobek points the .357 at the older one, and the younger one says, 'Yes.'

'Okay. Let's get a couple of chairs, and you two sit down.'

Sobek feels disoriented and nauseated from the chest trauma, but he taposes their wrists and ankles to two wooden dining-room chairs and puts more tape over their mouths. Then he peels off his shirt and vest to inspect his wounds. The entire center of his chest is a throbbing purple bruise. The bullets probably broke some ribs. Christ, that Pike can shoot. All three bullets would've been in his heart.

Sobek spits on Pike's body, and screams, 'FUCK YOU!'

The screaming makes his head spin worse, and he has to sit or throw up. When the spinning subsides, he considers the women.

'You're next.'

He is thinking about how best to kill them when he hears a car door out front and sees two deputies strolling toward the house.

Sobek drags the two women into a back room to hide them even as the doorbell rings. He puts on his shirt, not even thinking of the three bullet holes, and hurries to the door as it rings again. He plasters on a big smile, opens the door with a surprised expression, and says, 'Oh, wow, the Highway Patrol. Are we under arrest?'

The two deps stare at him for a moment, and then the closer one smiles. Friendly and getting the joke. 'Is Mrs Renfro at home?'

'Oh, sure. She's my aunt. Did you want to see her?'

'Yes, if we could.'

'Come on in out of that heat and I'll bring you back. She's in the pool.'

The other dep smiles then and takes off his campaign hat. He says, 'Man, I could go for some of that.'

Sobek nods, and smiles wider. 'Hey, why not? I'll get you guys a beer or a soft drink, if you like.'

He holds the door and lets them step past him into the living room, then closes the door, takes out his .357, and shoots both deputies in the back, puts the gun to their heads, and shoots them again.

38

Verdugo to Palm Springs was less than an hour. Paulette didn't answer when I called, which none of us liked, but I left word on her machine that she should drive directly to the Palm Springs Police Department and wait for us there.

During the drive, Krantz spoke several times on the radio, once getting a report that sheriffs had arrived on scene at Paulette's, and that everything was fine.

We left the interstate at North Palm Springs and drove directly to Paulette's house in the hills above the windmills. A clean new sedan that I didn't recognize was parked in the drive. The garage door was down, and no other cars were parked on the block. The house, like the neighborhood, was still.

I said, 'I thought the sheriffs were supposed to be here.'

'They were.'

Krantz got on his radio and told someone to confirm with the sheriffs, then have them send another car.

We parked beside the sedan, and got out.

Williams said, 'Goddamn. It's hot as hell out here.'

We didn't make it to the front door. We were passing the big picture window when all three of us saw the body in the family room, and a cold sweat broke over my back and legs even in the awful desert heat.

'That's Joe.'

Williams said, 'She-it.'

Krantz fumbled out his gun. 'Jerome, radio back. Tell'm we need cars right goddamned now. I don't care who. Tell'm to send an ambulance.'

Williams ran back to the unit.

Two swerving blood trails led out of the living room through the family room and into the kitchen. I couldn't see any other bodies, but I thought it might be Paulette and Evelyn. Then I saw that the sliding back doors were open.

'I'm going in, Krantz.'

'Goddamnit, we gotta wait for backup. He might still be in there.'

'Those people might be bleeding to death. I'm going in.'

The front door was locked. I trotted around the side of the house, popping fast peeks through every window I came to, not seeing anything unusual until I found Paulette and Evelyn in the rear corner bedroom. They were taped to chairs with duct tape covering their wrists and ankles and mouths, and struggling to get free. I tapped on the glass, and their eyes went wide. Evelyn struggled harder, but Paulette stared at me. I made a calming gesture, then spread my hands, asking if Sobek was in the house.

Paulette nodded.

I mouthed, 'Where?'

Paulette shook her head. She didn't know.

I moved along the rear of the house to the glass doors, dropped into a push-up position, and peeked inside. Joe was slumped on his side, the back of his shirt damp with blood. I was trying to see if his chest was moving when I heard a voice. The two blood trails ran past Pike through the kitchen and into the laundry room; that's where the voice came from. I looked at Pike again, and this time the tears started and my nose clogged, but I made the tears stop.

Krantz came toward me from the opposite side of the house, stopping on the other side of the doors. He had his gun out, holding it with both hands. 'I've got units and paramedics on the way.'

'Paulette and her daughter are alive in the room at the end of the hall. I'm hearing something in the garage. You get them out of here, okay? Get them safe.'

'What are you going to do?'

'Someone's in the garage.'

Krantz swallowed, and I could see then that he heard the voice. 'Ah, maybe I should do that.'

I liked him then, for maybe the first time. 'I'm better, Harvey. I'll do it. Okay?'

He stared at me, and then he nodded.

'Just get them out of the house. Where's Williams?'

'Covering the front.'

'He got a radio?'

'Yeah.'

'Tell him we're going inside and not to shoot me, then get those women.'

I stepped through the doors. The smell of blood was thin, and raw, and the great black desert flies had already found their way into the house. Pike was out in the center of the floor, but I did not go to him. I stayed near the walls, trying to see as many doors as possible.

I whispered, 'Just us, buddy.'

The blood trails arced through the kitchen and into a laundry room, where they stopped at a closed door. The voice was behind the door. Maybe Sobek was sitting in the garage talking to the bodies. Lunatics do that.

Here's what you do: You open the door, or you walk away and wait for the Palm Springs PD. If you walk away, then whoever is in the garage bleeds to death and you have to live with that, and with knowing you didn't go in because you were scared. These are the choices.

I closed my eyes, and whispered, 'I don't want to get shot.'

Then I hammered back my pistol, took six fast breaths, and went in.

Sobek's red Cherokee was parked directly in front of me, the sheriff's car next to it, both engines ticking. The two deps were in the front seat of their car, the remains of their heads slumped together in death. The voice was coming from their radio. I looked under both cars, then glanced into their back seats. Sobek wasn't there.

I closed the utility door behind me, and went back into the kitchen. Krantz had freed Paulette and her daughter. They were behind him, just coming into the family room from the hall. I thought we were going to make it. I thought that we'd get them out of there, and safe, but that's when Jerome Williams shouted something from somewhere outside, and two fast shots cracked through the house.

Krantz shouted, 'Jerome!'

Laurence Sobek ran out of a doorway at the end of the hall and in that crazy moment might have been Joe Pike; large and powerful, and dressed as Pike used to dress, even down to the sunglasses. But not. This was a mutant Pike, an anti-Pike, distorted and swollen and ugly. He didn't look like Curtis Wood now; he looked more like the inbred villain in a slasher movie.

Paulette, Evelyn, and Krantz were in the line of fire between me and Sobek. I yelled, 'DOWN! GET DOWN!'

Krantz shoved Paulette out of the way, aimed past Evelyn, and fired twice, hitting Sobek in the big torso both times.

Sobek came off the wall firing blindly, his bullets hitting the floor and the ceiling. One of his rounds caught me under the right arm with a hard slap, knocked away my gun, and spun me into the refrigerator.

Paulette ran to her daughter, again blocking Krantz's line of fire.

I yelled, 'Head shot, Krantz! The head! He's wearing a vest!'

Sobek charged straight down the hall, and barreled into Paulette, wrapping her in his arms and knocking Evelyn aside. He was crying, and his eyes were hopping as if his brain was on fire. He put his gun to her head.

'I'm not done yet. I'm not done.'

Krantz yelled, 'Drop your gun! Put it down, Curtis!'

My arm felt wet and tingly, as if worms were crawling beneath the skin. I tried to pick up my gun, but the arm wouldn't work.

Sobek jammed his weapon harder into Paulette's neck. 'You drop your own fuckin' gun, Krantz! You put it down or I'll kill this bitch. I'll do it, you bastard. I'll do it right fuckin' now!'

Krantz backed up, his gun shaking so badly that if he fired he would as likely hit Paulette as Sobek. I think Krantz knew that, too.

I tried to pick up my gun with my left hand. Sobek didn't even seem to know I was there anymore. He was focused on Krantz.

'I MEAN IT GODDAMNIT KRANTZ I'M GONNA DO IT I'M GONNA DO IT RIGHT NOW BLOW HER BRAINS OUT AND THEN I'M GONNA KILL MYSELF I DON'T CARE I DON'T CARE!'

It is against LAPD policy for an officer to give up his or her weapon. They teach that at the Academy, they live by it, and it is the right thing to teach and live by. You give up your weapon, and you're done.

But if you don't do what Laurence Sobek says, and someone dies, you will always wonder. It is another choice and another door, and you won't know what lies behind it until you go there.

He was going to kill her.

'Okay, Curtis. Just let her go and we'll talk. I'm putting the gun down like you want. Just don't hurt her, Curtis. Please do not hurt her.'

Krantz put his gun on the floor, and for the second time that day I liked Harvey Krantz.

I spoke quietly. 'Sobek? Why'd you kill Dersh? He wasn't part of this?'

Crazy eyes danced to me. 'Pike killed Dersh. Don't you watch the news?'

Krantz said, 'Shut up, Cole. Curtis, put down the gun. Please.'

Sobek walked Paulette closer to Krantz, shaking his head. 'I'm not done yet. They're going to pay for the Coopster. They're going to pay for that.'

Behind Sobek, Pike moved.

I said, 'Tell us about Dersh, Sobek. Tell us why you set up Pike.'

Sobek pointed his gun at me, and cocked the hammer. 'I didn't.'

Pike's eyes opened.

Krantz said, 'Damnit, Cole, shut up. Curtis, don't kill him. Let this woman go.'

Pike pushed himself up. His face was a mask of blood. His shirt was wet with it. He picked up his gun.

Sobek said, 'She's gotta die, and Wozniak's kid is gonna die, too. But you know what, Harvey?'

'What?'

Sobek aimed his .357 point-blank at Harvey Krantz.

'You're gonna die first.'

I said, 'DeVille isn't dead.'

Laurence Sobek stopped as if I'd hit him with a board. His face filled with rage, he aimed his gun at me again, then brought it back to Krantz. I could see his gun hand tighten.

He said, 'This is for killing my father.'

Krantz yelled, 'NO!'

Sobek was squeezing the trigger when Joe Pike brought up his weapon and fired one round through the back of Laurence Sobek's head. Sobek collapsed in a heap, and then there was silence.

Pike fell forward onto his hands, and almost at once tried to push himself up again.

Paulette said, 'Joe, lie down. Please lie down.'

Krantz just stood there. I could hear the sirens far away now, but drawing closer.

I struggled to my feet and went to Joe. Blood ran down my arm and dripped from my fingers.

'Stay down, Joseph. Got an ambulance on the way.'

Pike said, 'No. If I go down now, I'll spend the rest of my life in prison. Right, Krantz?'

Krantz said, 'You're going to bleed to death.'

Pike found his feet and stood, using Paulette to steady himself. He put his pistol into the waistband of his pants, then looked at me. 'You're shot.'

'You're shot twice.'

Pike nodded. 'It's so easy to show you up.'

He staggered then, but I caught him.

Paulette said, 'Please, Joe.' She was crying.

Pike was looking at me. 'Maybe there'll be something at Sobek's to put him with Dersh.'

'There wasn't.'

Pike looked tired. He took a handkerchief from his pants, but the blood had soaked through and it was red.

Paulette Wozniak said, 'Oh, damn.'

She pulled off her shirt and used it to wipe his face. She was wearing a white bra, but nobody looked or said anything, and I thought in that moment I could love her myself, truly and always.

The corner of Joe's mouth twitched, and he touched her face. 'Gotta go.'

Paulette blinked at the tears.

Joe let his fingers linger. 'You really are more beautiful.'

Then he turned away for the door, leaving his fingerprints in blood on her face.

Krantz said, 'I can't let you go, Pike. I appreciate what you did, and I'll stand up at your trial, but for now it's over.'

Krantz had his gun again. He was pale, and shaken, but he had the gun.

I said, 'Don't be stupid, Krantz.'

'It's over.'

Pike kept walking.

Krantz aimed his gun, but it was shaking as badly now as when he was aiming at Sobek. 'I mean it, Pike. You're a wanted man. You are under arrest, and you're going to stand trial. I won't let you leave this house.'

Krantz steadied the gun with his second hand, and pulled back the hammer, and that's when I twisted the gun away from him with my good hand. I shoved him against the wall.

Krantz screamed, 'You're interfering with an officer, goddamnit! You're obstructing justice!'

Pike walked out the front door without closing it, and then he was gone.

I said, 'Goodbye, Joe.'

Krantz slumped to the floor and put his face in his hands. The sirens were working their way up the hill and would soon arrive. They would probably pass Pike on their way up, and I wondered if any of them would notice the car driven by the bloody man. Probably not.

Krantz said, 'You shouldn't've done that, Cole. You aided and abetted his escape. I'm going to arrest you. It's going to cost your license.'

I nodded.

'You didn't help him, you asshole. He's going to bleed to death. He's going to die.'

The sirens arrived.

39

Of the two shots Sobek fired at Jerome Williams, only one connected, nipping an artery in his thigh. He would make it. My own wound was a bit more complicated. The bullet had torn through the outside of my right pectoral muscle, clipped the third lateral rib, then exited through my right latissimus dorsi. One of the hospital's resident surgeons came down to take a look, and said, 'Hmm.'

You have to worry when they say that.

'I can clean you up,' he said. 'But you're going to need some reconstructive surgery to the muscle group. Your pectoris attacher tendon is partially sheared, and the anterior joint capsule needs to be repaired.'

'How long will that take?'

'Four hours, tops.'

'Not how long will the surgery take. How long would I have to be here?'

'Three days.'

'Forget it.'

'Just want you to know the score. I gotta put you out anyway to take care of this.'

'Just give me a local. You're not putting me anywhere, and I'm not going out.' I wanted to be awake to find out about Pike. I figured they'd find him bled out on the side of a road. I wanted to be awake when the word came because I wanted to go to him.

'It's going to hurt like a sonofabitch with just a local.'

'Pretend you're a dentist and shoot me up, for chrissake.'

He gave me about two thousand injections, then cleaned the wound, and stitched the muscles and skin. It hurt worse than he said, but maybe it wasn't just the shoulder.

When he was done, he said, 'I'm giving you a Percocet script for the pain. You're going to need it. When the anesthetic wears off you're going to hurt even worse. This is strong stuff, so be sure you take just what I'm writing here. You need to see your own doctor tomorrow.'

'I'll be in jail.'

He sighed again and handed me the prescription. 'Take twice as much.'

He used thirty-two stitches to close the wound.

Krantz officially arrested me in the Palm Springs Hospital emergency room while Williams was in surgery. Stan Watts had driven out, and he stood there with a blank expression as Krantz read me the rights. Krantz said, 'Stan, I'm having him brought to County-USC so they can look at him. Maybe they'll want to book him in the jail ward there, and keep him overnight.'

Watts didn't answer.

'I want you to be there when they look at him. If they give him a pass, bring him over to Parker for the booking. I'll take care of it myself when I get back.'

Watts didn't answer again; he just kept staring at me with the blank look.

Krantz walked away to talk to the press.

When Krantz was gone, Watts said, 'I spent the whole ride out trying to figure out whether to blame you for Dolan.'

'I've been doing some of that myself.'

'Yeah, I imagine you would. But I know Dolan more than ten years, and I know what she was like. When she was hit, I saw how you went in. You didn't know what was in there, but you went right in. I saw how you covered her with your jacket.'

He stood there for a time like he didn't know what else to say, then put out his hand. I gave him my left, and we shook.

I said, 'Any word on Pike?'

'Not yet. Krantz said he was hit pretty bad.'

'Yeah. Bad. You guys finish going through Sobek's garage?'

'Most of it. SID's there now.'

'You see anything that clears Pike?'

Watts shook his head. 'No.'

I considered the Percocet script, wondering if it could take away this kind of hurt.

Watts said, 'C'mon, I'll take you back.'

'Krantz called a radio car.'

'Screw the radio car. You can ride with me.'

We didn't say ten words between Palm Springs and L.A. until we were approaching the exit for the County-USC Medical Center, where Krantz had ordered him to bring me.

'Where's your car?'

'Dolan's.'

'You drive with that arm?'

'I can drive.'

He continued past the County-USC exit without a word and brought me to Dolan's. We pulled into her drive, and sat there, staring at the house. Someone would have to go back to Sobek's garage for her Beemer. Someone would have to bring it home.

'I'm not going to book you tonight, but you gotta come in tomorrow.'

'Krantz will be pissed.'

'You let me worry about Krantz. You gonna come in or am I gonna have to go look for you?'

'I'll come in.'

He shrugged like he hadn't expected anything else, and said, 'I'll bet she's got a pretty good bottle of tequila in there. How about we tip one for her?'

'Sure.'

Dolan kept a spare house key beneath a clay pot in her backyard. I didn't ask Watts how he knew. When we got inside, Watts knew where she kept the tequila, too.

Her house was as quiet as any house could be, as if something had vanished from her home when she died. Maybe it had. We sat and drank, and after a while Stan Watts went back into her bedroom. He stayed there for a long time, then came out with a small onyx box, and sat with the box in his lap, and drinking. When he'd had enough to drink, he opened the box and took out a small blue heart. He slipped the heart into his jacket pocket, then put his face in his hands and cried like a baby.

I sat with him for almost an hour. I didn't ask him about the heart or the box, but I cried with and for him, and for Dolan, too. And for Pike, and me, because my life was falling apart.

The human heart is worth crying for, even if it's made of onyx.

After a while I used Dolan's phone to check my messages. Joe hadn't called, and neither had Lucy. The news of Laurence Sobek's identification and the events in Palm Springs had broken, and I hoped she would've called, but there you go.

I thought that I should call her, but didn't. I don't know why. I could shoot it out with Laurence Sobek, but calling the woman I loved seemed beyond me.

Instead, I went into Dolan's kitchen for the photograph she'd taken of me at Forest Lawn. I stared at it for a long time, and then I took it. It was right there on the refrigerator, but I hoped that Watts hadn't seen it. I wanted it to be between me and Samantha, and I didn't want it between Watts and her.

I went back into the living room and told Watts that I had to leave, but he didn't hear me, or, if he heard, didn't think I was worth answering. He was someplace deep within himself, or maybe in that little blue heart. In a way, I guess he was with Dolan.

I left him like that, got my prescription filled, then drove home, wishing I had a little blue heart of my own. A secret heart where, if I looked real hard, I could find the people who were dear to me.

40

My home felt large and hollow that evening. I phoned the guys who work for Joe, but they hadn't heard from him, and were upset by the news. I paced around the house, working up my nut to call Lucy, but thinking of Samantha Dolan. I kept seeing her earlier that morning, telling me she was going to stay after me, that she always got what she wanted, and that she was going to make me love her. Now she was dead and I would never be able to tell her that she already had.

My shoulder throbbed with a fierceness I didn't think possible. I took some of the Percocet, washed my hands and face, then called Lucy. Even dialing the phone hurt.

Ben answered on the third ring, lowering his voice when he realized it was me.

'Mom's mad.'

'I know. Will she speak to me?'

'You sure you want to?'

'I'm sure.'

I waited for her to come to the phone, thinking about what I would say and how I would say it. When Lucy picked up, her voice was more distant than I'd hoped.

She said, 'I guess you were right.'

'You heard about Joe?'

'Lieutenant Krantz called. He told me that Joe left the scene wounded.'

'That's right. I took away Krantz's gun so that Joe could leave. Officially, I'm under arrest. I have to go down to Parker Center tomorrow and turn myself in.'

'They call that aiding and abetting.'

I felt slow and stupid and sick to my stomach. My entire right side hurt.

'That's right, Lucy. I took Krantz's gun. I interfered. I committed a felony, and when I'm convicted I'll lose my license, and that's that. I'll get a job as a rent-a-cop, or maybe I can re-up with the Army. Be all I can be.'

Her voice softened. 'Were you going to tell me that you were shot?'

'Krantz tell you that?'

'Oh, Elvis.'

Sounding tired, she hung up.

I stood at the phone for a time, thinking that I should call her back, but I didn't.

Eventually, the cat came home, sniffing hopefully when he eased into the kitchen. I opened a can of Bumble Bee tuna, and sat with him on the floor. The Bumble Bee is his favorite. He lapped at it twice, then came to sniff my shoulder.

He licked at the bandages, and I let him.

There isn't so much love in the world that you can turn it away when it's offered.

The next morning, Charlie brought me to Parker Center, where Krantz and Stan Watts walked me through the booking process. Neither Krantz nor Watts mentioned that I had spent the night at home. Maybe they had worked it out between them.

I was arraigned that afternoon, a trial date was set in Superior Court, and I was released without bail. I wasn't really thinking about the proceedings; I was thinking about Joe.

Paulette Renfro and Evelyn Wozniak drove in from Palm Springs for the arraignment. After, they sat with Charlie and me to discuss what had occurred between me and Krantz. Paulette and Evelyn both offered to lie on my behalf, but I declined. I wanted them to tell the truth. Charlie listened to their version of events, which matched with mine. When they were done, Charlie leaned back and said, 'You're fucked.'

'That's what I like about you, Charlie. You're inspirational.'

'You want my legal advice, take them up on their offer to lie. We can cook up a good story, then it's the three of you against Krantz in court, and you'll skate.'

'Charlie, I don't want to play it that way.'

'Why not?'

That Charlie is something.

Later, Charlie spoke with the prosecutor handling the case, a young woman named Gilstrap out of USC Law who wanted to be governor. He came back and told me that I could plead guilty to the one felony charge of interfering with a police officer, and they would drop the obstruction of justice charge. If I took the plea, I would receive probation with no jail time served. I said, 'It's copping to a felony, Charlie. It means I lose my license.'

'You fight this, you're gonna lose your license anyway. You'll also do eighteen months.'

I took the plea, and became a convicted felon.

The next day I went into the hospital to have my shoulder rebuilt. It took three hours, not four, but left me in a cast that held my arm up from my body as if my shoulder were dislocated. I told the doctor that it made me look like a waiter. The doctor said another centimeter to the left, and

Sobek's bullet would've severed the nerve that controlled the small muscle groups in my hand and forearm. Then I would've looked like overcooked macaroni.

Thinking about that made me feel better about the cast.

That evening, Lucy brought flowers.

She let her fingers drift along the cast, then kissed my shoulder, and didn't look so mad anymore. A kindness came into her eyes that frightened me more than Laurence Sobek or getting shot or losing my license.

I said, 'Are we over?'

She stared at me for a long time before she shook her head. 'I don't know. It feels different.'

'Okay.'

'Let's be honest: This job was an excuse to come here. I came to Los Angeles because I love you. I changed my life to be with you, but also because I wanted to change. I had no promises or expectations about where we would go with this, or when, or even if any of it would work out. I knew what you were and what it meant the first time we met.'

'I love you.' I didn't know what else to say.

'I know, but I don't trust that love as much as I used to. Do you see?'

'I understand.'

'Don't just say that.'

'I get it, Lucy, but I couldn't have done anything else. Joe needed me. If he's not dead, he still needs me, and I will help him.'

'You're angry.'

'Yeah. I'm angry.'

Neither of us said very much more, and after a while she left. I wondered if I would see her again, or ever feel the same about her, or she about me, and couldn't believe that I was even having such thoughts.

Some days really suck.

The next morning, Abbot Montoya wheeled Frank Garcia into my room. Frank looked withered and old in the chair, but he gripped my leg in greeting, and his grip was strong. He asked about my arm, and about Joe, but after a while he seemed to drift, and his eyes filled with tears.

'You got that sonofabitch.'

'Joe got him.'

'You and Joe, and the woman who came to my house.'

'Her name was Samantha Dolan.'

His face screwed up, concerned. 'They haven't heard anything about Joe?'

'Not yet, Frank.'

'Anything you need, you let me know. Lawyers, doctors, I don't care what. Legal, illegal, it doesn't matter. My heart belongs to you now. If I can do it for you, I'll do it.'

He started to sob, and I felt embarrassed.

'You don't owe me anything, Frank.'

He squeezed my leg harder, so hard I thought the bone might break. 'Everything I have is yours. You don't have to understand that, or me. Just know that it's so.'

I thought about Rusty Swetaggen, and understood.

When they were leaving, Abbot Montoya stepped back through the door.

'Frank means it.'

'I know.'

'No. You don't know, but you will. I mean it, too. You are ours now, Mr Cole. Forever and always. That is a blood oath. Perhaps we are not so far from the White Fence, even after all these years.'

When he left I stared at the ceiling.

'Latins.'

Later that afternoon, Charlie Bauman was filling my room with cigarette smoke when Branford, Krantz, and Stan Watts dropped by.

Krantz stood at the end of my bed with his hands in his pockets, saying, 'A couple of kids found Pike's car outside Twentynine Palms.' Twentynine Palms is a barren, rugged place northeast of Palm Springs where the Marines have their Ground Combat Center. They do live-fire exercises out there, bringing in the fast movers to napalm the sand.

Charlie sat up.

I said, 'Was Pike in it?'

Branford glanced at my cast. 'Nope. Just a lot of his blood. The whole front seat was soaked. We've got the States out there doing a sweep.'

They were staring at me like I had helped him park the car.

Bauman said, 'You're not still going to prosecute Pike for this Dersh thing, are you, Branford?'

Branford just looked at him.

'Oh, for chrissake.'

I said, 'Krantz, you know better. You saw how Sobek was dressed, just like Pike. He's who the old lady saw.'

Krantz met my eyes. 'I don't know anything like that, Cole. Mrs Kimmel saw arrow tattoos. Sobek didn't have tattoos.'

'So he painted them on, then washed them off.'

'I heard you ask Sobek if he did Dersh. I heard Sobek deny it.'

Charlie waved his cigarette, annoyed. 'You want a signed confession? What are we talking about here?'

'I want facts. We haven't been sitting on our asses with this, Bauman. We ran everything Pike said about his alibi through the system, and it came back just the way I thought it would: bullshit. No hits on a black minivan, Trudy, or Matt. We flashed Sobek's picture in a six-pack for Amanda Kimmel, but she *still* puts the finger on Pike.'

Branford said, 'We've got the murder weapon, the GSR, and the motive; that gives us Pike.'

Charlie said, 'Pike's statement wasn't a secret. Sobek could've tossed the gun off the pier to match with Pike's story. If Sobek didn't kill Dersh, why was Jesus Lorenzo killed just a few hours later? You writing that off as a coincidence?'

'I'm writing it off as something I can't ask Sobek because Sobek is dead. Look, Pike saved Krantz's life, and those two women's, but I can't just forget about Dersh because we owe him one. You give me some proof that he didn't do it, or that Sobek did, I'll think it over.'

Charlie Bauman waved his cigarette like he didn't believe Branford for a second, then considered Krantz. 'Tell me something, Lieutenant? You really draw down on Pike after Pike saved you?'

'Yes, I really did that.'

'Even after he saved your life?'

'He murdered Eugene Dersh, and he's going to answer for it. What I feel doesn't matter.'

'Well, at least you feel something.'

No one said much after that, and pretty soon everybody left but Watts. He said, 'We buried Samantha this morning. Had over a thousand officers in the ranks. It was nice.'

'I'll bet it was.'

'We get any word on Pike, I'll let you know.'

'Thanks, Stan. I appreciate it.'

Thinking back, I'm sure the only reason Stan Watts tagged along with Krantz and Branford that day was to share Samantha Dolan's final moment with me, and to tell me that a thousand officers had seen her off.

I don't think he would've come for any other reason.

I wish I could have been there to see her off with them.

I left the hospital the next day.

The doctors raised hell, but I couldn't take lying in bed with Joe still missing. I hoped that Joe was alive, and thought that if anyone could survive it would be him, but I also knew that if Pike had found his way into the ravines and arroyos of the desert, his body might not be discovered for years.

I took too many painkillers, but still couldn't drive with the cast, so I hired a cab to take me out to the desert. I went back to Paulette's house, then up to Twentynine Palms, and tried to imagine what Joe might've been thinking, and where he might've gone, but couldn't.

I checked all the nearby motels and service stations, and ate so many Percocet that I threw up twice.

I went back to the desert the next day, and the next, but never found a trace. The cab fares totaled eight hundred dollars.

Perhaps if I were a better detective I could have gotten a line on him, or found his body, though not if Joe was alive and covering his tracks.

Telling myself that was better than thinking him dead.

When I wasn't at the desert I haunted Santa Monica, walking Joe's route both during the day and at night, talking to clerks and surfers and gangbangers and bodybuilders and maintenance people and food vendors and the limitless armies of street people. I walked the night route so often that the hookers who worked Ocean Avenue brought home-baked pie for me and Starbucks coffee. Maybe it was the cast. They all wanted to sign it.

My friends at the FBI and the DMV ran still more searches for black minivans, and people named Trudy and Matt, and I even got them to badger their friends in other states to do the same. Nothing turned up, and after a while my friends stopped returning my calls. I guess our friendship had its limits.

Eight days after I left the hospital I phoned Stan Watts. 'Is there anything on Joe?'

'Not yet.'

'Has SID finished with Sobek's garage?'

He sighed. 'Man, you don't give up, do you?'

'Not even after I'm dead.'

'They finished, but you're not going to like it much. They got this sharp kid over there named Chen. He tied Sobek to all of the vics except Dersh. I'm sorry.'

'Maybe he missed something.'

'This kid is *sharp*, Cole. He lasered Dersh's place looking for fibers that could've come from Sobek's, but found nothing. He lasered Sobek's, looking for something that might've come from Dersh, but that was a bust, too. He doped both places, and ran gas chromes, but struck out all the way around. I was hoping he'd find something that put Sobek with Dersh, too, but there's nothing.'

Chen was the guy who'd done the work up at Lake Hollywood. I remember being impressed when I'd read it. 'Think you could send over these new reports?'

'Shit, there's gotta be two hundred pages here.'

'Just the work he did on Dersh's place, and Sobek's garage. I don't need the others.'

'You got a fax there?'

'Yeah.' I gave him the number.

He said, 'You really been taking a cab out to the desert?'

'How'd you hear about that?'

'You know something, Cole? You and Dolan were of the same stripe. I can see why she liked you.'

Then he hung up.

While I waited for the fax, I reread Chen's Lake Hollywood report, and was again impressed with its detail. By the time I finished, the new reports had arrived, and I found them exhaustive. Chen had collected over one hundred separate fiber and soil samples from Dersh's home and property, and compared them with samples taken from Sobek's apartment, clothing, shoes, and vehicle, but found nothing that would tie the two together. No physical evidence tied Dersh to Joe Pike, either, but that didn't seem to bother Krantz.

I read the new report twice, but by the end of the second reading felt as if I was wasting my time – no matter how often I turned the pages, no new evidence appeared, and Chen's evidentiary conclusions remained unchanged. I was thinking that my time would be better spent looking for Trudy, or going back to the desert, when I realized that something was different between the work that Chen had done at Lake Hollywood and the work he'd done at Dersh's house.

I had read these reports hoping to find something exculpatory for Pike, but maybe what I was looking for wasn't something that was in the report. Maybe it had been left out.

I phoned the SID office, and asked for John Chen.

The woman who answered the phone said, 'May I tell him what it's regarding?'

I was still thinking about what the report didn't say when I answered her.

'Tell him it's about Joe Pike.'

41

The New, Improved John Chen

John Chen had leased the Porsche Boxster – also known as the 'tangmobile – on the very day he was promoted for his exemplary performance in the Karen Garcia homicide. He couldn't afford it, but John had decided that one could either accept one's miserable place in life (even if, like John, one was born to it) or defy it, and you could defy it if you just had the balls to take action. This was the new, improved John Chen, redefining himself with the motto: *If I can take it, it's mine.*

First comes the 'tangmobile, then comes the 'tang.

Just as John Chen had had his eye on the Boxster, so had he been head over heels in heat for Teresa Wu, a microbiology graduate student at UCLA and part-time assistant at SID. Teresa Wu had lustrous black hair, skin the color of warm butter, and professorial red glasses that John thought were the sexiest thing going.

Still flush with the accolades he'd garnered for his work at Lake Hollywood, John drove back to the office, made sure everyone there knew about the Boxster, then asked Teresa Wu for a date.

It was the first time he had asked her out, and only the second time he'd spoken to her. It was only the third time he'd been brave enough to ask out *anyone,*

Teresa Wu peered at him over the top of the red glasses, rolled her eyes as if he'd just asked her to share a snot sandwich, and said, 'Oh, please, John. No way.'

Bitch.

That was a week ago, but part of John's new-found philosophy was a second motto: *No guts, no nookie.* John had spent the next seven days working up his nut to ask her out again, and was just about to do so when some guy named Elvis Cole called, wanting to speak with him.

Now Teresa had left for school, and John put down the phone with a feeling of annoyance. Not only had the incoming call blown today's chance at Teresa Wu, but Chen didn't like it that Cole implied he had missed something at the crime scene. Chen liked it even less that he'd allowed the guy to badger him into meeting back at the Dersh house. Still, Chen was curious to hear what Cole had to offer; after all, if Chen could make a headline breakthrough on the Dersh case, Teresa Wu might change her mind about going out with him. How could she turn down a guy with a Boxster *and* his name on the front page of the *L.A. Times*?

Forty minutes later, John Chen tooled his 'tangmobile into Dersh's drive beside a green-and-white cab. The police tape had been removed from Dersh's door, and the house long released as a crime scene. Now it was nothing more than bait for the morbid.

As Chen shut down the Boxster, a man whose arm stuck from his body in a shoulder cast climbed out of the cab. He looked like a waiter.

The man said, 'Mr Chen. I'm Elvis Cole.'

There's a dorky name for you. Elvis.

Chen eyed Cole sourly, thinking that Cole probably wanted him to falsify or plant evidence. 'You're Pike's partner?'

'That's right. Thanks for coming out.'

Cole offered his good hand. He wasn't as big as Pike, but his grip was uncomfortably hard – like Pike, he was probably another gym rat with too many Y chromosomes who played private eye so he could bully people. Chen shook hands quickly and stepped away, wondering if Cole was dangerous.

'I don't have a lot of time, Mr Cole. They're expecting me back at the office five minutes ago.'

'This won't take long.'

Cole started down the alley alongside Dersh's home without waiting, and Chen found himself following. John resented that: Ballsy guys lead; they don't follow.

Cole said, 'When you covered the Lake Hollywood scene, you backtracked the shooter to a fire road and found where he'd parked his car.'

Chen's eyes narrowed. He automatically didn't like this, because Pike had done the tracking and he'd only tagged along. Chen, of course, had left that part out of his report.

'And?'

'There's no mention of the shooter's vehicle in the Dersh report. I was wondering if you looked for it.'

Chen felt a flood of relief and irritation at the same time. So that was the guy's big idea; that was why he'd wanted to meet. Chen put an edge in his voice, letting this guy know he wasn't just some a-hole with a pocket caddy.

'Of course, I looked for it. Mrs Kimmel heard the shooter's car door slam in front of her next-door neighbor's house. I checked the street and the curbs there and in front of the next house for possible tread marks, too, but there was nothing.'

'Did you look for oil drips?'

Cole said it just like that, without accusation, and Chen felt himself darken.

'What do you mean?'

'The Lake Hollywood report mentions oil drips that you found at the scene. You took samples up there and identified the oil.'

'Penzoil 10–40.'

'If the shooter's car was leaking up at the lake, it probably left drops here, too. If we found them, maybe you could prove they'd come from the same vehicle.'

Chen darkened even more, his face burning at the same time he felt a grim excitement. Cole had something here. Chen could compare brand, additives, and carbon particulate concentration to match the two samples. If he got a match, it would break open the Dersh case and guarantee headline coverage!

But when they reached the street, Chen's enthusiasm waned. The tarmac had last been refreshed in the sixties, and showed pothole plugs, the scorched weathering of L.A.'s inferno heat, and a webwork of tiny earthquake cracks. In the general area where Chen reasoned that the shooter had parked, any number of drips dotted the road, and they might've been anything: transmission fluid, power steering fluid, oil, brake fluid, antifreeze, the hawked lugey of a passing motorist, or bird shit.

Chen said, 'I don't know, Cole. It's been two weeks; anything that dripped that night has been weathered, dried, driven over, maybe contaminated with other substances. We won't be able to find anything.'

'We won't know if we don't look, John.'

Chen walked along the edge of the street, kicking pebbles and frowning. The damned street was so speckled it looked like measles. Still, it was an interesting idea, and if it panned out, the benefits might be enormous. Sex with Teresa Wu.

Chen dropped down into a push-up position the way Pike had shown him and considered the light on the road's surface. He let everything blur except the light, and noticed that some drips shined more than others. Those would be fresher. Chen moved to the curb, and imagined a car parked there, an SUV like the one at Lake Hollywood. He went low again in that place, looking for drip patterns. A vehicle parked for a time would not leave a single drip, but several, the dots overlapping.

Cole said, 'What do you think?'

John Chen, lost in the street, did not hear him.

'John?'

'Huh?'

'What do you think?'

'I think it's a long shot.'

'Is there any other kind?'

John Chen went back to the Boxster for his evidence kit, then spent the rest of the afternoon taking samples, and daydreaming about Teresa Wu.

42

Exactly twenty-four days after the City of Los Angeles district attorney's Office registered my conviction with the state, I received a letter from the California State Licensing Board revoking my investigator's license. In the same mail, the California Sheriffs Commission revoked my license to carry a firearm. So much for the Elvis Cole Detective Agency. So much for being a detective. Maybe I could become a sod farmer.

Two days later the doctors cut off my cast, and I began physical therapy. It hurt worse than any physical pain I'd ever felt, even worse than being shot. But my arm worked, and I could drive again. Also, I no longer looked like a waiter.

I drove to my office for the first time since the desert, walked up the four flights, and sat at my desk. I had been in that office for over ten years. I knew the people who worked in the insurance office across the hall, and I used to date the woman who owned the beauty supply company next door. I bought sandwiches from the little deli in the lobby, and did my banking in the lobby bank. Joe had an office there, too, though it was empty. He had never used it, and now perhaps never would.

I watched Pinocchio's eyes move from side to side, and said, 'I guess I could hang you in the loft.'

When the phone rang, I said, 'Elvis Cole Detective Agency. We're out of business.'

Frank Garcia said, 'What do you mean, out of business?'

'Just a joke, Frank. How you doing?' I didn't want to get into it.

'How come you haven't called? How come you and that pretty lady haven't come see me?'

'Been busy. You know.'

'What's that pretty lady's name? The one works for Channel 8?'

'Lucy Chenier.'

'I want you two to come have dinner. I'm lonely, and I want my friends around. Will you?'

'You mind if it's just me, Frank?'

'Is something wrong? You don't sound so good.'

'I'm worried about Joe.'

Frank didn't say anything for a while, but then he said, 'Yeah, well, some things we can control, and some we can't. You sure you're all right?'

'I'm fine.'

I spoke to Lucy every day, but over time our calls grew shorter and less frequent. I didn't enjoy them, and felt worse after we had spoken. It was probably the same for Lucy, too.

Stan Watts called, time to time, or I called him, but there was still no word about Joe. I phoned John Chen on eight separate occasions to see if he'd gotten anything from the tests he'd run, but he never returned my calls. I still don't know why. I stayed in touch with Joe's gun shop, and went through the motions of searching for the mysterious girl in the black van, but without real hope of finding anything. After a time, I felt like a stranger in my own life; all the things that had been real to me were changing.

On Wednesday of that week, I phoned my landlady and gave up my office. The Elvis Cole Detective Agency was out of business. My partner, my girlfriend, and now my business were gone, and I felt nothing. Maybe when I lost my license I had gone, too, and that was why I didn't feel anything. I wondered if they were hiring at Disneyland.

On Thursday, I parked in Frank Garcia's drive, and went to the door expecting dinner. Abbot Montoya answered, which surprised me.

He said, 'Frank and I had a little business, and he invited me to stay. I hope you don't mind.'

'You know better than that.'

He led me into the living room, where Frank was sitting in his chair. I said, 'Hi, Frank.'

He didn't answer; he just sat there for a moment, smiling with a warmth that reached all the way into my heart.

He said, 'How come I gotta find out from other people?'

'What?'

'You weren't kidding about being out of business. You lost your license.'

'There's nothing to be said for it, Frank. How'd you find out?'

'That pretty lady, Ms Chenier. She called me about it.'

'Lucy called you?' That surprised me.

'She explained what happened. She said you lost it helping Joe get away.'

I shrugged, giving his own words back to him. 'There's things we can control, things we can't.' I wasn't comfortable talking about it, and didn't want to.

Frank Garcia handed me an envelope.

I held it back without opening it. 'I told you. You don't owe me a nickel.'

'It's not money. Open it.'

I opened it.

Inside, there was a California state investigator's license made out in my name, along with a license to carry a concealed weapon. There was also a brief, terse letter from a director of the state board, apologizing for any inconvenience I might've suffered for the temporary loss of my licenses.

I looked at Frank, then at Abbot Montoya. I looked at the license again. 'But I'm a convicted felon. It's a state law.'

A fierce pride flashed in Abbot Montoya's eyes then, and I could see the strength and the muscle and the power that had been used to get these things. And I thought that maybe he was right, maybe he and Frank weren't so far from the White Fence gang-bangers they'd been as younger men.

He said, '*Temos tu corazón y tu el de nosotros. Para siempre.*'

Frank gripped my arm, the same fierce way he had gripped me before. 'Do you know what that means, my friend?'

I couldn't answer. All I could do was shake my head.

'It means we love you.'

I nodded.

'That pretty woman, she loves you, too.'

I cried, then, and couldn't stop, not for what I had, but for what I didn't.

43

Two days later I was hanging a framed copy of the new license in my office when the phone rang. My first thought was that it was John Chen or Stan Watts, but it was neither.

One of the guys who worked in Joe's gun shop said, 'You know who I am?'

My heart rate spiked. Just like that, and a cold sweat filmed my chest and back.

'Is this about Joe?'

'You ever been to the old missile control base above Encino? The one they turned into a park? You'll like the view.'

'Is Joe okay? Did you hear from him?'

'No way. Joe's probably dead. I just thought we might get together up at the park, maybe raise one for an old friend.'

'Sure. We could do that.'

'I'll give ya a call sometime. Bring a six-pack.'

'Anytime you want.'

'Sooner the better.'

He hung up.

I locked the office, and drove hard west through the city, and up to Mulholland.

It was a beautiful, clear Friday morning. The rush hour had passed, letting me make good time, but I would've made the time even if the streets had been crushed. It had to be Joe, or word of him, and I drove without thinking or feeling, maybe because I was scared the word would be bad. Sometimes, denial is all you have.

The government had built a missile control base high in the Santa Monica Mountains during the Cold War years. Then it was a top secret radar installation on the lookout for Soviet bombers coming to nuke Los Angeles. Now it was a beautiful little park that almost no one knew about except mountain bikers and hikers, and they only went on weekends.

When I reached the park, a Garcia tortilla company truck was parked off the road. I left my car behind it, hurried into the park, and made my way up the caged metal stairs to the top of the tower. The observation tower had once been a giant radar dome, and from it you could see south to the ocean and north across the San Fernando Valley.

Joe Pike was waiting on the platform.

He stiffened even though I didn't hug him hard. He was pale, and thinner than I'd ever seen him, though the white Garcia bakery shirt made him seem dark.

I said, 'Took you long enough to call, goddamnit. Can you spell "worry"?'

'I was down in Mexico, getting better.'

'You got to a hospital?'

Pike's mouth twitched. 'Not quite. How's the arm?'

'Stiff, but it's okay. I'm more concerned about you. You need anything?'

'I need to find Trudy.'

'I've been looking.' I told him what Watts had reported, and what my own searches had confirmed. Nothing on a black minivan or Trudy or Matt existed anywhere in the system. I also told him that I had no leads.

Pike took that in, and went to the rail. 'The police are on my house and the gun shop. They've frozen my accounts, and flagged my credit cards. They've been to see Paulette.'

'Maybe you should go south again. Sooner or later I'll get a hit that we can work with.'

Pike shook his head. 'I won't go south to hide, Elvis. I'm going to live it out here, one way or the other.'

'I'm not saying go south to hide. Go to stay free. Coming up here is too big a risk.'

'I'm willing to risk it.'

'And go back to jail?'

Pike's mouth flickered in an awful way. 'I'll never go to jail again.'

Then he looked past me, and straightened in a way that made my scalp prickle. 'They're on us.'

A flat blue detective sedan and an LAPD radio car slid to a stop by the Garcia van. A second radio car barreled in from the opposite direction, stopping in the center of the road. We didn't wait to see who they were or what they were planning.

Pike went low fast, and snaked down the twisting metal stair toward the ground. I was right behind him. We couldn't see the stair from the platform, or the ground from the stair, but if we could get away from the observation tower, the park opened onto miles of undeveloped mountains that stretched south to Sunset Boulevard and west to the sea. If Pike could get into the sage, there was no way the police could follow him without dogs or helicopters.

As we banged down the stairs, I said, 'There's a trail works south through the mountains to a subdivision above the Sunset Strip.'

'I know it.'

'If you follow the trail down, I can pick you up there later.'

It was planning done for nothing.

When we reached the bottom of the stair, Harvey Krantz and two SWAT cops with M16s were waiting.

The SWAT cops covered Joe Pike like he was a coiled cobra. They spread to the sides for crossing fire, their black rifles zeroed on Pike's chest even from ten feet away. Behind them, a cop shouted our location to the people on the road.

Krantz wasn't holding a gun, but his eyes were on Pike as if he were a down-range target. I expected him to start with our rights, or tell us we were under arrest, or maybe even gloat, but he didn't.

Krantz said, 'Go for it, Pike. Shoot it out, and you might get away.'

The SWAT cops shifted.

Pike stood with his weight on the balls of his feet, hands away from his body, as relaxed as if he were in a Zen rock garden. He would have a gun somewhere, and he would be wondering if he could get to it, and fire before the SWAT cops cut loose. Even wounded and weak, he would be thinking that. Or maybe he wasn't thinking anything at all; maybe he would just act.

Krantz took a step forward, and spread his hands. 'I don't have a gun, Pike. Maybe you'll get me.'

I looked from Krantz to Joe, and knew in that moment that something more than an arrest was happening. The SWAT cops traded an uncertain glance, but didn't lower their guns.

'What's wrong with you, Krantz?' I put up my hands. 'Raise your hands, Joe. Goddamnit, *raise them*!'

Pike didn't move.

Krantz smiled, but it was strained and ugly. He took another step. 'Time's running out, Joe. More officers are on the way.'

'Raise your hands, damnit! If you don't, then Krantz *wins*!'

Pike took a single breath, then looked past Krantz to the SWAT cops, talking to them now. 'My hands are going up.'

He raised them.

'Gun in my waistband under my shirt.'

Krantz didn't move.

One of the SWAT cops said, 'Krantz, get his damned gun.'

Krantz took out his own gun.

Stan Watts trotted up the path, breathing hard, and stopped when he saw us.

The SWAT cops said, 'Hey, Watts, get this bastard's gun.'

Stan Watts took Pike's gun, then took mine, and he stared at Krantz, standing there with his gun at his side. 'What in hell's going on, Krantz? Didn't you tell them?'

Krantz's jaw rippled as if he were chewing hard candy, and still his eyes didn't leave Pike. 'I wanted Pike to spook. I was hoping he'd give us the excuse.'

I said, 'Take his gun, Stan. Please take his gun.'

Watts stared at Krantz, then the gun Krantz held. Krantz's fingers worked at the gun like they had a life of their own. They kneaded and gripped the gun, and maybe wanted to raise it. Stan Watts went over and pried the gun away, and then pushed Krantz back hard.

'Go wait in the car.'

'*I'm your superior officer!*'

Watts told the SWAT cops they were done, then told us to put our hands down. He wet his lips like his mouth was dry. 'You're not under arrest. Branford's dropping the charges. You hear that, Pike? Branford's with your attorney right now. SID put Sobek's vehicle at Dersh's house. That's enough to get you off the hook.'

I gripped Pike's arm, and held it. John Chen had come through.

Krantz pushed past Watts and jabbed his finger at Pike. It was exactly the same move he'd made at Lake Hollywood the first time I saw him. 'I don't give a rat's ass what SID says, Pike; you're a murderer.'

Watts said, 'Stop it, Harvey.'

Krantz jabbed again.

'You killed Wozniak, and I still believe you killed Dersh.'

Krantz jabbed again, and this time Pike grabbed his finger so quickly that Harvey Krantz did not see him move. Krantz shrieked as he dropped to the ground, screaming, 'You're under arrest, goddamnit! That's assaulting an officer! You're under arrest.'

Pike and Watts and I stared at him there on the ground, red-faced and screaming, and then Watts helped him up, saying, 'We're not going to arrest anyone, Harvey. Go back to the car and wait for me.'

Krantz shook him off, and walked away without another word.

I said, 'Get him off the street, Watts. He came up here to murder Pike. He meant what he said.'

Watts pursed his lips, watching until Krantz was gone, then considered Pike. 'You could make a complaint, I guess. There's grounds.'

Pike shook his head.

I said, 'That's it? We're just going to forget what happened here?'

Watts put the frying pan face on me. 'What happened, Cole? We came up to give you the word, we did.'

'How'd you know we were here?'

'We've been running taps twenty-four/seven on phones Pike's employees are known to use. The wire guys heard Pike's boy tell you about this place, and figured it out.'

Watts glanced back to the road where Harvey Krantz was waiting in their car, alone.

Watts handed back our guns, holding on to Pike's as Pike reached for it. 'What Krantz said about hoping you'd give us an excuse, that's bullshit.

He's just upset. I don't play it that way, and he wouldn't either. Bauman said you hadn't been in touch, so we figured if there was a shot at reaching you up here, we should take it.'

I said, 'Sure, Watts.'

'Screw you, Cole. That's the way it is.'

'Sure.'

Watts followed after Krantz, and pretty soon the police mounted their cars, and left great brown clouds of dust as they drove away. I guess Harvey Krantz hated Pike so much he had to believe Pike was guilty no matter what. I guess that kind of hate can make you do things you ordinarily wouldn't do.

'Watts can say whatever he wants, but Krantz wanted it. You don't bring tactical officers to tell some guy he's off the hook. You don't even roll out. If Krantz didn't want it, he could've put the word through me and Charlie and the guys at your shop. You would've heard.'

Pike nodded without comment, and I wondered if he even gave a damn. Maybe it was better not to.

I said, 'What are you going to do?'

'Call Paulette.'

'Does it bother you, what Krantz said about Wozniak? That you're still carrying the blame?'

Pike shrugged, and this time I knew he didn't give a damn.

'Let Krantz and everyone think what they want. What I think, and do, is more important.'

Pike took a deep breath then, and cocked the dark glasses my way.

'I missed you, Elvis.'

That made me smile.

'Yeah, Joseph, I missed you, too. It's good to have you back.'

We shook hands then, and I watched him walk down to the Garcia bakery truck and drive away. I stood in the hot wind for a time, telling myself that it was over, that Pike was home, and safe, but even as I told myself these things, it was without a sense that any of it was finished, or resolved.

We were different now. The world had changed.

I wondered if our lives would ever be the same, or as good, and if we were less than we had been.

The devils take their toll, even in this angel town.

Maybe here most of all.

I have lived in my house for many years, but it wasn't my house anymore. It wasn't the cozy A-frame that wrapped me in warm woods and copper sunset light, hanging there off the side of a mountain. It had become a great cavern that left me listening to echoes as I walked from room to room searching for something I could not find. Climbing to the loft took days. Going into the kitchen weeks. Funny, how the absence of a friend can do that. Funny, how it takes a woman three beats of a heart to walk out a door, but the man she's walking away from can't make that same trip in a lifetime.

Guess that's why you're smiling, Cole. It's so damned funny.

That night, I locked my door, and worked my way down the crooked mountain streets into Hollywood. It gets dark in the canyons first, shadows pooling in the deep cuts as the high ridges hide the sun. Here's a tip: If you leave the canyons you can find the light again, and get a second chance at the day. It doesn't last long, but nobody said second chances will wait for you.

The Sunset Strip was a carnival of middle-aged hipsters rat-racing Porsches, and goateed Val-dudes smoking twenty-dollar Cubano Robustos, and a couple of million young women with flat bellies flashing Rodeo Drive navel rings. I didn't see any of it. Shriners from Des Moines were lined up outside House of Blues like catalog models for JCPenney. Yellow-haired kids clumped outside Johnny Depp's Viper Room, laughing with LAPD motorcycle cops about the latest acid casualty. Didn't see it; didn't hear it. Twilight faded to full-on night, and the night grew later. I drove all the way to the water, then north through the steep mountain passes of Malibu, then back along the Ventura Freeway, just another mass of speeding metal. I felt edgy and unsettled, and thought that maybe if I drove long enough I might find a solution.

I love L.A.

It's a great, sprawling, spread-to-hell city that protects us by its sheer size. Four hundred sixty-five square miles. Eleven million beating hearts in Los Angeles County, documented and not. Eleven million. What are the odds? The girl raped beneath the Hollywood sign isn't your sister, the boy backstroking in a red pool isn't your son, the splatter patterns on the ATM machine are sourceless urban art. We're safe that way. When it happens it's going to happen to someone else. Only thing is, when she walks out of your door, it isn't someone else. It's you.

I let myself off the freeway at the top of the Santa Monica Mountains and turned east along Mulholland. It's quiet up there, and dark; a million miles from the city even though it lies in the city's heart. The dry air breezed over me like sheer silk, and the desert smells of eucalyptus and sage were strong. A black-tailed deer flashed through my headlights. Coyotes with ruby eyes watched me from the grass. I was tired, and thought I should go home because this was silly, all this aimless driving. Just go home and go to sleep and get on with my life. You can save the world tomorrow. Find all the answers you want tomorrow.

After a time I pulled off the road, cut the engine, and stared at the lights that filled the valley floor. Two million people down there. Put them end to end and they would wrap around the moon. Red taillights lit the freeways like blood pumping through sluggish arteries. An LAPD helicopter orbited over Sherman Oaks, spotlighting something on the ground. Another opera I didn't want to be part of.

I got out of my car and sat cross-legged on the hood. The barrel shape of an owl sat atop a power pole, watching me.

The owl said, 'Who?'

You get that from owls.

A month ago, I had almost been killed. My best friend and partner had almost died, too, and I'd spent every day since then thinking that he was gone. Today, he came very close to dying again. Samantha Dolan was dead, my girlfriend had walked out on me, and here I was sitting in the dark with an owl. The world had changed, all right. Some great large place inside me was empty, and I didn't know if I could fill it again. I was scared.

The air was sultry, and felt good. When I first came here, I fell in love with this place. During the day, Los Angeles is a great playful puppy of a town, anxious to please and quick with a smile. At night, it becomes a treasure chest filled with magic and dreams. All you have to do is chase your dreams. All you need is the magic. All you have to do is survive, but it's that way anywhere. That's what I found here when I first came; that's what more and more people find here every day, always had and always would. It's why they come; that treasure chest of hope.

I could make it right with Lucy. I could pull my life together again and fill that empty place.

The owl said, 'Who?'

I said, 'Me.'

I climbed back in the car, but I didn't go home. I turned on the radio and made myself comfortable. I didn't need to go home anymore. I was already there.

L.A. isn't the end; it's the beginning.

So was I.

Demolition Angel

Acknowledgements

The author wishes to thank the following people for their help: Det. John Petievich, LAPD (retired); Det. Paul Bishop, LAPD; Det. Bob Nelson, Criminal Conspiracy Section, LAPD (retired); Lt Mike DeCoudres, commanding officer, LAPD Bomb Squad; Sgt Joe Pau, supervisor, LAPD Bomb Squad; Lt Anthony Alba, LAPD Public Affairs; Special Agent Charles Hustmyer, ATF; Stephen B. Scheid, Explosives Specialist, ATF; Marc Scott Taylor, Technical Associates, Inc.; Steven B. Richlin, OD; Jane Bryson, Ph.D.; Angela Donahue, Ph.D., Behavioral Science Unit, LAPD; Patricia Crais; Celia Gleason; Clay Fourrier; Leslie Day; Tami Hoag; Gerald Petievich; Shawn Coyne; Steve Rubin; Gina Centrello; Aaron Priest; Norman Kurland; Emile Gladstone; Tricia Davey; Jonathan King; and Laurence Mark.

The explosives experts and bomb technicians with whom I spoke were justifiably concerned that this book neither be instructional, nor reveal the exact capabilities by which bomb techs ply their trade. To that end, I have changed certain facts and procedures and fictionalized others. Professionals knowledgeable in the field should note that the technical and procedural inaccuracies contained in this work are the author's responsibility, and his alone.

For Jeffrey and Celia

PROLOGUE

To be disrupted: when the human body is
blown apart; as by the pressure force of a bomb.
– *Gradwohl's Legal Medicine*

Code Three Roll Out
Bomb Squad
Silver Lake, California

Charlie Riggio stared at the cardboard box sitting beside the Dumpster. It was a Jolly Green Giant box, with what appeared to be a crumpled brown paper bag sticking up through the top. The box was stamped GREEN BEANS. Neither Riggio nor the two uniformed officers with him approached closer than the corner of the strip mall there on Sunset Boulevard; they could see the box fine from where they were.

'How long has it been there?'

One of the Adam car officers, a Filipino named Ruiz, checked his watch. 'We got our dispatch about two hours ago. We been here since.'

'Find anyone who saw how it got there?'

'Oh, no, dude. Nobody.'

The other officer, a black guy named Mason, nodded.

'Ruiz is the one saw it. He went over and looked in the bag, the crazy Flip.'

'So tell me what you saw.'

'I told your sergeant.'

'Tell *me*. I'm the sonofabitch who's gonna approach the damned thing.'

Ruiz described seeing the capped ends of two galvanized pipes taped together with silver duct tape. The pipes were loosely wrapped in newspaper, Ruiz said, so he had only seen the ends.

Riggio considered that. They were standing in a strip mall on Sunset Boulevard in Silver Lake, an area that had seen increasing gang activity in recent months. Gangbangers would steal galvanized pipe from construction sites or dig up plastic PVC from some poor bastard's garden, then stuff them with bottle rocket powder or match heads. Riggio didn't know if the Green Giant box held an actual bomb or not, but he had to approach it as if it did. That's the way it was with bomb calls. Better than ninety-five percent turned out to be hairspray cans, some teenager's book bag, or, like his most recent call-out, two pounds of marijuana wrapped in Pampers. Only one out of a hundred was what the bomb techs called an 'improvised munition'.

A homemade bomb.

'You hear ticking or anything like that?'

'No.'

'Smell anything burning?'

'Uh-uh.'

'Did you open the bag to get a better look?'

'Hell, no.'

'Did you move the box or anything?'

Ruiz smiled like Riggio was nuts.

'Dude, I saw those pipes and shit my pants. The only thing I moved was my *feet!*'

Mason laughed.

Riggio walked back to his vehicle. The Bomb Squad drove dark blue Suburbans, rigged with a light bar and crammed with all the tools of the bomb technician's trade, except for the robots. You wanted the robots, you had to call them out special, and he wasn't going to do that. The goddamned robot would just get bogged down in all the potholes around the box.

Riggio found his supervisor, Buck Daggett, instructing a uniformed sergeant to evacuate the area for a hundred yards in all directions. The fire department had already been called, and paramedics were on the way. Sunset Boulevard had been closed and traffic rerouted. All for something that might turn out to be some do-it-yourself plumber's cast-off drain trap.

'Hey, Buck, I'm ready to take a look at that thing.'

'I want you in the suit.'

'It's too hot. I'll use the chest protector for the first pass, then the suit if I have to bring out the de-armer.'

All Riggio would be doing on the first pass was lugging out a portable X-ray to see inside the bag. If the contents appeared to be a bomb, he and Daggett would formulate a game plan and either de-arm the device or explode it in place.

'I want you in the suit, Charles. I got a feeling about this one.'

'You've always got a feeling.'

'I've also got the sergeant stripes. You're in the suit.'

The armored suit weighed almost ninety pounds. Made of Kevlar plates and heavy Nomex batting, it covered every part of Riggio's body except his hands, which remained bare. A bomb tech needed the dexterity of unencumbered fingers.

When the suit was in place, Riggio took the Real Time RTR3 X-ray unit and lumbered toward the package. Walking in the suit was like walking with his body wrapped in wet quilts, only hotter. Three minutes in the armor, and sweat was already running into his eyes. To make it worse, a safety cable and hardwire dragged behind him, the hardwire connecting him to Daggett via a Telex communicator. A separate wire linked the Real

Time to a computer in the Suburban's cargo bay. He felt like he was pulling a plow.

Daggett's voice came into Riggio's ear. 'How you doing out there?'

'Sweating my ass off, thanks to you.'

Riggio hated this part the most, approaching an object before he knew what it was. Every time was the same: Riggio thought of that unknown object as a living beast with a life and a mind. Like a sleeping pit bull. If he approached it carefully and made the right moves, everything would be fine. If he startled the dog, the damn thing would rip him apart.

Eighty-two slow-motion paces brought him to the box.

It was unremarkable except for a wet stain on one corner that looked like dog piss. The brown paper bag, crumpled and uneven, was open. Riggio peered into the bag without touching it. Leaning over was hard, and when he did, sweat dripped onto the Lexan faceplate like rain.

He saw the two pipes that Ruiz had described. The pipe caps appeared to be about two and a half inches in diameter and taped together, but nothing else about them was visible. They were loosely wrapped with newspaper, leaving only the ends exposed. Daggett said, 'How's it look?'

'Like a couple of pipes. Stand by. I'll get us a picture.'

Riggio placed the Real Time RTR3 on the ground at the base of the box, aimed for a side view, then turned on the unit. It provided the same type of translucent shadow image that security personnel see on airline baggage units, reproducing the image on two screens: one for Riggio on top of the RTR3 and another on the computer back at the Suburban.

Charlie Riggio smiled.

'Sonofabitch. We got one, Buck. We got us a bomb.'

'I'm seeing it.'

The two pipes were impenetrable shadows with what appeared to be a spool of wire or fuse triangled between them. There didn't appear to be a timer or an initiator of a more sophisticated nature, leading Riggio to believe that the bomb was a garage project made by an enterprising local gangbanger. Low-tech, dirty, and not particularly difficult to de-arm.

'This one's going to be a piece of cake, Buck. I make a basic fuse of the light-it-and-run-like-hell variety.'

'You be careful. Might be some kind of motion switch tucked away in there.'

'I'm not gonna touch it, Buck. Jesus. Gimme some credit.'

'Don't get cocky. Take the snaps and let's figure out what's what.'

The procedure was to take a series of digital computer snaps of the device via the Real Time at forty-five-degree angles. When they had the device mapped, Riggio would fall back to the Suburban, where he and Daggett would decide how best to destroy or de-arm it.

Riggio shuffled around the box, aiming the Real Time over the different angles. He felt no fear as he did this because he knew what he was dealing with now and trusted he could beat it. Riggio had approached over forty-eight suspicious packages in his six years with the Bomb Squad; only nine had been actual explosive devices. None of those had ever detonated in a manner that he did not control.

'You're not talking to me, Charlie. You okay?'

'Just got to work around the potholes, Sarge. Almost done. Hey, you know what I'm having? I'm having a brainstorm.'

'Stop. You'll hurt yourself.'

'No, listen to this. You know those people on the infomercials who make all that money with the stupid shit they sell? We could sell these damned suits to fat people, see? You just wear it and you lose weight.'

'Keep your damned head with that bomb, Riggio. How's your body temp?'

'I'm okay.'

In truth, he was so hot that he felt dizzy, but he wanted to make sure he had good clean shots. He circled the box like a man in a space suit, getting front, side, and off angles, then pointed the Real Time straight down for a top view. That's when he saw a shadow that hadn't been visible in the side views.

'Buck, you see that? I think I got something.'

'What?'

'Here in the overhead view. Take a snap.'

A thin, hairlike shadow emerged from the side of one pipe and extended up through the spool. This wire wasn't attached to the others, which confused Riggio until a sudden, unexpected thought occurred to him: Maybe the spool was there only to hide this other wire.

In that moment, fear crackled through him and his bowels clenched. He called out to Buck Daggett, but the words did not form.

Riggio thought, *Oh, God.*

The bomb detonated at a rate of twenty-eight thousand feet per second, twenty-two times faster than a nine-millimeter bullet leaves the muzzle of a pistol. Heat flashed outward in a burst of white light hot enough to melt iron. The air pressure spiked from a normal fifteen pounds per square inch to twenty-two hundred pounds, shattering the iron pipes into jagged shrapnel that punched through the Kevlar suit like hyperfast bullets. The shock wave slammed into his body with an overpressure of three hundred thousand pounds, crushing his chest, rupturing his liver, spleen, and lungs, and separating his unprotected hands. Charlie Riggio was lifted fourteen feet into the air and thrown a distance of thirty-eight feet.

Even this close to the point of detonation, Riggio might have survived if this had been, as he first suspected, a garage bomb cooked up by a gangbanger with makeshift materials.

It wasn't.

Bits of tarmac and steel fell around him like bloody rain, long after Charlie Riggio was dead.

Part One

1

'Tell me about the thumb. I know what you told me on the phone, but tell me everything now.'

Starkey inhaled half an inch of cigarette, then flicked ash on the floor, not bothering with the ashtray. She did that every time she was annoyed with being here, which was always.

'Please use the ashtray, Carol.'

'I missed.'

'You didn't miss.'

Detective-2 Carol Starkey took another deep pull on the cigarette, then crushed it out. When she first started seeing this therapist, Dana Williams wouldn't let her smoke during session. That was three years and four therapists ago. In the time Starkey was working her way through the second and third therapists, Dana had gone back to the smokes herself, and now didn't mind. Sometimes they both smoked and the goddamned room clouded up like the Imperial Valley capped by an inversion layer.

Starkey shrugged.

'No, I guess I didn't miss. I'm just pissed off, is all. It's been three years, and here I am back where I started.'

'With me.'

'Yeah. Like in three years I shouldn't be over this shit.'

'So tell me what happened, Carol. Tell me about the little girl's thumb.'

Starkey fired up another cigarette, then settled back to recall the little girl's thumb. Starkey was down to three packs a day. The progress should have made her feel better, but didn't.

'It was Fourth of July. This idiot down in Venice decides to make his own fireworks and give them away to the neighbors. A little girl ends up losing the thumb and index finger on her right hand, so we get the call from the emergency room.'

'Who is "we"?'

'Me and my partner that day, Beth Marzik.'

'Another woman?'

'Yeah. There's two of us in CCS.'

'Okay.'

'By the time we get down there, the family's gone home, so we go to the house. The father's crying, saying how they found the finger, but not the thumb, and then he shows us these homemade firecrackers that are so damned big she's lucky she didn't lose the hand.'

'He made them?'

'No, a guy in the neighborhood made them, but the father won't tell us. He says the man didn't mean any harm. I say, your daughter has been *maimed*, sir, other children are at *risk*, sir, but the guy won't cop. I ask the mother, but the guy says something in Spanish, and now she won't talk, either.'

'Why won't they tell you?'

'People are assholes.'

The world according to Carol Starkey, Detective-2 with LAPD's Criminal Conspiracy Section. Dana made a note of that in a leatherbound notebook, an act which Starkey never liked. The notes gave physical substance to her words, leaving Starkey feeling vulnerable because she thought of the notes as evidence.

Starkey had more of the cigarette, then shrugged and went on with it.

'These bombs are six inches long, right? We call'm Mexican Dynamite. So many of these things are going off, it sounds like the Academy pistol range, so Marzik and I start a door-to-door. But the neighbors are just like the father – no one's telling us anything, and I'm getting madder and madder. Marzik and I are walking back to the car when I look down and there's the thumb. I just looked down and there it was, this beautiful little thumb, so I scooped it up and brought it back to the family.'

'On the phone, you told me you tried to make the father eat it.'

'I grabbed his collar and pushed it into his mouth. I did that.'

Dana shifted in her chair, Starkey reading from her body language that she was uncomfortable with the image. Starkey couldn't blame her.

'It's easy to understand why the family filed a complaint.'

Starkey finished the cigarette and crushed it out.

'The family didn't complain.'

'Then why—?'

'Marzik. I guess I scared Marzik. She had a talk with my lieutenant, and Kelso threatened to send me to the bank for an evaluation.'

LAPD maintained its Behavorial Sciences Unit in the Far East Bank building on Broadway, in Chinatown. Most officers lived in abject fear of being ordered to the bank, correctly believing that it called into question their stability and ended any hope of career advancement. They had an expression for it: 'Overdrawn on the career account.'

'If I go to the bank, they'll never let me back on the Bomb Squad.'

'And you keep asking to go back?'

'It's all I've wanted since I got out of the hospital.'

Irritated now, Starkey stood and lit another cigarette. Dana studied her, which Starkey also didn't like. It made her feel watched, as if Dana was waiting for her to do or say something more that she could write down. It was a valid interview technique that Starkey used herself. If you said nothing, people felt compelled to fill the silence.

'The job is all I have left, damnit.'

Starkey regretted the defensive edge in her voice and felt even more embarrassed when Dana again scribbled a note.

'So you told Lieutenant Kelso that you would seek help on your own?'

'Jesus, no. I kissed his ass to get out of it. I know I have a problem, Dana, but I'll get help in a way that doesn't fuck my career.'

'Because of the thumb?'

Starkey stared at Dana Williams with the same flat eyes she would use on Internal Affairs.

'Because I'm falling apart.'

Dana sighed, and a warmth came to her eyes that infuriated Starkey because she resented having to reveal herself in ways that made her feel vulnerable and weak. Carol Starkey did not do 'weak' well, and never had.

'Carol, if you came back because you want me to fix you as if you were broken, I can't do that. Therapy isn't the same as setting a bone. It takes time.'

'It's been three years. I should be over this by now.'

'There's no "should" here, Carol. Consider what happened to you. Consider what you survived.'

'I've had enough with *considering* it. I've *considered* it for three fucking years.'

A sharp pain began behind her eyes. Just from *considering* it.

'Why do you think you keep changing therapists, Carol?'

Starkey shook her head, then lied.

'I don't know.'

'Are you still drinking?'

'I haven't had a drink in over a year.'

'How's your sleep?'

'A couple of hours, then I'm wide awake.'

'Is it the dream?'

Carol felt herself go cold.

'No.'

'Anxiety attacks?'

Starkey was wondering how to answer when the pager clipped to her waist vibrated. She recognized the number as Kelso's cell phone, followed by 911, the code the detectives in the Criminal Conspiracy Section used when they wanted an immediate response.

'Shit, Dana. I've gotta get this.'

'Would you like me to leave?'

'No. No, I'll just step out.'

Starkey took her purse out into the waiting room, where a middle-aged woman seated on the couch briefly met her eyes, then averted her face.

'Sorry.'

The woman nodded without looking.

Starkey dug through her purse for her cell phone, then punched the speed dial to return Kelso's page. She could tell he was in his car when he answered.

'It's me, Lieutenant. What's up?'

'Where are you?'

Starkey stared at the woman.

'I was looking for shoes.'

'I didn't ask what you were doing, Starkey. I asked where you were.'

She felt the flush of anger when he said it, and shame that she even gave a damn what he thought.

'The west side.'

'All right. The bomb squad had a call-out, and, um, I'm on my way there now. Carol, we lost Charlie Riggio. He was killed at the scene.'

Starkey's fingers went cold. Her scalp tingled. It was called 'going core'. The body's way of protecting itself by drawing the blood inward to minimize bleeding. A response left over from our animal pasts when the threat would involve talons and fangs and something that wanted to rip you apart. In Starkey's world, the threat often still did.

'Starkey?'

She turned away and lowered her voice so that the woman couldn't hear.

'Sorry, Lieutenant. Was it a bomb? Was it a device that went off?'

'I don't know the details yet, but, yes, there was an explosion.'

Sweat leaked from her skin, and her stomach clenched. Uncontrolled explosions were rare. A Bomb Squad officer dying on the job was even more rare. The last time it had happened was three years ago.

'Anyway, I'm on my way there now. Ah, Starkey, I could put someone else on this, if you'd rather I did that.'

'I'm up in the rotation, Lieutenant. It's my case.'

'All right. I wanted to offer.'

He gave her the location, then broke the connection. The woman on the couch was watching her as if she could read Starkey's pain. Starkey saw herself in the waiting-room mirror, abruptly white beneath her tan. She felt herself breathing. Shallow, fast breaths.

Starkey put her phone away, then went back to tell Dana that she would have to end their session early.

'We've got a call-out, so I have to go. Ah, listen, I don't want you to turn in any of this to the insurance, okay? I'll pay out of my own pocket, like before.'

'No one can get access to your insurance records, Carol. Not without your permission. You truly don't need to spend the money.'

'I'd rather pay.'

As Starkey wrote the check, Dana said, 'You didn't finish the story. Did you catch the man who made the firecrackers?'

'The little girl's mother took us to a garage two blocks away where we found him with eight hundred pounds of smokeless gunpowder. Eight hundred pounds, and the whole place is reeking of gasoline because you know what this guy does for a living? He's a gardener. If that place had gone up, it would've taken out the whole goddamned block.'

'My Lord.'

Starkey handed over the check, then said her good-byes and started for the door. She stopped with her hand on the knob because she remembered something that she had intended to ask Dana.

'There's something about that guy I've been wondering about. Maybe you can shed some light.'

'In what way?'

'This guy we arrested, he tells us he's been building fireworks his whole life. You know how we know it's true? He's only got three fingers on his left hand and two on his right. He's blown them off one by one.'

Dana paled.

'I've arrested a dozen guys like that. We call them chronics. Why do they do that, Dana? What do you say about people like that who keep going back to the bombs?'

Now Dana took out a cigarette of her own and struck it. She blew out a fog of smoke and stared at Starkey before answering.

'I think they want to destroy themselves.'

Starkey nodded.

'I'll call you to reschedule, Dana. Thanks.'

Starkey went out to her car, keeping her head down as she passed the woman in the waiting room. She slid behind the wheel, but didn't start the engine. Instead, she opened her briefcase and took out a slim silver flask of gin. She took a long drink, then opened the door and threw up in the parking lot.

When she finished heaving, she put away the gin and ate a Tagamet.

Then, doing her best to get a grip on herself, Carol Starkey drove across town to a place exactly like the one where she had died.

Helicopters marked ground zero the way vultures circle roadkill, orbiting over the crime scene in layers like a cake. Starkey saw them just as the traffic locked down, half a mile from the incident site. She used her bubble flasher to edge into an Amaco station, left her car, and walked the remaining eight blocks.

A dozen radio units were on the scene, along with two Bomb Squad Suburbans and a growing army of media people. Kelso was standing near the forward Suburban with the Bomb Squad commander, Dick Leyton, and three of the day-shift bomb techs. Kelso was a short man with a droopy mustache, in a black-checked sport coat. Kelso noticed Starkey, and waved to catch her eye, but Starkey pretended she didn't see him.

Riggio's body lay in a heap in the parking lot, midway between the forward Suburban and the building. A coroner investigator was leaning against his van, watching an LAPD criminalist named John Chen work the body. Starkey didn't know the CI because she had never before worked a case where someone had died, but she knew Chen.

Starkey badged her way past the uniforms at the mouth of the parking lot. One of the uniforms, a younger guy she didn't know, said, 'Man, that dude got the shit blown out of himself. I wouldn't go over there, I was you.'

'You wouldn't?'

'Not if I had a choice.'

Smoking at a crime scene was against LAPD policy, but Starkey fired up before crossing the parking lot to confront Charlie Riggio's body. Starkey had known him from her days on the squad, so she expected this to be hard. It was.

Riggio's helmet and chest protector had been stripped off by the paramedics who had worked to revive him. Shrapnel had cut through the suit, leaving bloody puckers across his chest and stomach that looked blue in the bright afternoon sun. A single hole had been punched in his face, just beneath the left eye. Starkey glanced over at the helmet and saw that the Lexan faceplate was shattered. They said that the Lexan could stop a bullet from a deer rifle. Then she looked back at his body and saw that his hands were missing.

Starkey ate a Tagamet, then turned away so that she wouldn't have to see the body.

'Hey, John. What do we have here?'

'Hey, Starkey. You got the lead on this one?'

'Yeah. Kelso said that Buck Daggett was out, but I don't see him.'

'They sent him to the hospital. He's okay, but he's pretty shook. Leyton wanted him checked.'

'Okay. So what did he say? You got anything I can use?'

Chen glanced back at the body, then pointed out the Dumpster.

'The device was over by that Dumpster. Buck says Riggio was over it with the Real Time when it went off.'

Starkey followed his nod to a large piece of the Real Time portable X-ray that had been blown out into the street. She considered the Dumpster again, and guessed that the Real Time had been kicked more than forty yards. Riggio himself lay almost thirty yards from the Dumpster.

'Did Daggett or the medics pull him over here?'

Anytime there was an explosion, bomb techs were trained to expect a secondary device. She figured that Daggett would have pulled Riggio away from the Dumpster for that reason.

'You'd have to ask Daggett. I think this is where he fell.'

'Jesus. We gotta be, what, thirty yards from the detonation point?'

'Buck said it was a helluva blast.'

She guesstimated the distance again, then toed the body armor to examine the blast pattern. The suit looked as if twenty shotguns had been fired into it point-blank. She'd seen similar suit damage when 'dirty' bombs had gone off with a lot of fire and shrapnel, but this bomb had pushed the shrap through twelve layers of armor and had thrown a man thirty yards. The energy released must have been enormous.

Chen took a plastic bag from his evidence kit, pulling the plastic tight to show her a piece of blackened metal about the size of a postage stamp.

'This is kind of interesting, too. It's a piece of the pipe frag I found stuck in his suit.'

Starkey looked close. A squiggly line had been etched into the metal.

'What is that, an *S*?'

Chen shrugged.

'Or some kind of symbol. Remember that bomb they found in San Diego last year, the one with dicks drawn all over it?'

Starkey ignored him. Chen liked to talk. If he got going about a bomb with dicks on it, she would never get her work done.

'John, do me a favor and swab some of the samples tonight, okay?'

Chen went sulky.

'It's going to be really late when I finish here, Carol. I've got to work the Dumpster, and then there's going to be whatever you guys find in the sweep. It's going to take me two or three hours just to log everything.'

They would search for pieces of the device everywhere within a hundred-yard radius, combing nearby rooftops, the faces of the apartment buildings and houses across the street, cars, the Dumpster, and the wall behind the Dumpster. They would search for anything and everything that might help them reconstruct the bomb or give them a clue to its origins.

'Don't whine, John. It's not cool.'

'I'm just saying.'

'How long does it take to cook through the gas chrom?'

The sulk became sullen and put-upon.

'Six hours.'

Residue from the explosive would be present on any fragments of the bomb they found, as well as in the blast crater and on Riggio's suit. Chen would identify the substance by cooking it through a gas chromatograph, a process which took six hours. Starkey knew how long it would take when she asked, but asked anyway to make Chen feel guilty about it taking so long.

'Couldn't you swab a couple of samples first, just to start a chrom, then log everything after? An explosive with this kind of energy potential could really narrow down the field of guys I'm looking at, John. You could give me a head start here.'

Chen hated to do anything that wasn't methodical and by the book, but he couldn't deny her point. He checked his watch, counting out the time.

'Let me see what time we finish here, okay? I'll try, but I can't guarantee anything.'

'I gave up on guarantees a long time ago.'

Buck Daggett's Suburban sat forty-eight paces from Riggio's body. Starkey counted as she walked.

Kelso and Leyton saw her coming and moved away from the others to meet her. Kelso's face was grim; Leyton's tense and professional. Leyton had been off shift when he'd gotten the call and had rushed over in jeans and a polo shirt.

Leyton smiled softly when their eyes met, and Starkey thought there was a sad quality to it. Leyton, the twelve-year commander of the Bomb Squad, had selected Carol Starkey for the squad, just as he'd selected Charlie Riggio and every other tech below the rank of sergeant-supervisor. He had sent her to the FBI's Bomb School in Alabama and had been her boss for three years. When she had been in the hospital, he had come every day after his shift to visit her, fifty-four consecutive days, and when she had fought to stay on the job, he had lobbied on her behalf. There wasn't anyone on the job she respected as much, or cared for as much.

Starkey said, 'Dick, I want to walk the scene as soon as possible. Could we use as many of your people as you can get out?'

'Everyone not on duty is coming out. You've got us all.'

She turned to Kelso.

'Lieutenant, I'd like to talk to these Rampart guys to see if we can't conscript some of their uniforms to help.'

Kelso was frowning at her.

'I've already arranged it with their supervisor. You shouldn't be smoking here, Starkey.'

'Sorry. I'd better go talk to him, then, and get things organized.'

She made no move to put out her cigarette, and Kelso ignored the obvious rebellion.

'Before you do, you'll be working with Marzik and Santos on this.'

Starkey felt another Tagamet craving.

'Does it have to be Marzik?'

'Yes, Starkey, it has to be Marzik. They're inbound now. And something else. Lieutenant Leyton says we might have a break here before we get started: 911 got a call on this.'

She glanced at Leyton.

'Do we have a wit?'

'An Adam car took the call, but Buck told me they were responding to Emergency Services. If that's the case, then we should have a tape and an address.'

That was a major break.

'Okay. I'll get on it. Thanks.'

Kelso glanced toward the press again, frowning when he saw an LAPD media officer approaching them.

'I think we'd better go make a statement, Dick.'

'Be right there.'

Kelso scurried over to intercept the media officer while Leyton stayed with Starkey. They waited until the other man was gone, then Leyton considered her.

'How you doing, Carol?'

'I'm fine, Lieutenant. Kicking ass and taking names, like always. I'd still like to come back to the squad.'

Leyton found it within himself to nod. They had weathered that pounding three years ago, and both of them knew that the LAPD Personnel Unit would never allow it.

'You were always a tough girl. But you were lucky, too.'

'Sure. I shit luck in the morning.'

'You shouldn't curse like that, Carol. It's not attractive.'

'You're right, Boss. I'll straighten out as soon as I kick the smokes.'

She smiled at him, and Leyton smiled back, because they both knew that she would do neither.

Starkey watched him walk away to join the press conference, then noticed Marzik and Santos talking to a uniformed sergeant amid a group of people outside one of the apartment buildings across the street. Marzik was looking over at her, but Starkey walked around to the front of the Suburban and examined it. The Suburban had faced the blast at about sixty-five yards away. The telex cables and security line that Riggio had pulled out with him still trailed from the rear of the Suburban to Riggio's armored suit, tangled now from the explosion.

The Suburban appeared undamaged, but on closer inspection she saw that the front right headlight was cracked. She squatted to look more closely. A piece of black metal shaped like the letter E was wedged in the glass. Starkey did not touch it. She stared until she recognized that it was part of a metal buckle from the straps that had held Riggio's armor suit. She sighed deep and long, then stood and looked back at his body.

The coroner's people were placing him into a body bag. John Chen had outlined the body's location on the tarmac with white chalk and now stood back, watching with an expression of profound disinterest.

Starkey wiped her palms on her hips and forced herself to take deep breaths, stretching her ribs and her lungs. Doing this hurt because of the scars. Marzik, still across the street, was waving. Santos looked over, maybe wondering why Starkey was just standing there.

Starkey waved back, the wave saying that she would join them in a moment.

The mall was a small strip of discount clothing shops, a used-book store, a dentist who advertised 'family prices' in Spanish, and a Cuban restaurant, all of which had been evacuated before Riggio approached the bomb.

Starkey forced herself toward the restaurant, moving on legs that were suddenly weak, as if she'd found herself on a tightrope and the only way off was that singular door. Marzik was forgotten. Charlie Riggio was forgotten.

Starkey felt nothing but her own hammering heart; and knew that if she lost control of it now, and of herself, she would certainly fall to her death.

When Starkey stepped into the restaurant, she began to shake with a rage beyond all hope of control. She had to grip the counter to keep her feet. If Leyton or Kelso walked in now, her career would be finished. Kelso would order her into the bank for sure, she would be forced to retire with the medical, and all that would be left of Carol Starkey's life would be fear, and emptiness.

Starkey clawed open her purse for the silver flask, feeling the gin cut into her throat in the same moment she cursed her own weakness, and felt ashamed. She breathed deep, refusing to sit because she knew she would not be able to rise. She took a second long pull on the flask, and the shaking subsided.

Starkey fought down the memories and the fear, telling herself she was only doing what she needed to do and that everything would be all right. She was too tough for it. She would beat it. She would win.

After a while, she had herself together.

Starkey put away the flask, sprayed her mouth with Binaca, then went back out to the crime scene.

She was always a tough girl.

Starkey found the two Adam car officers, who gave her the log time of their original dispatch call. She used her cell phone to call the day manager at Emergency Services, identified herself, provided an approximate time, and requested a tape of the call as well as an address of origin. What most people didn't know was that all calls to 911 were automatically taped and recorded with the originating phone number and that phone number's address. It had to be this way because people in an emergency situation, especially when threatened or dying, couldn't be expected to provide their location. So the system took that into account and provided the address for them.

Starkey left her office number, and asked the manager to provide the information as quickly as she had it.

When Starkey was finished with Emergency Services, she walked across to the apartment buildings where Marzik and Santos were questioning the few residents who had been let back into the area. They saw her coming, and walked out to meet her by the street.

Jorge Santos was a short man with a quizzical expression who always looked as if he was trying to remember something that he'd forgotten. His name was pronounced 'whore-hey', which had earned him the dubious nickname of Hooker. Beth Marzik was divorced, with two kids who stayed with her mother when she was on the job. She sold Amway products for the extra money, but she pushed it so hard that half the detectives at Spring Street would duck when they saw her approaching.

Starkey said, 'Good news. Leyton says the call-out was responding to a 911.'

Marzik smirked.

'This good citizen happen to leave a name?'

'I already put in a call to Emergency Services. They'll run the tapes and have something for us as soon as they can.'

Marzik nudged Santos.

'Bet you a dollar to a blow job there's no name.'

Santos darkened. He was a religious man, married with four children, and hated it when she talked like that.

Starkey interrupted her.

'I've gotta get the uniforms set up for the sweep. Dick says the Rampart detectives offered to help with the door-to-door.'

Marzik frowned as if she didn't like that idea.

'Well, we're not going to get to most of these people tonight. What I'm hearing is that a lot of the people who were evacuated went to relatives or friends after the damned thing blew.'

'You're getting a list of residents from the managers, right?'

'Yeah. So?'

Marzik looked suspicious. Her attitude made Starkey tired.

'Get the managers to pull the rental apps, too. They should be on file. Most of the rental applications I used to fill out wanted the name of a relative or somebody to vouch for you. That's probably where those people went.'

'Shit, that'll take forever. I *used* to have a date tonight.'

Santos's face grew longer than ever.

'I'll do it, Carol.'

Starkey glanced toward the Dumpster, where Chen was now picking at something on the ground. She gestured back toward the apartment buildings behind them.

'Look, Beth, I'm not saying do everybody on the goddamned block. Just ask if they saw something. Ask if they're the one who called 911. If they say they didn't see anything, tell'm to think about it and we'll get back to them in the next few days.'

Marzik still wasn't happy, but Starkey didn't give a damn.

She went back across the street to the Dumpster, leaving Marzik and Santos with the apartments. Chen was examining the wall behind the Dumpster for bomb fragments. Out in the parking lot, two of the Bomb Squad technicians were adjusting radial metal detectors that they would use when they walked the lawns out front of the surrounding apartment buildings. Two more off-duty bomb techs had arrived, and pretty soon everyone would be standing around with their thumbs up their asses, waiting for her to tell them what to do.

Starkey ignored all of them and went to the crater. It was about three feet across and one foot deep, the black tarmac scorched white by the heat.

Starkey wanted to place her hand on the surface, but didn't because the explosive residue might be toxic.

She considered the chalk outline where Riggio's body had fallen, then paced it off. Almost forty paces. The energy to kick him this far must have been incredible.

Starkey impulsively stepped into Riggio's outline, standing exactly where his body had fallen, and gazed back at the crater.

She imagined a slow-motion flash that stretched through three years. She saw her own death as if it had been filmed and later shown to her on instant replay. Her shrink, Dana, had called these 'manufactured memories'. She had taken the facts as they had later been presented to her, imagined the rest, then saw the events as if she remembered them. Dana believed that this was her mind's way of trying to deal with what had happened, her mind's way of removing her from the actual event by letting her step outside the moment, her mind's way of giving the evil a face so that it could be dealt with.

Starkey sucked deep on the cigarette, then blew smoke angrily at the ground. If this was her mind's way of making peace with what had happened, it was doing a damned shitty job.

She went back across the street to find Marzik.

'Beth? I got another idea. Try to locate the people who own all these shops and see if anyone was threatened, or owed money, or whatever.'

Marzik nodded, still squinting at her.

'Carol, what is that?'

'What is what?'

Marzik stepped closer and sniffed.

'Is that Binaca?'

Starkey glared at Marzik, then went back across the street and spent the rest of the evening helping the search team look for pieces of the bomb.

In the dream, she dies.

She opens her eyes on the hard-packed trailer-park earth as the paramedics work over her, their latex hands red with blood. The hum in her ears makes her think of a Mixmaster set to a slow speed. Above her, the thin branches of winter gum trees overlap in a delicate lace still swaying from the pressure wave. A paramedic pushes on her chest, trying to restart her heart. Another inserts a long needle. Cold silver paddles press to her flesh.

A thousand miles beyond the hum, a voice yells, 'Clear!' Her body lurches from the jolt of current.

Starkey finds the strength to say his name.

'Sugar?'

She is never certain if she says his name or only thinks that she says it.

Her head lolls, and she sees him. David 'Sugar' Boudreaux, a Cajun long out of Louisiana but still with the soft French accent that she finds so sexy. Her sergeant-supervisor. Her secret lover. The man to whom she's given her heart.

'Sugar?'

The faraway voices shout. 'No pulse!' 'Clear!' The horrible electric spasm.

She reaches toward Sugar, but he is too far away. It is not fair that he is so far. Two hearts that beat as one should not be so far apart. The distance saddens her.

'Shug?'

Two hearts that no longer beat.

The paramedics working on Sugar step away. He is gone.

Her body jolts again, but it does no good, and she is at peace with it.

She closes her eyes and feels herself rise through the branches into the sky, and all she knows is relief.

Starkey woke from the dream just after three that morning, knowing that sleep was beyond her. She lit a cigarette, then lay in the dark, smoking. She had finished at the crime scene just before midnight, but didn't get home until almost one. There, she showered, ate scrambled eggs, then drank a tumbler of Bombay Sapphire gin to knock herself out. Yet here she was, wide awake two hours later.

After another twenty minutes of blowing smoke at the ceiling, she got out of bed, then went through the house, turning on every light.

The bomb that took Starkey had been a package bomb delivered by a meth dealer to murder the family of an informant. It had been placed behind heavy bushes on the side of the informant's double-wide, which meant Sugar and Starkey couldn't use the robot to wheel in the X-ray or the de-armer. It was a dirty bomb, made of a paint can packed with smokeless powder and roofing tacks. Whoever had made the bomb was a mean sonofabitch who wanted to make sure he got the informant's three children.

Because of the bushes, Starkey and Sugar both had to work the bomb, Starkey holding aside the brush so that Sugar could get close with the Real Time. When two uniformed patrol officers had called in the suspicious package, they had reported that the package was ticking. It was such a cliché that Starkey and Sugar had burst out laughing, though they weren't laughing now because the package had stopped ticking. The Real Time showed them that the timer had malfunctioned; the builder had used a hand-wound alarm clock as his timing device, but, for some inexplicable reason, the minute hand had frozen at one minute before reaching the lead that would detonate the bomb. It had just stopped.

Sugar made a joke of it.

'Guess he forgot to wind the damned thing.'

She was grinning at his joke when the earthquake struck. An event every bomb tech working in Southern California feared. It would later be reported as 3.2 on the Richter scale, hardly noticeable to the average Angeleno, but the minute hand released, contact was made, and the bomb went off.

The old techs had always told Starkey that the suit would not save her from the frag, and they were right. Sugar saved her. He leaned in front of her just as the bomb went off, so his body caught most of the tacks. But the Real Time was blown out of his hands, and that's what got her. Two heavy, jagged pieces sliced through the suit, ripped along her right side, and dug a gaping furrow through her right breast. Sugar was knocked back into her, microseconds behind the Real Time. The force of him impacting into her felt as if she had been kicked by God. The shock was so enormous that her heart stopped.

For two minutes and forty seconds, Carol Starkey was dead.

Two teams of emergency medical personnel rushed forward even as pieces of the trailer and torn azalea bushes fell around them. The team that reached Starkey found her without a pulse, peeled away her suit, and injected epinephrine directly into her heart as they administered CPR. They worked for almost three minutes around the blood and gore that had been her chest and finally – heroically – restarted her heart.

Her heart had started again; Dave 'Sugar' Boudreaux's had not.

Starkey sat at her dinette table, thinking about the dream, and Sugar, and smoking more cigarettes. Only three years, and the memories of Sugar were fading. It was harder to see his face, and harder still to hear his soft Cajun accent. More often than not, now, she returned to their pictures to refresh her memories and hated herself for having to do that. As if she was betraying him by forgetting. As if the permanence she had once felt about their passion and love had all been a lie told by someone else to a woman who no longer lived.

Everything had changed.

Starkey had started drinking almost as soon as she got out of the hospital. One of her shrinks – she thought it was number two – had said that her issue was survivor's guilt. Guilt that her heart had started, and Sugar's had not; guilt that she had lived, and he had not; guilt that, down deep, down in the center of herself where our secret creatures live, she was *thankful* that she had lived, even at the price of Sugar's life. Starkey had walked out of the therapist's office that day and never went back. She had gone to a cop bar called the Shortstop and drank until two Wilshire Division robbery detectives carried her out of the place.

Everything had changed.

Starkey pulled away from people. She grew cold. She protected herself with sarcasm and distance and the single-minded pursuit of her job until the job was all that she had. Another shrink – she thought it was number three – suggested that she had traded one armored suit for another, then asked if she thought she would ever be able to take it off.

Starkey did not return to answer.

Tired of thinking, Starkey finished her cigarette, then returned to her bedroom to shower. She pulled off her T-shirt and looked at herself with an absence of feeling.

The right half of her abdomen from her breast to her hip was rilled and cratered from the sixteen bits of metal that had punched into her. Two long furrows roped along her side, following her lower ribs. Once tanned a walnut brown, her skin was now as white as a table plate because Starkey hadn't worn a bathing suit since it happened.

The worst of it was her breast. A two-inch piece of the Real Time had impacted on the front of her right breast just beneath the nipple, gouging out a furrow of tissue as it followed the line of her ribs before exiting her back. It had laid her open as if a river valley had been carved in her chest, and that is the way it healed. Her doctors had discussed removing the breast, but decided to save it. They had, but even after the reconstruction, it looked like a misshapen avocado. Her doctors had told her that further cosmetic surgeries could, in time, improve her appearance, but after four operations, Starkey had decided that enough was enough.

She had not been with another man since Sugar had left her bed that morning.

Starkey showered, dressed for the day, then called her office and found two messages.

'It's me, Starkey, John Chen. I got a pretty good swab from the blast crater. I'll set it up in the cooker, but that means I won't be out of here until after three. We should have the chrom around nine. Gimme a call. You owe me.'

The Emergency Services manager had left the second message, saying that she'd duped the tape of the 911 call reporting the suspicious device.

'I left the tape at the security desk, so you can pick it up anytime you want. The call was placed from a pay phone on Sunset Boulevard at one-fourteen, that would be yesterday afternoon. I've got a street address here.'

Starkey copied the information into a spiral casebook, then made a cup of instant coffee. She swallowed two Tagamet, then lit a cigarette before letting herself out into the sultry night air.

It was not quite five, and the world was quiet. A kid in a beat-up red hatchback was delivering the L.A. *Times,* weaving from side to side in the street as he tossed out the papers. An Alta-Dena dairy truck rumbled past.

Starkey decided to drive back to Silver Lake and walk the blast site again. It was better than listening to the silence in her still-beating heart.

Starkey parked in front of the Cuban restaurant next to a Rampart radio car watching over the scene. The mall's parking lot was otherwise deserted, except for three civilian vehicles that she remembered from the night before.

Starkey held up her badge before she got out.

'Hey, guys, everything okay?'

They were a male/female team, the male officer a skinny guy behind the wheel, the female short and chunky with mannish blond hair. They were sipping minimart coffee that probably hadn't been hot for hours.

The female officer nodded.

'Yeah. We're good, Detective. You need something?'

'I've got the case. I'm gonna be walking around.'

The female officer raised her eyebrows.

'We heard a bomb guy got creamed. That so?'

'Yeah.'

'Bummer.'

The male officer leaned past his partner.

'If you're gonna be here a few, you mind if we Code Seven? There's an In-'n-Out Burger a couple blocks over. We could bring you something.'

His partner winked at Starkey.

'Weak bladder.'

Starkey shrugged, secretly pleased to be rid of them.

'Take twenty, but you don't have to bring me anything. I won't be out of here before then.'

As the radio car pulled away, Starkey clipped her pistol to her right hip, then crossed Sunset to look for the address that the Emergency Services manager had provided. She brought her Maglite, but didn't turn it on. The area was bright from surrounding security lights.

A pay phone was hanging on the side of a Guatemalan market directly across from the mall, but when Starkey compared it to the address, they didn't match. From the Guatemalan market, she could look back across Sunset at the Dumpster. She figured out which way the numbers ran and followed them to find the pay phone. It was housed in one of the old glass booths that Pac Bell was discontinuing, one block east on the side of a laundry, across the street from a flower shop.

Starkey copied the names of the laundry and flower shop into her notebook, then walked back to the first phone and checked to see if it worked. It did. She wondered why the person who called 911 hadn't done so from here. The Dumpster was in clear view, but wasn't from the other phone. Starkey thought that the caller might've been worried that whoever set the bomb could see them, but she decided not to worry about it until she heard the tape.

Starkey was walking back across Sunset when she saw a piece of bent metal in the street. It was about an inch long and twisted like a piece of bow-tie pasta, one side rimed with gray residue. She had picked up nine similar pieces of metal the night before.

She brought it to her car, bagged it in one of the spare evidence bags she kept in the trunk, then walked around the side of the building to the Dumpster. Starkey guessed that the bomb hadn't been placed to damage the building, but wondered why it had been set beside the Dumpster. She knew that satisfying reasons for questions like this often couldn't be found. Twice during her time with the Bomb Squad, she had rolled out on devices left on the side of the freeway, far away from overpasses or exits or anything else they might harm. It was as if the assholes who built these things didn't know what else to do with them, so they just dropped them off on the side of the road.

Starkey walked the scene for another ten minutes and found one more small bit of metal. She was bagging it when the radio car returned to the lot, and the female officer got out with two cups.

'I know you said you didn't want anything, but we brought a coffee in case you changed your mind.'

'That was nice. Thanks.'

The female officer wanted to chat, but Starkey closed the trunk and told her she needed to get into the office. When the officer went back to her unit, Starkey walked around the far side of her own car and poured out the coffee. She was heading back to the driver's side when she decided to look over the civilian cars again.

Two of the cars had been pinged by bomb frag, the nearest of which had lost its rear window and suffered substantial damage. Parked closest to the blast, it belonged to the man who owned the bookshop. When the police let him back into the area, he had stared at his car, then kicked it and walked away without another word.

The third car, the one farthest away, was a '68 Impala with bad paint and peeling vinyl top. The side windows were down and the rear window had been replaced by cloudy plastic that was brittle with sun damage. She looked beneath it first, found nothing, and was walking around the front of the car when she saw a starburst crack on the windshield. She flashed the Maglite inside and saw a round piece of metal on the dash. It looked like a disk with a single fine wire protruding. Starkey glanced toward the Dumpster and saw it was possible that a piece of frag had come through the open windows to crack the windshield. She fished it out, examined it more closely with no idea what it might be, then dropped it into her pocket.

Starkey climbed back into her car without looking at the uniformed officers, then headed downtown to pick up the audiotape before reporting to her office. The sun was rising in the east, filling the sky with a great red fireball.

Mr Red

John Michael Fowles leaned back on the bench across from the school, enjoying the sun and wondering if he had made the FBI's Ten Most Wanted List. Not an easy thing to do when they didn't know who you were, but he'd been leaving clues. He thought he might stop in a Kinko's later, or maybe the library, and use one of their computers to check the FBI's web page for the standings.

The sun made him smile. He raised his face to it, letting the warmth soak into him, letting its radiation brown his skin, marveling at the enormity of its exploding gases. That's the way he liked to think of it: one great monstrous explosion so large and bright that it could be seen from ninety-three million miles away, fueled so infinitely that it would take billions of years to consume itself, so fucking cool that the very fact of it spawned life here on this planet and would eventually consume that life when it gave a last flickering gasp and blew itself out billions of years from now.

John thought it would be seriously cool to build a bomb that big and set the sucker off. How cool it would be to see those first few nanoseconds of its birth. Way cool.

Thinking about it, John felt a hardening in his groin of a kind that had never been inspired by any living thing.

The voice said, 'Are you Mr Red?'

John opened his eyes. Even with his sunglasses, he had to shield his eyes. John flashed the big white teeth.

'I be him. Are you Mr Karpov?'

Making like a Florida cracker talking street, even though John was neither from Florida, nor a cracker, nor the street. He enjoyed the misdirection.

'Yes.'

Karpov was an overweight man in his fifties, with a heavily lined face and graying widow's peak. A Russian emigrant of dubious legality with several businesses in the area. He was clearly nervous, which John expected and enjoyed. Victor Karpov was a criminal.

John scooted to the side and patted the bench.

'Here. Sit. We'll talk.'

Karpov dropped like a stone onto the bench. He clutched a nylon bag with both hands the way an older woman would hold a purse. In front, for protection.

Karpov said, 'Thank you for doing this, sir. I have these awful problems that must be dealt with. These terrible enemies.'

John put his hand on the bag, gently trying to pry it away.

'I know all about your problems, Mr Karpov. We don't need to say another word about'm.'

'Yes. Yes, well, thank you for agreeing to do this. Thank you.'

'You don't have to thank me, Mr Karpov, you surely don't.'

John would have never even spoken to the man, let alone agreed to do what he was about to do and meet Karpov like this, if he had not thoroughly researched Victor Karpov. John's business was by referral only, and John had spoken with those who had referred him. Those men had in fact asked John's permission to suggest his name to Karpov, and were in a position to assure Karpov's character. John was big on character. He was big on secrecy, and covering one's ass. Which is why these people did not know him by his real name or know anything about him at all except for his trade. Through them, John knew the complete details of Karpov's problem, what would be required, and had already decided that he would take the job before their first contact.

That was how you stayed on the Most Wanted List, and out of prison.

'Leave go of the bag, Mr Karpov.'

Karpov let go of the bag as if it were stinging him.

John laughed, taking the bag into his own lap.

'You don't have to be nervous, Mr Karpov. You're among friends here, believe you me. It don't get no friendlier than what I'm feeling for you right now. You know how friendly it gets?'

Karpov stared at him without comprehension.

'I think we're such good friends, me and you, that I'm not even gonna look in this bag until later. That's how such good friends we are. We're so fuckin' tight, you and me, that I know there is *exactly* the right amount of cash in here, and I'm willing to bet your life on it. How's that for friendly?'

Karpov's eyes bulged large, and he swallowed.

'It is all there. It is exactly what you said, in fifties and twenties. Please count it now. Please count it so that you are satisfied.'

John shook his head and dropped the sack onto the bench opposite Karpov.

'Nope. We'll just let this little scenario play out the way it will and hope you didn't count wrong.'

Karpov reached across him for the sack.

'Please.'

John laughed and pushed Karpov back.

'Don't you worry about it, Mr Karpov. I'm just funnin' with you.'

Funnin'. Like he was an idiot as well as a cracker.

'Here. I want to show you something.'

He took a small tube from his pocket and held it out. It used to be a dime-store flashlight, the kind with a push-button switch in the end opposite the bulb. It wasn't a flashlight anymore.

'Go ahead and take it. The damned thing won't bite.'

Karpov took it.

'What is this?'

John tipped his head toward the schoolyard across the street. It was lunchtime. The kids were running around, playing in the few minutes before they would have to troop back into class.

'Lookit those kids over there. I been watchin'm. Pretty little girls and boys. Man, look at how they're just running around, got all the energy in the world, all that free spirit and potential. You're that age, I guess everything's still possible, ain't it? Lookit that little boy in the blue shirt. Over there to the right, Karpov, Jesus, right there. Good-lookin' little fella, blond, freckles. Christ, bet the little sonofabitch could grow up fuckin' all the cheerleaders he wants, then be the goddamned President to boot. Shit like that can't happen over there where you're from, can it? But here, man, this is the fuckin' US of A, and you can do any goddamned thing you want until they start tellin' you that you can't.'

Karpov was staring at him, the tube in his hand forgotten.

'Right now, anything in that child's head is possible, and it'll stay possible till that fuckin' cheerleader calls him a pizzaface and her retarded fullback boyfriend beats the shit out of him for talking to his girl. Right now, that boy is happy, Mr Karpov, just look at how happy, but all that is gonna end just as soon as he realizes all those hopes and dreams he has ain't never gonna work.'

John slowly let his eyes drift to the tube.

'You could save that poor child all that grief, Mr Karpov. Somewhere very close to us there is a device. I have built that device, and placed it carefully, and you now control it.'

Karpov looked at the tube. His expression was as milky as if he were holding a rattlesnake.

'If you press that little silver button, maybe you can save that child the pain he's gonna face. I'm not sayin' the device is over there in that school, but I'm sayin' maybe. Maybe that whole fuckin' playground would erupt in a beautiful red firestorm. Maybe those babies would be hit so hard by the pressure wave that all their shoes would just be left scattered on the ground, and the clothes and skin would scorch right off their bones. I ain't sayin' that, but there it is right there in that silver button. You can end that boy's pain. You have the power. You can turn the world to hell, you want, because you have the power right there in that little silver button. I have created it, and now I've given it to you. You. Right there in your hand.'

Karpov stood and thrust the tube at John.

'I want no part of this. Take it. *Take it.*'

John slowly took the tube. He fingered the silver button.

'When I do what you want me to do, Mr Karpov, people are gonna die. What's the fuckin' difference?'

'The money is all there. Every dollar. All of it.'

Karpov walked away without another word. He crossed the street, walking so fast that his strides became a kind of hop, as if he expected the world around him to turn to flame.

John dropped the tube into the nylon bag with the money.

They never seemed to appreciate the gift he offered.

John settled back again, stretched his arms along the backrest to enjoy the sun and the sounds of the children playing. It was a beautiful day, and would grow even more beautiful when a second sun had risen.

After a while he got up and walked away to check the Most Wanted List. Last week he wasn't on it.

This week he hoped to be.

2

The Criminal Conspiracy Section where Starkey worked is housed on the fifth floor of an eight-story office building on Spring Street, just a few blocks from the LAPD's seat of power, Parker Center. LAPD's Fugitive Section and Internal Affairs Group are also housed there, on the fourth and sixth floors. The building is known to have the most congested parking of any building in city government, with the detectives on each floor having to wedge their cars together with barely enough room to open their doors. The officers who work there nicknamed the building 'Code Three' because, if they had to respond to an actual emergency, they would make better time running out of the building on foot to grab a cab.

Starkey parked on the third floor after ten minutes of maneuvering, then climbed the steps to the fifth floor. She noticed Marzik watching her as soon as she walked in, and decided to see if Marzik wanted to make something of the Binaca. Starkey went over, stopping in Marzik's face.

'What?'

Marzik met her gaze without looking away.

'I got those rental apps, like you wanted. I figure most of those people will go home today, and we can talk to them first. If anyone doesn't show, we can use the apps to find them.'

'Is there anything else?'

'Like what?'

'Like whatever you need to say?'

'I'm fine.'

Starkey let it go. If Marzik confronted her about the drinking, she didn't know what she could do except lie.

'Okay. I've got the 911 call. Is Hooker in?'

'Yeah. I saw him.'

'Let's listen to the tape, then I want to get over to Glendale. Chen's gonna have the chrom, and I want to see how they're coming with the reconstruction.'

'They just started. How far could they be?'

'Far enough to know some of the components, Beth. We get some manufacturers, we get the chrom, we can get going here.'

'We got all these interviews to do.'

Marzik made her tired. It was a shitty way to start the day.

'You guys can start in with the interviews while I'm over there. Round up Jorge and come to the desk.'

'I think he's in the crapper.'

'Knock on the door, Beth. Jesus Christ.'

Starkey borrowed a cassette player from the section sergeant, Leon Tooley, and brought it to her desk. Each CCS detective had a desk in a partitioned cubicle in the larger main room. There was the illusion of privacy, but the partitions were just low dividers, meaning that there was no real privacy. Everyone spoke in whispers unless they were showing off for Kelso, who spent most of his time hidden behind his office door. Rumor had it that he spent his day on the Internet, trading his stock portfolio.

Marzik and Santos showed up a few minutes later with coffee, Santos saying, 'Did you see Kelso?'

'No. Should I?'

'He asked to see you this morning.'

Starkey glanced at Marzik, but Marzik's face was unreadable.

'Well, Jesus, Jorge, nice of someone to tell me. Look, let's listen to this before I see him.'

Santos and Marzik pulled up chairs as Starkey turned on the tape. The sound started with the Emergency Services operator, a black female, and was followed by a male voice with a heavy Spanish accent.

EMS: 911. May I help you?

CALLER: 'aullu?

EMS: May I help you, sir?

CALLER: Eh ... se habla español?

EMS: I can transfer you to a Spanish speaker.

CALLER: Eh ... no, is okay. Lissen, you better sen' a man to look here.

Santos leaned forward and stopped the tape.

'What's that behind him?'

Starkey said, 'It sounds like a truck or a bus. He's calling from a pay phone just off Sunset, a block east of the mall.'

Marzik crossed her arms.

'Isn't there a pay phone right there outside that Cuban restaurant?'

'Yeah, and there's another across the street at that little food store, the Guatemalan place. But he walked down a block.'

Santos looked at her.

'How do you know that?'

'EMS called back with the address. I walked the scene again this morning.'

Marzik made a grunt, staring at the floor. Like only a loser without a life would do something like that.

Starkey started the tape again.

EMS: Look at what, sir?
CALLER: Eh ... I look in dis box, and I tink dere's a bomb in dere.
EMS: A bomb?
CALLER: Dese pipes, see? I dunno. It made me scared.
EMS: Could I have your name, sir?
CALLER: Is by the trash dere, you know? The beeg can.
EMS: I need your name, sir.
CALLER: You better come see.

The line clicked when the man hung up. That was the end of the tape. Starkey turned off the machine.

Marzik frowned.

'If it's legit, why wouldn't he leave his name?'

Santos shrugged.

'You know how people are. Could be he's illegal. He's probably just some neighborhood guy, around there all the time.'

Starkey scrounged for something to write on. The best she could do was a copy of *The Blue Line*, the LAPD's union newspaper. She drew a rough street map, showing the mall and the location of the phones.

'He says he looked in the bag. Okay. That means he's here at the mall. He says it scared him, seeing the pipes like that, so why not just use the phone right here outside the Cuban place or over here across the street? Why walk another block east?'

Marzik crossed her arms again. Every time Marzik didn't like something, she crossed her arms. Starkey could read her like the daily news.

'Maybe he wasn't sure it was a bomb, and then he wasn't sure he wanted to call. People have to talk themselves into things. Christ, sometimes I gotta talk myself into taking a shit.'

Santos frowned at Marzik's mouth, then tapped the phone outside the laundry.

'If I found something I thought was a bomb, I'd want to get as far away from it as possible. I wouldn't want to stand next to it. Maybe he was scared it would explode.'

Starkey considered that, and nodded. It made sense. She tossed *The Blue Line* into her wastebasket.

'Well, whatever. We've got the time of the call. Maybe someone around there saw something, and we can straighten this out.'

Santos nodded.

'Okay. You want to do that while we get the apartment houses?'

'One of you guys swing past, okay, Hook? I've gotta meet Chen over in Glendale.'

Starkey gave them the addresses, then went in to see Kelso. She walked in without knocking.

'Hooker said you wanted to see me.'

Kelso jerked away from his computer and swiveled around to peer at her. He had stopped telling her not to barge in over a year ago.

'Would you close the door, please, Carol, then come sit down.'

Starkey closed the door, then marched back across his office and stood at his desk. She was right about that cow Marzik. She didn't sit.

Kelso squirmed behind his desk because he wasn't sure how to come at what he wanted to say.

'I just want to make sure you're okay with this.'

'With what, Barry?'

'You seemed just a little, ah, strained last night. And, ah, I just want to be sure you're okay with being the lead here.'

'Are you replacing me?'

He began to rock, his body language revealing that that was exactly what he was thinking.

'Not at all, Carol. No. But this case strikes close to home with you, and we've had these, ah, episodes recently.'

He let it hang as if he didn't know how to carry it further.

Starkey felt the shakes coming on, but fought them down. She was furious with Marzik and terrified that Kelso might reconsider ordering her to the bank.

'Did Marzik say that I was drinking?'

Kelso showed both palms.

'Let's leave Marzik out of this.'

'You saw me at the crime scene, Barry. Did I act drunk or unprofessional to you?'

'That's not what I'm asking. You've been wound a little on the tight side, Carol. We both know that because we've talked about it. Last night you were confronted with a situation very similar to one that you yourself barely survived. Perhaps you were unnerved.'

'You're talking about replacing me.'

'I left our conversation last night thinking that I smelled gin. Did I?'

Starkey met his eyes.

'No, sir. You smelled Binaca. I ate Cuban for lunch, and I was blowing garlic all day. That's what you and Marzik smelled.'

He showed his palms again.

'Let's leave Marzik out of this. Marzik didn't say anything to me.'

Starkey knew he was lying. If Kelso had smelled gin on her breath, he would've said something at the scene. He was running with Marzik's complaint.

Starkey was very careful in how she stood. She knew he would be reading her body language the same way she read his. He would look for any sign of defensiveness.

Finally, he settled back, relieved that he'd said what he needed to say and had been the responsible commander.

'All right, Carol, this is your case. I just want you to know I'm here for you.'

'I need to get over to Glendale, Lieutenant. The quicker I can get hard news on the bomb, the faster we can bag this puke.'

Kelso leaned back, dismissing her.

'All right. If you need anything, you know I'm here. This is an important case, Carol. A human being died. More, an officer died, which makes it personal.'

'It's personal to me and the guys on the Bomb Squad, Lieutenant. Believe it.'

'I imagine it would be. Just take it easy, Carol, and we'll get through this all right.'

Starkey went back into the squad room, looking for Marzik, but she and Santos had already left. She gathered her things, then wrestled her car out of the parking lot jockeying spots with a fat IAG detective named Marley. It took her almost fifteen minutes to get out of the building, and then she pulled to the curb, so angry at Marzik that her hands were shaking.

The flask of gin was beneath her seat, but Starkey didn't touch it. She thought about it, but she didn't touch it.

Starkey lit another cigarette, then drove like a bat out of hell, blowing smoke like a furnace.

It was only eight-thirty when Starkey pulled into the Glendale PD parking lot. Chen had said he'd have the chromatograph by nine, but Starkey figured that he'd built a fuck-up and paperwork cushion into that estimate.

She sat in her car smoking for five minutes before using her cell phone to call SID.

'John, it's Starkey. I'm out here in the lot. You have the results?'

'You're outside right now?'

'Affirmative. I'm on my way in to see Leyton.'

Instead of giving her attitude or excuses, Chen said, 'Give me two minutes and I'll be right down. You're gonna love this.'

The LAPD Bomb Squad is based in a low-slung modern building adjacent to the Glendale police substation and piggybacked with the Scientific Investigation Division.

The building is built of red brick and snuggled behind a stand of rubber trees, most people would mistake it for a dental office, except that it is also snuggled behind a ten-foot fence topped with concertina wire. The parking lot is dotted with dark blue Bomb Squad Suburbans.

Starkey let herself into the Bomb Squad reception area and asked for Lieutenant Leyton. He'd stayed out with the others at the crime scene, walking the sweep like everyone else. Dark rings had set in around his eyes,

making him look older than she'd ever seen him, even after Sugar
Boudreaux died.

Starkey handed over the baggie.

'I walked the scene again this morning and found these. You got
someone on the reconstruction yet?'

Leyton held up the baggie to look. All three bits would have to be logged
into the evidence records, then tested to see if they were actually part of the
device.

'Russ Daigle. He came in early to start sorting what we recovered last
night.'

'Chen's on his way down with the chrom. I was hoping to snatch
whatever component manufacturers you have, so I can get rolling with
this.'

'Sure. Let's see what he has.'

She followed Leyton down a long hall past the ready room and the
sergeants' offices to the squad room. It didn't look like any other squad
room in the department; it looked like a high school science lab, all small
cramped desks and black Formica workbenches.

Every surface in the squad room was covered with de-armed bombs or
bomb facsimiles, from pipe bombs and dynamite bombs to canister bombs
and large military ordnance. An air-to-air missile hung from the ceiling.
Trade journals and reference books cluttered any surface not sporting a
bomb. FBI wanted posters were taped to the walls.

Russ Daigle was perched on a stool at one of the workbenches, sorting
pieces of metal. Daigle was one of the squad's three sergeant-supervisors,
and the man who had the most time on the squad. He was a short, athletic
man with a thick gray mustache and blunt fingers. He was wearing latex
gloves.

He glanced up when he heard them, nodding toward a smudged
computer at the end of his workbench. It was covered with *Babylon 5*
stickers.

'We got the snaps up. You wanna see?'

'You bet.'

She moved behind him to see the monitor.

'End and side view. We got others, but these are the best. It's a classic
goddamned pipe bomb. Betcha some turd built it in his garage.'

The digital snapshots that Riggio had taken were displayed on the
screen. They showed the two pipes as impenetrable black shadows neatly
taped together with a spool of wire fixed to the cleft between them. All four
pipe ends were capped. Starkey studied the images, comparing them to the
bits of jagged black metal that were spread on white butcher's paper. One
of the end caps was still intact, but the others were broken. Daigle had
divided them by size and conformation, exactly the way you would the
pieces in any other puzzle. He already had the major parts of all four caps

separated and had made good progress with the tubes, but it was clear that forty or fifty percent of the pieces were still missing.

'What do we have, Sarge? Looks like typical galvanized iron pipe, two-inch diameter?'

He picked up a piece of end cap that showed a letter *V* cast into the iron.

'Yeah. See the *V*? Vanguard pipe company. Buy it anywhere in the country.'

Starkey made note of it in her pad. She would compile a list of components and characteristics, and feed them through the National Law Enforcement Telecommunications System to the FBI's Bomb Data Center and the ATF's National Repository in Washington. The BDC and NR would search for signature matches with every bomb report in their systems.

Daigle ran his finger up under the edge of the cap, flaking off something brittle and white.

'See that? Plumber's joint tape. We got us a neat boy, here. Very precise. Even taped the joints. What does that tell you?'

Starkey knew that the old sergeant had already drawn a conclusion and was testing her. He'd done the same thing a hundred times when she was on the squad.

'You're plumbing your sink, you maybe want to tape the joints, but you sure as hell don't need to tape a bomb.'

Daigle grinned, proud that she'd seen it.

'That's right. No reason to tape it, so maybe he does it out of habit, you know? Could be he's a plumber or a building contractor of some kind.'

Another note for the feds.

'Both pipes are the same size, as near as I can measure from the snaps. He either cut or had'm cut to length, and he was particular. You see the tape shadow here, how careful he wrapped the tape? We got us a particular boy here, and he's good with his hands. Very precise.'

Already Starkey was getting a picture of the builder. He might be a skilled tradesman or a machinist or a hobbiest who took pride in precision, like a model builder or woodworker.

'Did Chen show you the *5*?'

'What *5*?'

Daigle placed a piece of the tube frag under the glass. It was the S that Chen had pulled from Riggio's armor.

'It looks like an *S*.'

Leyton said, 'We're not sure what it is, an *S*, or a *5*, or some kind of symbol.'

Daigle peered close at the glass.

'Whatever it is, he cut it in with a high-speed engraving tool.'

Chen came in while they were discussing the snaps. Like the others, he looked as if he hadn't slept much, but he was excited when he handed Starkey the chrom results.

'I can tell you right now I'm cooking another sample to confirm, but the explosive was something called Modex Hybrid. He didn't buy this at the local hardware store.'

They looked at him.

'The military uses it in artillery warheads and air-to-air missiles. We're talking about a burn rate of twenty-eight thousand feet per second.'

Daigle grunted. The burn rate was a measure of how fast the explosive consumed itself and released energy. The more powerful the explosive, the faster the burn rate.

'TNT goes, what, twenty thousand feet per second?'

Starkey said, 'Twenty, twenty-one, something like that.'

Leyton nodded.

'If we're talking about a military explosive, that's good for us. It should narrow the field, Carol. We see who's missing some, then find out who had access.'

Chen cleared his throat.

'Well, it won't be that simple. The chrom showed a lot of impurities in the chemical signature, so I phoned the manufacturer back in Pennsylvania. Modex comes in three forms: military grade, which is made under government contract, commercial grade, which is made for foreign export only – EPA won't let anyone use it here – and homegrown.'

Daigle scowled.

'What's that mean, homegrown?'

'The company rep thought a kitchen chemist might've cooked up this batch. It's not that hard to do if you've got the components and the right pressure equipment. The guy says it's about as hard as cooking up a batch of crystal meth.'

Starkey glanced over the chromatograph printout, but it didn't tell her what she wanted to know.

'Okay. If you can make the stuff by hand, I need the component list and the recipe.'

'The rep's going to put it together and fax it. I asked him for manufacturers, too. As soon as I get'm, they're yours.'

Starkey folded the page and put it with her notes. A unique explosive was a plus for the investigation, but she didn't like what it implied.

'If this stuff is a military explosive or needs some kind of high-end lab work, it changes my picture of the builder. We can't be talking about a guy who just wanted to see if he could do it. This is a serious bomb.'

Leyton frowned and leaned against the bench.

'Not necessarily. If the Modex turns out to be stolen, that's true – a backyard nutcase wouldn't know how to get his hands on something like that. But if he made it himself, he could've pulled the formula off the Internet. Maybe he figured that using a more powerful explosive like this was part of the challenge.'

Daigle crossed his arms, not liking it.

'Starkey's right about this being a serious bomb. So tell me this: Why does he build a device like this and just leave it by a Dumpster? There's gotta be more to it.'

'We talked to every one of the shop owners, Sarge. Nobody says they were threatened. The bomb didn't damage the building.'

Daigle scowled deeper.

'One of those fuckers is lying. You don't build a bomb this powerful just to play with yourself. You watch what I'm saying. One of those fuckers screwed somebody over and this thing is payback.'

Starkey shrugged, thinking maybe Daigle was right as she studied the snaps.

'Sarge, I'm looking at this thing, but I don't see a detonator. No batteries. No power source. How did it go off?'

Daigle slid off the stool to stretch his back and tapped the picture on the screen.

'I got a theory. One pipe holds the explosive, the other the detonator. Look here.'

He picked up two of the larger pieces of pipe, holding them for her and Leyton to see.

'See the white residue here on the inside of the curve?'

'Yeah. From when the explosive burned off.'

'That's right. Now look at this other piece. Nothing in here. Clean. Makes me think maybe he had the detonator in this pipe, along with a battery or whatever.'

'You think it was hooked to a timer?'

Daigle looked dubious.

'And the timer just happened to let go when Riggio was standing over it? I don't buy that for a second. We haven't found anything yet, but I'm thinking Riggio set off some kind of balance switch.'

'Buck said Charlie never touched the package.'

'Well, that's what Buck saw, but Charlie must've done something. Bombs don't just go off for no reason.'

Everyone suddenly grew silent, and Daigle flushed. Starkey realized it was because of her, then she flushed, too.

'Jesus, Carol. I'm sorry. I didn't mean it that way.'

'You've got nothing to be sorry for, Sarge. There was a reason. It's called an earthquake.'

Starkey remembered the twisted disk she'd found, took it from the baggie, and showed it to the others.

'I found this at the crime scene this morning. I don't know if it came from the bomb, but there's a good chance. It could be part of the initiator.'

Daigle put it under a magnifying glass for a closer look, chewing his lower lip, squinting and puzzled.

'Something electrical. Looks like we got a circuit board in here.'

Chen crowded in and peered at it. He pulled on a pair of Daigle's gloves, then selected a narrow screwdriver and pried open the disk like a clamshell.

'Sonofabitch. I know what this is.'

A single word was printed inside the disk, a word they all knew, that was so out of place it seemed absurd: MATTEL.

Chen put down the disk and stepped away. The others gathered closer for a better look, but Starkey was watching Chen. He looked stricken.

'What is it, John?'

'It's a radio receiver like they put in those remote-control cars for kids.'

Now all of them stared at him because what John Chen was saying changed everything they'd been thinking about this bomb and the anonymity of its explosion.

'Charlie Riggio didn't set off this device, and it didn't just happen to explode. It was radio-controlled.'

Starkey knew what he was saying at the same time as everyone else, but she was the one who said it.

'The lunatic who built this bomb was right there. He waited until Charlie was over the bomb, and then he set it off.'

John Chen took another breath.

'Yes. He wanted to see someone die.'

3

Kelso tasted the coffee he had just poured, making a face as if he'd sipped Drano.

'You really think the bastard triggered the device from the scene?'

Starkey showed him a fax she had received from a sales rep working for the radio control's manufacturer. It listed the receiver's performance specs and operating requirements.

'These little receivers operate on such low voltage that they're only tested out to sixty yards. The guy I spoke with gives us a ballpark maximum distance between transmitter and receiver of about a hundred yards. That's a line-of-sight distance, Barry. That puts our guy in open view.'

'Okay. So what's your idea?'

'Every TV station in town had a helicopter overhead, broadcasting the scene. They had cameras on the ground, too. Maybe one of those tapes caught this mutt at the scene.'

Kelso nodded, pleased.

'Okay, I like that. That's good thinking, Starkey. I'll talk to Media Relations. I don't see why there'd be a problem with that.'

'One other thing. I had to split up Marzik and Hooker. Marzik is interviewing the residents, and Hooker is talking to the police and fire personnel who were at the scene. It would help if I could get more people to help with the field interviews.'

He made the sour face again.

'Okay. I'll see what I can do.'

Kelso started away, but turned back.

'You're still okay with this, right? You can handle it?'

Starkey felt herself flush.

'Asking for more bodies isn't a sign of weakness, Barry. We're making progress.'

Kelso stared at her for a moment, then nodded.

'Yes. You are. I didn't mean to imply otherwise.'

That surprised Starkey and pleased her.

'Did you talk with Sergeant Daggett yet?'

'No, sir.'

'You should talk to him. Get him to thinking about the people he might've seen in that parking lot. When we get these tapes, you're going to want him to look at them.'

When Kelso closed his door, Starkey went back to her cubicle with her stomach in knots. Daggett would be confused and angry. He would be shaken because of what happened; second-guessing every decision that he'd made, every action, and every movement. Starkey knew he would be feeling these things because she had felt them, too, and didn't want to revisit them.

Starkey sat in her cubicle for twenty minutes without moving, thinking about the flask in her purse and staring at Buck Daggett's address in her Rolodex. Finally, she couldn't stand it anymore and stalked down to her car.

Daggett lived in a cramped Mediterranean-style home in the San Gabriel Valley, identical with its beige stucco and tile roof to a hundred others in the low-cost housing development just east of Monterey Park. Starkey had been there once, for a Bomb Squad cookout three months before Sugar died. It wasn't much of a house. A sergeant-supervisor's pay would cover something nicer, but Starkey knew that Daggett had been divorced three times. The alimony and child support probably ate him alive.

Five minutes after she left the freeway, Starkey pulled into Daggett's drive and went to the door. A black ribbon had been tied to the knocker.

Daggett's fourth and current wife answered. She was twenty years younger than Buck and attractive, though today she seemed vague and distracted. Starkey showed her badge.

'Carol Starkey, Mrs Daggett. I used to work with Buck on the squad. You and I have met, haven't we? I'm sorry, but I don't remember your name.'

'Natalie.'

'Natalie. Sure. Could I see Buck, please?'

'I had to stay home from work, you know? Buck's so upset.'

'That's right, Natalie. It's terrible, isn't it? Now, is Buck home?'

Natalie Daggett led Starkey through the house to their backyard, where Buck was changing the oil in his Lawn-Boy. As soon as Starkey stepped out into the yard, Natalie vanished back into her house.

'Hey, Buck.'

Daggett glanced up like he was surprised to see her, then scrambled to his feet. Just looking at him caused an ache in Starkey's chest.

He shrugged at the Lawn-Boy and seemed embarrassed.

'I'm trying to keep busy. I'd hug you, but I'm all sweaty.'

'Busy is good, Buck. That's okay.'

'You want a soda or something? Didn't Natalie offer you anything?'

He came over, wiping his hands on a greasy orange cloth that soiled his hands as much as cleaned them. It was hot in the tiny backyard. Sweat dripped from his hair.

'I don't have much time. We're running short.'

He nodded, disappointed, then opened a couple of lawn chairs that had been leaning against the house.

'I heard you caught the case. You doing okay over there on CCS?'

'I'd rather be back on the squad.'

Daggett nodded without looking at her. She suddenly thought that if she was still on the squad it might've been her down in Silver Lake instead of Riggio. Maybe he was thinking that, too.

'Buck, I've got to ask you some questions about what happened.'

'I know that. Sure. Hey, I don't think I ever told you, but the guys in the squad are really proud you made the move to become a detective. That's real police work.'

'Thanks, Buck. I appreciate that.'

'What are you, a D-3 now?'

'A D-2. I don't have enough time in grade for the promotion.'

Buck shrugged.

'You'll get there. Here you are with the lead, and only a D-2.'

Starkey worried he might be wondering if she was up to the job. She liked Buck, and didn't want him to doubt her. She got enough doubt from Kelso.

'Anyone call you about the bomb? You hear about that?'

'No. Hear about what?'

He was searching her face, and it took all of her strength not to look away. He knew it was going to be bad. She could see the fear of it blossom in his eyes.

'What about the bomb, Carol?'

'It was detonated by remote control.'

He stared at her without expression for a time, then shook his head, something like desperation edging into his voice.

'That can't be. Charlie made some good snaps with the Real Time. We didn't see a radio device. We didn't see *any* kind of detonator. If we'd seen anything like that, I would've yanked Charlie out of there. He would've come running.'

'You couldn't have seen it, Buck. The power pack and initiator were inside one of the pipes. The explosive was in the other. Something called Modex Hybrid.'

He blinked hard to hold back the tears, but they came anyway. Starkey felt her own eyes fill and put a hand on his arm.

'I'm okay.'

She let go of his arm, thinking the two of them were a fine pair.

Buck cleared his throat, took a breath and let it out.

'Modex. That's military, right? I know that name.'

'They use it in warheads. Almost ten thousand feet faster than TNT. But we're thinking maybe this batch was homemade.'

'Jesus. You're sure about the remote? You're sure it was radio-controlled?'

'We found the receiver. The person who set it off was somewhere in the area. He could've set it off anytime he wanted, but he waited until Charlie was right over the bomb. We think he was watching.'

He rubbed at his face and shook his head as if all of this was too much to bear.

She told him about the videotapes.

'Listen, Buck, I'm getting together the videos that the TV stations took. When we have everything together, I'd like you to come in and take a look. Maybe you'll see someone in the crowd.'

'I don't know, Carol. My head was on the bomb. I was worried about Charlie's body temp and about getting good snaps. We thought we had some gangbanger over there, you know? A *pachuco* showing off for the homeboys. It was just a couple of goddamned pipes, for Christ's sake.'

'It'll be another day or two before we get all the tapes. I want you to think about it, okay? Try to recall anyone or anything that stood out.'

'Sure. I got nothing else to do. Dick made me take three days.'

'It's good for you, Buck. Hey, you can take care of the weeds here in your yard. The place looks like shit.'

Daggett grudged a wan smile, and the two of them fell into silence. After a time, he said, 'You know what they're making me do?'

'What?'

'I gotta go to the bank. Shit, I don't want to talk to those people.'

Starkey didn't know what to say.

'They call it "trauma counseling". We got all these new rules now. You're in a shooting, you gotta go in. You get in a car wreck, you gotta go in. Now I guess I've got to tell some headshrinker what it feels like seeing my partner get blown to shit.'

Starkey was still trying to think of something to say when she felt her pager vibrate. It was Marzik's number, followed by 911.

Starkey wanted to return the call, but she didn't want to leave Buck Daggett so quickly, or like this.

'Don't worry about the bank. It's not like you're being ordered in.'

'I just don't want to talk to those people. What's there to say about something like this? What did *you* say?'

'Nothing, Buck. There's nothing to say. Just tell'm that. There's nothing to say. Listen, I've got to return this call. It's Marzik.'

'Sure. I understand.'

Daggett walked her out through the house and to the front door. His wife was nowhere around.

'Natalie's upset, too. I'm sorry she didn't offer you anything.'

'Don't worry about it, Buck. I didn't want anything anyway.'

'We were pretty tight, the three of us. She liked Charlie a lot.'

'I'll call you about the videos. Think about it, okay?'

She was stepping through the door when Buck stopped her.
'Detective?'
She looked back at him, smiling at his use of her title.
'Thanks for not asking. You know what I mean? Everyone asks you how you are, and there's nothing to say to that, either.'
'I know, Buck. It used to drive me crazy, everyone asking that.'
'Yeah. Well, I guess we're a pretty small club, me and you.'
Starkey nodded at him, and then Buck Daggett closed the door.
Starkey was paged a second time as she walked out to her car. This time it was Hooker. She called Marzik first because of the 911, using her cell phone as she sat in Daggett's drive.
Marzik got it on the first ring, as if she'd been waiting.
'Beth Marzik.'
'It's Starkey. What's up?'
Marzik's voice was excited.
'I got something here, Starkey. I'm down by that flower shop, the one across from the phone? 911 gets the call from the phone at one-fourteen, right? Well, the owner's kid is out front, getting ready to deliver some flowers, and he sees a guy on the phone.'
Starkey's pulse quickened.
'Tell me he saw a car, Beth. Say we've got a license plate.'
'Carol, listen to this. It's even better. He said it was an Anglo guy.'
'The caller was Latino.'
'Listen to me, Starkey. This kid is solid. He's sitting in his truck, listening to the fuckin' Gipsy Kings while they load the flowers. He's there from a little after one to exactly one-twenty. I know he was there during the call because they logged his departure time. *He says it was a white guy.*'
Starkey tried not to let herself get excited, but it was hard.
Marzik said, 'Why would a white guy pretend to be Latino unless it was the guy who set the bomb, Carol? If it was some white guy pretending to be Latino, then he was trying to hide, for Christ's sake. We could have an eye-wit to the fuckin' asshole who set the bomb.'
Starkey saw the possibilities, too, but she knew that investigations often took turns that seemed to be sure things only to have them fall apart.
'Let's take it a step at a time, Beth. I think this is a good thing, and we're going to go with it, but let's not get ahead of ourselves. Your wit only thinks the guy he saw was Anglo. Maybe the guy was Anglo, but maybe he only looked Anglo to the kid. We'll just have to see.'
'Okay. That's right. I know you're right, but the kid comes across solid. You need to come talk to him.'
'Is he there now, Beth?'
'Well, for a while. He's got more deliveries to make and it's getting late.'
'Okay. Keep him there. I'm coming down.'
'I can't just keep him here. If they get an order, he's got to make the delivery.'

'*Ask* him, Beth. Say pretty please.'

'What do you want me to do, suck his dick?'

'Yeah. Try that.'

Starkey broke the connection, then punched in Santos's number. When he answered, his voice was so soft that she could barely understand him.

'What are you whispering for?'

'Carol, is that you?'

'I can barely hear you. Speak up.'

'I'm at the office. An agent from the ATF is here. He flew in from Washington this morning.'

Starkey felt a burst of tension in her stomach and reached into her purse for a Tagamet.

'You're sure it's Washington? He didn't just drive over from the L.A. field office?'

She had submitted the preliminary bomb component information through the NLETS only yesterday. If this guy came from Washington, he must have hopped on the first jet.

'He's from Washington, Carol. He went in there with Kelso, and now Kelso wants to see you. He's been asking for our reports. I think they're going to take over our case. Look, I've gotta go. I've been stalling, but Kelso wants me to give him what we have.'

'Waitaminute, Jorge, did the guy say that? Did he *say* he wanted the case?'

'I've got to go, Carol. Kelso just stuck his head out. He's looking at me.'

'Stall longer, Jorge. I'm coming in. Marzik turned up something good for us.'

'From the looks of the guy in with Kelso, it's going to be something good for him.'

Starkey ate a Tagamet, then drove back to Spring Street with her dash bubble flashing.

Starkey made it back to her office in twenty-five minutes. Santos caught her eye from the coffee machine and nodded toward Kelso's door. It was closed.

'Did you give him the reports?'

Her look made him cringe.

'What could I do, tell Kelso no?'

Starkey set her jaw and stalked to Kelso's door. She knocked hard three times, then opened the door without waiting.

Kelso gestured wearily toward her as he spoke to the man seated across from his desk.

'This is Detective Starkey. She comes in whenever she wants. Starkey, this is Special Agent Jack Pell from—'

'The ATF. I know. Is he taking over this case?'

Pell was leaning forward with elbows on knees as if he were about to leap forward. Starkey guessed him to be in his mid-thirties, but if he was older, it wouldn't have surprised her. He had pale skin and intense gray eyes. She tried to read the eyes, but couldn't; they seemed guarded.

Pell turned to Kelso without acknowledging her.

'I need a few more minutes with you, Lieutenant. Have her wait outside until we're ready.'

Her. Like she wasn't standing there.

'Out, Starkey. We'll call you.'

'This is my case, Lieutenant. It's *our* case. One of *our* people died.'

'Wait outside, Detective. We'll call you when we want you.'

Starkey waited outside his door, fuming. Santos started over, saw her scowl, and veered away. She was cursing Kelso for giving away the CCS investigation when her pager buzzed on her hip.

'Oh, shit. Marzik.'

Starkey phoned Marzik from her cubicle.

'Carol, I'm standing here with this kid and he's got deliveries to make. Where in hell are you?'

Starkey kept her voice low, so the other detectives couldn't hear.

'Back at the office. The ATF is coming in.'

'You're shitting me? What's happening?'

'All I know is that an agent is in there with Kelso now. Look, I'll talk with the kid when I'm done here. Tell him to make his damned deliveries.'

'It's almost five, Carol. He's got deliveries, then he's going home. We can catch him tomorrow.'

Starkey checked her watch and thought it through. She wanted to talk to the kid now because she knew that time was a witness's enemy; people forgot details, people grew confused, people had second thoughts about cooperating with the police. Starkey finally decided that she was getting ahead of herself and pressing too hard. She wouldn't help herself with this kid by making him wait around for another couple of hours.

'Okay, Beth. Set it up. Is he working tomorrow morning?'

Marzik told her to hang on. The kid must have been standing there with her.

'He's in at eight. His father owns the store.'

'Okay. We'll get him tomorrow morning.'

'Us or the ATF?'

'I'm about to find out.'

Kelso stuck his head out, looking for her. Starkey put down the phone, wishing she'd used the time to eat more Tagamet. Sometimes she thought she should buy stock in that company.

When she reached Kelso, he whispered, 'Just relax, Carol. He's here to help us.'

'My ass he is.'

Kelso closed the door behind them. Pell was still poised forward in the chair, so Starkey gave him her best scowl. Those damned gray eyes were the coldest eyes she'd ever seen, and she had to fight the urge to look away.

Kelso returned to his desk.

'Agent Pell flew in from D.C. this morning. The information you fed into the system raised some eyebrows back there.'

Pell nodded.

'I don't have an interest in taking over your investigation, Detective. This is your town, not mine, but I do think I can help you. I flew out because we flagged some similarities between your bomb and some others we've seen.'

'Like what?'

'The Modex is his explosive of choice: fast, sexy, and elite. He also likes to use this particular type of radio detonator, hiding it in one of the pipes so you can't see it with the X-ray.'

'Who are we talking about?'

'If your guy is our guy, he uses the name Mr Red. We don't know his true name.'

Starkey glanced at Kelso, but his expression told her nothing. She figured he would be relieved to hand over the case to the feds, so he wouldn't have to worry about clearing it.

'What are we talking about here? Mr *Red*? Is this guy some kind of serial bomber? Is he a terrorist? What?'

'No, Detective, this mutt isn't a terrorist. As far as we know, he doesn't care about politics or abortion or any of that. Over the past two years, we've had seven bombings that show Modex Hybrid and a radio-triggering device similar to the one used here. Because of the nature of the targets and the people involved, we believe that four of them were done for criminal profit. He blows up something or someone probably because he's being paid to do it. This is how he makes his money, Starkey, blowing up things. He's a hit man with a bomb. But he also has a hobby.'

'I'm dying to know.'

Kelso snapped, surprising the hell out of her.

'Shut up, goddamnit, and listen.'

Starkey turned back to Pell, and the gray eyes were as depthless as stillwater pools. She found herself wondering why they might be so tired.

'He hunts bomb technicians, Starkey. He baits them, then he murders them. He's killed three so far, if we count your man, all with identical devices.'

Starkey watched the gray eyes. They did not blink.

'That's insane.'

'The profilers say it's a dominance game; I think he sees it as a competition. He makes bombs, bomb techs like you de-arm them, so he tries to beat you.'

Starkey felt a chill; Pell clearly read it.

'I know what happened to you. I looked you up before I flew out.'

Starkey felt invaded, and the invasion angered her. She wondered what he knew about her injuries and suddenly felt embarrassed that this man might know those things. She made her voice cool.

'Who and what I am is none of your business except for this: I am the lead investigator on this case.'

Pell shrugged.

'You signed the NLETS request. I like to know who I'm dealing with.'

Thinking about it now, Starkey had a recollection of reading an ATF flyer on an unknown suspect who might have been identified as Mr Red. It was the kind of flyer that passed through their office on a routine basis, but bore little relevance, as the subject was operating in other parts of the country.

'I would have remembered this, Pell, some nut murdering bomb technicians. No one here has heard of this asshole.'

Kelso shifted.

'They've kept that part of his activities on a need-to-know basis.'

'We don't want copycats, Starkey. We've kept all the details of his M.O. and bomb designs classified except the components that we list through NLETS.'

'So you're saying that your guy is our guy on the strength of a components list?'

'I'm not saying anything yet, but the Modex and the radio receiver are persuasive. The other design signatures are distinctive. And you have this letter you've found.'

Starkey was confused.

'What letter? What are you talking about?'

Kelso said, 'The number we found etched into the frag. The 5. Agent Pell thinks it might be the letter S.'

'Why do you think it's a letter?'

Pell hesitated, leaving Starkey to wonder what he was thinking.

'We've found etchings in Mr Red's work before. What I'll need to do is read your reports and compare your reconstruction with what we know. Then I'll make a determination whether or not your bomber is Mr Red.'

Starkey could see her case slipping away.

'Pardon me if I make up my own mind. But if you get to see mine, then I want to see yours. I want to compare whatever you have with what we find here.'

Kelso showed his palms.

'Now, Starkey, we don't need to be adversaries here.'

She wanted to kick him. That was just the kind of mealymouthed thing Kelso would say.

Pell gathered together a short stack of papers and gestured with them.

'That's not a problem, Detective. Lieutenant Kelso was kind enough to share your case reports; I'll be happy to give you copies of mine. They're at my hotel now, but I'll get them to you.'

Pell rolled the reports that Kelso had given him into a tube, then stood.

'I skimmed through these. They look pretty good, but I want to read them more carefully now.'

Pell turned to Kelso and gestured with the reports.

'Could you set me up with a place to read these, Lieutenant? I'd like to cover as much ground this evening as I can before Detective Starkey and I get down to business.'

Starkey blinked hard twice, then also faced Kelso.

'What does *that* mean? I've got my hands full with this investigation.'

Kelso came around his desk to open the door.

'Just relax, Carol. We're all on the same side here.'

As Pell walked past with the reports, he stopped beside Starkey, well into her personal space. She would have bet a thousand dollars that he did it on purpose.

'I won't bite, Detective. You don't have to be afraid of me.'

'I'm not afraid of anything.'

'I wish I could say the same.'

Kelso called Santos to take care of Pell, then came back into his office and closed the door. He wasn't happy, but Starkey didn't give a damn. Her hands were shaking so badly that she put them in her pockets so that he wouldn't see.

'You couldn't have been any less helpful.'

'I'm not here to be helpful. I'm here to find whoever killed Riggio, and now I've got to worry about the ATF second-guessing what I do and stealing my case.'

'Try to remember that it's a team effort, Detective. It can't hurt to let him look. If he can't tie our bomb to his man, he'll go back to Washington and be out of our hair. If our bomber and his bomber are one and the same, we might be damned lucky to have his help. I've already spoken to Assistant Chief Morgan about this. He wants us to extend our full cooperation.'

Starkey thought that was just like Kelso, call the brass and cover his ass.

'Marzik found a wit who might've seen our guy make the 911 call. He says that the person making the call was an Anglo guy.'

That stopped Kelso, who fidgeted with his pencil as he considered it.

'I thought the caller was Hispanic.'

'So did I.'

Starkey didn't add anything more. She figured that even Kelso was smart enough to see the implication.

'Well, I guess you'd better see to it. Call me at home to tell me what develops.'

'I was going to go see about it, Lieutenant, but I had to come meet Mr Pell instead. Now it has to keep until tomorrow. The witness had plans.'

Kelso looked disappointed.

'It couldn't be helped, then. See about it tomorrow and keep me informed. You're going to close this case, Starkey. I have every faith in that. So does the A-chief.'

Starkey didn't answer. She wanted to get out of there, but Kelso looked nervous.

'You're doing okay with this, aren't you, Carol? You're okay?'

Kelso came around his desk again, getting close to her, as if he was trying to smell her breath.

'I'm fine.'

'Good. Go home and get a good night's sleep. Rest is important to keep your mind sharp.'

Starkey let herself out, hoping that she wouldn't see Pell when she left. It was after six when she pulled out into the downtown traffic, but she didn't head home. She turned her car west toward a bar called Barrigan's in the Wilshire Division.

Less than twelve hours ago, she had emptied her flask and promised herself that she would ease up on the drinking, but to hell with that. She ate two Tagamet and cursed her rotten luck that the ATF was involved.

Special Agent Jack Pell

Pell sat in a small white room not much bigger than a coffin to read the reports. He had been provided with the initial findings from the Bomb Squad, SID, and the autopsy of the deceased officer.

After reading them, he felt that LAPD's Scientific Investigation Division and Bomb Squad had done an excellent job of forensics and analysis, though he was disappointed that only a single letter – the S – had been recovered. Pell was certain there would be more, but had a high degree of confidence that the criminalist over there, Chen, would not have overlooked anything. Pell wasn't so certain about the Medical Examiner's office. An important step had not been noted in the autopsy protocol.

He brought the reports into the hall and found Santos waiting.

'Do you know if the medical examiner took a full X-ray of Riggio's body?'

'I don't know. If it's not in the protocol, they probably didn't do it.'

'It's not, but it should be.'

Pell paged open the autopsy protocol and found the attending medical examiner's name. Lee Richards.

'Is Starkey still here?'

'She's gone.'

'I'd better see Lieutenant Kelso.'

Twenty minutes later, after Kelso had made two phone calls to locate Richards, Santos drove Pell around behind the rear of the County-USC Medical Center to the Medical Examiner's building.

When Santos started to get out with him, Pell said, 'Take five and grab a smoke.'

'Don't smoke.'

'You're not coming in there with me.'

Pell could tell that Santos was bothered by that, but Pell didn't care.

'You think I wanna watch an M.E. dig around in a friend of mine? I'll grab a cup of coffee and wait in the lobby.'

Pell couldn't object to that, so they crunched across the gravel toward the door.

Inside, Santos identified them to the security guard, then went for his coffee. Richards appeared a few minutes later, Pell following him into a cold tile X-ray room where they waited while two technicians wheeled in Riggio's body. The body was zipped into an opaque plastic bag. Pell and Richards stood silently as the technicians took the body from the bag and positioned it on the X-ray table. The great Y incision down the chest and abdomen that Richards had made during the autopsy was stitched closed, as were the wounds where the frags had done their worst damage.

Richards eyed the body as if he was assessing his work and liking it.

'The entry wounds were fairly obvious, as you can see. We took area X-rays wherever the entries appeared to be of a significant nature, and that's where we removed the fragments.'

Pell said, 'That's the problem. If you only look where you see an entry wound, you'll miss something. I've seen cases where shrapnel bounced off a pelvis and followed the femur down to a knee.'

Richards looked dubious.

'I guess it's possible.'

'I know it's possible. Where are his hands?'

Richards frowned.

'Hm?'

'Were his hands recovered?'

'Oh, yes. I examined them. I know I examined them.'

Richards peered at the bony stubs of the wrists, then squinted at the technicians.

'Where are the goddamned hands?'

The technicians fished around in the bag and came out with the hands. Scorched from the heat flash and macerated by the pressure wave. Richards looked relieved.

'See? We've got the hands. It's all here.'

Like he was proud of himself that all the body parts were accounted for.

Richards said, 'What we'll do is look over the body with the scope first. We see anything, we'll mark it, okay? That'll be faster than screwing around with the X-ray.'

'Fine.'

'I don't like the X-ray. Even with all the shielding, I worry about the cancer.'

'Fine.'

Pell was given a pair of yellow goggles to wear. He felt nothing as he watched them wheel Riggio's body behind a chromatic fluoroscope. The fluoroscope looked like an opaque flat-screen television, but when Richards turned it on, it was suddenly transparent. As the body disappeared behind the screen, its flesh was no longer flesh but transparent lime Jell-O, the bones impenetrable green shadows. Richards adjusted the screen.

'Pretty cool, huh? This won't scramble your 'nads the way an X-ray will. No cancer.'

At Richards's direction, the techs pushed the body slowly past the screen, revealing three sharply defined shadows below the knee, two in the left leg, one in the right, all smaller than a BB.

Richards said, 'Sonofabitch, here you go. Right here.'

Pell had expected to find even more, but the armored suit had done its work well. Only those fragments with a significant mass had carried enough inertia to punch through the Kevlar.

Richards peered at him.

'You want these?'

'I want it all, Doc.'

Richards marked the spots on the body with a felt-tipped pen.

By the time they finished scanning the body, they had found eighteen metal fragments, only two of which had any real size: one, an inch-long piece of twisted metal that had lodged in Riggio's hip joint; the other, a half-inch rectangular fragment that Richards had overlooked when he'd removed a cluster of fragments from the soft tissue of Riggio's right shoulder.

As Richards removed them, the taller technician rinsed them of clotted blood and placed them in a glass tray. Pell inspected each bit of metal, but he found no etches or markings.

Finally, Richards turned off the light screen, and lifted his goggles.

'That's it.'

Pell didn't say anything until the last of the fragments had been rinsed. It was the largest piece, and he wanted there to be something so badly that his heart was hammering, but when he examined it, he saw that there was nothing.

'Does any of this help, you think?'

Pell didn't answer.

'Agent?'

'I appreciate your staying, Doc. Thanks.'

Richards peeled off his gloves to glance at his watch. It was a Mickey Mouse watch.

'We'll send these over to SID in the morning. We have to deliver them under seal to maintain the chain of evidence.'

'I know. That'll be fine, thanks.'

It wasn't fine and Pell didn't like it. A cold rage of frustration threatened to spill out of him.

Pell was already thinking that he was too late, that Mr Red might have come and gone and be on to another city or maybe had never been here at all, when the taller technician mentioned the hands.

'Doc, you gonna scope the hands or should I bag this stuff and get out of here?'

Richards grunted like they might as well, then brought over the hands and placed them under the scope. Two bright green shadows were wedged among the metacarpal bones in the left hand.

'Shit. Looks like we missed a couple.'

Richards removed them with the forceps, passing them to the tech, who rinsed them and put them with the others.

Pell inspected them as he had done the others, turning over both pieces without hope when he felt an adrenaline jolt of rage surge through his body.

The larger piece had five tiny letters etched into its surface, and part of a sixth, and what he saw there stunned him. It wasn't what he expected. It wasn't anything that he had expected. His heart was beating so hard that it seemed to echo off the walls.

Behind him, Richards said, 'Find anything?'

'No. Just more of the same stuff, Doc.'

Pell palmed the shard with the letters and returned the remaining piece to the tray with the other recovered fragments. The lab technician did not notice that he had returned one piece and not two.

Richards must've read something in his eyes.

'Are you all right, Agent Pell? You need a drink of water or something?'

Pell put away those things he felt and carefully blanked his face.

'I'm fine, Doc. Thanks for your time.'

Special Agent Jack Pell walked back into the outer hall, where the security guard stared at him with goldfish eyes.

'You looking for Santos?'

'Yeah.'

'He took his coffee out to the car.'

Pell turned toward the door and was halfway down the hall when crimson starbursts appeared in the air before him, followed by a sharp wave of nausea. The air around the starbursts darkened and was suddenly alive with wormy shapes that writhed and twisted.

Pell said, 'Shit, not now. Not now.'

Behind him, the guard said, 'What?'

Pell remembered a bathroom. A men's room off the hall. He blinked hard against the darkening stars and shoved his way through the door. A cold sweat sprouted over his back and chest.

The dizziness hit him as he reached the sink, and then his stomach clenched and he barfed into the sink. The room felt as cold as a meat locker.

Closing his eyes didn't stop him from seeing the shapes. They floated in the air on a field of black, rising and twisting in slow motion as if filled with helium. He turned on the cold water and vomited again, spitting out the foul taste as he splashed water into his eyes. His stomach heaved a third time, and the nausea passed.

He heard voices in the hall and thought one of them might be Santos.

Pell clawed a towel from the rack, wet it with cold water, and staggered into the stall. When he straightened, his head spun.

He slumped onto the toilet and pressed the towel hard to his eyes, waiting.

He had done this before. He had done it many times and was scared because the time between bouts was shrinking. He knew what that meant, and it scared him more than anything in his life had ever scared him.

He sat on the floor, breathing through the wet towel until the floating monsters that haunted him vanished. When they were gone, he took out the piece of metal he had stolen and read the letters there, squinting to make his eyes work.

Pell hadn't told Kelso and Starkey everything about Mr Red. He hadn't told them that Mr Red didn't just kill random bomb techs. He chose his targets, usually senior techs with headline cases under their belts. He didn't kill just anyone; he killed only the very best.

When Pell learned of the S, he thought it would be from Charles.

It wasn't.

Pell read the fragment again.

TARKEY

Red Rage

CRIME BOSS DIES IN FIERY BLAST
Innocents Die Also
By Lauren Beth
Exclusive to the *Miami Herald*

Diego 'Sonny' Vega, the reputed chief enforcer of an organized Cubano crime empire, died early Thursday morning when a warehouse he owned was destroyed by a series of bomb blasts. The explosions occurred just after three A.M. It is not known whether Mr Vega was intentionally murdered, or if his presence in the building was coincidental.

The industrial park warehouse was the site of a 'knockoff' apparel operation, employing undocumented workers to manufacture counterfeit designer goods. Five of these workers were also killed, and nine others wounded.

Police spokesman Evelyn Melancon said, 'Obviously, this was a sweatshop operation. We do not at this time know if Mr Vega was the intended target, or if the warehouse itself was the target. We have no leads at this time as to who planted the bombs.'

Arson investigators and bomb technicians from the Bureau of Alcohol, Tobacco, and Firearms are sifting through the rubble in an effort to—

John Michael Fowles was disappointed that the article was on page three, but decided not to show it. He was also pissed off that there was no mention of Mr Red, nor of the fine work he had done in destroying the building. He folded the newspaper and handed it back to Angelo Rossi, the man who had put him in touch with Victor Karpov.

Rossi looked surprised when John returned the paper.

'There's more on the next page.'

367

'It's just an article, Mr Rossi. I'd rather be readin' the papers you got in that bag, if you know what I mean.'

'Well, sure.'

Rossi nervously handed over the bag with the money Karpov owed John. Karpov himself had refused to come meet John here at the library. He claimed illness, like a kid cutting class, but John knew the real reason: he was scared.

As before, John didn't bother to count it, or even open the bag. He put the money into his backpack, and lowered the pack to the floor. When John had told Rossi to meet him here in the periodicals section of the West Palm Beach Public Library, he had to explain what 'periodicals' were.

John gave Rossi the cracker's hayseed grin as he leaned back against the reading table.

'Take it easy, Mr Rossi. We're okay. You don't have an overdue book, do ya?'

Rossi glanced over his shoulder as if the book police were hot on his trail, clearly nervous and out of place. John wondered if the fat bastard had even been in a library except when he'd been sent there on high school detention.

'This is foolish, Red, meeting in a library like this. What kinda mook talks about shit like this in a library?'

'A mook like me, I guess. I like the order you find in a library, Angelo. It's the last place left where people behave with manners, don't you think?'

'Yeah. Whatever. Why'd you do your hair like that?'

'So people will remember it.'

Rossi's eyes narrowed. John pictured rusty gears turning in Rossi's head, and had to bite his tongue to keep from laughing, though he knew Rossi to be a smart man.

'Don't you worry about it, partner. Mr Red has his reasons.'

'Oh, I get it. Mr Red. The red hair.'

'There you go.'

Today, John's hair was cut way short and dyed a vivid red the colorist had called Promise of Passion. Contact lenses gave him green eyes. His sideburns were long and pointed, and he'd fit cotton wads into his lower cheeks to make his jaw appear more square. He was also wearing lifts that made him three inches taller.

If Rossi knew the real reason John had made himself up this way, the man would shit a Buick.

'Listen, my friends up in Jersey got another job I wanna talk to you about.'

'Down here or up there?'

'We got a fuckass Cuban pirate knocking over our ganja boats down off Key West.'

John shook his head before Rossi finished.

'No can do, Mr Rossi. I'd like to oblige, but things are gonna be heating up for me around here now, so I've gotta split.'

'Just listen a minute, okay, Red? What I'm talking about here won't take long at all. We just wanna kill a nigger, is all.'

'So go shoot him. You done it before.'

Rossi seemed agitated, and John wondered about that. He hadn't expected Rossi to pitch him another gig, and he was growing concerned with all the time he was wasting. He wanted Rossi to leave so that he could get on with his business. The real reason he had come to the library.

'Well, it's more than just walking up to some nigger and shooting him. I could get one'a these kids around here to do that. We wanna get him, his family, the whole damned nest of'm, you know. Kinda send a message, the way you're good at doing.'

'Can't help you, Mr Rossi. You had a job in another state, we could talk about it. But not here. I got some personal business I wanna take care of.'

Rossi nervously glanced around again, then scooted his chair closer. He wasn't taking the hint to leave, which made John figure that he'd probably already told the Jersey people that Mr Red would go along.

'Shit, the cops got nothing on you, and no way to connect you to that bastard Vega. You saw the paper. They don't know shit yet.'

'Don't believe everything you read, Angelo. Now I got other stuff I need to do, so if you'll excuse me, get the fuck outta here.'

In fact, John knew far more than Rossi or the press about what the blast investigators had gathered. At some time around eleven P.M. the night before, the Broward County Sheriff's laboratory had found his little calling card. They had entered their preliminary lab results and materials findings into the FBI's Bomb Data Center computer system. The BDC's computer had matched these findings with other known explosive devices that had been used around the country, and an alert had been kicked back to the sheriff and the local ATF office, as well as to the national FBI and ATF offices in Washington. John did not know, but he surmised, that while he and Angelo Rossi sat here in the coolness of the air-conditioned library, agents from the local ATF field office were scrambling to act on this information. Which was exactly what he wanted them to do.

'Look, Red, please. I'm telling you you can make a sweet buck here. How's twice what Karpov paid you sound?'

'Sorry, sir. Just can't.'

'You got us over a barrel.'

'Nah. I think *you're* the one over a barrel, right? You shot off your mouth to those wops up north, and now you can't deliver.'

Rossi glanced around again.

'Do me this as a favor, okay? I can give you everything you need to know about this nigger right now. Shit, I'll drive you there myself, you want.'

'Nope. No niggers on the menu today. Now get the fuck outta here, okay?'

Rossi's nostrils flared and his hand slipped beneath his jacket. Ninety degrees and a hundred percent humidity, and this dumb guinea was wearing a sport coat like he just came out of a double bill of *Goodfellas*.

John rolled his eyes.

'Oh, please, Mr Rossi. Let's not be small. What the fuck you think you're gonna do with that here in the library? Here in "periodicals"? Jesus Christ, you're so dumb you think "periodicals" is something a whore gets.'

Rossi's jaw worked as if he was chewing gum.

John grinned wider, then let the smile fall away and leaned toward Angelo Rossi. He knew Rossi feared him. He knew Rossi was about to fear him more.

'Here's a tip, Angelo: Pretend that you dropped something on the floor and bend down to pick it up. When you're down there, you look up under the bottom of this table.'

Rossi's eyes flickered.

'What you got down there?'

'You look, Angelo. You won't get bit.'

John took the newspaper from the table and let it slip to the floor.

'You go on and look now, okay? You just look.'

Rossi didn't bend down for the paper. Slowly, never taking his eyes from John, he slipped from the chair and squatted to the floor. When he rose again, Rossi's face was white.

'You crazy fuck.'

'That might be, Angelo. Now you go on and kill your own damned nigger. Me and you will work together again another time.'

Rossi showed his palms and backed away, bumping into two teenage girls who were trying to figure out how to use a reference computer.

When Rossi was gone, John considered the people at the surrounding tables. Mostly old people, reading newspapers and magazines. A group of preschool kids here on some kind of kindergarten field trip. A soft-looking man behind the research desk, reading a Dean Koontz novel. All of them just going along with their lives, oblivious.

John swung around to face the library's Internet research computer and tapped in the address for the FBI's web site: *www.fbi.gov*.

When the home page came up, he clicked on the Ten Most Wanted Fugitives icon and watched the page load.

Ten small pictures appeared, each with a link to its own page. John had checked the site before Rossi arrived, hoping to find his picture there. It wasn't then, and still wasn't.

A perfect example, John felt, of government inefficiency.

Disappointed, John went back to the home page, and clicked on the Unknown Suspects icon. Nine pictures appeared, three of which were artists' sketches. One of the sketches showed a studious young man with a balding pate, rim of brown hair, brown eyes, and dorky glasses. John had starved himself for two weeks before letting himself be seen that time, and the witnesses had certainly noticed: the sketch showed him to be gaunt and undernourished. He was also shown wearing a white button-down shirt and thin dark tie. It was a sketch that looked nothing like his true self, just as today he looked nothing like his true self.

He clicked on the sketch, which brought him to a page showing a brief (though inaccurate) description of himself, along with a catalog of the crimes he was suspected of committing. These charges included multiple counts of criminal bombing and murder. John was pleased to note that the feds considered him extremely dangerous, and that he used 'sophisticated explosive devices for criminal gain'. It wasn't as cool as being in the Top Ten, but it was better than getting piss on your shoe.

John felt that the FBI's refusal to include him in the Ten Most Wanted List was both cheesy and disrespectful. And lazy. The Top Ten was loaded with raghead terrorists, right-wing political kooks, and drug addicts who had murdered police officers. John had killed far more people than most of them. He believed himself to be the most dangerous man walking free in open daylight, and expected to be treated as such.

John guessed he would just have to up the stakes.

Beneath the table was a small device he had built for this library, specifically to be used as a message. It was simple, elegant, and, like every device he built, bore his signature. The local authorities would know within hours that Mr Red had come to call.

'Excuse me. Are you finished using that?'

An older woman with a body like a squash stood behind him. She was holding a spiral notebook.

'You want to use the computer?'

'Yes. If you're finished with it.'

John flashed the big grin, then scooped up his backpack and held the chair for her. Just before he stood, he reached beneath the table and turned on the timer.

'Yes, ma'am, I am. You sit right here. This chair's so comfy it'll make your butt smile.'

The older woman laughed.

John left her there and walked out into the sun.

4

Starkey woke the next morning on the couch, her body clenched into a fist. Her neck was stiff, and her mouth tasted as if it were lined with sheep's wool seat covers. It was four-twenty in the morning. She had gotten two hours' sleep.

Starkey felt disquieted by the dreams. A different quality had been added. Pell. In her dreams, he chased her. She had run as hard as she could, but her movements were sluggish and slow, while his were not. Starkey didn't like that. In the dream, his fingers were bony and sharp, like claws. She didn't like that, either. Starkey's dreams had been a constant since her injury, but she found herself feeling resentful of this addition. It was bad enough that the sonofabitch was invading her investigation; she didn't need him in her nightmares.

Starkey lit a cigarette, then gimped into the kitchen, where she found a small amount of orange juice that didn't smell sour. She tried to remember the last time that she'd been to the market, but couldn't. The only things she bought in quantity were gin and cigarettes.

Starkey downed the juice, then a glass of water, then got herself together for the day. Breakfast was two aspirin and a Tagamet.

Marzik had left word on her voice mail that they could meet the wit, a kid named Lester Ybarra, at the flower shop when it opened at nine. By five-thirty, Starkey was at Spring Street, climbing the stairs to her office. Spring Street was quiet. Neither CCS, Fugitive Section, nor IAG maintained a night shift. Their commanders and sergeant-supervisors were on pagers. They, in turn, would contact the officers and detectives in their commands on an as-needed basis. Fugitive Section, by the nature of their work as manhunters, often started their days as early as three a.m. in order to bag their mutts in bed. But today the stairs were empty, and her steps echoed in the silent altar of the stairwell.

Starkey liked that.

She had once told Dana that she enjoyed being awake before everyone else because it gave her an edge, but that had been a lie. Starkey enjoyed the solitude because it was easier. No one intruded. No one stared behind her back, thinking that she was the one, the tech who'd been blown apart and stitched back together like Frankenstein's monster, the one who had lost her partner, the one who had escaped, the one who had died. Dana had called her on it, offering Starkey the truth by asking if Carol ever felt the weight of their stares or imagined that she could hear their thoughts. Starkey, of course, denied all of it, but she thought about it later and admitted that Dana was right. Solitude was a spell that freed her.

Starkey opened the CCS office, then put on the Mr Coffee. As the coffee dripped, she went back to her desk. Like all the CCS detectives, she kept reference manuals and sourcebooks for explosives manufacturers, but, unlike the others, Starkey also had her texts and manuals from the FBI's Redstone Arsenal Bomb School, and the technical catalogs that she had collected during her days as a bomb technician.

Starkey brought a cup of coffee back to her desk, lit a fresh cigarette, then searched through her books.

Modex Hybrid was a trinary explosive used as a bursting charge in air-to-air missiles. Hot, fast, and dangerous. Trinary meant that it was a mixture of three primary explosives, combined together to form a compound more powerful and stable than any of the three alone. Starkey took out her case notebook and copied the components: RDX, TNT, ammonium picrate, powdered aluminum, wax, and calcium chloride. RDX, TNT, and ammonium picrate were high explosives. The powdered aluminum was used to enhance the power of the explosion. The wax and calcium chloride were used as stabilizers.

Chen had found contaminants in the Modex, and, after consulting with the manufacturer, had concluded that the Modex used in Riggio's bomb wasn't part of a government production. It was homemade, and therefore untraceable.

Starkey considered that, then searched through her books for information on the primary components.

TNT and ammonium picrate were available to the civilian population. You could get it damned near anywhere. RDX was different. Like the Modex, it was manufactured for the military only under government contract, but, unlike the Modex, it was too complicated to produce without industrial refining equipment. You couldn't cook up a batch in your microwave. This was the kind of break Starkey was hoping to find in her manuals. Someone could make Modex if they had the components, but they couldn't make the components. They would have to acquire the RDX, which meant that the RDX could be traced back to its source.

Starkey decided that this was a good angle to work.

She brought her notes to the NLETS computer, poured herself a fresh cup of coffee, then punched up a request form asking for matches with RDX. By the time she finished typing the form and entering the request, a few of the other detectives had begun to drift in for the start of the shift. The silence was gone. The spell was broken.

Starkey gathered her things and left.

*

Marzik was loading Amway products into her trunk when Starkey parked behind her outside the flower shop. Marzik carried the damned stuff everywhere and would make her pitch at the most inappropriate times, even when interviewing witnesses and, twice, when questioning potential suspects.

Starkey felt her stomach tighten. She had decided not to call Marzik on ratting her out to Kelso, but she now felt a wave of irritation.

They met on the sidewalk, Marzik saying, 'Is the ATF going to take over the case?'

'He says no, but we'll see. Beth, tell me you weren't in there with the Amway.'

Marzik slammed the trunk and looked annoyed.

'Why shouldn't I? They didn't mind. I made a good sale.'

'Do me a favor and leave it in the trunk. I don't want to see that again on this case.'

'Oh, for Christ's sake. I got two children to feed.'

Starkey was going to say more when a short, thin Latino teenager stepped out of the flower shop and looked at Marzik. 'Detective? My dad says I got to get going soon. We got morning deliveries.'

Marzik introduced her to Lester Ybarra as the lead investigator on the case.

Starkey offered her hand. Lester's felt clammy from being inside the flower shop. He smelled of chemicals and baby's breath.

'Hi, Lester. I really appreciate your helping us out like this.'

Lester glanced at Marzik, flashing a shy smile.

''s no pro'lem.'

Marzik said, 'Lester saw someone using the phone across the street between one and one-fifteen the day the bomb went off, right, Lester?'

Lester nodded, and Marzik nodded with him.

'Can you describe that person to Detective Starkey?'

Lester glanced at Starkey, then snuck a quick peek back at Marzik. His eyes went to Marzik so much that Starkey figured he had probably developed a crush on her, which made Starkey wonder if he had fabricated parts of his story to impress her.

Starkey said, 'Before we get to that, Lester, how about helping me set the scene, okay? So I can picture it?'

' 's no pro'lem.'

'Your van was where? About here where my car is?'

'Yeah.'

Starkey was parked directly outside the florist's front door in a red No Parking zone about fifteen feet from the corner.

'You always load the van out here in the street, bringing the flowers through the front door?'

'We got three vans. The other two was using the alley, so I had to be out here. I was supposed to leave by twelve-thirty, but we got this big order right when I was set to go. A funeral set, you know? Twelve sprays. We make a lotta money from funerals. My dad said I hadda wait, so I brought the van around front here.'

'You were sitting in the van, waiting, or you were loading flowers?'

'When I saw the guy, I was sitting there behind the wheel. Nothing to do, you know? My sisters hadda make the sprays. So I was just sitting there in case the cops come and I hadda move.'

Marzik said, 'He was in the red zone.'

Starkey nodded. Standing there listening, she had noticed that very few cars turned off Sunset onto the little side street. Lester would have an easy, unobstructed view of the pay phone hanging on the laundry across the street. She watched an older couple emerge from the laundry with a pink box and made a note to herself to mention it to Marzik.

'Okay, Lester, would you describe him for me? I know you described him for Detective Marzik, but now for me.'

Starkey and Marzik locked eyes. They were getting down to it now. Whether the caller was Anglo or Latino.

Lester launched into his description, describing an Anglo man of medium height and build, wearing a faded blue baseball cap, sunglasses (probably Wayfarers), dark blue trousers, and a lighter blue work shirt. Lester's impression was that the man was wearing some kind of a uniform, such as a gas station attendant or bus driver. Starkey took notes, not reacting to Lester's statement that the caller was an Anglo. Lester had not heard the man's voice. He thought the guy had to be in his forties, but admitted to being a lousy judge of age. As Lester spoke, Starkey felt the pager at her hip vibrate and checked the number. Hooker.

When Lester finished, Starkey folded her pad on a finger.

'If you saw this guy again, you think you'd recognize him?'

Lester shrugged.

'I don't think so. Maybe. I didn't really look at him, you know? Just for a couple seconds.'

'Did you see which way the man came from when he went to the phone?'

'I didn't notice.'

'How about when he left? You see where he went?'

'I wasn't paying attention, you know? He was just some guy.'

'He get out of or into a car?'

Lester shrugged.

Starkey put away the pad.

'Okay, Lester, I've got just one problem with this. We have reason to believe that the person making the call was Latino. You sure this guy was Anglo?'

'I'm pretty sure. His hair was light, you know? Not gray, but light.'

Starkey and Marzik traded another look, neither as enthusiastic as they had been yesterday. 'Pretty sure' was an equivocation.

'Light brown?'

'Yeah. A light brown. Kinda sandy.'

Marzik frowned. 'You could tell that with the cap?'

Lester touched his own ears.

'The part I could see down here, you know?'

That made sense to Starkey. She brought out the pad again and made another note. As she wrote, she had another thought.

'Okay. One more thing. Do you recall any identifying characteristics? A scar, maybe? A tattoo on his arm?'

'He was wearing long sleeves.'

'He was wearing a long-sleeved shirt?'

'Yeah. That's why I couldn't see his arms. I remember it was greasy and old, like he'd been working on a car or something.'

Starkey glanced at Marzik and found her staring. Marzik was clearly unhappy with Lester's uncertainty. When Starkey glanced back at Lester, he was watching Marzik.

'One last thing. You were out here, about, what? Fifteen minutes?'

'You keep sayin' that, one last thing. My old man's gonna kick my ass. I gotta go make these deliveries.'

'I mean it this time, Lester. Just this last question. Anyone else make a call from that phone while you were out here?'

Starkey already knew that no other calls had been made from that phone. She wanted to see if he would lie about it to impress Marzik or to make himself more important.

'I didn't see anyone else. No.'

Starkey put away her pad.

'Okay, Lester, thanks. I want you to come in with Detective Marzik and work with a sketch artist, see if we can't build a picture of this guy, okay?'

'That sounds pretty cool to me. My dad ain't gonna like it, though. He gonna raise hell.'

'You go take care of your deliveries, and we'll square it with your father, maybe get you down there later this morning. Detective Marzik will buy you lunch.'

Lester nodded his head like a collie.

'Okay. Sure.'

Lester vanished into the flower shop, but Marzik and Starkey stayed on the sidewalk.

'Why'd you have to tell him that, for Christ's sake? I don't want to spend all day with him.'

'Somebody has to be with him. You've set up the rapport.'

'It's not going to do any good. You hear that, "pretty sure"? The guy's wearing a cap, sunglasses, and a long-sleeved shirt on a day it's ninety-five fuckin' degrees. If it's our guy, he's wearing a goddamned disguise. If he's not, he's just some asshole.'

Starkey felt the urge for more antacid.

'Why do you always have to be so negative?'

'I'm not being negative. I'm just stating what's obvious.'

'Okay, then try this for obvious: *If* he's our guy, and *if* he's wearing the same clothes when he set off the bomb, and *if* he's on the news tape, the goddamned hat and sunglasses and long-sleeved shirt should make him easier to spot.'

'Whatever. I'll go talk to the kid's father. He's a bastard.'

Marzik stalked into the shop without another word. Starkey shook out a cigarette, lit it, and went to her car. She was so angry that she was trembling. First Pell, now this. She was trying to get past it because she had a job to do, and she knew the anger was getting in her way. She tried to remember some of the techniques that Dana had told her for setting aside her anger, but couldn't remember any of them. Three years in therapy, and she couldn't remember a goddamned thing.

Just as Marzik reappeared, Starkey was considering the people coming and going from the laundry, and how many of them passed the pay phone. She took a breath, calming herself.

'Beth, you talked to the people at the laundry, right?'

Marzik answered without looking at her. Sulking.

'I told you I did.'

'Did you run the time and description by them? I'm thinking that one of their customers might've seen our guy.'

Marzik pulled her pad from her purse, opened it to a list of names, then held it out with the same sulky indifference.

'I asked them for any customers they recalled between noon and two. I'm not stupid, Carol.'

Starkey stared at Marzik, then dropped her cigarette and crushed it.

'Okay. I wasn't going to say anything about this, but I think you and I need to clear the air.'

'About what? Your busting my balls about the Amway or because the kid isn't as solid as I thought he was?'

'You told Kelso that you thought I was drinking on the job.'

Marzik went a bright crimson, confirming Starkey's suspicion.

'No, I didn't. Did Kelso say that?'

'Beth, this is hard enough. If you're going to lie to me, do me the kindness of not saying anything and just listen.'

'I don't like being accused.'

'If you don't want to work with me, let's go to Kelso and tell him we can't work together. I'll tell him it's mutual, and neither of us will lose points.'

Marzik crossed her arms, then uncrossed them and squared herself in Starkey's face.

'If you want to talk about this straight-up, then let's get straight-up. Everyone on the squad knows you have a drinking problem. Jesus Christ, we can smell it. If you don't reek of gin, you're blowing Altoids to cover it.'

Starkey felt herself redden and fought the urge to step away.

'Everybody feels sorry for you because of what happened. They set you up over here in CCS and took care to bring you along, but you know what? That shit doesn't cut any ice with me. No one set me up, and no one is looking out for me, and I got two kids to raise.'

'No one's looking out for me.'

Starkey felt as if she was suddenly on the spot, and defensive.

'My ass there isn't. Everybody knows that Dick Leyton used his clout at Parker to make Kelso take you, and he's *still* watching out for you. I've got these two kids to raise, and I gotta have this job. That job isn't babysitting you, and it sure as hell doesn't include taking a career fall to cover your bad habits.'

'I'm not asking you to cover for me.'

'Good, because I won't. I also won't ask off this case because this is the kind of case that leads to a promotion. If this thing about the guy being Anglo turns out to be real, I want the credit. I've been a D-2 for too damned long. I need the bump to D-3. I need the money. If you can't handle it, then *you* ask off, because I need the money.'

Starkey felt her pager vibrate again, and, again, it was Hooker. She went into her car for her cell phone, thankful for the excuse, and berating herself for bringing up the business about the drinking. She knew that Marzik would deny ratting to Kelso, and as long as Marzik denied it, it was a no-winner. Now Marzik was openly hostile.

'Hook, it's me.'

'You and Marzik get anything from the flower kid?'

'Marzik's going to bring him in to work with an artist. Can you get that set up?'

'Right away. Listen, we got the news tapes you wanted. From three of the stations, anyway. You want me to set up the room for us to watch?'

'It's the tape they shot from the helicopters over the parking lot?'

'Yeah. There are a lot of tapes here. You want me to set up the room?'

Starkey flashed on the images trapped on the tape. She would see the bomb explode. She would see Charlie Riggio die.

'Set up the room, Jorge. I want the kid to look at them, too, but only after he's done with the artist, okay? I don't want him seeing the videos first, then describing someone he's seen just because he thinks they look suspicious.'

'I'll get it set up.'

'One more thing. What happened with Pell last night?'

'He didn't like something in the coroner's report. Kelso had me take him over there.'

Starkey felt her stomach knot.

'What didn't he like?'

'The M.E. hadn't done a full body X-ray, so Pell made him do it.'

'Jesus, Kelso's letting him work the case like he's local?'

'I can't talk, Carol. You know?'

'Did he find anything?'

'They found some more frag, but he said it didn't amount to very much.'

Starkey felt herself breathe easier. Maybe Pell would lose interest and go back to Washington.

'Okay, arrange for the artist and lock down the room for the tapes. I'll be there in a few minutes.'

She ended the call, then went back to Marzik. She had decided that she needed to smooth over things.

'Beth? We've got the videotape. Jorge's going to set up the artist for you. After that, how about you bring Lester back to watch the tapes? Maybe he'll pick out the hat man.'

'Whatever.'

'Look, I didn't mean to step on your toes about the laundry people. That was good thinking, getting the customer names.'

'Thank you too much.'

If that's the way she wanted it, Starkey thought, fine.

She got into her car and left Marzik waiting in the heat for Lester Ybarra.

Starkey intended to drive back to Spring Street, but as she passed the site where Riggio died, she slowed and turned into the parking lot.

Hearing that the videotapes had arrived had gotten her thinking. The remote-control manufacturer had told her that the maximum possible range for the transmitter was one hundred yards. Per Bomb Squad policy, the area had been cleared out to one hundred yards, which meant that whoever had the transmitter would have to be right at the edge of the boundary. Starkey thought that maybe the news tape would show the crowd where someone had been close enough to pull the trigger.

The parking lot had been released as a crime scene, and all of the shops except for the bookstore were once more open for business. Two young Latinos were painting the damaged wall, the Dumpster had been replaced, and the blast crater was now a black patch against gray tarmac. Life was moving on.

Starkey parked on the street, then walked over to the patch. She stared across Sunset Boulevard, trying to figure how far one hundred yards was, then looked south up the little side street past the apartment buildings, trying to gauge the distance. The sun beat down on her dark gray pants suit, making the fabric hot and uncomfortable. She took off her jacket and folded it across her arm. The painters stared at the pistol on her hip, so she unclipped it and held it in the fold of her jacket.

Starkey crossed Sunset at the light, then continued north past the Guatemalan market, counting paces until she reached one hundred and thirty. She figured this to be about a hundred yards. She was standing six parking meters north of Sunset Boulevard, about a car length north of a telephone pole. She noted the telephone pole in her casebook, figuring it would be easy to spot on the news video, then went back to the patch and counted the same number of paces south. She found herself beside a tall, spindly palm tree. With so many palms in the area, it would be hard to spot the right one. The apartment building across the street had a blue tile roof, so she noted that in her book. Starkey returned to ground zero twice more, counting paces east and west to fix obvious landmarks. When she was done, she lit a cigarette, then sat in her car, smoking.

She thought that somewhere within these boundaries the killer had watched, and waited, and murdered a man.

She wondered if he was the man that Lester Ybarra had described, if it was Pell's Mr Red, or if it was someone else.

Hooker was sorting through the tapes in a cardboard box when Starkey reached CCS.

First thing he said was, 'The ATF guy called.'

'Pell called?'

'Yeah. I put it on your desk.'

'Screw'm. Did you get Marzik set up with the sketch artist?'

'They don't have a computer free until later. She wanted me to ask if they can't come here and start on the tapes while they wait.'

'No, I told her why not. I want the kid to describe who he saw before we show him any faces. Marzik knows better than that.'

'I told her you'd say that. She wasn't happy about it.'

'Marzik complains about everything.'

Starkey saw a short stack of pink message slips as she dropped her purse into her file drawer. Chester Riggs, who was working out of Organized Crime, and Warren Perez, a D-3 in Rampart Bunco, were both returning her calls. Riggs and Perez were profiling the minimall shopkeepers to look for motives behind the bomb. Neither of them expected to find a link, and neither did Starkey. She didn't bother to read the message from Pell.

Starkey returned to Santos and fingered through the cassettes. They were in two sizes, big three-quarter-inch master tapes and half-inch VHS dubs that could be played on home machines.

Santos saw her frowning.

'These are only from three of the stations, Carol. We got more coming in. Man, it's hours. The running times are written on the outside, along with whether it's a close-up or the wide-angle.'

Starkey turned the tapes so that she could see what he was talking about. The shortest tape showed a recorded time of seventy-four minutes. The longest, one hundred twenty-six minutes. Each tape was also marked CLOSE or WIDE.

'What does that mean, close or wide?'

'Some of the helicopters carry two cameras mounted on a swivel that pokes out the bottom of the nose, just like a couple of guns. Both cameras focus on the same thing, but one of the cameras is zoomed in close, and the other is pulled back for a wider field of view. They record both cameras up in the chopper and also back at the studio.'

'I thought they show this stuff live.'

'They do, but they record it at the same time. We've got both the wide shots and the close shots, so that means there's twice as much to watch.'

Starkey was already thinking that the close shots wouldn't give her what she wanted. She pulled out the wide-angle VHS cassettes and brought them to her desk. She considered calling Buck Daggett, but decided that she should review the tapes first.

Behind her, Santos said, 'I've got us set up in the TV room upstairs. We can go up as soon as I'm done.'

Spring Street had one room that contained a television and VCR. CCS and Fugitive Section rarely needed or used it; much of the time it was used by IAG investigators watching spy tapes of other cops, and most of the time the VCR was vandalized because of that. Chewing gum, tobacco, and other substances were found jammed into the tape heads, even though the room was kept locked. Once, the hindquarters of a rat were found wedged in the machine. Cops were creative vandals.

'You sure the machine up there is working?'

'Yeah. I checked less than an hour ago.'

Starkey considered the tapes. Three different views of Charlie Riggio being killed. Anytime there was a bomb call-out, the newspeople got word fast and swarmed the area with cameras. Camera crews and newspeople had been at the trailer park the day she and Sugar had rolled out. She suddenly recalled joking with Sugar about putting on a good show for the six o'clock. She had forgotten that moment until now.

Starkey took a cigarette from her purse and lit up.

'Carol! Do you want Kelso to send you home?'

She glanced over at Hooker, not understanding.

'The cigarette.'

Starkey crushed it with her foot as she fanned the air. She felt herself flush.

'Didn't even realize I was doing it.'

Hooker was watching her with an expression she read as concern.

Starkey felt a stab of fear that he might be wondering if she was drunk, so she went over to his desk and squatted beside him so that he could smell her breath. She wanted him to know that she wasn't blowing gin.

'I'm worried about this ATF guy, is all. Did he say anything last night when he finished with the medical examiner?'

'Nothing. I asked him if he found what he was looking for, but all he said was that they found some more frag.'

'He didn't say anything else?'

'Nothing. He spent today over in Glendale, looking at the reconstruction.'

Starkey went back to her desk, making a mental note to phone the medical examiner to see what they'd found and also to call John Chen. Whatever evidence was recovered would be sent to Chen for examination and documentation, though it might take several days to work its way through the system.

Hooker finished logging the tapes and put the box under his desk. Official LAPD filing. He waved one of the three-quarter-inch tapes.

'I'm done. We'd better get started unless you want to wait for Marzik.'

Starkey's hands grew damp. She leaned back, her swivel chair squeaking.

'Jorge, look, I'd better return these calls. You start without me, okay?'

Hooker had spent a lot of time getting the tapes together. Now he was disappointed.

'I thought you wanted to see this. We've only got the room for a couple of hours.'

'I'll watch them at home, Jorge. I've got these calls.'

Her phone rang then. Starkey snatched it up like a life preserver.

'CCS. Starkey.'

'Don't you return your calls?'

It was Pell.

'I've been busy. We've got a wit who might have seen the man who placed the 911 call.'

'Let's meet somewhere. We need to discuss how we're going to handle the case.'

'There is no "we", Pell. If my guy isn't your Mr Red, then it doesn't matter to me. I still want to see what you have on the first seven bombings.'

'I have the reports. I have something else, too, Starkey. Let's get together and talk about it. This is important.'

She wanted to brush him off, but she knew that she would have to talk with him and decided to get it done. Starkey told him how to get to Barrigan's, then hung up.

Santos had been watching her. He came over with a handful of cassettes.

'Are the feds taking the case?'

'I don't know. He didn't say.'

'I guess it's just a matter of time.'

She looked at him. Santos shrugged and gestured with the tapes.

'I'm gonna go up. You sure you don't want to come?'

'I've got to meet Pell.'

Starkey watched Santos walk away, embarrassed that she had not been able to look at them with him. She had been to the bomb site, she had seen Riggio's body, she had smelled the heat and the blast in the hot air. After that, her fear of seeing the tapes seemed inexplicable, though she understood it. Starkey wouldn't be seeing only Riggio on the tape; she would see herself, and Sugar. She had imagined the events of her own death a thousand times, but she had never seen tape of the actual event or even thought that the moments had been recorded until now: joking with Sugar, the news crews watching with electronic eyes, tape reels spinning for the six o'clock news. Memories of those things had vanished with the explosion until now.

Starkey fingered the three cassettes, wondering if that tape of her own death still existed.

After a time, she told herself to stop thinking about it, gathered her things, and left to meet Pell.

Barrigan's was a narrow Irish bar in Wilshire Division that had catered to police detectives since 1954, when suits from the Homicide Bureau had held court with tales of blackjacking New York mobsters as they deplaned at LAX. The walls were covered with four-leaf clovers, each bearing the name and date of an officer who'd killed a man in the line of duty. Until only a handful of years ago, female police detectives were discouraged as customers, conventional wisdom being that the presence of female officers would discourage the emotionally dysfunctional secretaries and nurses who flocked to the bar eager to dispense sexual favors to any man with a badge. Though there was some truth to this, the female detectives replied, 'Tough shit.' The gender barrier was finally broken the night a Robbery–Homicide detective named Samantha Dolan shot it out toe-to-toe with two rape suspects, killing both. As is the custom after such incidents, a party was held for her at Barrigan's that same night. Dolan invited every female detective of her acquaintance, and the women decided they liked the place and would return. They informed the owner that they would be accorded proper service, else they'd have the good sisters over in the Department of Health close his ass down for health violations. That ended that. Starkey had never met Dolan, though she knew the story. Samantha Dolan had later been killed when she'd stepped through a doorway that had been booby-trapped with a double-barreled shotgun.

When Starkey entered Barrigan's late that afternoon, the bar was already lined with detectives. Starkey found a bench between a couple of Sex Crimes D-2s, struck up a fresh cigarette, and ordered a double Sapphire.

She was taking her first sip when Pell appeared beside her and put a heavy manila envelope on the bar.

'You always drink like that on the job?'

'It's none of your goddamned business what I do. But for the record, Special Agent, I'm off duty. I'm here as a favor to you.'

The D-2 next to her glanced over, eyeing Pell. He tinkled the ice in the remains of his double scotch, offering Pell the opportunity to comment on his drink, too.

Starkey offered to buy Pell a drink, but Pell refused. He slid onto the bench next to her, uncomfortably close. Barrigan's didn't have stools; the bar was lined with little benches hooked to a brass rail that ran along the bottom of the bar, each wide enough for two people. Starkey hated the damn things because you couldn't move them, but that's the way it had been since 1954, and that's the way it was going to stay.

'Move away, Pell. You're too close.'

He edged away.

'Enough? I could sit at another table if you like.'

'You're fine where you are. I just don't like people too close.'

Starkey immediately regretted saying it, feeling it revealed more of herself than she cared to share.

Pell tapped the manila envelope.

'These are the reports. I've got something else here, too.'

He unfolded a sheet of paper and put it on the bar. Starkey saw that it was a newspaper article that he had printed off the net.

'This happened a few days ago. Read it.'

BOMB HOAX CLEARS LIBRARY
By Lauren Beth
Miami Herald

The Dade County Regional Main Library was evacuated yesterday when library employees discovered what appeared to be a bomb.

When a loud siren began wailing, librarians found what they believed to be a pipe bomb fixed to the underside of a table.

After police evacuated the library, the Dade County Emergency Response Team recovered the device, which contained the siren, but no explosives. Police officials are calling the incident a hoax.

Starkey stopped reading.

'What is this?'

'We recovered an intact device in Miami. It's a clone of the bomb that killed Riggio.'

Starkey didn't like the news about this Miami device. If the bombs were clones like Pell said, that would give him what he needed to jump the case. She knew what would happen then: the ATF would form a task force, which would spur the FBI to come sniffing around. The Sheriffs would want to get their piece of the action, so they would be included, and before the day was done, Starkey and her CCS team would be relegated to gofer chores like overnighting the evidence to the ATF lab up in San Francisco.

She pushed the article away.

'Okay. A hoax. If your boy Mr Red is in Miami, why aren't you on a plane headed east?'

'Because he's here.'

'It looks to me like he's in Miami.'

Pell glanced at the D-2.

'Could we move to a table?'

Starkey led him to a remote corner table, taking the outside seat so that she could see the room. She figured that it would annoy him, having his back to the crowd.

'Okay, no one can hear you, Pell. We're free to be spies.'

Pell's jaw flexed with irritation, which pleased her. She struck a fresh cigarette, blowing smoke past his shoulder.

'The Miami police didn't give the full story to the papers. It wasn't a hoax, Starkey, it was a message. An actual note. Words on paper. He's never done that before, and he's never done anything like this. That means we have a chance here.'

'What did he say?'

'He said, "Would the deaths of these people put me in the Top Ten?"'

Starkey didn't know what in the hell that meant.

'What does that mean?'

'He wants to be on the FBI's Ten Most Wanted List.'

'You're kidding me.'

'It's a symbol, Starkey. He's some underachieving nobody who resents being an asshole. He's not on the list because we don't know who the hell he is; no one makes that list unless we have an ID. We don't, so he's getting frustrated. He's taking chances he didn't take earlier. That means he's destabilizing.'

Starkey's jaw felt like an iron clamp, but she understood why Pell was on it. When a perp changed his pattern, it was always good for the case. Any change gave you a different view of the man. If you could get enough views, pretty soon you had a clear picture.

'You said he's here. How do you know that? Did his message say that he was coming to Los Angeles?'

Pell didn't answer. He stared at her as if he was searching for something in her eyes, leaving her feeling naked and uncomfortable.

'What?'

'I didn't tell you and Kelso everything. When Mr Red goes hunting, he does not hunt randomly. He picks his targets, usually senior people or a tech who's been in the news; he goes after the big dog. He wants to say he beats the best a Bomb Squad has to offer. It's the ego thing.'

'That what he told you in his little note?'

'We know because he etches the target's name on the bomb casing. The first two techs he killed, we found their names in the frag during the reconstruction. Alan Brennert in Baltimore; Michael Cassutt in Philadelphia; both sergeant-supervisors who'd been involved in big cases.'

Starkey didn't say anything. She drew a large 5 in the water rings on the table, then changed it to an S. She guessed it came from 'Charles'. Charlie Riggio wasn't exactly the big dog of the LAPD Bomb Squad, but she wasn't going to say that.

'Why are you telling me this here in a bar and not in Kelso's office?'

Now Pell glanced away. He seemed nervous about something.

'We try to keep that information on a need-to-know basis.'

'Well, I'm honored, Pell. I sure as hell have a need to know, wouldn't you say?'

'Yes.'

'Makes me wonder what else you might be holding back.'

Pell glanced back sharply.

'As the lead, you could make statements to the press to help advance his destabilization. These aren't just little machines that he's building. These bombs are who he is, and he's meticulous about them. They are very precise, very exact. We know he takes pride in them. In his head, it could become a one-on-one game that keeps him in Los Angeles and gives us a better shot to nail him.'

'Me versus him.'

'Something like that. What do you say?'

Starkey didn't have to think about it.

'I'm in.'

Pell sighed deeply, his shoulders sagging as he relaxed, as if he had been afraid that she wouldn't go along. She smiled to herself, thinking how little he knew.

'All right, Starkey. All right. We believe that he builds the bombs locally. He'll go into an area, acquire the things that he needs, and build the bomb there, so he doesn't have to transport anything, risking capture on the airlines. I put a list of the Modex components in with the reports. I want you to run a local check for people with access to RDX.'

Even though Starkey was already running the search, it irritated her that he was giving instructions.

'Listen, Pell, if you want to run a search, do it yourself. You're not giving the orders here.'

'It's important, Starkey.'

'Then *you* do it!'

Pell glared at her, then seemed to reconsider. He showed his palms and relaxed.

'I guess you could look at it this way, Detective: if I do it, I'm taking over your case; if you do it, I'm only advising you. Which do you want it to be?'

Starkey looked smug.

'It's already happening, Pell. I punched it in today.'

He nodded without expression and went on. She found herself irritated that he didn't acknowledge that she was ahead of him.

'Do we have a photograph of this guy? There must've been a security camera.'

'There aren't any security cameras in the downtown branch, but I'll have a sketch by tomorrow. The wits described a white male in his twenties with bright red hair. We also have two other sketches from previous incidents. I can already tell you that all three look different. He changes his appearance when he lets himself be seen.'

Starkey shrugged noncommittally. Lester had described an older man, nothing even close to young, but she decided not to mention Lester until they had the sketch.

'Whatever. I want a copy of all three of your sketches when you have them, and I want something else, too. I want to see the bomb.'

'As soon as I get the report, you'll get the report.'

'You didn't hear me. I want the bomb. I want it in my hands. I'm a bomb technician, Pell. I want to break it down myself, not just accept someone else's report. I want to compare it to the Silver Lake bomb and learn something. I know we can do this because I've traded comparative evidence with other cities before.'

Pell seemed to consider her again, then nodded.

'Okay, Starkey, I think that's a good idea. But I think you should arrange it.'

Starkey frowned, wondering if Pell was going to be deadwood.

'*Your* people have the damned thing. It would be easier for you to get it.'

'The more I do, the more pressure I'll get from Washington to take over the case before the FBI comes in.'

'Who's talking about the FBI? We're not dealing with a terrorist here. This is domestic.'

'A terrorist is whoever the FBI says is a terrorist. You're worried about me coming in, I'm worried about the FBI. We all have something to worry about.'

'Jesus Christ, Pell.'

He showed his palms again, and she nodded.

'Okay. I'll do it myself.'

Pell stood, then gave her a card.

'This is the motel where I'm staying. My pager number is on the back.'

Starkey put it away without looking at it.

'Anything comes up, I'll give you a call.'

Pell was staring at her.

'What?'

'Mr Red is dangerous, Starkey. A guy like this in town, you don't want to be too drunk to react.'

Starkey rattled the ice in her glass, then took a sip.

'I've already been dead once, Pell. Believe me, there are worse things.'

Pell considered her another moment, Starkey thinking he wanted to say something, but then he left. She watched him until he stepped out of the bar into a wedge of blinding light and was gone. Pell had no fucking idea.

Starkey returned to her bench at the bar and ordered a refill. She was convinced that Pell knew more than he was saying.

The Sex Crimes dick leaned close.

'Fed?'

'Yeah.'

'They're all pricks.'

'We'll see.'

*

Starkey spent most of the afternoon thinking about the tapes that waited in her car. Those tapes and what was on them were real. After a while, it was the weight of the tapes that pulled her from the bar. It was almost eight when she left Barrigan's and drove home.

Starkey's head hurt from the gin. She was hungry, but there was nothing to eat in her house and she didn't want to go out again. She put the tapes in her living room by the VCR, but decided to shower first, then read the reports.

She let the water beat into her neck and skull until it ran cold, then dressed in a black T-shirt and panties. She found a box of raisins, ate them standing at the kitchen sink. When she was finished, she poured a glass of milk, struck a fresh cigarette, and sat at the kitchen table to read.

The manila envelope contained seven ATF explosives profiles written at the ATF's National Laboratory Center in Rockville, Maryland. Each report contained an analysis of a device that was attributed to an unidentified suspect known only as Mr Red, but each was heavily edited. Pages were missing, and several paragraphs in each report had been deleted.

Starkey grew angry at the deletions, but she found herself interested in the details that were present and read with clear focus. She took notes.

Every one of the devices had been built of twin pipe canisters capped and sealed with plumber's tape, one pipe containing the radio receiver (all receivers identified as being from the WayKool line of remote-control toy cars) and 9-volt battery, one the Modex Hybrid explosive. None of the reports mentioned the etched names that Pell had described. She thought that the deleted material probably referenced that.

When she finished with the reports, she went into her living room and stared at the tapes. She knew that she had been avoiding them, evidence that could potentially offer a breakthrough in her case. But even now, her stomach knotted at the thought of seeing them.

'Oh, goddamnit. This is stupid.'

She went into the kitchen, poured herself a stiff gin, then loaded the first tape into the machine. She could have watched the tapes with Buck Daggett or Lester Ybarra, or with Marzik and Hooker, but she knew she had to see them alone. At least, this first time. She had to see them alone because she would be seeing things that none of the rest of them would see.

The image was a wide shot of the parking lot. The Bomb Squad Suburban was in place, the parking lot and the nearby streets cordoned off. The frame did not move, telling Starkey that the helicopter had been in a stationary hover. Riggio, already in the suit, was at the rear of the Suburban, talking with Daggett. Seeing them like that chilled her. Seeing Daggett pat Riggio's helmet, seeing Riggio turn and lumber toward the bomb was like watching Sugar.

'How you doin', cher? You gettin' a good air flow?'

'Got a windstorm in here. You?'

'Wrapped, strapped, and ready to rock. Let's put on a good show for the cameras.'

They checked over each other's armor suit and cables. Sugar looked okay to her. She patted his helmet, and he patted hers. That always made her smile.

They started toward the trailer.

Starkey stopped the tape.

She took a breath, realizing only then that she had stopped breathing. She decided that her drink needed more lime, brought it into the kitchen, cut another slice, all the while knowing that she was simply avoiding the video.

She went back into the living room and restarted the tape.

Riggio and the Suburban were in the center of the screen. The bomb was a tiny cardboard square at the base of the Dumpster. The shot was framed too tightly on the parking lot to reveal any of the landmarks she had paced off that morning. The only figures visible were Riggio, Daggett, and a uniformed officer standing at the edge of the building in the bottom of the frame, peeking around the corner.

When Riggio started toward the bomb, the frame shifted, sliding above the minimall to reveal a small group of people standing between two apartment houses. Starkey focused on them, but they were too small and shadowed to tell if any wore long-sleeved shirts and baseball caps.

Starkey was cursing the tiny image when suddenly the frame shifted down, centering on Riggio and losing the people. The camera operator in the helicopter must have adjusted the shot, losing everything except the side of the mall, the bomb, and Riggio.

Riggio reached the bomb with the Real Time.

Starkey knew what was coming and tried to steel herself.

She had more of the drink, feeling her heart pound.

She glanced away and crushed out her cigarette.

When she looked at the screen again, Riggio was circling the box.

They were in the azaleas, wrestling the heavy branches aside so that Sugar could position the Real Time. Sugar looked for all the world like some kind of Star Trek space invader with a ray gun. She had to twist her body to see him.

Her eyes blurred as the white flash engulfed her . . .

Starkey strained to see into the shadows and angles at the outer edge of the frame, between cars, on roofs, in garbage cans. She wondered if the bomber was somehow underground, peering out of a sewer drain or from the vent of a crawl space beneath a building. Riggio circled the bomb, examining it with the Real Time. She put herself in the killer's head and tried to see Riggio from the ground level. She imagined the radio control in her hand. What was he waiting for? Starkey felt anxious and wondered if the killer was growing frightened at the thought of murdering another human being, or excited. Starkey saw the switch as a TV remote, held in the killer's pocket. She saw his eyes on Riggio, unblinking. Riggio finished his circle, hesitated, then leaned over the box. In that moment, the killer pressed the switch and . . .

. . . the light hurled Charlie Riggio away like an imaginary man.

Starkey stopped the tape and closed her eyes, her fist clenched tight as if it was she who had clutched the switch and sent Charlie Riggio to hell.

She felt herself breathe. She felt her chest expand, her body fill with air. She gripped her glass with both hands and drank. She wiped at her eyes.

After a while, she pressed the 'play' button and forced herself to watch the rest of the tape.

The pressure wave flashed across the tarmac, a ripple of dust and debris sucked up after it. The Dumpster rocked backwards into the wall. Smoke rose from the crater, drifting lazily in a swirl as Buck Daggett rushed forward to his partner and pulled off the helmet. An Emergency Services van screeched into the lot beside them, two paramedics rushing in to take over. Buck stood watching them.

Starkey was able to pick out the boundaries she had marked and several times found knots of people at the edge of the hundred-yard perimeter who were hidden behind cars or buildings. She froze the image each time, looking for long-sleeved males in blue baseball caps, but the resolution was too poor to be of much use.

She watched the other two tapes, drinking all the while. She examined the murky images as if willing them to clear, thinking that any of those shadowed faces might belong to the man or woman who had built and detonated the bomb.

Later that night, she rewound the tapes, turned off her television, and fell into a deep sleep there on her couch.

She is kicked away from the trailer by a burst of white light.

The paramedics insert their long needle.

She reaches for Sugar's hand as his helmet is pulled free.

His head lolls toward her.

It is Pell.

5

The next morning, Marzik walked through CCS like a shy student handing back test papers, passing out copies of the suspect likeness that had been created from Lester Ybarra's description. Kelso, the last to get one, scowled as if it were his daughter's failing exam.

'There's nothing here we can use. Your wit was a waste of time.'

Marzik, clearly disappointed, was stung by Kelso's words.

'Well, it's not my fault. I don't think Lester really saw anything. Not the face, anyway.'

Starkey was at her desk when Kelso approached with the picture. She kept her eyes averted, hoping that neither he nor Marzik would notice their redness. She was sure the gin was bleeding through her pores and tried not to blow in their faces when she commented on the likeness.

'It's a ghost.'

Marzik nodded glumly, agreeing.

'Casper all the way.'

The portrait showed a white male approximately forty years of age with a rectangular face hidden by dark glasses and a baseball cap. His nose was undistinguished in shape and size, as were his lips, ears, and jaw. It worked out that way more times than not. If a wit saw no identifying characteristics, the portrait ended up looking like every other person on the street. The detectives called them 'ghosts' because there was nothing to see.

Kelso scowled at the portrait some more, then shook his head and sighed deeply. Starkey thought he was being an ass.

'It's nobody's fault, Barry. We're still interviewing people who were in the laundry at about the same time. The portrait is going to develop.'

Marzik nodded, encouraged by Starkey's support, but Kelso didn't look impressed.

'I got a call from Assistant Chief Morgan last night. He asked how you were doing as the lead, Carol. He's going to want a report soon.'

Starkey's head throbbed.

'I'll go see him whenever he wants. That's not a problem.'

'He won't just want to look at you, Carol; he'll want *facts*, as in *progress*.'

Starkey felt her temper starting to fray.

'What do you want me to do, Barry, pull the perp out of my ass?'

Kelso's jaw knotted and unwound like he was chewing marbles.

'That might help. He suggested that we could forestall the ATF taking over this case if we had something to show for our efforts. Think about it.'

Kelso stalked away and disappeared into his office.

Starkey's head throbbed worse. She had gotten so drunk last night that she scared herself and had spent most of the morning worried that her drinking was finally out of hand. She woke angry and embarrassed that Pell had once more been in her dreams, though she dismissed it as a sign of stress. She had taken two aspirin and two Tagamet, then pressed into the office, hoping to find a kickback on the RDX. She hadn't. Now this.

Marzik said, 'Kelso's a turd. Do you think he talks to us like that because we're women?'

'I don't know, Beth. Listen, don't sweat the picture. Pell has three other likenesses that he's going to deliver. We can show those to Lester. Maybe something will click.'

Marzik didn't leave. Starkey was certain that she needed another breath mint, but wouldn't take one with Marzik standing over her.

'Even though Lester didn't get a face, he's solid on the cap and long-sleeved shirt.'

'Okay.'

'I've got him set up to come in this afternoon to look at the tapes. You see anything last night?'

Starkey leaned back to stay as far from Marzik as possible.

'Not on the wide shots. Everything is so murky you can't really see. I think we need to have them enhanced, see if that won't give us a better view.'

'I could take care of that, you want.'

'I already talked to Hooker about it. He's had tapes enhanced before when he was working Divisional Robbery over in Hollenbeck. Listen, I need to check the NLETS, okay? We'll talk later.'

Marzik nodded, still not moving. She looked like she wanted to say something.

'What, Beth?'

'Carol, listen. I want to apologize for yesterday. I was a bitch.'

'Forget it. Thanks for saying so, but it's okay.'

'I felt bad all night and I wanted to apologize.'

'Okay. Thanks. Thank you. Don't sweat the picture.'

'Yeah. Kelso's such a turd.'

Marzik took her portrait and went back to her desk. Starkey stared after her. Sometimes Marzik surprised her.

When Marzik wasn't looking, Starkey popped a fresh Altoid, then went for the coffee. When she checked the NLETS system on the way back to her desk, this time something was waiting.

Starkey had expected one or two hits on the RDX, but nothing like what she found.

The California State Sheriffs reported that Dallas Tennant, a thirty-two-year-old white male, was currently serving time in the California State Correctional Facility in Atascadero, a facility for prisoners receiving treatment for mental disorders. On three separate occasions two years ago, Tennant had exploded devices made with RDX. Starkey smiled when she saw it was three devices. RDX was rare; three devices meant that Tennant had had access to a lot of it. Starkey printed off the computer report, noting that the case had been made by a Sheriff's Bomb and Arson sergeant-investigator named Warren Mueller out of the Central Valley office in Bakersfield. Back at her desk, she looked up the phone number in her State Law Enforcement Directory, then called the Central Valley number, asking for the Bomb and Arson Unit.

'B and A. Hennessey.'

'Warren Mueller, please.'

'Yeah, he's here. Stand by.'

When Mueller came on, Starkey identified herself as a Los Angeles police officer. Mueller had an easy male voice with a twang of the Central Valley at the edges. Starkey thought he had probably grown up downwind of one of the meatpacking plants up there.

'I'm calling about a perp you collared named Dallas Tennant.'

'Oh, sure. He's enjoying a lease in Atascadero these days.'

'That's right. Reason I'm calling is I got a kicker saying that he set off three devices using RDX. That's a lot of RDX.'

'Three we know of, yeah. Coulda been more. He was buying stolen cars from some kids up here, hundred bucks, no questions, then driving'm out into the desert to blow'm up. He'd soak'm in gas first so they'd burn, you know? Crazy fool just wanted to see'm come apart, I guess. He blew up four or five trees, too, but he used TNT for that.'

'It's the RDX that interests me. You know where he got it?'

'Well, he claimed that he bought a case of stolen antipersonnel mines from a guy he met at a bar. You believe that, I got some desert land up here I'll sell you. My guess is that he bought it off one of these meth-dealing biker assholes, but he never copped, so I couldn't tell you.'

Starkey knew that the vast majority of bombings were the result of drug wars between rival methamphetamine dealers, many of whom were white bikers. Meth labs were chemical bombs waiting to happen. So when a meth dealer wanted to eliminate a rival, he often just blew apart his Airstream. Starkey had rolled out on almost a hundred meth labs when she was a bomb tech. Bomb Squad would roll even for a warrant service.

'So you think you could still have a guy up there with RDX to sell?'

'Well, that's possible, but you never know. We didn't have a suspect at the time, and we don't have one now. All we had was Dallas, blowing up his goddamned cars. The guy's your classic no-life, loner bomb crank. But the guy stood up, though, I'll give'm that. Wherever he got it, he didn't roll.'

'Did he have any more RDX in his possession at the time of his arrest?'

'Never found any of his works. Said he made everything at home, but there was no evidence of it. He had this shithole apartment over here out past the meat plant, but we didn't find so much as a firecracker. We couldn't find any evidence of these mines he claimed to have bought, either.'

Starkey considered that. Building bombs for bomb cranks like Dallas Tennant was a way of life. It was their passion, and they inevitably had a place where they built their bombs, in the same way that hobbiests had hobby rooms. Might be a closet or a room or a place in their garage, but they had a place to store their supplies and practice their craft. Such places were called 'shops'.

'Seems like he would've had a shop.'

'Well, my personal feeling is that he was butt-buddies with the same guy sold him the RDX, and that guy packed up when Dallas was tagged, but like I say, that's just my feeling.'

Starkey put that in her notes, but didn't think much of Mueller's theory. As Mueller had already pointed out, bomb cranks were introverted loners, usually with low self-esteem and feelings of inadequacy. They were often extremely shy and almost never had relationships with women. Sharing their toys didn't fit with the profile. Starkey suspected that if Tennant didn't cop to his shop, it was because he didn't want to lose his toys. Like all chronics, he would see explosions in his dreams, and probably spent much of every day fantasizing about the bombs he would build as soon as he was released.

Starkey closed her pad.

'Okay, Sergeant, I think that about does it. I appreciate your time.'

'Anytime. Could I ask you something, Starkey?'

'I've asked you plenty.'

He hesitated. She knew in that moment what was coming and felt her stomach knot.

'You being down there in L.A. and all, you the same Starkey got blown up?'

'Yeah. That was me. Listen, all I've got here is what the Sheriffs put out on the kicker. Could you fax your casework on Tennant to give me a little more?'

'This about that thing happened down there in Silver Lake?'

'Yes, sir.'

'Sure. It's only a few pages. I can get to it right away.'

'Thanks.'

Starkey gave him the fax number and hung up before Mueller could say any more. It was always like that, even more so from the bomb techs and bomb investigators, from the people who lived so close to the edge but never looked over, in a kind of awe that she had.

Starkey refilled her coffee and brought it into the stairwell where she stood smoking with three Fugitive Section detectives. They were young, athletic guys with short hair and thick mustaches. They were still enthusiastic about the job and hadn't yet let themselves go, the way most cops did when they realized that the job was bureaucratic bullshit that served no purpose and did no good. These guys would bag their day at two in the afternoon, then head over to Chavez Ravine to work out at the Police Academy. Starkey could see it in their tight jeans and forearms. They smiled; she nodded back. They went on with their discussion without including her. They had made a collar that morning in Eagle Rock, a *veterano* gang member with a rep as a hard guy who was wanted for armed robbery and mayhem. The mayhem charge meant he'd bitten off a nose or an ear during one of the assaults. The three Fugitive cops had found him hiding under a blanket in a garage when they made the pinch. The tough *veterano* had pissed his pants so badly that they wouldn't put him in the car until they'd found a plastic trash bag for him to sit on. Starkey listened to the three young cops relive their story, then crushed out her cigarette and went back to the fax machine. Another cop story. One of thousands. They always ended well unless a cop took a bullet or got bagged in an unlawful act.

When Starkey got back to the fax machine, Mueller's casework was waiting in the tray.

Starkey read it back at her desk. Tennant had an arrest history of fire starting and explosives that went back to the age of eighteen and had twice received court-mandated psychiatric counseling. Starkey knew that the arrests had probably started even earlier, but weren't reflected in the case file because juvenile records were sealed. She also knew this because Mueller's notes indicated that Tennant was missing two fingers from his left hand, an explosives-related injury that occurred while he was a teenager.

Mueller's case involved interviewing a young car thief named Robert Castillo, who had stolen two of the three cars that Tennant destroyed, along with photographs of the demolished cars. Mueller had been summoned to the Bakersfield Puritan Hospital Emergency Room by patrol officers, where he found Castillo with a windshield wiper blade through his cheek. Castillo, having delivered a late-model Nissan Stanza to Tennant, had apparently stood too close when Tennant destroyed it, caught the blade through his face, and had been rushed to the hospital by his friends. Starkey read Mueller's interview notes several times before she caught something in the Castillo interview that reinforced her belief that Tennant still maintained his shop. She decided that she wanted to speak with him.

Starkey looked up the phone number for Atascadero, called, and asked for the law enforcement liaison officer. Police officers couldn't just walk in off the street to speak with prisoners; the prisoner had the right to have counsel present and could refuse to speak with you. Atascadero was a long way to drive just to be told to fuck off.

'You have an inmate up there named Dallas Tennant. I'm working an active case here in Los Angeles that he might have information relating to. Would you see if he'd talk to me without counsel?'

'Would you still want to see him if he demands counsel?'

'Yes. But if he wants to play it that way, I'll need the name of his attorney.'

'All right.'

She could tell by the way the man paused that he was writing. Soft music played behind him.

'When would you want to see him, Detective?'

Starkey glanced at the clock on the wall and thought about Pell. 'Later today. Ah, say about two this afternoon.'

'All right. He's going to want to know what it's about.'

'The availability of an explosive called RDX.'

The liaison officer took her number and told her he'd call back as soon as possible.

After she hung up, Starkey got a fresh cup of coffee, then went back to her desk, thinking about what to do. LAPD policy required detectives always to work in pairs, but Marzik had interviews and Hooker was going to see about the tape. Starkey thought about Pell. There was no reason to call him, no reason to tell him any of this until it was over and she had something to say.

She found his card in her purse and paged him.

Starkey completed the evidence transfer request, which she faxed to the ATF regional office in Miami, then waited for Pell in the lobby. The drive from downtown L.A. to Atascadero was going to be just over three hours. She had thought that Pell would want to drive, because men always wanted to drive, but he didn't. Instead, he said, 'I'll use the time to read Tennant's case file, then we can work out a game plan.'

There he was with the game plan again.

She gave him the report, then maneuvered out of the city and up the coast along the Ventura Freeway. He read without comment, seeming to take forever to get through the six pages. She found his silence irritating.

'How long is it going to take you to read that, Pell?'

'I'm reading it more than once. This is good stuff, Starkey. We can use this. Searching for the RDX paid off.'

'I wanted to mention that to you. I want to make sure we don't get off on the wrong foot here.'

Pell looked at her.

'What wrong foot?'

'I know you think you were advising me, but I don't need it. You come in, start telling me what to do and how to do it, and expect me to hop to it. It doesn't work that way.'

'It was just a suggestion. You did it anyway.'

'I just want to get things straight. Don't expect that I'll get coffee for you.'

Pell stared at her, then glanced back at the pages.

'You spoke with the arresting officer?'

'Yeah. Mueller.'

'Can I ask you to tell me what he said, or is that too much like asking you for a mocha?'

'I'm not trying to fight with you. I just wanted to set the ground rules.'

She went through her conversation with Mueller, recounting pretty much everything that had been said. Pell stared at the passing scenery, so silent that she wondered if he was even listening. But when she finished, he glanced through the pages again, then shook his head.

'Mueller dropped the ball about Tennant not having a shop. According to this, Tennant was buying stolen cars to destroy them. Three cars, three explosions. The car thief—'

'Robert Castillo.'

'Yeah, Castillo. Castillo said that Tennant had asked him to steal a fourth car. He wouldn't need another car if he didn't have more RDX to destroy it or knew how to get more.'

Starkey's grip tightened on the wheel.

'That's what I figured.'

Pell shrugged and put the pages aside.

It sounded so lame. That was exactly what Starkey had reasoned, and she wished that she had said it before Pell. Now it looked like he was the one who'd found the hole in Tennant's denials.

'You said you had a suspect likeness coming from Miami. Did you get it for me?'

'Yeah. That, and the first two we have.'

He slipped them from his jacket and unfolded them for her.

'Can you see?'

'Yeah.'

'There were enough people in the library to put together a pretty good composite. Our guy shows to be six feet, one-eighty or so, but he's probably wearing lifts and padding. The wits from the earlier sightings made him at five ten. He had a square jaw, bright red hair, sideburns. That doesn't square with the earlier sightings, either.'

Starkey glanced at the three sheets as she drove. Pell was right, none of the three looked very much alike, and none of them looked like the man Lester Ybarra described. The Miami likeness was as Pell said, the second likeness showed a balding, professorial-looking man with glasses, and the third, which was the first description that the feds had, showed a much heavier man with woolly Rasta braids, sunglasses, and a beard.

She handed them back to Pell.

'This last one looks like you in drag, Pell.'

Pell put the sheets away.

'What about your guy? He match any of these?'

Starkey told him to open her briefcase, which was on the backseat. When Pell had it, he shook his head.

'How old is this guy supposed to be?'

'Forty, but our wit isn't dependable.'

'So he might've made himself up to look older.'

'Maybe. If we're talking about the same guy.'

'Mr Red is in his late twenties, early thirties. That's about all we know for sure. That, and him being white. He lets himself be seen, Starkey. He changes his look to fuck with us. That's how he gets off, fucking with us.'

After that, they drove in silence for a while, Starkey thinking about how she was going to approach Tennant. She happened to glance over and found Pell staring at her.

'What?'

'You said you had gotten videotapes from the Silver Lake event. Did you look at them yet?'

Starkey put her eyes on the road. They had passed Santa Barbara; the freeway was curving inland toward Santa Maria.

'Yeah. I looked at them last night.'

'Anything?'

Starkey shrugged.

'I've gotta have them enhanced.'

'That must've been hard for you.'

'What?'

'Looking at what happened. It must've been hard. It would be for me.'

Pell met her eyes, then went back to staring out the window. She thought he might be pitying her and felt herself flush with anger.

'Pell, one more thing.'

'What?'

'When we get there with Tennant, it's my show. I'm the lead here.'

Pell nodded without expression, without looking at her.

'I'm just along for the ride.'

Starkey drove the remaining two hours in silence, pissed off that she had invited him along.

The Atascadero Minimum Security Correctional Facility was a village of brown brick buildings set in the broad open expanse of what used to be almond groves in the arid ranchland south of Paso Robles. There were no walls, no guard towers; just a ten-foot chain-link fence and a single front gate with two bored guards who had to slide a motorized gate out of the way.

Atascadero was used to house nonviolent felons who the court deemed unsuitable for the general prison population: ex-police officers, white-collar criminals convicted of one-shot paper crimes, and vacationing celebrities who'd wrung out the eight or nine chances the courts inevitably gave them on drug charges. No one ever got knifed or gang-raped at Atascadero, though the inmates did have to maintain a three-acre truck garden. The worst that could happen was heatstroke.

Starkey said, 'They're going to make us check our guns. Be faster with the paperwork if we leave'm in the car.'

'You going to leave yours?'

'It's already in my briefcase. I never carry the damned thing.'

Pell glanced over, then pulled an enormous Smith 10mm autoloader and slipped it under the seat.

'Jesus, Pell, why do you need a monster like that?'

'No one gets a second shot.'

Starkey badged the gate guards, who directed her to the reception area. They left the car in a small, unshaded parking lot, then went inside to find the law enforcement liaison officer, a man named Larry Olsen, waiting for them.

'Detective Starkey?'

'Carol Starkey. This is Special Agent Pell, with the ATF. Thanks for setting this up.'

Olsen asked for identification and had them sign the log. He was a bored man who walked as if his legs hurt. He led them out the rear through double glass doors and along a walk toward another building. From back here, Starkey could see the truck garden and two basketball courts. Several inmates were playing basketball with their shirts off, laughing and enjoying themselves. They missed easy shots and handled the ball poorly. All of them except one were white.

Olsen said, 'I should tell you that Tennant is currently being medicated. These are court-mandated therapies. Xanax for anxiety and Anafranil to help regulate his obsessive-compulsive disorder. He's required to take them.'

'Is that going to give us a problem with him agreeing to have no lawyer present?'

'Not at all. They don't affect his judgment, just his compulsions. He was off the meds for a while, but we had a problem recently and had to resume the treatment.'

Pell said, 'What kind of problem?'

'Tennant used cleaning products and some iodine he stole from the infirmary to create an explosive. He lost his left thumb.'

Pell shook his head.

'What an asshole.'

'Well, this is a minimum-security installation, you know. The inmates have a great deal of freedom.'

Dallas Tennant was an overweight man with pale skin and large eyes. He was sitting at a clean Formica table that had been pushed against the wall, but stood when Olsen showed them into the interview room. His left hand was bandaged, strangely narrow without its thumb. Tennant's eyes locked on Starkey and stayed there. He barely glanced at Pell. The index and middle fingers of his right hand were missing at the second joint, the caps of scar old and worn. This was the injury that Starkey had read about in Mueller's case file.

Tennant said, 'Hello, Mr Olsen. Is this Detective Starkey?'

Olsen introduced them, Tennant offering his hand, but neither Starkey nor Pell taking it. You never shook their hand. Shaking hands put you on an equal basis, and you weren't equals. They were in prison; you weren't. They were weak; you were strong. Starkey had learned that it was a game of power when she was still in uniform. Assholes in prison thought of a friend as someone it was easy to manipulate.

Olsen put his clipboard on the table and opened a felt-tipped pen.

'Tennant, this form says that you have been advised of your right to have an attorney present for this interview, but that you have declined that right. You have to sign it here on this line, and I will witness.'

As Tennant signed the forms, Starkey noticed a thick plastic book on the corner of the table. Two screw-thread hasps kept it fastened at the spine; the cover was of a tropical island at sunset with script letters that read *My Happy Memories*. It was the kind of inexpensive photo album you could buy at any dime store.

When Starkey glanced up, Tennant was staring at her. He smiled shyly.

'That's my book.'

Olsen tapped the form.

'Your signature right here, Detective.'

Starkey forced her eyes away from Tennant and signed. Olsen signed beneath her signature, dated the page, then explained that a guard would be outside the room to remove Tennant when they were finished. After that, he left.

Starkey directed Tennant where to sit. She wanted to be across from him, and she wanted Pell at his side so that Tennant would have to look at one or the other, but not both. Tennant slid his scrapbook across the table when he changed seats to keep it near him.

'First off, Dallas, I want to tell you that we're not investigating you. We're not looking to bring charges against you. We're going to overlook any crimes you admit to, as long as they don't include crimes against persons.'

Tennant nodded.

'There won't be any of that. I never hurt anyone.'

'Fine. Then let's get started.'

'Can I show you something first? I think it might help you.'

'Let's not get sidetracked, Dallas. Let's stay with the reason we're here.'

He turned his book for her to see, ignoring her objection.

'It won't take long, and it's very important to me. I wasn't going to see you at first, but then I remembered your name.'

He had marked a place in the book with a strip of toilet tissue. He opened to the marked page.

The newspaper clip was yellow from being smothered by the plastic for three years, but the below-the-fold two-column headline was still readable. Starkey felt her skin grow cold.

OFFICER KILLED IN BOMB BLAST; SECOND OFFICER CRITICAL

It was an L.A. *Times* article about the trailer-park bombing that had killed Sugar and wounded Starkey. Above the headline was a grainy black-and-white picture that showed the two EMP teams, one team working on Sugar, the other on Starkey, as firefighters hosed the flaming trailer behind them. She had never read the article or the three follow-up articles. A friend of Starkey's named Marion Tyson had saved them and had brought them to Starkey in the week after her release from the hospital. Starkey had thrown them away and had never spoken to Marion Tyson again.

Starkey took a moment to make sure her voice would not waver, that she wouldn't give away her feelings.

'Are all the articles in this book bomb-related?'

Tennant flipped the pages for her to see, revealing flashes of death and devastated buildings, crumpled cars, and medical text photographs of severed limbs and disrupted bodies.

'I've collected these since I was a child. I wasn't going to talk to you, but then I remembered who you are. I remember watching the news the day you were killed, and what an impression that made on me. I was hoping I could get you to autograph it.'

Before she could respond, Pell reached across the table and closed the book.

'Not today, you piece of shit.'

Pell pulled the book close and laid his arm across it.

'Today, you're going to tell us where you got the RDX.'

'That's mine. You can't take that. Mr Olsen will make you give it back.'

Starkey was inwardly livid with Pell for intruding, but she kept her manner calm. The change in Pell was dramatic; in the car, he'd seemed distant and thoughtful; this Pell was poised in his chair like a leopard anxious to pounce.

'I'm not going to sign your book, Dallas. Maybe if you tell us where you got the RDX and how we could get some, maybe then I might sign it. But not now.'

'I want my book. Mr Olsen is going to make you give it back.'

'Give it back, Pell.'

Starkey eased the book away from Pell and slid it across the table. Tennant pulled the book close again and covered it with his hands.

'You won't sign it?'

'Maybe if you help us.'

'I bought some mines from a man I didn't know. Raytheons. I don't remember the model number.'

'How many mines?'

He had told Mueller that he'd bought a case, which, she knew because she had phoned Raytheon, contained six mines.

'A case. There were six in the case.'

Starkey smiled; Tennant smiled back at her.

Pell said, 'What was this man's name?'

'Clint Eastwood. I know, I know, but that was how he identified himself.'

Starkey took out a cigarette and lit up.

'How could we find Clint?'

'I don't know.'

'How did *you* find Clint?'

'You're not supposed to smoke in here.'

'Mr Olsen gave me special permission. How did you find Clint? If we let you out today and you wanted more RDX, how would you reach him?'

'I met him in a bar. That's all there was to it. Like I told them when they arrested me. He had a case of antipersonnel mines, I bought it, and then he was gone. I didn't want *mines*; I mean, I wasn't going to put them out in a field and watch cows walk on them or anything. I bought them to scavenge the RDX.'

Starkey believed that Tennant was telling the truth about salvaging his RDX from stolen mines; high-order explosives were almost always acquired that way, from mortar shells or hand grenades or other military gear. But she also believed that his source wasn't some nameless yahoo in a roadhouse. Bomb cranks like Tennant were low self-esteem loners; you wouldn't find 'Plays well with others' on his report cards. Starkey knew that, as with arsonists, Tennant's obsession with explosives was a sublimated sexuality. He would be awkward with women, sexually inexperienced in the normal sense, and find his release in a large pornography collection devoted to deviant practices such as sadomaso-chism and torture. He would avoid face-to-face confrontations of any kind. He would lurk in hobby shops like the one where he had been employed and swap meets; he would be far too afraid to connect in a biker bar. Starkey decided to change her approach and come at him from a different direction. She took out the photographs of the three cars and the interview pages from Mueller's case file. The same things that Pell had read and understood on the drive up.

'All right, Dallas. I can buy that. Now tell me this, how much RDX do you have left?'

Tennant hesitated, and Starkey knew that Mueller had never asked that.

'I don't have any left. I used it all.'

'Sure you do, Dallas. You only blew up three cars. I can look at these pictures and tell that you didn't use all the RDX. We can calculate things like that, you know? Start with the damage, then work backwards to estimate the amount of the charge. It's called an energy comparison.'

Tennant blinked his eyes blandly.

'That's all I had.'

'You bought the cars from a young man named Robert Castillo. Mr Castillo said that you asked him for a fourth car. Why would you need a fourth car if you only had enough pop for three?'

Tennant wet his lips and made the shy smile. He shrugged.

'I had some dynamite. You soak the interior with enough gasoline, they go fine even with the dynamite. Not as good as with the RDX, but that's special.'

Starkey knew he was lying, and Tennant knew she knew. He averted his eyes and shrugged.

'I'm sorry. There's nothing to say.'

'Sure there is. Tell us where we can find your shop.'

Starkey was certain that if they could find his shop, they would find evidence that would lead to his source of the RDX or to other people with similar sources.

'I didn't have a shop. I kept everything in the trunk of my car.'

'Nothing was found in the trunk of your car except a few clips and wire.'

'They kept asking me about that, but there was nothing to say. I'm a very neat person. They even offered to reduce my time and give me outpatient status, but I had nothing to trade. Don't you think I would have made a deal if I could?'

Pell leaned forward and put his hands close to Tennant's book.

'I think you jerk off every night about using the rest of your stuff when you get out of here, but you're here on a mental. That's a one-way ride until the headshrinkers decide that you're sane, which figures to be never. Does a sane man blow off his own thumb?'

Tennant flushed.

'It was an accident.'

'I represent the United States Government. Detective Starkey here represents the Los Angeles Police Department. Together, with a little cooperation from you, we might be able to help get your time reduced. Then you won't have to mess around popping off fingers with window cleaner, you can go for the whole hand, maybe even an arm.'

Starkey stared at Tennant, waiting.

'I never hurt anybody. It's not fair they keep me here.'

'Tell that to the kid with the windshield wiper through his face.'

Starkey could see that Tennant was thinking. She didn't want to give him much time, so she stepped in, trying to appear sympathetic.

'That's right, Dallas. You didn't intend to hurt that boy, you even tried in your own way to keep him safe.'

'I told him to take cover. Some people just won't listen.'

'I believe that, Dallas, but the thing is, you see, this is why we're here, we've got someone out there who doesn't care about people the way you do. This person is trying to hurt people.'

Tennant nodded.

'You're here because of the officer who was killed. Officer Riggio.'

'How do you know about Riggio?'

'We have television here, and the Internet. Several of the inmates are wealthy people, bankers and lawyers. If you have to be in prison, this is the place to be.'

Pell snorted.

'Officer Riggio was killed with RDX?'

'RDX was a component. The charge was something called Modex Hybrid.'

Tennant leaned back and laced his fingers. The missing thumb must have hurt because he winced and drew back his hand.

'Did Mr Red set that bomb?'

Pell came out of his chair so suddenly that Starkey jumped.

'How do you know about Mr Red?'

Tennant glanced nervously from Starkey to Pell.

'I don't, really. People gossip. People share news, and lies. I don't even know that Mr Red is real.'

Pell reached across the table and gripped Tennant's wrist above his bandaged hand.

'Who, Tennant? Who's talking about Mr Red?'

Starkey was growing uncomfortable with Pell's manner. She was willing to let him play bad guy to her good guy, but she didn't like it that he was touching Tennant, and she didn't like the intensity she saw in his eyes.

'Pell.'

'What do they say, Tennant?'

Tennant's eyes grew larger and he tried to twist away.

'Nothing. He's a myth, he's someone who makes wonderful elegant explosions.'

'He *kills* people, you sick fuck.'

Starkey pushed out of her chair.

'Leave go of him, Pell.'

Pell's face was bright with anger. He didn't leave go.

'He knows that Red uses Modex, Starkey. We've never released that information to the public. How does he know?'

Pell gripped Tennant's bandaged hand. Tennant went white and gasped.

'Tell me, you sonofabitch. How do you know about Mr Red? What do you know about him?'

Starkey shoved Pell hard, trying to move him away, but couldn't. She was terrified that the guard would hear and burst in.

'Damnit, Pell, leave go! Step away from him!'

Tennant slapped at Pell without effect, then fell backward out of the chair.

'They talk about him on Claudius. That's how I know! They talk about the bombs he builds, and what he's like, and why he's doing these things. I saw it on Claudius.'

'Who the fuck is Claudius?'

'Goddamn you, Pell. Get back.'

Starkey shoved at Pell again, and this time he moved. It was like pushing a house.

Pell was breathing hard, but he seemed in control again. He stared at Tennant in a way that Starkey read with certainty that if Pell had his gun, he would be holding it to the man's head.

'Tell me about Claudius. Tell me how you know about Mr Red.'

Tennant whimpered from the floor, cradling his hand.

'It's an Internet site. There's a chat room for people . . . like me. We talk about bombs and the different bombers and things like that. They say that Mr Red even lurks there, reading what they say about him.'

Starkey turned away from Pell, staring at Tennant.

'Have you had contact with Mr Red?'

'No. I don't know. It's just a rumor, or maybe it isn't. I don't know. If he's there, he uses a different name. All I'm saying is what the others say. They said the Unabomber used to come around, too, but I don't know if that was true.'

Starkey helped Tennant to his feet and put him in the chair. A red flower blossomed on the bandage; his wound was seeping.

'You okay, Tennant? You all right?'

'It hurts. Goddamn, it hurts. You bastard.'

'You want me to get the guard? You want the doctor?'

Tennant glanced at her and picked up his book with his good hand.

'I want you to sign.'

Starkey signed Tennant's book, and then she called the guard and got Pell out of there. Tennant seemed fine when they left, but she wasn't sure what he might say once they were gone.

Pell moved like an automaton, stalking out ahead of her, stiff with tension. Starkey had to walk hard to keep up, growing angrier and angrier. Her face felt like a ceramic mask, so brittle that if he stopped walking before they reached the car, it might shatter and, with it, her control.

She wanted to kill him.

When they reached the parking lot, Starkey followed him to his side of the car and shoved him again. She caught him from behind, and this time he wasn't ready. He stumbled into the fender.

'You crazy bastard, what was that all about? Do you *know* what you did in there? Do you *know* what kind of trouble we could be in?'

If she had her Asp from her uniform days, she would happily beat him stupid.

Pell glared at her darkly.

'He gave us something, Starkey. This Claudius thing.'

'I don't give a *shit* what he gave us! You touched a prisoner in there! You tortured him! If he files a complaint, it's over for me. I don't know about the motherfucking ATF, but let me tell you something, Pell, *LAPD will have my hide on the barn!* That was wrong, what you did in there. That was *wrong.*'

She was so angry that she wanted to throttle him. All he did was stand there, and that made her feel even angrier.

Pell took a deep breath, spread his hands, and looked away as if whatever had driven him inside was leaching away.

'I'm sorry.'

'Oh, that's great, Pell, thanks. You're sorry.'

She walked away from him, shaking her head. She could still feel last night's drunk, and suddenly she realized that she was already thinking about getting there again, blasting back a couple of quick shots to kill the knots in her neck. She was so damned angry that she didn't trust herself to speak.

That's when Pell said, 'Starkey.'

Starkey turned back just in time to see Pell stagger against the car. He caught himself on the fender, then collapsed to one knee.

Starkey ran to him.

'Pell, what's wrong?'

He was as pale as milk. He closed his eyes, hanging his head like a tired dog. Starkey thought he was having a heart attack.

'I'm going to get someone. You hang on, okay?'

Pell caught her arm, holding tight.

'Wait.'

His eyes were clenched shut. He opened them, blinked, then closed them again. His grip on her was so strong that it hurt.

'I'm okay, Starkey. I get these pains sometimes. It's a migraine, that's all. Like that.'

He wasn't letting go of her.

'You look like shit, Pell. I'd better get someone. Please.'

'Just give me a minute.'

He closed his eyes, taking deep breaths. Starkey had the frantic thought that he was dying right here in the damned parking lot.

'Pell?'

'I'm okay.'

'Let go of me, Pell, or I might have to smack you again.'

He held her with a grip like pliers, but when she said it, his face softened, and he let go. Color began to return to his face.

'Sorry. I didn't mean to hurt you.'

He looked at her then. She was very close to him. His closeness embarrassed her, and she scooted away.

'Let me just sit here for a second. They can't see us, right?'

She had to stand to peer over the car at the reception building.

'Not unless they can see through the car. If they saw what happened, they probably think we're down here making out.'

Starkey flushed, surprised that she'd said something like that. Pell seemed not to notice.

'I'm okay now. I can get up.'

'You don't look okay. Just sit here for a minute.'

'I'm okay.'

He stood, balancing himself against the car, then used the door for support as he climbed in. By the time she went around the other side and got behind the wheel, he had more color.

'Are you okay?'

'Close enough. Let's go.'

'You really fucked us up in there.'

'I didn't fuck us up. He gave us Claudius. That's something we didn't have before.'

'If he files a complaint, you can use that to explain to Internal Affairs why they shouldn't bring me up on charges.'

Pell reached across the seat and touched her thigh. His expression surprised her; his eyes were deepened with regret.

'I'm sorry. If he files a complaint, I'll take the bullet. It wasn't you in there, Starkey, it was me. I'll tell them that. Just drive, would you, please? That isn't an order; it's a request. It's a long ride home.'

She stared at him a moment longer, then she started the car and pulled away, her leg feeling the weight of his hand as if it were still there.

6

It was after seven when Starkey let Pell off at the curb outside Spring Street. The summer sun was still high in the west, resting on the crown of a palm. Soon, the sky would purple.

Starkey struck a fresh cigarette, then turned into the traffic. Hooker and Marzik had long since gone home. Even Kelso was gone, probably eating dinner about now. Starkey passed an In-'n-Out Burger, her stomach clenching at the thought of food. She hadn't eaten anything since breakfast, so she made do with a couple of antacids.

In the long silence coming back to L.A., Starkey had decided that Pell was dangerous to her case and to her chances of reclaiming her career. If Tennant filed a complaint or squawked to his attorney, she was done. Olsen might be on the phone with Kelso right now; Kelso might be filing for an IAG investigation. A lot could happen in three hours.

Starkey flicked her cigarette out the window, hard. Trading her job for this Claudius thing seemed like a sour deal. The only way Starkey could protect herself was to report Pell and file an officer complaint. She could call Kelso at home and explain what happened. Tomorrow morning, he would walk her up to IAG, where she would be interviewed by a lieutenant, who would then phone Olsen and ask him to interview Tennant. By mid-afternoon, the lines between Spring Street and the ATF field office would burn. Washington would jerk Pell from the case, and her own ass would be covered. Then, if Tennant squawked, Starkey would be clear. She would have acted accordingly and by the book. She would be safe.

Starkey lit a second cigarette, thankful for the slow pace of the traffic. Around her, cars pulsed from parking garages like the life bleeding from a corpse. Going to Kelso was not an acceptable option. Even thinking about it made her feel cheesy and low.

She couldn't get Pell out of her head.

Starkey didn't know anything about migraine headaches, but what had happened in the parking lot had scared her even more than Pell losing control with Tennant. She fretted that beating the hell out of suspects was Pell's ATF way of doing things, and that meant he would do it again, placing her in even greater legal jeopardy. She was certain that he was hiding something. She had enough secrets of her own to know that people didn't hide strengths; they guarded their weaknesses. Now she feared Pell's. The bomb investigators that she had known were all detail people; they moved slowly and methodically because they built puzzles often made of many small pieces over investigations that lasted weeks, and often months. Pell didn't act like a bomb investigator. His manner was predatory and fast, his actions with Tennant extreme and violent. Even his gun didn't fit the profile, that big ass Smith 10.

She drove home, feeling as if she was in a weakened position and angry because of it. She thought about calling Pell at his hotel and raising more hell, but knew that would do no good. She could either call Kelso or move on; anything else was just jerking off.

At home, Starkey filled her tub with hot water for a bath, then poured a stiff gin and brought it to her bedroom where she took off her clothes.

Naked, she stood at the foot of her bed, listening to the water splash, sipping the gin. She was intensely aware of the mirror on the closet. It was behind her, almost as if it were waiting. She took a big slug of the drink, then turned and looked at herself. She saw the scars. She saw the craters and rills and valleys, the discolorations and the pinhole stitching. She looked at her thigh, and saw the print of his hand as clearly as if she bore a brand.

Starkey sighed deeply and turned away.

'You must be out of your goddamned mind.'

She finished the drink in a long series of gulps, stalked into the bath, and let the heat consume her.

7

'Tell me about Pell.'

'He's a fed with the ATF. That's Alcohol, Tobacco, and Firearms.'

'I know.'

'If you knew, why did you ask?'

'I meant I know what the acronym stands for, that ATF is the Bureau of Alcohol, Tobacco, and Firearms. You seem irritable today, Carol.'

'How inconsiderate of me. I must have forgotten to take my daily dose of mellow.'

Starkey was annoyed with herself for mentioning Pell to Dana. On the drive to Santa Monica, she had mapped out what she wanted to talk about in today's session, which had not included Pell, yet Pell was the first damned thing that popped from her mouth.

'I put myself at risk for this guy, and I don't even know him.'

'Why did you do that?'

'I don't know.'

'If you had to guess.'

'Nobody likes a rat.'

'But he violated the law, Carol. You said so yourself. He laid hands on this prisoner, and now you are in jeopardy for not reporting him. You clearly don't approve of what he did, yet you are conflicted about what to do.'

Starkey lost track of Dana's voice. She stood at the window, watching the traffic on Santa Monica Boulevard, smoking. A cluster of women waited at the crosswalk below, anxiously watching their bus idle on the other side of six lanes of bumper-to-bumper morning rush-hour traffic. From their squat Central American builds and plastic shopping bags, Starkey made them for housekeepers on their way to work in the exclusive homes north of Montana. When the light changed, the bus began to rumble away. The women panicked, charging across the street even as cars continued through the red. Horns blew, a black Nissan swerving, almost nailing two of the women, who never once looked at the car as it passed. They ignored it in their need to catch the bus, giving themselves up to chance. Starkey knew she could never do that.

'Carol?'

Starkey didn't want to talk about Pell anymore or watch a bunch of women with nothing more on their minds than catching a goddamned bus.

She went back to her seat and crushed out her cigarette.

'I want to ask you a question.'

'All right.'

'I'm not sure if I want to do this or not.'

'Do what, Carol? Ask me the question?'

'No, do what I'm about to tell you about. I got these tapes of what happened to Charlie Riggio, the news video that the TV stations took. You know what I realized? The TV station has tapes of me, too. They have videotape of what happened to me and Sugar. Now I can't stop thinking about it, that it's out there right now, trapped on a tape, and I could see it.'

Dana wrote something on her pad.

'When and if you decide that you're ready for something like that, I think it would be a good idea.'

Starkey's stomach went cold. Part of her had wanted Dana's permission; part of her had wanted to be let off the hook.

'I don't know.'

Dana put her pad aside. Starkey didn't know whether to be frightened by that or not. She had never known Dana to put aside the pad.

'How long have you had the dreams, now, Carol?'

'Almost three years.'

'So you see Sugar's death, and your own, almost every night for three years. I had a thought about this the other day. I don't know if it's right or not, but I want to share it with you.'

Starkey eyed her suspiciously. She hated the word 'share'.

'Do you know what a perception illusion is?'

'No.'

'It's a drawing. You look at it, and you see a vase. But if you look at it with a different mind-set, you see two women facing each other. It's like a picture hidden within a picture. Which you see depends upon the perceptions and predispositions you bring to the viewing. When a person looks at a picture over and over again, maybe they're trying to find that hidden picture. They keep looking, hoping that they'll see it, but they can't.'

Starkey thought this was all bullshit.

'You're saying that I'm having the dream because I'm trying to make sense of what happened?'

'I don't know. What do you think?'

'I think that if you don't know, I sure as hell don't. You're the one with a Ph.D.'

'Fair enough. Okay, the Ph.D. suggests that we have to deal with the past in order to heal the present.'

'I do that. I try to do that. Christ, I think about that goddamned day so much I'm sick of it.' Starkey raised a hand. 'And, yes, I know that thinking about it isn't the same as dealing with it.'

'I wasn't going to say that.'

'Right.'

'This isn't a criticism, Carol. It's an exploration.'

'Whatever.'

'Let's get back to the perception illusion. The notion I had is that your dream is the first picture. You return to it because you haven't found the second picture, the hidden picture. You can only see the vase. You're looking for the two women, you suspect that they're there, but you haven't been able to find them. It occurred to me that maybe this is because what you're seeing isn't what really happened. It's what you imagined happening.'

Starkey felt her irritation turning to anger.

'Of course it's what I imagined. I was fucking dead, for Christ's sake.'

'The tape would show what really happened.'

Starkey drew a deep breath.

'Then, if there are two women to be found, you might be able to find them. Maybe what you would discover is that there is only the vase. Whichever you find, maybe that knowledge would help you put this behind you.'

Starkey looked past Dana to the window again. She pushed to her feet and went back to the window.

'Please come back to your seat.'

Starkey shook out a cigarette, lit up. Dana wasn't looking at her. Dana faced the empty seat as if Starkey were still there.

'Carol, please come back to your seat.'

Starkey blew out a huge screen of smoke. She sucked deep, filled the air with more.

'I'm okay over here.'

'Have you realized that whenever we come to something that you don't want to hear or that you want to avoid, you escape through that window?'

Starkey stalked back to the chair.

'The dream changed.'

'How so?'

Starkey crossed her legs, realized what she was doing, uncrossed them.

'Pell was in the dream. They took off Sugar's helmet, and it was that bastard Pell.'

Dana nodded.

'You're attracted to him.'

'Oh, for Christ's sake.'

'Are you?'

'I don't know.'

'A little while ago, you told me that he scared you. Maybe this is the true reason why.'

'The two faces?'

'Yes. The hidden picture.'

Starkey tried to make a joke of it.

'Maybe I'm just a freak who likes to put herself at risk. Why else would I work the Bomb Squad?' -

'You haven't seen anyone since it happened?'

Starkey felt herself flush. She averted her eyes, hoping she looked thoughtful instead of sick to her stomach with fear.

'No. No one.'

'Are you going to act on this attraction?'

'I don't know.'

They sat quietly until Dana glanced at her clock.

'Looks like our time is almost up. I'd like to leave you with something else to think about for next time.'

'Like I don't have enough?'

Dana smiled as she picked up the pad, laying it across her legs as if she was already considering the notes she would write.

'You made a joke about working on the Bomb Squad because you enjoyed the risk. I remember something that you said when we were first seeing each other. I had said that being a bomb technician seemed like a very dangerous profession.'

'Yeah?'

Starkey didn't remember.

'You told me that it wasn't. You told me that you never thought of bombs as dangerous, that a bomb was just a puzzle that you had to solve, all neat and contained and predictable. I think you feel safe with bombs, Carol. It's people who scare you. Do you think that's why you enjoyed the Bomb Squad so much?'

Starkey glanced at the clock.

'Looks like you were right. Time's up.'

After leaving Dana, Starkey worked her way through the crosstown traffic toward Spring Street with a growing sense of inevitability. She told herself it was resolve, but she knew it was as much about resolve as a drunk falling down stairs. He was going to hit the bottom whether he resolved to or not. She was on the stairs. She was falling. She was going to see herself die.

By the time Starkey reached CCS, she felt numb and fuzzy, as if she were a ghost come back to haunt a house, but was now separate from it, unseen and weightless.

Across the squad room, Hooker was screwing around with the coffee machine. She watched him, thinking that Hooker had the phone numbers for the TV news departments. She told herself to get the numbers, start calling, and find the goddamned tapes of herself. Do it *now*, before she chickened out.

She marched to the coffee machine.

'Jorge, did you set it up to have those tapes enhanced?'

'Yeah. I told you I'd take care of it, remember?'

'Mm. I just wanted to be sure.'

'It's a postproduction company in Hollywood that the department uses. We should have them in two or three days.'

'Right. I remember. Listen, did we get any of those tapes from channel eight?'

'Yeah. You took one of them home, Carol. Don't you remember?'

'For Christ's sake, Jorge, I took a shitload of tapes home. Can I remember where they all came from?'

Hooker was staring at her.

'No. I guess not.'

'Who'd you talk to over there at channel eight? To get the tapes?'

'Sue Borman. She's the news director.'

'Lemme have her number, okay? Something I want to ask her about.'

'Maybe I can help. What do you want to know?'

Nothing was easy. He couldn't just say, sure, and go get the goddamned number.

'I want to talk to her about the tapes, Jorge. Now, could I please have her number?'

Starkey followed Hooker back to his desk for the number, then went directly to her phone where she called channel eight. She punched the number mechanically, without thought of what she would say or how she would say it. She didn't want to think. She didn't want to give herself time to not do it.

Channel eight was the only television station that she recalled at the trailer park. She knew that others had been there, but she did not remember which others and didn't want to call around, asking. Channel eight she remembered because of their station ID letters. KROK. The bomb techs used to call the KROK remote vehicle the shitmobile.

'This is Detective Carol Starkey with LAPD. I'd like Sue Borman, please.'

When Borman came on, she sounded harried. Starkey guessed that probably went with the job.

'We sent tapes over there. Is everything all right with them? You don't have a playback problem, do you?'

'No, ma'am. The tapes are fine. We appreciate your cooperation. I'm calling about another set of tapes.'

'What you got are the only tapes we have. We sent you everything.'

'These are older tapes. They'd probably be in your library. Three years ago, an officer was killed at a trailer park in Chatsworth, and another officer was injured. Do you remember that?'

'No. Was that another bomb thing?'

Starkey closed her eyes.

'Yes. It was a bomb thing.'

'Waitaminute. It wasn't just one guy; both guys were killed, but they brought back one of them at the scene, right?'

'That's the one.'

'I was a news writer back then. I think I wrote the story.'

'It's been three years. Maybe you don't keep the tapes.'

'We keep everything. Listen, what did you say your name is?'

'Detective Starkey.'

'You're not who I talked to about the Silver Lake thing, right?'

'No, that was Detective Santos.'

'Okay, what I'll have to do is check our library. I'll do that and get back to you. Gimme the date of the incident and your phone number.'

Starkey gave her the date and phone number.

'You want the tape if we have it?'

'Yes, ma'am.'

'Is this connected to what happened in Silver Lake?'

Starkey didn't want to tell this woman that she was one of the officers on the tape.

'We don't believe that they're connected, but we're checking. It's just something we have to follow up.'

'If there's a story here, I want in.'

'If there's a story, you can have it.'

'What did you say your name was?'

'Starkey.'

'I'll get back to you.'

Starkey was shaking when she put down the phone. She put her hands flat on the desk and tried to still them. She couldn't. She thought she should feel elated or proud of herself for taking this step, but all she felt was sick to her stomach.

She dry-swallowed a Tagamet and was waiting for the nausea to pass when Pell called.

'Can you talk?'

'Yes, I can talk.'

'I wanted to apologize again about yesterday, up there with Tennant. I hope that what happened hasn't created a problem for you.'

'I haven't been marched upstairs to Internal Affairs yet, if that's what you mean. Tennant could still change his mind and destroy my career, but so far I'm safe.'

'Did you report me?'

'Not my style, babe. Forget it.'

'Okay. Well, like I said yesterday, if it comes to that, I'll take the hits.'

She felt herself flush with an anger that seemed more aimed at herself than him.

'You can't take the hits, Pell. I guess you're being noble or something, but I'm fucked for not reporting you whether you take the hits or not. That's the way it works here on the local level.'

'Okay. Listen, there's another reason I called. I've got someone who can help us with this Claudius thing.'

'What do you mean?'

'If it's true what Tennant said, that Mr Red goes there, I'm thinking we can use that. The ATF has a guy at Cal Tech who knows about this stuff. I've set it up, if you're game.'

'You're damn right I am.'

'Great. Can you pick me up?'

The card from Pell's hotel was on her desk. She looked at it and saw that he was staying in Culver City near LAX. A place called the Islander Palms.

'You mean you want me to come get you? Why don't we just meet there? You're way the hell in the wrong direction.'

'I'm having trouble with my damned rental car. If you don't want to pick me up, I'll take a cab.'

'Take it easy, Pell. I'll see you in twenty minutes.'

The Islander Palms was a low-slung motel just off Pico Boulevard, a couple of blocks west of the old MGM Studio. It was two floors, with neon palm trees on a large sign overlooking the parking lot, sea-green trim, and an ugly stucco exterior. Starkey was surprised that Pell was staying in such a dump and thought he'd probably picked it out of a low-end tour book. It was the kind of place that screamed 'family rates'.

Pell stepped out of the lobby when she turned into the parking lot. He looked pale and tired. The dark rings under his eyes made her think that the trouble wasn't with his car; he was probably still shaken from whatever had rocked him up at Atascadero.

He got in without waiting for her to shut the engine.

'Jesus, Pell, is the ATF on a budget? LAPD would put me up in a better place than this.'

'I'll call the director and tell him you said to shape up. You know how to get there?'

'I was born in L.A. I got freeways in my blood.'

As they drove back across the city, Pell explained that they were meeting a man named Donald Bergen, who was a graduate student in physics. Bergen was one of several computer experts employed by the government to identify and monitor potential presidential assassins, militia cranks, pedophiles, terrorists, and others who used the Internet as a source of communication, planning, and execution of illegal activity. This was a gray area of law enforcement, and getting darker every day. The Internet wasn't the US Postal Service, and chat rooms weren't private phone calls, yet law enforcement agencies were increasingly limited as to what they could and could not do on the Internet.

'Is this guy some kind of spook?'

'He's just a guy. Do me a favor, okay, and don't ask him about what he does, and don't tell him too much about what we're doing. It's better that way.'

'Listen, I'm telling you right now that I'm not going to do anything that's illegal.'

'This isn't illegal. Bergen knows why we're coming, and he knows about Claudius. His job is to get us there. After that, it's up to us.'

Starkey considered Pell, but didn't say any more. If Bergen and Claudius could help close her case, then that's what she wanted.

Twenty minutes later, they found a spot in visitors' parking and entered the Cal Tech campus. Even though Starkey had spent her life in L.A., she'd never been there. It was pretty; earth-colored buildings nestled in the flats of Pasadena. They passed young men and women who looked normal, but, she thought, were probably geniuses. Not many of the kids here would choose to be cops. Starkey thought that if she were smarter, neither would she.

They found the Computer Sciences building, went down a flight of stairs, and walked along a sterile hall until they found Bergen's office. The man who opened the door was short and hugely muscular, like a bodybuilder. He smelled, faintly, of body odor.

'Are you Jack Pell?'

'That's right. Mr Bergen?'

Bergen peered at Starkey.

'Who's she?'

Starkey badged him, already irritated.

'*She* is Detective Carol Starkey, LAPD.'

Bergen looked back at Pell, suspicious.

'Jerry didn't say anything about this. What's the deal with her?'

'We're a matched set, Bergen. That's all you need to know. Now open the door.'

Bergen leaned out to see if anyone else was in the hall, then let them in, locking the door after them. Starkey smelled marijuana.

'You can call me Donnie. I'm all set up for you.'

Bergen's office was cluttered with books, software manuals, computers, and pinups of female bodybuilders. Bergen told them to sit where two chairs had been set up in front of a slim laptop computer. Starkey was uncomfortable, sitting so close to Pell that their arms touched, but there wasn't room to move away. Bergen pulled up a tiny swivel chair to sit on the other side of Pell, the three of them hunched in front of the small computer as if it were a window into another world.

'This isn't going to take long. It was pretty easy, compared to some of the stuff I do for you guys. But I'm kinda curious about something.'

Starkey noted that Bergen talked to Pell without looking at her. She thought that he was probably uncomfortable around women.

Pell said, 'What's that?'

'When I get jobs like this, I file a voucher back through Jerry, but this time he said leave it alone.'

'We'll talk about that later, Donnie. That isn't Detective Starkey's concern.'

Bergen turned a vivid red.

'Okay. Sure. Whatever you say.'

'Show us about Claudius, Donnie.'

'Okay. Sure. What do you want to know?'

'Show us how to find Claudius.'

'It's already found. I was there this morning.'

Bergen, who was sitting on the far side of Pell, as far from Starkey as he could get, reached over and punched several computer keys.

'First thing I did was run a search for web sites about bombs, explosives, improvised munitions, mass destruction, things like that. There are hundreds of them.'

As Starkey watched, the screen filled with the home page of something called GRAVEDIGGER, showing a skull with atomic bomb mushroom clouds in the eye sockets. Bergen explained that it was built and maintained by a hobbiest in Minnesota and was perfectly legal.

'A lot of the more elaborate sites have message boards so people can post notes to each other or get together in a chat room so they can talk in real time. Do you know how we run the assassination scans?'

Starkey said, 'Donnie?'

Bergen cleared his throat, glancing at her quickly before looking away. 'Yes, ma'am?'

'You don't have to ma'am me. But I want you to talk to me, too, okay? I'm not going to bust you for smoking pot or whatever it is you're worried about, okay?'

'I wasn't smoking pot.'

'Just talk to me, too. I have no idea how you run the assassination scans. I don't even know what assassination scans are.'

Pell said, 'Maybe we shouldn't get into this.'

Bergen turned red again.

'Sorry.'

'Just tell us how you found Claudius and bring us there.'

Bergen twisted around to point out a stack of bright blue PowerMacs wired together on a metal frame.

'What you do is search for word combinations. Say your combination is President, White House, and kill. I've got software that floats on forty service providers, constantly searching for that combination of words on message boards, newsgroups, and in chat rooms. If the combination shows up, the software copies the exchange and the e-mail addresses of the people involved. What I did was task the software with looking for the word "Claudius", along with a few others, and this is what we found. It's as easy as keeping the world safe for democracy.'

Bergen clicked another button, and a new page appeared. His chest swelled expansively.

'You can run but you can't hide, motherfuckers. That's Claudius.'

It was a face with a head of flames. The face was tortured, as if in great pain. Starkey thought it looked Roman. Along the left side was a navigation bar that showed different topics: HOW TO, THE PROS, MILITARY, GALLERY, LINKS, MOST WANTED, and several others.

Starkey leaned toward the screen.

'What are all these things?'

'Pages within pages. The gallery is pictures of blast victims. It's pretty gruesome. The how-to pages have articles about bomb construction and a message board where these a-holes can talk about it with each other. Here, let's take a tour.'

Bergen used a mouse control to click them through a tour of hell. Starkey watched diagrams of improvised munitions flick past on the screen, saw articles on substituting common household products for their chemical counterparts in order to create explosives. The gallery contained photographs of destroyed buildings and vehicles, medical text pictures of people that had been killed by explosive blasts, endless shots of Third World people missing feet and legs from land mines, and photos of animals that had been blown apart in wound research studies.

Starkey had to look away.

'These people are fucking nuts. This is disgusting.'

'But legal. First Amendment, babe. And if you read close, you'll note that nothing posted on these pages, which we call public pages, is legally actionable. No one is admitting to crimes or to buying and selling illegal items. They're just hobbiests. Ha.'

Pell said, 'We're looking for someone who calls himself Mr Red. They talk about him here. We were told that he might even visit himself.'

Bergen was nodding again before Pell finished, letting them know that he was still ahead of them. He checked his watch, then glanced over at a large desktop Macintosh.

'Well, if he's been here since eleven-oh-four last night, he's calling himself something else. I'm charting the sign-ons.'

He swiveled back to the laptop and used the mouse control to open the message boards.

'As far as people posting about him, you got a lot of that. A bunch of these freaks think he's a fucking hero. Red, and these other assholes. We've got discussion threads here about the Unabomber; that guy out in California they called the IRS Bomber, Dean Harvey Hicks; that asshole down south who was trying to kill judges and lawyers; those Oklahoma pricks; and a *ton* of stuff about Mr Red.'

Starkey said, 'Show us.'

Bergen punched up a thread devoted to Mr Red, explaining that a thread was a string of messages posted on a particular bulletin board and how she could move sequentially from message to message to follow the exchange. She said, 'Where do I start?'

'Start anywhere. It won't matter. The thread goes on forever.'

Starkey chose a message at random and opened it.

SUBJECT: Re: Truth or Consequences
FROM: BOOMER |
MESSAGE-ID: >187765.34 @ zipp<
>> . . . that the Unabomber did his thing for so many years without being caught proves his superiority . . . <<

Kaczynski was lucky. His devices were simple, crude, and embarrassing. If you want elegance, look to Mr Red.

The Boomster
(often mistaken, but never wrong)

Starkey opened the next message of the thread.

SUBJECT: Re: Truth or Consequences
FROM: JYMBO4
MESSAGE-ID: >222589.16 @ nomad<
>> If you want elegance, look to Mr Red. <<

What elegance, Boom? So he uses a schmantzy goo like Modex, and nobody knows who he is. The Unabomber wasn't identified for seventeen frigging years. Red's only been around for two. Let's see if he's smart enough to stay uncaught.

But I do have to admit that his nonpolitical nature appeals to me. Ragheads and terrorists give bombers a bad name . . . ha! I dig it that he's a straight-ahead asskicker.

Rock on,
J

Starkey looked at Pell.

'None of these people should be allowed to breed.'

Pell laughed.

'Don't worry about that, Starkey. I'd guess most of these people have never had a date.'

Starkey glanced at Bergen.

'That's what they do here, they leave messages back and forth like this?'

'Yeah. That's why they call it a message board. But these guys are the lightweights. No one here is gonna admit to anything criminal. If you want the real kooks, you've got to go to the chat room. See, most anyone can get where we are now if you know where to look, but the chat room here is different. You can't just sign on, you know, like, knock, knock, here I am.

You've got to be invited.'

'How did you get invited?'

Bergen looked smug.

'I didn't need an invitation; I broke in. But normal people need what's called a hot ticket, that's special software that someone has to send to you via e-mail. It's like a key to get in. These guys want to talk about things they can be arrested for, so they want their privacy. They know that I'm out here, man, the guys like me. But they think they're safe in the chat room.'

Bergen hit more keys, after which a window on the screen opened, showing two names having a conversation, ALPHK1 and 22TIDAL. They weren't discussing bombs, or explosives, or anything even remotely related; they were discussing a popular television series.

Pell said, 'They're talking about a goddamned actress.'

'They can talk about anything they want in a chat room. It's real time. They're having a conversation just like we are, only they're typing it. These guys could be anywhere on the planet.'

Starkey watched their exchange with a growing sense that she might be discovered, that either one might suddenly look through the computer screen and see her.

'Can they see us?'

'Nope, not now. We are cloaked, man, absolutely invisible. There are no walls on the Internet, no walls at all when I am at play.'

Bergen laughed again, and Starkey thought he was probably as crazy as the loons they were watching.

Pell sighed deeply, then nodded at her.

'I can see him here, Starkey. These people would appeal to his ego. He would come here, read all this crap about how great he is, it's just the kind of thing a guy like this would do. We can reach him here.'

Starkey was swept by the realization that any of these people could be Mr Red himself.

She looked past Pell to Bergen.

'We can leave messages here if we have a screen name?'

'Sure. Post messages, come here into the chat room, anything you want if I set you up for it. That's why we're here, right?'

She looked at Pell, and Pell nodded.

'That's what we want.'

'No problemo. Let's get to it, and you can get on your way.'

Pell

They chose the name HOTLOAD. Pell thought it was silly, but, as they sat there working, he decided that there was a subliminal sexuality to it that could work for them.

He watched Starkey out the corner of his eye, admiring her intensity. Bergen's office was small and cramped; barely big enough for the three of them to fit in front of the computer. Bergen smelled so bad that Pell kept leaning away from him into Starkey. Every time Pell touched her, Starkey shrank away. Once, when their thighs touched, he thought she was going to fall out of her chair.

Pell wondered about that, thinking that maybe she had an aversion to men or hated being touched, but he decided that this was unlikely. When he'd had the damned spell in Atascadero, she had expressed a surprising warmth that he'd found moving ... even as she chewed his ass about Tennant.

'Earth to Pell.'

Starkey and Bergen were both staring at him. He realized that he hadn't been paying attention, that he had been thinking about Starkey.

'Sorry.'

'Well, Jesus Christ, Pell, pay attention. I don't want to spend the night here.'

Bergen showed them how to use the little computer, how to turn it on and off, and set them up with an Internet address through an anonymous provider owned and operated by the government. Then he showed them how to get to Claudius once they had accessed the Internet. They talked over how to proceed and decided to do something that Bergen called 'trolling'. Writing as Hotload, they posted three messages about Mr Red on the message boards: two affirming Hotload's status as a fan and one reporting a rumor that Mr Red had struck again in Los Angeles, asking if anyone knew if this was true. Bergen explained that the idea was to provoke a response and establish a presence on the boards.

When they finished, Pell told Bergen that he would be back in a few minutes, then walked Starkey out.

Starkey said, 'Why do you have to go back?'

'ATF business. Don't worry about it.'

'Oh, fuck yourself, Pell. Jesus.'

'This annoyance? Is it perpetual with you?'

Starkey frowned without answering. She shook out a cigarette and lit up. Pell thought about all the smoking and drinking, wondering if she had always been this way or if this Starkey had been born that day in the trailer park. Like the tough talk and bad attitude. Sometimes, as he drove around the city or lay in his shitty hotel room, Pell wanted to ask her those things, but knew it wouldn't be appropriate. He knew too damned much for his own good, such as how something like the trailer park could change a person, like if your inside was weak, you covered it with a hard outside. He forced himself to stop thinking these things.

She waved the cigarette like she wasn't happy with the way it was lit, then stared past him.

'I've got to get back to Spring Street. I'm supposed to go out with Marzik, looking for people who saw our guy.'

'You take the computer. We can get together at your place later to see if anyone responded.'

She glanced at him, then shrugged.

'Sure. We can do it at my place. I'll wait in the car.'

Pell watched Starkey walk away until she was gone, then went back to Bergen's office. He knocked again, and Bergen peered past him down the hall just like before, making sure that the coast was clear. Pell hated dealing with people like this.

When the door was closed, Bergen said, 'I hope I didn't say anything wrong in front of her.'

Pell took out an envelope containing twelve hundred dollars, then watched as Bergen counted it.

'Twelve hundred. Jerry said to leave it alone, but I was just curious, you know? This is the first time you guys have paid me in cash.'

'If Jerry said to leave it alone, you should leave it alone.'

Bergen shrugged, nervous.

'Right. You want a receipt?'

'What I want is a second computer.'

Bergen stared at him.

'You want another one? Just like the one I gave you?'

'Yes. Set up so I can reach Claudius.'

'What do you need a second one for?'

Pell stepped closer, met Bergen's eyes in a way that made the muscular man flinch.

'Can you fix me up with a second computer or not?'

'It's another twelve hundred.'

'I'll come back later. Alone.'

8

After Starkey dropped Pell back at his motel, she and Marzik spent the afternoon interviewing customers of the Silver Lake laundry with no success. No one recalled seeing a man in a baseball cap and long-sleeved shirt making a call. Starkey dreaded reporting to Kelso that the suspect likeness would remain unresolved.

At the end of the day, they swung past the flower shop to show Lester Ybarra the three likenesses that Starkey had gotten from Pell.

Lester considered the three pictures, then shook his head.

'They look like three different guys.'

'They're the same guy wearing disguises.'

'Maybe the guy I saw was wearing a disguise, too, but he looked older than these guys.'

Marzik asked to bum one of Starkey's Tagamet.

Starkey drove home that night determined to give herself a break from the gin. She made a large pitcher of iced tea. She sipped it as she tried to watch television, but spent most of the evening thinking about Pell. She tried to focus on the investigation instead, but her thoughts kept returning to Pell and their earliest conversation that day, Pell saying that he would take the bullets if Tennant filed the charge, Pell saying he would take the hits.

Starkey shut the lights, went to bed, but couldn't sleep. Not even her usual pathetic two hours.

Finally, she took Sugar's picture from her dresser, brought it into the living room, and sat with it, waiting for the night to end.

One man had already taken the hits for her. She would never allow another man to do that again.

At ten minutes after nine the next morning, Buck Daggett called her at Spring Street.

'Ah, Carol, I don't want to be a pest, but I was wondering if you've had any breaks.'

Starkey felt a wave of guilt. She knew what it was like to be in Buck's position, feeling that you were on the outside of something so devastating. She had felt that way after the trailer park. She still did.

'Not really, Buck. I'm sorry.'

'I was just wondering, you know?'

'I know. Listen, I should call to keep you up on this. I've just been so busy.'

'I heard they found some writing in the frag. What's that about?'

'We're not sure what we found. It's either a 5 or an S but, yeah, it was cut into the body of the pipe.'

Starkey wasn't sure how much she should tell him about Mr Red, so she let it go at that.

Buck hesitated.

'A 5 or an S? What in hell is that, part of a message?'

Starkey wanted to change the subject.

'I don't know, Buck. If anything develops, I'll let you know.'

Santos waved at her, pointing at the phone. A second line light was blinking.

'Listen, Buck, I got a call. As soon as we get anything, I'll call.'

'Okay, Carol. I'm not nagging or anything.'

'I know. I'll see you later.'

Starkey thought he sounded disappointed, and felt all the more guilty for avoiding him.

The second call was John Chen.

'We got an evidence transfer here in your name from the ATF lab in Rockville.'

'Is it bomb components from Miami?'

'Yeah. You should've told me it was coming, Starkey. I don't like stuff just showing up like this. I got court today, and now I have to take care of all this chain of evidence paperwork. I've gotta be at court by eleven.'

Starkey glanced at her watch.

'I'll be there before you leave. I want to look at it.'

To maintain the chain of evidence, Chen or another of the criminalists would personally have to log over the components into Starkey's possession.

'I've got court, Carol. Make it later today or tomorrow.'

He had this whiny quality to his voice that annoyed the hell out of her.

'I'm leaving now, John. I'll be there in twenty minutes.'

She was on her way out when Kelso's door opened, and she remembered Tennant. For a few brief minutes, she had forgotten Atascadero.

'Starkey!'

Kelso steamed across the squad room, carrying a coffee cup that read WORLD'S SEXIEST LOVER. Starkey watched him without expression, thinking, Fuck it, if Olsen had made the call filing a complaint, it was too late to worry about it.

'Assistant Chief Morgan wants to have a meeting this afternoon. One o'clock in my office.'

Starkey felt the ground fall away beneath her.

'About what?'

'What do you think, Detective? He wants to know what we're doing down here about Riggio. Dick Leyton will be here, too. You will advise them on the status of the investigation, and I hope to hell you have something to say.'

Starkey felt her panic ease; apparently, no one was complaining to Internal Affairs.

Kelso spread his hands.

'So? Would you care to give me a preview?'

Starkey told him about Claudius, explaining that Tennant had learned about Mr Red there, and that she felt it was a possible source of information.

Kelso listened, somewhat mollified.

'Well, that's something, I guess. At least it looks like we're doing something.'

'We *are* doing something, Barry.'

Even with nothing to drink, he made her head throb.

Starkey was still shaking when she left CCS, hoping to reach Chen before he left for court. She did, catching him coming down the stairs with a sport coat draped over his arm. He wasn't happy to see her.

'I told you I had court, and you said you'd be here in twenty minutes.'

'Just get me squared away, then you can leave me to it.'

She preferred being alone when she worked. It would be easier to concentrate if Chen wasn't watching over her shoulder, being male and offering his help.

Chen grumped about it, but turned and two-stepped the stairs, bringing her back along the hall and into the lab. Two techs were eating sandwiches between plastic bags containing what appeared to be human body parts. The smell of preservative was strong.

Chen said, 'They sent two devices, Starkey. It isn't just the library device like you said.'

That surprised her.

'All I expected was the library device.'

'We got that, but we also got the frag from a detonation they had down there. The reports say they're pretty much the same design, only one was really a bomb and the other wasn't.'

Starkey recalled what Pell had told her about a sweatshop bombing, which was described in one of the seven reports he had provided. She had already read the Dade County report on that device and thought that having it might prove useful.

Chen led her to a corner of the lab where two white boxes rested on the black lab table. Both boxes had been opened.

Chen said, 'Everything's bagged, tagged, and logged. You've gotta sign here, then the ATF says you're clear to do whatever you want, up to and including destructive testing.'

Destructive testing was sometimes necessary to separate components or obtain samples. Starkey didn't anticipate having to do that and would refer to those results that the Miami authorities had found.

Starkey signed four federal evidence forms where Chen indicated, then gave them back to him.

'Okay. Can I work here at your table?'

'Just try not to make a mess. I know where everything is, so put it back in its proper place. I hate when people move things.'

'I won't move anything.'

'You want me to tell Russ Daigle you're up here? He'll probably want to see this.'

'I'd rather work the bomb by myself, John. I'll get him when I'm done.'

When Chen was finally gone, Starkey took a breath, closed her eyes, and felt the tension melting away with the glacial slowness of ice becoming water. This was the part of the job that she loved, and had always loved. This was her secret. When she touched the bomb, when she had its pieces in her hands, when they pressed into the flesh of her fingers and palms, she was part of it. It had been that way since her first training exercise at the Redstone Arsenal Bomb School. The bomb was a puzzle. She became a piece in a larger whole that she was able to see in ways that others couldn't. Maybe Dana was right. For the first time in three years, she was alone with a bomb, and she felt at rest.

Starkey pulled on a pair of vinyl gloves.

The ATF had sent both devices along with their respective reports, one each from the Dade County Bomb Squad and the ATF's National Laboratory Center in Rockville, Maryland. Starkey put the reports aside. She wanted to come at the material with a fresh eye and draw her own conclusions. She would read their reports later to compare the conclusions of the bomb techs in Maryland and Miami with her own.

The exploded device was the usual scorched and twisted frag, the fragments in twenty-eight Ziploc bags, each bag labeled with a case number, an evidence number, and description.

#3B12:104/galvanized pipe
#3B12:028/detonator end plug
#3B12:062–081/assorted pipe

Starkey glanced at the contents of each without opening the bags because she saw no need; her interest was in the intact device. The largest fragment was a twisted, four-inch piece of pipe that flattened into a perfect rectangle, its edges as perfect as if they had been cut with a machinist's tool. Explosions could do that, changing the shape of things in unexpected and surprising ways, ways that often made no sense because every distortion was not only the result of the explosive, but was also predicted by the inner stresses of the material being changed.

She returned the bags to their box, pushed that box aside. The second box contained the disassembled parts of the device that had been recovered from the library. She laid these bags out on the bench, organizing them by components. One bag contained the siren that had sounded to draw attention, another the timer, another the siren's battery pack. The siren had been crushed and two of three AA batteries ruptured when Dade County de-armed the device with its water cannon. Starkey thought she would not have recognized the siren if the bag hadn't been labeled.

When the bomb components were laid out, Starkey opened the bags.

The two galvanized pipe cylinders had been blown open like blooming flowers, but were otherwise intact. The duct tape that had joined the pipes had been scissored, but was still in place. The scent of the glue that Dade County had used in their attempt to bring up fingerprints still clung to the metal. Starkey knew that the Dade County forensics team would have expected to find print fragments, even though they might not have belonged to Mr Red. Salespeople, store clerks, the person who rang up the sale. But nothing had been found. Mr Red had cleaned the components, leaving nothing to chance.

Starkey assembled the pieces with little effort. Some of the pieces would no longer fit together because they were misshapen by the de-armer, but Starkey had everything close enough. Outwardly, the only difference between this device and the one that had killed Charlie Riggio was the addition of the timer. Red had placed the device, then, when he was ready, pressed the switch to start the countdown. She guessed by the looks of it that the timer was probably good for an hour, counting down from sixty minutes. The police report, if it was thorough, would have constructed a timeline built from witness reports to try to establish how long between the time Red was last seen near the table and the siren going off. This didn't interest Starkey.

She placed her hands on the components, feeling the substance of them. The gloves hid much of the texture, but she kept them on. These were the same pieces of metal and wire and tape that Mr Red had touched. He had acquired the raw components, cut them, shaped them, and fitted them together. The heat of his body had warmed them. His breath had settled over them like smoke. Oils from his skin stained them with unseeable shadows. Starkey knew that you could learn much about a person by the way they kept their car and their home, by the way they ordered the events of their life or covered canvas with paint. The bomb was a reflection of the person who built it, as individual as their face or their fingerprints. Starkey saw more than pipe and wire; she saw the loops, arches, and whorl patterns of his personality.

Mr Red was proud of his work to the point of arrogance. He was meticulous, even obsessive. His person would be neat, as would his home. He would be short-tempered and impatient, though he might hide these things from other people, often by pretending to be someone else. He would be a coward. He would only let out his rage through the perfect devices that he constructed. He would see the devices as himself, as the self he wished to be – powerful, unstoppable. He was a creature of habit because the structure of it gave him comfort.

Starkey examined the wiring, noting that where the wires were joined, each had been connected with a bullet connector of a type available in any hobby store. The connector sleeves were red. The wires were red. He wanted people to see him. He wanted people to know. He was desperate for the attention.

Starkey put the bullet connectors under a magnifying glass and used tweezers to remove the clips. She found that the wire was looped around the connector three times in a counterclockwise direction. Every wire. No bullet connectors from Riggio's bomb had been found, so she had nothing to compare it with. She shook her head at Mr Red's precision. Every wire, three times, counterclockwise. The structure gave him comfort.

Starkey examined the threads cut into the pipe ends and the white plastic plumber's tape that had been peeled away. Starkey hadn't removed the tape from Riggio's bomb because she hadn't thought it necessary, but now she realized that this was a mistake. The plumber's tape was a completely unnecessary part of the bomb, and therefore potentially the most revealing. It occurred to Starkey that if Mr Red liked to write messages, he might write them on the tape, which had started out as a clean white surface.

She examined the tape fragments that the ATF people had stripped, but found nothing. The tape, designed to be crushed to make the pipe joint airtight, had been shredded when it was removed. Even if something had been written there, she couldn't have found it.

Deciding to examine the tape from the remaining joints, Starkey brought the pipes to a vise at the end of Chen's bench. She fit rubber pads on the vise jaws so that the pipe wouldn't be marred, then used a special wrench with a rubber mouth to unscrew the end cap. It wasn't particularly tight and didn't take much effort.

The plumber's tape was cut deep into the threads. She brought the magnifying glass over and, using a needle as a probe, worked around the root of the threads until she found the end of the tape. Working this close made her eyes hurt. Starkey leaned away, rubbing her eyes with the back of her wrist. She noticed the black tech smiling at her, gesturing with her own reading glasses. Starkey laughed. That would come soon enough.

Starkey worked the tape for almost twenty minutes before she got it free. She found no writing or marks of any kind. She switched the pipes in the vise, then went to work on the second tape. This one didn't take as long. Ten minutes later, Starkey was unpeeling the tape when she realized that both joints had been wrapped the same way. Mr Red had pressed the tape onto the top of the pipe, then wrapped away from himself, winding the tape over and down and around before bringing it under the pipe and back up again. Clockwise. Just as he had wound the wire to the bullet clips the same way every time, he had wrapped the plumber's tape to the threads the same way every time. Starkey wondered why.

Starkey's eyes were killing her, and the beginnings of a headache pulsed behind her forehead. She peeled off the gloves, got a cigarette, and went out to the parking lot. She leaned against one of the blue Bomb Squad Suburbans, smoking. She stared at the red brick garages at the back of the facility where bomb techs practiced aiming and firing the de-armer. She remembered the first time she had fired the de-armer, which was nothing more than a twelve-gauge water cannon. The noise had scared the hell out of her.

Mr Red thought about his bombs and built them carefully. She suspected that he had a reason for wrapping the tape clockwise around the pipe threads. It bothered her that she didn't see it. If he saw a reason that she couldn't see, it meant he was better than her, and Starkey could not accept that. She flicked away her cigarette, pretended to hold the pipe and wrap it. She closed her eyes and pretended to screw on the end cap. When she opened her eyes, two uniformed officers heading out to their cars were laughing at her. Starkey flipped them off. The third time she assembled her imaginary pipe, she saw the reason. He wrapped the tape clockwise so that when he screwed on the end cap – also clockwise – the tape would not unwind and bunch. If everything went clockwise, the cap would screw on more easily. It was a small thing, but Starkey felt a jolt of fierce pride like nothing she had known in a long time. She was beginning to see how his mind worked, and that meant she could beat him.

Starkey went back inside, wanting to check the taping on the sweatshop bomb, but found only a fragment of an end cap. There would be a sample of joint tape in the threads, but not enough to tell her the direction of the winding. She went downstairs to the Bomb Squad, looking for Russ Daigle. He was in the sergeants' bay, eating a liverwurst sandwich. He smiled when he saw her.

'Hey, Starkey. What are you doing here?'

'Upstairs with Chen. Listen, we got an end cap off Riggio's bomb, right?'

He took down his feet and swallowed as he nodded.

'Yep. Got one intact and a piece of another. I showed you the joint tape, remember?'

'You mind if I take apart the one that's intact?'

'You mean you want to unscrew it?'

'Yeah. I want to look at the tape.'

'You can do whatever you want with it, but that's going to be hard.'

He brought her out to his workbench where the pieces of the Silver Lake bomb were locked in a cabinet. Once Chen had released them, they were Daigle's to use in the reconstruction.

'See here? The pipe is still mated to the cap, but they bulged from the pressure so you can't unscrew them.'

Starkey saw what he meant and felt her hopes sag. The pipe wasn't round; it had been distorted by gas pressure into the shape of an egg. There was no way to unscrew it.

'Can I take it upstairs and play with it?'

Daigle shrugged.

'Knock yourself out.'

Starkey brought the cap upstairs, fit it into the vise, then used a high-speed saw to cut it in half. She used a steel pick to pry the inner pipe halves away from the outer cap halves, then fitted the two inner pipe halves together again in the vise. Daigle would probably be irritated because she had cut the cap, but she couldn't think of another way to reach the tape.

It took Starkey almost forty minutes to find the end of the tape, working with one eye on the clock and a growing frustration. Later, she realized that it took so long because she thought it would be wrapped overhand like the tape on the Miami device. It wasn't. The tape on this joint had been wrapped underhand.

Counterclockwise, not clockwise.

Starkey stepped away from the bench.

'Jesus.'

She flipped through the report that had been sent from Rockville and found that it had been written by a criminalist named Janice Brockwell. She checked the time again. Three hours later in D.C. meant that everyone back there should have returned from lunch, but not yet left for the day. Starkey searched through the lab until she found a phone, called the ATF's National Laboratory, and asked for Brockwell.

When Janice Brockwell came on, Starkey identified herself and gave the case number of the Miami hoax device.

'Oh, yeah, I just sent that out to you.'

'That's right. I have it here now.'

'How can I help you?'

'Are you familiar with the first seven devices?'

'The Mr Red bombs?'

'That's right. I read those reports, but don't remember seeing anything about the tape on the pipe joints.'

Starkey explained what she had found on the library device.

'You were able to unwrap the tape?'

Starkey could hear the stiffness in Brockwell's voice. She felt that Starkey was criticizing her.

'I unscrewed one of the end caps, and the tape darn near unwrapped itself. That got me to thinking about it, so I worked the other loose. Then I started wondering about the caps on the other bombs.'

Starkey waited, hoping her lie would soften the sting.

The defensiveness in Brockwell's voice eased.

'That's a pretty cool notion, Starkey. I don't think we paid attention to the tape.'

'Could you do me a favor and check? I want to know if they match.'

'You say they're clockwise, right?'

'Yeah. Both windings were clockwise. I want to see if the others match.'

'I don't know how many intact end caps we have.'

Starkey didn't say anything. She let Brockwell work it through.

'Tell you what, Starkey. Let me look into it. I'll get back to you, okay?'

Starkey gave Brockwell her number, then returned the bomb components to their boxes and locked them beneath Chen's bench.

Starkey arrived back at Spring Street with ten minutes to spare. She was harried by the rush to get back, so she stopped on the stairs, smoking half a cigarette to give herself a chance to calm down. When she had herself composed, she went up and found Marzik and Hooker in the squad room. Marzik arched her eyebrows.

'We thought you were blowing off the meeting.'

'I was at Glendale.'

She decided that she didn't have time to tell them about the Miami bomb. They could hear it when she went over it for Kelso.

'Is Morgan here yet?'

'In there with Kelso. Dick Leyton's in there, too.'

'Why are you guys still out here?'

Marzik looked miffed.

'Kelso asked us not to attend.'

'You're kidding.'

'The prick. He probably thinks his office will look smaller with too many bodies in there.'

Starkey thought Marzik's guess was probably true. She saw that she still had a minute, so she asked Marzik and Santos if they had anything new. Marzik reported that the Silver Lake interviews were still a bust, but Santos had spoken with the postproduction facility and had some good news.

He said, 'Between all the tapes, we've got pretty much of a three-hundred-sixty-degree view of the area around the parking lot. If our caller is there, we should be able to see him.'

'When can we have the tape?'

'Day after tomorrow at the latest. We're going to have to go see the tape on their machine for the best possible clarity, but they say it's looking pretty good.'

'Okay. That's something.'

Marzik came closer to her, glancing around to make sure no one could overhear.

'I want to warn you about something.'

'You're always hearing these things you warn me about.'

'I'm just telling you what I heard, all right? Morgan's thinking about turning over the investigation to Robbery–Homicide.'

'You're shitting me.'

'It makes sense, doesn't it? A man died. It's a murder. You have Homicide investigate. Look, I'm just telling you what I heard, is all. I don't want to lose this investigation any more than you.'

Starkey could tell by Santos's expression that he took it seriously, too.

'Okay, Beth. Thanks.'

Starkey checked her watch again. All this time she'd been worried about losing the case to a federal task force, and now this. She decided not to think about it because there was nothing that she could say. She would either convince Morgan that she was on top of the case or she wouldn't. She popped an Altoid and a Tagamet, then steeled herself and knocked on Kelso's door exactly at one o'clock.

Kelso answered with his smarmiest smile, putting on a show for the A-chief. Dick Leyton smiled as he greeted her.

'Hi, Carol. How you doing?'

'Fine, Lieutenant. Thanks.'

Her palms were wet when she shook his hand. He held on to her an extra moment, giving her hand a squeeze to show his support.

Kelso introduced her to Assistant Chief of Police Christopher Morgan, an intense, slender man sporting a charcoal suit. Like most officers, Starkey had never met Morgan, or any of the other six assistant chiefs, though she knew them by reputation. Morgan was reputed to be a demanding executive who micromanaged his domain with a violent temper. He had run in twelve consecutive Los Angeles City Marathons, and he demanded that his staff run, also. None of them smoked, drank, or were overweight. Like Morgan, all of them were immaculately groomed, wore charcoal suits, and, outside the office, identical military-issue sunglasses. Officers in the lower ranks called Morgan and his staff the Men in Black.

Morgan shook her hand without emotion, bypassing pleasantries by asking her to bring him up to date.

Leyton said, 'Carol, why don't you start by describing the device, since your investigation stems from there?'

Starkey briefed Morgan on the Silver Lake bomb's configuration, how it had been detonated, and how they knew that the builder had been on the scene within one hundred yards. She used these descriptions to brief him on Mr Red. When she was explaining his use of radio detonation and why they believed he had been within one hundred yards of the bomb, Morgan interrupted.

'The TV stations can help you with that. They can provide videotape.'

Starkey told him that she had already acquired the tapes and was currently having them enhanced. Morgan seemed pleased with that, though it was hard to tell because his expression never changed.

It took her less than five minutes to describe everything that had been done, including their development of Claudius as a possible source of information about RDX and Mr Red. All in all, she felt that she had done a pretty good job.

'This bomb couldn't have been placed in Silver Lake as a threat to one of the businesses there?'

'No, sir. Detectives from the OC Bureau and Rampart did background checks on all the businesses in the mall, and the people who work in them. Nothing like that came up. No one was threatened, and, so far, no one has taken credit for the bombing.'

'So what's the line of your investigation?'

'The components. Modex Hybrid is an elite explosive, but it's not complicated to make if you have the components. TNT and ammonium picrate are easy to come by, but RDX is rare. The idea now is to use the RDX as a way to backtrack to whoever built the bomb.'

Morgan seemed to consider her.

'What does that mean, "whoever"? I thought it was understood that Mr Red built the bomb.'

'Well, we're working under the assumption that he did, but we also have to consider that it might have been built by someone else, too.'

Dick Leyton shifted on the couch, and Kelso frowned.

'What are you talking about, Starkey?'

Starkey described comparing the joint tape from both end caps of the Miami device and the surviving end cap from the Silver Lake device.

'Each of the bombs that has been linked to Mr Red has been designed and constructed the same way. Even the way he binds the wire to the bullet connectors, three clockwise twists. Same way every time. He's a craftsman, he probably even thinks of himself as an artist. There's something different about the Silver Lake bomb. It's small, but people like this are creatures of habit.'

Dick Leyton appeared thoughtful.

'Was that noted in the seven earlier bombs?'

'I called Rockville and asked about it. No one thought to check the direction of the wrapping before.'

Morgan crossed his arms.

'But you did?'

Starkey met his eyes.

'You have to check everything, Chief. That's the way it works. I'm not saying we have a copycat; the security around the Mr Red investigation has been tight. All I'm saying is that I found this difference. That bears consideration.'

Starkey wished that she'd never brought it up. Morgan was frowning, and Kelso looked irritated. She felt like she was digging a hole for herself. Dick Leyton was the only one in the room who seemed interested.

'Carol, if this were the work of a copycat, how would that affect your investigation?'

'It expands. If you assume that this bomb wasn't built by Mr Red, you have to ask who *did* build it? Who knows enough about Mr Red to duplicate his bombs, and how would they get the components? Then you start to wonder, why? *Why* copycat Mr Red? Why kill a bomb tech, or anyone else, especially if you're not taking credit for it?'

Morgan heard her out, his face an impenetrable mask. When she was done, he glanced at his watch, then at Kelso.

'This sounds like a Homicide investigation. Barry, I'm thinking we should let Robbery–Homicide take over. They have the experience.'

There it was. Even with Marzik's warning, Starkey's breath caught. They were going to lose the case to the Homicide Bureau.

Kelso wasn't happy with that.

'Well, I don't know, Chief.'

Dick Leyton said, 'Chief, I think that would be a mistake.'

His statement surprised her.

Leyton spread his hands reasonably, looking for all the world like the calm, assured professional.

'The way to get to this guy is through a bomb investigation. Following the RDX, just as Detective Starkey is doing. It takes a bomb investigator to do that, not a homicide cop. Starkey's doing a good job with that. As for this difference she's found, we have to recognize it, but not get carried away with it. Serial offenders like Mr Red undergo evolutions. Yes, they're creatures of habit, but they also learn, and they change. We can't know what's in his mind.'

Starkey stared at him, feeling a warmth that embarrassed her.

Morgan seemed thoughtful, then checked his watch again and nodded.

'All right. We've got a cop killer out there, Detective Starkey.'

'Yes, sir. We're going to find him. I am going to clear this case.'

'I hope so. Those are all fine questions you raise. I'm sure you could spend a very long time finding answers for them. But, considering what we know, it seems like a long shot. Long shots are enormous time wasters. All the evidence seems to point to Mr Red.'

'The tape was just something that didn't fit, that's all.'

Her voice came out defensive and whiny. Starkey hated herself for saying it.

Morgan glanced at Kelso.

'Well, as long as we don't get sidetracked chasing theories that don't pan out. That's my advice to you, Detective. Listen to Lieutenant Leyton. Keep your investigation moving forward. Investigations are like sharks. If they stop moving forward, they sink.'

Kelso nodded.

'It will move forward, Chief. We're going to lock down this sonofabitch. We're going to get Mr Red.'

Morgan thanked everyone for the fine jobs they were doing, then glanced at his watch again and left. Dick Leyton winked at her, then followed Morgan out. Starkey wanted to run after him and kiss him, but Kelso stopped her.

Kelso waited until Morgan and Leyton were gone, then closed the door.

'Carol, forget this copycat business. You were doing fine until you said that. It sounds like nonsense.'

'It was only an *observation*, Barry. Did you want me to ignore it?'

'It made you sound like an amateur.'

Southern Comfort

John Michael Fowles bought the 1969 Chevelle SS 396 from a place called Dago Red's Used Cars in Metairie, Louisiana. The SS 396 sported a jacked-up rear end, big-assed Goodyear radials with raised letters, and rust rot along the fenders and rocker panels. The rust rot was extra; John bought it because the damned thing was red. A red car from Dago Red's for Mr Red. John Michael Fowles thought that was a riot.

He used the Miami money, paying cash with a false Louisiana driver's license that gave his name as Clare Fontenot, then drove to a nearby mall where he bought new clothes and a brand-new Apple iBook, also for cash. He got the one colored tangerine.

He drove across Lake Pontchartrain to Slidell, Louisiana, where he ate lunch at a diner called Irma's Qwik Stop. He had seafood gumbo, but didn't like it. The shrimp were small and shriveled because they'd been simmering all day. This was the first time John Michael Fowles had been to Louisiana. He didn't think much of the place. It was as humid as Florida, but not nearly so pretty. Most of the people were fat and looked retarded. Too much deep-fried food.

Irma's Qwik Stop was across a narrow two-lane road from a titty bar called Irma's Club Parisienne. John was going to meet a man there at eight that night who called himself Peter Willy, Peter Willy being a play on Willy Peter, military slang for white phosphorous explosive. Peter Willy claimed to have four Claymore antipersonnel mines to sell. If this was true, John would buy the mines for one thousand dollars each in order to recover the half-pound of RDX housed in them. RDX, which he needed for the Modex Hybrid he used in his bombs, was harder than hell to find, so it was worth the effort to come to Louisiana for it, even though Peter Willy was probably full of shit.

John had 'met' Peter Willy, as with many of his contacts, in an Internet chat room. Peter Willy purported to be a death-dealing ex-Ranger and former biker who now worked the offshore oil platforms for Exxon, two weeks on, two weeks off, and occasionally spent his off time hiring out as a mercenary in South America. John knew this was bullshit. Using what was known as a 'Creeper' program, John had backtraced Peter Willy's screen name to an Earthlink member named George Parsons and to the Visa card number with which Parsons paid for his account. Once John had the Visa number, it was easy to establish Parsons's true identity as an FAA flight controller employed at New Orleans International Airport. Parsons was married with three daughters, had never been convicted of a crime, and was not a veteran of military service, let alone being a death-dealing ex-Ranger and part-time mercenary. Maybe he would show tonight, but maybe he wouldn't. People like Peter Willy often chickened out. Big talk on the Net, but short of action in the real world. This, John knew, is what separated the predators from the prey.

John sat in the diner, sipping iced tea until six women rose from a corner booth and left. The alpha female, a busted-out Clairol blonde with cratered skin and an ass as wide as a mobile home, had put the bill on her charge card. Now, as they herded out, John ambled past their table. He made sure that no one was looking, then palmed the credit card slip and tucked it into his pocket.

As it was only a little after two in the afternoon, John had time to kill and was curious to learn what the ATF had made of his little love letter in the Broward County Library. John had been moving steadily since then, working Claudius to locate a new source of RDX, but was now anxious to read the alerts that had been written about him in the ATF and FBI bulletins. He knew that his little stunt at the library would not place him on the Ten Most Wanted List, but he expected that field offices around the country would be buzzing with alerts. Reading them gave him a serious boner.

John laughed at the absurdity.

Sometimes he was so goddamned bizarre that he amazed himself.

John paid for his meal without leaving a tip (the crappy shrimp), saddled up the big 396, and rumbled down the road back to the Blue Bayou Motel, where he had acquired a room for twenty-two dollars. Once in his room, John plugged the new iBook into the phone line and dialed up AOL. Typically, he would sign on to Claudius to read what the geeps posted about him, and sometimes he would even pretend to be someone else, dropping hints about Mr Red and enjoying his mythic status. John ate that stuff up: John Michael Fowles, Urban Legend, Rock God. But not tonight. Using the Visa card slip and the Clairol blonde's name, he joined AOL, signed on to the Internet, then typed in the URL address for a web site he maintained under the name Kip Russell. The web site, housed in a server in Rochester, Minnesota, was identified by a number only and had never been listed on any search engine. It could not be found on Yahoo!, AltaVista, HotBot, Internet Explorer, or anything else. John's web site was a storage facility for software.

John Michael Fowles traveled light. He moved often, abandoned those possessions and identities by which he could be tracked, and often carried no more than a bag of cash. He was without bank accounts, credit cards (except those he stole or bought for temporary use), and real property. Wherever he relocated, he acquired the things he needed, paid cash, then abandoned them when he moved. One of the things he often needed but never carried was software. His software was indispensable.

Before John built bombs, he wrote software. He hacked computer systems, networked with other hackers, and was as deeply into that world and its ways as he was into explosives. He wasn't as good at it as he was with explosives, but he was good enough. The software that waited for him in Rochester was how he was able to run background checks on doofballs like Peter Willy, and how he knew what the feds knew about Mr Red. With the software that rested in Rochester, he could open doors into credit card companies and banks, telephone systems and the National Law Enforcement Telecommunications System, including the FBI's Bomb Data Center, the ATF's National Repository, and some branches of the Defense Department, which he often scanned for reports of munitions thefts.

When John had accessed his web site, he downloaded an assault program named OSCAR and a clone program named PEEWEE. The downloading took about ten minutes, after which John hand-dialed the phone number for a branch of Bank of America in Kalamazoo, Michigan, and used OSCAR to hack into their system. PEEWEE piggybacked on OSCAR and, once in the B of A system, cloned itself into a free entity that existed only within the B of A branch in Kalamazoo. PEEWEE, from Kalamazoo, then dialed into the ATF's National Repository. As expected, PEEWEE was stopped at a gate that demanded a coded password. PEEWEE then imported OSCAR to assault the gate. Start to finish, the process took two minutes and twelve seconds, whereupon John Michael Fowles, also known as Mr Red, had access to everything within the government's database of information on bombs and bombers.

John smiled to himself as he always did, and said, 'Piece a' fuckin' cake.'

The most recent entry was from Los Angeles, which surprised John. It should have been from Miami, but it wasn't.

John Michael Fowles had not been to Los Angeles in almost two years.

John stared at the entry for several seconds, curious, then opened the file. He skimmed the summary remarks, learning that an LAPD bomb technician named Charles Riggio had died in a Silver Lake parking lot. John scanned the summary, the last lines of which hit him with all the impact of a nuclear device.

... *analysis finds residue of the trinary explosive Modex Hybrid ... Initial evidence suggests that the perpetrator is the anonymous bomber known as 'Mr Red'.*

John walked across the room, leaned against the wall and stared at nothing. He was breathing harder now, his back clammy. He stalked back to the iBook.

John's eye zoomed into the components of the bomb until they filled his screen.

He wondered for a crazy, insane moment if he had built the bomb and somehow forgotten it, laughed aloud at that, then threw the iBook across the room as hard as he could, gouging a three-inch rent in the wall and shattering the plastic case.

John shouted, 'You MOTHERFUCKER!'

John Michael Fowles grabbed his bag of cash and ran out of the motel. Peter Willy would have a long night at the titty bar, waiting for someone who would not show. John barrel-assed the big red SS 396 along the edge of the lake, pushing the gas-guzzling engine hard and making the fat, low-class tires squeal. He stopped on the side of the causeway long enough to throw the iBook into the water, then drove like a motherfucker all the way back to the airport. He put the car in long-term parking, wiped down the interior and doors to remove his fingerprints, then paid cash for a one-way ticket to Los Angeles.

No one knew better than John Michael Fowles what it took to make Modex Hybrid or how to find those things within the bomb community. John Michael Fowles had resources, and he had clues.

Somebody had stolen his work, which meant someone was trying to horn in on his glory.

John Michael Fowles was not going to tolerate that.

He was going out there to get the sonofabitch.

Part Two

I Luv L.A.

John Michael Fowles got off the plane with twenty-six thousand dollars, three driver's licenses, and four credit cards, two of which matched with names on the licenses. He also had the phone number of a twenty-eight-year-old flight attendant with dimples deep enough to swallow you and a tan warmer than a golden sunset. She lived in Manhattan Beach. Her name was Penny.

Just being in Los Angeles made John smile.

He loved the dry sunny weather, the palm trees, the good-looking babes in their skimpy clothes, the cool people, the slick cars, the hunger for wealth, the asshole movie stars, that the whole damned place was so big and flat and spread to hell, the La Brea Tar Pits, hot dog stands that looked like hot dogs, that big-ass Hollywood sign spread across that friggin' mountain, earthquakes and firestorms, the funky clubs on the Sunset Strip, sushi, the caramel tans, Mexicans, the tour buses filled with people from Iowa, the glittering swimming pools, the ocean, Arnold Schwarzenegger, the G's with their forties, and Disneyland.

It was a great place for devastation.

First thing he did was rent a convertible from Hertz, strip off his shirt, slip on his shades, and cruise up Sepulveda Boulevard, looking good. He was past his mad now, over his snit; now was the time for cold calculation and furious vengeance. Mr Red had arrived.

John dropped the shitkicker persona and went black. He loved white guys who acted black. M&Ms. Light on the outside, dark on the inside. *Yo, G, 'sup?* L.A. was the perfect place for this. Everyone was always pretending to be something they weren't.

John bought oversized clothes from a secondhand shop two blocks up from the beach in Venice, a new iBook, and the other things he needed, then took a room at a small motel called the Flamingo Arms. It smelled of foreigners. John shaved his head, draped himself with faux gold chains, then signed on to the Internet. This time he didn't bother with cracking into the NLETS system. He searched for news stories on the Silver Lake bomb, finding three pieces. The first two articles contained pretty much the same thing: the LAPD Bomb Squad had rolled out to investigate a suspicious package, whereupon Officer Charles Riggio, thirty-four, a nine-year veteran of the squad, was killed when the package exploded. None of the news stories gave details of the device, though the detective leading the investigation, a woman named Carol Starkey, was quoted as attributing the bomb, 'a crude, poorly made device', to 'an infantile personality'. John laughed when he read that. He knew that the ATF suspected him, and that, therefore, LAPD suspected him, also.

John said, 'The dumb bitch is trying to play me.'

John was especially intrigued by the third story, a sidebar article on Starkey herself, who had once been a bomb tech until she had been caught in an explosion. The article said that Starkey had actually died, but had been revived at the scene. John was fascinated by that. There was a photograph of Starkey and some other cops at the scene, but the picture was small and the resolution was poor. John stared at Starkey, trying to see through the murk, and touched the screen.

'Well.'

In the final paragraph, Starkey vowed to find the person or persons responsible for Riggio's death.

John smiled at that one.

'Not if I find the motherfucker first.'

John dumped the news stories and went to his web site in Rochester for the list of phone numbers, e-mail addresses, and other things he often needed but didn't carry. He copied the phone number of a man he knew as Clarence Jester, who lived in Venice. Jester owned a small pawnshop as his primary occupation, but was an arsonist. Now in his late fifties, Jester had once served twelve years of federal time for starting fires and was an on-again, off-again psychiatric patient. His hobby was adopting dogs from the pound, dousing them with gasoline, and watching them burn. In the past, John had found him an excellent source of information about those in the bomb community.

'Clarence. It's LeRoy Abramowicz, my man. I'm in L.A.'

'Yeah?'

Clarence Jester spoke with the careful hesitancy of a paranoid, which he was.

'Thought I might swing by and do a little business. That cool?'

'I guess.'

Anxious to get going, but hungry, John scarfed a Big Kahuna burger on the way, ambling into Clarence Jester's pawnshop a few minutes later.

Jester was a small, nervous man, with badly thinning hair. He would not shake hands, explaining that he had a thing about germs.

'Hey, Clarence. Let's go for a walk.'

Clarence, ready for him, closed the shop without a word.

Outside, Clarence eyed him carefully.

'You look different.'

'I went black. Everybody's doing it.'

'Mm.'

Business was always done outside, John knowing that Clarence would be more than happy to trade customers for prison time. Twice before, John had bought ammonium picrate from Jester. In addition to being an arsonist, Jester bought and sold explosives, extreme pornography, and the occasional automatic assault weapon. John knew that whoever duplicated his bomb would have to mix their own Modex Hybrid, which meant they would have had to acquire RDX.

'Clarence, I'm looking for a little RDX. You help me with that?'

'Ha.'

'What's the "ha" mean, my man?'

'You don't sound black. You sound like a white man trying to talk nigger.'

'Stay with the RDX, Clarence. Do me that courtesy.'

'Nobody has RDX. I see some RDX once every couple of years, that's it. I got some TNT and PETN, though. That PETN will blow your ass off.'

Clarence brushed his fingers across his mouth as he said it, mumbling his words. He probably thought John was wired.

'Gotta be RDX.'

'I can't help you with that.'

'That's you. There's gotta be someone else. Hell, you're not living in Buttcrack. This is L.A. You got everydamnthing out here.'

A girl in a Day-Glo green bikini bladed past, her ears wrapped in headphones. She had a tattoo of a sun rising out of her pants and a yellow cocker spaniel on a leash. John noticed that Clarence watched the dog.

'Just point the way, Clarence. I find what I'm looking for, I'll kick back a finder's fee to you. I won't leave you cold.'

The dog disappeared around a corner.

'The RDX is ringing a bell.'

'There you go.'

'Don't get excited just yet. When I say it's hard to find, I mean it's hard to find. Just a few years ago, there was a fellow up north who got busted for blowing up cars. He was using RDX. I can maybe put you in touch with him.'

John began to feel jazzed. Connections lead to connections.

'A customer of yours?'

'He didn't get the RDX from me, I'll tell you that.'

Clarence proceeded to tell him about a man named Dallas Tennant, who was now serving time. John stopped him when he got to the part about prison, irritated.

'Hold on. What in hell good does it do me if he's in the goddamn prison?'

'You can talk to him on Claudius.'

'In prison?'

'Like that means shit. You wouldn't believe the stuff I did when I was in prison. Listen, somehow this guy turned enough RDX to blow up three cars. If he can't help you, maybe he can put you with someone who can.'

His irritation lifted, and John began to feel jazzed again. This was the way he knew it had to be, all the way out from New Orleans. He wondered if Detective Starkey was smart enough to backtrack the RDX. And if their paths would cross.

'Do you know Mr Tennant's screen name?'

'Got it back in my computer. You know how to get on Claudius?'

'I know.'

John clapped Jester on the back, just to see him flinch.

'Thanks, Clarence.'

'Don't touch me. I don't like that.'

'Sorry.'

'Hey, you heard the big rumor we got out here?'

'No. What rumor?'

'Mr Red came to town. They're saying he blew up some cop in Silver Lake.'

His mood ruined, John clapped Clarence Jester on the back again.

Atascadero

When the last of the inmates had left the library, Dallas Tennant gathered the magazines and books from the tables, stacking them on his cart. The library wasn't very big, only six tables, but the reading selection was current and varied. Several of the inmates at Atascadero were millionaires who had arranged for generous donations of books so that they would have something to read. The Atascadero library was the envy of the California state prison system.

Mr Riley, the civilian employee who managed the library, turned out the light in his office. He was a retired high school history teacher.

'Are you almost done here, Dallas?'

'I just have to put these away, then dust the stacks. It won't take long.'

Mr Riley hesitated in his door. He was never comfortable leaving the inmate employees unattended, though there was nothing in the rules against it.

'Well, maybe I should stay.'

Dallas smiled pleasantly. Earlier, Dallas had overheard Mr Riley say that his son and daughter-in-law were coming for dinner, so he knew that Riley was anxious to leave.

'Oh, that's all right, Mr Riley. We got that box of new books today. I thought I would enter them into the computer tonight so I'd have more time to restack the shelves tomorrow. That might keep me here later than I thought.'

'Well, as long as the door is closed by nine. You have to be at the infirmary by nine or they'll come looking for you.'

Inmates at Atascadero had enormous freedom, but there was still oversight. Dallas, for example, could work late at the library, but was required to stop by the infirmary for his nightly meds. If he didn't report there by nine P.M., the nurse would notify the duty guard, who would set about finding him.

'I know, sir. I will. Would you tell the guard that I'll be in your office, please, just in case he walks by and sees me in there?'

'I will. You have a good evening, Dallas.'

'You too, sir.'

447

Not wanting to linger, Mr Riley left, thanking Dallas for his good work just as he thanked him every evening.

Dallas Tennant was a good boy. Always had been and still was, even in Atascadero. He was polite, well mannered, and even tempered. He was also a bright boy, way bright enough not only to mix chemicals and construct intricate devices, but also to manipulate others.

As soon as Dallas arrived at Atascadero, he had arranged for a job in the kitchen, which not only gave him access to things like baking soda and match heads, but also gave him an unlimited supply of snack foods. He was then able to trade the snacks with inmates working in Janitorial Services for certain cleaning products, which, when combined with things pilfered from the kitchen, created dandy little explosives.

His little accident and the loss of his thumb had ruined that, getting him banned from any area containing chemical supplies, but this library job was almost as good for a different kind of access.

The ironic part of being banned from kitchen and cleaning duty was that Dallas did not create that particular explosive from supplies found within the prison. He had traded for that explosive with someone from the outside.

Dallas still smiled, thinking about it, even with the loss of his thumb. Some things were worth a small sacrifice.

Dallas cleared the remainder of the magazines and books, but didn't take the time to put them in their proper places. He stepped out into the hall, making sure that Mr Riley was gone, then checked the time. A guard would be along in about twenty minutes to see if Dallas was where he was supposed to be. Dallas went into Riley's office, broke out the box of books that the guard would be expecting to see, then recovered the software diskette that he kept hidden behind Riley's file cabinet. Though Atascadero was a modern facility and was linked to the California prison system via the Internet, no computer that prisoners could access was supposed to have Internet software installed; that was reserved for secure office machines and the computers belonging to the administrators.

Dallas had acquired his own software, arranging for his attorney to pay his monthly service charges from his rental income.

He loaded the software onto Riley's hard drive, connected the modem to the phone line, and signed on. When he was finished for the evening, he would un-install, and Mr Riley would be none the wiser.

In moments, Dallas Tennant was home again.

Claudius.

It was the one place where Tennant felt comfortable, an anonymous world where he was not judged or ridiculed, but embraced as one of a like tribe. His only friends were there, other anonymous screen names with whom he shared posts in the public areas and often chatted in the secret chat room. His instant-messaging list showed several who were currently signed on: ACDRUSH, who loved to post intricate chemical formulas that were, Tennant believed, always wrong; MEYER2, who shared Tennant's admiration for Mr Red; RATBOY, who had written a fourteen-page treatise on how the Oklahoma City bomb could have generated forty percent more explosive force with a few small enhancements; and DEDTED, who believed that Theodore Kaczynski was not the Unabomber.

Tennant posted under the name BOOMER.

Careful to keep an eye out for the guard, he scanned a message board thread that he had created about Mr Red's appearance in Los Angeles. He was writing an addition when a messaging window appeared on his screen.

WILL YOU ACCEPT A MESSAGE FROM NEO?

Tennant did not know a 'Neo', but was curious. He clicked the button to accept, and the instant-messaging window opened.

NEO: **You don't know me, but I know you.**

Tennant glanced toward the hall again, nervous because he knew that the guard was due soon, and his time on-line was short. He typed a response.

BOOMER: **Who are you?**

Neo's response came back quickly.

NEO: **Someone who admires your use of RDX. I want to discuss it.**

Tennant, like all habitués of Claudius, was aware that law enforcement agents often trolled to entrap people into saying something incriminating. He was careful never to post anything incriminating outside of the secure chat area.

BOOMER: **Good night.**
NEO: **Wait! You want to meet me, Dallas. I am giving you an opportunity tonight that others only dream about.**

Tennant felt a flush of fear at the use of his true name.

BOOMER: **How do you know my name?**
NEO: **I know many things.**
BOOMER: **You think highly of yourself.**
NEO: *You* **think highly of me, Dallas. You have written many posts about me. Come to the chat room.**

Tennant hesitated. This changed things. If Neo had a key to the chat room, then someone had vouched for him. He was as safe as safe could be in this uncertain world.

BOOMER: You have a key?
NEO: I. do. I am in the chat room now. Waiting.

Tennant used his own key and opened the chat-room window. It was empty except for Neo.

BOOMER: Who are you?
NEO: I am Mr Red. You have something that I want, Dallas. Information.

Tennant stared at the name ... incredulous ... disbelieving ... hopeful. Then he typed:

BOOMER: What do you have to trade?

9

As soon as Starkey walked through her door that night, she regretted
agreeing to let Pell come to her home. She scooped magazines and
newspapers off the floor, policed up a Chinese food carton, and fretted that
the air smelled. She tried to remember the last time that she had cleaned
the kitchen and the bathroom, but couldn't. There was nothing in the
house to drink except gin, tonic, and tap water. You could write your name
in the dust on top of the television. She grabbed a fast shower, dressing in
jeans and a black T-shirt, then made a half-hearted attempt to make her
house presentable. The last guest that she'd had was Dick Leyton, almost a
year ago. He'd stopped by to catch up with her, and stayed for a drink.

You really should get a life, Starkey. Maybe they sell'm at the Best Buy.

Whatever Kelso thought, Starkey had a good feeling about the
investigation. Having her hands on the Miami bomb had been good for
her; it was concrete and real and had led to her learning something new,
something she would not have otherwise known, about the Silver Lake
bomb. Maybe Kelso and the others couldn't see it, but Starkey was a bomb
tech; she believed that the pieces added up, and now she had another piece.
She was anxious to see if Claudius would yield anything useful, and was
encouraged by Hooker's report from the postproduction facility. She also
felt that there was more to be had from Dallas Tennant.

Starkey set up the laptop on her dining-room table, figuring that was the
best place for them to work. She had plugged it in and turned it on when
she heard Pell's car turn into her drive.

When she opened the door, he was carrying a pizza and a white bag.

'It's the dinner hour, so I thought I would bring something. I've got a
pizza here and an antipasto. I hope you didn't make something.'

'Crap. I've got a duck baking.'

'I guess I should've called.'

'Pell, I'm joking. My usual dinner is a can of tuna fish and some tortilla
chips. This will be great.'

She brought the food into the kitchen, feeling doubly embarrassed that
there was nothing to drink. She wasn't even sure she had clean dishes.

'You don't drink gin and tonic, do you?'

'Maybe some tonic without the gin. Where's the computer?'

'It's on the table in the dining room, through there. You want to eat first?'

'We can eat while we work.'

Starkey thought he was probably anxious to leave. She found that her glasses were spotted and hoped he wouldn't notice. She filled two glasses with ice and tonic. She felt a fierce urge to add gin to her glass, but resisted.

When she turned to hand him the glass, he was watching her.

'I didn't know what you liked, so I got half veggie, half pepperoni and sausage.'

'Either way is fine, but thanks. That was thoughtful.'

Just hearing the words come out made her groan to herself. The two of them sounded like a couple of social misfits on an awkward first date. She reminded herself that this was work, not a date. She didn't date. She still needed to go to Best Buy to pick out a life.

As she got out plates and silverware, she considered telling him what she had learned about the joint tape, but she decided against it. She would wait until she heard from Janice Brockwell. She told herself that then she would know whether or not she had something, but part of her didn't want Pell to dismiss her discovery out of hand the way Kelso had.

They divided the antipasto and pizza, then brought their plates and glasses into the dining room. They put two chairs together, just like in Bergen's office, then Starkey signed on to Claudius. She sat with an uncomfortable awareness of Pell's proximity, then edged her chair away.

'Maybe we should eat first. So we don't get grease on the keys.'

'Let's not worry about the keys. I want to see if anyone responded.'

Starkey shifted her chair next to him again, and they opened the door into Claudius.

With Bergen, they had posted three messages, two expressing enthusiastic admiration for Mr Red, one asking if the rumor that Mr Red had struck again in Los Angeles was true. This last message had drawn several responses, one of which reproduced a story from the *Los Angeles Times*, but most of which doubted Mr Red's appearance, citing his recent criminal blast in Miami and growing status as 'Urban Legend'. One poster compared Mr Red to Elvis, suggesting that pretty soon he was going to be seen working in every Denny's in America.

Starkey used the mouse control to advance from message to message, reading, waiting for Pell's grunt, then clicking to the next message. As she concentrated on the bizarre nature of the posts, her awareness of Pell lessened until he reached across her and abruptly took the mouse.

'Hang on. I want to read the last one again.'

In the moment when his hand covered hers, she drew away from him as if she'd received an electrical charge, then felt herself flush with embarrassment. She covered it by taking back the mouse and asking a question.

'What did you see?'

'Read it.'

SUBJECT: Re: Truth or Consequences

FROM: AM7TAL

MESSAGE-ID: >9777721.04 @ selfnet<

>> truth to the rumor? <<

My sources inform me that The Man recently laid waste in south Florida, and that is confirmed. History tells us that he waits a while between gigs. The practical reality is that nobody shits Modex in the morning. Anybody got some for sale?

Ha ha. Just kidding, federal motherfuckers!

Am7

Starkey reread the message.

'You think he's Mr Red?'

'No. He's making the joke about buying Modex, but Mr Red mixes his own. Red wouldn't expect to buy it, he would buy the components. What if we post back to this guy, making a joke of our own, saying something like we don't have any Modex, but we could probably help him out with some RDX?'

'Throw bait on the water.'

'For him, and anyone else reading this stuff.'

Pell turned the keyboard and shifted in his seat. His knee touched her knee, his right arm touched her left. Starkey didn't jerk away this time; she let the touch linger. She glanced at Pell, but Pell seemed lost in composing the message. Pictures flashed in her mind: *She touches his arm, their eyes lock, they kiss.* Her heart pounded, thinking about it. *She takes his hand, leads him to the bedroom, he sees her scars.*

Starkey felt sick to her stomach and eased away.

I'm not ready for this.

She stared at her pizza, but couldn't eat it.

Pell, oblivious, said, 'What do you think?'

SUBJECT: Re: Truth or Consequences

FROM: HOTLOAD

MESSAGE-ID: >5521721.04 @ treenet<

>> nobody shits Modex in the morning. Anybody got some for sale? <<

RDX is the best laxative! I might be willing to share for the right price. Ha ha yourself!

HOTLOAD

'It looks good.'

Starkey glanced over and saw that he was rubbing his eyes and squinting.

'You okay?'

'Pretty soon I'm going to need reading glasses, then a cane.'

'I have some drops, if you want.'

'That's okay.'

They posted the message.

'Anything else?'

'Just wait and see, I guess.'

Pell closed the laptop.

'I don't want you to think I'm telling you what to do, but could I ask you to run another NLETS search on the RDX? See if we get a hit on anyone other than Tennant?'

'I already did, and we didn't. The only name that comes up is Tennant.'

'We've already gotten what we're going to get from him.'

'Maybe from Tennant, but not from Tennant's case.'

'What does that mean?'

'I reread Mueller's case notes again. It's clear that he didn't need to find Tennant's shop or recover additional explosives to make his case, so he let a lot of stuff slide. His interview notes indicate that he didn't spend much time with Tennant's landlady or Tennant's employer. He had pictures of the three cars Tennant destroyed and the statement from the kid who stole the cars; that was all he needed. If he blew off the other wits, there still might be something to find.'

'That's good thinking, Starkey. That could pay off.'

Starkey realized that she was smiling at him, and that Pell was smiling back. The house was silent. With the computer off, Starkey was all the more aware that she and Pell were alone. She wondered if he felt that, too, and suddenly wished for other sounds: the television, the radio, a car on the street. But there was only the two of them, and she didn't know what to do with that.

She abruptly cleared the plates, taking them into the kitchen.

'Thanks again for the pizza. Next time has to be on me.'

When the plates were in the sink, she returned to the dining room, but didn't go to her chair. She didn't offer more tonic, and hoped it was apparent that she wanted him to leave. Pell looked like he wanted to say something, but she didn't give him the chance. She wedged her hands in her pockets.

'So I guess we'll check back tomorrow. I'll call you about it.'

Pell finally stood. She walked him to the door, then stepped well back from him.

'I'll see you, Pell. We'll catch this bastard.'

'Good night, Starkey.'

As soon as he stepped through the door, she shut it. Starkey didn't feel better with the door closed; she felt stupid and confused. She was still feeling that way when she went to bed, where she stared at the ceiling in the darkness and wondered why she felt so lost. All she had was the job. All she had was the investigation. That was her life these past three years. That was all it would ever be.

Pell

In his motel, Pell was staring at the computer when the monsters came. They floated up out of the keyboard like writhing segmented worms swarmed by fireflies. He closed his eyes, but still could see them, floating in the blackness. He stumbled into the bathroom for the ice and wet towels that were still in the lavatory, then lay on the bed, the cool towels on his face, his head aching from a pain so great that it left him gasping, and fearful.

He wanted to call Starkey.

He cursed himself for that and concentrated on the pain instead, on this place. He listened to the evening commuter traffic outside his window, the stop-and-go noise of people struggling upstream against the weight of the city; squealing brakes, revving engines, the rumble of overloaded trucks. It was like being on the edge of hell.

He was getting to know her, and that was bad. Every time they were together, he saw a deeper side of her, a surprising side, and his guilt was growing because of it. Pell was too good at reading people, at seeing the hidden face that all people secretly wear, their true face. Pell had learned long ago that everyone is really two people: the person they let you see and the secret person within. Pell had always been able to read the secret person, and the secret person within Starkey's tough-cookie exterior was a little girl who was trying hard to be brave. Inside the little girl was a warrior heart, trying to rebuild her life and career. He hadn't counted on liking her. He hadn't counted on her liking him. It ate at him. It was growing.

But there was nothing to be done for it.

After a time, the pain passed and his vision cleared. Pell glanced at the clock. An hour. Pell covered his face with his hands. Five minutes, maybe ten, but it couldn't have been an hour.

He climbed off the bed and went back to the computer. The flaming head stared out at him from the screen. Pell pushed the guilt he felt about Starkey to the side and opened the door into Claudius. Her name had been on the bomb. Mr Red wanted her. He could work that.

Pell used a different screen name, one that Starkey didn't know, and began to write about her.

10

The next morning, Starkey was the first detective in the office as usual. She figured that Mueller probably didn't get into his office at six A.M., so she killed time with paperwork. Hooker arrived at five after seven, Marzik drifting in about twenty minutes later. Marzik had Starbucks.

Marzik was stowing her briefcase when she glanced over.

'How'd the big meeting with the A-chief go?'

'He told me to keep the case moving forward. That was his contribution.'

Marzik dropped into her seat, sipping the coffee. Starkey smelled chocolate. Mocha.

'I hear Dick Leyton saved your ass in there.'

Starkey frowned, wondering what Marzik had heard.

'What does that mean? What did you hear?'

Marzik pried the lid from her cup, blew to cool the coffee.

'Kelso told Giadonna. He said you floated some notion about Silver Lake being a copycat. I'm kinda curious when you were planning on telling me and Hooker about it.'

Starkey was pissed off that Kelso would say anything, and pissed that Marzik thought she'd been keeping something from them. She explained about the Miami device and the difference she had found in the direction of the tape.

'It's not the big headline you're making it sound. I wanted to talk it over with you guys today. I didn't get a chance yesterday.'

'Well, whatever. Maybe you were too busy thinking about Pell.'

'What does that mean?'

'Hey, he's a good-looking guy. For a fed.'

'I haven't noticed.'

'He got you in on that Claudius thing, right? All I'm saying is when a guy does you a turn like that, you should think about paying him back. Give the man a blow job.'

Hooker lurched to his feet and walked away. Marzik laughed.

'Jorge is such a goddamned tightass.'

Starkey was irritated.

'No, Beth. He's a gentleman. You, you're trailer trash.'

Marzik wheeled her chair closer and lowered her voice.

'Now I'm being serious, okay? It's pretty obvious you're attracted to him.'

'Bullshit.'

'Every time somebody mentions the guy, you look like you're scared to death. And it's not because he might take the case.'

'Beth? When's the last time you were choked out?'

Marzik arched her eyebrows knowingly, then rolled her chair back to her desk.

Starkey went for more coffee, ignoring Marzik, who sat on her fat ass with a smugfuckingsmile. Hooker, still embarrassed by Marzik's remark, lingered on the far side of the squad room, too humiliated to meet Starkey's eye.

Starkey went back to her desk, scooped up the phone, and dialed Mueller. It was still early, but it was either call Mueller or shoot Marzik between the eyes.

When Mueller came on the line, he sounded rushed.

'I gotta get movin' here, Starkey. Some turd put a hand grenade in a mailbox.'

'I just have a couple of questions, Sergeant. I spoke with Tennant, and now I need to follow up a few things with you.'

'He's a real piece of work, ain't he? He loses any more fingers, pretty soon he'll be countin' on his toes.'

Starkey didn't think it was funny.

'Tennant still denies that he had a shop.'

Mueller interrupted her, annoyed because she was wasting his time.

'Waitaminute. We talked about this, didn't we?'

'That's right.'

'There's nothing new to cover. If he's got a shop, we couldn't find it. I been thinking about this since you called. I've got to tell you I think the guy is probably telling the truth. A pissant like this wouldn't have the balls to hold out when he could trade for time.'

She didn't bother pointing out that for a pissant like Tennant, his shop would be the most important thing in the world.

Instead, she told him that she had reason to believe that Tennant had a shop and more RDX, also. This time when he spoke, his voice was stiff.

'What reason?'

'Tennant told us the same thing he told you, that he salvaged the RDX from a case of Raytheon GMX antipersonnel mines. That's six mines.'

'Yeah. That's what I remember.'

'Okay. I looked up the GMX in our spec book down here. It says that each GMX carries a charge of 1.8 pounds of RDX, which means he would have had a little over ten pounds. Now, I'm looking at the pictures of these three cars you sent. They're fairly light-bodied vehicles, but most of the damage seems to be from fire. I ran an energy calc on the RDX, and it seems to me that if he had used a third of his load on each car, the damage would've been much greater than it is here.'

Mueller didn't answer.

'Then I saw here in your interview notes with Robert Castillo that Tennant asked him to steal a fourth car. That implies to me that Tennant had more RDX.'

When Mueller finally spoke, his tone was defensive.

'We searched that rathole he was living in. We searched every damned box and cubbyhole in the place. We had his car impounded for three months and even stripped the damned rocker panels. We searched the old lady's house, and her garage, and I even had the Feebs bring out a god-damned dog for the flower bed, so don't try to make out that I fucked up.'

Starkey felt her voice harden and regretted it.

'I'm not trying to make out anything, Mueller. Only reason I called is that there aren't many notes here from your interviews with his landlady or employer.'

'There was nothing to write. The old bat didn't want to talk to us. All she gave a shit about was us not tromping on her flower beds.'

'What about his employer?'

'He said what they all say, how surprised he was, how Dallas was such a normal guy. We wear cowboy boots up here, Starkey, but we're not stupid. You just remember. That sonofabitch is sitting in Atascadero because of me. I made my case. When you make yours, call me again.'

He hung up before she could answer, and Starkey slammed down her phone. When she looked up, Marzik was staring at her.

'Smooth.'

'Fuck him.'

'You're really pissed off today. What got up your ass?'

'Beth. Just leave it alone.'

Starkey shuffled through the casework again. Tennant's landlady had been an elderly woman named Estelle Reager. His employer had been a man named Bradley Ferman, owner of a hobby shop called Robbie's Hobbies. She found their phone numbers and called both, learning that Robbie's Hobbies was out of business. Estelle Reager agreed to speak with her.

Starkey gathered her purse, and stood.

'Come on, Beth. We're going up there to talk to this woman.'

Marzik looked shocked.

'I don't want to go to Bakersfield. Take Hooker.'

'Hooker's busy with the tapes.'

'So am I. I'm still talking to the laundry people.'

'Get your shit together and put your ass in the car. We're taking the drive.'

Starkey left without waiting.

*

The Golden State Freeway ran north out of Los Angeles, splitting the state through the great, flat plain of the Central Valley. Starkey believed it to be the finest driving road in California, or anywhere; long, straight, wide, and flat. You could set the cruise control at eighty, put your brain on hold, and make San Francisco in five hours. Bakersfield was less than ninety minutes.

Marzik sulked, bound up tight on the passenger side with her arms and legs crossed like a pouting teenager. Starkey wasn't sure why she had made Marzik come, regretting it even as they left Spring Street. Neither of them spoke for the first half-hour until they crested the Newhall Pass at the top of the San Fernando Valley, the great roller coasters and spires of the Magic Mountain amusement park appearing on their left.

Marzik shifted uncomfortably. It was Marzik who spoke first.

'My kids want to go to that place. I keep putting them off because it costs so much, but, Jesus, they see these damned commercials, these people on the roller coasters. The commercials never say how much it costs.'

Starkey glanced over, expecting Marzik to look angry and resentful, but she didn't. She looked tired and miserable.

'Beth, I want to ask you something. What you said about me and Pell, is it really that obvious?'

Marzik shrugged.

'I don't know. I was just saying that.'

'Okay.'

'You never talk about your life. I just kinda figured you don't have one.'

Marzik looked over at her.

'Now can I ask you something?'

Starkey felt uncomfortable with that, but told Marzik she could ask whatever she wanted.

'When's the last time you had a man?'

'That's a terrible thing to ask.'

'You said I could ask. If you don't want to talk about it, fine.'

Starkey realized that she was gripping the steering wheel so hard her knuckles were white. She took a breath, forcing herself to relax. She grudgingly admitted that she wanted to talk about this, even though she didn't know how. Maybe that was why she had made Marzik come with her.

'It's been a long time.'

'What are you waiting for? You think you're getting younger? You think your ass is getting smaller?'

'I don't know.'

'I don't know what you want because we never talk. Here we are, the only two women in the section, and we never talk about anything but the goddamned job. Here's what I'm saying, Carol, you do this damned job, but you need something else, because this job is shit. It takes, but it doesn't give you a goddamned thing. It's just shit.'

Starkey glanced over. Marzik's eyes were wet and she was blinking. Starkey realized that suddenly everything had turned; they were talking about Marzik, not Starkey.

'Well, I'll tell you what *I* want. I want to get married. I want someone to talk to who's taller than me. I want someone else in that house even if he spends all his time on the couch, and I have to bring him the beer and listen to him fart at three in the morning. I am sick of being alone, with no one for company but two kids eating crackers. Shit, I want to be married so bad they see me coming a mile away and run.'

Starkey didn't know what to say.

'I'm sorry, Beth. You're dating, right? You'll find someone.'

'You don't know shit about it. I hate this fucking job. I hate my rotten life. I hate these two kids. Isn't that the most horrible thing you've ever heard? I hate these two kids, and I don't know how I'm gonna get them up here to Magic Mountain.'

Marzik ran out of gas and lapsed into silence. Starkey drove on, feeling uncomfortable. She thought that Marzik must want something for having said all that, but didn't know what. She felt that she was letting Marzik down.

'Beth, listen.'

Marzik shook her head, not looking over, clearly embarrassed. Starkey was embarrassed, too.

'I'm not very good at girl talk. I'm sorry.'

They lapsed into silence then, each of them lost in her own thoughts as they followed the freeway down from the mountains into the great Central Valley. When Bakersfield appeared on the flat, empty plain, Marzik finally spoke again.

'I didn't mean that about my kids.'

'I know.'

They left the freeway a short time later, following directions that Estelle Reager had given until they came to a prewar stucco home between the railroad transfer station south of Bakersfield, and the airport. Mrs Reager answered the door wearing jeans, a checked shirt, and work gloves. She bore the lined, leathery skin of a woman who had spent much of her life in the sun. Starkey guessed that Mueller had come in like a cowboy, thinking he could ride roughshod over the old woman, who had gotten her back up. Once up, she would be hard to win over.

Starkey introduced herself and Marzik.

Reager eyed them.

'A couple of women, huh? I guess none of the lazy men down there wanted to drive up.'

Marzik laughed. When Starkey saw the twinkle that came to Estelle Reager's eye, she knew they were home free.

Mrs Reager showed them through the house and out the back door to a small patio covered by a translucent green awning. The awning caught the sun, washing everything with a green glow. The driveway ran along the side of the house to a garage, behind which sat a small, neat guest house. A well-maintained vegetable garden filled the length of the yard between the patio and the guest house.

'We appreciate your seeing us like this, Mrs Reager.'

'Well, I'm happy to help. I don't know what I can tell you, though. Nothing I ain't already said before.'

Marzik went to the edge of the patio to look at the guest house.

'Is that where he lived?'

'Oh, yes. He lived there for four years, and you couldn't ask for a better young man. I guess that sounds strange, considering what we know about him now, but Dallas was always very considerate and paid his rent on time.'

'It looks empty. Is anyone living there now?'

'I had a young man last year, but he married a teacher and they needed a bigger place. It's so hard to find quality people in this price range, you know. May I ask what it is you're hoping to find?'

Starkey explained her belief that Tennant still had a store of bomb components.

'Well, you won't find anything like that here. The police searched high and low, let me tell you that. They were all in my garden. I was happy to help, but they weren't very nice about it.'

Starkey knew that her guess about Mueller had been right.

'If you want to look through his things, you can help yourself. They're all right there in the garage.'

Marzik turned back, glancing at Starkey.

'You've still got Tennant's things?'

'Well, he asked me to keep them, you know, since he was in jail.'

Starkey looked at the garage, then at Mrs Reager.

'These were things that were here when the police searched?'

'Oh, yes. I got'm in the garage, if you want to look.'

She explained that Tennant had continued to pay rent on his guest house for the first year that he was in prison, but that he had finally written to her, apologizing that he would have to stop and asking if she would be willing to store his things. There weren't very many. Only a few boxes.

Starkey asked the older woman to excuse them, and walked with Marzik to the garage.

'If she says we can go into the garage, we're okay with that because it's her property. But if we go into his boxes and find anything, we could have a problem with that.'

'You think we need a search warrant?'

'Of course we need a search warrant.'

They would need a search warrant, but they were also out of their operating area, Los Angeles police in the city of Bakersfield. The easiest thing to do would be to call Mueller and have him come out with a request for a telephonic warrant.

Starkey went back to Mrs Reager.

'Mrs Reager, I want to be clear on something. These things in your garage, they are things that the police have already looked at?'

'Well, they were in the guest house when the police came. I would guess they looked.'

'All right. Now, you said that Tennant asked you to store his things. Did you pack them?'

'That's right. He didn't have very much, just clothes and some of those adult movies. I didn't pack those. I threw them away when I found them. The furniture was mine. I rented it furnished in those days.'

Starkey decided that there was nothing to be gained by searching the boxes. Her real hope was in identifying people with whom Tennant might have stored his components well before the time of his arrest.

'Did you know any of his friends or acquaintances?'

'No one ever came here, if that's what you're asking. Well, I take that back. One young man did come by a few times, but that was long before Dallas was arrested. They worked together, I think. At that hobby shop.'

'How long before?'

'Oh, a long time. At least a year. I think they were watching those movies, you know?'

Marzik took out the three suspect sketches.

'Do any of these look like the man?'

'Oh, Lord, that was so long ago and I didn't pay attention. I don't think so.'

Starkey let it go, thinking that she was probably right.

Marzik said, 'That was Tennant's only job, the hobby shop?'

'That's right.'

'Did he have any girlfriends?'

'No. None that I knew.'

'What about family?'

'Well, all I knew of was his mother. I know she died, though. Tennant came into my house and told me that. He was heartbroken, you know. We had coffee, and the poor boy just cried.'

Starkey wasn't thinking about the mother. Something about the boxes bothered her.

'Tennant continued paying rent to you for a year, even after he was in prison?'

'That's right. He thought he might be released, you know, and wanted to come back. He didn't want me to rent the house to anyone else.'

Marzik raised her eyebrows.

'Imagine that. Is anyone renting it from you now?'

'No. I haven't had a guest in there since my last young man.'

Starkey glanced over, and Marzik nodded. They were both thinking the same thing, wondering why Tennant didn't want to give up his apartment even when he had no use for it. If Tennant wasn't paying rent now and wasn't the occupant of record, they could legally enter and search the premises with the owner's permission.

'Mrs Reager, would you give us permission to look inside?'

'I don't know why not.'

The guest house was musty and hot, revealing one large main room, a kitchenette, bath, and bedroom. The furniture had long since been removed, except for a simple dinette table and chairs. The linoleum floor was discolored and dingy. Starkey couldn't remember the last time she had seen linoleum. Mrs Reager stood in the open door, explaining that her husband had used the building as an office, while Starkey and Marzik went through the rooms, checking the flooring and baseboards for secret cubbyholes.

Mrs Reager watched with mild amusement.

'You think he had a secret hiding place?'

'It's been known to happen.'

'Those police who were here, they looked for that, too. They tried looking under the floor, but we're on a slab. There's no attic, either.'

After ten minutes of poking and prodding, both Starkey and Marzik agreed that there was nothing to find. Starkey felt disappointed. It looked as if the drive up to Bakersfield was a waste, and her trail backwards to the RDX was at an end.

Marzik said, 'You know, this is a pretty nice guest house, Mrs Reager. You think I could send my two kids up here to live with you? We could put iron bars on the windows.'

The older woman laughed.

Starkey said, 'Beth, can you think of anything else?'

Marzik shook her head. They had covered everything.

Something about Tennant continuing to pay rent still bothered Starkey, but she couldn't decide what. After thanking Mrs Reager for her cooperation, Starkey and Marzik were walking through the gate when it came to her. She stopped at the gate.

Marzik said, 'What?'

'Here's a guy who worked at a hobby shop. He couldn't have made very much money. How do you figure he could afford paying rent while he was in prison?'

They went back around the side of the house to the back door. When Mrs Reager reappeared, they asked her that question.

'Well, I don't know. His mother died just the year before all that mess came up. Maybe he got a little money.'

Starkey and Marzik went back to their car. Starkey started the engine, letting the air conditioner blow. She recalled that Mueller had noted that

Tennant's parents were deceased, but nothing more had been written about it.

'Well, that was a bust.'

'I don't know. I'm having a thought here, Beth.'

'Uh-oh. Everyone stand back.'

'No, listen. When Tennant's mother died, he could have inherited property, or used some of the money to rent another place.'

'When my mother died, I didn't get shit.'

'That's you, but say Tennant got something. I'll bet you ten dollars that Mueller didn't run a title search.'

It would take a day or two to run the title check, but they could have a city prosecutor arrange it through the Bakersfield district attorney's office. If something was identified, Bakersfield would handle the warrant.

Starkey felt better as they drove back to Los Angeles, believing that she had something that kept her investigation alive. The A-chief had told her to keep the case moving forward; now, if Kelso asked, she could point to a direction. If she and Pell could turn a second lead through Claudius, fine, but now they didn't need it.

By the time they reached Spring Street, Starkey had decided to call Pell. She told herself that it was because she had to arrange a time for visiting Claudius tonight, but she finally realized that she wanted to apologize for the way she had acted last night. Then she thought, No, she didn't want to apologize, she wanted another chance to show him that she was human. Another chance at a life. Maybe talking with Marzik had helped, even though they had mostly talked about Marzik.

Starkey saw the manila envelope waiting on her desk all the way from the door. It was like a beacon there, hooking her eye and pulling her toward it. Giant letters on the mailing label read KROK-TV.

Starkey felt her stomach knot. She could tell by the way the envelope bulged that it was a videocassette. After ordering it, she had put it out of her mind. She had refused to think of it. Now, here it was.

Starkey tore open the envelope and lifted out the cassette. A date was written on the label. Nothing else, just the date three years ago on which she died. The noise of her breathing was loud and rasping, her skin cold, and getting colder.

'Carol?'

It took her forever to look over.

Marzik was next to her, her expression awkward. She must have seen the date, recognized it.

'Is that what I think it is?'

Starkey would have spoken, but couldn't find her voice.

'What are you going to do with it?'

Her voice came from a million miles away.

'I'm going to watch it.'

Marzik touched her arm.

'Do you want someone with you?'

Starkey couldn't take her eyes from the cassette.

'No.'

Driving home from Spring Street, the tape was a presence in Starkey's car. It sat on the passenger seat like a body brought back from the dead, breathing so deeply to fill long-empty lungs that it threatened to draw all the air from the car and suffocate her. When traffic forced her to stop, she looked at it. The tape seemed to be looking back. She covered it with her briefcase.

Starkey did not drive directly home. She stopped at a coffee shop, bought a large black coffee, and drank it leaning on a little counter that looked toward the street. Her neck and shoulders were wound tight as metal bands; her head ached so badly that her eyes felt as if they were being crushed. She thought about the bad stools at Barrigan's and how a double gin would ease the pressure on her eyes, but she refused to do that. She told herself no; she would see this tape sober. She would witness the events of that moment and her final time with Sugar Boudreaux sober. No matter how terribly it hurt, or how difficult it was. She was sober on that day. She would be sober now.

Starkey decided that the way to play it was not to race home and throw herself into the tape, but to act as if her life were normal. She would pace herself. She would be a mechanical woman feeling mechanical emotions. She was an investigator; this was the investigation of herself. She was a police detective; you do your job, leave it at the office, go home and live your life.

Starkey stopped at the Ralphs market. There was no food in the house, so she decided this was the time to stock up. She pushed the buggy up and down the aisles, filling it with things she had never eaten and probably would never eat. Canned salmon. Creamed corn. Brussels sprouts. Standing in the checkout line, she lost her appetite, but bought the food anyway. What in hell would she do with creamed corn?

Starkey fought an overpowering urge for a drink as soon as she stepped through the door. She told herself it was a habit, a learned pattern. You get home, you have a drink. In her case, several.

She said, 'After.'

Starkey brought her briefcase and three bags of groceries into the kitchen. She noticed that there were two messages on her answering machine. The first was from Pell, asking why he hadn't heard from her and leaving his pager number. She shut him out of her thoughts; she couldn't have him there now. The second call was from Marzik.

'Ah, Carol, it's me. Listen, ah, I was just, ah, calling to see if you were okay. Well. Okay. Ah, see ya.'

Starkey listened to it twice, deeply moved. She and Beth Marzik had never been friends, or even had much to do with each other in a personal way. She thought that she might phone Marzik later and thank her. After.

Starkey set the cassette on the kitchen table, then went about putting away the groceries. She had a glass of water, eyeing the cassette as she drank, then washed the glass and put it on the counter. When the last of the groceries were away, she picked up the cassette, brought it into the living room, and put it into her VCR. Marzik's offer to be with her flashed through her head. She reconsidered, but knew this was just another ploy to avoid watching the tape.

She pressed the 'play' button.

Color bars appeared on the screen.

Starkey sat cross-legged on the floor in front of her television. She was still wearing her suit; hadn't taken off the jacket or removed her shoes. Starkey had no recollection of when KROK arrived on the scene; when they had started taping or for how long. They might have gotten everything or they might only have the end. She recalled that the cameraman had been on top of their van. That was all. The camera was on top of the van and had a view of everything.

The tape began.

She was pulling the straps tight on Sugar's armor suit. She was already strapped in, except for the helmet. Buck Daggett and another sergeant-supervisor, Win Bryant, who was now retired, moved at the back of the truck, helping them. Starkey hadn't worn the suit since that day, but now felt the weight of it, the heavy density and the heat. As soon as you put the damned thing on, it turned your body's heat back at you, cooking you. Starkey, tall and athletic, had weighed one hundred thirty-five pounds; the suit weighed ninety-five pounds. It was a load. Starkey's first thought: *Why do I look so grim?* Her expression was somber, almost scowling; wearing her game face. Sugar, naturally, was smiling his movie star smile. Once, not long after they had begun sleeping together, she confessed to him that she was never scared when she was working a bomb. It sounded so much like macho horseshit that she had to work up her courage to say it, but it was true. She used to think that something was wrong with her because she felt that way. Sugar, in turn, had confessed that he was so terrified that as soon as they received a call out he would pop an Immodium so he wouldn't crap in the suit. Watching the tape, Starkey thought how relaxed Sugar looked, and that it was she who looked scared. Funny, how what you see isn't always what's there.

They were talking. Though the tape had sound, she could hear only the ambient noise around the microphone. Whatever she and Sugar were saying to each other was too far away for the mike to pick up. Sugar must have said something funny; she saw herself smile.

Daggett and Bryant helped them on with their helmets, then handed the Real Time to Sugar. Sugar smacked her helmet, she smacked his, then they lumbered toward the trailer like a couple of spacewalking astronauts.

The field of view gave her the full length of the trailer, the overhanging trees, and a prime view of the thick azaleas that made a thready, matted wall around the trailer. Sugar had cut away part of the bushes on an earlier trip out, leaving a bare spot to work through. As she now watched, they each pointed at different parts of the bush, deciding how to approach the device. The plan was for Starkey to hold the limbs aside so that Sugar could get the snaps with the Real Time.

Starkey watched the events with a sense of detachment she found surprising.

Sugar had less than thirty seconds to live.

She leaned into the bush first, using the weight of the suit to help her shove the limbs aside. She watched herself step away, then move in again for a better position. She didn't recall that, and marveled at it. In her memory, she had not made that second move. Sugar leaned past her with the Real Time, and that's when the camera bounced from the earthquake, not a big one, a pretty damned small one by L.A. standards, 3.2 centered just north of them in Newhall. The picture bounced, and she heard the cameraman mutter.

'Hey, was that—?'

The sound of the bomb going off covered his words. On television, it was a sharp *crack!* like a gunshot.

It happened so fast that all Starkey saw was a flash of light and the Real Time spinning lazily end around end through the air. She and Sugar were down. There were shouts and frantic cries from behind the camera.

'You gotta get this! Don't fuck up! Keep rolling!'

The picture was small and far away. It was like watching someone else.

Daggett and Bryant ran to them, Daggett to her, Bryant to Sugar, Buck dragging her away from the trailer. One of the things they drilled into you at Bomb School was to fear a secondary explosion. When there was one explosion, there might be another, so you had to clear the wounded from the area. Starkey had never known that she had been moved. She was dead when it happened.

The tape ran for another nine minutes as the paramedics raced forward, stripped away the armor suits, and worked to resuscitate them. In the dreams, Starkey was beneath a canopy of branches and leaves that covered her like lace, but now she saw that there was nothing above her. In the dreams, she was close enough to Sugar to reach out and touch him. Now, she saw that they were ten yards apart, crumpled like broken dolls, separated by a wall of sweating, cursing EMTs desperate to save them. There was no beauty in this moment. The tape ended abruptly as an ambulance was turning into the shot.

Starkey rewound the tape to a point where she and Sugar were both on the ground and pressed the 'pause' button. She touched the screen where Sugar lay.

'You poor baby. You poor, poor baby.'

After a while, she rewound the tape, ejected it from the VCR, then turned off her television.

Twice during the evening, the phone rang again. Both times the caller left a message. She didn't bother to check.

She went to bed without having a drink, slept deeply, and did not dream.

Manifest Destiny

'And you are?'

'Alexander Waverly, attorney at law. I phoned about Dallas Tennant.'

The guard inspected the California State Bar card and the driver's license, then handed them back, making a note in his log.

'Right. You're Tennant's new attorney.'

'Yes, sir. I phoned to arrange the interview.'

'Have you seen clients here at Atascadero before, Mr Waverly?'

'No. I've never been to a facility like this before. My specialty is medical malpractice and psychiatric disorders.'

The guard smiled.

'We call this "facility" a prison. But it's more like a country club, if you ask me. You gonna talk to Tennant about why he's crazy?'

'Well, something like that, but I shouldn't discuss that with you, should I?'

'No, I guess not. Okay, what you do is sign here and here in the register. I'll have to inspect your briefcase, and then you come around here through the metal detector, okay?'

'All right.'

'Do you have any weapons or metal objects on you?'

'Not today.'

'A cell phone?'

'Yes. Can't I bring my cell phone?'

'No, sir. Your pager is okay, but not the cell. We'll have to hang on to it here. What about a tape recorder?'

'Yes. I have this little tape recorder. It's okay to have this, isn't it? I'm the worst at taking notes.'

'The tape recorder's okay. I just need to look at it, is all.'

'Well, all right, but about my phone. What if I'm paged and need to make a call? I have an associate in court.'

'You let us know and we'll get you to a phone. Won't be a problem.'

He signed the register where instructed, careful to use his own pen, careful not to touch the counter or logbook or anything else that might be successfully lasered for a fingerprint. He didn't bother to watch as the guard inspected his briefcase and tape recorder. Instead, he passed through the metal detector, smiling at the guard who waited on the other side. He traded the cell phone for the briefcase and recorder, then followed the second guard through double glass doors and along a sidewalk to another building. He was aware that a security camera had recorded him. The videotape would be studied and his picture reproduced, but he had a high level of confidence in his disguise. They would never be able to recognize his true self.

John Michael Fowles was delivered to a small interview room where Dallas Tennant was already waiting. Tennant was seated at a table, his good hand covering his damaged hand as if he was embarrassed by it. Tennant smiled shyly, then forgot himself and rested the good hand on a thick scrapbook.

The guard said, 'You've got him for thirty minutes, Mr Waverly. You need anything, I'll be at the desk down the hall. Just stick out your head and give a shout.'

'That's fine. Thank you.'

John waited until the door was closed, then set his briefcase on the table. He gave Tennant the big smile, spreading his hands.

'Tah-DAH! Mr Red, at your service.'

Tennant slowly stood.

'This is . . . an honor. That's what it is, an honor. There's no other way to describe it.'

'I know. This world is an amazing place, isn't it, Dallas?'

Tennant offered his hand, but John didn't take it. He found Tennant's personal hygiene lacking.

'I don't shake hands, m'man. For all I know, you were just playing with your pecker, toying with your tool, commingling with your cockster, know what I mean?'

When Tennant realized that John wasn't going to shake hands, he pushed the heavy book across the table. His awkward, shuffling manner made John want to kick him.

'I'd like to show you my book. You're in here, you know?'

John ignored the book. He slipped off his suit coat, folded it over the back of the chair, then unbuckled his belt. He moved the chair with his toe.

'We'll get to the book, but first you have to tell me about the RDX.'

Tennant watched John like a dog waiting for his master to spoon out the kibble.

'Did you bring it? What we talked about, did you bring it?'

'You don't have to stand there drooling, Dallas. You think I'm taking off my clothes because I want to flash my pecker?'

'No. No, I'm sorry.'

'Mr Red is a man of his word. You just remember that. I expect that you'll be a man of his word, too, Dallas. That's very important to me, and to our future relationship. You're not gonna get carried away and brag to anyone that Mr Red came to see you, now, are you?'

'No. Oh, no, never.'

'You do that, Dallas, and there'll be hell to pay. I'm just warning you, okay? I want that to be clear between us.'

'I understand. If I told, then you couldn't come see me again.'

'That's right.'

John smiled, absolutely certain that Dallas Tennant couldn't go the week without telling someone of their encounter. John had planned for that.

'The police were already here, and, you know, they might come back. I don't want you to find out and think I told them anything. I can't help it that they came.'

'That's fine, Dallas. Don't you worry about it.'

'They came about the RDX. I didn't tell them anything.'

'Good.'

'One of them was a woman. Her name was Carol Starkey. She's in my book, too. She was a bomb technician.'

Tennant pushed the book across the table, desperate for John to look.

'She wasn't alone. She brought an ATF agent named Pell or Tell or something like that.'

'Jack Pell.'

Tennant looked surprised.

'You know him?'

'You might say that.'

'He was mean. He grabbed my hand. He hurt me.'

'Well, you just forget about them. We got our own little business here, you and me.'

John dropped his trousers, pulled down his shorts, and untaped two plastic bags from his groin. One contained a thin gray paste, the other a fine yellow powder. John placed them on top of Tennant's book.

'This oughta wake'm up out in the vegetable garden, you set it off.'

Tennant massaged each bag, inspecting the contents through the clear plastic.

'What is it?'

'Right now, just a couple of chemicals in bags. You mix'm together with a little ammonia like I'm gonna tell ya, Dallas, and you're going to end up with what we in the trade call a very dangerous explosive: ammonium picrate.'

Tennant held the two bags together as if he could imagine them mixing. John watched him closely, looking for signs that Tennant knew what he held in his hands. He figured that Tennant had heard of ammonium picrate, but probably had no experience with it. He was counting on that.

'Isn't that what they call Explosive D?'

'Yeah. Nice and stable, but powerful as hell. You ever work with D before?'

Dallas considered the chemicals again, then put the bags aside.

'No. How do I detonate it?'

John smiled widely, pleased with Tennant's ignorance.

'Easy as striking a match, Dallas. Believe me, you won't be disappointed.'

'I won't tell where I got it. I promise. I won't tell.'

'I ain't worried about that, Dallas. Not even a little bit. Now, you tell me who has the RDX, then I'll tell you how to mix these things.'

'I won't forget this, Mr Red. I'll help you out any way I can. I mean that.'

'I know you do, Dallas. Now you just tell me about the RDX, and I am going to give you the power of life and death, right there in those little bags.'

Dallas Tennant stuffed both bags down the front of his pants, then told Mr Red who had the RDX.

Later, John took his time signing out, but once he was in his car and past the security gate, he pushed hard toward the freeway. He had made Tennant promise not to mix the components for at least two days, but he didn't trust in that any more than he trusted Tennant not to tell anyone about his visit. He knew that Dallas would mix the damned stuff as soon as possible; a goof like Tennant couldn't help himself. John was counting on that, too, because he had lied about what the chemicals were and how they would react.

They weren't Explosive D, and they were anything but stable.

It was the only way he had to make sure that Tennant kept his mouth shut.

11

Starkey woke at her usual early hour, but without the sense of anxiety she often felt. She made a cup of instant coffee, then sat smoking in the kitchen, trying to figure out how she felt about the tape. She knew she felt differently, but she wasn't sure how. There had been no revelations, no surprises, no hidden truths to be found. She had witnessed no mistakes on her part or Sugar's that would have sealed the curse of guilt, but also no heroic action that would remove it. Finally, it came to her. Every day for three years the trailer park had ridden her like a yoke, been immediate to her thoughts. Now the trailer park was farther away.

Starkey showered, put on the same suit that she had worn the day before, then went outside and positioned her car so that the headlights lit the white gardenia bush on the side of her house. She cut three flowers.

The Los Angeles National Cemetery in Westwood didn't open its gates until six A.M., but Starkey found a security guard, badged him, and told him she needed to go in. He was an older man, uncertain and insecure, but Starkey kept the flat cop eyes on him until he relented.

Starkey wasn't one for visiting the dead. She had trouble finding Sugar's grave, her flashlight darting over the uniform white grave markers like a lost dog trying to find her master. She walked past it twice, then doubled back, found it, and put the flowers beneath his name. Sugar had grown up with the scent of gardenias in Louisiana.

She wanted to tell him something about moving beyond it all, but didn't know that there was really anything to say. She knew that she would be saying it more for herself than him, anyway. Life was like that.

Finally, Starkey took a deep breath.

'We were something, Shug.'

The old man watched her wordlessly from the gatehouse as she left the cemetery, driving away to start her day.

Starkey spent her first hour at Spring Street organizing her casebook, then made a list of things to cover with Marzik and Hooker. Hooker got there before Marzik, sidling up to her as if he expected her to spray the office with gunfire. Starkey could tell by his expression that Marzik had told him about the tape. She felt disappointed, but that was Marzik.

'Morning, Carol. Ah, how's it going?'

'I'm okay, Jorge. Thanks.'

'You doing all right?'

'I saw the tape. I'm okay with it.'

Hooker nodded nervously.

'Well, if there's anything I can do.'

Starkey stood and kissed his cheek.

'You're a sweet man, Jorge. Thank you.'

Hooker showed enormous white teeth.

'Now get out of my face and lemme get back to work.'

Hooker laughed and went back to his desk. He was still laughing when Starkey's phone rang.

'Detective Starkey.'

'It's Warren Mueller, up here in Bakersfield.'

Starkey was surprised, and told him so. She asked why he was calling.

'Your people down there had our city attorney run a property check on Tennant's mother, a woman named Dorothea Tennant.'

'That's right.'

'You scored, Starkey. I wanted to be the one to tell you that. I'm standing outside the place right now. The old lady died owning a little duplex up here that's still in her name. Tennant must have never brought the issue to probate court.'

Starkey felt a tremendous rush of energy. Marzik walked in as Mueller was saying it. Starkey waved her over, cupping the mouthpiece to tell her the news.

'It's Bakersfield. We got a hit, Beth. Tennant has property.'

Marzik pumped her fist.

Mueller said, 'What's that? I didn't hear you.'

'I was telling the people here. Listen, Mueller, you need to have your Bomb Squad roll. There might be explosive materials on the site—'

Mueller cut her off.

'Throttle back, Detective. We're two jumps ahead of you. You didn't just score on the property; you got his shop. This is where he kept his goods, Starkey. Our bomb people are securing the location now.'

Hooker and Marzik were both spreading their hands, wanting to know what was going on. She asked Mueller to hold on, told them what she knew, then got back to Mueller.

'Okay, Sergeant. I'm with you. What do you have?'

'This place his mother owned is a little duplex house. One's empty, but the other has people living in it.'

'Jesus. Was his shop next door?'

Starkey was thinking this was how Tennant continued to pay rent on his own apartment even from prison.

'No, it wasn't like that. He's got a converted garage here in back of the place that he kept locked. That's where he kept the goods.'

'You find the RDX?'

'Negative on the RDX, but we got some TNT and about twenty pounds of black powder.'

'We're hoping that there might be evidence that links Tennant with his source for the RDX. This has a direct bearing on the Silver Lake investigation, Mueller. If you find anything like papers, correspondence, pictures, anything that gives us a trail, I want it secured. I'll drive up there to inspect it.'

'Will do, but there's more. These people in the house said they had a prowler back here about a month ago.'

'Wait. Someone went into the shop?'

'They didn't see him enter or leave the building. All they saw was some guy looking around. The old man who lives up at the house called out, but the guy takes off over the fence. My wit says it looked like he was carrying something.'

'You're thinking the RDX?'

'Well, if there *was* RDX inside, he could have taken it.'

'You get a description?'

'White male between forty and fifty, five ten to six feet, one-eighty, baseball cap, and sunglasses.'

She cupped the phone to fill in Marzik and Hooker. The man in the baseball cap had them trading high fives.

'Sergeant, we have a similar suspect from Silver Lake. If we fax our likeness up there, would you run it past those people, see what they say?'

'You bet.'

'Give me your fax.'

Starkey passed the number along to Marzik, then got back to Mueller.

'One more thing. Was there any sign of forced entry? If the guy went in, did he have to break in?'

'I know what you meant. No. Tennant had the place locked up with a couple of heavy-duty Yale padlocks. We had to cut'm off with bolt cutters. They hadn't been forced. So if this guy went in there and took the RDX, he had a key.'

Starkey couldn't think of anything else to ask.

'Mueller, I know you didn't have to make this call. It shows class.'

'Well, you were right, Starkey. I might be a hardhead, but I'm also a gentleman.'

'You are. This is good work, Sergeant. This is going to help us down here.'

Mueller laughed.

'How about that? I guess me and you're just about the best two cops ever to strut the earth.'

Starkey smiled as she hung up.

Marzik said, 'Fuckin' A! Are we detectives or what?'

Starkey asked Hooker to see about getting them a look at the enhanced tape. She wanted to see it as quickly as possible because the similar description of the man in the baseball cap gave weight to their 911 caller as the bomber. She had a strong feeling that the man in the long-sleeved shirt would be on the tape. If Hooker was right about the three-hundred-sixty-degree view, he had to be. He had to be within the hundred-yard perimeter to detonate the bomb.

As Hooker set it up, Starkey filled in Kelso, then paged Jack Pell. She felt a powerful urge to share the news with him, which surprised her. She left her own pager number as the return.

The postproduction facility was a block south of Melrose, in an area saturated with Japanese tourists and used-clothing stores. Starkey and Santos drove over together where a thin young man named Miles Bennell met them in the lobby.

Starkey said, 'Thanks for making the time for us.'

Bennell shrugged.

'Well, you guys are trying to solve a crime. That's probably more important than editing a toilet paper commercial.'

'Some days it is.'

She was thinking that she would want Lester to see the tape, too, and probably Buck Daggett. She asked Bennell if they could have a copy when they left.

'You mean to play on a home machine?'

'That's right.'

Bennell looked pained.

'Well, I can make a copy like that, but you're going to lose resolution. That's why you guys had to come here to see it. Do you know anything about how we do this?'

'I can't even program my VCR.'

'A TV picture is made up of little dots called pixels. When we blow up the images on the tape, they get blurry because the pixels, which contain a set amount of information, expand and the information becomes diluted. What we do is take that pixel, break it into more pixels, then use the computer to extrapolate the missing content. It's kind of like making high-definition television in reverse.'

'You mean the computer just colors in the space?'

'Well, not really. The computer measures the difference in lights and darks, determines where the shadow lines are, then makes the lights lighter and the darks darker. You end up with really sharp lines and concentrated colors.'

Starkey didn't understand what he was saying and didn't care. All she cared about was whether or not it worked.

They walked along a hall past other editing bays, from which she could hear the voices of popular television series, and into a dark room with a console facing a bank of television monitors. The room smelled of daisies.

'How much tape do we have?'

'Eighteen minutes.'

Starkey was surprised.

'Out of almost six hours, we got just eighteen minutes?'

Bennell sat at the console and pushed one of the green backlit buttons. The center TV monitor flashed with color bars.

'If the only people who were in the shot were the two Bomb Squad guys, we cut it. That was most of the tape. We only get to see bystanders when the cameras changed angles or the helicopters rotated out of position.'

Starkey remembered that from when she viewed the tapes.

'Okay. So what are we going to see?'

'Short clips. Anytime an angle caught a view of the crowd, or the people hiding behind buildings, or things like that, we clipped them. That's what we enhanced. We got kinda lucky with the angles, too. Jorge said you guys wanted to see pretty much the entire perimeter.'

'That's right.'

'Between the different helicopters, I think we've got that. You're looking for a man in a baseball cap and sunglasses, right?'

'That's right, wearing a long-sleeved shirt.'

Starkey put the likeness drawing on the console for Bennell to see.

'Hey, that looks like my roommate.'

'Your roommate been to Miami recently?'

'Nah. He never gets out of bed.'

Bennell continued adjusting his console.

'We've got a couple guys in caps, I can tell you that. Let's see what they look like. I can go as fast or slow as you like. We can freeze frame. When we freeze, it will appear to lose some clarity, but I can help that.'

He pressed another button, and the tape started. There was a hyper-real quality to the image that Starkey thought made the objects in the picture look metallic. The blues were a brilliant blue; the grays almost glowed; the shadows were as sharply defined as the shadows on the moon.

Santos said, 'It looks like a Maxfield Parrish painting.'

Bennell grinned.

'You got it, dude. Okay, I left a few seconds' lead on the camera swings to give our eyes time to keep up with the picture. See, right now there's no one but the cop—'

'His name is Riggio.'

'Sorry, Officer Riggio. Now, watch, the camera is about to move.'

The angle suddenly shifted, revealing several people clumped behind the cordon tape north of Sunset Boulevard by the Guatemalan market. Starkey recognized the landmarks she noted when she was pacing off distances. The people she was seeing were within that distance and therefore could have been the bomber.

The technician froze the tape, then tickled a joystick to brighten the image.

Santos pointed at a figure.

'Here. Man here in a cap.'

Starkey counted eight people in this slice of the crowd. The image quality was still indistinct, but far crisper than the images she'd seen on her television when she was half in the bag from too many gins. The man Santos pointed out was wearing a red or brown cap with the bill forward. Lester Ybarra had described a man in a blue cap, like a Dodgers cap, but Starkey had enough experience with eyewitnesses to know that this meant little. It was easy to misremember a color. Because of the angle, it was impossible to see if the man was wearing sunglasses or a long-sleeved shirt.

Starkey said, 'Does the shot stay on these people for long?'

Bennell checked a clipboard with his notes.

'They're in the frame for sixteen seconds.'

'Let's advance it and see what happens. I want a look at this guy's arms if we have it.'

Bennell showed her a large dial on the console for controlling the frame advance.

'Here, you can advance it however fast or slow you want by twisting this dial. Clockwise is forward. You want to back up, turn it the other way.'

Starkey turned it too much on her first try, making the tape blur forward. The technician brought it back and let her have the knob again. The second time went better. Twelve seconds into the shot, the man in the hat turned to look at the man behind him and could be seen wearing a short-sleeved shirt.

They worked back and forth through the tape for almost an hour, isolating on everyone within the perimeter. Finally, Santos had to pee. Starkey called a cigarette break and was standing in the parking lot, smoking, when her pager buzzed. She felt a jolt of excitement when she saw it was Pell. Santos stuck his head out the door.

'We're ready to go, Carol.'

'Be there in a minute.'

She called Pell from the front seat of her car and told him what Mueller had found in Tennant's shop. When she was done with that, there was a silence on the phone until she said, 'Pell, listen, you got the pizza last time. I'll take care of dinner tonight.'

She thought that he was going to say no or bring up what she'd said last night, but there was only a silence for a time that grew until he finally broke it.

'What time you want me over there?'

'How about seven?'

When they ended the call, Starkey asked herself what in hell was she doing. She hadn't intended to bring up dinner or get together with Pell or any of that; that she said those things had surprised her as much as they had probably surprised Pell.

Starkey finished her cigarette, then returned to the editing bay. Watching the eighteen minutes of enhanced tape took almost two hours. As they worked through the clips, Starkey charted the remaining perimeter landmarks, and, by the time they finished, was satisfied that they had a three-hundred-sixty-degree view of the scene, and a fairly complete picture of everyone within the maximum range of the radio transmitter.

But she was also disappointed because the man in the baseball cap was not to be found.

They finished on a wide shot that showed most of the area. Riggio was over the bomb in the instant before the detonation. Buck Daggett was by the Suburban. The parking lot looked wide and empty. Starkey crossed her arms and considered that this particular search had come to nothing.

Santos looked crestfallen.

'I was sure he would be here. He had to be.'

'He is, Jorge. Somewhere. If he took off his cap and rolled up his sleeves, he could be any of these people, and we wouldn't know it, but he has to be here somewhere.'

Bennell seemed as disappointed as Santos. With all his work enhancing the film, he wanted to be a part of cracking the case.

'He could be on the other side of any of these buildings. He could be sitting on the sidewalk behind one of these cars, and we'd never see him.'

Starkey shrugged, but she knew that wasn't likely. The representative from the radio-control manufacturer had said that the transmitter had to 'see' the receiver, which meant that it had to have a clear line of sight.

Bennell said, 'Do you still want a copy of the tape?'

'That would be good. Maybe I'll look at it again later.'

'It won't be as sharp on your home machine.'

'Right now, the sharpness isn't helping much.'

Bennell made a copy for each of them.

Starkey and Santos drove back to Spring Street in silence, the enthusiasm of only three hours ago diminished, but not gone. Mr Red had to be somewhere. The only question was ... where?

Starkey's Mirror

John Michael Fowles was liking the Beverly Hills Library just fine except for the Arabs. It didn't matter if they called themselves Arabs, Iranians, Persians (which was just another name for the goddamned Iranians), Iraqis, Saudis, sand niggers, dune coons, shade spades, or Kuwaitis; a raghead was a raghead. John hated the goddamned camel jockeys because they had such an easy time getting on the Ten Most Wanted List. You take an Arab, he farts sideways, and the feds put him on the list. A real American like John had to bust his ass to get there. Beverly Hills was crawling with Arabs.

John closed his eyes and meditated, trying to manage the stress. He pretended that the Arabs weren't swarming through the stacks like Guccied locusts. It wasn't easy being the world's most dangerous man walking free in open sunlight. You had to cope.

John knew where to find the remains of the RDX now and would soon recover it, though that would keep for a day or two. Tennant had been helpful that way, the creepy doof. John hated the socially disgusting, fingerless misfits like Dallas Tennant who inhabited his world. They gave the serious explosives hobbiest a bad name.

After John had learned what he needed to know about the RDX, he had enjoyed hearing about Carol Starkey. Tennant described her as a tough cookie, which John liked a lot. Tennant talked about her so much that John found himself asking questions, and even looking in Tennant's book just to see the articles on Starkey. After he had finished with Tennant, John had driven back to Los Angeles and here to the library. He spent several hours reading old newspaper stories about Starkey, searching for pictures of her, wondering if she was as good a bomb technician as the stories portrayed.

Tough break, that earthquake.

John had laughed aloud when he'd read that, causing a couple of Iranians to look. *Man*, John had thought, *if there is a God, He is one mean-spirited sonofabitch.*

A goddamned earthquake.

Only in California.

John was fascinated that Starkey had actually been killed by a bomb and had then returned from death. He marveled at the experience, and couldn't stop thinking about it. To have been so close to the blast, to have been washed by the energy, to feel it press over the totality of her body like some insane kiss, to be lifted and caressed that way.

He thought that he and Carol Starkey might be soul mates.

When he left the library, John returned to his room at the Bel Air Hotel, a lovely romantic bungalow renting for eight hundred dollars per night, thanks to his latest American Express Gold card and false identity. He signed on to Claudius. The past few days he had noticed an increased number of posts about himself, and about RDX. Several of the posters were even spreading the same rumor that Jester had said, that Mr Red was behind Silver Lake. John didn't like that. Now that John knew Tennant had told Starkey and Pell about Claudius, he realized what was happening: Starkey thought that he had killed Riggio and was baiting him. She had fallen for the copycat's ploy. John was both annoyed and elated. He enjoyed the idea of Starkey thinking about him, of her trying to catch him.

John read through the new posts and found that they were no longer only about him. Many were about Starkey, some saying that the former bomb tech and poster girl of the bomb crank crowd was now in charge of the investigation. It was like she had her own cheering section.

John scrolled through the thread of posts until he came to the last one:

SUBJECT: **Showdown**
FROM: **KIA**
MESSAGE-ID: **136781.87 @ lippr**

They caught the Unabomber. They caught Hicks, and McVey, and the rest. If anyone can take Red down, it's Starkey. I heard he already tried to get her, and missed.
Ha. You only get one shot.
Good-bye, Mr Red.

John wondered what Kia had heard that made him think Mr Red had tried to kill Starkey. Did these people shit rumors when they woke in the morning? John snapped off his computer and sulked. These people were out of their friggin' minds. Starkey was becoming the star and he was becoming . . . the other guy.

After he calmed down, John rebooted the iBook and dialed on to his site in Minnesota. When he had the software he wanted, he hacked into the local telephone company and downloaded Carol Starkey's address.

The bathroom window was louvered glass, dark green and pebbled, one of those narrow windows that go from the floor to the ceiling that you open to let out the steam from your bath. It had probably been in the house since the fifties. He used a shim to slip the latches on the screen, set it aside, then worked out the first piece of glass. The first was the hardest; he anchored the pane with a loose strip of electrician's tape so it wouldn't fall, then worked it free using a screwdriver and his fingertips. When the first was out, he reached inside, groped around until he found the lever, then opened the window. After that, the other panes came easily.

John Michael Fowles took out enough of the panes to make an opening about two feet high, then stepped through the window and was inside Carol Starkey's home.

He took a breath. He could smell her. Soap and cigarettes. He allowed himself a moment to enjoy the feeling of being here in her personal place. Here he was in her house, her home. Here he was, smelling her smells, breathing the air she breathed; it was like being inside her.

First thing John did was take a fast pass through the house, making sure there were no dogs, no guests, nothing that he hadn't foreseen. The air conditioner running made him edgy; he wouldn't be able to hear a car pull in, or hear a key slipping into a lock. He would have to hurry.

John unlocked the back door in case he had to leave fast, then returned to the bathroom. He pulled the screen back into place, latched it, then replaced the panes. That done, he gave himself a longer moment; he took a deeper breath. The bathroom counter was a clutter of jars and bottles: Alba Botanica lotion, cotton puffs in a glass jar, soap balls, a basket of dusty pinecones, a blue box of Tampax Super Plus, an LAPD coffee mug holding a toothbrush and a wilted tube of Crest. The mirror above the lavatory was spotted and streaked; the grout between the tile dark with fungus. Carol Starkey, John thought, had not paid attention in Home Ec. He found this disappointing.

John looked at himself in Starkey's mirror. He made a wide monkey smile, inspecting his teeth, then considered her toothbrush. He put it in his mouth, tasting the Crest. Mint. He worked it around his teeth and gums, brushed his tongue, then put it back in the jar.

He moved through the living room, shooting a quick peek out the window to check for her car. Clear. He sat on the couch, running the flat of his palms along the fabric. He imagined Starkey doing the same thing, their hands moving in unison. The living room was no cleaner than the bathroom. John was particular about his personal grooming and thought it reflected poorly on the character of people who weren't.

He found her computer on the kitchen table, its modem plugged into the phone line there. The computer was what he wanted, but he passed it now, moving through the kitchen to her bedroom. The bedroom was dark, and cooler than the rest of the house. He stood at the foot of the bed, which was unmade, the sheet and duvet mounded like a nest. This bitch lived like a pig. John knew it was crazy. He knew it was insane, that if she came home now, he would either have to kill her or pay a heavy price, but, Jesus Christ, man, here was her FUCKING BED. John took off his clothes. He rubbed his body over the sheets, his face into her pillow. He flapped his arms and legs like he was making a snow angel. He was hard, but he didn't want to take the time for that now. He climbed out of the bed, rearranged the mound as it had been, then dressed and returned to the kitchen.

John came prepared for both PC and Macintosh, but was still disappointed to find that she used a PC. It was like the sloppy house; it spoke poorly of her.

He booted the laptop, expecting the usual array of personal icons to appear on the screen, but was surprised to find only one. It hit him then, and John laughed out loud; Starkey didn't know a goddamned thing about computers. When Tennant told them about Claudius, Pell must have set her up through the feds. She probably didn't even know how to work the damned thing.

It only took moments after that. John hooked his zip drive to the laptop, installed the necessary software to copy her files, then uninstalled the software to remove all traces of what had happened. Later, at the hotel, he would open her files to confirm the screen name that she used on Claudius.

Now, he was inside her house. When he had her screen name, he would get inside her mind.

12

Starkey dropped off Hooker at Spring Street, then turned toward home. She stopped at a Ralphs market, where she picked up a roasted chicken, mashed potatoes, and some diet soda. When she was waiting in line, it occurred to her that Pell might not drink soda, either, so she picked up a quart of milk, a bottle of merlot, then added a loaf of French bread. She couldn't remember the last time she'd had a dinner guest. When Dick Leyton dropped by that evening a year ago, he'd only stayed for a drink.

The traffic moving out of downtown was brutal. Starkey wallowed along in it, feeling stupid. She hadn't planned on asking Pell over and hadn't thought it through. The words had just spurted out, and now she felt obvious and embarrassed. Once, when Starkey was sixteen years old, a boy she barely knew named James Marsters had invited her to the junior–senior prom. On the day of the dance, Starkey had put on the gown she was borrowing from her older sister and thought herself so fat and ugly that she was convinced James Marsters would run screaming. Starkey had vomited twice and had been unable to eat anything all day. She felt like that now. Starkey could disarm a case of dynamite wired to a motion sensor, but things like this held a different potential for destruction.

She was late getting home. Pell was already there, parked on the street in front of her house. He got out as she pulled into her drive and walked over to meet her. When she saw the expression on his face, she wanted to reach for her Tagamet. He looked like he wasn't sure if he wanted to be here.

She got out with the bags.

'Hey.'

'Help you with those?'

She gave him one of the two bags, telling him about Bakersfield as she let them into the house. When she told him that a man was seen at Tennant's shop who could have been the same man making the 911 call, Pell seemed interested, but when she described the suspect as a man in his forties, Pell shrugged.

'It's not our guy.'

'How do you know it's not our guy?'

'Mr Red is younger. This is Los Angeles; everyone here wears sunglasses and baseball caps.'

'Maybe our guy isn't Mr Red.'

Pell's face darkened.

'It's Mr Red.'

'What if it isn't?'

'It is.'

Starkey felt herself growing irritated at Pell's certainty, like he had inside information or something. She thought again of telling him about the joint tape, but she still wanted to wait for Janice Brockwell.

'Look, maybe we shouldn't talk about it. I think we've got something good here, and you're shitting on it.'

'Then maybe we shouldn't talk about it.'

They put the two bags on the counter near her sink. Starkey took a deep breath, then faced him, squaring off as if she was about to ask to see some identification. She decided that the only way to survive the evening was to get it out in the open.

'Tonight is a date.'

She felt stupid. Here they were, standing in her kitchen, and she pops with that like it was a confession.

Pell looked so uncomfortable that Starkey wanted to crawl into the oven. He searched her eyes, then stared at the bags.

'I don't know about this, Carol.'

Now she felt humiliated; three inches tall and kicking herself for being such an ass.

'I understand if you want to leave. I know this looks stupid. I've got to tell you, I *feel* really stupid right now, so if you think I'm as stupid as I'm thinking I am, I wish the hell you would leave.'

'I don't want to leave.'

'It's only a date, for Christ's sake. That's all it is.'

She stared past him at the floor, thinking this was the biggest botch job anyone could imagine.

Pell started taking things from the bags.

'Why don't we put these things away and have dinner?'

He worked for several minutes while she stood there. Finally, she pitched in, taking the things from the bags, putting the milk in the refrigerator, taking freshly washed plates and silverware from the dishwasher. Some date. Nobody was saying anything.

Starkey put the chicken and mashed potatoes to one side, wondering what she should do with them. They looked pathetic in their foil and plastic containers.

'Maybe we should heat them.'

Pell put his palm on the carton with the chicken.

'Feels warm enough.'

Starkey got out plates and a knife to cut the chicken, thinking that she should have gotten stuff for a salad. She felt thoroughly dispirited, which Pell seemed to read. It made him look even more awkward.

He said, 'Why don't I help? I'm a pretty good cook.'

'I can't cook worth a shit.'

'Well, since it's already cooked, you probably can't mess it up too badly. All we have to do is put it on plates.'

Starkey laughed. Her body shook with it and she feared she might cry, but she refused to let herself. *You were always a tough girl.* Pell put down the food and came to her, but she held up a hand, stopping him. She knew that doors were opening. Maybe because of what had happened to Charlie Riggio; maybe because she had seen the tape of the events in the trailer park; but maybe just because it had been three years and she was ready. She thought, then, that it didn't matter why. It just was.

'I'm not very good at this, Pell. I'm trying to let myself feel something again, but it isn't easy.'

Pell stared at the chicken.

'Damnit, why don't you say something? I feel like I'm stuck out here all alone and you're just watching me.'

Pell stepped closer and put his arms around her. She tensed, but he did nothing more than hold her. She allowed it. Slowly, she relaxed, and when her arms went around him, he sighed. It was as if they were giving themselves over to each other. Part of her wanted it to grow into more, but she wasn't ready for that.

'I can't, Jack.'

'Shh. This is good.'

Later, they brought the food into the dining room and spoke of inconsequential things. She asked him about the ATF and the cases he had worked, but he often changed the subject or turned his answer into a question.

Later still, when the dishes were cleared and cleaned and put away, he stepped away from her, still awkward, and said, 'I guess I should go.'

She nodded, walking him to the front door.

'I hope it wasn't too awful.'

'No. I hope we can do it again.'

Starkey laughed.

'Man, you must be a glutton for punishment.'

Pell stopped in the door and seemed to struggle with what he wanted to say. He had been struggling for all of their time together, and now she wondered why.

'I like you, Starkey.'

She felt herself smile.

'Do you?'

'This isn't easy for me, either. For a lot of reasons.'

She took heart in that.

'I like you, too, Pell. Thanks for coming by tonight. I'm sorry it got kinda weird.'

Pell stepped through the door and was gone. Starkey listened as his car pulled away, thinking that maybe a little weirdness was good for people.

Starkey finished straightening the kitchen, then went back to her bedroom, thinking to get undressed and crawl into bed. She decided the bed was a mess, so she stripped the sheets and pillowcases, stuffed them in the wash, and put on fresh. Her whole damned house was a mess and needed to be scoured. She showered, instead.

After the shower, she checked her messages at work, and found that Warren Mueller had called. His was the only message.

'Hey, Starkey, it's Warren Mueller. I ran that crappy picture you faxed past the old man at Tennant's place. He couldn't tell one way or the other, but he thought they kinda looked alike, white guy around forty, the hat and the glasses. I'm gonna have our artist work with him, see if we can't refine the picture. We get anything, I'll fax it down. You take care.'

Starkey deleted the message, then hung up, thinking that their picture might be crappy, but everyone was seeing someone who looked more or less like the same guy, and nothing like Mr Red.

Starkey decided that she might as well check Claudius. She went back into the dining room, turned on the computer, and signed on. She reread the message boards, noting that AM7 had responded to their post about RDX with a long, meandering story about his time in the army. Several other people had responded also, though no one offered to buy or sell RDX or even hinted that they knew how. A lot of people were posting about her.

Starkey was reading when a message window appeared on her screen.

WILL YOU ACCEPT A MESSAGE FROM MR RED?

A tingle of fear rippled up her back. Then she smiled because it had to be a joke, or some Internet weirdness that she had no chance of understanding.

The window hung there.

WILL YOU ACCEPT A MESSAGE FROM MR RED?

Starkey opened the window.

MR RED: You've been looking for me.

Starkey knew it had to be a joke.

HOTLOAD: Who is this?

MR RED: Mr Red.
HOTLOAD: That isn't funny.
MR RED: No. It is dangerous.

Starkey went for her briefcase. She looked up Pell's hotel number and called him there. Getting no answer, she phoned his pager.

MR RED: Are you calling for help, Carol Starkey?

She stared at the words, then checked the time and knew that it couldn't be Pell; he didn't have a computer. It must be Bergen. Bergen was probably a pervert, and he was the only other person besides Pell who knew about Hotload.

HOTLOAD: Bergen, you asshole, is this you?
MR RED: You doubt me.
HOTLOAD: I know exactly who you are, you ASSHOLE. I'm telling Pell about this. You'll be lucky if the ATF doesn't fire your ass.
MR RED: HAHAHAHAHA! Yes, tell Mr Pell. Have him fire me.
HOTLOAD: You won't be laughing tomorrow, you prick.

Starkey stared at the message, irritated.

MR RED: You do not know who ANYONE is, Carol Starkey. I am not Bergen. I am Mr Red.

Starkey's phone rang, Pell calling back.
She said, 'I think we've got a problem with Bergen. I'm on Claudius. This window just pops up, and whoever it is knows that I'm Hotload. He says that he's Mr Red.'
'Blow him off, Carol. It must be Bergen. I'll see about him tomorrow.'

MR RED: Where are you, Carol Starkey?

When Starkey put down the phone, the message was hanging there, waiting. She stared at it, but made no move to respond.

MR RED: Okay, Carol Starkey, you're not having any, so I will be gone. I will leave you with the World According to Mr Red.
MR RED: I did not kill Charles Riggio.
MR RED: I know who did.
MR RED: My name is Vengeance.

City Lights

John Michael Fowles signed off Claudius. He broke the cell-phone connection through which he had signed on to the Net and settled back, pushing the iBook aside. The moonlit shade felt good after the heat of the day, sitting there on the quiet street.

His car was parked just up the block from Starkey's house, in the dense shadows of an elm tree heavy with summer leaves. He could see her house from here. He could see the lights in her windows. He watched.

Brimstone

Dallas Tennant carried the ammonia in a paper cup, pretending it was coffee. He blew on it and pretended to sip, the sharp fumes cutting into his nose, making his eyes water.

'Night, Mr Riley.'

'Good night, Dallas. I'll see you tomorrow.'

Mr Riley was still at his desk, finishing the day's paperwork. Dallas raised the cup to him.

'Is it all right if I take the coffee back to my cell?'

'Oh, sure. That's fine. Is there any more in the pot?'

Dallas looked pained, and held out the cup.

'This was the last, Mr Riley. I'm sorry. I've washed the pot. Would you like me to make another before I go? Would you like this one?'

Riley waved him off and turned back to his work.

'That's all right. I'll be leaving soon enough. You enjoy it, Dallas.'

Dallas bid Riley good night again, then let himself out. He hid the ammonia in a supply closet long enough to stop at the infirmary for his meds, then continued on to his room, walking more quickly because he was anxious to make the explosive. True, he had promised Mr Red that he would wait for a few days, but Dallas would have mixed the Explosive D yesterday as soon as Mr Red had gone, if he had had the ammonia and a detonation system. He didn't, so, earlier this morning when Mr Riley was gone for lunch, Dallas had signed on to the Internet and printed out pornographic pictures from web sites in Amsterdam and Thailand. He had traded photographs of whores having sex with horses for the ammonia, and Asian women fisting each other for the match heads and cigarettes that he would use as a detonator. Once those things were in his possession, he had spent the rest of the day growing so anxious to mix his new toy that he was damn near running by the time he reached his cell.

Dallas waited long minutes by the door, making sure that no one was coming along the hall, then huddled at the foot of his bed with the two plastic bags and the cup of ammonia. Mr Red's instructions were simple: Pour the ammonia in the bag with the powder, mix it well until the powder was dissolved, then pour that mixture into the bag with the paste.

Mr Red had warned him that this second bag would get warm as the two substances mixed, but that the mixture would stiffen to a tacky paste, sort of like plastique, and the explosive would then be active.

Dallas poured the ammonia into the first bag, zipped the top, and kneaded it to dissolve the powder. He planned to make the explosive, then spend the rest of the night fantasizing about setting it off in one of the metal garbage cans behind the commissary. Just thinking about the can coming apart, the crack of thunder that was going to snap across the yard, made him aroused.

When the powder was dissolved, Dallas was preparing to pour the solution into the second bag when he heard the guard approaching.

'Tennant? You get your meds okay?'

Dallas pushed the bags under his legs, bending like he was untying his shoes. The guard was staring in at him through the bars.

'Sure did, Mr Winslow. You can check with'm, if you want. I went by there.'

'No problem, Tennant. I'll see them later this evening. I just wanted to make sure you remembered.'

'Yes, sir. Thank you.'

The guard started away, then paused and frowned. Dallas's heart hammered; sweat sprouted over his back.

'You okay in there, Tennant?'

'Yes, sir. Why?'

'You're bent over all hunched.'

'I have to poo.'

The guard considered that, then nodded.

'Well, don't shit your pants, Dallas. You've got about an hour till lights out.'

Dallas listened as the footsteps faded, then went to the door to peek up and down the hall before resuming his work. He opened the second bag, balanced it between his legs, then added the powder solution. He sealed the top and kneaded the second bag. Just as Mr Red had told him, the bag grew warm.

What Mr Red hadn't told him was that the contents would turn bright purple.

Tennant was excited, and concerned. Earlier that day, when he had finished downloading the pornography, he had web-searched a couple of explosives sites and read about ammonium picrate. He had learned that it was a strong, stable explosive, easy to store and use, and safe (as far as such things go) because of its stability. But both articles had also described ammonium picrate as a white, crystalline powder; not a purple paste.

The bag grew warmer.

Tennant stopped kneading. He looked at the paste in the bag. It was swelling the way yeasty bread dough swells, as if it was filling with tiny bubbles of gas.

Tennant opened the bag and sniffed. The smell was terrible.

Two thoughts flashed in Dallas Tennant's mind. One, that Mr Red couldn't have been wrong; if he said this was ammonium picrate, then it must be ammonium picrate. Two, that some explosives don't require a detonator. Dallas had read about that once, about substances that explode just by being mixed together. There was a word for reactions like that, but Dallas couldn't remember it.

He was still trying to recall that word when the purple substance detonated, separating his arms and rocking Atascadero so deeply that all the alarms and water sprinklers went off.

The word was 'hypergolic'.

13

Starkey tried to ignore the way Marzik was staring at her. Marzik had finished interviewing the laundry people without finding anyone else who had seen the 911 caller and was supposed to be writing a report to that effect, but there she was, kicked back, arms crossed, squinting at Starkey. She had been watching Starkey for most of the morning, probably hoping that Starkey would ask why, but Starkey ignored her.

Finally, Marzik couldn't stand it anymore and wheeled her chair closer.

'I guess you're wondering why I'm looking at you.'

'I hadn't noticed.'

'Liar. I've been admiring that Mona Lisa smile you're sporting today.'

'What are you talking about?'

'That smile right there beneath your nose, the one that says you bit the bullet and got yourself a fed-kabob.'

'You always take something sweet and make it gross.'

Marzik broke into a nasty grin.

'*I WAS RIGHT!*'

Every detective in the squad room looked. Starkey was mortified.

'You're not right. Nothing like that happened.'

'*Something* must've happened. I haven't seen you this mellow since I've known you.'

Starkey frowned.

'The change has come early. You should try it.'

Marzik laughed, and pushed her chair back to her desk.

'I'd be willing to try whatever put that grin on your face. I'd try it *twice*.'

Starkey's phone rang while Marzik was still smirking. It was Janice Brockwell, calling from the ATF lab in Rockville, Maryland.

'Hi, Detective. I'm phoning about the matter we discussed.'

'Yes, ma'am.'

'In the seven bombing events that we attribute to Mr Red, we have six usable end caps, out of an estimated twenty-eight end caps used in the devices. I broke the six and determined that the joint tape was wrapped in a clockwise direction each time.'

'They were all wrapped in the same direction?'

493

'Clockwise. That's right. You should know that the six end caps are from five different devices used in three cities. I consider this significant, Detective. We're going to include this as part of Mr Red's signature in the National Repository and forward it along as an alert to our field offices. I'll copy my report to you via snail mail for your files.'

Starkey's palms were cold, and her heart pounded. If Mr Red wrapped the joint tape in the same direction every time, why had the Silver Lake bomb been wrapped in the *opposite* direction?

Starkey wanted to shout at Hooker and Marzik.

Brockwell said, 'You did good, Detective Starkey. Thanks for the assist.'

Starkey put down the phone, trying to decide what to do. She was excited, but she wanted to be careful and not overreact. A small thing like the direction in which that tape was wrapped might have meant nothing, but now meant everything. It did not fit within the pattern. It was a difference, and therefore it meant that the Silver Lake bomb was different.

Starkey paced to the coffee machine to burn off energy, then returned to her desk. Mr Red was smart. He knew that his devices were recovered, that the analyses were shared. He knew that federal, state, and local bomb investigators would study these things and build profiles of him. Part of the thrill for him was believing that he was smarter than the men and women who were trying to catch him. That was why he etched the names, why he hunted bomb technicians, why he had left the false device in Miami. He would enjoy playing with their minds, and what better way to play than change a single small component of his signature just to create doubt, to make investigators like Carol Starkey *doubt*.

If the bomb was different, you had to ask *why?* And the most obvious answer to that was also the most terrible. *Because a different person had built it.*

Starkey wanted to think it through. She wanted to be absolutely certain before she brought it back to Kelso.

'Hey, Beth?'

Marzik glanced over.

'I've got to get out of here for a few minutes. I'm on pager, okay?'

'Whatever.'

Starkey walked the few short blocks to Philippe's, smoking. She knew bombs, she knew bombers. She decided that Mr Red would not change his profile, even to taunt the police. He was too much about being known; he didn't want them to doubt who they were dealing with; he wanted them to *know* it. The very fact of his signature screamed that he wanted the police to be absolutely certain with whom they were dealing. Mr Red wanted his victory to be clear.

At Philippe's, Starkey bought a cup of coffee, sat alone at one of the long tables, and lit a fresh cigarette. It was illegal to smoke in the restaurant, but the customer load was light and no one said anything.

I did not kill Charles Riggio.

The feds had multiple suspect descriptions from the Miami library as well as earlier sightings, all of which described Red as a man in his late twenties. Yet Lester Ybarra had described a man in his forties, as had the old man in Tennant's duplex. If Mr Red had not built this bomb, then someone else had built it, someone who had gone to great lengths to make the bomb appear to be Mr Red's work. Starkey finally said the word to herself: *Copycat.*

Copycats were most common in serial killer and serial rapist crimes. Hearing frequent news coverage of such crimes could trigger the predisposed into thinking they could get away with a one-shot homicide, using the copycat crime to cover a motive that was far removed from an insane desire to kill or an overpowering rage against women. The perpetrator almost always believed that the cover of the other crimes would mask his true intent, which was typically revenge, money, or the elimination of a rival. In almost all cases, the copycat did not know the full details of the crimes because those details had not been released. All the copycat knew was what he or she had read in the papers, which was invariably wrong.

Yet this copycat knew all the details of how Mr Red constructed his bombs except for the one thing that had never appeared in the bomb analysis reports: the direction in which Mr Red had wrapped the plumber's tape.

Starkey watched the smoke drift off her cigarette in a lazy thread, uncomfortable with the direction of her thoughts. The pool of suspects who knew the exact components of Mr Red's bombs, and how he put those components together, was small.

Cops.

Bomb cops.

Starkey sighed.

It was hard to think about. The person who murdered Charlie Riggio had been within one hundred yards. He had seen Riggio arrive at the scene, watched him strap into the armor, waited as Riggio approached the device. He knew who he was killing. In the two and a half years that she had served as a bomb investigator, she had made exactly twenty-eight cases, none of those against people with access to the details of Mr Red's bombs or with the acumen to pull it off.

Starkey dropped her cigarette into the coffee, its life extinguished in a sharp hiss.

Starkey took out her cell phone. She caught Jack Pell at his motel.

'Pell? I need to see you.'

'I was getting ready to call. I spoke with Bergen this morning.'

They agreed to meet at Barrigan's. Starkey wanted to see him with an urgency that surprised her. It had occurred to her, late last night and again early this morning, that she might be falling in love with him, but she wasn't sure and wanted to be careful. The past three years had left an emptiness within her that longed to be filled. She told herself that it was important not to confuse that longing with love, and not to let that need distort friendship and kindness into something it wasn't.

The morning crowd at Barrigan's was the usual assortment of Wilshire detectives, sprinkled with drifters from the Rampart table and a clique of Secret Service agents who kept to themselves at the end of the bar. Even at ten in the morning, the place was loaded with cops. Starkey shoved through the door and, when she saw Pell sitting at the same table where they had sat before, felt a flush of warmth.

'Thanks. I really need to see you about this.'

He flashed a smile, clearly pleased to see her. He looked happy. She hoped it was because he was seeing her.

'Jack, it's time for you to take the case.'

He smiled the way somebody smiles when they think you're joking, but aren't sure.

'What are you talking about?'

It wasn't easy to say.

'I'm talking about you – the ATF – taking over the investigation into Charlie Riggio's murder. I cannot carry it forward, Jack. Not effectively. I now believe that what happened in Silver Lake to Charlie involves the Los Angeles Police Department.'

He glanced toward the bar, probably to see if anyone was listening.

'You think one of your people is Mr Red?'

'I don't think Mr Red is behind this. I could go over Kelso's head to Parker, or go to IAG, but I am not prepared to do that until I have more evidence.'

Pell leaned forward and took her hand. She felt encouraged. It was funny how you could draw strength from someone you cared about.

'Waitaminute. Hold on. I spoke with some people about Bergen this morning. Bergen was with other clients last night at exactly the time you called me. You had Mr Red last night, Carol. We've got the bastard. We can use this to bring him in.'

Pell was so excited she thought he was going to fall out of his chair.

'That can't be. He knew my name. He knew that Hotload is Carol Starkey. How could he know that?'

Pell answered slowly.

'I don't know.'

'He told me that he didn't kill Riggio. He said that he knew who did.'

Pell stared at her.

'Is that what this is about? He tells you he didn't kill Riggio, and you believe him?'

'He didn't build the Silver Lake bomb.'

'Did he tell you that, too?'

'The ATF lab in Rockville, Maryland, told me that.'

She told him about the call from Janice Brockwell, and how the Silver

Lake bomb differed from every other bomb that had been attributed to Mr Red.

Pell grew irritated, staring at the Secret Service agents until she finished. 'It's just tape.'

Pell's voice had taken on a note of impatience. Her own voice came out harder.

'Wrong, Jack, it is forensic evidence, and it shows that *this* bomb is different. It's different in the one way that no one knew about because it had never been in any of the bomb analysis reports. Every other component could have been copied from a police report. He cut Riggio's name in the bomb to make us think it was Mr Red.'

Pell stared at the bar again. With that one turn of his head, she felt a chill of loneliness that left her confused and frightened.

'It's Mr Red. Trust me on this, Starkey, it's Mr Red. Everything we're doing here is working. We're flushing out the sonofabitch. Don't get sidetracked. Keep your eye on the ball.'

'The people in the Miami library described a man in his twenties. The other descriptions you had were also of men in their twenties. But here in L.A., we've got two descriptions of men in their forties.'

'Mr Red changes his appearance.'

'Damnit, Pell, I need your help with this.'

'Every investigation turns up contradictory evidence. I've never seen an investigation that didn't. You've grabbed onto a few small bits and now you're trying to turn the whole investigation. It's Mr Red, Carol. That's who you need to have in your head. That's who we're going to catch. Mr Red.'

'You're not going to help me, are you?'

'I want to help you, but this is the wrong direction. It's Mr Red. That's who did this. Please just trust me.'

'You're so fixated on Mr Red that you won't even look at the facts.'

'It's Mr Red. That's why I'm here, Starkey. That's what I'm about. Mr Red.'

The warm feelings that she had felt were gone. It should have helped, she later thought, that he seemed to be in as much pain as she, but it didn't.

She was alone with it. She told herself that was okay; she had been alone for three years.

'Pell, you're wrong.'

Starkey walked out, and drove back to Spring Street.

'Hook, you have the casebook?'

Hooker looked up at her, eyes vague from his paperwork.

'I thought you were gone.'

'I'm back. I need to see the casebook.'

'Marzik had it. I think it's on her desk.'

Starkey found the book on Marzik's desk and brought it to her own. One of the pages contained a list of all police officers at the Silver Lake parking lot on the day Riggio died. She felt surreal looking at the list. These people were friends and co-workers.

'You find it?'

Hooker was staring at her. She started at his voice, closing the book, then tried to cover her embarrassment.

'Yeah. Thanks.'

'Marzik had it, right?'

'It was on her desk. Thanks.'

The book contained the names of those Bomb Squad officers present at the time of the call-out and also listed those officers who checked in on the scene after the event. Buck, Charlie, Dick Leyton, and five other members of the day-shift Bomb Squad. Eight out of the fourteen-person squad. Herself, Hooker, Marzik, and Kelso. The uniformed officers and detectives from Rampart. What the list could not say, and what she could not know for sure, was when those people had arrived or who else might have been at the scene, hidden by cover or disguise.

Starkey removed the page from the binder, made a copy of it, then returned the book to Marzik's desk.

The drive north to Glendale happened in slow motion. Starkey constantly questioned her actions and conclusions, both about Riggio and about Pell. She wasn't a homicide investigator, but she knew the first rule of any homicide investigation: look for a link between the victim and the killer. She would have to look to Charlie Riggio and hope that something in his life would lead to who killed him. She felt sick about Pell. She wanted to call him; she wanted him to call her. She was certain that he felt something for her, but no longer trusted her certainty.

Starkey pulled into the police parking lot, but did not leave her car. She stared at the modern brick Bomb Squad building, the day bright and hot. The parking lot, the great dark Suburbans, the laughing techs in their black fatigues; everything was different. She was suddenly within the perception puzzle that Dana had described, one view giving her a picture of police officers, another the faces of suspects and murderers. Starkey stared at the building and wondered if she were out of her mind for thinking these things, but either she was right about what the plumber's tape meant or she was wrong. She hoped that she was wrong. She sat smoking in the car, staring at the building where she had felt most alive and at home, most a part of something, and knew that if she was wrong she had to prove it to herself.

'How're you holding up, kiddo?'

Starkey nearly jumped out of her skin.

'You scared me.'

'I saw you sitting out here and thought you saw me. If you're coming in, you can walk with me.'

Dick Leyton was smiling his kindly smile, the tall benevolent older brother. She got out and walked with him because she didn't know what else to do.

'Has Charlie's desk been cleared yet?'

'Buck came by and boxed it for the family. Charlie had two sisters. Did you know that?'

She didn't want to talk about Riggio's sisters or walk with Dick Leyton, who had come to see her every night when she was in the hospital.

'Ah, no, no, I didn't. Listen, Dick, are Charlie's things still here?'

Leyton didn't know, asking why she was interested. She was so embarrassed at the lie that she thought he must surely see it, but he didn't.

'I didn't know about the sisters. You work on something like this, you see the case, but you never see the man. I guess I was hoping to look at his things to get to know him a little better.'

Leyton didn't answer. They walked together into the squad room where Russ Daigle pointed out the box of Riggio's things beneath his desk. Riggio's locker had been cleared also, his sweats and a change of clothes and toiletry items bagged and secured with the box. Waiting for his sisters.

Starkey carried the box into the suit room where she could be alone. Buck had been complete and careful in packing Riggio's things: pens and pencils were bound together with a rubber band, then secured in the LAPD Bomb Squad coffee cup that had probably held them; two powerboat magazines and a James Patterson paperback were protecting a short stack of snapshots. Starkey examined the snapshots, one showing Riggio on a motorcycle, another of Riggio as a whitewalled Marine, three showing Riggio posing with a trophy deer. Starkey recalled that Riggio was a hunter, who often bragged of being a better shot than the two SWAT buddies with whom he hunted every year. She doubted that any of them concealed a motive for Charlie Riggio's death. The street clothes that Riggio had probably worn to work on the day he died were neatly folded and placed to cover everything else. A Motorola cell phone was wrapped in a black T-shirt to keep it safe. Starkey looked through the clothes for a wallet, didn't find it, and figured that Riggio had probably had the wallet in his fatigues when he died. The coroner's office either still had it or would release it directly to the next of kin. Starkey finished with the box in less than ten minutes. She was hoping for a desk calendar or day book that might give her an insight into his life over the past few months, but there wasn't anything like that. She was surprised at how little of a personal nature Riggio had brought to the job.

She brought the box back out to the squad room and stowed it beneath the now empty desk.

Russ Daigle nodded at her, his face tired.

'Pretty sad, isn't it?'

'Always, Russ. Has the family set a date for the funeral yet?'

'Well, you know, the coroner hasn't released the body.'

She hadn't known. She'd been so busy with the investigation that she hadn't paid attention.

Daigle had turned back to his paperwork, his heavy shoulders hunched over the black desk. His gray hair was cropped short, the back of his neck was creased and stubbled. The oldest of the sergeant-supervisors, he had been on the squad longer than anyone. Last year an officer named Tim Whithers had transferred in from Metro, the elite uniform division. Whithers was a tough, cocky young guy, who insisted on calling Russ 'Dad' even though Russ repeatedly asked him to stop. Whithers called him Dad until Russ Daigle coldcocked him one morning out in the parking lot. One punch below the ear. Knocked him out. Whithers went back to Metro.

'Hey, Russ?'

He glanced over.

'Were you at Silver Lake when it happened?'

'I was at home. Something like this happens, you always wish you had been there, though. You think you maybe could have done something. You feel that, too?'

'Yeah. I feel like that, too.'

'Are you okay, Carol? You look like something's on your mind.'

Starkey walked away without answering, feeling a sudden swell of panic as if she were trapped in a den of killers, and hated herself for it. Russ Daigle was happily married, had four adult children and nine grandchildren. Their pictures were a forest on his desk. To think he might have killed Charlie Riggio was absurd.

'Carol?'

She didn't look back.

14

Starkey left Glendale without knowing where she would go or what she would do. That was bad. Working an investigation was like working a bomb. You had to keep your focus. You had to have a clear objective and work to that end, even when you were drinking sweat and pissing blood.

If this were a normal investigation, Starkey would have questioned Riggio's co-workers about his friends and relationships, but now she couldn't do that. She considered contacting his two SWAT hunting buddies, but worried that word of it might get back to the Bomb Squad.

Leyton had said that Riggio had two sisters. Starkey decided to start there.

Every casebook included a page on the victim. Name, address, physical description, that kind of thing. On the night of Riggio's death, Starkey had assigned Hooker the task of gathering this information, and he had done his usual thorough job. She looked up the page and saw that Riggio was the middle child between two sisters, Angela Wellow and Marie Riggio. The older of the sisters, Angela, lived in Northridge, which wasn't far from Charlie's apartment in Canoga Park. The other sister lived south of Los Angeles in Torrance.

Starkey phoned Angela Wellow, identified herself, and expressed her condolences.

Angela's voice was clear, but tired. Jorge had listed her age as thirty-two.

'You worked with Charlie?'

Starkey explained that she had, but that now she was a bomb investigator with the Criminal Conspiracy Section.

'Mrs Wellow, there are some—'

'Angela. Please, I get enough of that missus from the kids. If you were a friend of Charlie's, I don't want you calling me missus.'

'You live near Charlie's apartment, don't you, Angela?'

'That's right. It's just over here.'

'Has anyone from the department talked to you?'

'No, not to me. Someone called our parents about Charlie, then Mom and Dad called me. They live in Scottsdale. I had to call my sister.'

'Reason I'm calling now is because you live so close to Charlie's. We think that Charlie had some files that we need on two other cases. We think he brought them home. Now we need them back. Could you meet me at his apartment, and let me see if I can find them?'

'Charlie had files?'

'Bomb reports on older cases. Nothing to do with Silver Lake. Now we need them back.'

A note of irritation crept into Angela's voice.

'I was already there. I've been there every day, trying to get his things packed. Oh, for God's sake.'

Starkey made herself hard and detached, even though she felt like a dog for lying.

'I appreciate your feelings, Angela, but we really need those files.'

'When do you have to do this?'

'I'm available right now. The sooner the better from our end.'

They agreed to meet in an hour.

With the traffic, it took Starkey almost that long to get to Northridge, high in the San Fernando Valley. Riggio's apartment building was on a busy street three blocks south of the Cal State campus. It was a great cave of a building, an upscale stucco monster that had probably been rebuilt after the big earthquake in '94. Starkey left her car in a red zone, then went to the glass security doors where she and Angela had agreed to meet. Two young women on their way out with book bags held the door, but Starkey waved them off, telling them that she was meeting someone. Starkey watched them heading toward the campus and smiled. This was just the kind of place where Charlie Riggio would live. Inside, there would be a pool and Jacuzzi, probably a game room with a pool table, cookouts every night, and plenty of young women.

Now, a thin young woman with the harried look of a mother opened the glass door and looked out. She was carrying a little boy who couldn't have been more than four.

'Are you Detective Starkey?'

'Mrs Wellow? Sorry, Angela?'

'That's right.'

Angela Wellow must have parked beneath the building and entered through the inside. Starkey showed her badge, then followed Angela through the central courtyard and up a flight of stairs to a second-floor apartment. The little boy's name was Todd.

'I hope this won't take long. My older boy gets home from school at three.'

'It shouldn't, Angela. I appreciate your going to this trouble.'

Riggio's apartment was nice, a two-bedroom loft with a high arched ceiling and an expensive big-screen television. A mounted deer head stared down at her from the wall. Starkey wondered if it was the same deer she'd seen in the pictures. The couch was lined with large boxes, and more boxes were in the kitchen. It would be a sad job, packing the belongings of the dead.

Angela put down her little boy, who ran to the television like it was a close and trusted friend.

'What do your files look like? Maybe I've seen them.'

Starkey cringed at the lie.

'They look like three-ring binders. They're probably black.'

Angela stared at the boxes as if she were trying to remember what was in them.

'Well, I don't think so. These are his clothes, mostly, and things from the kitchen. Charlie didn't keep anything like an office. There's his bedroom upstairs. He has one of those weight machines in the other bedroom.'

'Do you mind if I look?'

'No, but I really don't have very long.'

Starkey hoped that she would have Riggio's bedroom to herself, but Angela picked up the little boy and showed her up the stairs.

'It's this way, Detective.'

'Were you and Charlie close?'

'He was probably closer to Marie, she's the youngest, but our family was a good one. Did you know him well?'

'Not as well as I would have liked. Something like this happens, you always wish you'd taken the time.'

Angela didn't answer until they reached the top of the stairs.

'He was a good guy. He had a stupid sense of humor, but he was a good brother.'

The bed had already been stripped of linen. More boxes waited on the floor, some empty, others partially filled. A dresser stood against one wall, a jumble of pictures wedged into the mirror frame. Most of the pictures were of an older couple that Starkey took to be his parents.

'Is this your sister?'

'That's Marie, yes. These here are our parents. We haven't taken down the pictures yet. It's just too hard.'

The little boy upended a box and climbed inside. Angela sat on the bed, watching him.

'I guess you can look through these boxes. They're mostly clothes, but I remember some papers and books and things.'

Starkey used her body to block Angela's view as she went through the boxes. Having Riggio's sister three feet behind her left her with the feeling that even if something was here, she would not find it. There was a heavy photo album that she wanted to look through, and a notepad, and, in the corner of the room, a Macintosh computer that might contain anything at all. There was too much, and here she was, going through it under false pretenses with the dead man's sister staring at her back. What a half-assed, pathetic way to conduct an investigation.

Angela said, 'You were a bomb technician like Charlie?'

'I used to be. Now I'm a bomb investigator.'

'Could I ask you something about that?'

Starkey said that she could.

'They won't release Charlie's body. They haven't even let us go see him. I keep seeing these pictures in my head, you see? About why they won't let us have him.'

Starkey turned, feeling awkward with this woman's discomfort.

'Is Charlie, you know, in pieces?'

'It's not like that. You don't have to worry about Charlie being like that.'

Angela nodded, then looked away.

'You think about these things, you know? They don't tell you anything, and you imagine all this stuff.'

Starkey changed the subject.

'Did Charlie talk about his job?'

She laughed and wiped at her eyes.

'Oh, God, when didn't he talk about it? You couldn't shut him up. Every call out was either an atom bomb or a practical joke. He liked to tell about the time they rolled out on a suspicious package that someone had left outside a barber shop. Charlie looked inside and he sees that it's a human head, just this head. When Charlie's supervisor asks what's in the box, Charlie tells him it looks like the barber took too much off the top.'

Starkey smiled. She had never heard that story, and thought that Riggio had probably made it up.

'Charlie loved working with the Bomb Squad. He loved the people. They were like a family, he said.'

Starkey nodded, remembered that feeling, and the pang of loss that came with losing it. And now she suspected that family of murder.

Starkey finished with the boxes, then went through the dresser and the closet without finding anything helpful. She had lost confidence that, working alone, she could discover something that would suggest a motive for Riggio's death. Maybe there was nothing to be found, and never had been.

'Well, maybe I was wrong about those reports. It doesn't look like Charlie brought them home after all.'

'I'm sorry.'

Starkey couldn't think of anything else to say or ask and was ready to leave. Angela had been saying how she was in a hurry to get home for her son, but now she lingered on the bed.

'Detective, could I ask you something else?'

'Of course.'

'Were you and Charlie girlfriend and boyfriend?'

'No. I didn't know Charlie had a girlfriend.'

Starkey glanced at the pictures in the mirror: Riggio and his parents, Riggio with his sisters and nieces and nephews.

'He had a girlfriend, but he never brought her to meet us. Here's this nice Italian boy, you're supposed to be married and have a million kids. My parents were always after him, you know, when are you going to get married, when are you going to settle down, when do we get to meet this girl?'

'What did Charlie say?'

Angela seemed embarrassed again.

'Well, some of the things he said, I got the impression she was married.'

'Oh.'

Angela nodded.

'Yeah. *Oh.*'

'I'm sorry. I didn't mean it like that.'

'No, I understand. But it happens, right? I think it was hard for Charlie. Here's this young, good-looking guy, but he was heartfelt. I think she was married to someone Charlie worked with.'

Angela met Starkey's eyes as if she was waiting for a reaction, but then she looked away.

'I probably shouldn't have said that, but if it's not you, I thought you might know her. I'd like to talk to her. I wouldn't make a problem with her husband or anything like that. I just thought we could talk about Charlie. It might be good.'

'I'm sorry. I don't know anything about that.'

Starkey wondered if the photo album held pictures that Riggio had wanted to keep hidden, pictures of a woman who was married to someone else that he couldn't keep out on the mirror.

Angela suddenly glanced at her watch and jumped up.

'Oh, shit. Now I really am late. I'm sorry, but I have to go. My son will be home soon.'

'It's all right. I understand.'

Starkey followed Angela down, but now her mind was racing for a way to get a view of Riggio's photo album.

By the time they reached the door, Todd was squirming in his mother's arms. He was tired and cranky and overdue for his nap. When Starkey saw the time Angela was having with him at the door, Starkey took her keys.

'Here, I'll get the door. That boy's a handful.'

'It's like trying to hold a fish.'

Starkey held the door to let Angela through. She pretended to lock the door, but unlocked it, instead. She closed it, then rattled the knob as if checking to make sure it was secure. Angela's arms still filled with squirming child, Starkey placed the keys in Angela's purse.

'Thanks again for trying to help, Angela. I feel a little silly that I got you out here and couldn't find the files. I was sure Charlie brought them home.'

'If they turn up, I'll call.'

Angela saw Starkey to the glass doors and let her out. Starkey walked out to her car, climbed behind the wheel, but did not start her car. Her heart was hammering. She told herself that what she was about to do was insane. Worse, it was illegal. A D.A. out to make an example of her could press for breaking and entering.

Five minutes later, Angela Wellow appeared on the service drive at the side of the apartment building in a white Honda Accord, turned south, and drove away. Starkey flicked her cigarette out the window, then crossed back to the apartment building just as a young man with a book bag was wrestling a mountain bike through the glass door. Starkey held the door for him.

'Don't be late for class.'

'I'm always late. I was born late.'

Starkey walked calmly to the second floor, where she let herself into Charlie Riggio's apartment. She took the stairs two at a time, going directly to the box with the photo album. Now that she was thinking in terms of an illicit affair, she wanted Riggio's phone bills and charge receipts, but had no idea which box held those things and was too frightened to take the time to find them. Starkey smiled grimly; she might have been a fearless bomb technician, but she was a chickenshit crook. She found the photo album, but didn't dare look at it there. It was too thick, and held too many photographs.

She took the book, this time locking the door behind herself, and hurried down to her car. She drove straight home and brought the photo album inside under her jacket as if it were pornography.

She sat with the album at the dining-room table, turning the pages slowly, telling herself that the odds were so long as to be unimaginable, that Angela Wellow was probably wrong, and that tomorrow she would be back to square one, all alone in her belief that someone other than Mr Red was behind Charlie's death.

Page after page were pictures that charted Charlie Riggio's life: Charlie playing high school football, Charlie with his buddies, Charlie with pretty young girls who looked anything but like the wives of cops, Charlie hunting, Charlie at the Police Academy, Charlie with his family. They were happy pictures; the type of pictures that a man kept because they made him smile.

It was near the end of the book where she found a picture taken at last year's Bomb Squad Chili Cookoff. She found the second like it taken at the Christmas party, and then, two pages later, a third that had been taken at a CCS barbeque that Kelso had thrown on the Fourth of July.

Starkey peeled the pictures from the album and put them on the table side by side, asking herself if they could really mean what she thought they meant. She told herself they couldn't; she told herself she was wrong, and reading too much into them, but what Angela Wellow had said hung over her like an ax.

... she's married to someone he works with.

The pictures were all the same, a man and a woman, arms around each other, smiling, a little too close, a little too familiar, a little too friendly.

Charlie Riggio and Suzie Leyton.

Dick Leyton's wife.

Starkey poured a tall gin and tonic, drank most of it. She felt angry, and betrayed. Leyton being a suspect was too big to get her arms around. Just thinking about it wore her down. Starkey decided to deal with it as if Leyton were just another part of the investigation. There was no other way to see it.

She went to her own collection of pictures and found a shot of Leyton that she'd taken at an LAPD Summer Festival Youth Camp. It was a crisp shot, a close-up showing Leyton in civilian clothes and sunglasses. She brought it to Kinko's, made several copies, adjusting the contrast until she had one that showed the best detail, then returned home where she phoned Warren Mueller. She didn't expect him to be in his office, but she tried him anyway. To Starkey's surprise, she got him on the first ring.

'I've got a favor to ask, Sergeant. I have a photograph that I want you to show the old man who lives in Tennant's duplex.'

'Is it the guy in the hat?'

'It could be. Here's the thing, I don't want anyone else to see the picture. I want this kept between me and you.'

Mueller hesitated.

'I'm not liking the way this sounds.'

'It's about tracing Tennant's RDX. I don't want to tell you any more than that, and I am asking you not to ask.'

'All this makes me wonder who's in your picture.'

'Look, Mueller, if this is too hard, I'll drive up there and do it myself.'

'Now, hold on.'

'It's someone who would be hurt badly by this if I'm wrong, and I might be wrong. I'm asking you for a favor here, goddamnit, so what's it going to be?'

'This guy in your picture, he's LAPD, isn't he?'

Starkey couldn't bring herself to speak.

'Okay. Okay, I'll take care of it. You know what you're doing down there, Starkey? You gonna be okay with this?'

'I'm okay.'

'All right. You fax up your picture. I'll go wait by the machine. If you're expecting to use this ID in court, I'm gonna have to make up a six-pack.'

The suspect picture was never shown to witnesses by itself; the courts ruled this to be leading. Detectives were required to show a spread of pictures, hoping that the witness would identify the right one.

'That's fine. Now, one more thing. If we get a confirmation from your wit, I'm going to want to see Tennant about this. I'd like to do that tomorrow.'

Mueller cleared his throat, hesitating.

'Hell, Starkey, I guess you didn't hear. Tennant's dead. I called Atascadero today to set up a little interview about his shop, you know? The silly sonofabitch blew his damned arms off and bled to death.'

Starkey didn't know what to say.

'He blew off his arms? His arms were separated?'

The energy it took to do that was tremendous.

'Yeah. Man I talked to over there said it was a real mess.'

'What did he use, Mueller? Christ, you can't make anything like that out of cleaning products.'

'Sheriff's EOD is running the analysis. Guess we'll know in a day or two. Whatever the case, you can forget about getting anything from Tennant. He's a memory.'

Starkey was slow to answer.

'I'll fax that picture now. If it doesn't come through clear, call back and I'll try again.'

She gave him her home phone.

'Owe you one, Sergeant. Thanks.'

'I'll collect. You can bet your split-tail bottom on that.'

'Mueller, you're the most charming man I know.'

'Kinda grows on you, doesn't it?'

'Yeah. Like anal warts.'

Starkey gave Mueller a minute, then put the photocopy of Leyton through her fax. She waited for his call, but after a few silent minutes had passed, she figured that the photo had gone through okay.

She didn't know what else to do. She could take the photo to Lester Ybarra, but if he told Marzik she would have to explain. She needed to put Leyton in Silver Lake at the time of the detonation, but that meant questioning more people whom she couldn't question. She knew that Leyton was at the scene when she arrived, but had he been there in the moment when someone had triggered the device?

Starkey's eye kept going to the computer, waiting silently on her dining-room table. She had not turned it on since she turned it off last night. Now it seemed to watch her.

I did not kill Charles Riggio.

I know who did.

Starkey lit a cigarette, then went into the kitchen and made herself another drink. Sobriety had lasted all of two days. She went back into the dining room, turned on the computer, and signed on to Claudius.

Mr Red did not jump out at her. The chat room was empty. She sipped her drink, smoked, and read through the boards. There were new posts, but nothing beyond the mundane chitchat of defective personalities. She finished her second drink, then made another. She left the computer on with Claudius's flaming head like a painting on her wall. She smoked a second cigarette. Starkey walked through her house, once stepping out the back door, twice stepping out the front. She thought about Pell, and she thought that she might one day like a persimmon tree. She didn't know what persimmons were like, but that didn't stop her from wanting the tree. Outside, the eastern sky purpled and time passed.

Starkey floated like that for almost two hours as the purple dimmed to black, and then she was rewarded.

WILL YOU ACCEPT A MESSAGE FROM MR RED?

She opened the window.

MR RED: Am I Bergen?

She stared at the line, then typed her answer.

HOTLOAD: No. You are Mr Red.
MR RED: THANK YOU!!! We're finally on the same page.
HOTLOAD: Is that important to you? Us being on the same page?

Red's hesitation left her with a grim satisfaction.

MR RED: Are you alone?
HOTLOAD: Room full of cops here, babe. It's a spectator sport.
MR RED: Ah. Then you must be naked.
HOTLOAD: If you start talking trash, I'll go away.
MR RED: No, you won't, Carol Starkey. You have questions.

She did. She drew deep on the cigarette, then typed her question.

HOTLOAD: Who killed Riggio?
MR RED: Didn't I?
HOTLOAD: You said no.
MR RED: If I tell you, it will spoil the surprise.
HOTLOAD: I already know. I just want to see if our answers match.
MR RED: If you knew, you would have made an arrest. You might suspect, but you don't know. I would tell you if you and I were the only ones here ... but not in front of a room filled with cops.

Starkey laughed at the way he wrapped the conversation around to force her admission.

HOTLOAD: They left. We're alone now.

He hesitated again, and she felt a stab of hope that he might actually tell her.

MR RED: Are we? Are we really alone?
HOTLOAD: I wouldn't lie.
MR RED: Then I will tell you a secret. Just between you and me.
HOTLOAD: What?

She waited, but nothing came back. She thought he might be typing a long reply, but the minutes stretched until she finally realized that he wanted her to beg. His need to manipulate and control was textbook.

HOTLOAD: What's the big secret, Crimson Boy? I'm on a timer here.
MR RED: It isn't about Riggio.
HOTLOAD: Then what?
MR RED: It will scare you.
HOTLOAD: WHAT?????

He paused again, and then his message appeared.

MR RED: Pell is not who he seems. He is using you, Carol Starkey. He has been playing us against each other.

The statement struck her like a board. It came from nowhere, jolting her like a head-on collision.

HOTLOAD: What do you mean?

He didn't answer.

HOTLOAD: What does that mean, Pell is not who he seems?

No answer.

HOTLOAD: How do you know Pell?

Nothing.

HOTLOAD: Answer me!

No answers came back. The window hung there, unchanging. His statement that Pell was not who he seemed haunted her. Her first impulse was to phone Pell, but she felt caught between them like a ship between the ocean and a storm, Mr Red on one side, Pell the other.

During the days when Starkey served on the Bomb Squad, the ATF had maintained a liaison agent with LAPD in an office housed with CCS. Three weeks after Starkey returned from Bomb School in Alabama, Sugar had introduced her to Regal Phillips, the ATF liaison agent. Phillips was an overweight man with a friendly smile, who had retired near the end of Starkey's first year; they had worked together only occasionally during that year, but Sugar loved the older man, and Starkey sensed then that the feelings had run deep both ways. Phillips had visited Starkey twice during her time in the hospital, both visits ending with Phillips weeping after recounting stories about Sugar's exploits on the squad.

That final visit had been the last time Starkey had seen Regal Phillips, almost three years ago. She hadn't phoned him after the hospital because she couldn't be with Regal without being with Sugar, and that hurt too much.

Now, after all this time, she felt embarrassed as she listened to his phone ring.

When Regal answered, she said, 'Reege, it's Carol Starkey.'

'Lord, girl, how are you? I had it in my head that you didn't talk to black people anymore.'

He sounded like the same old Reege, the warm voice revealing only a hint of surprise.

'Pretty good. Working. I'm with CCS now.'

'I heard that. I still got friends over there. I'm keeping tabs on you.'

He laughed softly when he said it, his voice so full of affection that she felt ashamed of herself.

'Reege, ah, listen, I'm really sorry I haven't stayed in touch. It's hard for me that way.'

'Don't worry about it, Carol. Things changed for a lot of people that day in the trailer park.'

'You know about Charlie Riggio?'

'What I see on the news. You working on that?'

'That's right. Reege, this is an awkward thing for me to ask.'

'Ask it.'

'I'm working with an ATF agent that I, ah, have my doubts about. I was wondering if you could look into him for me. You know what I mean?'

'No, Carol, I don't think that I do.'

'I want to know who he is, Reege. I guess I'm asking you if I can trust him.'

'What's his name?'

'Jack Pell.'

Phillips told her that it might take a day or two, but that he would call back soon. Starkey thanked him, then hung up and doused the lights. She did not sleep. She didn't even get into bed. Starkey stayed on the couch in the dim light, waiting until morning, wondering how a man she now trusted so little could mean so much to her.

Pell

Earlier that day, when Pell left Barrigan's, he squinted against the nuclear California sun. The light was so bright that it felt like an ax blade wedged between his eyes. Even the sunglasses didn't help.

Pell sat in his car, trying to figure out what to do. The look of hurt on her face had left him feeling like a dog. He knew that she was right: He was so obsessed by Mr Red that he couldn't see anything else, but he had the fragment with her name on it. He had wanted to reach across the table and tell her everything, tell her the truth. He had wanted to open himself, because he had also been closed, and thought that she might be the only one who could understand, but he couldn't be sure. He had wanted to tell her of his growing feelings for her, but there was only Mr Red. He no longer knew where Red ended and he began.

His head began to throb.

'Jesus. Not again.'

Soft gray shapes floated up from the dashboard, from the windows, from the hood of his car.

It was happening more frequently now. It would only get worse.

15

Starkey left her house well before dawn. She had had it with the emptiness of the quiet rooms, the conflicting thoughts about Pell and Dick Leyton and her shitty life. She told herself to get her head in the case, so she left the thoughts and emptiness, and made her way across town.

She needed to determine Dick Leyton's whereabouts at the time of the blast and thought that Hooker might have noted Leyton's TOA in the casebook. Starkey didn't bother to shower. She changed clothes, lit a fresh cigarette, and drove.

Spring Street was a tomb. Hers was the only car on the parking level. Not even the Fugitive Section had shown for work.

Starkey said fuck it and brought her cigarette into the office. She could always blame the cleaning crew.

The casebook was on Marzik's desk where she remembered it, but Hooker had made no note of Leyton's arrival time, just that he was present. Starkey pulled the box of videotapes from under Hooker's desk. She found the copy of the enhanced tape that Bennell had made for them, along with the news tape she remembered as having the widest angles, and brought them upstairs to the video room. She had watched those damned tapes so many times she knew them by heart, but she had always been looking for the man in the baseball cap; she had never looked at the cops.

The image quality of the enhanced tape was crappy on the VCR just as Bennell had warned, but she watched it anyway, searching the perimeter of the cordon for Dick Leyton. She remembered that he was wearing a polo shirt, that he looked as if he'd just come from home.

She watched the tape, then watched it again, but it was always the same: Riggio approached the box, the explosion, then Buck ran forward to strip away his partner's helmet. Starkey gave up trying to find Leyton in the moments prior to the explosion because the clips were too short and indistinct. She concentrated on that time after the blast, figuring that if Leyton were at the scene, he would have run forward to see about his man. She keyed the tape to the explosion, and watched again. *Bang!* For almost twelve seconds of real time after the blast, Buck and Charlie were alone in the frame. Then the paramedics' ambulance raced up beside them from the bottom of the picture. Two LAFD paramedics jumped out, taking Buck's place. Four seconds later, a single uniformed officer ran forward from the left side of the frame, and two more uniformed officers entered from the right. The officer from the left appeared to be trying to get Buck to sit down or move away, but Buck shook him off. Three more officers entered the frame from the bottom, turning back almost at once to head off two men in street clothes. Other men in street clothes entered from the right. Now a second ambulance moved into the frame, followed by more people on foot. Two of the figures appeared to be wearing polo shirts, but she didn't recognize them. Then the tape ended.

'Shit!'

Something about the tape bothered her, but she wasn't sure what. She was seeing something, yet not seeing it. The answer was in the tape, Starkey cursed the news station for not running the camera longer, then went back to CCS.

Starkey decided to ask Buck. She left CCS before the other detectives arrived and made her way to Glendale. She didn't know whether or not Buck had duty that day, so she stopped at a diner to wait until seven when the Bomb Squad receptionist, Louise Mendoza, arrived. Mendoza, who would know the duty roster, usually arrived before the bomb techs.

At five minutes before seven, Starkey phoned.

'Louise, it's Carol Starkey. Does Buck have duty today?'

'He's back in the shed. You want me to put you through?'

'I just wanted to know if he was there. I'm on my way over to see him.'

'I'll let him know.'

'One other thing, Louise. Ah, is Dick there?'

'Yeah, but if you want to talk to him you'd better let me put you through. He has to go down to Parker this morning.'

'That's okay. It'll keep.'

Starkey pulled into the Glendale PD parking lot ten minutes later. She found Buck and Russ Daigle in the shed, the brick building at the ass end of the parking lot where the squad practiced with the de-armer and the robots. They were standing over the Andrus robot, drinking coffee and frowning. Both men smiled when they saw her.

'Damn thing's pulling to the right. You try to make the damn thing go straight ahead, it veers off to the right. You got any idea what's wrong?'

'It's a Republican.'

Daigle, a staunch Republican, laughed loudly.

'Buck? Could I see you for a moment?'

Buck joined her at the door, the two of them stepping outside.

She told him that she had come about the enhanced tape, that they were ready for him to take a look. That was her excuse for the conversation.

'I'll look if you want, but I didn't see anything in those other tapes. Jesus, I don't know if I can stomach it again, seeing Charlie like that.'

She wanted to turn the conversation to Leyton.

'There's no rush. Maybe I should ask Dick if he saw anything. He might be able to pick out someone.'

Daggett nodded.

'You might. He was back there behind the cordon.'

Starkey felt sick. She told herself to be professional. This is why she was here. This is why she was a cop.

'When did he get on scene?'

'I dunno, maybe twenty minutes before Charlie went out, something like that.'

'I'll talk to him about it.'

Starkey walked back across the parking lot, feeling as if her legs were enormous stilts, pushing her to a height that left her dizzy. She could barely get into her car, taking forever to fold the stilts the way a mantis folds its legs. Nothing fit anymore. She stared at the Bomb Squad. Leyton's office was there. The box with Charlie Riggio's things was still beneath Daigle's desk. She thought of his cell phone there. If Riggio and Susan Leyton had been lovers, Starkey thought that he would probably have called her often. He would have snuck calls to her during the day when Dick was at work, and there would be the record of it in his phone bills. Starkey was surprised at how uninvolved she felt when that thought came to her. Maybe it was just another step along the case. It was as if nothing mattered very much except building the evidence that she could bring to Kelso, and prove Pell wrong.

She took out her own cell phone, and called Angela Wellow. This time she told her the truth.

Starkey sat with Angela Wellow in the quiet of her home, the two of them sitting on the edge of a tattered couch. Riggio's photo album was on the couch between them; Todd was sleeping facedown on the floor. Angela glanced at the album again and again, as if there were some explanation beyond what Starkey was giving. She rubbed her palm on her thigh.

'I don't know about this. I don't know what to think when someone says something like this. You're telling me that Charlie was murdered?'

'I'm investigating that possibility. That's why I need Charlie's phone bills, Angela. I need to see who he was calling.'

Angela stared at her. Starkey knew what was coming. When Starkey gave back the album and explained that she had gone to Charlie's condo under false pretenses, Angela had listened to it all without saying a word. Now she was about to say it.

'Why did you have to lie to me yesterday? Why couldn't you just say?'

Starkey tried to look her in the eyes, but couldn't.

'I don't know what else to do. I'm sorry.'

'Jesus.'

Angela walked over to her little boy, stared down at him like she wasn't sure who he was.

'What do I tell my parents?'

Starkey ignored that. She didn't want to talk about the details of what was happening. She didn't want to get sidetracked. She wanted to keep moving forward until this thing was tied down, and she could bring it to Kelso.

'I need his phone bills, Angela. Can we please go look for his phone bills.'

Angela said, 'Todd? Todd, wake up, honey. We have to go out.'

Angela lifted her sleeping boy onto her shoulder, then turned on Starkey with angry eyes.

'You can follow me over there. I don't want you going in Charlie's house again.'

Starkey waited outside Riggio's building for almost an hour until Angela Wellow came out the glass doors with a handful of white envelopes.

'It took me forever to find them. I'm sorry.'

'That's all right. I appreciate this, Angela.'

'No, you don't. I don't know what you're doing or why, but you don't know me well enough to appreciate what I'm doing.'

Angela left her with the envelopes, walking away without another word.

Starkey struck a cigarette, exhaling a cloud that settled in the car even with the windows open. She liked the taste of it, and the way smoking made her feel. She didn't see what all the whining was about. So what if you got cancer.

She opened Charlie Riggio's phone bills and there it was, so obvious that it jumped out at her. She didn't know the Leytons' home number, but she didn't need to know it. Charlie had called the same number in the same 323 area code two and three times every day, sometimes as many as six or seven calls, going back for months.

Starkey put the bills aside, finished her cigarette, then took out her own phone. She checked the number again, then dialed.

A familiar woman's voice.

'Hello?'

'Hello, Susan.'

Starkey felt tired.

'I'm sorry. Who?'

Starkey paused.

'Susan?'

'I'm sorry. You have the wrong number.'

Starkey looked at the number again, making sure she had dialed correctly. She had.

'This is Carol Starkey. I'm calling for Susan Leyton.'

'Oh, hi, Detective Starkey. You dialed the wrong number. This is Natalie Daggett.'

16

Natalie Daggett said, 'Are you still there? Hello?'

Starkey checked the phone numbers again. It was the same number; multiple calls every day for months.

'I'm here. I'm sorry, Natalie. I was expecting someone else. It's taking me a minute to switch gears.'

Natalie laughed.

'That happens to me, too. I have these senior moments all the time.'

'Are you going to be home for the next hour or so?'

'Buck isn't home. He went back to work.'

'I know. I'll be stopping by to see you. It won't take long.'

'What do you want to see me about?'

'It won't take long, Natalie. I'll see you in a few minutes.'

'What is this about?'

'It's about Buck. I'm working on a little surprise for him. Because of what happened to Charlie. Sort of a welcome back party.'

'Is that why you were calling Susan?'

'That's right. Dick is the one who suggested it.'

'Oh. Oh, okay. I guess so.'

'I'll see you in a few minutes.'

'Okay.'

Starkey closed her phone, then put it aside. Not Dick, but Buck Daggett. She had searched the tapes for the killer again and again, and he was right there in plain sight every time, hiding in open view, waiting for his partner to get over the bomb. Starkey thought about Dana again, and the perception puzzle. It was all in how you looked at it. Now she realized what had bothered her about the tape. Buck hadn't cleared the area for a secondary device. He should have pulled Riggio away from the scene before stripping off his armor, just as he had pulled Carol away from the trailer; she'd seen that on the tape of her own death, but he hadn't pulled Riggio. All bomb techs were trained to clear the area for a secondary, but Buck knew there wasn't a secondary. It was always there, glaring at her, and she'd missed it.

Starkey made the long drive to Monterey Park in good time. She didn't hurry. Starkey was confident that Natalie did not know that her husband had murdered her lover. Buck had planned the murder far too carefully to risk confessing to his wife, even if to punish her.

Starkey was still relieved when she pulled into the Daggetts' drive and saw that Buck's Toyota 4-Runner wasn't home. She put on her best cop face before she went to the door, the same face that she had used when she confronted the father in Venice with his little girl's thumb.

Starkey rang the bell.

Natalie looked drawn when she answered the door. Starkey thought that she probably hadn't been sleeping.

'Hi, Natalie. Thanks for seeing me.'

Starkey followed her into a small dining room, where they sat at a bare table. The Lawn-Boy mower was still sitting in the backyard. Buck had never mowed the lawn. Natalie didn't offer something to drink, just as she hadn't offered anything the last time Starkey was there.

'What kind of surprise did you have in mind?'

Starkey took the phone bills from her purse and put them on the table. Natalie glanced at them without comprehension.

'Natalie, I'm sorry, but I'm not here about a party. I went through Charlie's things and found some things I need to ask you about.'

Starkey could see the fear rise when she mentioned Charlie's name.

'I thought this was about Buck?'

Starkey pushed the bills across the table, turning them so that Natalie could read them.

'These are Charlie's cell-phone bills. You see your number there? You see how many calls he made? Now, I already know the answer to this, but I need to hear you say it, Natalie. Were you and Charlie having an affair?'

Natalie stared at the pages without touching them. She sat absolutely still as her nose turned red and tears bled from her eyes.

'Natalie, were you? Were you and Charlie in love?'

Natalie nodded. She looked twelve years old, and Starkey's heart filled with an embarrassing ache, and shame.

'How long were you involved?'

'Since last year.'

'Please speak up.'

'Since last year.'

'Does Buck know?'

'Of course not. He would be so hurt.'

Starkey took back the telephone bills and returned them to her jacket.

'Okay. I'm sorry I had to ask, but there it is.'

'Are you going to tell Buck?'

Starkey stared at the woman, then lied.

'No, Natalie. This isn't something I'm going to tell Buck. You don't have to worry about that.'

'I just made a mistake with Charlie. That's what it was, a mistake. Everybody's entitled to a mistake.'

Starkey left her like that, walking out to her car in the fierce heat, then driving away to Spring Street.

Buck

Buck Daggett didn't like it that Starkey had been spending so much time in Glendale. Her asking so many questions about that bastard, Riggio, made him nervous. Especially when he'd heard about her wanting to get to know Riggio now that Riggio was dead. What in hell was that about? Starkey had never given a damn about Riggio or anyone else since that fucking bomb in the trailer park. She had turned into a lush and a has-been, and now she was supposed to be Ms. Maudlin?

Buck had been proud of himself that he'd built in the connection between Mr Red and Starkey. He had wanted to keep the investigation as far from Riggio as possible, but just his rotten luck the only piece of her name that had been found was the goddamned S, letting them think it was part of Charles. Still, he'd thought everything was going to be fine when the feds rolled in and everyone started chasing their tails about Mr Red, but now it looked as if that bitch, Starkey, had tumbled to the truth anyway. Or at least suspected it.

Buck Daggett had still been fucking around with the Andrus robot when Natalie called. The stupid bim couldn't help telling him that Starkey was coming by because they were going to toss a surprise party for him. To cheer him up. Ha. Buck had hung up and barely made it to the toilet before he'd puked up his guts, then he'd raced home to see for himself.

As Starkey drove away from his house, Buck crouched in his neighbor's yard, watching her. He didn't know how much she had on him yet, but he knew she suspected him, and that was enough.

Buck decided to kill her.

17

Starkey phoned Mueller from her car, trying to catch him at his office, but he was gone. She left word on his voice mail that the man in the photo was no longer a suspect, and that she would be faxing up a new image. She phoned Beth Marzik next.

'Beth, I want you to get together a six-pack and meet me at the flower shop. Call Lester and make sure he's there. If he's on a delivery, tell them to have him come back.'

'I was just getting ready to go to lunch.'

'Damnit, Beth, lunch will keep. I want a mix of Anglos and Latins in their forties, just as Lester described. Don't tell anyone, Beth. Just get it together and meet me at Lester's.'

'Listen, you can't just drop this on me. Who am I putting together the six-pack for? Do you have a suspect?'

'Yes.'

Starkey hung up before Marzik could ask who. Time was now a factor. She could not trust that Natalie wouldn't tell Buck about her visit, or about her interest in Charlie Riggio. She didn't fear that Buck would flee; her concern was that he would move to destroy evidence that might be necessary in the case against him.

She drove faster now, swinging past her house for a snapshot of Buck Daggett before turning toward Silver Lake. Like the shot of Dick Leyton, it was a picture of Buck in civilian clothes. When she reached the flower shop, Marzik and Lester were talking together on the sidewalk. Marzik left Lester, and walked over as Starkey got out of her car. She had the six-pack sheet in a manila envelope.

'You want to tell me what's going on here? That kid's old man is raising nine kinds of hell.'

'Let me see the sheet.'

The six-pack was a paper sandwich with places for six photographs like a page from a photo album. Detective bureaus kept files of them based on age, race, and type, most of the pictures being file photos of police officers. Starkey pulled out one of the six pictures, then fitted in the picture of Buck Daggett.

Marzik gripped Starkey's arm.

'Tell me you're joking.'

'I'm not joking, Beth.'

Starkey brought the sheet to Lester. She explained that she wanted him to look at each picture carefully before making his decision, then asked if any of the men pictured here was the man that Lester saw using the telephone. Marzik watched Lester so closely that Lester asked her what was wrong.

'Nothing, pal. Just look at the pictures.'

'None of these guys are wearing hats.'

'Look at their faces, Lester. Think back to the guy you saw on the phone. Could any of these men be him?'

'I think it's him.'

Lester pointed out Buck Daggett.

Marzik walked away.

'Is she okay?'

'She's fine, Lester. Thanks.'

'Did I pick the right one?'

'None of the answers are right, Lester. Some are just more wrong than others.'

Marzik was staring at the sidewalk when Starkey joined her.

'You going to tell me now?'

Starkey laid it out, and then they called Kelso, telling him that they were on their way in. Starkey asked if he would have Hooker meet them. Kelso demanded to know why Starkey wanted to see them together.

'I have some additional evidence in the case, Barry. I need your advice on how to proceed with it.'

The ploy of asking for his guidance worked. Kelso told her that he and Santos would be waiting.

Marzik was still leaning against her car when Starkey got off the phone.

Marzik said, 'This is going to sound stupid, Carol, but can we take one car? I don't want to ride back alone.'

'It doesn't sound stupid.'

When they reached Spring Street, Starkey didn't bother wrestling her car in the parking garage. They left it in the red zone out front and used the elevator.

For the first time that she could remember, Kelso's computer was turned off. He was waiting behind his desk with his fingers steepled, as if he had been like that since she called. Santos was on his couch, looking like a kid who'd been called in to see the principal. Carol thought he looked tired. They probably all looked tired.

Kelso said, 'What is it, Carol?'

'It isn't Mr Red, Barry. It was never Mr Red.'

Kelso raised his hands, shaking his head even as she spoke.

'We covered that, didn't we? The signatures are identical—'

Marzik snapped, 'Barry, just *listen.*'

Santos arched his eyebrows, surprised. Kelso stared at her, then spread his hands.

'I'm listening.'

Starkey went on.

'Barry, the signatures are *not* identical. Almost, but *not.* If you don't believe me, call Rockville yourself and ask the ATF.'

Santos said, 'What will they tell him?'

'That the Silver Lake bomb is *different.* They will *suggest* that the person who built the Silver Lake device was working from an ATF bomb analysis because the one deviation from the other devices was an element that was *not* included in those reports.'

Starkey took it one step at a time, never mentioning Buck Daggett until the end. She went through the difference in the bomb devices, then the similarities, and that the builder would need to find a source of RDX in order to mix the Modex Hybrid that Mr Red favored.

'RDX is the hardest of the components to find, Barry. The only person in this area in recent history who's had any was Dallas Tennant. If you were looking to find some, you would go to him. Beth and I found Tennant's shop. A man similar in description to the individual who made our 911 report was seen there about a month ago. I believe he went there for Tennant's RDX. I don't know how this man learned of Tennant's shop. I don't know if he discovered it the way Beth and I did, through a property search, or if he made a deal of some kind with Tennant. We can't ask Tennant because Tennant is now dead.'

'What man?'

Starkey plowed on without answering. She believed that if she accused Buck Daggett before laying out the supporting evidence, the meeting would become a shouting match.

Starkey held up the six-pack, but didn't yet give it to him.

'We showed this six-pack to Lester Ybarra. Lester identified one of these men as the man who placed the call. We'll have to show a similar six-pack to the witness up in Bakersfield to see if they confirm.'

She handed the sheet to Kelso and pointed out Buck Daggett's picture. 'Lester identified that man.'

Kelso shook his head and looked up.

'He made a mistake. That's all there is to it.'

Starkey put Riggio's phone bills on top of the six-pack.

'These are Charlie Riggio's cell-phone bills. Look at every phone number I've marked. That's Buck Daggett's home phone number. Riggio and Natalie Daggett were involved. Natalie Daggett confirmed this involvement to me less than an hour ago. I believe that Buck found out, and murdered Charlie because of it.'

Hooker sighed loudly.

'Oh, my Lord.'

Kelso's jaw flexed. He went to the window, looked out, then came back and leaned against his desk with his arms crossed.

'Who else knows this, Carol?'

'Only the people in this room.'

'Did you tell Natalie that you suspect Buck of the murder?'

'No.'

Kelso sighed again, then went back behind his desk.

'Okay, we can't let this sit. If Buck has explanations for these things, he can make them and clear this up.'

Marzik grunted, and Kelso's eyes flashed angrily.

'You think this is easy, Detective? *I've known this man for ten years.* This isn't just some fucking collar.'

Starkey had never heard Barry Kelso swear.

Jorge said, 'No, sir. It's not.'

Kelso glanced at Santos, then took another breath and leaned back.

'I'll have to notify Assistant Chief Morgan. Starkey, I'll want you with me. He might want to see us, and I'm damned well sure he'll have questions. This is goddamned terrible, a Los Angeles police officer involved in something like this. We'll have to bring in Dick Leyton. We're not going to roll over there and arrest one of his people without telling him what's happening. As soon as I talk to Morgan and Leyton, we'll get this done.'

Starkey found herself liking Barry Kelso. She wanted to say something.

'Lieutanant, I'm sorry.'

Kelso rubbed at his face.

'Carol, you don't have anything to be sorry for. I want to tell you that this is good work, but it doesn't seem like the thing to say.'

'Yes, sir. I understand.'

Penance

Buck didn't go back to Glendale. He phoned Dick Leyton to tell him that he'd left early for the day and wouldn't be back. The real reason for the call was to get a sense of what Leyton knew. If Leyton considered Buck a suspect, Buck was going to hire the best damned attorney he could find and ride it out straight down the middle. But Leyton was relaxed and friendly, and Buck was willing to bet the farm that Starkey had kept her suspicions to herself.

And that's what he was doing, betting the farm.

Buck still had almost seven pounds of Modex Hybrid, plus components left over from copycatting Mr Red's bomb. He convinced himself that Starkey hadn't yet gathered enough evidence to make her move, which gave him hope. If he acted fast enough and took her out before she could develop her case, he might still get out of this.

After he spoke with Leyton, Buck concocted an elaborate list of errands to get Natalie out of the house, then went home. She seemed strained, probably from Starkey's visit and questions, but he pretended not to notice. He gave her the list, kicked her out, then forced himself to calm down and think it through again. He was desperate, and scared; he knew that desperate and scared men make mistakes.

When Buck felt composed, and absolutely convinced that killing Starkey was the only way out, he said, 'Well, get to it, then.'

Buck kept the Modex Hybrid and the remaining components in a large Igloo cooler out in the garage. He backed his 4-Runner out to give himself room, then shut the overhead door so no one could see him from the street. He opened the side door that let onto his backyard for air and turned on a utility fan; the Modex sublimated vapors that were toxic.

Buck pulled the cooler from the high shelf where it was out of Natalie's reach and brought it to his workbench. The remaining Modex was in a large, nonreactive glass jar. It was dark gray in color and looked like window putty. He wore vinyl gloves as he laid out the components so as not to leave fingerprints, but also to avoid getting the Modex on his skin. The shit could kill you dead as lead just from handling it.

The sudden voice in Buck's backyard damn near made him piss his pants.

'Yo yo yo, whasup, whasup? Anybody home?'

Buck threw a towel over his bench, and went to the door. He had thought it was a black guy from the voice, but this kid was white.

'What do you want?'

'Be lookin' to earn a little extra bank, my man. Saw the yard was in, shall we say, disarray? Thought I'd offer my landscaping services.'

'I'll mow it myself, thanks anyway. Now I've got to get back to work.'

'Looks like that ain't exactly on your immediate agenda, if you see what I'm sayin'. Help a brother who wants to earn a living instead of do crime.'

Buck's head began to throb. Now that he looked at him, this kid wasn't a kid. He looked to be in his late twenties.

'Help yourself by getting out of here, asshole. I said I was busy.'

The kid took a step back, but didn't look scared.

'Yowza! Guess you be handin' out walkin' papers. Feets, do yo stuff!'

'Are you fuckin' crazy?'

'Nah, Mr Daggett, I'm just tryin' to have a good time. Sorry I bothered you.'

Buck caught the name right away.

'How'd you know my name?'

'Chinaman across the street told me. I tried to cut his place first, but he told me to come over here. He said your place always looks like shit.'

'Well, fuck him, too. Now let me get back to work.'

Buck watched the kid walk away, then went back into his garage, hating the Chinaman across the street. Buck didn't see the kid come back, didn't see the hard thing that knocked him to his knees. Even if he had seen it coming, it would not have mattered. It was already too late.

Buck was never fully unconscious. He knew that something had hit him, and that he was hit twice more after he went down. He saw the kid over him, but he couldn't raise his arms to protect himself. The kid handcuffed him to the workbench, then disappeared from view.

Buck tried to speak, but his mouth didn't work any better than his arms and legs. Buck grew frightened that he was paralysed, and cried.

After a while, the kid came back and shook him.

'You awake?'

The kid looked into his eyes, then slapped him. The kid had a thin, gaunt face like a ferret. Buck noticed now for the first time that his scalp was very pale; he hadn't been bald for long.

'You awake? C'mon, I know I didn't hit you hard enough to kill you. Get your fuckin' act together.'

'I don't have any money.'

'I don't want your money, dumbass. You should be so lucky, I only wanted your money.'

Buck's ears were ringing, a steady high-pitched sound that did not diminish. Once, during a high school baseball game, he had collided with another player and gotten a concussion. He remembered it feeling like this.

'Then what do you want? You want the truck, the keys are in my pocket. Take it.'

'What I'm going to *take* is the rest of this Modex. What I *want* is to teach you a lesson.'

Buck wasn't thinking at his best. It surprised him that this kid made up like some kind of black rapper would know about the Modex, or even what it was.

'I don't understand.'

The kid took Buck's face in his hands and leaned close.

'You stole my fucking work, you cocksucker. You *pretended* to be me. Can you spell . . . *error in judgment*?'

'I don't know what in hell you're talking about.'

'Maybe this will help you understand.'

The kid went to the other end of the bench. When he came back, he had one of the pipes. Wires led into an open end; the other end had been capped. He waved it under Buck's nose to let Buck catch the sharp smell of the Modex inside, and in that moment, Buck grew scared.

'*Now* do you know who I am?'

Buck knew, and felt so scared in that moment of knowing that the urine ran out of him in a rush of warmth.

'Please don't kill me. Please. Take the fucking Modex and go. Please don't kill me. I'm sorry I pretended I was you but you see I had to kill that motherfucker who was fucking my wife and—'

Mr Red put a hand over Buck's mouth.

'Chill. Just be cool. Relax.'

Buck nodded.

'You okay now?'

Buck nodded.

'Okay. Now listen.'

Mr Red sat cross-legged on the hard concrete in front of him, holding the bomb in his lap as if it was a playful kitten.

'You listening?'

'Yes.'

'I'm not going to kid you about this, I am seriously pissed off you tried to make everyone think it was me who killed that guy, but here's your shot. You got one shot, and here it is.'

Buck waited, but Mr Red was waiting for him to ask.

'What? What's my shot?'

'Tell me what Carol Starkey knows.'

John walked out to the stolen car he'd left on the street. The Chinaman was nowhere to be seen. He had left Buck at his bench, very much alive, but unconscious. John had splashed some water on Daggett and slapped his face to bring him around. When he saw that Buck was waking up, he left.

John climbed behind the wheel, started his car, and shook his head. It was a hot day on a crappy street in the middle of Shitsville, USA. How could people live like this? John let his car creep down the street as he counted to a hundred. When he reached one hundred, he figured Buck was fully awake.

That's when he pressed the silver button.

Spring Street

Marzik and Santos phoned their homes, Santos telling his wife and Marzik her mother that they would be late. Starkey could tell from Marzik's reaction that her mother wasn't happy about it. After those calls, the three detectives sat at their desks, alone with their thoughts. At one point, Jorge asked if anyone wanted a fresh pot of coffee, but neither Starkey nor Marzik answered. He did not make the coffee.

Marzik was the first one bored with the wait, and expressed her annoyance.

'What in hell is taking so long? We don't need Parker Center to rubber-stamp this thing. Let's just go pick up the sonofabitch.'

Santos frowned at her.

'He wants Morgan to sign off, is all. It's politics.'

'Kelso's such a chickenshit.'

'Maybe Morgan isn't there. Maybe he can't reach Lieutenant Leyton.'

'Oh, screw that.'

Starkey had decided to head for the stairwell with a cigarette when Reege Phillips called. The tone of his voice was careful and measured, which immediately put her on edge. She didn't want Hooker and Marzik to hear.

Starkey said, 'I don't know that I can talk right now, Reege. Will this keep?'

'I don't think so, Carol. You got a problem on your hands.'

'Ah, can I call you right back?'

'You want to change phones?'

'That's right. I've got your number.'

'Okay. I'm right here.'

Starkey hung up, told Santos and Marzik she was going for a smoke, and brought her purse. When she was in the stairwell, she called Phillips on her cell phone. Just pressing the numbers left her feeling sick.

'What do you mean, that I have a problem?'

'Jack Pell isn't an ATF agent. He used to be, but not anymore.'

'That can't be right. Pell had bomb analysis reports from Rockville. He had a spook at Cal Tech doing work for us.'

'Just listen. Pell was an ATF field agent working for the Violent Crime Task Force, attached to the Organized Crime Division of the Justice Department. Twenty months ago, he was in a warehouse in Newark, New Jersey, trying to get the goods on some Chinese AKs coming up from Cuba. You read those reports he gave you?'

'Yes.'

'Think Newark.'

'Mr Red's first bomb.'

'Pell was in that warehouse when it went off. The concussion caused something in his eyes called commotio retinae. You catch it in time, you can fix it with the laser. Pell's didn't show up until later, and then it was too late.'

'What does that mean, too late?'

'He's going blind. Way the man explained it is that the retinas are pulling away from his optic nerves, and there's nothing they can do to stop it. So the Bureau retired him. Now you're telling me he's acting like he's still on the job. You got a rogue agent on your hands, Carol. He's hunting down the bastard who took his eyes. You call the FO and get them in on this before Pell hurts somebody.'

Starkey leaned against the wall, feeling numb.

'Carol? You there?'

'I'll take care of it, Reege. Thank you.'

'You want me to get the office on this?'

'No. No, I'll do it. Listen, I've gotta go, Reege. We have something here.'

'You watch out for that guy, Carol. He's looking to kill that sonofabitch. No tellin' what he might do. He might even kill you.'

After she ended the call, Starkey finished her cigarette, then went back into the squad room. She must have looked odd.

Marzik said, 'What's wrong with you?'

'Nothing.'

Finally, Kelso's door opened and Kelso stepped out. Starkey could see that something was wrong with him, but Marzik was already halfway to the stairs, muttering.

'It's about goddamned time.'

'Beth, wait.'

Kelso stared at them. He didn't speak; he didn't move for the longest time.

Santos said, 'What is it, Lieutenant?'

Kelso cleared his throat. His jaw worked as if he were trying to make spit.

'Detectives, the San Gabriel police were notified that an explosion occurred at Buck's home. He was pronounced dead at the scene.'

18

By the time they reached Daggett's home, the San Gabriel Fire Department had the fire out. The garage and the back side of the house were still venting steam, but the Sheriff's bomb investigators were already walking the scene. Starkey wanted to walk with them, but the commander of the Sheriff's Bomb Squad refused to clear her onto the site until the body had been removed. Only Kelso was allowed in the rear. Dick Leyton had arrived a few minutes before them.

Starkey, Marzik, and Santos stood in a tight knot in the front yard, Santos talking to burn off the nervous energy.

'Do you think he killed himself? That's what happens when you get close, you know?'

'I don't know.'

'You hear that a lot with officers. They realize they're about to take the fall, bang, they kill themselves.'

Starkey, feeling bad enough, walked away.

'I wonder if he killed his wife, too.'

Marzik put a hand on his shoulder.

'Jorge? Shut the fuck up.'

Starkey's first thought had also been suicide, but that was something they might never know unless Daggett left a note. If he didn't, the rubble would be sifted, the frag collected, the device reconstructed as with any other bomb. They would try to place the moment of detonation and determine if it had been accidental, or by design. Starkey knew it would all be a matter of guesswork.

Waiting there on the street, Starkey's thoughts drifted back to Pell. She considered paging him, but didn't know what she would say if he returned her call. She put it out of her head. She was getting good at that, putting things out of her head.

After a while, Kelso came up the drive past Buck's 4-Runner and waved them to join him.

'How many bodies?'

'Just Buck. It looks like Natalie wasn't home. We don't yet know if she left before it happened or after, but her car is missing.'

Starkey felt some of her tension ease, though not much. She had been worried that Buck and Natalie had gone together.

Kelso looked at Starkey.

'The thinking now is that it was a suicide. I want you to be ready for that, Carol. We can't be sure yet, but that's what it looks like.'

Marzik said, 'Why?'

'He wrote something on the wall above his workbench. The spray paint is still tacky. We can't be sure it's a suicide note, but it could be.'

Starkey took a deep breath.

'Does it mention me?'

'No. All it says is, "The truth hurts." That's all it says.'

The San Gabriel coroner investigators wheeled a gurney bearing a blue plastic body bag to their van. The bag was misshapen and wet.

Kelso started back down the drive.

'Come on. We can go back now. I want to warn you all that it's a mess. His body was badly dislocated. Also, I want you to remember that this is not our crime scene. The Sheriff's investigators are talking to Dick Leyton now, and they will want to talk to us. Stay close.'

Santos looked sad.

'So Carol was right.'

Marzik frowned at him.

'Of course she was right, you idiot.'

'I was hoping that ... even with everything we know, I guess I was hoping she was wrong.'

Marzik stopped, and waved them on.

'Screw it. I don't want to see all that blood. I'm going to stay out here.'

They walked back along the drive past the firemen and the San Gabriel Bomb Squad. Under other circumstances, at another crime scene, Starkey would have talked to these people, but she ignored them. Dick Leyton was in the backyard with a couple of San Gabriel suits that Starkey took to be Sheriff's investigators. Kelso and Santos joined them, leaving Starkey alone. She was glad for that. She didn't want to look at these things, and think the things that she was thinking, and have to talk to anyone. She wished she hadn't heard all that crap about suicide because now she was feeling guilty about it.

The drive and the buildings were wet. The firemen were cranking in their hoses, moving in teams around Buck's 4-Runner and away from the garage. Starkey stepped off the drive to make way for them and felt the water squish up around her shoes. The aluminum garage door had been pulled out of its frame by the fire department. Starkey could see that it had been down at the time of the detonation by the way the aluminum panels were bowed outward. The firemen would have wanted to raise it to get water on the flames, but couldn't; they had probably set grappling hooks to pull it away. Inside the garage, the Sheriff's bomb investigators were sifting and photographing the debris exactly as Starkey and her people had done in Silver Lake. The air in the garage was damp, and heavy with the scent of burned wood.

The spray-painted words were above his bench.

THE TRUTH HURTS

They were red.

'You one of the L.A. people?'

Starkey showed her badge.

'Yeah. CCS. You mind if I look?'

'Just tell us before you touch anything, okay?'

Starkey nodded.

A half-moon shape like a jagged crown of splinters was blown out of Buck's workbench. Wooden shrapnel sprouted from the inner garage walls like porcupine quills. Much of the bench was charred from the fire, but not the area shattered by the blast. Something had hit the far wall and left a red smear. Starkey concentrated on the painted words. THE TRUTH HURTS. It could mean anything or nothing. What truth? The truth that was about to come out? The truth that his wife loved another man? That Pell had lied to Starkey, and used her?

Starkey said, 'How do you call the scene?'

'Too early for that.'

'I know it's too early, but I haven't seen the body. You have, so you probably have an idea.'

The investigator didn't stop what he was doing to offer his opinion. Like any investigator, he wanted to finish his work and get the hell out.

'Judging from the way he came apart, I'd say he was right on top of it, there at his bench. His lower extremities are fine except for the wood frag they caught. Most of the damage was in his chest and abdomen. He was damn near eviscerated, which suggests he had the device against his stomach when it went off. If it was a suicide, well, I guess he figured tucking it into his stomach was the way to go. If it was accidental, he was probably setting the leg wires into the detonator and he caught a spark. That would be my guess.'

Starkey tried to picture Buck Daggett stupid enough to wire a charge with the batteries connected, but couldn't. Of course, she also couldn't picture Buck building bombs to murder someone.

Starkey walked back out onto the drive to consider the scene. She tried to get a sense of the pressure release. The garage door had been bowed, the side door blown out, and Buck Daggett seriously injured, but the structural damage was minor. She guessed the energy released was about as much as two hand grenades. Big enough, but not on the order of what killed Charlie Riggio or what Tennant was using to blow apart cars.

Kelso called out to her.

'Starkey, come over here.'

'Just a minute.'

The side door had been blown off its hinges and cracked by the pressure change, which meant the door had been closed. She could understand that Buck would want the garage door closed so that his neighbors couldn't see what he was doing, but it didn't make sense that he would close the side door. She knew that he was working either with Modex or RDX, and either one threw some pretty nasty fumes.

Starkey went back inside to the investigator.

'Your Bomb Squad recover any undetonated explosive?'

'Nope. What was here is what went up. They ran a dog through, too, before they let in the coroner's people. You just missed him. Those dogs are something to see.'

'What about his hands?'

'You mean the injuries?'

'Yeah.'

'They were intact. We noted some lacerations and tissue loss, but they were still on. I know what you're thinking, that the hands should've gone, but if he was hunched over it, it kinda depends what he was doing when the charge let go.'

Starkey couldn't see it. If Buck had committed suicide, she thought that he would have been gripping the bomb, holding it tight against his body to make sure he died quickly. His hands would have been gone. If he was seating a detonator in the charge and the explosive had set off accidentally, his hands would still be gone.

'Starkey.'

Starkey had an uneasy feeling as she joined Kelso and the others in the yard. She kept thinking about the red paint, and that Mr Red claimed to know who had imitated him. How could Mr Red know that? From Tennant?

The two suits were Sheriff's Homicide detectives named Connelly and Gerald. Connelly was a large, serious man; Gerald had the empty eyes of a man who had been on the job too long. Starkey didn't like being around him.

After the introductions, Kelso told Starkey that Connelly and Gerald wanted to interview her. They exchanged cards, Connelly saying that they would be in contact sometime within the next few days.

Gerald said, 'Maybe there's something you can help us with right now.'

'If I can.'

'Did you see Sergeant Daggett earlier today?'

'Not today. I saw him yesterday.'

'You see any bruises or contusions on his face or head?'

Starkey glanced at Kelso, who was staring at her.

'I didn't see anything like that. I can't say about today, but there was nothing like that yesterday.'

Gerald touched the left side of his forehead.

'Daggett has a lump here that shows edema and bruising. We're wondering when he got it.'

'I don't know.'

She wasn't liking this. First Tennant blows up, now Daggett blows himself up. Mr Red claims he knows the copycat, and how could he know except through Tennant?

Starkey looked back at the garage.

'It wasn't a very big charge.'

Gerald made a grin like a nasty shark.

'You didn't see the body. It blew that poor fucker to shit.'

Starkey forgot about Gerald and spoke to Kelso.

'I got a description from the bomb investigator in there, Barry. Daggett shows the injuries because of his proximity, but I don't think it was much of a blast. I can't know for sure how much RDX Tennant had, but it was more than this.'

Kelso squinted at her.

'Are you saying that some explosive is missing?'

'I don't know.'

Starkey walked back to the street to smoke. Everything had come to an end that wasn't really an ending. She kept thinking about the contusion on Buck's head, and about his hands. His hands should be gone. She found herself wondering what Tennant had used to blow himself up, and how he had gotten it. It took enormous energy to blow a man's arms off. She didn't like the little questions that had no answers. They were like reconstructing a bomb, only to find that there are wires that lead nowhere. You couldn't pretend they didn't exist. Wires always led somewhere. When you were dealing with bombs, wires always led to someplace bad. She thought about Pell.

Marzik came up, shaking her head.

'Was it bad?'

'Not too bad. We've both seen worse.'

'It must have been pretty goddamned bad. You're crying.'

Starkey turned away.

Marzik cleared her throat, embarrassed.

'I didn't want to see all that mess. I've got enough mess to last me into my next life. Let me have a cigarette.'

Starkey looked at her, surprised.

'You don't smoke.'

'I haven't smoked in six years. Are you going to give me one of those things or do I have to buy it from you?'

Starkey gave her the pack.

They heard Natalie's screams before they saw her, coming from the cordon at the end of the street. Natalie tried to push past the officers, struggling to get to her home. An older woman, probably a neighbor, wrapped Natalie in her arms as Dick Leyton ran to her from the front of the house. Later, Starkey knew, a San Gabriel detective would question her, asking about the explosives, asking if Buck had talked about suicide. Starkey was relieved that she would not have to ask those questions, and guilty for feeling that relief.

Marzik shook her head.

'Could this get any worse?'

Starkey knew that it could. She crushed out her cigarette.

'Beth, get a ride back with Kelso, okay? I'm taking the car.'

'Where are you going?'

Starkey walked faster.

All the small, odd things about Pell made sense now; the shitty motel, him needing her to run the NLETS search and the evidence transfer, the way he had lost it with Tennant. Driving to his motel, Starkey tried to put herself into the same mind-set that she used when she was de-arming bombs. It had always felt to her, then, as a kind of separation. As if she was in some other dimension, safe and secure, from where she used her body to handle the bomb like a flesh-and-bone robot, devoid of feelings. She tried to get to that place, but failed. It wasn't so easy to separate herself from her feelings anymore.

Starkey parked outside the motel, used her cell phone to call him. The phone rang ten times before the hotel operator, a tired male voice, asked if she'd like to leave a message. Starkey hung up, then went inside, walking past the lobby as if she knew where she was going. She knew Pell's room number from calling him there, found the room, then searched the halls until she found a housekeeper. Starkey tried to make herself look pleasant, an expression she didn't trust herself to pull off.

'Hi, I'm Mrs Pell, in 112. My husband has both keys, and he's not here right now. Could you let me in?'

'Wass you name?'

'Pell. P-e-l-l. It's room 112.'

The housekeeper, a young Latina, looked up the room on her clipboard. 'Shoe. I let you in.'

The housekeeper keyed the lock, then stepped out of the way as Starkey entered. Mr Red's words echoed in her brain.

He is using you, Carol Starkey. He has been playing us against each other.

The computer was sitting on a spindly desk against the wall. Identical to her computer. The same. She turned it on. The same icons on the screen. She opened them. The same doorway to Claudius.

Starkey turned to the bed. It was rumpled, and smelled of sweat. A thought came: *I would have slept in that bed.* Words lost like a whisper on a breeze.

She searched the room. She did not know what she was looking for, nor what she might find, but she went through the bathroom, the chest and desk, and his suitcase without finding anything more. Again in the center of the room, she tried to decide if she should wait or go. She was walking to the door when she turned to the closet, and searched the pockets of his clothes there. A plastic Ziploc baggie was in the inner pocket of his leather jacket. A piece of frag. She unzipped the plastic, dropped the fragment into her palm, and saw the letters:

TARKEY

Her hands and forearms tingled as if the blood had been cut off. It didn't matter that it was Buck Daggett who had etched her name to mislead them; Pell had thought that Mr Red had built the bomb. Sitting in Barrigan's, he had *known*. That night in her house, holding her, he had believed that she was the target. And he had hidden that from her. He had used her.

'What are you doing here?'

Pell stood in the door. His face was pale, cut with hollows. He looked like a hundred-year-old man waiting for his second stroke. Now that she understood that he was a victim just as she was a victim, some deep part of her felt the urge to soothe him. She called herself a fool.

'You bastard.'

She didn't slap him. She used her fist. She hit him hard in the mouth, making him bleed.

Starkey held up the bit of black metal.

'Where did you get this? The medical examiner? The *first* goddamned day you were here?'

Pell didn't move. He didn't even seem to feel the blow.

'Carol, I'm sorry.'

'What was I, Jack? Bait? All along you thought he was after me, and you didn't warn me?' She pointed at the computer. 'You've been on that damned thing trying to make him come for me, *and you didn't warn me!*'

He shook his head, his silence making her even more angry.

'*IT WASN'T MR RED!* Buck Daggett killed Riggio, and now Buck is dead!'

'It's Mr Red.'

She hit him again.

'*STOP SAYING THAT.*'

The housekeeper appeared in the hall, staring with wide eyes. Starkey forced herself to calm.

'Charlie was having an affair with Buck's wife, so Buck killed him. An eyewitness in Bakersfield put Buck at Tennant's shop. That's where Buck got the materials to make the bomb. We were on our way to arrest Buck when he was killed in his own garage with those same materials. *IT WASN'T MR RED.*'

Pell moved past her to sit on the edge of his bed.

'Is that why you came here? To tell me that?'

'No. I know that you're not on active duty anymore, and I know why. I'm sorry about your eyes. I really am, Jack, but you're already blind. You can't even see that we're killing people.'

'What are you talking about?'

'Dallas Tennant. Buck Daggett. If they didn't do it to themselves, then someone did it to them. What if we drew Mr Red here, and they're dead because of us?'

'If he's here, then we can catch him.'

Starkey felt sad for him.

'Not you, Jack. That part of it is over. I'm going to tell Barry. He's going to call the ATF field office. What you do about that is up to you. I wanted you to know it was coming.'

Pell started toward her, but Starkey shook her head.

'Don't.'

'I wasn't going to ask you not to.'

'It doesn't matter what you were going to do. What matters is what you did. I have tried for so long to feel nothing, but I opened myself to you, and you used me. Three years, I finally take a step, and it was a lie.'

'That isn't true.'

'Don't say that. It doesn't matter if you felt something for me. Don't tell me if you did, because that will just make this harder.'

To his credit, he nodded.

'I know.'

It was harder than Starkey thought it would be, to tell him these things. More difficult because she had expected that he would argue with her, or be defensive, but he wasn't. He seemed hurt and confused.

'I believe that everyone has a secret heart, a heart deep down inside where we keep our secret selves. I think our secret hearts see things that our eyes can't. Maybe mine saw that you had been hurt the way I had been hurt. Like we were kindred spirits. Maybe that's why I let myself feel again. I only wish mine could have seen that you were lying to me.'

When she looked at him again, tears had filled his eyes. She had to turn away from him. All of this was so much harder than it should have been.

'That's what I came here to say. Good-bye, Jack.'

Starkey put the fragment bearing her name on the desk, then walked out.

Starkey signed on to Claudius as soon as she reached home. The chat-room occupancy counter showed four people, none of whom was Mr Red. She didn't bother to read what they were writing. She typed three words.

HOTLOAD: **Talk to me.**

The others responded, but no message from him appeared.

HOTLOAD: I know you're there. TALK TO ME!

The window appeared. He was waiting for her.

WILL YOU ACCEPT MESSAGES FROM MR RED?

Starkey slapped the mouse to open the message window. The conversation would be between only them. Private.

MR RED: Hello, Carol Starkey. I have been waiting for you.

Starkey closed her eyes to calm herself. She waited until she was ready.

HOTLOAD: Did you kill him?
MR RED: I have smoked much ass in my time. Be specific.
HOTLOAD: You know who I mean, you fuck. Daggett.
MR RED: Oooo. I like it when you talk dirty.
HOTLOAD: DID YOU KILL HIM?
MR RED: Now she's shouting. If I shout back, you won't like it, babe.
   My voice is EXPLOSIVE.

Starkey went into the kitchen, mixed a tall drink. She downed two Tagamet, telling herself that she had to stay calm and control the conversation.
She returned to the computer.

HOTLOAD: Did you kill him?
MR RED: Do you want the truth, Carol Starkey? Or do you want me to
   tell you what you want to hear?
HOTLOAD: The truth.
MR RED: The truth is real. Real things are a commodity. If I answer
   this question for you, you must answer a question for me. Do you
   agree?
HOTLOAD: Yes.
MR RED: The truth hurts.

She knew that he had given his answer. He had written that on Buck Daggett's wall. *The truth hurts.*
Calmly, she typed.

HOTLOAD: Fuck you.
MR RED: In my dreams, you do.
HOTLOAD: Why did you do this?
MR RED: He took my name in vain, CS. You're smart enough to know
   that he murdered Riggio, aren't you?

HOTLOAD: I know what he did.

MR RED: Do you know this? He was building a second bomb when I found him. He was going to do to you exactly what he had done to Riggio.

HOTLOAD: You can't know that.

MR RED: He gave his confession. Moments before I knocked him out, laid him across the device he had built, and set it off.

The screen blurred through Starkey's tears. She had more of the drink, then wiped her eyes.

HOTLOAD: Is this my fault?

MR RED: Do I detect the faint aroma of . . . guilt?

HOTLOAD: Was it because of me and Pell? Did we draw you here?

MR RED: You've had your question. Now it's time for mine.

Starkey composed herself.

HOTLOAD: All right.

MR RED: By now, you must know that Pell is not who he claims. You know that he is one of my first victims. You know that he is outside the law.

HOTLOAD: I know.

MR RED: You know he was using you.

It took Starkey a moment to compose herself.

HOTLOAD: Get to your question.

He let her wait. Starkey knew that he wanted her to ask again, but she didn't. She decided that she would sit there the rest of her life and not ask him. She was tired of being manipulated.

Finally, he couldn't stand it anymore.

MR RED: How does it feel to be used by a man you love?

Starkey read the question and felt nothing. She knew that he wanted a reaction, but she would not give him the satisfaction.

HOTLOAD: I am going to arrest you.

MR RED: I am laughing. Ha ha.

HOTLOAD: Laugh now, cry later.

MR RED: My work here is done, Carol Starkey. I have enjoyed you. Good-bye.

Starkey knew that there would be no more messages that night. She turned off the computer, then sat in her silent house, smoking. She went to her answering machine and played the messages that Pell had left. She played them over and over, listening to his voice. It hurt.

19

Starkey drank for most of the night, smoking an endless chain of cigarettes that left her home cloudy and gray. She fell asleep twice, both times dreaming of Sugar again and the day in the trailer park. The sleep was anguished, only lasting for a few minutes at a time. Once, she woke seeing the trailer with red words painted on its side: THE TRUTH HURTS. That was the end of the sleep.

She decided that she would tell Kelso first thing in the morning. There wasn't anything else to do. The investigation had to turn back to Mr Red, and it had to turn quickly if they were to have any chance of catching him. She thought she knew how.

At ten minutes after five that morning, she paged Warren Mueller. She was too drunk to give a damn about the time. Her phone rang twelve minutes later, a groggy voice on the other end of the line.

'Damn, Mueller, I didn't expect you to call until later. I guess you sleep with your pager right there by your bed.'

'Starkey? Do you know what time it is?'

'Listen, I know how Tennant got the explosives that he blew himself up with. He got them from Mr Red. Red went in there to see him.'

She could hear Mueller clearing his throat.

'How do you know that?'

'He told me.'

'Tennant?'

'No, Warren, Mr Red. There's two things you need to do. First, you want to check the video record for whoever went in there to see him in the past couple of days. And here's the other thing, and this is important. You know Tennant's scrapbook?'

'I don't know what in hell you're talking about.'

'You never went to see Tennant there?'

'Why in the hell would I go see him?'

'He had a scrapbook, Mueller. A collection of clippings and junk about bomb incidents. Anyone who went in there to see him had to look at that damned book. Get the book. Have it printed and run every print you find. There's no way Red went to see him and didn't touch that book.'

She described the book in detail, giving Mueller the rest of the facts. After that, she showered, dressed, and packed up the computer. She would need it when she explained to Kelso about Claudius. The last things she did before leaving were fill her flask and drop a fresh pack of Tagamet into her purse.

Starkey timed her arrival at Spring Street so that Kelso would be in his office. She didn't want to get into the office first and have to make conversation with Marzik and Hooker. She wedged her car into the parking lot next to Marzik's, gathered up the computer, and brought it with her.

Hooker was at his desk.

'Hey, Hook. Is Kelso in?'

'Yeah.'

'Where's Beth?'

'The ladies' room.'

Starkey loved Jorge. He was the last man in America who called it the ladies' room.

Starkey went out to the bathroom, where she found Marzik smoking. Marzik fanned the air before she realized it was Starkey, and looked guilty.

'This is your fault.'

'Why don't you just go in the stairwell?'

'I don't want anyone to know. Six years I've been off these damned things.'

'Throw it away and come inside. I've got to see Kelso, and I want you and Hooker with me.'

'Jesus, I just lit the damned thing.'

'For God's sake, Beth, please.'

Even when Starkey was loving Marzik, she hated her.

Starkey didn't wait for Hooker and Marzik to get themselves together; she didn't want the three of them trooping into his office like a bunch of ducks in a row. She knocked on the door, then pushed her way inside with the computer. Kelso eyed it because he knew that Starkey didn't own a computer and knew nothing about them.

'Barry, I need to see you.'

'You and I have a meeting with Chief Morgan later. He wants to be briefed before the press conference. He also wants to congratulate you, Carol. He told me that. Everyone except you was running off half-cocked about Mr Red, and you broke this case. I think he's going to bump you to D-3.'

Starkey put the computer on his desk. Both Marzik and Hooker came in behind her.

'Okay, Barry, we can do that. But I have to tell you some things first, and I want Beth and Jorge to hear it, too. Buck didn't kill himself. It wasn't an accident. Mr Red killed him.'

Kelso glanced at Marzik and Santos, then frowned at Starkey.

'Maybe I'm confused. Weren't you the one who said that Mr Red wasn't involved here?'

'Mr Red did not kill Charlie Riggio. That was Buck. Buck copycatted Red's M.O. to cover the murder, just like we proved.'

'Then what in hell are you talking about?'

'Mr Red didn't like someone pretending to be him. He came here to find that person. He did.'

Santos said, 'Carol, how do you know that?'

Starkey pointed at the computer.

'He admitted it to me on that through Claudius. Mr Red and I have been in personal contact now for almost a week.'

Kelso's face closed into an unreadable scowl as she told them about the entire avenue of the investigation that she had held secret, and how, through Claudius, it had led to her contact with Mr Red. Kelso only stopped her once, when she was telling them about Jack Pell.

'How long have you known that Pell is not a representative of the ATF?'

'Since yesterday. I confronted him about it last night.'

'You are sure about this? You are *positive* that this man is functioning without authority?'

'Yes.'

Kelso's jaw flexed. His nostrils flared as he drew a deep breath. When Starkey glanced at Hooker and Marzik, they both stared at the floor.

She said, 'Barry, I'm sorry. I was wrong for playing it this way, and I apologize. But we still have a shot at Mr Red. Buck had more Modex. I'm sure he had more, and I think Red took it.'

'Did Red tell you this?'

'We don't have conversations. It's not like we tell each other secrets; he taunts me, he teases me. We have this, I don't know what you would call it, a relationship. That's why Pell and I went on-line like this, to try to bring him out. I'm sure I can contact him again. We can work him, Barry. We can catch the sonofabitch.'

Kelso nodded, but he wasn't nodding agreement. She could see that in his face. He was angry, and probably nodding to something he had thought.

'We look like fools.'

Starkey took a breath.

'You don't, Barry. I do.'

'That's where you're wrong, Detective. I'm going to call Morgan. I want you to wait outside. Don't go anywhere. Don't do anything. Marzik, Santos, that's you, too.'

They nodded.

'Did either of you know about this?'

Starkey said, 'No.'

'Goddamnit, I'm not asking you.'

Marzik said, 'No, sir.'

'No, sir.'

'Wait outside.'

As Starkey was walking out, Kelso stopped her.

'One more thing. At any time during your, I don't know what to call them, conversations? At any time when you were talking to that murderer, did you impart or reveal any, and I mean anything at all, information about this investigation?'

'No, Barry, I did not.'

'Starkey. Never call me by my first name again.'

Outside, Starkey apologized to Santos and Marzik. Santos nodded glumly, then went to his desk and lapsed into silence. Marzik was livid and didn't try to hide it.

'If you cost me a promotion, I'm going to kick your drunken ass. I knew you were fucking that bastard.'

Starkey didn't bother to argue. She sat at her desk and waited.

Kelso's door remained closed for almost forty-five minutes. When it opened, Starkey, Marzik, and Santos all rose, but Kelso froze Marzik and Santos with a glance.

'Not you. Starkey, inside.'

When she went in, he closed the door. She had never seen him as angry as he was right now.

He said, 'You're finished. You are suspended immediately, and you will be brought up on professional-conduct charges, as well as charges of compromising this investigation. I have already spoken to IAG. They will contact you directly, and you will be subject to their administrative orders. If any criminal charges arise from the subsequent investigation, you will be prosecuted to the full extent of the law. I would advise you to contact a lawyer today.'

Starkey went numb.

'Barry, I know I fucked up, but Mr Red is still out there. He has more Modex. We can't just stop; we can't just end it like this.'

'The only thing at an end is you. You're done. The rest of us are going to continue doing our jobs.'

'Damnit, I *am* the investigation. *I can get to him*, Barry. You want to fire me, fine, fire me after we get the sonofabitch!'

Kelso slowly crossed his arms, considering her.

'*You* are the investigation? That's the most arrogant, self-centered statement I've ever heard from a detective on this department.'

'Barry, I didn't mean it like that. You know I didn't mean it like that.'

'I *know* you took it upon yourself to conduct an investigation independent of my office. I know – because you told me so – that you secretly set about baiting the murderer we were all supposed to be trying to find. Maybe, if you had come to me, we would have done that anyway, but we don't *know* that. And now, according to you, I know that Buck Daggett is dead by that man's hand. How does that feel, Carol, knowing that you may have cost Buck his life?'

Starkey blinked hard, trying to stop the tears that filled her eyes. *The truth hurts.* But there it was.

'It feels just like you think it feels. Please don't, Barry. Please let me stay and help you catch this guy. I need to.'

Kelso took a deep breath, stood, then went behind his desk and took his seat.

'You're dismissed.'

Starkey moved for the computer. She needed the computer to get to Mr Red.

'That stays.'

Starkey left the computer on his desk and walked out.

20

Marzik was at her desk; Santos wasn't in the squad room. Starkey thought about telling Marzik what had happened, but decided to hell with it. Later, when everyone had calmed, she thought she might call.

'Good-bye, Beth.'

Marzik didn't respond. So far as Starkey could tell, she didn't even look.

Starkey worked her car out of the parking garage and drove out into the city with no idea of what to do or where to go. She had expected that Kelso would punish her, that there would be a suspension and loss of pay, but she never thought that he would jerk her from the investigation. She was too much a part of it, had too much of herself invested in it. Everything she had was invested in it. In Mr Red. Thinking that, she felt the tears, and angrily fought them back. Pell was probably telling himself the same thing.

Starkey fished her flask from beneath the seat, propped it between her legs. She lit a cigarette, blowing a geyser of smoke out the window. The flask was real. She wanted the drink. She squeezed the flask hard between her legs and thought, *Oh, for Christ's sake.* She shoved it back under the seat.

She drove to the top of Griffith Park. The place was crawling with tourists. It was hot; the smog was so thick it hung like a mist, hiding the buildings. Starkey watched the tourists trying to see the city through the curtain of crap in the air. They probably couldn't see more than two or three miles out into the basin. It was like staring at lung cancer. Starkey thought, *Here, here's some more.* She lit a fresh cigarette.

She told herself to stop it. She was acting like an ass. She knew that it was Buck Daggett. Whatever Buck had done, it was eating her up that she might have played a role in his death. It was Pell, because the rotten prick had meant something to her, even more than she cared to admit.

Starkey bought a Diet Coke at the concession stand and was walking to the top of the observatory when her pager buzzed. She recognized Mueller's number by the area code. When she reached the top, she called him.

'It's Starkey.'

'You're gonna be the FBI's cover girl.'

'The book?'

'Oh, baby. Was that a call, or was that a call? We got a clean set, eight out of ten digits, both thumbs. You know the bastard went in there posing as Tennant's attorney? Can you believe the balls?'

'Warren? Is there a surveillance tape?'

'Yeah. We've got that, too. The SLO field office is all over this thing. Starkey, the feds up here are creaming their pants. We got his ID. Listen to this, John Michael Fowles, age twenty-eight. No criminal record of any kind. Had his prints in the federal casket because he enlisted in the Navy when he was eighteen, but washed out as unsuitable for service. He used to start fires in the goddamned barracks.'

Starkey was breathing hard, like a horse wanting to get into the race.

'Warren, listen, I want you to call CCS down here and give them this information, okay? I'm off the investigation.'

'What in hell are you talking about?'

'I fucked up. It's my fault. I would tell you about it, but I just can't right now. Would you call them, please? They're going to need this.'

'Listen, Starkey, whatever you did, they gotta be crazy. I just want you to know that. You're a top cop.'

'Will you call them?'

Starkey felt as if the world was shifting away beneath her feet, sliding out to sea and leaving her behind.

'Yeah. Yeah, sure, I'll do that.'

'I'll talk to you later about it.'

'Starkey?'

'What?'

'Look, you just take care of yourself, okay?'

'Good-bye, Sergeant.'

Starkey closed her phone and watched the tourists putting dimes into the telescopes so they could get a better view of the smog. John Michael Fowles. She saw John Michael hunched over his computer, waiting for Hotload to sign on. She saw him building his bomb with Buck Daggett's leftover Modex. She saw him targeting another bomb technician and waiting to punch the button that would tear someone apart. She wanted to be on that computer with him. She wanted to finish the job she had started, but Kelso had cut her out of it.

No.

There was another way.

She opened her phone again, and called Pell.

Pell

Pell left the motel. He knew that once the local ATF field office was informed that an agent was illegally prosecuting a case, they would act quickly to investigate. He assumed that Starkey would identify his hotel, so he moved. He didn't know what he would do or where he would go, but he was certain that his pursuit of Mr Red was at its end. Now that he was found out, the local field offices around the country would be notified, as well as the bomb units of every police force in America. He was done.

He decided not to run. His retinas would soon detach completely, and irreparably – and that would be that. He thought he might wait a day or two, hoping that Starkey and the L.A. cops could bag Mr Red, and then he would turn himself in. Fuck it. There ain't no prize for second place.

He felt no loss at missing Mr Red. That part of it surprised him. For almost two years, his private pursuit had been his consuming passion. Now, well, it just didn't matter. The loss he felt was for Starkey. The regret he felt was for the pain he had caused her.

Pell checked into a different hotel, then drove aimlessly until he found himself at a diner on the water in Santa Monica. He had gone there to see the ocean. He thought that he should probably try to see as many things as possible while he was still able, but once there he hadn't even bothered to get a table facing outward. He sat at the counter, thinking that he might try to stay in Los Angeles. At least long enough to try to make peace with Starkey. Maybe he could apologize. If he couldn't make it right, maybe he could make her hate him less.

When his pager vibrated, he recognized her number, and thought that she might be calling to tell him to turn himself in. He thought that he might do that.

He returned her call.

'You calling to arrest me?'

What she said surprised him.

'No. I'm calling to give you one last chance to catch this bastard.'

Starkey found him at a rathole diner, waiting in a booth. Her heart felt heavy when she saw him, but she pushed that aside.

'You might as well know. You're not the only one on the wrong side of the law.'

'What does that mean?'

She told him what had happened. She kept it short. She was uneasy being around him.

'Here's the deal, Pell, and you have to agree to it. If we get this guy, we are not going to kill him, we are going to arrest him. This is no longer your personal vendetta. Agreed?'

'Yes.'

'If we get this set up, we are going back to Kelso. I am not a goddamned cowboy like you. I want to do this the right way, and I want to make sure it works.'

'You want to save your job.'

'Yes, Pell, I want to save my job. They might fire me anyway, but I want to go out as the police officer I am, and not some half-cocked asshole who got Buck Daggett killed.'

Pell stared out the window. She thought he was trying to memorize whatever he saw out there.

'If I go in with you, I might be taken into custody.'

'You don't have to go. Come if you want, or not. I'm just telling you how it has to be played.'

Pell nodded again. She knew that was hard for him. He would be taking himself out of the play.

'Then what do you need me for?'

'Mr Red waits for me. He's got this ... fixation. I can use that. But I need your computer to get back on Claudius. Kelso took mine.'

Pell glanced away again.

'I should have told you what I was doing. I'm sorry I didn't.'

'Stop. I don't want to hear it.'

'I've been living with one thing in my life for a long time. You get used to doing things a certain way.'

'Is this what you've been doing for two years, Pell? Bullshitting your way from city to city after this guy?'

Pell shrugged, as if it embarrassed him.

'I have a badge and an ID number. I know the procedure, and I have friends. Most people don't question the badge. Cops never question it.'

'Look, I don't care, and I don't want to talk about it. You want to do this or not?'

He looked at her.

'I want to do it.'

'Then let's go.'

She started to slide out of the booth. He took her arm, stopping her. 'Carol?'

'What? Don't touch me like that, Pell. I don't like it.'

'I fell in love with you.'

She hit him again, so fast that she didn't even know she was doing it. The people at the surrounding tables looked at them.

'Don't you say that.'

Pell felt his face.

'Jesus, Starkey, that's three.'

'Don't you say that.'

He shoved himself out of the booth.

'The computer is in my car.'

They went to her place.

It was hard looking at Pell. It was difficult being in the same room with him, but she told herself to be strong. They had brought themselves down this road together. There was no other way to play it, but she was uncomfortably aware of the feelings she'd had when they'd been in this position before.

They set up the computer at the dining-room table, and Starkey signed on as before. It was earlier than the previous times she'd had contact with Mr Red, but she couldn't just sit. When the flaming head stared out at her, she entered the chat room, which was empty.

Pell said, 'What are you going to say?'

'This.'

HOTLOAD: John Michael Fowles.

'Who's John Michael Fowles?'

'Mr Red. Warren Mueller got his prints off Tennant's book. I knew that if Red had gone in there, Tennant would have made him look at that damned book.'

Pell stared at the screen. Starkey saw his lips move, as if he were reading the name silently to himself, branding it into his cells.

Starkey didn't expect Fowles to be waiting for her, not this early in the day. He might come anytime, or no time; they might have a long wait. She struck a cigarette, and told Pell that if he wanted anything in the kitchen, he could find it for himself. Neither of them left the computer.

Fowles was there almost at once.

WILL YOU ACCEPT A MESSAGE FROM MR RED?

Starkey smiled. Pell shifted forward, Starkey thinking he might fall into the computer.

'Fast.'

'He's been waiting.'

She opened the window.

MR RED: Excellent, Detective Starkey. You rock.

HOTLOAD: Your praise makes me blush.

MR RED: How did you learn my name?

HOTLOAD: Ah . . . a question. Do you want the truth, or do you want me to tell you what you want to hear?

MR RED: I am laughing, Carol Starkey. Well done.

Starkey did not answer.

Pell said, 'Why aren't you answering him?'

'Let him wait. It's a game he plays.'

Finally, another message appeared.

MR RED: The truth is a commodity. What will you want in return?

HOTLOAD: You will have to answer a question of mine. Do you agree?

MR RED: Within reason. I will not tell you my whereabouts or answer
    questions of that nature. All else is fair game.
HOTLOAD: Agreed.
MR RED: Agreed.
HOTLOAD: Tennant's book. When I realized that you had seen him, I
    knew he would have made you look at the book.

Fowles again fell silent. It was several moments before he replied.

MR RED: Fuck.
HOTLOAD: Only in your dreams.

'Christ, Starkey, how close *are* you two?'
'Shut up.'

MR RED: Do you know why I looked at his book, Carol Starkey?
HOTLOAD: To read the articles about yourself?
MR RED: To read the articles about you.

Pell shifted again. Starkey watched the screen, thinking, then typed:

HOTLOAD: Now, my question.
MR RED: Yes.

Starkey hesitated. Her fingers trembled, and she thought of the flask
again. She lit a fresh cigarette.
Pell saw the tremble.
'You okay?'
She didn't answer him.

HOTLOAD: I ask you again: Would you have come to Los Angeles if we
    had not baited you?
MR RED: The truth, or what you want to hear?
HOTLOAD: Answer my question.

Fowles paused again.
'What's he doing?'
'He's thinking. He wants something. He's trying to figure out how to get
it.'
'What does he want?'
'Pay attention, Pell. He wants me.'

MR RED: I will answer your question in person. Give me your phone
    number.
HOTLOAD: You must be nuts.

MR RED: I AM MR RED! OF *COURSE*, I'M NUTS!

HOTLOAD: Don't have a cow, John.

MR RED: Don't call me John. I am Mr Red.

HOTLOAD: I still won't give you my number. That is farther than I'm willing to go.

MR RED: I've had more than a few fantasies about you going all the way, Carol Starkey.

HOTLOAD: Remember the ground rules, John. You get graphic, I'm gonna sign off and go take a cold shower.

MR RED: What's in it for you is . . . the truth.

HOTLOAD: The truth hurts.

MR RED: The truth can also set you free.

She leaned back, letting it sit. She needed to think. She knew that they would have only one shot to bring him in; if he figured out what she was trying to do, her chance would be gone, and so would he.

Pell said, 'Be weak.'

Starkey glanced over and found Pell watching her.

He said, 'He's male. If you want him, need him. Let him take care of you.'

'That isn't me.'

'Pretend.'

She turned back to the keyboard.

HOTLOAD: I am afraid.

MR RED: Of the truth?

HOTLOAD: You want to be in the Ten Most Wanted. I am afraid you will use me to get there.

MR RED: There are things I want more than being on that list.

HOTLOAD: Like what?

MR RED: I want to hear your voice, Carol Starkey. I want to have a conversation. Not like this. I want to see your expressions. I want to hear your inflections.

HOTLOAD: Do you see how weird this is? I am a police officer. You are Mr Red.

MR RED: We are both in Tennant's book.

She didn't respond.

MR RED: We are the same.

She hesitated again. She knew what she wanted, but she could not suggest it. He had to suggest it. It had to be his idea or he would never go for it.

HOTLOAD: I will not give you my phone number.

MR RED: Then I will give you a number.

HOTLOAD: I am laughing. If you give me a number, I will know your location.

MR RED: Perhaps that is my idea. Perhaps I would like you to, ah, cum.

HOTLOAD: Don't be crude.

MR RED: Crude, but not stupid. Let us do this: Sign on to Claudius later today at exactly three p.m. I will be here. I will give you a phone number. If my phone doesn't ring in fifteen seconds, I will leave, and you will never hear from me again. If you call, we will talk for exactly five minutes, and I will answer your question. No more than five minutes. I would like a longer conversation, but we both know what you'll be doing.

HOTLOAD: Yes. I will be tracing the call.

MR RED: Perhaps. But perhaps I can convince you that we were meant for better things.

HOTLOAD: Don't count on it.

MR RED: Fair enough. I will beat you at that, you know. You won't catch me.

HOTLOAD: We'll see.

'You've got him, Starkey.'

'Maybe.'

She had what she needed to go back to Kelso, but everything depended on Mr Red. A large part of her was scared that if he signed off now, he would not return. He would not be there at three o'clock. She knew better than to type this, but something in her wanted to know. She told herself that if she brought him to this point, he would be hers. He would not vanish, he would not disappear. He would return to her, and she would catch him.

It was such an intimate thing that she felt embarrassed writing it in front of Pell.

HOTLOAD: When you're having your fantasies of me, what do you think about?

He hesitated so long that she grew scared that he had gone. When his answer came, she regretted having asked.

MR RED: Death.

Starkey did not reply. She signed off Claudius, then turned off the machine.

Pell was staring at her.

She said, 'Stop looking at me like that. We've got a lot to do.'

Mr Red

John Michael Fowles was parked less than two blocks up the street from Starkey's house. He closed the iBook and smiled.

'DAMN, I'm good! I am so fucking good that somebody should tattoo "Mr Irresistible" on both cheeks of my ass.'

He pushed the iBook aside and patted the jar of Modex. He liked having it with him, the gray explosive in its jar like a big glob of toothpaste. It was better than having a goldfish. You didn't have to feed it.

He waited until Starkey and Pell left, then drove back to his hotel to work on the new bomb. He was building a different kind of bomb this time, one just for Carol Starkey. He didn't have much time.

21

Starkey wanted to maneuver John Michael Fowles into revealing his location so that she could bag him. To do that, she needed phone traps in place in the event they spoke on a land line, and the cell companies standing by for a triangulation in the more likely event that his number linked to a cell phone. Once his position was fixed, she needed bodies to close the perimeter. Since the target was John Michael Fowles, AKA Mr Red, she feared that he would have explosives on his person, which required a call-out from the Bomb Squad. All of this meant that she needed Kelso's help.

She phoned Dick Leyton.

When he came on the line, he sounded distant, but concerned. She knew from his tone that he'd heard the news.

'Dick, I need your help.'

'I don't know that I'm in a position to give it. I spoke with Barry. What in hell were you thinking, Carol?'

'Did Barry tell you that I was in contact with Mr Red?'

'Of course he told me. You're in serious trouble because of this. Serious. I don't think you'll get off with just a suspension.'

'Dick, I know I'm in trouble. Please listen to me. I am *still* in contact with Mr Red. I was just on-line with him.'

'Damnit, Carol, you're only making it worse for yourself. You need to—'

Starkey interrupted him.

'I *know* Barry fired me, I *know* that I'm not part of the team, but I can get this guy, Dick. I have a relationship with him whether Barry likes it or not, and we can use that to bag this mutt. I have him set up, Dick. I have the guy set up.'

Leyton didn't say anything. She knew he was thinking, so she pressed ahead to convince him.

'At exactly three o'clock, he's going to be on-line again. He's going to give me a phone number to call. I will call it. Dick, I think I can arrange a face-to-face. If I can't, maybe we can still trap the call. This is Mr Red, for God's sake, do you think we should walk away from an opportunity like this? Take me to Barry, Dick. Please.'

They spoke about it for another ten minutes, Leyton asking questions, Starkey answering. They both knew that Leyton would have to call Morgan. He needed to convince the A-chief before Kelso would go for it. They would also need Morgan's horsepower to get everything set up in time. Starkey immediately regretted agreeing with Fowles to do this today; she kicked herself for not putting him off until tomorrow, but it was too late for that now. Leyton finally said that he would do it, telling Starkey to meet him at Spring Street by two o'clock.

When she hung up, she looked at Pell.

'You heard.'

'We're on.'

'If Morgan goes for it, I would guess that he's going to alert the ATF and the Feebs. They might be there.'

'They probably will. Those boys don't like to sit out the dance.'

'Maybe you shouldn't come.'

'I didn't come this far to quit, Starkey.'

'Well, let's go. You want to get something to eat?'

'I don't think I could.'

'You want some Tagamet?'

Pell laughed.

She brought him back to the diner for his car, and then they went their separate ways.

Starkey put her car in the red zone outside Spring Street at five minutes before two, and went up with the second computer. Leyton was already present, as were Morgan and two of his Men in Black. Pell hadn't yet arrived. Starkey found herself hoping that he would change his mind about coming. Kelso was outside his office with two suits whom Starkey took to be federal agents. Marzik was talking up one of the Men in Black and ignored her.

Everyone in the room stopped what they were doing and looked at her.

Dick said, 'Carol, why don't we go into Barry's office.'

Starkey followed them into Kelso's office, where Morgan nodded politely.

'Looks like you're in some trouble, Detective.'

'Yes, sir.'

'Well, let's see how this turns out.'

Kelso wasn't happy about any of it, but he wasn't stupid, either. He wanted Mr Red, and if this was their best shot, he was game to take it. Three representatives from the phone company had set up a computer of their own, feeding into Barry's phone jack.

Leyton said, 'Carol, I sketched out our discussion both to Chief Morgan and to Lieutenant Kelso. They're on board with this. The dispatch office is standing by with secure communication to the patrol division. SWAT has been alerted, and the Bomb Squad is, as always, ready to roll.'

Starkey nodded, smiling at the 'as always'.

'All right.'

Secure communication meant that all directions to patrol units would be transmitted through the computers in the black and whites. No one wanted to use radio calls because those could be intercepted by the media and private citizens.

'Where do you want to do this?'

Kelso said, 'Here in my office. Do you need anything special for the computer?'

'Just a phone line. I'll use my cell phone to make the voice call.'

One of the Men in Black said, 'Shouldn't she use a hard line for the trap?'

One of the phone company people said, 'Negative. He's providing the number. We'll work the address from that unless he's on a cell. If he's mobile, it doesn't matter what she's on.'

Kelso cleared his desk so that Starkey could set up the computer. She caught a glimpse of Pell out in the squad room, talking with the federal suits.

At ten minutes before three, Starkey was waiting to sign on with an audience crowded around her. Leyton came up behind her and rubbed her shoulders.

'We've still got a few minutes. Get a cup of coffee.'

Starkey left for the squad room, glad for the break. Pell was still with the two suits, but he wasn't in handcuffs. She didn't go for a cup of coffee. She went over to Pell.

'Are these people with the ATF?'

The shorter of the two introduced himself as Assistant Special Agent-in-Charge Wally Coombs and the taller as Special Agent Burton Armus, both of the Los Angeles field office.

'Is Mr Pell under arrest?'

'Not at this time. We'd like to ask you a few questions about all this.'

'You'll have to ask me later.'

'We understand that.'

'I will need Mr Pell's assistance in the other room.'

The two agents traded a look, then Coombs shrugged.

'Sure.'

Pell followed her back to Kelso's, walking very close behind her.

'Thanks.'

At two fifty-nine, Starkey was again in front of the computer.

She said, 'Are we ready?'

Morgan met the eyes of the section leaders and the phone company people. One of the phone people murmured something into his private line, then gave a thumbs-up. Morgan nodded at her.

'Go.'

Starkey opened the door into Claudius. Almost at once, the words appeared.

WILL YOU ACCEPT A MESSAGE FROM MR RED?

Kelso said, 'Jesus.'
Morgan frowned.
'No talking.'
When the window appeared, it wasn't what any of them expected.

MR RED: **Sorry, babe. Changed my mind.**

Kelso said, 'Damnit!'
Morgan shushed him. He nodded to Starkey, encouraging.
'Play it as you would, Detective Starkey. You know what they say, shit happens.'
Starkey glanced up at him, and the Man in Black smiled.
Starkey typed.

HOTLOAD: **You're an asshole.**
MR RED: **I have been thinking.**
HOTLOAD: **Don't bruise yourself.**
MR RED: **A conversation isn't going to be enough for me. I am a man of LARGE appetites, if you catch my drift.**
HOTLOAD: **We had a deal.**
MR RED: **Your point?**
HOTLOAD: **You said you would answer my question.**
MR RED: **What I said was, I will answer your question in person. I will still do that.**
HOTLOAD: **I think you're jerking me around. You know I won't meet you. No way am I going to do that.**

Kelso said, 'Ah, Carol—'
Pell said, 'She knows what she's doing.'

MR RED: **Then you will never know why Buck Daggett died.**

Starkey leaned back, waiting. She could feel Kelso, Leyton, and the others shifting behind her, and didn't like it.

MR RED: **Meet me, Carol Starkey. I will not hurt you.**
HOTLOAD: **Where?**
MR RED: **Don't say it if you don't mean it.**
HOTLOAD: **Where?**
MR RED: **Echo Park. You know the big fountain.**

Morgan quietly told his assistants to have plainclothes units position themselves around Echo Park. She heard Dick Leyton speaking softly into his cell phone, alerting the Bomb Squad. She ignored them.

HOTLOAD: Yes.

MR RED: Park on the south side of the pond and walk toward the concession stand. Walk all the way to the concession stand, and only from that direction. I will be watching you. If you come alone, we will meet. If not, I will think less of you.

HOTLOAD: You're a fool.

MR RED: Am I, Carol Starkey? I am Mr Red. The truth is out there.

They set it up on the roll, coordinating SWAT and the Bomb Squad to meet in a parking lot six blocks east of Echo Park. Plainclothes spotters of Latin descent were posted on the streets surrounding the park, equipped with radios. All uniformed officers and black and white radio cars were pulled.

The phone people wrapped a wire on Starkey there in Kelso's office, even as the orders were being given. Starkey was to drive to the park in her own car and do exactly as John Michael Fowles had instructed. Once in the park, if and when he approached her and identified himself, the area would be sealed. Snipers would be in position if needed.

Pell said, 'You okay with this?'

It was happening so fast that she wanted to throw up.

'Sure.'

They hustled her out to her car less than eight minutes after the computer was off.

Starkey drove to Echo Park, pretending that none of this was happening. She knew that this was the best approach. Forget about all the activity in support of her, just like approaching a bomb. Do it that way, and she wouldn't be caught looking for the snipers or the plainclothes people, and give herself away.

The drive from Spring Street to Echo Park took twelve minutes. She parked on the south side like he said, fighting the urge to throw up. He wouldn't be standing there with a grin and a hot dog in his hand. He was Mr Red. There would be a surprise.

'Radio check.'

'One two three, three two one.'

'You're clear.'

'I'm pulling the plug.'

'Rog.'

She took the plug from her ear. If he saw it, he would know she was wired. The mike taped between her breasts would pick up her voice. If she said, 'Hello, Mr Red,' they would hear.

The plan was simple. Point him out, hit the ground, let everyone else do their jobs.

Starkey locked her car and walked toward the concession stand. It was a weekday summer afternoon. The park was jammed with families, kids with balloons, bladers and boarders and plenty of ice cream. It was so hot that the tarmac beneath her feet was soft. Starkey hoped that it wouldn't get hotter.

A long line waited at the concession stand. She had to cover about sixty yards, which she did slowly so that she could search each face in the area. She didn't care if Fowles thought she was being careful, but she didn't want him to think she was stalling to give other officers a chance to set up.

When she reached the concession stand, she stopped. No one approached her, and no one even looked like they could be Mr Red. The crowd was mostly Latin, with a smattering of blacks and Asians. She was one of the few Anglos that she could see.

Starkey shook out a cigarette and lit up. The minutes stretched. He could be anywhere, he could be nowhere. She wondered if he had changed his mind again.

A short, squat woman and her children joined the line. She reminded Starkey of the women she had seen from Dana's window, the women trying to catch their bus. This woman had four children, small ones, all boys, all short, squat, and brown like their mother. The oldest boy stood close by his mother's side, but the other three ran pell-mell in circles, chasing each other and screaming. Starkey wished that they would shut the hell up. All the screaming was getting on her nerves. The two smallest boys raced behind the concession stand, came out from around the other side, and skidded to a stop. They had found the bag. At first, Starkey wasn't sure what they were doing or what they had, but then the earth heaved up against her feet and she knew.

The two smallest boys looked in the bag. Their older brother joined them. A plain paper shopping bag that someone had left at the corner of the concession stand.

Starkey wished she had eaten more Tagamet.

'Get away from there.'

She didn't shriek or rush forward. This was Mr Red. He would have a remote. He was watching, and he could fire the charge whenever the fucking hell he wanted.

Starkey dropped her cigarette and crushed it. She had to get those kids away from there.

She walked toward the bag.

'We have a possible device. I say again, possible device. I gotta get these kids away.'

When she was closer, she raised her voice, made it sharp and angry. 'Hey!'

The boys looked. They probably spoke no English.

'Get the fuck away from that.'

The boys knew she was talking to them, but stared at her without comprehension. Their mother said something in Spanish.

Starkey said, 'Tell them to get away from that.'

The mother was chattering in Spanish when Starkey reached the bag and saw the pipes.

'BOMB!'

She grabbed two of the boys, she could only get two, and lunged backwards, screaming, 'BOMBBOMBBOMB! POLICE OFFICER, CLEAR THE AREA, MOVE MOVE MOVE!'

The boys screamed, their mother lit into Starkey like a mama cat, the people in the line milled in confusion. Starkey pushed and shoved, trying to get the people to move even as police units bucked over the curb and roared toward her across the park –

– and nothing happened.

Russ Daigle, wet with sweat, his face drawn in the way a person's face can be drawn only when they work a bomb, said, 'There's no charge in the pipes.'

Starkey had guessed that forty minutes ago. If Mr Red had wanted to blow it, he would have blown it when she was standing there. Now she was sitting in the back of Daigle's Suburban, just as she used to sit when she was on the squad, and winding down from de-arming a device. Daigle had sent the Andrus robot forward with the de-armer to blow the pipes apart.

'There was a note.'

Daigle handed her the red 3 x 5 index card. Dick Leyton and Morgan had walked over with him.

The note said: *Check the list.*

Starkey looked at them.

'What the fuck does this mean?'

Leyton squeezed her arm.

'He's on the Ten Most Wanted List. As soon as the Feebs had his identity, they added him.'

Starkey laughed.

'I'm sorry, Carol. It was a good try. It was a really good try.'

They were done. Any relationship she'd had with Mr Red was history. He would've seen what they had tried to do. Wherever he was, he was no doubt laughing his ass off. She might sign on to Claudius again, and he might be there, but any hope of baiting him into a trap was gone. He had what he wanted.

Kelso came over and told her pretty much the same thing. He even managed to look embarrassed.

'Listen, Carol, we're still going to have to deal with what happened, but, well, maybe we can work out something to keep you on the job. You won't be able to stay with CCS, but we'll see.'

'Thanks, Barry.'

'You can even call me by my first name.'

Starkey smiled.

The two ATF agents hovered around Pell like his personal guards. Starkey caught Pell's eye. Pell spoke to the agents, then walked over.

'How you doing?'

'Been better. But I've been worse, too. You hear they put him on the list?'

'Yeah. Maybe he'll retire. The sonofabitch.'

Starkey nodded. She didn't know what to think about that. Would Mr Red stay in Los Angeles? Would he continue to kill, or would he simply vanish? She thought about the Zodiac Killer up in San Francisco, who had murdered a string of people, and then simply stopped.

She looked at the two feds.

'What's going to happen with your friends?'

'They're not going to drag me away in chains. They want me to come in to the FO for an interview, but they advised me of my rights, and told me to get an attorney. What does that tell you?'

'That you're fucked?'

'You have such a way with words.'

Starkey smiled, even though she didn't feel much like smiling.

'That's a nice smile.'

'Don't.'

'I need to talk to you, Carol. We have to talk about this.'

Starkey shoved off the back of the Suburban.

'I don't want to talk. I just want to go somewhere and heal.'

'I don't mean talk about what's going to happen to me. I mean talk about us.'

'I know what you meant. Good-bye, Jack. If I can help you when they interview me, I will.'

Starkey looked deeply into the two dimming eyes, then walked away so that he could not see how very much she wanted that time with him.

22

Starkey did not drive back to Spring Street. The summer sun was still high in the west, but the air was clear, and the heat felt good. She drove with the windows down.

Starkey stopped at an A.M./P.M. minimart, bought a jumbo iced tea, then took a turn through Rampart Division. She watched the citizens and enjoyed the play of traffic. Every time she saw a black and white, she tipped her head at them. The pager at her waist vibrated once, but she turned it off without checking the number. Pell, she figured. Or Kelso. Either way, it didn't matter. She was done with the bombs. She could walk away and live without working the bombs or being a bomb investigator and get along just fine. She was heartened by what Kelso had said. She thought that she might like working Homicide, but most detectives wanted Homicide. It was a tough billet to get, and she hadn't done all that well at CCS. When word got out that she had withheld information from her own detectives, she'd be lucky to find a spot in Property Crimes.

Starkey thought about these things until she realized that she was doing it so she wouldn't think about Pell, and then she couldn't get him out of her head. The tea was suddenly bitter, and the knowledge of how Red had played her was a jagged pill that cut at her throat. She threw away the tea, popped two Tagamet, then turned for home, feeling empty, but not so empty that she wanted to fill that lost place with gin.

That was something, and, she guessed, maybe she had Pell to thank for it, though she was in no mood to do so.

By the time Starkey reached her house, she was hoping that she would find Pell waiting in the drive, but she didn't. Just as well, she thought, but in that same moment her chest filled with an ache of loss that she hadn't known since Sugar had died. Realizing that did not improve her spirits, but she forced away the thought of it and what it meant. She was better now. She had grown. She would spend the rest of her day trying to save her job, or deciding how best to leave it and the memory of Jack Pell behind.

Starkey shut her engine and let herself into her home. The message light was blinking by the front phone, but she did not see it, nor would it have mattered if she had.

The first and only thing she saw, the thing that caught her eye as if it had reached out with claws, was the device on her coffee table. An unexpected visual jolt of twin galvanized pipes duct-taped to a small black box, red and blue and yellow wires neatly folded along its length. Alien and mechanical, stark and obvious as it rested on a stack of *Glamour* and *American Crime Scene*; everything about it screaming BOMB in a way that flushed acid through Starkey's soul in the same moment her world exploded in a white fury.

'Can you hear me?'

His voice was surprisingly mellow. She could barely understand him over the shrill ringing in her ears.

'I can see your eyes moving, Carol Starkey.'

She heard footsteps, heavy heels on hard floor, then smelled the overripe odor of what she thought was gasoline. The footsteps moved away.

'You smell that? That's charcoal starter fluid I found in your pantry. If you don't wake up, I'm going to set your leg on fire.'

She felt the wet on her leg, the nice Donna Karan pants and the Bruno Magli shoes.

The sharp throb behind her right ear was a swelling spike that made her eyes water. She could feel her heart beating there, strong and horrible. When she opened her eyes, she saw double.

'Are you okay, Carol Starkey? Can you see me?'

She looked toward his voice.

He smiled when their eyes met. A black metal rod about eighteen inches long sprouted from his right hand. He'd found her Asp in the closet. He spread his hands, gesturing wide and presenting himself.

'I'm Mr Red.'

She was seated on the hearth, arms spread wide, handcuffed to the metal frame surrounding her fireplace. Her legs were straight out before her, making her feel like a child. Her hands were numb.

'Congratulations, John. You finally made the list.'

He laughed. He had beautiful even teeth, and didn't look anything like she'd imagined or anything like the grainy photos that she'd seen. He looked younger than his twenty-eight years, but in no way the shabby misfit that most bombers were. He was a good-looking man; he had all his fingers.

'Well, now that I'm there, it ain't so much, you know? I've got bigger fish to fry.'

She thought to keep him talking. As long as he was talking, her odds of survival increased. The device was no longer on the coffee table. Now, the device was sitting on the floor inches beyond her feet.

She tried not to look at it.

'Look at it, Carol Starkey.'

Reading her mind.

He came over and sat cross-legged on the floor, patting the device like a friend.

'The last of Daggett's Modex Hybrid. It's not the mix I prefer, but it'll get the job done.' He stroked the device, proud of it. 'And this one really is for you. Got your name on it and everything.'

She looked at it just to watch his hand; the fingers were long and slender and precise. In another life, they could have belonged to a surgeon or watchmaker. She looked at the bomb. The two pipes were the same, but the black box was different. A switch topped the box, with two fine wires leading to a battery pack. This bomb was different. This bomb was not radio-controlled.

She said, 'Timer.'

'Yeah. I gotta be somewhere else when this one goes off. Celebrating my ascension to the Ten. Isn't this cool, Carol Starkey? They wouldn't put me on the list until they knew my name, and you're the one who identified me. You made my dream come true.'

'Lucky me.'

Without another word, he reached to the black box, pressed the side, and a green LED timer appeared, counting down from fifteen minutes. He grinned.

'Kinda hokey, I know, but I couldn't resist. I wanted you to watch the damned thing.'

'You're insane, Fowles.'

'Of course, but couldn't you be more original than that?'

He patted her leg, then went to her couch and came back with a wide roll of duct tape.

'Look, don't do anything chicken and close your eyes, okay? I mean, why waste the moment? This is my gift to you, Carol Starkey. You're going to see the actual instant of your destruction. Just watch the seconds trickle down until that final second when you cease. Don't sweat being wounded or anything like that. You'll reach death as we know it in less than a thousandth of a second. Oblivion.'

'Fuck you.'

He tore off a strip of tape, but stopped on his knees and smiled.

'In a way, that's what I'm doing to you.'

'I want the truth about something.'

'The truth is a commodity.'

'Answer me, you bastard. Did all of this happen . . . did Buck die because I brought you here?'

He settled back on his heels to consider her, then smiled.

'Do you want the truth?'

'Yes.'

'You'll have to answer one of mine.'

'I'll tell you whatever you want.'

'All right. Then here's the truth. Spend your guilt on other matters,

Detective Starkey. I learned about the Silver Lake bomb on the NLETS system before you and Pell ever started playing your little game. Daggett brought me here, not you.'

Starkey felt a huge wedge of tension ease.

'Now you answer mine.'

'What?'

'How did it feel?'

'How did what feel? Being used?'

He leaned closer, like a child peering into an aquarium.

'No, no, no. The trailer park. You were right on top of it. Even though it was just black powder and dynamite, it had to hit you with an overpressure of almost sixty thousand pounds.'

His eyes were alive with it. She knew then that this was what he wanted, to be the person in that moment, to feel the force of it. Not just control it, but feel it, to take it into himself and be consumed by it.

'Fowles. It felt like . . . nothing. I lost consciousness. I didn't feel anything until later.'

He stared at her as if he was still waiting for her answer, and she felt her anger rage. It had been the same with everyone since the day it had happened; friends, strangers, cops, now even this maniac. Starkey had had enough of it.

'What, Fowles? Do you think a window opens so that you see God? It's a fucking explosion, you moron. It happens so fast you don't have time even to know it's happening. It's about as mystical as you hitting me when I walked through that door.'

Fowles stared without blinking. She wondered if he was in a fugue state.

'Fowles?'

He frowned, irritated.

'That's because you had nothing but a low-end piece of bullshit, Starkey. Homemade crap thrown together by some ignoramus. Now you're dealing with Mr Red. Two kilos of Modex boiling out at twenty-eight K. The pressure wave is going to sweep up your legs in one ten-thousandth of a second, smashing the blood up into your torso just like a steamroller driving right up to your hips. The hydrostatic shock is going to blow out every capillary in your brain in about a thousandth of a second. Instant brain death at just about the same time as your lower legs separate. You'll be dead, though, so you won't feel it.'

'You should stay and enjoy the show. You could sit on my lap.'

Fowles grinned.

'I like you, Starkey. Too bad I didn't know you when you worked the bombs. I would've gotten it right the first time.'

He grabbed her hair with his left hand, forced her head back, and pressed the tape over her mouth. She tried to twist away, but he pressed the tape down hard, then added a second piece. She opened her mouth as far as she could, letting the skin pull. She felt the tape loosen, but it didn't pull free.

The timer was down to thirteen minutes and forty-two seconds. Fowles checked his watch.

'Perfect.'

She tried to tell him to fuck himself, but it came out a mumble.

John Michael Fowles squatted beside her and gently touched her head. 'Save a place in hell for me, Carol Starkey.'

He stood then and went to the door, but she did not see him. She watched the timer, the green LED numbers spinning down toward eternity.

Pell

Coombs and Armus were gentlemen about it. They could have brought him in like just another mutt, but they played it straight. They wanted his gun and his badge, which he had left in his motel, and they wanted to talk to him. He asked if he could meet them at the field office, and they said fine. It helped that Dick Leyton told them that Pell had been instrumental in getting them this close to Mr Red.

Pell drove back to his motel, got the ID and the big Smith 10, then checked out. He sat in his car for a long time, listening to his heart beat and feeling sweat run down his chest. He did not think about John Michael Fowles, or about Armus and Coombs; he thought about Starkey.

Pell cranked his car and went after her, having no idea what he would say or do, only knowing that he could not let her go this easily. Coombs and Armus could wait.

Pell parked on the street in front of her house, relieved when he saw her car in the drive. Funny, he thought, that his heart beat now with the same kind of intensity as when he was facing a mutt in a life-or-death situation.

When Starkey didn't answer, his first thought was that she'd seen him approach, and was ignoring him.

He knocked, and called through the door.

'Carol, please. I want to talk.'

He tried to see through the little panes of glass that ran vertically beside her door, but they were crusted with dust. He rubbed at them, looked harder. He thought that she was sitting at the fireplace, but then he saw the tape, and her wrists and the handcuffs. Then he saw the device at her feet.

Pell slammed the door with his foot, and then he was in, going through the door when something heavy hit him from behind and the world blurred. He stumbled forward, seeing flashing bursts of light. Starkey's eyes were wild. Something exploded brilliantly in his head. A man was behind him, hitting him. The man was screaming.

'You fuck! You fuck!'

Pell clawed out his Smith as he was hit again. He could feel consciousness slipping away, but the Smith came out and the safety went off and he fired up into the shadow above him even as the light bled into darkness.

When Pell came to the door, Starkey tried to call through the tape, whipping her head from side to side. She kicked at the floor with her heels, trying to warn him with the noise. She raked her face on her shoulders, tearing at the tape, and jerked at the handcuffs, letting them cut into her wrists.

Fowles jumped behind the door with the Asp just as Pell crashed through. Pell saw only her, and even as Starkey tried to warn Pell with her eyes, Fowles nailed him with the Asp. Fowles hit him again and again, the hard weight of the Asp crashing down like a cinder block.

Pell went down, woozy and blank. Starkey saw him reach out his gun, that monster ugly autoloader, and then he was shooting, shooting up into Fowles, who flipped back and sideways, then crawled toward her couch.

Starkey raked her face against her shoulders, feeling the tape work free, even as she watched the timer. It was winding down so fast the numbers blurred.

Fowles tried to rise, but couldn't.

Pell moaned.

Starkey worked at the tape, stretching her jaw and raking her face until finally one end of the tape came free and she found her voice.

Starkey screamed, 'Pell! Pell, get up!'

6:48.47.46.

'Pell. Get up and get the keys! Wake up, Pell, goddamnit!'

Pell pushed himself onto his back. He stared straight up at the ceiling, blinking his eyes again and again as if he were seeing the most amazing thing.

'Damnit, Pell, we've got six minutes, this thing is gonna explode! Come over here.'

Pell pushed onto his side and blinked some more, then rubbed at his face.

'I can't see you. I can't see anymore. There's nothing left but light and shadows.'

Starkey's blood drained. She knew what had happened. The fight had finished the work on his eyes, caused the damaged retinas to separate and fold away, severing their final fragile connection to the optic nerves.

She felt herself hyperventilating and forced herself to hold her breath, to stop breathing just long enough to get herself under control.

'You can't see, Jack? How about up close? Can you see your hand?'

He held his hand in front of his face.

'I see a shadow. That's all I see. Who hit me? Was it him?'

'You shot him. He's on the couch.'

'Is he dead?'

'I don't know if he's dead or not, Jack, but forget him! This bomb is on a timer. The goddamned timer is running down, you understand?'

'How much time do we have?'

'Six minutes, ten seconds.'

Not enough time for the police to respond. She knew it was the first thing he would think.

'I can't see, Carol. I'm sorry.'

'Goddamnit, Jack, I'm handcuffed to this fucking fireplace. You get me loose and I can de-arm that bomb!'

'I CAN'T SEE!'

She could see the sweat leaking from his short hair down his face. He rolled onto his side and pushed himself up onto his hands and knees. Facing away from her. Across the room, Fowles tried to rise once more, failed, and whatever life was left seemed to drain from him.

'Jack.'

Pell turned.

She forced her breathing to even out. When you work the bomb, you stay calm. Panic kills.

'Jack, quick now, okay? Turn toward my voice.'

'This is pathetic.'

But he did it.

6:07.06.05.

'Straight ahead of you is twelve o'clock. Fowles is at eight o'clock, right? Just across the room. Maybe fourteen feet. He's on a couch behind the coffee table, and I think he's dead. The keys might be in his pockets.'

She could see the hope flicker on his face.

'MOVE, damnit!'

He crawled, two knees and a hand, the other feeling ahead for the table.

'That's it, Jack. Almost at the table and he's right behind it.'

When Pell reached the table, he shoved it aside. He found the couch before Fowles's leg, then walked his hands up the legs to the pockets. Fowles's shirt was wet, and the blood had soaked down along his thighs. Pell's hands grew red as he worked.

4:59.58.57.

'Find it, Jack! GET THE DAMNED KEYS!'

'They're not here! They're not in his pockets!'

'You missed them!'

'THEY'RE NOT HERE!'

She watched him dig in both pants pockets and the back pockets, then run his fingers around Fowles's waist just as he'd frisk a suspect.

'The socks! Check his socks and shoes!'

She searched the room with her eyes, thinking maybe Fowles had tossed the keys. You didn't need keys to lock handcuffs, only to remove them. He had never intended to remove them. She didn't see them, and it would only be wasting time for him to feel his way around the room searching for something so small.

'I CAN'T FIND THEM!'

Fowles moaned once, and shifted.

'He's still alive!'

3:53.52.51.

Her eyes went back to the flashing timer and watched the seconds trickle away.

'Is he armed? Does he have a gun?'

'No, no gun.'

'Then forget him! Five o'clock now. Come around to five o'clock.'

Pell continued ripping at Fowles's clothes.

'JACK, GODDAMNIT, DO IT! FIVE O'CLOCK!'

Pell turned toward her voice.

3:30.29.28.

'The door's at five o'clock. Get out of here.'

'No.'

'Romantic, Jack. Very romantic.'

'I'M NOT LEAVING YOU!'

He crawled toward her, covering the ground without concern for obstacles, veering far to the right.

'Here.'

Changing course to find her foot, barely missing the device, then walking his hands up her legs.

'Talk to me, Carol. You're handcuffed to what?'

'An iron fire grate. The frame is set into the bricks.'

His hands slid across her body, jumped to her arms and found her right hand, felt over the cuffs and her wrist to the iron frame. He gripped the frame with both hands and pulled, his face going red. He swung around and wedged his feet against the wall and pulled even harder until the veins bulged huge and swollen in his face.

'It's solid, Jack. The bolts are set deep.'

He crabbed across her and tried the other bar. She found herself, strangely, growing calm. She wondered what Dana would say about that. Acceptance? Resignation?

Pell's voice was frantic.

'A lever. Maybe I can pry it out. There's gotta be something I can use.'

'The Asp.'

The Asp had rolled against the far wall. They lost almost a minute as she directed him to it, then back. He wedged it behind the rail and pulled.

The Asp bent at its joint, useless, and fell free.

'It broke.'

Pell threw it aside.

'Something stronger, then! A fireplace poker! A log!'

'I DON'T HAVE ANY OF THAT, PELL!! THERE'S NOTHING IN MY

GODDAMNED HOUSE!!! I'M A ROTTEN HOMEMAKER!! NOW GET OUT OF HERE!'

He stopped then, and looked toward her face with eyes so gentle and open that she felt sure he could see.

'Where's the door, Carol?'

She didn't hesitate, and loved him for going, loved him for sparing her the final three minutes of guilt that she had caused his death, too.

'Behind you, seven o'clock.'

He touched her face, and let his fingers linger.

'I did you wrong, Carol. I'm sorry about that.'

'Forget it, Jack. I absolve you. Hell, I friggin' love you. Now please go.'

He followed her leg down to the device, cradled it under his arm, and began navigating toward the door.

Starkey realized what he was doing and screamed in a rage.

'GODDAMNIT, NO!!! PELL, DON'T YOU DO THAT!!! DON'T YOU KILL YOURSELF FOR ME!!'

He crawled for the door, carrying the device under his left arm, moving well right of the door as he'd lost his bearings.

'You're doing me a favor, Starkey. I get to go out a hero. I get to die for the woman I love. That's the most a guy like me can ever hope to do.'

He bumped into the nest of tables, lost his balance, and dropped the bomb. She could see the lights in the timer blurring.

As he fumbled to pick it up, Starkey knew that he was going to do it. He was going to carry the damned thing outside and blow himself to hell and leave her in here to carry the weight of it just as she'd done with Sugar, and then, only then, her eyes filled and the only possible way to save them both came to her.

'Pell, listen.'

He had the bomb again and was feeling for the door.

'Pell, LISTEN! We can de-arm the bomb. I know how to de-arm the fuckin' bomb!'

He paused, and looked at her.

'How much time?'

'I can't see it. Turn it to the right and put it on its side.'

2:44.43.42.

'Bring it over here, Jack. Let me look close at it, and I'll tell you what to do.'

'That's bullshit, Starkey. You just want to die.'

'I want to live, Pell! Goddamn you, I want to live and I want you to live, too, and you're wasting time! We can do this!'

'I CAN'T SEE!'

'I CAN TALK YOU THROUGH IT! Pell, I'm serious. We've still got a little time, but we're losing it. Bring it over here.'

'Shit!'

Pell followed her directions until he was next to her, breathing hard and sweating so much that his shirt was wet.

'Put it on the floor. Next to me. A little farther away.'

He did as she said.

'Now rotate it. C'mon. I want to see the time.'

2:33.32.31.

'How long?'

'We're doing great.'

She once more forced herself to hold her breath. It reminded her of the first time she had walked a bomb, and then she remembered that it had been Buck Daggett who'd been her supervisor that day, and who had told her the trick of holding her breath as they had buttoned her into the suit.

'Okay. Now turn it over. Lemme look at the bottom.'

'I got no clippers. I got no pliers. I think I have a knife.'

'Shut up and let me think.'

You make choices. The choices can haunt you forever, or they can set you free.

'Tell me what you see, Carol. Describe it.'

'We've got a black Radio Shack timer fastened on top of a translucent Tupperware food-storage container. Looks like he melted holes in the lid to drop the leg wires. Typical Mr Red ... the works are hidden.'

'Battery pack?'

'Gotta be inside with everything else. The top isn't taped. It's just snapped on.'

She watched his fingers feel lightly over the timer, then around the edges of the lid. She knew that he would be thinking exactly what she was thinking: that Red could've built a contact connection into the lid that would automatically trigger the explosive if the lid were removed.

You make choices. The choices can haunt you forever, or they can set you free.

'Open it, Jack. From the corners. Just pop up the corners. Slow.'

She could feel the sweat creep down from her hair.

Pell was blinking at the Tupperware, trying to see it, but then he wet his lips and nodded. He was thinking it, too. Thinking that this could be it, but that, if it were, neither of them would know it. A ten-thousandth of a second was too fast to know much of anything.

1:51.50.49.

Pell opened the lid.

'Loose all four corners, but don't lift the lid away from the container. I want you to lift it just enough to test the tension on the wires.'

She watched him do as she instructed, sweat now running into her own eyes so that she had to twist her face into her shoulders to wipe it away. She was blinking almost as much as Pell.

'I can feel the wires pull against whatever's inside.'

'That's the explosive and the initiator. Is there play in the wire?'

He lifted the top a few inches away from the container.

'Yeah.'

'Lift the top until you feel the wire pull.'

He did.

1:26.25.24.

'Okay. Now tilt the container toward me. I want to see inside.'

When Pell tilted the Tupperware, she saw the contents slide, which was good. That meant it wasn't fastened to the container and could be removed.

A squat, quart-sized metal cylinder that looked like a paint can sat inside with the end plug of an electric detonator sticking up through the top. Red and white leg wires ran from the end plug to a shunt, from which another set of wires sprouted up through the lid to the timer, and off to the left to a couple of AA batteries that were taped to the side of the can. A purple wire ran directly from the batteries to the timer, bypassing the shunt, but connecting through a small red box that sprouted yet another wire that led back to the detonator. She didn't like that part. Everything else was simple and direct and she'd seen it a hundred times before ... but not the red box, not the white wire leading back to the detonator. She found herself staring at these things. She found herself scared.

'Tell me what to do, Carol.'

'Just hang on, Pell. I'm thinking. Lift it out, okay? It looks like everything is taped together in there, so you don't have to worry about it falling apart. Just cup it with your hands, support it from the bottom, and lift it out. Put it on the floor.'

He did as she instructed, handling it as gently as a lace egg.

'Can you see it okay?'

'Fine.'

1:01.00.

0:59.

'How're we doing with the time?'

'All the time in the world, Pell.'

'Are we going to be able to do this?'

'No sweat.'

'You don't lie worth shit, Starkey.'

With the bomb sitting openly on the floor, she could see the connections and wiring more clearly, but she still did not know the purpose of the tiny red box. She thought it might be a surge monitor, and that scared her. A surge monitor would sense if the batteries had been disconnected or the wiring cut and bypass the shunt and the timer. It would be a built-in defense trigger to prevent de-arming the bomb. If they cut the wires or pulled the timer, the shunt would automatically fire the detonator.

Her heart rate increased. She had to twist her head again to wipe away the sweat.

'Is there a problem, Carol?'

She could hear the strain in his voice. .

'No way, Pell. I live for this stuff.'

Pell laughed.

'Jesus Christ.'

'Wish He was here, pal.'

Pell laughed again, but then the laugh faded.

'What do I do, Carol? Don't lose it on me, babe.'

She guessed that he could hear the strain in her, too.

'Okay, Pell, here's what we're looking at. I think there's a surge monitor cut into the circuit. You know what that is?'

'Yeah. Auto-destruct.'

'We try to disconnect anything, it'll sense a change in something called the impedance and detonate the bomb. The timer won't matter.'

'So what do we do?'

'Take a big chance, buddy. Put your fingers on the timer, then find the wires that lead down through the lid. I want you to be on the bottom side of the lid, okay, so you're closest to the device.'

He did it.

'Okay.'

'There are five wires coming through the lid. Take one. Any one.'

He took the red wire.

'Okay, that's not the one we want, so separate it from the others, and take another.'

Purely by chance, he took the purple.

'That's it, babe. That's the one. Now follow it and you'll come to a little box.'

She watched the gentle way his fingers moved along the wire, and thought that he would have been equally gentle as his fingers moved along her scars.

'I'm there. Two wires lead out the other side.'

'Right, but don't worry about it. Before we can de-arm the timer, we've got to de-arm this thing, and I don't know how to do that. I'm telling you the truth now, Jack. I don't know what we're dealing with, so all I can do is guess.'

He nodded without saying anything.

'Real easy now, because I don't want you to accidentally pull loose a wire, I want you to separate the surge monitor from the rest of the device. Just kinda pull the wires to the side so that the box is off by itself and put it on the floor.'

'What do you want me to do with it?'

'You're going to stomp on it.'

He didn't bat an eye or tell her she was crazy.

'Okay.'

As he did that, she said, 'It could detonate, Jack. I'm sorry, but it could just fucking let go.'

'It's going to go anyway.'

'Yes.'

'We've both been through it before, Carol.'

'Sure, Pell. No sweat to people like us.'

When he had the monitor on the floor away from the other wires, he kept one hand on the surge monitor, then crabbed around into a squat to position, his heel over the monitor.

'Am I lined up over the damned thing?'

'Do it, Pell.'

One ten-thousandth of a second.

Pell brought his heel down hard.

Starkey felt her breath hiss out as if her chest had been wrapped in iron bands.

Nothing happened.

When Pell lifted his foot, the plastic square was in pieces. And they were still alive.

'I crushed it, right, Starkey? Did I get it?'

She stared at the broken pieces. A set of small silver keys were in the debris. The handcuff keys. That bastard had put the keys in the bomb.

'Starkey?'

She glanced at the timer.

0:36.35.34.

Something inside her screamed for him to scoop up the keys, unhook her, and let them both run. But she knew he couldn't. He could never find the keys and fumble to the cuffs and unlock her. There wasn't nearly enough time.

'What do I do? Talk to me, Carol. *Tell me what to do!*'

She didn't want him thinking about the keys. She didn't want him distracted.

'Find the batteries.'

His fingers traced over the device until they found the little 9-volt taped to the side of the paint can.

'Got it.'

'Feel the wires coming off the top? They're attached by a little snap at the top of the battery.'

'Got it. Now what?'

If she was working this bomb in a call-out, she would be in the armor and would've set up the de-armer and blown the bomb apart from the safety of the Suburban sixty yards away. They wouldn't be handling the bomb because you never knew what might set them off, or how stable they were, or what the builder might have rigged. Safety was in distance. Safety was in playing it safe, and taking no chances and thinking everything through before you did it.

'Take it off.'

Pell didn't move.

'Just take it off?'

0:18.17.16.

'Yes, take it off. Just unsnap the damned thing. That's all we can do. We have to break the circuit, and we don't have any other way to do it, so we're going to cut the battery out of the loop and pray there won't be a backcharge that fires the detonator. Maybe this sonofabitch didn't build in a second surge monitor that we can't even see. Maybe it won't go off.'

He didn't say anything for a while.

0:10.09.08.

'I guess this is it, then, right?'

'Pull it off in one clean move. Don't let the contacts brush together again after you separate them.'

'Sure.'

'Don't let it be halfway, Pell. One clean move. Cut the connection like your life depends on it.'

'How much time?'

'Six seconds.'

He tilted his head toward her, his eyes looking too much to the right. He smiled.

'Thanks, Starkey.'

'You, too, Pell. Now pull off the damned cap.'

He pulled.

0:05.04.03.

The timer continued reeling down.

'Is it safe, Starkey?'

The timer continued spinning, and Starkey felt her eyes well. She thought, *Oh, goddamnit,* but she said nothing.

'I'm sorry, Jack.'

0:02.01.

She closed her eyes and tensed for something she would never feel.

'Starkey? Are we okay, Starkey?'

She opened her eyes. The timer showed 00:00, but there was no explosion.

Pell said, 'I think we're still alive.'

John Michael Fowles did not want to die. His head grew light, even as his chest seemed to swell. He heard Starkey's voice, and Pell's. He realized that they were working to de-arm the bomb, and, in that moment, wanted to laugh, but he was bleeding to death. He could feel the blood filling his lungs. He passed out again, then once more heard their voices. He lifted his head just enough to see them. He saw the bomb. They had done it. They had de-armed it. John Michael Fowles laughed then, blowing red bubbles from his mouth and nose. They thought they had saved themselves. They didn't know that they were wrong.

Fowles summoned all of his strength to rise.

*

'Pell, my hands hurt.'

Pell was holding her. He had crawled to her when the moment had passed, put his arms around her, and held her close. Now, he pushed up onto his knees.

'Tell me how to get to the phone. I'll call 911.'

'Get the keys first and unhook me. There were keys in the surge monitor. I think they probably go to the handcuffs.'

Pell sat back on his heels.

'There were keys, and you didn't tell me?'

'We didn't have time, Jack.'

Pell sighed deeply, as if all of the tension was only then flooding out of him. He followed her directions to the keys, then back to her. When her hands were free, Starkey rubbed her wrists. Her hands burned as the circulation returned.

Beyond Jack, from the couch, Fowles made a sound like a wet gurgle, then rolled off the couch onto the floor.

Pell lurched around.

'What was that?'

Starkey felt no sense of alarm. Fowles was as limp as a wet sheet.

'It's Fowles. He fell off the couch.'

Starkey called to him.

'Fowles? Can you hear me?'

Fowles reached a hand toward her dining room. His legs slowly worked as if he was trying to crawl away, but he couldn't bring his knees beneath himself.

'What's he doing, Carol?'

'I'll call 911 and get an ambulance. He's still alive.'

Starkey rose, then helped Pell to his feet. Across the room, Fowles inched past the end of the coffee table, leaving a red trail.

Starkey said, 'Just lay there, Fowles. I'm getting help.'

She left Pell by the front door, then went back to Fowles just as he edged to the far end of the couch.

Starkey came abreast of him as he reached behind the end of the couch, his back to her.

'Fowles?'

Fowles slowly teetered onto his back, once more facing her. What Starkey saw then made all of her training as a bomb technician come screaming back at her: *Secondary! Always clear for a secondary!*

She should have cleared the area for a secondary, just as Buck Daggett had always preached.

Fowles was clutching a second device to his chest. He looked up at Starkey with a bloodstained smile.

'The truth hurts.'

Starkey pushed away from him, shoving hard against a floor that tried to anchor her, trapped in a nightmare moment with legs that refused to move, her heart echoing thunder in her ears as she rushed in a painful, panicked, horrible lunge for Pell and the door as –

John Michael Fowles gazed up through the red lens of his own blood at a crimson world, then pressed the silver button that set him free.

After

Starkey stood in the open front door of the house they were renting, smoking as she watched the house across the street. The people who lived there, whose name she didn't know, had a black Chihuahua. It was fat and, Starkey thought, ugly. It would sit in their front yard, barking at anyone or anything that passed, and stand in the middle of the street, barking at cars. The cars would blow their horns, but the damned Chihuahua wouldn't move, forcing the cars to creep around it in a wide berth. Starkey had thought that was funny until two days ago when the Chihuahua came over and shit on her driveway. She'd tried to chase it back across the street, but the dog had just stood there, barking. Now she hated the mean little sonofabitch.

'Where are you?'

'Smoking.'

'You're going to get cancer.'

She smiled.

'You say the most romantic things.'

Starkey couldn't wait to move back to her own house, though the repairs would take another month, what with the foundation work, the new floor, two new shear walls, and all the doors and windows being replaced. Not one window or door was square after the blast because of the overpressure. It could have been worse. Starkey had reached Pell in the doorway when the device detonated. The pressure wave had washed over her like a supersonic tidal wave, kicking her into Pell and both of them through the door. That's what saved them. Kicked out the door, off the porch, and into the yard. They had both been cut by glass and wood splinters, and neither of them could hear for a week, but it could have been worse.

Starkey finished the cigarette, then flicked the butt into the yard. She tried not to smoke in the house because it irritated his eyes. She had been twenty-three days without a drink. When she was done with that, maybe she would try to kick the smokes. Change wasn't just possible, it was necessary.

They weren't going to prosecute a blind man. The Bureau of Alcohol, Tobacco, and Firearms had made a lot of noise about it at first, but Starkey and Pell had gotten Mr Red, and that counted for a lot. They even let Jack keep the medical; no one would take health benefits from a guy who'd lost his eyes on the job.

Starkey was still waiting to hear about herself. She had a good Fraternal Order of Police lawyer and Morgan's support, so she would do all right. She had the month off, and then the hearing. Morgan had told her that he would take care of it, and she trusted him. Barry Kelso called from time to time, asking after her. She found that she liked hearing from him. Beth Marzik never called.

Pell said, 'Come here. I want you to see this.'

He always said things like that, as if by her seeing something, he could enjoy it. She found that she liked that, too. She liked it very much.

Jack had placed candles around the bedroom. He had them in little stubby candleholders and on saucers and plates, twinkling on the dresser and the chest and the two nightstands. She watched as he set the last one, tracing the wick with his fingers, lighting it with one of her Bic lighters, dripping the wax that he aimed so carefully with his fingers onto a plate, setting the butt of the candle into it. He never asked for help with anything. She would offer, from time to time, but she never pushed it. He even cooked. He scared the shit out of her when he cooked.

'What do you think?'

'They're beautiful, Jack.'

'They're for you.'

'Thank you.'

'Don't move.'

'I'm here.'

He followed her voice, edging around the bed to her. He would have missed her by a couple of feet, so she touched his arm.

Pell had been living with her since he left the hospital. His eyes were gone. That was it. Neither of them knew if his staying here would be permanent, but you never know.

Starkey pulled him close and kissed him.

'Get in the bed, Jack.'

He smiled as he eased himself into the bed. She went around, pulling the shades. It was still light out, but with the shades down, the candles cast them in a copper glow. Sometimes, after they had made love, she would make shadow creatures in the candlelight and describe them to him.

Starkey took off her clothes, dropping them to the floor, and moved into his arms. She allowed his hands to move over her body. His fingers brushed her old scars, and the new scars. He touched her in places where she liked being touched. She had been frightened, their first time together, even in the dark. He saw with his hands.

'You're beautiful, Carol.'

'So you say.'

'Let me prove it.'

She gasped at his touch, and at the things he did for her. Starkey had come a long way; there was farther still to go. Getting there would be a better thing with Pell in her life.

Hostage

To Frank, Toni, Gina, Chris, and Norma;
And to Jack Hughes, who enriched our lives.
For twenty years of friendship and laughter,
tacky though it may be.

PROLOGUE

The man in the house was going to kill himself. When the man threw his phone into the yard, Talley knew that he had accepted his own death. After six years as a crisis negotiator with the Los Angeles Police Department's SWAT team, Sergeant Jeff Talley knew that people in crisis often spoke in symbols. This symbol was clear: Talk was over. Talley feared that the man would die by his own hand, or do something to force the police to kill him. It was called suicide by cop. Talley believed it to be his fault.

'Did they find his wife yet?'

'Not yet. They're still looking.'

'Looking doesn't help, Murray. I gotta have something to give this guy after what happened.'

'That's not your fault.'

'It is my fault. I blew it, and now this guy is circling the drain.'

Talley crouched behind an armored command vehicle with the SWAT commander, a lieutenant named Murray Leifitz, who was also his negotiating team supervisor. From this position, Talley had spoken to George Donald Malik through a dedicated crisis phone that had been cut into the house line. Now that Malik had thrown his phone into the yard, Talley could use the public address megaphone or do it face-to-face. He hated the megaphone, which made his voice harsh and depersonalized the contact. The illusion of a personal relationship was important; the illusion of trust was everything. Talley strapped on a Kevlar vest.

Malik shouted through the broken window, his voice high and strained.

'I'm going to kill this dog! I'm going to kill it!'

Leifitz leaned past Talley to peek at the house. This was the first time Malik had mentioned a dog.

'What the fuck? Does he have a dog in there?'

'How do I know? I've got to try to undo some of the damage here, okay? Ask the neighbors about the dog. Get me a name.'

'If he pops a cap, we're going in there, Jeff. That's all there is to it.'

'Just take it easy and get a name for the dog.'

Leifitz scuttled backward to speak with Malik's neighbors.

George Malik was an unemployed housepainter with too much credit card debt, an unfaithful wife who flaunted her affairs, and prostate cancer. Fourteen hours earlier, at two-twelve that morning, he had fired one shot above the heads of the police officers who had come to his door in response to a disturbance complaint. He then barricaded the door and threatened to kill himself unless his wife agreed to speak to him. The officers who secured the area ascertained from neighbors that Malik's wife, Elena, had left with their only child, a nine-year-old boy named Brendan. As detectives from Rampart Division set about locating her, Malik threatened suicide with greater frequency until Talley was convinced that Malik was nearing the terminal point. When the Rampart detectives reported what they believed to be a solid location obtained from the wife's sister, Talley took a chance. He told Malik that his wife had been found. That was Talley's mistake. He had violated a cardinal rule of crisis negotiation: He had lied, and been caught. He had made a promise that he had been unable to deliver, and so had destroyed the illusion of trust that he had been building. That was two hours ago, and now word had arrived that the wife had still not been found.

'I'm gonna kill this fuckin' dog, goddamnit! This is her goddamned dog, and I'm gonna shoot this sonofabitch right in the head, she don't start talkin' to me!'

Talley stepped out from behind the vehicle. He had been on the scene for eleven hours. His skin was greased with sweat, his head throbbed, and his stomach was cramping from too much coffee and stress. He made his voice conversational, yet concerned.

'George, it's me, Jeff. Don't kill anything, okay? We don't want to hear a gun go off.'

'You liar! You said my wife was gonna talk to me!'

It was a small stucco house the color of dust. Two casement windows braced the front door above a tiny porch. The door was closed, and drapes had been pulled across the windows. The window on the left was broken from the phone. Eight feet to the right of the porch, a five-member SWAT Tactical Team hunkered against the wall, waiting to breach the door. Malik could not be seen.

'George, listen, I said that we'd found her, and I want to explain that. I was wrong. We got our wires crossed out here, and they gave me bad information. But we're still looking, and when we find her, we'll have her talk to you.'

'You lied before, you bastard, and now you're lying again. You're lying to protect that bitch, and I won't have it. I'm gonna shoot her dog and then I'm gonna blow my brains out.'

Talley waited. It was important that he appear calm and give Malik the room to cool. People burned off stress when they talked. If he could reduce Malik's level of stress, they could get over the hump and still climb out of this.

'Don't shoot the dog, George. Whatever's between you and your wife, let's not take it out on the dog. Is it your dog, too?'

'I don't know whose fuckin' dog it is. She lied about everything else, so she probably lied about the dog. She's a natural-born liar. Like you.'

'George, c'mon. I was wrong, but I didn't lie. I made a mistake. A liar wouldn't admit that, but I want to be straight with you. Now, I'm a dog guy myself. What kind of dog you got in there?'

'I don't believe you. You know right where she is, and unless you make her talk to me, I'm gonna shoot this dog.'

The depths to which people sank in the shadowed crevasses of desperation could crush a man as easily as the weight of water at the ocean floor. Talley had learned to hear the pressure building in people's voices, and he heard it now. Malik was being crushed.

'Don't give up, George. I'm sure that she'll talk to you.'

'Then why won't she open her mouth? Why won't the bitch just say something, that's all she's gotta do?'

'We'll work it out.'

'Say something, goddamnit!'

'I said we'll work it out.'

'Say something or I'm gonna shoot this damned dog!'

Talley took a breath, thinking. Malik's choice of words left him confused. Talley had spoken clearly, yet Malik acted as if he hadn't heard. Talley worried that Malik was dissociating or approaching a psychotic break.

'George, I can't see you. Come to the window so I can see you.'

'STOP LOOKING AT ME!'

'George, please come to the window!'

Talley saw Leifitz return to the rear of the vehicle. They were close, only a few feet apart, Leifitz under cover, Talley exposed.

Talley spoke under his breath.

'What's the dog's name?'

Leifitz shook his head.

'They say he doesn't have a dog.'

'OPEN YOUR GODDAMNED MOUTH RIGHT NOW OR I'M SHOOTING THIS DOG!'

Something hard pounded in the center of Talley's head, and his back felt wet. He suddenly realized that illusions worked both ways. The Rampart detectives hadn't found Malik's wife because Malik's wife was inside. The neighbors were wrong. She had been inside the entire time. The wife and the boy.

'Murray, launch the team!'

Talley shouted at Murray Leifitz just as a loud whipcrack echoed from the house. A second shot popped even as the tactical team breached the front door.

Talley ran forward, feeling weightless. Later, he would not remember jumping onto the porch or entering through the door. Malik's lifeless body was pinned to the floor, his hands being cuffed behind his back even though he was already dead. Malik's wife was sprawled on the living-room sofa where she had been dead for over fourteen hours. Two tac officers were trying to stop the geyser of arterial blood that spurted from the neck of Malik's nine-year-old son. One of them screamed for the paramedics. The boy's eyes were wide, searching the room as if trying to find a reason for all this. His mouth opened and closed; his skin was luminous as it drained of color. The boy's eyes found Talley, who knelt and rested a hand on the boy's leg. Talley never broke eye contact. He didn't allow himself to blink. He let Brendan Malik have that comfort as he watched the boy die.

After a while, Talley went out to sit on the porch. His head buzzed like he was drunk. Across the street, police officers milled by their cars. Talley lit a cigarette, then replayed the past eleven hours, looking for clues that should have told him what was real. He could not find them. Maybe there weren't any, but he didn't believe that. He had blown it. He had made mistakes. The boy had been here the entire time, curled at the feet of his murdered mother like a loyal and faithful dog.

Murray Leifitz put a hand on his shoulder and told him to go home.

Jeff Talley had been a Los Angeles SWAT officer for thirteen years, serving as a Crisis Response Team negotiator for six. Today was his third crisis call in five days.

He tried to recall the boy's eyes, but had already forgotten if they were brown or blue.

Talley crushed his cigarette, walked down the street to his car, and went home. He had an eleven-year-old daughter named Amanda. He wanted to check her eyes. He couldn't remember their color and was scared that he no longer cared.

Part One

The Avocado Orchard

1

Bristo Camino, California

Friday, 2:47 p.m.

Dennis Rooney

It was one of those high-desert days in the suburban communities north of Los Angeles with the air so dry it was like breathing sand; the sun licked their skin with fire. They were eating hamburgers from the In-N-out, riding along in Dennis's truck, a red Nissan pickup that he'd bought for six hundred dollars from a Bolivian he'd met working construction two weeks before he had been arrested; Dennis Rooney driving, twenty-two years old and eleven days out of the Antelope Valley Correctional Facility, what the inmates called the Ant Farm; his younger brother, Kevin, wedged in the middle; and a guy named Mars filling the shotgun seat. Dennis had known Mars for only four days.

Later, in the coming hours when Dennis would frantically reconsider his actions, he would decide that it hadn't been the saw-toothed heat that had put him in the mood to do crime: It was fear. Fear that something special was waiting for him that he would never find, and that this special thing would disappear around some curve in his life, and with it his one shot at being more than nothing.

Dennis decided that they should rob the minimart.

'Hey, I know. Let's rob that fuckin' minimart, the one on the other side of Bristo where the road goes up toward Santa Clarita.'

'I thought we were going to the movie.'

That being Kevin, wearing his chickenshit face: eyebrows crawling over the top of his head, darting eyeballs, and quivering punkass lips. In the movie of Dennis's life, he saw himself as the brooding outsider all the cheerleaders wanted to fuck; his brother was the geekass cripple holding him back.

'This is a better idea, chickenshit. We'll go to the movie after.'

'You just got back from the Farm, Dennis, Jesus. You want to go back?'

Dennis flicked his cigarette out the window, ignoring the blowback of sparks and ash as he considered himself in the Nissan's sideview. By his own estimation, he had moody deep-set eyes the color of thunderstorms, dramatic cheekbones, and sensuous lips. Looking at himself, which he did, often, he knew that it was only a matter of time before his destiny arrived, before the special thing waiting for him presented itself and he could bag the minimum-wage jobs and life in a shithole apartment with his chickenshit brother.

Dennis adjusted the .32-caliber automatic wedged in his pants, then glanced past Kevin to Mars.

'What do you think, dude?'

Mars was a big guy, heavy across the shoulders and ass. He had a tattoo on the back of his shaved head that said BURN IT. Dennis had met him at the construction site where he and Kevin were pulling day work for a cement contractor. He didn't know Mars's last name. He had not asked.

'Dude? Whattaya think?'

'I think let's go see.'

That was all it took.

The minimart was on Flanders Road, a rural boulevard that linked several expensive housing tracts. Four pump islands framed a bunkerlike market that sold toiletries, soft drinks, booze, and convenience items. Dennis pulled up behind the building so they couldn't be seen from inside, the Nissan bucking as he downshifted. The transmission was a piece of shit.

'Look at this, man. The fuckin' place is dead. It's perfect.'

'C'mon, Dennis, this is stupid. We'll get caught.'

'I'm just gonna see, is all. Don't give yourself a piss enema.'

The parking lot was empty except for a black Beemer at the pumps and two bicycles by the front door. Dennis's heart was pounding, his underarms clammy even in the awful dry heat that sapped his spit. He would never admit it, but he was nervous. Fresh off the Farm, he didn't want to go back, but he didn't see how they could get caught, or what could go wrong. It was like being swept along by a mindless urge. Resistance was futile.

Cold air rolled over him as Dennis pushed inside. Two kids were at the magazine rack by the door. A fat Chinaman was hunkered behind the counter, so low that all Dennis could see was his head poking up like a frog playing submarine in a mud puddle.

The minimart was two aisles and a cold case packed with beer, yogurt, and Cokes. Dennis had a flash of uncertainty, and thought about telling Mars and Kevin that a whole pile of Chinamen were behind the counter so he could get out of having to rob the place, but he didn't. He went to the cold case, then along the rear wall to make sure no one was in the aisles, his heart pounding because he knew he was going to do it. He was going to rob this fucking place. As he was walking back to the truck, the Beemer pulled away. He went to the passenger window. To Mars.

'There's nothing but two kids and a Chinaman in there, the Chinaman behind the counter, a fat guy.'

Kevin said, 'They're Korean.'

'What?'

'The sign says "Kim." Kim is a Korean name.'

That was Kevin, always with something to say like that. Dennis wanted to reach across Mars and grab Kevin by the fucking neck. He pulled up his T-shirt to flash the butt of his pistol.

'Who gives a shit, Kevin? That Chinaman is gonna shit his pants when he sees this. I won't even have to take it out, goddamnit. Thirty seconds, we'll be down the road. He'll have to wipe himself before he calls the cops.'

Kevin squirmed with a case of the chicken-shits, his nerves making his eyes dance around like beans in hot grease.

'Dennis, please. What are we going to get here, a couple of hundred bucks? Jesus, let's go to the movie.'

Dennis told himself that he might have driven away if Kevin wasn't such a whiner, but, no, Kevin had to put on the goddamned pussy face, putting Dennis on the spot.

Mars was watching. Dennis felt himself flush, and wondered if Mars was judging him. Mars was a boulder of a guy; dense and quiet, watchful, with the patience of a rock. Dennis had noticed that about Mars on the job site; Mars considered people. He would watch a conversation, say, like when two of the Mexicans hammered a third to throw in with them on buying some tamales. Mars would watch, not really part of it but above it, as if he could see all the way back to when they were born, see them wetting the bed when they were five or jerking off when they thought they were alone. Then he would make a vacant smile like he knew everything they might do now or in the future, even about the goddamned tamales. It was creepy, sometimes, that expression on his face, but Mars thought that Dennis had good ideas and usually went along. First time they met, four days ago, Dennis felt that his destiny was finally at hand. Here was Mars, charged with some dangerous electrical potential that crackled under his skin, and he did whatever Dennis told him.

'Mars, we're gonna do this. We're robbing this fuckin' store.'

Mars climbed out of the truck, so cool that even heat like this couldn't melt him.

'Let's do it.'

Kevin didn't move. The two kids pedaled away.

'*No one's here, Kevin!* All you have to do is stand by the door and watch. This fat fuck will cough right up with the cash. They're insured, so they just hand over the cash. They get fired if they don't.'

Dennis grabbed his brother's T-shirt. The Lemonheads, for chrissake. His fucking brother was a lemonhead. Mars was already halfway to the door.

'Get out of the truck, you turd. You're making us look bad.'

Kevin wilted and slid out like a fuckin' baby.

Junior Kim, Jr.
Kim's Minimart

Junior Kim, Jr., knew a cheese dip when he saw one.

Junior, a second-generation Korean-American, had put in sixteen years behind a minimart counter in the Newton area of Los Angeles. Down in Shootin' Newton (as the LAPD called it), Junior had been beaten, mugged, stabbed, shot at, clubbed, and robbed forty-three times. Enough was enough. After sixteen years of that, Junior, his wife, their six children, and all four grandparents had bailed on the multicultural melting pot of greater LA, and moved north to the far less dangerous demographic of bedroom suburbia.

Junior was not naïve. A minimart, by its nature, draws cheese dips like bad meat draws flies. Even here in Bristo Camino, you had your shoplifters (mostly teenagers, but often men in business suits), your paperhangers (mostly women), your hookers passing counterfeit currency (driven up from LA by their pimps), and your drunks (mostly belligerent white men sprouting gin blossoms). Lightweight stuff compared to LA, but Junior believed in being prepared. After sixteen years of hard-won inner-city lessons, Junior kept 'a little something' under the counter for anyone who got out of hand.

When three cheese dips walked in that Friday afternoon, Junior leaned forward so that his chest touched the counter and his hands were hidden.

'May I help you?'

A skinny kid in a Lemonheads T-shirt stayed by the door. An older kid in a faded black wife-beater and a large man with a shaved head walked toward him, the older kid raising his shirt to show the ugly black grip of a pistol. 'Two packs of Marlboros for my friend here and all the cash you got in that box, you gook motherfucker.'

Junior Kim could read a cheese dip a mile away.

His face impassive, Junior fished under the counter for his 9mm Glock. He found it just as the cheese dip launched himself over the counter. Junior lurched to his feet, bringing up the Glock as the black-shirted dip crashed into him. Junior hadn't expected this asshole to jump over the counter, and hadn't been able to thumb off the safety.

The larger man shouted, 'He's got a gun!'

Everything happened so quickly that Junior wasn't sure whose hands were where. The black shirt forgot about his own gun and tried to twist away Junior's. The big guy reached across the counter, also grabbing for the gun. Junior was more scared now than any of the other times he had pulled his weapon. If he couldn't release the safety before this kid pulled his own gun, or wrestled away Junior's, Junior knew that he would be fucked. Junior Kim was in a fight for his life.

Then the safety slipped free, and Junior Kim, Jr., knew that he had won. He said, 'I gotcha, you dips.'

The Glock went off, a heavy 9mm explosion that made the cheese dip's eyes bulge with a terrible surprise.

Junior smiled, victorious.

'Fuck *you*.'

Then Junior felt the most incredible pain in his chest. It filled him as if he were having a heart attack. He stumbled back into the Slurpee machine as the blood spilled out of his chest and spread across his shirt. Then he slid to the floor.

The last thing Junior heard was the cheese dip by the door, shouting, 'Dennis! Hurry up! Somebody's outside!'

Margaret Hammond, Witness

Outside at the second pump island, Margaret Hammond heard a car backfire as she climbed from her Lexus.

Margaret, who lived across the street in a tile-roofed home that looked exactly like a hundred others in her development, saw three young white males run out of the minimart and get into a red Nissan pickup truck, which lurched away with the jumpy acceleration that tells you the clutch is shot. It headed west toward the freeway.

Margaret locked the pump nozzle to fill her tank, then went into the minimart to buy a Nestlé's Crunch chocolate bar, which she intended to eat before she got home.

Less than ten seconds later, by her own estimation, Margaret Hammond ran back into the parking lot. The red Nissan had disappeared. Margaret used her cell phone to call 911, who patched her through to the Bristo Camino Police Department.

Dennis

Their voices overlapped, Kevin grabbing Dennis's arm, making the truck swerve. Dennis punched him away.

'You killed that guy! You *shot* him!'

'I don't know if he's dead or what!'

'There was fucking blood everywhere! It's all over you!'

'Stop it, Kevin! He had a fuckin' gun! I didn't know he would have a gun! It just went off!'

Kevin pounded the dash, bouncing between Dennis and Mars like he was going to erupt through the roof.

'We're fucked, Dennis, *fucked*! What if he's *dead?!*'

'*SHUT UP!*'

Dennis licked his lips, tasting copper and salt. He glanced in the rearview. His face was splattered with red dew. Dennis lost it then, certifiably freaked out because he'd eaten human blood. He swiped at his face, wiping the blood on his jeans.

Mars touched him.

'Dude. Take it easy.'

'We've gotta get away!'

'We're getting away. No one saw us. No one caught us. We're fine.'

Mars sat quietly in the shotgun seat. Kevin and Dennis were wild, but Mars was as calm as if he had just awakened from a trance. He was holding the Chinaman's gun.

'Fuck! Throw it out, dude! We might get stopped.'

Mars pushed the gun into his waistband, then left his hand there, holding it the way some men hold their crotch.

'We might need it.'

Dennis upshifted hard, ignoring the clash of gears as he threw the Nissan toward the freeway two miles ahead. At least four people had seen the truck. Even these dumb Bristo cops would be able to put two and two together if they had witnesses who could tie them to the truck.

'Listen, we gotta think. We gotta figure out what to do.'

Kevin's eyes were like dinner plates.

'Jesus, Dennis, we gotta turn ourselves in.'

Dennis felt so much pressure in his head that he thought his eyes were swelling.

'No one's turning themselves in! We can get outta this! We just gotta figure out what to do!'

Mars touched him again.

'Listen.'

Mars was smiling at nothing. Not even looking at them.

'We're just three guys in a red truck. There's a million red trucks.'

Dennis desperately wanted to believe that.

'You think?'

'They've got to find witnesses. If they find those two kids or the woman, then those people have to describe us. Maybe they can, but maybe they can't. When the cops get all that sorted out, then they have to start looking for three white guys in a red truck. You know how many red trucks there are?'

'A million.'

'That's right. And how long does all that take? The rest of the day? Tomorrow? We can be across the border in four hours. Let's go down to Mexico.'

The vacant smile was absolutely sure of itself. Mars was so calm that Dennis found himself convinced; it was as if Mars had run this path before and knew the turns.

'That's a fucking plan, Mars. That's a *plan*! We can kick back for a few days, then come back when everything blows over. It always blows over.'

'That's right.'

Dennis pushed harder on the accelerator, felt the transmission lag, and then a loud BANG came from under the truck. The transmission let go. Six hundred dollars. Cash. What did he expect?

'Mother*FUCK*ing piece of *SHIT*!'

The truck lost power, bucking as Dennis guided it off the road. Even before it lurched to a stop, Dennis shoved open the door, desperate to run. Kevin caught his arm, holding him back.

'There's nothing we can do, Dennis. We're only making it worse.'

'Shut up!'

Dennis shook off his brother's hand and slid out of the truck. He searched up and down the road, half expecting to see a highway patrol car, but the cars were few and far between and those were mostly soccer moms. Flanders Road from here to the freeway cut through an area of affluent housing developments. Some of the communities were gated, but most weren't, though most were hidden from the road by hedges that masked heavy stone walls. Dennis looked at the hedges, and the walls that they hid. He wondered if escape lay beyond them.

It was like Mars read his mind.

'Let's steal a car.'

Dennis looked at the wall again. On the other side of it would be a housing development filled with cars. They could crash into a house, tie up the soccer mom to buy some time, and *drive*.

Dennis didn't think about it any more than that.

'Let's go.'

'Dennis, please.'

Dennis pulled his brother out of the truck.

They crashed into the hedges and went up the wall.

Officer Mike Welch, Bristo Camino Police

Officer Mike Welch, thirty-two years old, married, one child, was rolling code seven to the Krispy Kreme donut shop on the west side of Bristo Camino when he got the call.

'Unit four, base.'

'Four.'

'Armed robbery, Kim's Minimart on Flanders Road, shots fired.'

Welch thought that was absurd.

'Say again, shots fired. Are you kidding me?'

'Three white males, approximately twenty years, jeans and T-shirts, driving a red Nissan pickup last seen west on Flanders Road. Get over there and see about Junior.'

Mike Welch was rolling westbound on Flanders Road. Junior's service station was straight ahead, less than two miles. Welch went code three, hitting the lights and siren. He had never before in his three years as a police officer rolled code three other than when he pulled over a speeder.

'I'm on Flanders now. Is Junior shot?'

'That's affirm. Ambulance is inbound.'

Welch floored it. He was so intent on beating the paramedics to Kim's that he was past the red truck parked on the opposite side of the road before he realized that it matched the description of the getaway vehicle.

Welch shut his siren and pulled off onto the shoulder. He twisted around to stare back up the street. He couldn't see anyone in or around the truck, but there it was, a red Nissan pickup. Welch waited for a gap in traffic, then swung around and drove back, pulling off behind the Nissan. He keyed his shoulder mike.

'Base, four. I'm a mile and a half east of Kim's on Flanders. Got a red Nissan pickup, license Three-Kilo-Lima-Mike-Four-Two-Nine. It appears abandoned. Can you send someone else to Kim's?'

'Ah, we can.'

'I'm gonna check it out.'

'Three-Kilo-Lima-Mike-Four-Two-Nine. Rog.'

Welch climbed out of his car and rested his right hand on the butt of his Browning Hi-Power. He didn't draw his weapon, but he wanted to be ready. He walked up along the passenger side of the truck, glanced underneath, then walked around the front. The engine was still ticking, and the hood was warm. Mike Welch thought, sonofabitch, this was it, this was the getaway vehicle.

'Base, four. Area's clear. Vehicle is abandoned.'

'Rog.'

Welch continued around to the driver's-side door and looked inside. He couldn't be sure that this was the getaway vehicle, but his heart was hammering with excitement. Mike Welch had come to the Bristo police department after seven years as a roofing contractor. He had thought that police work would be more than writing traffic tickets and breaking up domestic disturbances, but it hadn't worked out that way; now, for the first time in his career, he might come face-to-face with an actual felon. He looked either way up and down the road, wondering why they had abandoned the truck and where they had gone. He suddenly felt frightened. Welch stared at the hedges. He squatted again, trying to see under the low branches, but saw nothing except a wall. Welch drew his gun, then approached the hedges, looking more closely. Several branches were broken. He glanced back at the truck, thinking it through, imagining three suspects pushing through the hedges. Three kids on the run, shitting their pants, going over the wall. On the other side of the wall was a development of expensive homes called York Estates. Welch knew from his patrol route that there were only two streets out unless they went over the wall again. They would be hiding in someone's garage or running like hell out the back side of the development, trying to get away.

Welch listened to the Nissan's ticking engine, and decided that he was no more than a few minutes behind them. His heart rate increased. He made his decision. Welch burned rubber as he swung out onto the road, intent on cutting them off before they escaped the development, intent on making the arrest.

Dennis

Dennis dropped from the wall into a different world, hidden behind lush ferns and plants with leathery green leaves and orange trees. His impulse was to keep running, haul ass across the yard, jump the next wall, and keep going, but the siren was right on top of them. And then the siren stopped.

Kevin said, 'Dennis, *please*, the police are gonna see the truck. They're gonna know who we are.'

'Shut up, Kevin. I *know*. Lemme think!'

They were in a dense garden surrounding a tennis court at the rear of a palatial home. A swimming pool was directly in front of them with the main house beyond the pool, a big-ass two-story house with lots of windows and doors, and one of the doors was open. Just like that. Open. If people were home, there would be a car. A Sony boom box beside the pool was playing music. There wouldn't be music if no one was home.

Dennis glanced at Mars, and, without even looking back at him, almost as if he had read Dennis's mind again, Mars nodded.

Jennifer Smith

Sixty feet away through the open door, Jennifer Smith was thoroughly pissed off about the state of her life. Her father was behind closed doors at the front of the house, working. He was an accountant, and often worked at home. Her mother was in Florida visiting their Aunt Kate. With her mom in Florida and her dad working, Jen was forced 24/7 to ride herd on her ten-year-old brother, Thomas. If her friends wanted to go to the Multiplex, Thomas had to go. If she lied about going to Palmdale so she could sneak down to LA, Thomas would tell. Jennifer Smith was sixteen years old. Having a turd like Thomas grafted to her butt 24/7 was wrecking her summer.

Jen had been laying out by the pool, but she had come in to make tuna fish sandwiches. She would have let the turd starve, but she didn't mind making lunch for her father.

'Thomas?'

He hated it if you called him Tommy. He didn't even like Tom. It had to be Thomas.

'Thomas, go tell Daddy that lunch is ready.'

'Eat me.'

Thomas was playing Nintendo in the family room.

'Go tell Daddy.'

'Just yell. He'll hear you.'

'Go get him or I'll spit in your food.'

'Spit twice. It turns me on.'

'You are *so* gross.'

Thomas paused the Nintendo game and looked around at her. 'I'll get him if you ask Elyse and Tris to come lay out.'

Elyse and Tris were her two best friends. They had stopped coming over because Thomas totally creeped them out. He would wait in the house until everyone was lying by the pool, then he would appear and offer to rub oil on them. Even though everyone said ooo, yuck, go away, he would sit there and stare at their bodies.

'They won't lay out with you here. They know you watch.'

'They like it.'

'You are *so* gross.'

When the three young men stepped inside, Jen's first thought was that they were gardeners, but all the gardeners she knew were short, dark men from Central America. Her second thought was that maybe they were older kids from school, but that didn't feel right either.

Jennifer said, 'May I help you?'

The first one pointed at Thomas.

'Mars, get the troll.'

The biggest one ran at Thomas, as the first one charged into the kitchen.

Jennifer screamed just as the first boy covered her mouth so tightly that she thought her face would break. Thomas tried to shout, but the bigger boy mashed his face into the carpet.

The third one was younger. He hung back near the door, crying, talking in a loud stage whisper, trying to keep his voice down.

'Dennis, let's go! This is crazy!'

'Shut up, Kevin! We're here. Deal with it.'

The one holding her, the one she now knew as Dennis, bent her backwards over the counter, mashing the sandwiches. His hips ground against hers, pinning her. His breath smelled of hamburgers and cigarettes.

'Stop kicking! I'm not going to hurt you!'

She tried to bite his hand. He pushed her head farther back until her neck felt like it would snap.

'I said stop it. Relax, and I'll let you go.'

Jennifer fought harder until she saw the gun. The bigger boy was holding a black pistol to Thomas's head.

Jennifer stopped fighting.

'I'm going to take my hand away, but you better not yell. You understand that?'

Jennifer couldn't stop watching the gun.

'Close the door, Kevin.'

She heard the door close.

Dennis took away his hand, but kept it close, ready to clamp her mouth again. His voice was a whisper.

'Who else is here?'

'My father.'

'Is there anyone else?'

'No.'

'Where is he?'

'In his office.'

'Is there a car?'

Her voice failed. All she could do was nod.

'Don't yell. If you yell, I'll kill you. Do you understand that?'

She nodded.

'Where's his office?'

She pointed toward the entry.

Dennis laced his fingers through her hair and pushed her toward the hall. He followed so closely that his body brushed hers, reminding her that she was wearing only shorts and a bikini top. She felt naked and exposed.

Her father's office was off the entry hall behind wide double doors. They didn't bother to knock or say anything. Dennis pulled open the door, and the big one, Mars, carried in Thomas, the gun still at his head. Dennis pushed her onto the floor, then ran straight across the room, pointing his gun at her father.

'Don't say a goddamned word! Don't fucking move!'

Her father was working at his computer with a sloppy stack of printouts all around. He was a slender man with a receding hairline and glasses. He blinked over the tops of the glasses as if he didn't quite understand what he was seeing. He probably thought they were friends of hers, playing a joke. But then she saw that he knew it was real.

'What are you doing?'

Dennis aimed his gun with both hands, shouting louder.

'Don't you fucking move, goddamnit! Keep your ass in that chair! Let me see your hands!'

What her father said then made no sense to her.

He said, 'Who sent you?'

Dennis shoved Kevin with his free hand.

'Kevin, close the windows! Stop being a turd!'

Kevin went to the windows and closed the shutters. He was crying worse than Thomas.

Dennis waved his gun at Mars.

'Keep him covered, dude. Watch the girl.'

Mars pushed Thomas onto the floor with Jennifer, then aimed at her father. Dennis put his own gun in the waistband of his pants, then snatched a lamp from the corner of her father's desk. He jerked the plug from the wall, then the electrical cord from the lamp.

'Don't go psycho and everything will be fine. Do you hear that? I'm gonna take your car. I'm gonna tie you up so you can't call the cops, and I'm gonna take your car. I don't want to hurt you, I just want the car. Gimme the keys.'

Her father looked confused.

'What are you talking about? Why did you come here?'.

'*I want the fucking car, you asshole! I'm stealing your car! Now, where are the keys?*'

'That's what you want, the car?'

'Am I talking fucking Russian here or what? DO YOU HAVE A CAR?'

Her father raised his hands, placating.

'In the garage. Take it and leave. The keys are on the wall by the garage door. By the kitchen. Take it.'

'Kevin, go get the keys, then come help tie these bastards up so we can get outta here.'

Kevin, still by the windows, said, 'There's a cop coming.'

Jennifer saw the police car through the gaps in the shutters. A policeman got out. He looked around as if he was taking his bearings, then came toward their house.

Dennis grabbed her hair again.

'Don't fucking say a word. Not one fucking word.'

'Please don't hurt my children.'

'*Shut up.* Mars, you be ready! Mars!'

Jennifer watched the policeman come up the walk. He disappeared past the edge of the window, then their doorbell rang.

Kevin scuttled to his older brother, gripping his arm.

'He knows we're here, Dennis! He must've seen me closing the shutters!'

'Shut up!'

The doorbell rang again.

Jennifer felt Dennis's sweat drip onto her shoulder and wanted to scream. Her father stared at her, his eyes locked onto hers, slowly shaking his head. She didn't know if he was telling her not to scream, or not to move, or even if he realized that he was doing it.

The policeman walked past the windows toward the side of the house.

'He knows we're here, Dennis! He's looking for a way in!'

'He doesn't know shit! He's just looking.'

Kevin was frantic, and now Jennifer could hear the fear in Dennis's voice, too.

'He saw me at the window! He knows someone's here! Let's give up.'

'Shut up!'

Dennis went to the window. He peered through the shutters, then suddenly rushed back to Jennifer and grabbed her by the hair again.

'Get up.'

Mike Welch

Officer Mike Welch didn't know that everyone in the house was currently clustered less than twenty feet away, watching him through the gaps in the shutters. He had not seen Kevin Rooney or anyone else when he'd pulled up. He'd been too busy parking the car.

As near as Welch could figure, the people from the red Nissan had jumped the wall into these people's backyard. He suspected that the three suspects were blocks away by now, but he hoped that someone in this house or the other houses on this cul-de-sac had seen them and could provide a direction of flight.

When no one answered the door, Welch went to the side gate and called out. When no one responded, he returned to the front door and rang the bell for the third and final time. He was turning away to try the neighbor when the heavy front door opened and a pretty teenage girl looked out. She was pale. Her eyes were rimmed red.

Welch gave his best professional smile.

'Miss, I'm Officer Mike Welch. Did you happen to see three young men running through the area?'

'No.'

Her voice was so soft he could barely hear her. Welch noted that she appeared upset, and wondered about that.

'It would've been five or ten minutes ago. Something like that. I have reason to believe that they jumped the wall into your backyard.'

'No.'

The red-rimmed eyes filled. Welch watched her eyes blur, watched twin tears roll in slow motion down her cheeks, and knew that they were in the house with her. They were probably standing right on the other side of the door. Mike Welch's heart began to pound. His fingers tingled.

'Okay, miss, like I said, I was just checking. You have a good day.'

He quietly unsnapped the release on his holster and rested his hand on his gun. He shifted his eyes pointedly to the door, then mouthed a silent question, asking if anyone was there. She did not have time to respond.

Inside, someone that Mike Welch could not see shouted, 'He's going for his gun!'

Loud explosions blew through the door and window. Something hit

Mike Welch in the chest, knocking him backward. His Kevlar vest stopped the first bullet, but another punched into his belly below the vest, and a third slipped over the top of his vest to lodge high in his chest. He tried to keep his feet under him, but they fell away. The girl screamed, and someone else inside the house screamed, too.

Mike Welch found himself flat on his back in the front yard. He sat up, then realized that he'd been shot and fell over again. He heard more shots, but he couldn't get up or duck or run for cover. He pulled his gun and fired toward the house without thinking who he might be hitting. His only thought was to survive.

He heard more shots, and screaming, but then he could no longer hold his gun. It was all he could do to key his shoulder mike.

'Officer down. Officer down. Jesus, I've been shot.'

'Say again? Mike? Mike, what's going on?'

Mike Welch stared at the sky, but could not answer.

2

Friday, 3:24 p.m.

Jeff Talley

Two-point-one miles from York Estates, Jeff Talley was parked in an avocado orchard, talking to his daughter on his cell phone, his command radio tuned to a whisper. He often left his office in the afternoon and came to this orchard, which he had discovered not long after he had taken the job as the chief of Bristo Camino's fourteen-member police department. Rows of trees, each tree the same as the last, each a measured distance from the next, standing without motion in the clean desert air like a chorus of silent witnesses. He found peace in the sameness of it.

His daughter, Amanda, now fourteen, broke that peace.

'Why can't I bring Derek with me? At least I would have someone to hang with.'

Her voice reeked of coldness. He had called Amanda because today was Friday; she would be coming up for the weekend.

'I thought we would go to a movie together.'

'We go to a movie every time I come up there. We can still go to the movies. We'll just bring Derek.'

'Maybe another time.'

'When?'

'Maybe next time. I don't know.'

She made an exaggerated sigh that left him feeling defensive.

'Mandy? It's okay if you bring friends. But I enjoy our alone time, too. I want us to talk about things.'

'Mom wants to talk to you.'

'I love you.'

She didn't answer.

'I love you, Amanda.'

'You always say you want to talk, but then we go sit in a movie so we can't talk. Here's Mom.'

Jane Talley came on the line. They had separated five months after he resigned from the Los Angeles Police Department, took up residence on their couch, and stared at the television for twenty hours a day until

607

neither of them could take it anymore and he had moved out. That was two years ago.

'Hey, Chief. She's not in the greatest mood.'

'I know.'

'How you doing?'

Talley thought about it.

'She's not liking me very much.'

'It's hard for her right now. She's fourteen.'

'I know.'

'She's still trying to understand. Sometimes she's fine with it, but other times everything sweeps over her.'

'I try to talk to her.'

He could hear the frustration in Jane's voice, and his own.

'Jeffrey, you've been trying to talk for two years, but nothing comes out. Just like that, you left and started a new life and we weren't a part of it. Now you have this new life up there and she's making a new life down here. You understand that, don't you?'

Talley didn't say anything, because he didn't know what to say. Every day since he moved to Bristo Camino he told himself that he would ask them to join him but he hadn't been able to do it. He knew that Jane had spent the past two years waiting for him. He thought that if he asked right now she would come to him, but all he managed to do was stare at the silent, immobile trees.

Finally, Jane had had enough of the silence.

'I don't want to go on like this anymore, just being separated. You and Mandy aren't the only ones who need to make a life.'

'I know. I understand.'

'I'm not asking you to understand. I don't care if you understand.'

Her voice came out sharp and hurt, then both of them were silent. Talley thought of her on the day they were married; against the white country wedding gown, her skin had been golden.

Jane finally broke the silence, her voice resigned. She would learn no more today than yesterday; her husband would offer nothing new. Talley felt embarrassed and guilty.

'Do you want me to drop her at your house or at the office?'

'The house would be fine.'

'Six o'clock?'

'Six. We can have dinner, maybe.'

'I won't be staying.'

When the phone went dead, Talley put it aside, and thought of the dream. The dream was always the same, a small clapboard house surrounded by a full SWAT tactical team, helicopters overhead, media beyond the cordon. Talley was the primary negotiator, but the nightmare reality of the dream left him standing in the open without cover or protection while Jane and Amanda watched him from the cordon. Talley was in a life-or-death negotiation with an unknown male subject who had barricaded himself in the house and was threatening suicide. Over and over, the man screamed, 'I'm going to do it! I'm going to do it!' Talley talked him back from the brink each time, but, each time, knew that the man had stepped closer to the edge. It was only a matter of time. No one had seen this man. No neighbors or family had been found to provide an ID. The subject would not reveal his name. He was a voice behind walls to everyone except Talley, who knew with a numbing dread that the man in the house was himself. He had become the subject in the house, locked in time and frozen in place, negotiating with himself to spare his own life.

In those first weeks, Brendan Malik's eyes watched him from every shadow. He saw the light in them die over and over, dimming like a television with its plug pulled, the spark that had been Brendan Malik growing smaller, falling away until it was gone. After a while, Talley felt nothing, watching the dying eyes the same way he would watch *Wheel of Fortune*: because it was there.

Talley resigned from the LAPD, then sat on his couch for almost a year, first in his home and later in the cheap apartment he had rented in Silver Lake after Jane threw him out. Talley told himself that he had left his job and his family because he couldn't stand having them witness his own self-destruction, but after a while he grew to believe that his reasons were simpler, and less noble: He believed that his former life was killing him, and he was scared. The incorporated township of Bristo Camino was looking for a chief of police for their fourteen-member police force, and they were glad to have him. They liked it that he was SWAT, even though the job was no more demanding than writing traffic citations and speaking at local schools. He told himself that it was a good place to heal. Jane had been willing to wait for the healing, but the healing never quite seemed to happen. Talley believed that it never would.

Talley started the car and eased off the hard-packed soil of the orchard onto a gravel road, following it down to the state highway that ran the length of the Santa Clarita Valley. When he reached the highway, he turned up his radio and heard Sarah Weinman, the BCPD dispatch officer, shouting frantically over the link.

'... *Welch is down. We have a man down in York Estates*...'

Other voices were crackling back at her, Officers Larry Anders and Kenn Jorgenson talking over each other in a mad rush.

Talley punched the command freq button that linked him to dispatch on a dedicated frequency.

'Sarah, one. What do you mean, Mike's down?'

'Chief?'

'What about Mike?'

'He's been shot. The paramedics from Sierra Rock Fire are on the way. Jorgy and Larry are rolling from the east.'

In the nine months that Talley had been in Bristo, there had been only three felonies, two for nonviolent burglaries and once when a woman had tried to run down her husband with the family car.

'Are you saying that he was *intentionally* shot?'

'Junior Kim's been shot, too! Three white males driving a red Nissan pickup. Mike called in the truck, then called a forty-one fourteen at one-eight Castle Way in York Estates, and the next thing I know he said he'd been shot. I haven't been able to raise him since then.'

Forty-one fourteen. Welch had intended to approach the residence.

Talley punched the button that turned on his lights and siren. York Estates was six minutes away.

'What's the status of Mr. Kim?'

'Unknown at this time.'

'Do we have an ID on the suspects?'

'Not at this time.'

'I'm six out and rolling. Fill me in on the way.'

Talley had spent the last year believing that the day he became a crisis negotiator for the Los Angeles Police Department had forever changed his life for the worse.

His life was about to change again.

Jennifer

Jennifer had never heard anything as loud as their guns; not the cherry bombs that Thomas popped in their backyard or the crowd at the Forum when the Lakers slammed home a game-winning dunkenstein. The gunfire in movies didn't come close. When Mars and Dennis started shooting, the sound rocked through her head and deafened her.

Jennifer screamed. Dennis slammed the front door, pulled her backwards to the office, then pushed her down. She grabbed Thomas and held tight. Her father wrapped them in his arms. Layers of gun smoke hung in shafts of light that burned through the shutters; the smell of it stung her nose.

When the shooting was done, Dennis sucked air like a bellows, stalking back and forth between the entry and office, his face white.

'We're fucked! That cop is *down!*'

Mars went to the entry. He didn't hurry or seem scared; he *strolled.*

'Let's get the car before more of them get here.'

Kevin was on the floor beside her father's desk, shaking. His face was milky.

'You shot a cop. You shot a cop, Dennis!'

Dennis grabbed his brother by the shirt.

'Didn't you hear Mars? He was going for his gun!'

Jennifer heard a siren approaching behind the shouting. Then Dennis heard it, too, and ran back to the windows.

'Oh, man, they're coming!'

Jennifer's father pulled her closer, almost as if he was trying to squeeze her into himself.

'Take the keys and go. The keys are on the wall by the garage. It's a Jaguar. Take it while you still can.'

Dennis stared through the open shutters like prison bars, watching the street with fearful expectation. Jennifer wanted them to run, to go, to get out of her life, but Dennis stood frozen at the windows as if he was waiting for something.

Mars spoke from the entry, his voice as calm as still water.

'Let's take the man's car, Dennis. We have to go.'

Then the siren suddenly seemed to be in the house, and it was too late. Tires screeched outside. Dennis ran to the front door. The shooting started again.

Talley

York Estates was a walled development that had been named for the legendary walled city of York in England, a village that was protected from the world by a great stone wall. The developers built twenty-eight homes on one- to three-acre sites in a pattern of winding streets and cul-de-sacs with names like Lancelot Lane, Queen Anne Way, and King John Place, then surrounded it by a stone wall that was more decorative than protective. Talley cut his siren as he entered from the north, but kept the lights flashing. Jorgenson and Anders were shouting that they were under fire. Talley heard the pop of a gunshot over the radio.

When he turned into Castle Way, Talley saw Jorgenson and Anders crouched behind their car with their weapons out. Two women were in the open door of the house behind them and a teenaged boy was standing near the cul-de-sac's mouth. Talley hit the public address key on his mike as he sped up the street.

'You people take cover. Get inside your homes!'

Jorgenson and Anders turned to watch him approach. The two women looked confused and the boy stood without moving. Talley burped his siren, and shouted at them again.

'Get inside now! You people move!'

Talley hit the brakes hard, stopping behind Jorgenson's unit. Two shots pinged from the house, one snapping past overhead, the other thumping dully into Talley's windshield. He rolled out the door and pulled himself into a tight ball behind the front wheel, using the hub as cover. Mike Welch lay crumpled on the front lawn of a large Tudor home less than forty feet away.

Anders shouted, 'Welch is down! They shot him!'

'Are all three subjects inside?'

'I don't know! We haven't seen anyone!'

'Are civilians in the house?'

'I don't know!'

More sirens were coming from the east. Talley knew that would be Dreyer and Mikkelson in unit six with the ambulance. The shooting had stopped, but he could hear shouts and screaming inside the house. He flattened on the street and called to Welch from under the car.

'Mike! Can you hear me?'

Welch didn't respond.

Anders shouted, his voice frantic.

'I think he's dead!'

'Calm down, Larry. I can hear you.'

Talley had to take in the scene and make decisions without knowing who or what he was dealing with. Welch was in the middle of the front lawn, unmoving and unprotected. Talley had to act.

'Does this house back up on Flanders Road?'

'Yes, sir. The truck is right on the other side of the wall that runs behind the house, that red Nissan! It's the suspects who hit Kim's.'

The sirens were closer. Talley had to assume that innocents were inside. He had to assume that Mike Welch was alive. He keyed his transceiver mike.

'Six, one. Who's on?'

Dreyer's voice came back.

'It's Dreyer, Chief. We're one minute out.'

'Where's the ambulance?'

'Right behind us.'

'Okay. You guys set up on Flanders by the truck in case these guys go back over the wall. Send the ambulance in, but tell them to wait at Castle and Tower. I'll bring Welch to them.'

Talley broke the connection, then pushed himself up to a crouch.

'Larry, did you guys fire on the house?'

'No, sir.'

'Don't.'

'What are you going to do?'

'Stay down. Don't fire at the house.'

Talley climbed back into his car, keeping his head low and the driver's door open. He backed up, then powered into the yard, maneuvering to a stop between Welch and the house to use the car as a shield. Another shot popped the passenger-side window. He rolled out of the car almost on top of Welch. Talley opened the rear door, then dragged Welch to the car. It was like lifting two hundred pounds of deadweight, but Welch moaned. He was alive. Talley propped him upright in the open door, then lifted for all he was worth to fold Welch onto the backseat. He slammed the door, then saw Welch's gun on the grass. He went back for it. He returned to the car and floored the accelerator, fishtailing across the slick grass as he cut across the yard and into the street. He sped back along the cul-de-sac to the corner where the ambulance was waiting. Two paramedics pulled Welch from the rear and pushed a compress onto his chest. Talley didn't ask if Welch would make it. He knew from experience that they wouldn't know.

Talley stared down the length of the cul-de-sac and felt himself tremble. The first flush of panic was passing, and now he had time to think. Now he had time to acknowledge that what was happening here was what had cost him so much in Los Angeles. A hostage situation was developing. His mouth went dry and something sour flushed in his throat that threatened to make him retch. He keyed the mike again to call his dispatcher. He had exactly four units on duty and another five officers off. He would need them all.

'Chief, I pulled Dreyer and Mikkelson off the minimart. We've got no one on the scene now. It's totally unsecured.'

'Call the CHP and the Sheriffs. Tell them what's going on and request a full crisis team. Tell them we've got two men down and we have a possible hostage situation.'

Talley's eyes filled when he realized that he had used that word. Hostage.

He remembered Welch's gun. He sniffed the muzzle, then checked the magazine. Welch had returned fire, which meant that he might have wounded someone in the house. Maybe even an innocent.

He shut his eyes hard and keyed the mike again.

'Tell them to hurry.'

Jennifer

Jennifer whispered, 'Daddy.'

Her father held her head, whispered back.

'Shh.'

They snuggled closer. Jennifer thought her father might be trying to pull them through the floor, that if he could just make the three of them small enough they would disappear. She watched Mars peering through the shutters, his wide back hunched like an enormous swollen toad. When Mars glanced back at them, he looked high.

Kevin threw a *TV Guide* at him.

'What's wrong with you? Why'd you start shooting?'

'To keep them away.'

'We could've gotten out the back!'

Dennis jerked Kevin toward the entry.

'Get it together, Kev. They found the truck. They're already behind us.'

'This is bullshit, Dennis! We should give up!'

Jennifer wanted them to run. She wanted them to get away, if that's what it took; she wanted them *out.*

The words boiled out of her before she could stop them.

'We don't want you here!'

Her father squeezed her, his voice soft.

'Be quiet.'

Jennifer couldn't stop.

'You have no right to be here! No one invited you!'

Her father pulled her closer.

Dennis jabbed a finger at her.

'Shut up, bitch!'

He turned and shoved his brother into the wall so hard that Jennifer flinched.

'Stop it, Kevin! Go through the house and lock all the windows. Lock the doors, then watch the backyard. They're gonna come over that wall just like we did.'

Kevin seemed confused.

'Why don't we just give up, Dennis? We're caught.'

'It's going to be dark in a few hours. Things will change when it gets dark. Go do it, Kev. We're going to get out of this. We will.'

Jennifer felt her father sigh before he spoke. He slowly pushed to his knees.

'None of you are going to get out of this.'

Dennis said, 'Shut the fuck up. Go on, Kevin. Watch the back.'

Kevin disappeared toward the rear through the entry.

Her father stood. Both Dennis and Mars aimed their guns at him.

Jennifer pulled at his legs.

'Daddy! Don't!'

Her father raised his hands.

'It's okay, sweetie. I'm not going to do anything. I just want to go to my desk.'

Dennis extended his gun.

'Are you fuckin' nuts?! You're not going anywhere!'

'Just take it easy, son.'

'Daddy, don't!'

Her father seemed to be moving in a dream. She wanted to stop him, but she couldn't. She wanted to say something, but nothing came out. He walked stiffly, as if he was prepared to take a punch. It was as if this man in the dream wasn't her father, but someone she had never before seen.

He went behind his desk, carefully placing two computer disks in a black leather disk case as he spoke. Dennis followed along beside him, shouting for him to stop, shouting that he shouldn't take another step, and pointing the gun at his head. Dennis looked as scared as she felt.

'I'm warning you, goddamnit!'

'I'm going to open my desk.'

'*I'll fuckin' kill you!*'

'Daddy, *please!!!*'

Jennifer's father held up a single finger as if to show them that one tiny finger could do them no harm, then used it to slide open the drawer. He nodded toward the drawer, as if to show Dennis that nothing would hurt him. Her father took out a thick booklet.

'This is a list of every criminal lawyer in California. If you give up right now, I'll help you get the best lawyer in the state.'

Dennis slapped the book aside.

'Fuck you! We just killed a cop! We killed that Chinaman! We'll get the fuckin' death penalty!'

'I'm telling you that you won't, not if you let me help you. But if you stay in this house, I can promise you this: You'll die.'

'*Shut up!*'

Dennis swung his gun hard and hit her father in the temple with a wet thud. He fell sideways like a sack that had been dropped to the floor.

'*No!*'

Jennifer lunged forward. She pushed Dennis before she realized what she was doing.

'*Leave him alone!*'

She shoved Dennis back, then dropped to her knees beside her father. The gun had cut an ugly gouge behind his right eye at the hairline. The gouge pulsed blood, and was already swelling.

'Daddy? Daddy, wake up!'

He didn't respond.

'Daddy, *please!*'

Her father's eyes danced insanely beneath the lids as his body trembled.

'Daddy!'

Tears blurred her eyes as unseen hands lifted her away.

The nightmare had begun.

3

Friday, 3:51 p.m.

Talley

Talley wanted to stay with Welch, but he didn't have the time. He had to stabilize the scene and find out what was going on inside the house. He requested a second ambulance to stand by in case there were more casualties, then climbed back into his car and once more drove into the cul-de-sac. He brought his unit so close to Anders's vehicle that the bumpers crunched. He slipped out and hunkered behind the wheel again, calling over to Anders and Jorgenson.

'Larry, Jorgy, listen up.'

They were young guys. Men who would work as carpenters or salesmen if they weren't working as suburban policemen. They had never seen anything like what was now developing on Castle Way, and neither had any of Talley's other men. They had never pulled their guns. They had never made a felony arrest.

'We've got to evacuate these houses and seal the neighborhood. I want all the streets coming in here blocked.'

Anders nodded vigorously, excited and scared.

'Just the cul-de-sac?'

'All the streets coming into the neighborhood. Use Welch's unit to get back to the corner, then go from house to house here on the cul-de-sac through the backyards. Climb the walls if you have to, and move everyone out the same way. Don't expose yourself or anyone else to this house.'

'What if they won't leave?'

'They'll do what you say. But don't let anyone come out the front of their homes. Start with the house directly behind us. Someone could be wounded in there.'

'Right, Chief.'

'Find out who lives here. We need to know.'

'Okay.'

'One more thing. We might have one or more perps still on the loose. Have the other guys start a house-to-house. Warn everyone in the neighborhood to be on the lookout.'

Anders duckwalked to Welch's unit, the first car in the line, then swung it around in a tight turn and accelerated out of the cul-de-sac.

The first few minutes of any crisis situation were always the worst. In the beginning, you rarely knew what you were dealing with, and the unknown could kill you. Talley needed to find out who he was dealing with, and who was at risk in the house. Maybe all three perpetrators were in the house, but he had no way of knowing. They might have split up. They might have already murdered everyone inside. They might have killed the occupants, shot up the street, then committed suicide. Jeff Talley might be staring at a lifeless house.

Talley keyed his mike to talk to his other cars.

'This is Talley. Clear the freq and listen. Jorgenson and I are currently in front of the house at one-eight Castle Way in York Estates. Anders is evacuating the residents of the surrounding houses. Dreyer and Mikkelson are at the rear of the property on Flanders Road near a red Nissan pickup. We believe that one or more of the people who shot Junior Kim and Mike Welch are in the house. They are armed. We need an ID. Did Welch run the plates on that truck?'

Mikkelson came back.

'Chief, two.'

'Go, two.'

'The truck is registered to Dennis James Rooney, white male, age twenty-two. He has an Agua Dulce address.'

Talley pulled out his pad and scratched down Rooney's name. In another life he would dispatch a unit to Rooney's address, but he didn't have the manpower for that now.

His radio popped again.

'Chief, Anders.'

'Go, Larry.'

'I'm with one of the neighbors. She says the people in the house are named Smith, Walter and Pamela Smith. They've got two kids. A girl and a boy. Hang on. Okay, it's Jennifer and Thomas. She says the girl is about fifteen and the boy is younger.'

'Does she know if they're in the house?'

Talley could hear Anders talking with the neighbor. Anders was so anxious that he was keying his mike before he was ready. Talley told him to slow down.

'She says the wife is in Florida visiting a sister, but she believes that the rest of the family is at home. She says the husband works there in the house.'

Talley cursed under his breath. He had a possible three hostages inside. Three killers, three hostages. He had to find out what was happening inside the house and cool out the shooters. It was called 'stabilizing the situation.' That's all he had to do. He told himself that over and over like a mantra: *That's all you have to do.*

Talley took a deep breath to gather himself, then another. He keyed his public address system so that he could speak to the house. In the next moment he would engage the subjects. In that instant, the negotiation would begin. Talley had sworn that he would never again be in this place. He had turned his life inside out to avoid it, yet here he was.

'My name is Jeff Talley. Is anyone in the house hurt?'

His voice echoed through the neighborhood. He heard a police car pull up at the mouth of the cul-de-sac, but he did not turn to look; he kept his eyes fixed on the house.

'Everyone in the house relax. We're not in a hurry here. If you've got wounded, let's get them tended to. We can work this out.'

No one answered. Talley knew that the subjects in the house were now under incredible stress. They had been involved in two shootings, and now they were trapped. They would be scared, and the danger level to the civilians would be great. Talley's job was to reduce their stress. If you gave the subjects time to calm down and think about their situation, sometimes they realized that their only way out was to surrender. Then all you had to do was give them an excuse to give up. That was the way it worked. Talley had been taught these things at the FBI's Crisis Management School, and it had worked that way every time until George Malik had shot his own son in the neck.

Talley keyed the mike again. He tried to make his voice reasonable and assuring.

'We're going to start talking sooner or later. It might as well be now. Is everyone in there okay, or does someone need a doctor?'

A voice in the house finally answered.

'Fuck you.'

Jennifer

Her father's eyes flickered as if he were dreaming, back and forth, up and down. He made a soft whimpering sound, but his eyes didn't open. Thomas hunched beside her, whispering.

'What's wrong?'

'He's not waking up. He should be awake, shouldn't he?'

This wasn't supposed to be happening; not in her house, not in Bristo Camino, not on this perfect summer day.

'Daddy, *please!*'

Mars knelt beside her to feel her father's neck. He was large and gross. She could smell him. Sweat and vegetables.

'Looks like brain damage.'

Jennifer felt a rush of fear and nausea, then realized that he was toying with her.

'Fuck you.'

Mars blinked uncomfortably, as if she had surprised and embarrassed him.

'I don't do things like that. They're bad.'

Mars walked away.

Her father's wound pulsed steadily, but the bleeding had almost stopped, the clotted blood and injured flesh swelling into an ugly purple volcano. Jennifer stood, and faced Dennis.

'I want to get some ice.'

'Shut up and sit your ass down.'

'*I'm getting some ice. He's hurt.*'

Dennis glared at her, his face red and angry. He glanced at Mars, then at her father. Finally, he turned back to the shutters.

'Mars, take her into the kitchen. Make sure Kevin isn't fucking off back there.'

Jennifer left without waiting for Mars, and went to the kitchen. She saw Kevin hiding behind the couch in the family room so that he could see the French doors. She wanted the backyard to be crowded with police officers and vicious police dogs, but it was empty. The pool was clean and pure, the raft that she had been enjoying less than thirty minutes earlier motionless on the water, the water so clear that the raft might have been floating on air. Her radio sat on the deck beside the pool, but she couldn't hear it. It had all happened so fast.

Jennifer opened the cabinet beneath the sink. Mars kicked it shut.

'What are you doing?'

He towered over her, his groin only inches from her face. She slowly stood to her full height. He was still a foot taller, and so close that it hurt to look up. Jennifer smelled the sour vegetables again. It took all of her strength not to run.

'I'm getting a washcloth. Then I'm going to open the freezer for the ice. Is that all right with you?'

Mars edged closer. His chest brushed the tips of her breasts. She did not let herself look away or step back, but her voice was hoarse.

'Get away from me.'

Mars stared down at her, his eyes unfocused, almost as if he couldn't see her. A vacant smile played at his lips. He swayed, his chest massaging gently against her breasts.

She still would not let herself step back. She summoned her strength again, and spoke clearly.

'*Get away from me.*'

The vacant smile flickered, then his eyes focused as if he could once more see her.

She opened the cabinet again without waiting for him to answer, found a cloth, then went to the freezer for ice. It was a huge black Sub-Zero, the kind with a freezer drawer on the bottom. She pulled it open, then scooped ice into the washcloth. Most of it spilled onto the floor.

'I need a bowl.'

'So get one.'

Mars walked away as she got the bowl. He went into the family room, and asked if Kevin had seen anything. She couldn't hear Kevin's answer.

Jennifer chose a green plastic Tupperware bowl, then saw the paring knife on the counter, left from when she diced a slice of onion for the tuna. She glanced at Mars, but Mars was still with Kevin. She was terrified that if she reached for the knife they would see her, and then she thought that even if she had the knife what would she do with it? They were older and stronger. She glanced up again. Mars was staring at her. She averted her eyes, but saw from the corner of her eye that he stayed with Kevin. Her shorts didn't have pockets and her suit top didn't have enough material to cover the knife. Even if she took it, what would she do with it? Attack them? Puh-lease. Mars came back to the kitchen. Without thinking about it, she pushed the knife behind the Cuisinart mixer her mom kept on the counter.

Mars said, 'What's taking so long?'

'I'm ready.'

'Hang on.'

Mars went to the refrigerator and pulled it open. He took out a beer, twisted off the cap, and drank. He took a second bottle and tipped it toward her.

'You want one?'

'I don't drink beer.'

'Mommy won't know. You can do anything you want right now, and Mommy won't know.'

'I want to go back to my father.'

She followed him back to the office, where Mars gave the second beer to Dennis at the shutters. Jennifer joined Thomas at their father beside the desk. She scooped ice from the bowl into the washcloth, then made an ice pack and pressed it to her father's wound. She cringed when he moaned.

Thomas edged closer and spoke so softly that she could barely hear him.

'What's going to happen?'

Mars's voice cut across the room.

'*Shut up!*'

Mars was staring at her. Slowly, his gaze moved down along the lines of her body. She flushed again, forcing herself to concentrate on her father. She knew he was playing with her, just as he had before.

The phone rang.

Everyone in the room looked at the phone, but no one moved. The ringing grew louder and more insistent.

Dennis said, 'Jesus Christ!'

He stalked to the desk and scooped up the phone, but the ringing continued.

'What the fuck is this? Why won't it stop?'

Thomas said, 'It has more than one line. Press the blinking light.'

Dennis stabbed the blinking light, then slammed down the phone. The ringing stopped.

Dennis went back to the shutters, grumbling about rich people having more than one line.

The phone rang again.

'*Fuck!*'

The public address voice from the street echoed through the house.

'Answer the phone, Dennis Rooney. It's the police.'

Talley

Hunkered behind the front wheel of his radio car, Talley listened to the ringing in his ear as a helicopter appeared. It spiraled down for a closer look until Talley could see that it was from one of the Los Angeles television stations. They would have heard about Kim and Welch by monitoring police frequencies. If the helicopters were here, the vans and reporters would be close behind. Talley covered the phone and twisted around to see Jorgenson.

'Where are the Sheriffs?'

'Inbound, Chief.'

'Get back on the horn and request air cover. Tell them we have news choppers coming in.'

The phone inside the house was still ringing. Talley thought, *Answer the phone, you sonofabitch.*

'Tell Sarah to call the phone company. Get a list of all the lines to the house and have them blocked except through my cell number. I don't want these guys talking with anyone on the outside except for us.'

'Okay.'

Talley was still giving orders when the phone stopped ringing and a male voice answered.

'Hello?'

Talley waved Jorgenson quiet, then took a breath to center himself. He did not want his voice to reveal his fear.

'Is this Dennis Rooney?'

'Who are *you*?'

'My name is Jeff Talley. I'm with the Bristo Police Department, out here behind the car in front of you. Is this Dennis Rooney?'

Talley specifically did not identify himself as the chief of police. He wanted to appear to have a certain degree of power, but he also did not want to be seen as the final authority. The negotiator was always the man in the middle. If Rooney made demands, Talley wanted to be able to stall by telling him that he had to check with his boss. That way Talley remained the good guy. He could build a bond with Rooney through their mutual adversity.

'That cop was going for his gun. That Chinaman pulled a gun, too. No one wanted to shoot him. It was an accident.'

'Is this Dennis Rooney? I want to know with whom I'm speaking.'

'Yeah. I'm Rooney.'

Talley felt himself relaxing. Rooney wasn't a raving lunatic; he didn't start off by screaming that he was going to murder everyone in the house. Talley made his voice firm, but relaxed.

'Well, Dennis, I need to know whether or not anyone in there needs a doctor. There was an awful lot of shooting.'

'We're cool.'

'We can send in a doctor, if you need it.'

'I said we're cool. Aren't you listening?'

Rooney's voice was strained and emotional. Talley expected that.

'Everyone out here is concerned about who's in there with you, Dennis, and how they're doing. Do you have some people in there with you?'

Rooney didn't answer. Talley could hear breathing, then a muffled sound as if Rooney had covered the phone. He would be thinking it through. Talley knew that thinking things through logically would be hard for Rooney during these next few minutes. Rooney would be pumping on adrenaline, frantic, and scared. Finally, he came back on the line.

'I got this family. That isn't kidnapping, is it? I mean, they were already here. We didn't grab'm and take'm someplace.'

Rooney's answer was a good sign; by showing concern for the future, he revealed that he did not want to die and feared the consequences of his actions.

'Can you identify them for me, Dennis?'

'You don't need to know that. I've told you enough.'

Talley let that slide. The Sheriff's negotiator could press for their names later.

'Okay, you're not going to tell me their names right now. I hear that. Will you at least tell me how they're doing?'

'They're fine.'

'How about your two friends? You don't have a man dying on you, do you?'

'They're fine.'

Talley had gotten Rooney to admit that all three gunmen were in the house. He muted the phone and turned to Jorgenson.

'All three subjects are in the house. Tell Larry to call off the house-to-house.'

'Rog.'

Jorgenson radioed his call as Talley returned to Rooney. Overhead, a second helicopter joined the first and positioned itself in a hover. Another news crew.

Talley said, 'Okay, Dennis, I want to explain your situation.'

Rooney interrupted him.

'You been asking me questions, now I've got a question. I didn't shoot that Chinaman. He pulled a gun and we were wrestling and his own gun went off. That Chinaman shot himself.'

'I understand, Dennis. There'll probably be a security camera. We'll be able to see what happened.'

'The gun just went off, is what I'm saying. It went off and we ran and that's what happened.'

'Okay.'

'So what I want to know is, that Chinaman, is he okay?'

'Mr. Kim didn't make it, Dennis. He died.'

Rooney didn't respond, but Talley knew that images of shooting his way out and possibly even of suicide would be kaleidoscoping through his head. Talley had to give him a vent for the pressure.

'I won't lie to you, Dennis; you guys are in trouble. But if what you said about the struggle is true, that could be a mitigating circumstance. Don't make things worse than they already are. We can still work our way out of this.'

Kim having pulled a gun would mitigate nothing. Under California law, any death occurring during the commission of a felony was murder, but Talley needed to give Rooney some measure of hope. It did.

Rooney said, 'What about the police officer? He went for his gun, too.'

'He's still alive. You caught a break there, Dennis.'

'Don't you forget I've got these people in here. Don't you guys try to rush the house.'

Some of the edge had gone from Rooney's voice.

'Dennis, I'm going to ask you right now to let those people go.'

'No way.'

'You're ahead of the game as long as they're not hurt. The police officer is alive. You said Mr. Kim pulled a gun on you. Just let those people walk out.'

'Fuck that. They're the only thing keeping you from blowing us away. You'll kill us for shooting that cop.'

'I know you're feeling that way right now, Dennis, but I'm going to give you my word about something. We're not going to storm the house. We're not coming in there by force, okay?'

'You'd better not.'

'We're not. But I want you to know what you're facing out here. I'm not telling you to threaten you; I'm telling you to be straight up. We have officers surrounding the house, and this neighborhood is locked down. You can't escape, Dennis; that just isn't going to happen. The reason I'm out here talking to you is that I want to get out of this thing without you or the people in that house getting hurt. That's my goal here. Do you understand that?'

'I understand.'

'The best thing you can do to help yourself is to let those people go, Dennis. Let them go, then surrender, everything nice and peaceful and orderly. If you're cooperative now, it will look better for the judge later. Do you see that?'

Rooney didn't respond, which Talley took as a positive sign. Rooney wasn't arguing. He was thinking. Talley decided to terminate the contact and let Rooney consider his options.

'I don't know about you, Dennis, but I could use a break. You think about what I said. I'll call back in twenty minutes. If you want to talk before that, just shout, and I'll phone you again.'

Talley closed the phone. His hands were shaking so badly that he dropped it. He took another deep breath and then another, but they didn't help to steady him.

Jorgenson said, 'Chief? You okay?'

Talley waved that he was fine.

The helicopters were still up there. They had set up on fixed points in a hover. That meant they were using their cameras.

Talley put the phone in his pocket, told Jorgenson to call if anything changed, then backed his car out of the cul-de-sac. One conversation with a scared twenty-two-year-old kid, and Talley wanted to vomit. Larry Anders was waiting at the intersection along with two more of his officers: Scott Campbell and Leigh Metzger. Campbell was a retired Bakersfield security officer who signed on with Bristo to supplement his pension. Metzger was a single mother who had spent eight years on the San Bernardino Police Department as an instructional officer. She had almost no street time. Seeing them gave Talley no confidence.

'Jesus, Larry, are the goddamned Sheriffs coming here on foot? Where are they?'

'Sarah's been on the phone with them, Chief. She says you should call.'

Talley felt his stomach clench.

'What's wrong?'

'I don't know. She also says that the newspeople want to know what's happening. They've got reporters at the minimart, and they're on their way here.'

Talley rubbed his face, then checked his watch. It had been fifty-three minutes since Junior Kim was shot. Fifty-three minutes, and his world had collapsed to the size of a subdivision.

'When the newspeople get here, let them into the development, but don't let them come here to the cul-de-sac.'

'Ah, there's an empty lot by King and Lady, something like that. Can I put them over there?'

'Perfect. And don't let them wander around. I'll get over there in a few minutes and make a statement.'

Talley went to his car, telling himself that everything was fine. He had established contact, found out that all three subjects were in the house, and no one was shooting. He opened his car and felt the heat roll out as if from an oven. He was so drained that he didn't care. He radioed his office.

'Give me some good news, Sarah. I need it.'

'The Highway Patrol is sending six patrol units from Santa Clarita and Palmdale. They should be about ten minutes out, and inbound now.'

Patrol units.

'What about a tactical squad and the negotiation team? We need to get those people deployed.'

Talley sounded strident, but he didn't care.

'I'm sorry, Chief. Their response team is hung up in Pico Rivera. They said they'll get here as soon as possible.'

'That's just fucking great! What are we supposed to do until then?'

'They said you'll have to handle it yourself.'

Talley held the mike in his lap without the strength to lift it.

'Chief? You still there?'

Talley pulled the door shut, started the engine, and turned on the air conditioner. Anders and Campbell looked over when they heard the engine start, then seemed confused when he didn't pull away. He turned the vents so they blew the cold air into his face. Talley shook so badly that he pushed his hands under his legs, feeling frightened and ashamed. He dug his fingers into his thighs and told himself that this wasn't Los Angeles, that he was no longer a negotiator, that the lives of the people in the house did not rest with him. He only had to hang on until the Sheriffs took over, and then he could go back to his orchard and the perfect peace of its stillness. It was only a matter of minutes. Of seconds. He told himself that anyone could hang on for seconds. He told himself that, but he didn't believe it.

4

Friday, 4:22 p.m.

Dennis

Dennis slapped down the phone, livid with an anger he could barely contain, shouting, 'Fuck *you*!'

Talley thought he was an idiot, all that shit about wanting a peaceful resolution and promising not to storm the house. Dennis knew the score when it came to cops: A cop was down, so somebody had to pay. The bastards would probably assassinate him the first chance they got without ever giving him a chance to stand trial. That bastard Talley probably wanted to pull the goddamned trigger himself. Dennis was so pissed off that he felt sick to his stomach.

Mars said, 'What did they want?'

'What do you think they want, Mars? Jesus, they want us to give up.'

Mars shrugged, his expression simple.

'I'm not giving up.'

Dennis glared at the two kids huddled around their old man, then stalked out of the office. He needed to figure a way out of this fucking house, and away from the police. He needed a plan. Walking made it easier to think, like he could get away from the fear of being trapped; a big-ass house like this, and it felt as if the weight of it was crushing his breath away. If he threw up, he didn't want to do it in front of Mars.

Dennis crossed through the kitchen, searching for the garage. He found the keys on a Peg-Board in the pantry just like the man had said, and shoved open the door to the garage. A gleaming Jaguar sedan and Range Rover were waiting, neither more than a couple of years old. Dennis checked the gas in the Jaguar, and found the tank full. If his truck had broken down only five minutes sooner, if they had found this house only five minutes sooner, if they had driven away in this sweet Jaguar only five minutes sooner, they wouldn't be sweating out a murder count. They wouldn't be trapped.

Dennis smashed his fist into the steering wheel, shouting, 'SHIT!'

He closed his eyes.

Chill, dude.

Don't lose it.

There has to be a way out.

'Dennis?'

Dennis opened his eyes and saw Kevin in the door, squirming like he had to pee.

'You're supposed to be watching for the cops.'

'I need to talk to you. Where's Mars?'

'He's watching the front like you're supposed to be watching the back. Get out of here.'

Dennis shut his eyes tight. The cops were watching the front and back of the house, but it was a big house; there had to be a window or door that the cops couldn't see. The house was surrounded by trees and bushes and walls, all of which blended and merged with the heavy cover of the surrounding houses. When night came, the shadows between the houses would fall like heavy black coats. If he created a diversion – say, he dressed up the hostages to look like Mars, Kevin, and himself, tied them into the Jaguar, then used the remote control to raise the garage door – all the cops would be watching the garage as he slipped out the other side of the house and away through the shadows.

'Dennis?'

'We're looking at murder charges, Kevin. Let me *think*.'

'It's about Mars. We've got to talk about what happened.'

Kevin wore the pussy face again, the mewly lurching eyebrows and don't-kick-me expression that made Dennis want to punch him. Dennis hated his younger brother and always had; hated the suffocating weight of having to carry him through life. He didn't need the prison shrink to tell him why: Kevin was their past; he was their weak ineffectual mother who abandoned them, their brutal meth-head father who beat them, their pathetic and embarrassing place in life. Kevin was the shadow of their future failure, and Dennis hated him for it.

Dennis got out of the Jaguar and slammed the door.

'We've got to find a way out of here, Kevin, that's what we've got to do. It's that simple. We look for a way out of this goddamned house because I am *not* going back to jail.'

Dennis pushed past his brother, unable even to look at him. Kevin followed along behind. They went through a kitchen, then along a wide hall past a formal dining room to a den with lush leather couches and a beautiful copper bar. Dennis imagined himself serving drinks to beautiful guests who had stepped out of television commercials and porno tapes. He would be a player if he lived in a house like this. He would have become the man of his destiny.

They reached the master bedroom at the rear of the house. It was a huge room with sliding glass doors that looked out at the pool, this one room bigger than the apartment Dennis and Kevin shared. Dennis wondered if there was a bathroom window or some other way to sneak out.

Kevin plucked at his arm.

'Dennis, *listen.*'

'Look for a way out.'

'Mars lied about that cop who came to the door. That cop never pulled his gun. You didn't have to shoot him.'

Dennis grabbed Kevin's shirt.

'Stop it! We didn't have any choice!'

'I was standing right there. I was watching him, Dennis. He put his hand on his gun, but he didn't pull it. I'm telling you that cop never drew.'

Dennis let go of Kevin's shirt and stepped back, not knowing what to say.

'You just didn't see, is all.'

'I was *there.* Mars lied.'

'Why would he do that?'

'Something's wrong with that guy, Dennis. He *wanted* to shoot that cop.'

Dennis's throat felt tight. He was pissed off, thinking this was just like his fuckup brother, dishing out another helping of shit onto a plate that was already overflowing.

'You don't know what you're talking about. We're surrounded by cops and we're looking at a homicide charge. We've got to find a way out of this, so just *stop.*'

Three doors opened off the bedroom. Dennis thought they might lead to closets or bathrooms with maybe a window on the side of the house, but that isn't what he found.

Clothes hung on racks with shoes filling shoe stands beneath the clothes like any other large closet, but this room had something more: A bank of small black-and-white televisions filled the near wall; Mars and the two kids could be seen on one of the screens; another showed the cop car sitting out front in the cul-de-sac; the Jaguar and the Range Rover were revealed in the garage; every room, bathroom, and hall inside the house was visible, as well as views of the outside of the house, the pool, poolhouse, and even the area behind the poolhouse. Every inch of the property seemed to be watched.

'Kevin?'

Kevin came up behind him, and made a hissing sound.

'What is this?'

'It's a security system. Jesus, look at this stuff.'

Dennis studied the view of the master bedroom. The camera appeared to be looking from the upper left ceiling corner above the door through which he had just entered. Dennis went out and looked up into the corner. He saw nothing.

Still inside the room, Kevin said, 'Hey, I can see you.'

Dennis rejoined his brother. The monitors were above a long keyboard set with button pads, LED windows, and red and green lights. Right now, all of the lights glowed green. Rows of buttons were lined along the right side of the keyboard, the buttons labeled MOTION SENSORS, INFRA-RED, UPSTAIRS LOCKS, DOWNSTAIRS LOCKS, and ALARMS. Dennis felt creeped out. He turned back to the door and slowly pushed it. The door swung easily, but with a feeling of weight and density. A heavy throwbolt was set into the door so that it could be locked tight from the inside. Dennis rapped on the door with his knuckles. Steel.

He turned back to his brother.

'What the fuck is going on here? They've got this place stitched up like a bank.'

Kevin was on his knees at the back of the closet, partially buried by a wall of hanging clothes. He slowly rocked back on his heels, then turned around holding a white cardboard box about the size of a shoe box. Dennis saw that the wall behind the clothes was like a small metal garage door that could be raised or lowered. It was raised, and more white boxes were stacked behind it.

Kevin held out the box.

'Look.'

The box was filled with hundred-dollar bills. Kevin pulled out a second box, then a third. They bulged with money. Dennis opened a fourth box. Money.

Dennis and Kevin looked at each other.

'Lets get Mars.'

Jennifer

Jennifer was worried. Her father's breathing was raspy. His eyes jerked spastically beneath their lids like eyes do when someone is having bad dreams. She placed a pillow from the couch beneath his head, and sat beside him, holding the ice to his head. The bleeding had stopped, but the wound was red and inflamed, and an ugly bruise was spreading across his face.

Thomas nudged her knee, and whispered.

'Why won't he wake up?'

She glanced at Mars before she answered. Mars had pulled her father's desk chair across the room and was sitting so that he could watch the police.

'I don't know.'

'Is he going to die?'

Jennifer was worried about that, too, though she didn't want to say. She thought that her father might have a concussion, though the only thing she knew about concussions for real was that the catcher on her high school baseball team had gotten a concussion during a game when he had blocked home plate and a bigger player had bowled him over. Tim had to go to the hospital that night and missed two days of school. Jennifer was scared that her father needed a doctor, too, and might get worse without medical attention.

'Jen?'

Thomas nudged her again, his voice an insistent whisper.

'Jen?'

She finally answered, and tried to look upbeat.

'I think he has a concussion. That's all it is.'

The phone on her father's desk rang. Mars glanced over, but made no move to answer it. The phone stopped ringing just as Dennis and Kevin reappeared from the rear of the house. Dennis walked over and stared down at her father, then her. The expression on his face creeped her out. Kevin was staring, too.

Dennis squatted beside her.

'Your old man, what's he do for a living?'

'He's an accountant.'

'He does taxes for other rich people, he handle their money, what?'

'Duh. That's what accountants do.'

Jennifer knew she was taunting him, and she was ready for his anger, but Dennis seemed to consider her. Then he glanced at Thomas before smiling.

'What's your name?'

'Jennifer.'

'What's your last name?'

'Smith.'

'Okay, Jennifer Smith. And your old man?'

'Walter Smith.'

Dennis looked at Thomas.

'How about you, fat boy?'

'Eat me.'

Dennis grabbed Thomas's ear.

Thomas blurted out his name.

'Thomas!'

'Fat boy Thomas, you give me shit, I'm gonna beat your ass. Are we clear on that?'

'Yes, sir.'

Dennis let go of Thomas's ear.

'That's a good fat boy.'

Jennifer wished that he would just leave them alone, but he didn't. He smiled at her and lowered his voice.

'We're going to be here a while, Jennifer. Where's your bedroom?'

Jennifer blushed furiously, and Dennis smiled wider.

'Now don't think nasty thoughts on me, Jennifer. I didn't mean it like that. You look cold, wearing just the bikini top. I'll bring you a shirt. Cover up that fine body.'

She averted her eyes and blushed harder.

'It's upstairs.'

'Okay. I'll bring you something.'

Dennis told Mars to come with him, and then the two of them left. Kevin went to the window.

The phone rang again, but Kevin ignored it. The ringing went on forever.

Thomas nudged her knee again.

When she looked at him, his face was deathly white with pink blotches at the corners of his mouth. That was the face he got when he was angry. She knew he didn't like being called a fat boy.

He nudged her again, wanting to say something. She made sure that Kevin wasn't watching them, then mouthed the word more than spoke it.

'What?'

Thomas leaned close and lowered his voice even more. The pink spots at his mouth burned brightly.

'I know where Daddy has a gun.'

5

Friday, 5:10 p.m.

Glen Howell

Glen Howell closed his cell phone after fifteen rings. He didn't like that. He was expected, and he knew that this person always answered his phone, and was irritated that now, him running late like this, the sonofabitch would pick *now* not to answer. In Glen Howell's world, lateness was not tolerated and excuses were less than useless. Punishment could be severe.

Howell didn't know why the streets leading into York Estates were blocked, but the traffic was at a standstill. He figured it had to be a broken gas line or something like that for them to close the entire neighborhood, backing up traffic and wasting everyone's time. Rich people didn't like to be inconvenienced.

The window on his big S-class Mercedes slid down without a sound. Glen craned out his head, trying to see the reason for the delay. A lone cop was working the intersection, waving some cars away. He let a television news van through. Glen raised the window again, the heavy tint cutting the glare. He took the .40-caliber Smith & Wesson from his pocket and put it in the glove box. He had a valid California Concealed Weapon Permit, but thought it best not to draw attention to himself if he had to get out of the car.

Glen checked his watch again for the fourth time in five minutes. He was already ten minutes late. At this rate, he would be still later. Three of the cars ahead of him turned away, one car was let through, and then it was his turn. The cop was a young guy, tall and rectangular with a protruding Adam's apple.

Glen lowered the window. The heat ballooned in, making him wish he was back in Palm Springs, instead of being an errand boy. He tried to look professional and superior, working the class distinctions, rich successful business dude, lowly uneducated public servant.

'What's going on, Officer? Why the roadblock?'

'Do you live here in the neighborhood, sir?'

Glen knew that if he lied, the cop might ask to see his driver's license for the address. Glen didn't want to get caught in a lie.

'I have a business appointment. My associate is expecting me.'

'We've got a problem in the neighborhood, so we've had to close the area. We're only admitting residents.'

'What kind of problem?'

The cop looked uncertain.

'Do you have family in the development, sir?'

'Just my friends, like I said. You're making me worried about them, Officer.'

The cop frowned, and glanced back along the row of cars behind Glen.

'Well, what it is, we've got robbery suspects in one of the houses. We've had to evacuate several of the homes, and close off the development until we can secure the area. It could take a while.'

Glen nodded, trying to look reasonable. Ten seconds, he already knew that he couldn't flash a hundred at this guy to buy his way in. He would never go for it.

'Listen, my client is expecting me, Officer. It won't take long. Really. I just need a few minutes, then I'm gone.'

'Can't let you in, sir, I'm sorry. Maybe you could phone your party and have them come meet you, if they're still inside. We've had people going door to door, telling people to stay indoors or offering to escort them out. I can't let you in.'

Glen worked on staying calm. He smiled, and stared past the patrol car like he was thinking. His first impulse in any confrontation was to use his gun, put two hot ones square in the other guy's forehead, but he had a handle on that. Years of therapy had taught him that, even though he had an anger-based personality, he could control it. He controlled it now.

'Okay. That might work. Can I park over here to call?'

'Sure.'

Glen pulled his car to the side, then called the number again. This time, he let it ring fifteen times, but still didn't get an answer. Glen didn't like this. With all the cops around, his guy might have developed a case of the quivering shits and was laying low, or maybe he'd been forced from his home. He might even have a bunch of cops in his home, using it as a command post or something. Glen laughed out loud at that one; no fucking way. Glen figured the guy must've been evacuated, in which case he would probably call Palm Springs to arrange another meet location, and Palm Springs would phone Glen. The cop would probably know which families had been evacked, or could find out, but Glen didn't want to draw attention to his man by asking.

Glen wheeled around in a slow U and headed back up the street, still thinking about it, when he saw that another television news van had joined the line. Glen decided to take a flyer, and lowered his window when he reached the van. The driver was a balding guy with a rim of hair behind his ears and loose skin. A trim Asian woman with pouty lips perched in the passenger seat. Glen guessed her for the on-air talent, and wondered if the puffy lips were natural or man-made. Women who injected shit into their lips creeped him out. He decided that she was probably a spitter.

Glen said, 'Excuse me. They wouldn't tell me what's going on, just that some people in the neighborhood are being evacuated. Do you guys know anything about this?'

The woman twisted in her seat and leaned forward to see past the driver.

'We don't have anything confirmed, but it looks like three men were fleeing the scene of a robbery and took a family hostage.'

'No shit. That's terrible.'

Glen couldn't give less of a shit except that it was ruining his day. He wondered if he could talk the reporter into letting him come along.

'Do you live in the neighborhood?'

Glen knew that she was angling for something, and began to relax. If she thought he had something that she wanted, she might be willing to get him inside.

'I don't live here, but I have friends in there. Why?'

The line of cars had moved forward, but the news van stayed where it was. The reporter flipped through a yellow pad.

'We've got unconfirmed reports that there are children involved, but we can't get anyone to tell us anything about the family. It's a family named Smith.'

The big Mercedes sensed the heat. The air conditioner blew harder. Glen didn't feel it.

'What was the name again?'

'Mr. and Mrs. Walter Smith. We've heard they have two children, a boy and a girl.'

'They're being held hostage? These three guys have the Smiths?'

'That's right. Do you know them? We're trying to find out about the kids.'

'I don't know them. Sorry.'

Glen rolled up the window and pulled away. He drove slowly so as not to attract attention. He had the strange sensation of being removed from his body, as if the world had receded and he was no longer a part of it. The a.c. was roaring. Walter Smith. Three assholes had crashed into Walter Smith's home, and now the place was surrounded by cops and cameras, and their whole fucking neighborhood was sealed.

Three blocks later, Glen pulled into a parking lot. He took his gun from the glove box and put it back in his pocket. He felt safer that way. He opened his phone again, and dialed another number. This time, his call was answered on the first ring.

Glen spoke four words.

'We have a problem.'

Palm Springs, California
5:26 p.m.

Sonny Benza

Oxygen was the key. Sonny took a deep breath, trying to feed his heart. He was forty-seven years old, had high blood pressure, and lived in fear of the stroke which had claimed his father at fifty-five.

Benza stood in the games room of his mansion perched on a ridge above Palm Springs. Outside, his two kids, Chris and Gina, home from school, were splashing in the pool. Inside, Phil Tuzee and Charles 'Sally' Salvetti pulled an extra television next to the big screen, sweating like pigs, 36 inches, a Sony. They were rushed and frantic, anxious to get the set on. Between the big-screen projection TV with the picture-in-picture function and the Sony, they could watch all three major Los Angeles television stations. Two showed aerial views of Walter Smith's house, the third some pretty-boy talking head outside a gas station.

Sonny Benza still refused to believe it.

'What do we know? Not this TV bullshit. What do we know for *sure*? Maybe it's a different Walter Smith.'

Salvetti wiped the sweat from his forehead, looking pale under the Palm Springs tan.

'Glen Howell called it in. He's at the house, Sonny. It's *our* Walter Smith.'

Tuzee made a patting motion with his hands, trying to play the cooler.

'Let's everybody take it easy. Let's relax and walk through this a step at a time. The Feds aren't knocking on the door.'

'Not yet.'

Phil Tuzee was close to pissing himself. Sonny put his arm across Tuzee's shoulders, giving the squeeze, being the one in control.

'We got, what, ten or fifteen minutes before that happens, right, Phil?'

Tuzee laughed. Just like that, they were calmer. Still worried, still knowing they had a major cluster fuck of a problem, but the first bubble of panic had burst. Now, they would deal with it.

Benza said, 'Okay. What exactly are we dealing with here? What does Smith have in the house?'

'It's tax time, Sonny. We have to file the corporate quarterlies. He has our records.'

The bristly hairs on the back of Benza's head stood.

'You're sure? Glen hadn't made the pickup?'

'He was on his way to do that when this shit went down. He gets there and finds the neighborhood blocked off. He says Smith doesn't answer his phone, which you know he would do if he could, and then he gets the story

635

from some reporters. Three assholes broke into Smith's house to hide from the cops, and now they're holding Smith and his family hostage. It's our Walter Smith.'

'And all our tax stuff is still in that house.'

'Everything.'

Benza stared at the televisions. Stared at the house on the screens. Stared at the police officers crouched behind bushes and cars, surrounding that house.

Sonny Benza's legitimate business holdings included sixteen bars, eight restaurants, a studio catering company, and thirty-two thousand acres of vineyards in central California. These businesses were profitable in their own right, but they were also used to launder the ninety million dollars generated every year by drug trafficking, hijackings, and shipping stolen automobiles and construction equipment out of the country. Walter Smith's job was to create false but reasonable profit records for Sonny's legitimate holdings which Benza would present to his 'real' accountants. Those accountants would then file the appropriate tax returns, never knowing that the records from which they were working had been falsified. Benza would pay the appropriate taxes (taking every deduction legally allowable), then be able to openly bank, spend, or invest the after-tax cash. To do this, Walter Smith held the income records of all Benza businesses, both legal and illegal.

These records were in his computer.

In his house.

Surrounded by cops.

Sonny went over to the big glass wall that gave him a breathtaking view of Palm Springs on the desert floor below. It was a beautiful view.

Phil Tuzee followed him, trying to be upbeat.

'Hey, look, it's just three kids, Sonny. They're gonna get tired and come out. Smith knows what to do. He'll hide the stuff. These kids will walk out and the cops will arrest them, and that's that. There won't be any reason for the cops to search the house.'

Sonny wasn't listening. He was thinking about his father. Frank Sinatra used to live down the street. It was the house that Sinatra had remodeled to entertain JFK, spent a couple of hundred thousand to buff out the place so he and The Man could enjoy a little poolside poon as they discussed world affairs, sunk all that money into his nest only to have, after the checks were signed and the work was done, JFK blow him off and refuse to visit. Story goes that Sinatra went fucking nuts, shooting through the walls, throwing furniture into the pool, screaming that he was gonna take out a hit on the motherfucking President of the United States. Like what did he expect, Kennedy to be butt-buddies with a mobbed-up guinea singer? Sonny Benza's home was higher up the ridge than Frank's old place, and larger, but his father had been impressed as hell with Sinatra's place. First time his father had come out to visit, he'd walked down to Sinatra's place and stood in the street, staring at Sinatra's house like it held the ghost of the Roman Empire. His father had said, 'Best move I ever made, Sonny, turning over the wheel to you. Look how good you've done, living in the same neighborhood as Francis Albert.' The Persians who lived there now had gotten so freaked out by Sonny's dad, they had called the police.

'Sonny?'

Benza looked at his friend. Tuzee had always been the closest to him. They'd been the tightest when they were kids.

'The records don't just show our business, Phil. They show where we get the money, how we launder it, and our split with the families back east. If the cops get those records, we won't be the only ones who fall. The East Coast will take a hit, too.'

The breath flowed out of Phil Tuzee as if he were collapsing.

Sonny turned back to the others. They were watching him. Waiting for orders.

'Okay. Three kids like this, the cops will give'm time to chill, they'll see they're caught and that the only way out is to give up. Two hours tops, they'll walk out, hands up, then everybody goes to the station to make their statements. That's it.'

Hearing it like that made sense.

'But that's a best-case scenario. Worst case, it's a bloodbath. When it's over, the detectives go in for forensic evidence and come out with Smith's computer. If that happens, we go to jail for the rest of our lives.'

He looked at each man.

'If we live long enough to stand trial.'

Salvetti and Tuzee traded a look, but neither of them added anything because they knew it was true. The East Coast families would kill them.

Tuzee said, 'Maybe we should warn them. Call old man Castellano back there to let'm know. That might take off some of the edge.'

Salvetti raised his hands.

'Jesus, no fuckin' way. They'll go apeshit and be all over us out here.'

Sonny agreed.

'Sally's right. This problem with Smith, we've got to get a handle on it fast, solve the problem before those bastards back in Manhattan find out.'

Sonny looked back at the televisions and thought it through. Control and containment.

'Who's the controlling authority? LAPD?'

Salvetti grunted. Salvetti, like Phil Tuzee, was a graduate of USC Law who'd worked his way through school stealing cars and selling cocaine. He knew criminal law.

'Bristo is an incorporated township up by Canyon Country. They have their own police force, something like ten, fifteen guys. We're talking a pimple on LA's ass.'

Tuzee shook his head.

'That doesn't help us. If the locals can't handle this, they'll call in the

Sheriffs or maybe even the Feds. That's all we need, the Feebs rolling in. Either way, there'll be more than a few hick cops to deal with.'

'That's true, Phil, but it will all be processed back through the Bristo PD office because it's their jurisdiction. They've got a chief of police up there. It's his crime scene even if he turns over control.'

Sonny turned back to the televisions. A street-level camera was showing the front of the house. Sonny thought he saw someone move past a window, but couldn't be sure.

'This chief, what's his name?'

Salvetti glanced at his notes.

'Talley. I saw him being interviewed.'

The television shifted its shot to show three cops hunkered behind a patrol car. One of them was pointing to the side of the house like he was giving orders. Sonny wondered if that was Talley.

'Put our people on the scene. When the Feds and Sheriffs come in, I want to know who's running their act, and whether they've ever worked OC.'

If they had experience working Organized Crime, he would have to be careful who he deployed to the area.

'It's already happening, Sonny. I've got people on the way, clean guys, not anyone they would recognize.'

Benza nodded.

'I want to know everything that comes out of that house. I want to know about the three turds who started this mess. That bastard Smith might start talking just to cut a break for himself or his family. He might let them in on everything.'

'He knows better than that.'

'I want to know it, Phil.'

'I'm on it. We'll know.'

Sonny Benza watched the three cops hunkered behind the patrol car, the one he believed to be the chief of police talking on a cell phone. He had never murdered a police officer because killing cops was bad for business, but he would not hesitate to do so now. He would do whatever it took to survive. Even if it meant killing a cop.

'I want to know about this guy Talley. Find out everything there is to know about him, and every way we can hurt him. By the end of the day, I want to own him.'

'We'll own him, Sonny.'

'We better.'

Part Two

The Fly

6

Friday, 6:17 p.m.

Talley

Two of Talley's night-shift duty officers, Fred Cooper and Joycelyn Frost, rolled up in their personal cars. Cooper was breathless, as if he had run from his home in Lancaster, and Frost hadn't even taken the time to change into her uniform; she had strapped her vest and Sam Browne over a sleeveless cotton top and baggy shorts that showed off legs as pale as bread dough. They joined Campbell and Anders in the street.

Talley sat motionless in his car.

When Talley rolled to a barricade-hostage situation with SWAT, his crisis team had included a tactical team, a negotiating team, a traffic control team, a communications team, and the supervisors to coordinate their actions. The negotiating team alone included a team supervisor, an intelligence officer to gather facts and conduct interviews, a primary negotiator to deal with the subject, a secondary negotiator to assist the primary by taking notes and maintaining records, and a staff psychologist to evaluate the subject's personality and recommend negotiating techniques. Now Talley had only himself and a handful of untrained officers.

He closed his eyes.

Talley knew that he was in the beginning moments of panic. He forced himself to concentrate on the basic things that he needed to do: secure the environment, gather information, and keep Rooney cool. These three things were all he had to do until the Sheriffs took over. Talley began a mental list; it was the only way he could keep his head from exploding.

Sarah called him over his radio.

'Chief?'

'Go, Sarah.'

'Mikkelson and Dreyer got the security tape from the minimart. They said you can see these guys plain as a zit on your nose.'

'They inbound?'

'Five out. Maybe less.'

Talley felt himself relax as he thought about the tape; it was something concrete and focused. Seeing Dennis Rooney and the other subjects would

641

make it easier to read the emotional content in Rooney's voice. Talley had never bet a hostage on his intuition, but he believed there were subtle clues to emotional weakness – or strength – that an astute negotiator could read. It was something he knew. It was familiar.

His four officers were staring at him. Waiting.

Talley climbed out of his car and walked up the street. Metzger had a look on her face, the expression saying it was about goddamned time.

They needed a house in which to view the tape. Talley set Metzger to that, then divided more tasks among the others: Someone had to find out if the Smiths had relatives in the area, and, if so, notify them; also, they had to locate Mrs. Smith in Florida. The Sheriffs would need a floor plan of the Smith house and information on any security systems that were involved; if none were available from the permit office, neighbors should sketch the layout from memory. The same neighbors would be questioned to learn if any of the Smiths required life-sustaining medications.

Talley began to grow comfortable with the familiarity of the job. It was something that he'd done before, and he had done it well until it killed him.

By the time Talley finished assigning the preliminary tasks, Mikkelson and Dreyer had arrived with the tape. He met them at a large Mediterranean home owned by a bright sturdy woman who originally hailed from Brazil. Mrs. Peña. Talley identified himself as the chief of police and thanked her for her cooperation. She led them to the television in a large family room, where she showed them how to work the VCR. Mikkelson loaded the videotape.

'We watched the tape at Kim's to make sure we had something. I left it cued up.'

'Did you pull up anything on Rooney from traffic or warrants?'

'Yes, sir.'

Dreyer opened his citation pad. Talley saw that notes had been scrawled across the face of a citation, probably while they were driving.

'Dennis James Rooney has a younger brother, Kevin Paul, age nineteen. They live together over in Agua Dulce. Dennis just pulled thirty days at the Ant Farm for misdemeanor burglary and theft, knocked down from felony three. He's got multiple offenses, including car theft, shoplifting, drug possession, possession of stolen goods, and DUI. The brother, Kevin, did juvenile time on a car theft beef. At one time or another, both were in foster care or were wards of the state. Neither graduated from high school.'

'Any history of violent crimes?'

'Nothing in the record but what I said.'

'When we're done here, I want you to talk to their landlord. Guys like this are always behind on the rent or making too much noise, so the landlord has probably had to jam them. I want to know how they reacted. Find out if they threatened him or flashed a weapon or rolled over and made nice.'

Talley knew that a subject's past behavior was a good predictor of future behavior: People who had used violence and intimidation in the past could be expected to react with violence and threats in the future. That was how they dealt with stress.

'Find out from the landlord if they have jobs. If they work, ask their employers to come talk to me.'

'Got it.'

Mikkelson stepped away from the VCR.

'We're ready, Chief.'

'Let's see it.'

The screen flickered as the tape engaged. The bright color image of a daytime Spanish-language soap opera was replaced by the soundless black-and-white security picture of Junior Kim's minimart. The camera angle revealed that the camera was mounted above and to the right of the cash register, showing Junior Kim and a small portion of the clerk's area behind the counter. The counter angled up the left side of the frame, the first aisle angled along the right. The camera gave a partial view of the rest of the store. Small white numbers filled a time-count window in the lower right of the screen.

Mikkelson said, 'Okay. Here they come. The guy we think is Rooney entered a few minutes ago, then left. Here where the tape picks up, it's maybe five minutes later.'

'Okay.'

A sharp-featured white male matching Dennis Rooney's description opened the door and walked directly to Junior Kim. A larger white male with a broad face and wide body entered with him. The second man's hair was shaved down to his scalp in a fuzz cut.

'Is that Rooney's brother?'

'The third guy is about to come in. The third guy looks like Rooney.'

A third white male stepped inside before Mikkelson finished. Talley knew the third man was Rooney's brother from the resemblance, though Kevin was shorter, thinner, and wearing a Lemonheads T-shirt. Kevin waited by the door.

Talley studied their expressions and the way they carried themselves. Rooney was a good-looking kid, with eyes that were hard but uncertain. He walked with an arrogant, rolling gait. Talley guessed that he was posturing, but couldn't yet tell if Rooney was posturing for others or himself. Kevin Rooney shuffled from foot to foot, his eyes flicking from Dennis to the gas islands outside the store. He was clearly terrified. The larger man had a wide flat face and expressionless eyes.

'We have an ID on the big guy?'

'No, sir.'

'Was the camera hidden?'

'Hanging off the ceiling big as a wart on a hog's ass, and these guys didn't even bother to wear masks.'

Talley watched the video without a feeling of connection. During his time on LAPD he had seen three or four hundred such videos, all showing robberies gone bad just the way this one was about to go bad, and only one out of twenty perpetrators had bothered to don a mask. Mostly, they didn't care; mostly, they didn't think about it; geniuses didn't go into crime. Only the first tape had shocked him. He was still a probationary officer, twenty-two years old and fresh from the academy. He had watched a thirteen-year-old Vietnamese girl walk into a convenience store just like this one, shoot the elderly African-American clerk in the face at point-blank range, then turn her gun on the only other person in the store, a pregnant Latina named Muriel Gonzales who was standing next to her. The pregnant woman had fallen to her knees, thrusting her hands up as she begged for her life. The Vietnamese shooter touched the gun to Muriel Gonzales's forehead and let off a shot without hesitation, then calmly walked around behind the counter and cleaned out the cash register before walking out of the store. When she reached the door, she hesitated, then returned to the counter, where she stole a box of Altoids. After that she stepped over Muriel Gonzales and left. Seeing those murders had left Talley so shaken that he had spent the next two months thinking about resigning.

The events in Kim's Minimart happened as quickly: Rooney lifted his shirt to expose a gun, then vaulted over the counter. Kim stood with a gun of his own. Talley was relieved that Rooney had told the truth about Kim having a gun. It wouldn't help Rooney in court, but Talley could use what he was seeing to play on Rooney's sense of being the victim of bad luck. That was all Talley cared about right now, finding things he could use to manipulate Dennis Rooney.

The struggle between Rooney and Junior Kim lasted only seconds, then Kim staggered backward, dropped his pistol, and slumped against the Slurpee machine. Rooney was clearly surprised that Kim had been shot. He jumped back over the counter and ran to the door. The larger man didn't move. Talley found that odd. Kim had just been shot and Rooney was running, but the third man just stood there. Junior Kim's pistol had landed on the counter. The third man tucked it into his waist, then leaned over the counter, resting his weight on his left hand.

Mikkelson said, 'What's he doing?'

'He's watching Kim die.'

The big man's pasty Pillsbury Doughboy face creased.

Mikkelson said, 'Jesus, he's smiling.'

Talley's back and chest prickled. He stopped the tape, then rewound it until the unknown subject leaned forward on his hand.

'We need to confirm that the younger guy is Kevin Rooney, and we need to ID the third subject. Make hard-copy prints from the tape. Show them to Rooney's landlord, his neighbors, and the people at his job. We might get a fast ID on the third guy that way.'

Mikkelson glanced at Dreyer uncertainly.

'Ah, Chief, how do we make prints from the tape?'

Talley cursed under his breath. In Los Angeles, an officer would take the tape to the Scientific Investigations Division in Glendale, then return an hour later with however many prints were needed. Talley thought that the Palmdale PD probably had the necessary equipment to do that job, but Palmdale was a long drive in Friday-night traffic.

'You know the computer store in the mall?'

'Sure. They sell PlayStations.'

'Call first. Tell them we have a VHS videotape and ask if they know how to grab and print a frame. If they can, take it there. If they can't, call the camera store in Santa Clarita. If *they* can't help, call Palmdale.'

Talley pointed out the unknown subject's hand resting on the counter. He turned to Cooper and Frost.

'See here where he put his hand? I want you two to meet the Sheriff's homicide team at Kim's, and tell them about this. They'll be able to lift a good set of prints.'

'Yes, sir.'

Talley told them to get to it, then headed back out to the street and climbed into his car. He considered his impressions of Rooney from the videotape and from their conversation. Rooney wanted to be 'understood,' but he also wanted to be seen in exaggerated heroic terms: Tough, manly, and dominant. Talley decided that Rooney was a low-self-esteem personality who craved the approval of others while seeking to control his environment. He was probably a coward who covered his lack of courage with aggressive behavior. Talley decided that he could use Rooney's needs to his advantage. He checked his watch. It was time.

Talley opened his phone and punched the redial button. The phone in Smith's house rang. And rang. On the tenth ring, Rooney still hadn't answered. Talley grew worried, imagining a mass murder though he knew it was more likely that Rooney was just being a dick. He radioed Jorgenson.

'Jorgy, anything happening at the house?'

Jorgenson was still hunkered behind his car in the body of the cul-de-sac.

'Nada. It's quiet so far. I would've called you if I heard anything.'

'Okay. Stand by.'

Talley pressed the redial button again. This time he let the phone ring an even dozen times before he closed the phone. He went back on the radio.

'You hear anything from the house?'

'I thought I heard the phone ringing.'

'See any movement?'

'No, sir. It's quiet as a clam.'

Talley wondered why Rooney was refusing to answer the phone. He had seemed agreeable enough during their first contact. Talley keyed his radio again.

'Who's on with the CHiPs?'

The California Highway Patrol officers had been used to supplement his own people on the perimeter of the house. They worked off their own communication frequency, distinct from the Bristo freq.

'I am.'

'Tell them to advance to the property lines. I don't want them exposed to fire, but I want Rooney to see them. Put them at the east and west walls, and at the back wall.'

'Rog. I'll take care of it.'

If Rooney wouldn't answer the phone, Talley would force Rooney to call him.

Dennis

The money changed things. Dennis couldn't stop thinking about the money. It no longer was enough to escape; he was frantic to take the money with him. Dennis brought Mars to the closet, letting him see the boxes of cash that crowded the closet floor. Dennis laid his hands on the cash to savor the velvety feel. He lifted a pack of hundred-dollar bills to his nose and riffled the bills, smelling the paper and ink and the sweet human smell of cash. He tried to guess the number of bills in the pack. Fifty, at least; maybe a hundred. Five thousand dollars. Maybe ten thousand. Dennis couldn't stop touching the money, feeling it; softer than any breast, silkier than a woman's thigh, sexier than the finest ass.

He grinned up at Mars so wide that his cheeks cramped.

'There's gotta be a million dollars here. Maybe more. Look at it, Mars! This place is a bank!'

Mars barely glanced at the money. He went to the back of the little room, looking at the ceiling and the floor, tapping the walls, then studied the monitors. He pushed the boxes aside with his feet.

'It's a safety room. Steel door, reinforced walls, all the security; it's like a bunker. If anyone breaks into your house, you can hide. I wonder if they have sex in here?'

Dennis was irritated that Mars showed so little interest in the cash. Dennis wanted to dump the cash into a huge pile and dive in naked.

'Who gives a shit, Mars? Check out this cash. We're rich.'

'We're trapped in a house.'

Dennis was getting pissed off. This was the life-altering event that Dennis had always known was waiting for him: This house, this money, here and now – this was his destiny and his fate; the moment that had drawn him all the years of his life, plucked at him to take chances and commit outrageous acts, made him the star in the movie of his own life – all along it had been pulling him forward to the here and now, and Mars was harshing his mellow. He shoved a pack of cash into his pocket and stood.

'Mars, listen, we're going to take this with us. We'll put it in something. They must have suitcases or plastic bags.'

'You can't run with a suitcase.'

'We'll figure it out.'

'It's going to be heavy.'

Dennis was getting more pissed off. He slapped Mars in the chest. It was like slapping a wall, but Mars averted his eyes. Dennis had learned that Mars would go along if you knocked the shit out of him.

'We can carry it, we can even stuff it up our asses, but we're not leaving here without it.'

Mars nodded, rolling over just as Dennis knew he would.

'I'm glad you found the money, Dennis. You can have my share.'

Mars was depressing him. Dennis told Mars to go back to the office to make sure Kevin wasn't fucking up. When Mars left, Dennis felt relieved; Mars was fucking weird and getting weirder. If he didn't want the money, Dennis would keep it all for himself.

He searched through the other closets in the bedroom until he found a black Tumi suitcase, the kind with a handle and wheels. Dennis filled it with packs of hundreds; worn bills that had seen a lot of use, not a crisp new note among them. When the suitcase was full, Dennis wheeled it into the bedroom and parked it on the bed. Mars was right: He didn't know how he was going to get out of here lugging that big-ass case. He wouldn't be able to sneak out a window and run through backyards, but they had two cars and three hostages. Dennis refused to believe that he had come this close to his destiny to let it slip away.

Dennis returned to the office and found Mars watching the television. Mars turned up the volume.

'It's on every channel, dude. You're a star.'

Dennis saw himself on television. The newspeople had cut one of Dennis's old booking photos into the upper right corner of the screen. It was a shot that made him look like Charles Manson.

The picture changed to an aerial view of the house they were in. Dennis saw police cars parked in the street and two cops hunkered behind the wheels. A hot newschick was saying how Dennis had recently been released from the Ant Farm. Dennis found himself grinning again. Something smoky rushed through Dennis's veins just as it did when he got away with stealing a car: part anger and rage, part rush, part a groovy feeling like the whole fucking world was giving him high fives. Here he was with a million bucks for the taking, here he was on television. It was the big FUCK YOU to his parents, to his teachers, to the cops, to all the shitbirds who had kept him down. FUCK! YOU! He had arrived. He felt real. It was better than sex.

'Yeah! Fuckin' YEAH!'

He went to the door.

'Kevin! Come see this!'

The phone rang, spoiling the magic of the television. That would be Talley. Dennis ignored it, and returned to the television. The helicopters, the cops, the reporters – everyone was here because of him. It was *The Dennis Rooney Show*, and he had just figured out the ending: They would use the kids as hostages and boogie to the border in that big flashy Jaguar with the helicopters broadcasting every moment of the trip on live TV.

Dennis slapped Mars on the arm.

'I got it, dude. We'll use the Jaguar. We'll take the cash and the two kids, and leave their father here. The cops won't mess with us if we have those kids. We can boogie straight down to TJ.'

Mars shrugged blandly, his voice as quiet as a whisper.

'That won't work, Dennis.'

Dennis grew irritated again.

'Why not?'

'They'll shoot out the tires, and then a police sniper will put a bullet in your head from a hundred yards away.'

'Bullshit, Mars. O. J. Simpson drove around for *hours*.'

'O. J. Simpson didn't have hostages. They won't let us leave with these children. They'll kill us, and we won't even see it coming.'

The picture shifted again to an aerial view of the minimart surrounded by Highway Patrol cars. The view slowly orbited the cars. The movement made Dennis feel sick, like riding in the backseat of a car. He watched the cops crouched behind their cars, and worried that Mars was right about the snipers. That was just the kind of chickenshit double cross the cops would pull.

Dennis was still thinking about it when Kevin screamed from his position by the French doors.

'Dennis! There's cops all over the place out here! *They're coming!*'

Dennis forgot the snipers and ran to his brother.

Talley

Talley was in the cul-de-sac, waiting behind his car, when Dennis began shouting from the house. Talley let him rant, then opened his phone and called.

Dennis answered on the first ring.

'You fuck! You tell those fuckin' cops to move back! I don't like'm this close!'

'Take it easy, Dennis. Are you saying that you don't like seeing the officers on the perimeter?'

'Stop saying whatever I say back to me! You know what I mean!'

'I do that to make sure I understand you. We can't afford to misunderstand each other.'

'If these bastards try to come in·here, people are gonna die! Everybody's gonna die!'

'No one is going to hurt you, Dennis. I told you that before. Now give me a minute to see what's going on out here, okay?'

Talley hit the mute button on his phone.

'Jorgy, are you on with the perimeter?'

'Yes, sir.'

'Are they on the walls where we placed them?'

'Yes, sir. We've got two north on Flanders, and two more in each of the rear yards on either side. They're on the wall.'

Talley turned off the mute.

'Dennis, I'm checking into it, okay? Tell me what you see.'

'I see fuckin' cops! I'm looking right at'm. They're too close!'

'I can't see them from out here behind my car. Help me, okay? Where are they?'

Talley heard muffling sounds, as if Rooney was moving with the phone. Talley wondered if it was a cordless. Like all hostage negotiators, he hated cordless and cell phones because they didn't anchor the subject. You could fix a hardwired phone's location. Then you knew the subject's location whenever you had him on the line. If you launched a tactical breach, knowing the subject's location could save lives.

Rooney said, 'All the way around, goddamnit! These bastards over here at this white house. They're right on the goddamn wall! You make them get back!'

Talley hit the mute button again. The white house was a sprawling contemporary to Talley's left. A brushed-steel gate crossed the front drive. The house on the east side to Talley's right was dark gray. Talley counted to fifty, then opened the cell line again.

'Dennis, we got a little problem here.'

'Fucking right we got a problem. Make'm get back!'

'Those officers are Highway Patrolmen, Dennis. I'm with the Bristo Camino Police Department. They don't work for me.'

'Bullshit!'

'I can tell you what they're going to say.'

'Fuck what they say! If they come over that wall, people are going to die! I've got hostages in here!'

'If I tell these guys that you're being cooperative, they'll be more inclined to cooperate with you. You understand that, don't you? Everyone out here is concerned that the civilians in there with you are okay. Let me speak with Mr. Smith.'

'*I told you they're fine.*'

Talley sensed that everything inside wasn't as Rooney claimed, and that concerned him. Most hostage takers agreed to let their hostages say a few words because they enjoyed taunting the police with their control of the hostage; it made them feel powerful. If Rooney wouldn't let the Smiths talk, then he must be frightened of what they might say.

'Tell me what's wrong, Dennis.'

'Nothing's wrong! I'll let the sonofabitch talk when I get good and goddamned ready. I'm in charge of this shit, not you!'

Dennis sounded so stressed that Talley backed off. If anything was wrong in the house, he didn't want to make the situation worse. But having pressed Rooney for a concession, he had to get something or he would lose credibility.

'Okay, Dennis, fair enough for now, but you've still got to give me something if you want the patrolmen to back off. So how about this: You tell me who you have in there. Just tell me their names.'

'You know who owns the house.'

'We heard that those kids might have some friends over.'

'If I tell you, will you get these assholes to back off?'

'I can do that, Dennis. I just got word from their commander. He'll go along.'

Rooney hesitated, but then he answered.

'Walter Smith, Jennifer Smith, and Thomas Smith. There's no one else in here.'

Talley muted the phone again.

'Jorgy, tell the CHiPs to back off the wall. Tell them to find a position with a view of the house, but they can't be on the wall. Have them do it now.'

'Rog.'

Talley waited as Jorgenson spoke into his mike, then he went back to his phone.

'Dennis, what do you see?'

'They're pulling back.'

'Okay. We made it work, me and you. We did something here, Dennis. Way to go.'

Talley wanted Rooney to feel as if they had accomplished something together. Like they were a team.

'Just keep them away. I don't like them that close. They come over that wall, people are going to die in here. Do you understand what I'm saying? I'm not a guy you can fuck with.'

'I'll give you my word about that right now. We're not coming in there. We won't come over that wall unless we think you're hurting someone. I want to be up front about that. If it looks like you're going to hurt those people, we'll come in without warning.'

'I'm not going to hurt anyone if you stay away. That's all there is to it.'

'That's the way to play it. Just be cool.'

'You want these people, Talley? You want them safe and sound? Right now?'

Talley knew that Rooney was about to make his first demand. It could be as innocent as a pack of cigarettes or as outrageous as a phone call from the President.

'You know that I do.'

'I want a helicopter with a full tank of gas to take us to Mexico. If I get the helicopter, you get these people.'

During his time with SWAT, Talley had been asked for helicopters, jet aircraft, limousines, buses, cars, and, once, a flying saucer. All negotiators were trained that certain demands were non-negotiable: firearms, ammunition, narcotics, alcohol, and transportation. You never allowed a subject the hope of escape. You kept him isolated. That was how you broke him down.

Talley responded without hesitation, making his voice reasonable, but firm, letting his tone assure Rooney that the refusal wasn't the end of the world, and wasn't confrontational.

'Can't do that, Dennis. They won't give you a helicopter.'

Rooney's voice came back strained.

'I've got these people.'

'The Sheriffs won't trade for a helicopter. They have their rules about these things. You could ask for a battleship, but they won't give you that, either.'

When he spoke again, Rooney sounded weaker.

'Ask them.'

'It can't even land here, Dennis. Besides, Mexico isn't freedom. Even if you had a helicopter, the Mexican police would arrest you as soon as it landed. This isn't the Old West.'

Talley wanted to change the subject. Rooney would brood about the helicopter now, but Talley thought that he could give him something else to think about.

'I saw the security tape from the minimart.'

Rooney hesitated, as if it took him a moment to realize what Talley was saying, then his voice was anxious and hopeful.

'Did you see that Chinaman pull a gun? Did you see that?'

'It played out just the way you said.'

'None of this would've happened if he hadn't pulled that gun. I damn near shit my pants.'

'Then none of this was premeditated. That's what you're saying here, right? That you didn't premeditate what happened?'

Rooney wanted to be seen as the victim, so Talley was sending the subtle message that he sympathized with Rooney's situation.

'We just wanted to rob the place. I'll admit that. But, fuck, here comes the Chinaman pulling a gun. I had to defend myself, right? I wasn't trying to shoot him. I was just trying to get the gun away so he couldn't shoot *me*. It was an accident.'

The adversarial edge disappeared from Rooney's voice. Talley knew that this was the first indication that Rooney was beginning to see Talley as a collaborator. Talley lowered his voice, sending a subtle cue that this was just between them.

'Can the other two guys hear me?'

'Why do you want to know that?'

'I understand that they might be there with you, so you don't have to respond to what I'm about to say, Dennis. Just listen.'

'What are you talking about?'

'I know you're worried about what will happen to you because the officer was shot. I've been thinking about that, so I've got a question. Was anyone else in there shooting besides you? Just a yes or no, if that's all you can say.'

Talley already knew the answer from Jorgenson and Anders. He let the question hang in the air. He could hear Rooney breathe.

'Yes.'

'Then maybe it wasn't your bullets that hit the officer. Maybe it wasn't you who shot him.'

Talley had gone as far as he could. He had suggested that Rooney could beat the rap by shifting the blame to one of the other subjects. He had given Rooney a doorway out. Now, he had to back off and let Rooney brood over whether or not to step through.

'Dennis, I want to give you my cell phone number. That way you can reach me whenever you want to talk. You won't have to shout out the window.'

'That'd be good.'

Talley gave him the number, told Rooney that he was going to take another break, then once more backed his car out of the cul-de-sac. Leigh Metzger was waiting for him on the street outside of Mrs. Peña's home. She wasn't alone. Talley's wife and daughter were with her.

Santa Monica Hospital Emergency Room
Santa Monica, California
Fifteen years ago

Officer Jeff Talley, shirtless but still wearing his blue uniform pants even though they are ripped and streaked with blood, notices her calves first. He is a sucker for shapely calves. Talley is sitting on a gurney in the emergency room, his torn hand packed in a bowl of ice to reduce the swelling and kill the pain while he waits for them to take him to X-ray. His partner, a senior patrol officer named Darren Consuelo, is currently locking Talley's gun, radio, Sam Browne, and other equipment in the trunk of their patrol car for safekeeping.

The nurse comes out of a door across the room, lost in whatever she's scribbling on the clipboard, dressed in white with a pale blue apron, her dark hair pulled back into a ponytail. The calves get him first because they are not hidden by the clunky white stockings that nurses often wear; they are sleek, strong, and fiercely brown from much time in the sun. She has legs like a gymnast or sprinter, which Talley likes. He checks her out: tight ass, trim body, shoulders broad for her small stature. Then he sees her face. She appears to be about his age, twenty-three, twenty-four, something like that.

'Nurse?'

He winces when she glances over, trying to look like he's suffering intense pain. In truth, his hand is numb.

She recognizes the LAPD pants and shoes, smiles encouragingly.

'How's it going, Officer?'

She is not a beautiful woman, but she is pretty with healthy clean skin, and an expression of kindness that moves him. Her eyes glow with a warmth that fills him.

'Ah, Nurse –'

He reads her name tag. Jane Whitehall.

'Jane . . . they were supposed to bring me to X-ray, but I've been out here forever. Think you could check for me?'

He makes the grimace again, impressing her with his suffering.

'I know they're backed up tonight, but I'll see what I can do. What's wrong?'

He lifts his hand from the pink ice. The fleshy pad on the inside of his third finger is ripped and torn. The edges of the laceration are blue from the cold, but the bleeding has mostly stopped.

Nurse Whitehall grimaces sympathetically.

'Ow. That's nasty.'

Talley nods.

'I chased a rape suspect into a backyard in Venice, where the guy sicced his pit bull on me. I'm lucky I've still got a hand.'

Nurse Whitehall carefully places his hand back into the ice. Like her eyes, her touch is warm and certain.

'Did you catch him?'

'Yes, ma'am. He went down hard, but he went down. I always get my man.'

He smiles, letting her know that he is kidding her, and she returns his smile. Talley thinks that he is making great headway, and is about to tell her that he has just been accepted to become a Special Weapons and Tactics officer when Consuelo comes plopping around the corner with a Diet Coke and two PayDay candy bars. Consuelo, like always, smells of cigarettes.

'Jesus, you're still sittin' there? Haven't they snapped the picture yet?'

Talley takes the Diet Coke, wishing that Consuelo would go back to the candy machine. He wants to be alone with the nurse.

'They're backed up. You can hang out in the coffee shop, you want. I'll find you when I'm done here.'

Nurse Whitehall smiles politely at Consuelo.

'I'll see where we are with the X-ray.'

Consuelo grunts, gruff and pissed off about having to spend his day in the emergency room.

'While you're back there, snag a load of klutz pills for this guy, extra strength.'

Quickly, Talley says, 'I'll find you in the coffee shop.'

Nurse Whitehall cocks her head, clearly wondering what Consuelo means. 'Were you with him when the pit bull attacked?'

'That what he told you happened to his hand?'

Talley feels the flush creep up his neck. He meets Consuelo's eyes with a silent plea for help.

'Yeah, Consuelo was there. When we collared the rapist in Venice.'

Consuelo bursts out laughing, spraying peanuts and caramel all over the gurney.

'A rapist? A pit bull? Jesus, lady, this dumb putz slammed his finger in the car door.'

Consuelo walks away, gurgling his smoker's laugh.

Talley wants to crawl under the gurney and disappear. When he looks at Nurse Whitehall again, she is staring at him.

Talley shrugs, trying to make a joke.

'I thought it was worth the shot.'

'That really how you hurt your hand, you caught it in a car door?'

'Not very heroic, is it?'

'No.'

'Well, there you go.'

Nurse Whitehall walks three steps away, stops, turns back, and looks at him with an expression of profound confusion.

'I must be out of my mind.'

She kisses him just as two doctors and another nurse step off the elevator. Talley pulls her close, kissing her deeply, just as he does again that night after their date at the Police Academy's Rod and Gun Club, and every night thereafter. From the instant he sees the warmth in her eyes, Jeff Talley is in love.

Three months and one day later, they marry.

Talley

Talley felt embarrassed and angry with himself. He had been so consumed that he had forgotten about Jane and Amanda. He checked the charge on his cell phone battery, then pocketed the phone and joined them.

Amanda looked like her mother: both were short, though Amanda was a bit taller, and both were thin. They shared what Talley felt was their most telling feature: faces so expressive that they were open doors to their hearts. Talley had always been able to see whatever Jane felt; in the beginning when the feelings were good, this was good; but toward the end, the open reflections of pain and confusion added to a load he found impossible to bear.

Talley kissed his daughter, who was as responsive as a wet towel.

'Sarah told us that there are men with guns barricaded in a house! Where are they?'

Talley pointed toward the cul-de-sac.

'Just around the corner and up that street. You see the helicopters?'

The helicopters made it hard to hear. .

Amanda's eyes were wide and excited as she looked around at the police cars, but Jane looked drawn with dark rings circling her eyes. Talley thought that his wife looked tired. He felt a stab of guilt and shame.

'You been working overtime?'

'Not so much. Two nights a week.'

'You look tired.'

'Does it make me look older, too?'

'Jesus, Jane, I didn't mean it like that. I'm sorry.'

She closed her eyes and nodded, her expression saying that they were covering familiar ground.

Rather than stand outside, Talley brought them into the house. Mrs. Peña's kitchen was filled with the rich smells of brewing coffee and cheese enchiladas. She had put out pitchers of water and cans of soft drinks, insisting that the officers help themselves, and now she was cooking.

Talley introduced Jane and Amanda to Mrs. Peña, then led them into the family room. The big television was playing live coverage of the scene. Amanda went to the television.

'Sarah said they have hostages.'

'They have a father and two children. We think that's all, but we don't know. One of the kids is a girl. About your age.'

'This is *so* cool. Can we go see the house?'

'No, we can't go up there.'

'But you're the chief of police. Why not?'

Jane said, 'It's a crime scene, Mandy. It's dangerous.'

Talley turned to his wife.

'I should've called, Jane. This thing broke just after we spoke, then everything was happening so fast that I didn't even think of it. I'm sorry.'

Jane touched his arm.

'How are *you* doing?'

'I think the guy's going to come around. I've been on the phone with him; he's scared, but he's not suicidal.'

'I'm not asking about the situation, Chief. I mean *you.*'

She glanced at her hand on his arm, then looked up at him again.

'You're shaking.'

Talley stepped away just enough so that her hand fell. He glanced past her at the big television. He could see Jorgenson hunkered behind his radio car.

'The Sheriffs are taking over as soon as they get here.'

'But they're not here. You are. I know what this does to you.'

'They'll be here when they get here. I'm the chief of police, Jane. That's it.'

She stared at him the way she did when she was looking for meaning beyond his words. It used to infuriate him. Where Jane's face was a mirror to every emotion she felt, his face was flat and plain and revealed nothing. She had often accused him of wearing a mask, and he had never been able to explain that it wasn't a mask. It was a tightly held control that kept him from falling apart.

He looked away again. It hurt to see her concern.

'All right, Jeff. I'm just worried about you, is all.'

Talley nodded.

'You guys should have dinner up here before you head back. Let some of the traffic bleed out. Maybe that Thai place. You like that place, don't you?'

Jane grew serious, then nodded.

'We could do that. There's no point in rushing home.'

'Good.'

'I don't want to just drop her off at your place so she has to sit there all alone, so how about she and I go eat, then we'll both stay over. We'll rent a movie. If this thing blows over tonight, you and Mandy could be laughing about it tomorrow this time.'

Talley felt embarrassed. He nodded, but the nod was a stall because he didn't know what to say. He noticed that Jane had dyed her hair a new color. She had colored it the same rich chestnut for as long as Talley could remember, but now it was a deep red so dark that it was almost black. Her hair was cut shorter, too, almost a boy cut. Talley realized then that this woman deserved more than he would ever be able to give her. He told himself that if he cared for her and for whatever they once had, he had to set her free, not curse her with a man whose heart had died.

'What?'

He looked away again.

'You and I need to talk.'

She didn't say anything for a moment, just stared up at him until a faint smile touched the corners of her mouth. He could tell that she was frightened.

'All right, Jeff.'

'The Sheriffs will be here soon. When they get set up, I'll hand off the phone, and then I should be able to leave.'

She nodded.

Talley wanted to tell her then. He wanted to tell her that she was free, that he wouldn't hold her back any longer, that he finally knew that he was beyond redemption, but the words wouldn't come and their absence left him feeling cowardly.

He told Metzger to escort his wife and daughter out of the development, then he went back to his car to wait for the Sheriffs in the dimming light.

Santa Clarita, California
Six miles west of Bristo Camino
Chili's Restaurant
7:02 p.m.

Glen Howell

Glen Howell didn't have to warn his people to keep their voices down; they were surrounded by middle-class vanilla families come to sop up cut-rate frozen shrimp and fried cheese on their Friday night out; people Glen Howell thought of as zombies; irritated men and women at the end of another pointless week, pretending that their screaming, out-of-control, overfed children weren't monsters. Welcome to suburbia, Howell thought, and you can stuff it up your ass.

Howell didn't let the four men and two women get booze, or food that was made to order. He didn't have time to hustle after the parolee cooks in the kitchen, and booze would put his people to sleep. He needed them sharp. Howell had called in each of the six himself, running each name past Sonny Benza personally. They were longtime associates who could do what needed to be done without drawing attention to themselves, and they could do it quickly. From what Howell was learning, speed was going to be everything. Speed, and a total domination of the local scene. He accepted the fact that he would not sleep again until this was over.

Ken Seymore, who had spent the past two hours pretending to be a reporter from the *Los Angeles Times*, was saying, 'They requested a full crisis response team from the L.A. County Sheriff's Department. The Sheriffs are on the way now, but there's been some kinda problem, so they've been delayed.'

Duane Manelli fired off a question. Manelli spoke in abrupt bursts, the way an M16A2 coughed out three-shot groups.

'How many people is that?'

'In the Sheriff's team?'

'Yeah.'

When Duane Manelli was eighteen years old, a state judge had given him the choice between going into the service or pulling twenty months for armed robbery. Manelli had joined the army, and liked it. He spent twelve years in the service, going airborne, ranger, and finally special forces. He currently ran the best hijack crew in Sonny Benza's operation.

Seymore found his notes.

'Here's what we're looking at: A command team, a negotiating team, a tactical team – the tac team includes a perimeter team, the assault team, snipers, and breachers – and an intelligence team. Some of these guys might double up on what they do, but we're looking at about thirty-five new bodies on the scene.'

Somebody whistled.

'Damn, when those boys roll, they roll.'

LJ Ruiz leaned forward on his elbows, frowning. Ruiz was a quiet man with a thoughtful manner who worked for Howell as an enforcer. He specialized in terrorizing bar owners until they agreed to buy their booze from distributors approved by Benza.

'What's a breacher?'

'If they gotta blow open a door or a window or whatever, the breachers set the charge. They go to a special school for that.'

Howell didn't like that many more policemen coming in, but they had expected it. Seymore had reported that, so far, the federal authorities hadn't been requested, but Howell knew that the odds of this would increase as time passed.

Howell asked when the Sheriffs would arrive.

'Cop I talked to, he said they'll be here in three hours, maybe four tops.'

Howell checked his watch, then nodded at Gayle Devarona, one of the two women at the table. Like Seymore, she had pretended to be a news reporter in order to openly ask questions. If the questions were too blatant to ask, she used her skills as a thief.

'What's up with the local cops?'

'We got sixteen full- and part-time employees, fourteen police officers and two full-time office people. I got their names here, and most of the addresses. I could've gotten the others, but I had to come here.'

Seymore laughed.

'Bitch, bitch, bitch.'

'Fist yourself.'

Howell told them to knock it off. Bullshit took time.

Devarona tore a single sheet from a yellow legal pad and passed it across the table to Howell.

'I got the names from the Bristo police office. The addresses and phones I got from a contact at the phone company.'

Howell scanned a neatly hand-printed list. Talley's name was at the top, along with his address and two phone numbers. Howell guessed that one was the house phone, the other a cell.

'You get any background on these people, see what we have to deal with?'

She went through what she had, which made Bristo sound like a burial ground for retired meter maids and retards. Not that bad, really, but Howell thought that they'd caught a break. He knew of small towns in Idaho where half the population had pulled time on LAPD's Robbery-

Homicide Division and the other half were retired FBI. Try to fuck around up there, they'd hand you your ass. Howell checked his watch again. By midnight tonight, he could and would have credit checks and military records (if any) of each of these officers, as well as information about their families.

'What about Talley?'

Sonny Benza had specifically told him to zero in on Talley. You cut off the head, the body dies.

She said, 'I got what I could. Single, ex-LAPD. The condo he lives in is provided by the city.'

Seymore interrupted.

'Those cops I talked to out at Smith's place, they said Talley was a hostage negotiator in LA.'

Devarona scowled, like she hated him stepping on her goods.

'His last three years on the job. Before that, he was SWAT. There's a picture of him on the wall in their office, Talley in an assault suit, holding the big gun.'

Howell nodded at these last two bits of information. They were the first interesting things that he'd heard. He wondered how a SWAT-qualified crisis negotiator ended up crossing school kids in Beemerland. Maybe the free condo.

Devarona said, 'He was on LAPD a total of fourteen years, then he resigned. The woman I talked to didn't want to say, but I'd make him for a stress release. Something's hinky about why he hung it up.'

Howell made a note to pass that up to Palm Springs. He knew that Benza had people on the Los Angeles Police Department. If they turned something rotten on Talley, they might be able to use it as leverage. He had one last question about Talley.

'He work as a detective down there?'

'I asked about that. The girl didn't know, but it's still a good notion to follow up.'

When Devarona finished, Howell waited for more, but that was it. Everyone had given what they had. All in all, Howell couldn't kick. Start to finish, they'd had maybe two hours to get it together. Now there was more to do. He considered the sixteen names on Devarona's list. The list of bankers, lawyers, private investigators, and police officers owned by Sonny Benza and his associates was far longer; that list numbered in the hundreds, and all of those names could be brought to bear for the task at hand.

'Okay, get the rest of the addresses, then divide up the names and start digging. Gayle, you're on credit and finances. We get lucky, one of these clowns is gonna be in so deep that he's drowning. Maybe we can toss him a life preserver. Duane, Ruiz, find out where these people play. Some married doof is gonna keep a whore on the side; one of these turds is gonna like chasing the dragon with a fruit. Shovel dirt and find the skeletons. Ken, you're back at the house with the reporters. If anything breaks, I want to know about it before God.'

Seymore leaned back, irritated. Howell always got pissed off when he did that.

'Don't start with the faces, goddamnit. If you've got something to say, say it.'

'We're going to need more people. If this thing drags out a few days, we're gonna need a lot more.'

'I'm on it.'

Now Seymore leaned forward, and lowered his voice still more.

'If things get wet, we're going to need people who can handle that end.'

Wet work was blood work. Howell had already thought of that and had already made the call.

'The right people are on their way. You worry about your job. I got my side covered.'

Howell checked his watch again, then copied Talley's address and phone numbers on the bottom of the sheet. He tore off his copy, then stood.

'I want updates in two hours.'

Howell put Talley's address in his pocket as he walked out to his car. Not just anyone would murder a chief of police with an army of cameras and newspeople around. He needed someone special for a job like that.

7
Newhall, California Sundown
Friday, 7:39 p.m.

Marion Clewes

His name was Marion Clewes. He was waiting in a donut shop in Newhall, California, twelve miles west of Bristo Camino in an area where all of the signs were in Spanish. Marion was the only person in the shop other than the woman behind the counter who spoke no English and seemed uneasy about his being there. Even at sundown, the unairconditioned shop was hot, leaving her skin filmed with grease. It was a filthy place, with coffee rings on the broken Formica tables and a sticky floor. Marion didn't mind. He could feel the weight of the air, heavy with grease and cinnamon. He took a seat at a table facing the door to wait for Glen Howell.

Marion was used to meeting Howell in places like this. Howell was never comfortable with him, and was probably afraid of him. He suspected that Howell didn't even like him, but that was okay. They paid him well for doing what he enjoyed, and he did these things with a merciless dependability.

Marion stared at the woman. She crossed and recrossed her arms until she disappeared behind the fryer, frantic to escape his gaze. He shifted his stare to the parking lot. A fly droned past his ear. It was a black desert fly, fat with juice and thorny with coarse hair, kicking off green highlights in the cheesy fluorescent lights. It buzzed low over the table in an S-shaped course, swung slowly around, and landed in a sprinkle of sugar. Marion slapped it. He waited, holding his hand in place, feeling for movement. When Marion raised his hand, the fly oozed sideways, legs kicking, trying to walk. Marion watched it. The best it could do was drive itself in a pathetic circle. Marion examined his hand. A smear of fly goo and a single black leg streaked his third finger. He touched his tongue to the smear and tasted sugar. He watched the fly push itself in the circle. Gently, he held it in place with his left index finger, and used his right index fingernail to break away another leg. He ate it. Hmm. One by one, he broke away the

661

fly's legs and ate them. One wing was damaged, but the other beat furiously. He wondered what the fly was thinking.

Headlights flashed across the glass.

Marion glanced up to see Howell's beautiful Mercedes pull to a stop. It was a lovely car. Marion watched Howell get out of the car and come inside. Marion pushed the fly to the side as Howell took a seat opposite him.

'There's a woman in the back. I don't think she speaks English, though.'

'This won't take long.'

Howell spoke softly, getting down to business. He placed a slip of yellow paper on the table in front of Marion.

'Talley lives here. It's a condo. I don't have anything about what the place is like or if there's security or anything like that.'

'It doesn't matter.'

'Here's the drill: We have to own this guy – that's straight from the top – and we don't have a lot of time to mess around. I need you to find something we can use to twist him.'

Marion put the address away. He had done this kind of thing before, and knew what was needed. He would look for weakness. Everyone held their weakness close. He would copy bank account numbers; he would search for pornography and drugs, old love letters and sex toys, prescription medications and computer files. Maybe a lab report from a personal physician describing heart disease or phone records to another man's wife. It could be anything. There was always something.

'Is he there now?'

'Don't you listen to the news?'

Marion shook his head.

'He's not home, but I can't tell you when he will or won't get back there. So be ready for that.'

'What if he walks in on me?'

Howell averted his eyes, reached a decision, then looked back.

'If he's got you, kill him.'

'Okay.'

'Listen, we don't want him dead. We want to control him. We need to use him. But if you're caught, well, fuck it. Cap his ass.'

'What about later? After he's used?'

'That's up to Palm Springs.'

Marion accepted that. Sometimes they were kept alive because they could be used over and over, but most times he was allowed to finish the job. The finishing was his favorite part.

Howell said, 'You have my pager number and my cell?'

'Yes.'

'Okay. Page me when you're done. Whether you find something or not, keep me in the loop.'

'What if there's nothing in his home?'

'Then we'll hit his office. That'll be harder. He's the chief of police.'
Howell got up without another word.

Marion watched the beautiful Mercedes slide away into the deepening twilight, then looked back at the fly. Its legless body lay on its side, still. Marion touched it. The remaining wing fluttered.

Marion said, 'Poor fly.'

Marion carefully pulled out the remaining wing, then left to do his job.

8
Friday, 7:40 p.m.

Talley

The helicopters over York Estates switched on their lights to become brilliant stars. Talley didn't like losing the sun. The creeping darkness changed the psychology of hostage takers and police officers alike. Subjects felt safer in the dark, hidden and more powerful, the night allowing them fantasies of escape. Perimeter guards knew this, so their stress level would rise as their efficiency decayed. Night laid the foundation for overreaction and death.

Talley stood by his car, sipping Diet Coke as his officers reported. Rooney's employer, who believed that he could identify the unknown subject, had been located and was inbound; Walter Smith's wife had not yet been found; Rooney's parole officer from the Ant Farm had been identified but was in transit to Las Vegas for the weekend and could not be reached; ten large pizzas (half veggie, half meat) had just been delivered from Domino's, but someone had forgotten napkins. Information was coming in so fast that Talley began to lose track, and it would come faster. He cursed that the Sheriffs hadn't yet arrived.

Barry Peters and Earl Robb trotted up the street from their radio car. Robb was carrying his Maglite.

'We're set with the phone company, Chief. PacBell shows six hard lines into the house, four of them listed, two unlisted. They blocked all six in and out like you wanted. No one else can call in on those numbers, and the only number they can reach calling out is your cell.'

Talley felt a dull relief; now he didn't have to worry that some asshole would get the Smiths' number and convince Rooney to murder his hostages.

'Good, Earl. Did we get more bodies from the Highway Patrol?'

'Four more CHiPs and two cars from Santa Clarita.'

'Put them on the perimeter. Have Jorgenson do it, because he knows what I told Rooney.'

'Yes, sir.'

Robb trotted away as Peters turned on his Maglite, lighting two floor plan sketches that had been made on typing paper.

'I worked these out with the neighbors, Chief. This is the upstairs, this is the downstairs.'

Talley grunted. They weren't bad, but he wasn't confident that they were accurate; details like window placement and closet location could be critical if a forced entry was required. Talley asked about architectural drawings.

'These are the best I could do; there wasn't anything at the building commission.'

'There should be. This is a planned community. Every house plan in the development should be on file.'

Peters looked upset and embarrassed.

'I'm sorry, Chief. I called both the Antelope Valley and Santa Clarita building commissions, but they don't have anything, either. You want me to try something else?'

'The Sheriffs are going to need those plans, Barry. Get hold of someone from the mayor's office or one of the council people. Sarah has their home and work numbers. Tell them we need access to the permit office right away. Pull the permits you find and check the contractors. Somebody had to keep a set of file plans.'

As Peters hustled away, Larry Anders's car rolled around the corner and pulled to a stop beside Talley. A slim, nervous man climbed from the passenger side.

'Chief, this is Brad Dill, Rooney's employer.'

'Thanks for coming, Mr. Dill.'

'Okay.'

Talley knew that Dill owned a small cement-contracting business based in Lancaster. Dill had weathered skin from working in the sun and small eyes that kept glancing somewhere else. He had trouble maintaining eye contact.

'You know what's going on here, Mr. Dill?'

Dill glanced up the street past Talley, then inspected the ground. Nervous.

'Okay, the officer told me. I just want to say I didn't know anything about this. I didn't know what they were going to do.'

Talley thought that Dill probably had a criminal record.

'Mr. Dill, those two didn't know what they were going to do until they did it. Don't worry about it. You're here because you've worked with them and I'm hoping you can help me understand them. You see?'

'Okay. Sure. I've known Dennis for almost two years now, Kevin a little less.'

'Before we get into that, I want you to identify these guys. Officer Anders says you also know the third subject?'

'Okay. Sure. That would be Mars.'

'Let's look at the pictures. Larry, do you have them?'

Anders returned to the car and brought back the two 8 × 10 prints that had been made from the security tape. He had to return to his car a second time for his Maglite. Soon they would have to move into one of the houses. Talley wondered if Mrs. Peña would let them use hers.

'Okay, Mr. Dill. Let's take a look. Can you identify these people?'

The first picture showed a slightly fuzzy Kevin Rooney by the front door; Dennis and the third man were clearly visible in the second print. Talley was pleased with the prints. Anders had done a good job.

'Okay. Sure. That's Kevin, he's Dennis's kid brother. And that one is Dennis. He just come back from the Ant Farm.'

'And you know the third man?'

'That would be Mars Krupchek. He come on the job about a month ago. No, wait, not quite four weeks, I guess. Him, I don't know so well.'

Anders nodded along with Dill, confirming what he had heard earlier.

'I called Krupchek in to Sarah on the drive, Chief. She's running his name through DMV and the NCIC.'

Talley questioned Dill about how Dennis behaved on the job. Dill described a temperamental personality with a penchant for overstatement and drama. Talley grew convinced that his original impression was correct: Rooney was an aggressive narcissist with esteem problems. Kevin, on the other hand, showed evidence of concern for others; where Dennis would show up for work late and expend little effort on the job, Kevin showed up on time and was willing to help others; he was a passive personality who would take his cues from the stronger personalities in his sphere of influence. He would never drive an action, but would instead react to whatever was presented to him.

Talley paused to consider if he was missing an obvious avenue of questioning. He took the Maglite from Anders to look at the photograph of Kevin, then decided to move on to Mars Krupchek. He had been concerned about Mars since he had seen the unknown subject lean over the counter to watch Junior Kim die. Talley noticed something on the 8 × 10 of Mars that he hadn't seen in the security tape. A tattoo on the back of Mars's head that read: BURN IT.

'What can you tell me about Krupchek?'

'Not so much. He showed up one day looking for work when I needed a guy. He was well-spoken and polite; he's big and strong, you know, so I gave him a try.'

'Did he know the Rooneys before he came on the job?'

'No, I know that for a fact. I introduced them. You know, Mars this is Dennis, Dennis this is Mars. Like that. Mars just kinda stays by himself except for when he's with Dennis.'

Talley pointed out the tattoo.

'What's this mean, "Burn it"?'

'I dunno. It's just a tattoo.'

Talley glanced at Anders.

'Did you put out the tattoo as an identifier?'

'Yes, sir.'

Identities on the NCIC computer could be cross-checked by permanent identifiers like tattoos and scars. Talley turned back to Brad Dill.

'You know what he did before this?'

'No, sir. Nope.'

'Know where he's from?'

'He doesn't talk so much. You ask him, he doesn't say so much.'

'How does he get along with the other men?'

'Well enough, I guess. He never had much to do with anyone until Dennis came back. That was only a week or so ago. Before Dennis came back, he would just stay by himself and watch everyone else.'

'What do you mean, watch everyone else?'

'I don't know if I'm saying it right. When the guys go on a break, he doesn't sit with'm. He sits off by himself and watches them, kinda like he was keeping an eye on them. No, wait, that's not right. It was more like he's watching TV. Does that make sense? Sometimes it'd make me think he'd fallen asleep the way he'd do that. He was just, I dunno, staring.'

Talley didn't like what he was hearing about Krupchek, but he also didn't know what to make of it.

'Has he ever demonstrated violence or aggression toward the other men?'

'He just sits there.'

Talley handed the photograph back to Anders. Mars Krupchek might be retarded or suffer from some other mental impairment, but Talley didn't know. He had no sense of who Mars Krupchek was, what he was capable of, or how he might act. This left Talley feeling anxious and wary. The unknown could kill you, and was often worse than you imagined.

'Mr. Dill, do you have an address for Krupchek?'

Dill pulled a tiny address book from his back pocket and read off an address and phone number. Anders copied them.

Talley thanked Brad Dill for his help, told him that Anders would bring him home, then took Anders aside out of earshot.

'Check that Krupchek's address matches with the billing address listed with the phone. If it does, call the Palmdale City Attorney's office and ask for a telephonic search warrant, then head to his residence. After you've got the warrant, go in and see what you find. Take someone with you.'

As Anders and Dill drove away, Talley tried to recall the things that he still needed to do. Mrs. Smith had to be found, his officers had to be fed, and he wanted to check the perimeter positions of the newly arrived Highway Patrol officers to make sure that Jorgenson hadn't placed them too close to the house. When he realized that he would have to call Rooney again soon, a swell of panic threatened to overwhelm him. He would have to call Rooney every hour throughout the night; interrupt his sleep, break down his resistance, wear him down. A hostage barricade was a war of attrition and nerves. Talley didn't know that his own nerves were enough to see it through.

Metzger's voice cut through his radio.

'Chief, Metzger.'

'Go, Leigh.'

'The Sheriffs are inbound. Ten minutes out.'

Talley slumped against his car and closed his eyes. Thank God.

Dennis

Dennis tried not to look at Mars after his conversation with Talley, but he couldn't help himself. He thought about what Kevin had told him, about Mars wanting to shoot that cop who had come to the door, about Mars lying that the cop had pulled his weapon and Mars firing first. Maybe Talley had something; maybe Dennis could beat the rap if it was Mars who shot the officer, and not him. If Kevin backed him up, they might be able to cut a deal with the prosecutor for their testimony against Mars. Dennis felt a desperate hope, but then he remembered the money. If he cut a deal, he had to give up the money. He shoved the phone aside and turned back to the others. He wasn't ready to give up the cash.

Kevin looked at him anxiously.

'Are they giving us the helicopter?'

'No. We gotta find another way out of here. Let's start looking.'

The girl and her fat brother were still kneeling beside their father. She started on him right away.

'There's nothing to look for. You've got to do something to help my father.'

She still held the washcloth to her father's head, but now the ice was melted and the cloth was soaked. Dennis felt a flash of annoyance.

'Shut up, all right? I've got a situation here, in case you haven't noticed.'

Her face worked harder.

'All you're doing is watching yourself on TV. You hurt him. Look at him. He needs a doctor.'

'Shut up.'

'It's been hours!'

'Put more ice in the cloth.'

'Ice doesn't help!'

The fat boy started crying.

'He's in a coma!'

The girl surprised him. She lurched to her feet with the abrupt fury of a jack-in-the-box and stomped toward the door.

'I'm getting a doctor!'

Dennis felt outside of himself, as if the weight of the cops and his being trapped in this house were all suddenly real where they hadn't been before. He caught her in two steps, slapping her just the way his old man used to lay out the old lady, that shrill bitch. He caught the girl square on the side of the face with the weight of his hand, knocked her flat fucking down to the floor. The fat boy shouted her name and charged, pummeling Dennis like an angry midget. Dennis dug his fingers into the soft meat on the back of the boy's neck, and the fat boy squealed. Then Kevin was shoving him away.

'STOP IT!'

Kevin pushed the fat boy down with his sister, placing himself between them and Dennis.

'Just stop it, Dennis. Please!'

Dennis was in a blood fury. He wanted to beat Kevin down, to smash his face and kick him into a pulp. He wanted to beat the fat boy and the girl, then throw the cash in the Jaguar and crash out of the garage and shoot it out with the cops all the way down to Mexico.

Mars was staring at him, his face a shadow, his eyes tiny glints of strange light like ferrets peering from caves.

Dennis shouted, '*What?*'

Mars made the quiet smile and shook his head.

Dennis stepped back, breathing hard. Everything was coming apart. Dennis looked back at the television, half expecting to see the cops storming the house, but the scene outside was exactly as it had been minutes before. The girl was holding her face in her hands. The fat boy was glaring with hate-filled eyes like he wanted to cut Dennis's throat. Their father was breathing noisily through his nose. The pressure was making him crazy.

Dennis said, 'We gotta do something with them. I can't deal with this shit.'

Mars lumbered to his feet, large and gross.

'We should tie them up so we don't have to worry about them. We should have done that anyway.'

Dennis hooked his head toward the girl, speaking to Kevin.

'Mars is right. We can't leave these assholes running around like this, getting in the way. Find something to tie'm up with, and take them upstairs.'

'What do I use to tie them?'

'Look in the garage. Look in the kitchen. Mars, you find something, okay? You know what we need. This turd doesn't know anything.'

Mars disappeared toward the garage. Kevin took the girl's arm as if he was afraid that she would hit him, but she stood without resisting, her face working and the tears coming harder.

'What about my father? You can't just leave him like this.'

Her father was cold to the touch; every few seconds a tremor rippled through his body. Dennis took his pulse like he knew what he was doing, but he couldn't tell a goddamned thing. He didn't like how the man looked, but didn't say anything about it because there was nothing to say.

'We'll put him on the couch. That way he'll be more comfortable.'

'He needs a doctor.'

'He's just sleeping. You take a head shot, you gotta sleep it off, is all. My old man used to beat me worse than this.'

Dennis had Kevin help lift her father onto the couch.

When Mars returned, Dennis told them to take the kids upstairs. He was tired of thinking about them. He was tired of thinking about everything except the money. He needed a way out.

Jennifer

Mars opened the door to her room, then stepped aside so that she and Kevin could enter. He had come back from the garage with extension cords, duct tape, a hammer and nails. He gave two extension cords to Kevin.

'Put her in here. Tie her to the chair, and tie her *tight*. Tie her feet. I'll take care of the windows and the door when I finish with the boy.'

Mars looked at her with unfocused eyes, as if he were waking from a deep sleep and she was the memory of a dream.

'I'll check how you tie her when I come back.'

Mars pulled Thomas away as Kevin brought her into the room. The lights were on because she never turned them off; she fell asleep with them on, either talking on the phone or watching TV, and woke with them on, and never thought to turn them off when she left to start her day. The shades had been pulled and the phone was on the floor against the wall, its plug smashed so that it couldn't be used. Kevin dragged her desk chair into the middle of the floor. He avoided her eyes, nervous.

'Just let this happen and everything will be okay. You gotta pee or anything?'

She felt a flush of embarrassment. She had to use the bathroom so badly that she burned.

'It's in there.'

'Where? You got your own bathroom?'

'Uh-huh. It's right there.'

'Okay, come on.'

She didn't move.

'You can't come with me.'

He stood in the bathroom door, waiting.

'I'm not going to leave you alone.'

'I'm not going to the bathroom in front of you.'

'Would you rather pee on yourself?'

'I'm not letting you watch. I don't have guns or anything in there, if that's what you're worried about.'

He seemed annoyed, but she didn't care. He stepped into the bathroom to look around, then came back.

'Okay, I won't go in with you, but you can't close the door. I'll stand over here. That way I can't see you.'

'But you'll hear.'

'Look, piss or don't piss. I don't care. If you're not going to go, put your ass in the chair before Mars comes back.'

Jennifer had to pee so badly that she decided to go. She tried to pee quietly, but it seemed louder than ever. When she was finished, she returned to her room too embarrassed to make eye contact.

'You're disgusting.'

'Whatever. Sit here and put your hands behind the chair.'

'I don't see why you can't just lock me in. It's not like I can go anywhere.'

'Either I'm going to tie you or Mars will tie you.'

She perched on the chair, tense and wary.

Kevin had two long black extension cords. She cringed when he touched her, but he didn't treat her roughly or twist her arms.

'I don't want to make this too tight, but I got to tie you. Mars is going to check.'

His voice held a regret that surprised her. She knew that Kevin was scared, but now she wondered if he felt embarrassed at what they were doing. Maybe he even had a conscience. He finished with her wrists, then moved around in front of her to tie her ankles to the legs of the chair. She watched him, thinking that if there was a friend to be found among them it was him.

'Kevin?'

'What?'

She kept her voice soft, scared that Mars would hear.

'You're caught in this just like me.'

His face darkened.

'I've heard the three of you talking. You're the only one who seems to know that you're making it worse by being here. Dennis doesn't get that.'

'Don't talk about Dennis.'

'Why do you go along with him?'

'Things just happen, is all. Don't talk about it.'

'My father needs a doctor.'

'He's just knocked out. I've been knocked out.'

'You know it's worse than that. Think about what you're doing, Kevin, *please*. Make Dennis see. If my father dies they'll charge you with his murder, too. You know that.'

'There's nothing I can do.'

'You knew better than to rob that minimart, didn't you? I'll bet you tried to talk Dennis out of it, but he wouldn't listen and now you're all trapped in here and wanted for murder.'

He kept his face down, pulling at the extension cords.

'I'll bet that's true. You knew it was wrong, and it was. Now you know this is wrong, too. My daddy needs a doctor, but Dennis is just being stubborn. If you keep following Dennis and Mars, the police will kill you all.'

Kevin leaned back on his heels. He seemed tired, as if he had been worrying the problem for so long without solution that the worrying had worn him out. He shook his head.

'I'm sorry.'

A shadow moved behind Kevin, catching Jennifer's eye. Mars stood in the door, staring at them, his face blank. She didn't know how long he had been there, or what he had heard.

Mars didn't look at Kevin; he was staring at her.

'Never be sorry.'

Kevin stood so quickly that he almost fell.

'I tied her ankles too tight. I had to tie them again.'

Mars went to the windows. He hammered heavy nails into the sills so that the windows wouldn't open, then came back to stand in front of her. He stood very close, towering over her in a way that made him seem to reach the ceiling. He squatted between her legs, then tugged at the bindings on her ankles. The cord cut into her skin.

'This isn't tight enough. You tied her like a pussy.'

Mars wrapped the cord more tightly, then did the same at her wrists. The wire cut into her flesh so hard that she had to bite her tongue, but she was too scared to complain. He tore a strip of wide gray duct tape off the roll. He pressed it hard over her mouth.

Kevin worried his hands, fidgeting, clearly frightened of Mars.

'Make sure she can breathe, Mars. Don't put it so tight.'

Mars ran his fingers hard over the tape. She was so creeped out at his touch that she wanted to scream.

'Go downstairs, Kevin.'

Kevin hesitated at the door. Mars still knelt in front of her, pushing at the tape as if he wanted to work it into her pores. Pushing and pushing. Rhythmic. Pushing. Jennifer thought she might faint.

Kevin said, 'Aren't you coming?'

'I'll be along. Go.'

Jennifer looked at Kevin, pleading with him not to leave her alone with Mars.

Kevin left.

When she finally looked at Mars again, he was watching her. Mars brought his face level with hers, then leaned forward. She flinched, thinking he was going to kiss her, but he didn't. He didn't move for the longest time, staring first into her left eye, then into her right. He leaned closer, and sniffed. He was smelling her.

Mars straightened.

'I want to show you something.'

He pulled off his shirt, revealing a flabby body as pasty as an unwashed bedsheet. Tattooed across his chest in flowing script was:

A Mother's Son.

'You see? It cost two hundred forty dollars. That's how much I love my mom.'

Looking at him grossed her out. His chest and belly were specked with small gray knots as if he were diseased. She thought they might be warts.

She suddenly felt the weight of his eyes and glanced up to see him watching her. She realized that he knew she had been staring at the lumps. He touched one of them, a hard gray knot, then another, and the corner of his mouth curled into a smile that was almost too small to see.

'My mom burned me with cigarettes.'

Jennifer felt sick. They weren't lumps or warts; they were scars.

Mars pulled on his shirt, then leaned close, and this time she was certain that he would touch her. Her heart pounded. She wanted to turn away, but she couldn't.

He placed his hand on her shoulder.

Jennifer jerked against her binds, twisting her head, arching her back, feeling the bite of the extension cords in her wrists and ankles as she tried to scream through the tape.

Mars squeezed her shoulder once, firmly, as if he were testing the bone beneath her flesh, and then he drew away.

Mars made the little smile again, then went to the door. He paused there, staring at her with eyes so empty that she filled them with nightmares. He turned off the lights, stepped out, then pulled the door closed. The sound of his hammer was as loud as thunder, but not so loud as her fearful heart.

Dennis

Dennis was at the window, watching the police, when he heard the pitch of the helicopters change. That was the first thing, the helicopters repositioning themselves. Then one of the patrol cars out front fired up. The lead car swung around in a tight arc, roaring away as a new Highway Patrol car arrived. He couldn't tell if Talley was still outside or not. The cops were up to something, which made Dennis feel queasy and scared. They would have to leave soon or they might not be able to leave at all.

Mars settled onto the couch by Walter Smith. He put his hand on Smith's head as if he was stroking the soft fur between a dog's ears.

'They didn't give you the helicopter because they don't believe you're serious.'

Dennis paced away from the window, irritated. He didn't like Mars's smug I-know-something-that-you-don't smile. Mars had egged him on about robbing the minimart, and Mars had shot the cop at the front door.

'You don't know what you're talking about. They've got rules about this stuff. Fuck them anyway. I never thought we'd get a helicopter. I just thought it would be worth a try.'

Mars stroked Smith's head, running his fingers slowly over the man's scalp as if he was probing the contours of his skull. Dennis thought it was weird.

'You don't see the big picture, Dennis.'

'You want a picture, Mars? Here it is: We've gotta find a way out of here with that cash.'

Mars patted Smith's head.

'Our way out is right here. You don't understand the power we have.'

'The hostages? Jesus, they're *all* we have. If we didn't have these people, the cops would be all over us.'

When Mars looked up again, Dennis thought his eyes were brighter, and somehow now watchful.

'What we have is the fear they feel. Their fear gives us power. The police will only take us seriously if they're scared we'll kill these people. It isn't the people that we have to trade, Dennis. It's their death.'

Dennis thought he was kidding.

'Okay, dude. Mars, you're creeping me out.'

'The police have no reason to deal with us unless they take us seriously. All they have to do is wait until we get tired, and then we'll give up. They know that, Dennis. They're counting on it.'

Dennis felt his chest expand against a tight pressure that filled the room. Mars continued to watch him, his eyes now focused into hard, dark beads. Dennis had the vague feeling that somehow the power between them was shifting, that Mars was leading him somewhere and waiting to see if Dennis would follow.

'So how do we convince them?'

'Tell them we're going to let the fat boy go as a sign of good faith.'

Dennis didn't move. He could see Kevin from the corner of his eye, and knew that Kevin was feeling the same awful pressure.

'We send the fat boy out the front door. We don't go with him, we just open it and tell him to go. He just has to walk across the yard here and out to the cars, and he'll be fine. Your pal, Talley, he'll probably call the kid over, saying something like, "C'mon, son, everything is fine."'

Dennis's back felt wet and cold.

'We wait until he's about halfway across the yard, then we shoot him.'

Dennis heard his own heartbeat. He heard his breath flow across his teeth, a faraway hiss.

Mars spread his hands at the simple beauty of it.

'Then they'll know we mean business, and we'll have something to trade.'

Dennis tried to tell himself that Mars was kidding, but he knew that Mars was serious. Mars meant every word.

'Mars. We couldn't do something like that.'

Mars looked curious.

'I could. I'll do it, if you want.'

Dennis didn't know what to say. Overhead, the helicopters beat louder. He went to the shutters and pretended to look out, but the truth was that he couldn't look at Mars any longer. Mars had scared him.

'I don't think so, dude.'

'You don't?'

'No. We couldn't do that.'

The bright intensity in Mars's eyes faded like a candle losing its flame, and Mars shrugged. Dennis felt relieved. He told them to watch out for the cops, then he once more walked through the house. He went into every downstairs room around the perimeter of the house, checking each window to see if he could use it to sneak out, but all of the windows were in plain view of the cops. Dennis knew that his time was running out. If he was going to get out, he had to do it soon, because more cops were on the way. He moved along the rear of the house, through the family room and into the garage. He hoped to find some kind of side door, but instead he came to a small utility bathroom at the end of a workshop off the garage. A sliding window with frosted glass was let into the wall above the sink. Dennis opened it, and saw the heavy leaves of an oleander bush, dark green and pointed, thick against the dusty screen. He pressed his face to the screen and peered out, but it was impossible to see very much in the growing darkness. The window was on the street side of the wall that enclosed the backyard, but was hidden by the oleander. If the oleander wasn't there the cops out front would be able to see him. Dennis pushed out the screen, taking care to do it quietly. He opened the window wider, crawled up onto the sink, and leaned out. He would never have done this in the daylight, but the darkness gave him confidence. The ground was four feet below. He worked his shoulders through the window. The row of oleanders followed the wall, but he couldn't tell how far. He was growing excited. He pushed himself back into the house, then turned around so that he could step through feet first, one leg and then another. He lowered himself to the ground. He was outside the house.

Dennis crouched on the ground beneath the oleander, his back pressed to the high stucco wall, listening. He could hear the police radios from the cars parked at the front of the house. He caught tiny glimpses of the two cars through the leaves, glinting in the streetlight. He couldn't see the cops, but he knew they would be watching the front of the house, not the row of shrubs along the side wall. Dennis lay down at the base of the wall and inched along its length. The oleanders were thicker in some places and thinner in others, but the police didn't see him. He came to the end of the wall and saw that the oleanders continued into the neighbor's front yard. Dennis grew more excited. They could bag the cash, drag it along behind the oleanders, then slip away while the cops were watching the house, right under their noses!

Dennis worked his way back to the window and climbed into the house. Dennis was pumped! He was going to beat this thing! He was going to beat Talley, beat the murder rap, and cruise south to TJ in style.

He ran back to the office to tell Kevin and Mars that he had found the way out.

Marion Clewes

The planet Venus hung low in the blackening western sky, racing toward the ridge of mountains and the edge of Talley's roof. The stars were not yet out, but here in the high desert, away from the city, the sky would soon be washed with lights.

Talley's condominium was one of forty-eight stucco and stained-wood units spread over four buildings arranged like the letter H. Mature eucalyptus and podocarpus trees shouldered over the buildings like drunks leaning over a rail. Marion guessed that the condos had at one time been apartments, then converted and sold. Each unit had a small fenced patio at ground level, and centered between the four buildings was a very nice pool; small, unprotected parking lots were on either side of each building for the residents. It seemed like a pleasant place to live.

Marion walked through the grounds, hearing music and voices. Cars were turning into the parking lots, men and women still arriving from work; an older woman was methodically swimming laps, the pool's lone occupant; charcoal grills were smoking on several of the patios, filling the air with the smells of burning flesh.

Marion circled the building with Talley's unit. Because the buildings were of older construction (Marion guessed they had been built in the seventies), the gas meters, electric meters, and junction boxes for both telephones and cable TV were clustered together at an out-of-the-way spot opposite the parking lots. Any individual security systems would be junctioned with the telephone lines. Marion was pleased to see that the building had no alarms. Marion was neither surprised nor shocked; being a sleepy small town so far from LA, the greatest security the condo association might buy would be having a rent-a-cop cruise the parking lots every hour. If that.

Marion found Talley's unit, let himself through the gate to the front door. He clenched his jaw so as not to laugh; the patio and door were hidden by a six-foot privacy fence. He couldn't have asked for anything easier. He rang the bell twice, then knocked, already knowing that no one was home; the house was dark. He pulled on latex gloves, took out his pry bar and pick, then set to work. Four minutes later, the deadbolt slipped. Eighty seconds after that, he let himself in.

'Hello?'

He didn't expect an answer, and none came. Marion shut the door behind him, but did not lock it.

The kitchen was to the left, a small dining room to the right. Sliding glass doors offered a view of the patio. Directly ahead was a large living room with a fireplace. Marion looked for a desk or work space, but saw none. He unlatched the glass doors, then crossed the living room to open the largest window. He would relock everything if he left at his leisure, but for now he arranged fast exits. Howell did not want Talley dead, so Marion would try not to kill him even if Talley surprised him.

Marion climbed steep stairs to a second-floor landing with doors leading to a bathroom and two other rooms, the room to his right the master bedroom. He turned on the light. Marion expected to search every closet and drawer in the house for something that could be used as leverage, but there it was as soon as he entered, right there, waiting. It happened that way, sometimes.

A desk rested against the far wall, scattered with papers and bills and receipts, but that isn't what caught Marion's eye. Five photographs waited at the back of the desk, Talley with a woman and girl, the woman and Talley always the same, the girl at different ages.

Marion kneeled, brought the frame to his face.

A woman. A girl.

A wife. A daughter.

Marion considered the possibilities.

9

Friday, 8:06 p.m.

Talley

The Los Angeles County Sheriff's Department Crisis Response Team came around the corner like a military convoy. A plain Sheriff's sedan led the file, followed by a bulky Mobile Command Post vehicle that looked like a bread truck on steroids. The Sheriffs wouldn't need Mrs. Peña's home; the van contained its own power generator, a bathroom, uplinks for the Intelligence Officer's computers, and a communications center for command and control coordination. It also had a Mr. Coffee. The Sheriff's SWAT team followed in two large GMC Suburbans with a second van containing their weapons and support gear. As the convoy stopped, the SWAT cops un-assed, already geared out in dark green tactical uniforms. They hustled to the second van, where a senior sergeant-supervisor passed out radios and firearms. Four radio cars followed the tactical vehicles with uniformed deputies who clustered around their own sergeant-supervisor. Talley heard a change in the helicopters' rotor turbulence as they repositioned to broadcast the Sheriffs' arrival. If Rooney was watching television, his stress level would soar. During periods like this the possibility of the subject panicking and taking action increased. Talley hurried to the lead car.

A tall, slender African-American officer climbed out from behind the wheel as a blond officer with thinning hair climbed from the passenger side.

Talley put out his hand.

'Jeff Talley. I'm the chief here. Are you the team commander?'

The tall man flashed a relaxed smile.

'Will Maddox. I'll be the primary negotiator. This is Chuck Ellison, my secondary. The commander would be Captain Martin. She's back in the van.'

As Talley shook their hands, Ellison winked.

'She likes to ride in the van instead of with us negotiators. Lots of pretty lights in there.'

'Chuck.'

Ellison looked innocent.

'Something I said?'

The energy on the street changed dramatically; Talley had felt that he was hanging from a ledge by his fingers, but now an organized military weight was settling over York Estates. A brilliant pool of white light swept over them on its way along the convoy. All three of them held up their hands to cut the glare. The different teams breaking up into their components with well-rehearsed efficiency felt comforting. Talley no longer felt alone. In a matter of minutes, this man Will Maddox would take the responsibility of other lives from his shoulders.

Talley said, 'Mr. Maddox, I am damned glad to see you here.'

'Will. Mr. Maddox is my wife.'

Ellison laughed loudly.

Maddox smiled absently at the lame joke, glancing at the mouth of the cul-de-sac a half-block away.

'The barricade up there?'

'Up at the end. I've got two men directly out front, three men spread across the property on either side, and another three beyond the back wall on Flanders Road. We have two people on each entrance here into York and three with the media. We could use more with the media right away before they start leaking through the development.'

'You can brief the Captain on those kinds of things, but there are a couple of points that I need to hit before we get into all that.'

'Go.'

Talley walked with them back toward the control van to find the Captain. He knew from his own experience that Maddox and Ellison would want a virtual replay of his conversations with Rooney.

'It's you who's had direct contact with the subjects?'

'Yes. Only me.'

'Okay. Are the innocents under an immediate threat?'

'I don't believe so. The last contact I had with Rooney was about twenty minutes ago. Way I left it, he's in there thinking that he has outs both for Kim's murder and the attempt on the officer. You know about that?'

While inbound, the Sheriffs had received a radio briefing on the events leading up to the barricade situation. Maddox confirmed that they knew the bare bones.

'Okay. Turns out Kim had a gun, and more than one of the subjects besides Rooney fired upon the officer. I left him thinking that a sharp lawyer could cut a deal on both counts.'

'Has he made any demands?'

Talley told him about Rooney demanding that the perimeter be pulled back and the deal that they'd made, the hostage names for the pullback. Getting the first concession was often the most difficult, and how it was gotten could set the tone for everything that was to follow.

Maddox walked with his hands in his pockets, his expression knowing and thoughtful.

'Good job, Chief. Sounds like we're in pretty good shape. You used to be with LAPD SWAT, weren't you?'

Talley looked more closely at Maddox.

'That's right. Have we met?'

'I was on LAPD as a uniform before I went with the Sheriffs, which put us there about the same time. When we got the call here today, your name rang a bell. Talley. You did the nursery school.'

Talley felt uncomfortable whenever someone mentioned the nursery school.

'That was a long time ago.'

'That had to be something. I don't think I would've had the balls.'

'It wasn't balls. I just couldn't think of anything else.'

On a bright spring morning in the Fairfax area of Los Angeles, a lone gunman invaded a Jewish day-care center, taking an adult female teacher and three toddlers hostage. When Talley arrived, he found the gunman confused, incoherent, and rapidly dissociating. Fearing that the subject had suffered a psychotic break and the children were in imminent danger, Talley offered himself in trade for the children; this was against direct orders from his crisis team captain and in violation of LAPD policy. Talley approached the day-care center unarmed and unprotected, surrendering himself to the gunman, who simultaneously released the children. As the gunman stood in the door with one arm hooked around Talley's neck and a 9mm Smith & Wesson pistol pressed to Talley's head, Talley's best friend during those days, Neal Craimont, dropped the subject with a sixty-yard cortical brain shot, the 5.56mm hypervelocity bullet passing only four inches to the left of Talley's own brain stem. The newspapers had made Talley out to be a hero, but Talley had considered the events of that morning a failure. He had been the primary negotiator, and for a negotiator, it is always a failure when someone dies. Success only comes with life.

Maddox seemed to sense Talley's discomfort. He dropped the subject.

When they reached the rear of the command van, a woman wearing a green tactical uniform stepped from among a knot of sergeants to meet them. She had a cut jaw, smart black eyes, and short blond hair.

'Is this Chief Talley?'

Maddox nodded.

'This is him.'

She put out her hand. Now closer, Talley saw the captain's insignia on her collar. She had a tough grip.

'Laura Martin. Captain. I'm the field commander in charge of the crisis response team.'

Where Maddox and Ellison were relaxed and loose, Martin was as taut as a power cable, her manner clipped and humorless.

'I'm glad you've met our negotiators. Sergeant Maddox will take over as the primary.'

'We were just discussing that, Captain. I think we're in pretty good shape with that. The subjects seem calm.'

Martin keyed the radio transceiver strapped to her harness and called for a communications check of her supervisors in five minutes, then looked back at Talley.

'Do you have a perimeter in place around the house?'

'Yes, ma'am.'

'How many men?'

'Eleven. A mix of my people and the Highway Patrol. I put the men in close, then pulled them back to get things going with Rooney, so you'll have to be careful with that.'

As Talley spoke, Martin didn't seem to be paying attention. She glanced both ways along the street, leading Talley to think that she was measuring the scene and more than likely sizing up his officers. He found himself irritated. The command van was being repositioned farther down the block over an access point to the underground power and phone lines that ran under the streets. If they wanted to tap into the phone lines that ran to the house, they could do it from there. They could also tap power for the van. Talley had already called PacBell and the Department of Water and Power to the scene.

'I'll get my supervisors together so you can brief everyone at once. I want to rotate my tactical people into the perimeter as soon as we've stabilized the situation.'

Talley felt another flash of irritation; it was clear that the scene was stable. He suggested that Martin assemble her supervisors in Mrs. Peña's home, but Martin thought that would take too much time. As she called her people together under a streetlight, Talley radioed Metzger for copies of the floor plan. He passed them out as everyone assembled, and gave a fast overview of his conversations with Rooney, describing what he knew of the house and the people within it.

Martin stood next to him, arms crossed tightly, squinting at him with what Talley began to feel was a critical suspicion.

'Have you cut the power and phones?'

'We blocked the phones. I didn't see any reason to cut the power until we knew for sure what we were dealing with.'

Martin told her intelligence officer, a sergeant named Rojas, to have someone from the utility companies standing by if they needed to pull the plug.

Metzger pointed up the street.

'They're already standing by. See that guy in the Duke cap? That's him.'

The tactical team supervisor, a veteran sergeant named Carl Hicks, studied the floor plan sketches, and seemed irritated when Talley couldn't produce actual city floor plans.

'Do we know where they're keeping the hostages?'

'No.'

'How about the location of the subjects?'

'The room immediately to our right of the front door is the father's office. Rooney is usually in there when he talks to me, but I can't say if he sticks. I know he moves through the house to keep an eye on the perimeter, but he's buttoned up pretty well. The shades are down over every window except the French doors overlooking the pool in back. They don't have drapes back there, but he's got the lights off.'

Hicks frowned at Martin.

'Sucks for us, but what can you do? We might be able to get heat images.'

If they had to breach the house, it was safer for everyone if the breaching team knew the location of everyone in the environment.

Maddox tipped his chin toward Talley.

'The Chief here worked Rooney into admitting that all three perps are inside. I might be able to work him for the locations.'

Martin didn't look impressed with that.

'Hicks, float two men around the perimeter to find out exactly what we're dealing with here. Let's make sure this place is secure.'

Talley said, 'Captain, be advised that he's hinky about the perimeter. I pulled back the line to start the negotiation. That was part of the deal.'

Martin stepped away to stare up the street. Talley couldn't tell what she might be looking at.

'I understand that, Chief. Thank you. Now, will you be ready to hand off the phone to Maddox and Ellison as soon as we're in place?'

'I'm ready right now.'

She clicked her tongue curtly, then glanced at Maddox.

'Sounds good, Maddox. The three of you should get into position at the front of the house.'

Maddox's face was tight. Talley thought he was probably irritated with her manner, also.

'I'd like to spend some time going over the Chief's prior conversations with these guys.'

Martin checked her watch, impatient.

'You can do that while we rotate into the perimeter; I want to get the show on the road. Chief Talley, I have seven minutes after the hour. Do I now have command of the scene?'

'Yes, ma'am. It's yours.'

Martin checked her watch again. Just to be sure.

'Then log it. I now have command and control. Sergeant Maddox, get into position. Sergeant Hicks, you're with me.'

Martin and Hicks trotted away into the milling SWAT officers.

Maddox stared after her for a moment, then looked at Talley.

'She's wound kinda tight.'

Talley nodded, but said nothing. He had thought that he would feel relieved when he turned over command of the scene.

He didn't.

Thomas

Alone in his dark room, Thomas held his breath, better to hear past the changing whup-whup-whup of the helicopters. He feared that Mars might pretend to leave, then creep back to see if he was trying to get untied. Thomas knew every squeak in the upstairs hall because Jennifer liked to spy on him; one squeaky spot was right outside his door, the other about halfway to Jennifer's room. So he listened.

Nothing.

Thomas was spread-eagle on his lower bunk, face up, his wrists and ankles tied so tightly to the corner bedposts that his feet felt numb. After Mars had finished tying him, he stood by the bed, towering over him like some kind of retard with his slack jaw hanging open like one of those public-bathroom perverts his mother always warned him about every time he went to the mall. Then Mars had taped over his mouth. Thomas was SCARED; sweat gushed from him like he was a lawn sprinkler and he thought he was going to suffocate. He struggled and pulled at the wires that held him, straining to get free until he felt Mars's breath on his cheek. Then he couldn't move at all, like his mind and body had disconnected and all he could do was just lie there like a turtle waiting for a car to squash it flat.

Mars placed a hand on his chest, and now the breath went to his ear. Warm and moist. Then, a whisper.

'I will eat your heart.'

Thomas's body burned from the inside out, a kind of wet heat that grew hotter and hotter. He messed his pants.

Mars went to the door, shut the lights, and left, pulling the door closed. Thomas waited, counting slowly to one hundred. Then he set about working his way free.

Thomas was good at working his way free. He was also good at sneaking out of his house, which he had done almost every night this summer. He would sneak out after his parents had gone to bed to hook up with Duane Fergus, who lived in a big pink house on King John Place. Sometimes they threw eggs and wads of wet toilet paper at the cars passing on Flanders Road. When that got old, they would sneak across Flanders to a development that was still under construction where teenagers parked to make out. Duane Fergus (who was a year older and claimed to shave) once threw a rock at a brand-new Beemer because (he said) the lucky turd behind the wheel was getting 'road head.' They both shit a brick when the car roared to life, bathing them in its lights. They ran so hard back across

Flanders that a monster 18-wheeler had almost turned them into blacktop pie.

Thomas had perfected the art of moving through his home without being seen because he had changed some of the camera angles. Just a bit, just a nudge, so that his mom and dad couldn't see *everything*. He knew that most people didn't live in houses where every room was watched by a closed-circuit television system. His father explained that they had such a system because he handled other people's financial records and someone might want to steal them. It was a big responsibility, his father had said, and so they had to protect those records as best they could. His father often warned both Thomas and Jennifer to be careful of suspicious characters, and to never discuss the alarms and cameras with their friends. His mother was fond of saying that she thought the whole mess was nonsense and just their father's big toy. Duane thought they were da bomb.

The wire holding his left wrist was slack.

When Mars was tying Thomas's right wrist to the post, Thomas had scrunched away just enough so that now the cord held a little bit of play. Now he worked harder at it, pulling the knots tighter but creating enough slack to touch the knot that held him to the post. The knot was *tight*. Thomas dug at it so hard that the pain in his fingertips brought tears, but then the knot loosened. He worked frantically, terrified that Mars or one of the others would throw open the door, but then the knot gave and his left hand was free. The tape hurt coming off his mouth worse than getting a cavity filled. He untied his right hand, then his feet, and then he was free. Like Duane said, you had to risk being street pizza if you wanted to see a guy getting road head.

Thomas stayed on the bed, listening.

Nothing.

I know where Daddy has a gun.

Thomas felt calm and certain in what he needed to do. He knew exactly what the cameras could see and what they couldn't. He wanted to go to his bathroom to clean himself, but knew he would be visible on the monitor if he did. He pulled off his pants, used his underwear to clean off the poo as best he could, then balled the underwear and pushed them under the bed. He slipped to the floor and crawled along the wall toward his closet, passing under his desk. Someone had ripped his phone out of the wall, leaving the plug in the socket but tearing free the wires. Turds.

In *The Lion, the Witch, and the Wardrobe*, the children found a secret door at the rear of their wardrobe that let them escape the real world into the magical land of Narnia. Thomas had his own secret door at the back of his closet: an access hatch to the attic crawl space that ran beneath the steep pitch of the roof. It was his own private clubhouse (his and Duane's), through which he could move along the eaves to the other access hatches dotted around the house.

Thomas pulled open the hatch and wiggled into the crawl space, being careful not to bump the rafters with his head. The heat in the closed space of the attic enveloped him like a gas. He found the flashlight that he kept just inside the hatch, turned it on, then pulled the hatch closed. The crawl space in this part of the house was a long triangular tunnel that followed the back edge of the roof. Where windows were cut into the roof, the triangle became a low rectangle, forcing Thomas to crawl on his belly. He worked his way along until he came to a second access hatch, this one in Jennifer's closet. He listened until he grew satisfied that the turds weren't in her room, then he pushed it open, knocking over a tumble of shoes.

The closet was dark, its door closed.

He eased his way out over the shoes and through a rack of her dresses, then turned off his flashlight. He listened at the closet door, and again heard nothing. He eased open the door. The lights in Jennifer's room were off; that was good because he knew that most of her room could be seen on the monitors. He opened the door so slowly that it seemed to take forever to get it open enough for him to stick out his head. The room was lit by pale blue moonlight. He could see Jennifer bound to the chair near the front of the room, her back to him.

'Jen?'

She lurched in the chair and mumbled. He called to her, his voice low.

'I'm in your closet. Just relax, okay? If they're watching, they can see you on the monitors.'

She stopped struggling.

Thomas tried to remember what the camera saw of Jennifer's room. He and Duane sometimes went into the security room when his parents were away so that Duane could see her naked. He was pretty confident that if he crept out of the closet on his belly, then hugged the wall beneath the windows where the shadows were darkest, he could get pretty close to the chair. If he heard Mars or those other turds coming, he could haul ass back into the crawl space, then go back to his room or run for the garage.

'Jen, listen up, okay? I'm going to come over there.'

She shook her head wildly, mumbling frantically into the tape.

'Be *QUIET!* I can untie you.'

He pushed open the closet a few inches wider, then edged forward on his elbows into the shadows. As he passed her desk, he saw that her phone had also been torn from the plug. Turds.

Thomas worked his way around the perimeter of the room, and soon he was stretched out beside her bed, using deep shadows as cover. He was about four feet from her now, and could see that her mouth was taped. He looked up at the corner of the ceiling where the camera was located. These cameras didn't hang down visible to anyone in the room; they were what his father called 'pinhole cameras,' set in the crawl space behind the wall where they peeked out through tiny holes. He slithered out to the chair and worked his way behind her. He figured that the camera could probably see her from the waist up, but not very well in the darkness. He decided to take a chance. He snaked his hand up behind her, then quickly yanked the tape from her mouth before ducking down to the floor again.

'Shit! Ow!'

'Be quiet! *Listen!*'

'They're going to catch you!'

'Shhhh! *Listen!*'

Thomas strained his ears again, concentrating past the helicopters and the sounds of the police outside.

Nothing.

'It's okay, Jen. They didn't see, and they can't see me now. Don't look around. Just listen.'

'How did you get in here?'

'I used the crawl space. Now *listen* and *hold still.* I'm going to untie you. They nailed the windows shut, but I think we can use the crawl space to get downstairs. If we sneak to the garage, we can open the garage door and run for it.'

'No!'

Thomas worked frantically at the knots binding her. The cords weren't that tight around her wrists and ankles, but the knots had been pulled *hard.*

'Thomas, *stop!* I mean it! Don't untie me.'

'Are you on dope? We might be able to get away!'

'But Daddy will still be in here! I'm not going to leave him.'

Thomas settled back on his heels, confused.

'But, Jen –'

'*No!* Thomas, if you can get out, then go, but I'm not leaving without my father.'

Thomas was so angry he wanted to punch. Here they were, locked in the dark with three psychokillers who probably drank human blood, one maniac who wanted to eat their hearts *for sure,* and she wouldn't leave. But then, as Thomas thought about it, he knew she was right. He couldn't leave their father, either.

'What are we gonna do, Jen?'

She didn't answer for a time.

'Call the police.'

'The house is surrounded by police.'

'Call them anyway! Maybe they have an idea. Maybe if we tell them exactly what's going on in here it will help them.'

Thomas glanced toward her desk, recalling the wires ripped from the plug.

'They broke the phones.'

Jennifer fell silent again.

'Then I don't know. Thomas, you should get out.'

'No!'

'I mean it. If you can get to the police, maybe you can help them. You know all about the alarms and the cameras. You know that Daddy is hurt. That asshole, Dennis, lied to them about Daddy. He's telling them we're all fine.'

'Let me untie you. We can hide in the walls.'

'No! They might hurt Daddy! Listen, if they find out that you're not in your room, I'm going to tell them that you got out. They won't know you're still in the walls. They'll never even think of that! But if both of us are gone, they'll take it out on Daddy. They might hurt him!'

Thomas thought about it.

'Okay, Jen.'

'Okay, *what*?'

'We're not going to leave him. I'm going to get us out of here.'

Jennifer jerked so hard against the cords that she almost tipped over the chair.

'You leave that gun alone! They'll kill you!'

'Not if I have the gun! We can hold them off long enough to let in the police, that's all we have to do.'

She twisted hard in the chair, trying to see him.

'Thomas, don't you dare! They're adults! They're criminals and they've got guns, too!'

'Don't talk so loud or they'll hear you!'

'I don't care! It's better than you getting killed!'

Thomas reached up, pulled the tape back over her mouth, and rubbed it hard so that it would stick. Jennifer squirmed, trying to shout through the tape. Thomas hated the thought of leaving her tied, but she just didn't see that he had no other choice.

'I'm sorry, Jen. I'll untie you when I get back. Then we can get Daddy out of here. You'll see. I won't let them hurt us.'

Jennifer was still struggling as Thomas worked his way back through the shadows. When he reached the closet he could still hear her trying to shout through the tape. She was shouting the same thing over and over. He could understand her, even though her words were muffled.

They're going to kill you.

They're going to kill you.

Thomas slipped back into the crawl space, working his way carefully through the dark.

Dennis

The little bathroom off the garage was as dark as a cave when Dennis showed them the window, telling Mars and Kevin that they could work their way into the neighbor's yard and then around the side of that house to slip past the cops. Mars seemed thoughtful, but Dennis couldn't be sure with all the dark shadows.

'This could work.'

'Fuckin' A, it could work.'

'But you never know what the police are doing or where they might be. We have to give them something to think about besides us.'

'They'll be watching this house. They got nothing else to do.'

Kevin said, 'I don't like any of it. We should give up.'

'Shut up.'

Mars went into the garage and stood by the Range Rover. Dennis was scared that Mars would suggest killing the kid again.

'C'mon, Mars, we've got to get goin' here. We don't have all the time in the world.'

Mars turned back to him, his face lit by the dim light from the kitchen.

'If you want to get away, we should burn the house.'

Dennis started to say no, but then he stopped. He had been thinking of putting the kids in the Jaguar and opening the garage door with the remote as a diversion, but a fire made better sense. The cops would shit their pants if the house started to burn.

'That's not a bad idea. We could start a fire on the other side of the house.'

Kevin raised his hands.

'You guys are crazy. That adds arson to the charges against us.'

'It makes sense, Kevin. All the cops will be watching the fire. They won't be looking at the neighbor's yard.'

'But what about these people?'

Kevin was talking about the Smiths.

Dennis was about to answer when Mars did it again. His voice was quiet and empty.

'They'll burn.'

The back of Dennis's neck tingled as if Mars had raked a nail across a blackboard.

'Jesus, Mars, nobody has to burn. We can put'm here in the garage before we take off. We'll figure somethin' out.'

They decided to use gasoline to start the fire. Dennis found a two-gallon plastic gas can that the family probably kept for emergencies, but it was almost empty. Mars used the plastic air hose from the family's aquarium to siphon gas from the Jaguar. He filled the two-gallon can, then a large plastic bucket that was stained by detergent. They were carrying the gasoline into the house when they heard the helicopters again change pitch and more cars pull into the cul-de-sac.

Dennis stopped with the bucket, listening, when suddenly the front of the house was bathed in light, framing the huge garage door and spilling into the bathroom window even through the oleanders.

'What the fuck?! What's going on?'

They hurried to the front of the house, gasoline splashing from the bucket.

'Kevin! Watch the French doors!'

Dennis and Mars left the gasoline in the entry, then ran into the office where Walter Smith still twitched on the couch. Spears of light cut through the shutters, painting them with zebra stripes. Dennis opened the shutters and saw that two more police cars filled the street. All four cars had trained their spotlights on the house and a great pool of light from the helicopters burned brilliantly on the front yard. More cars arrived.

'Holy shit.'

The television showed the L.A. County Sheriffs rolling through the dark streets of York Estates. Dennis watched a group of SWAT assholes trot through an oval of helicopter light as they deployed through the neighborhood. Snipers; stone-cold killers dressed in ninja suits with rifles equipped with night-vision scopes, laser sites, and – for all he knew – motherfucking death rays. Mars had been right; these bastards would drop them cold if they tried to drive away with the kids.

'This is *fucked*. Look at all those cops.'

Dennis peeked out the shutters again, but so many floodlights had been set up in the street that the glare was blinding; a thousand cops could be standing sixty feet away, and he wouldn't know.

'*Fuck!*'

Everything had once more changed. One minute he had a great plan to slip away, but now all sides of the house were lit up like the sun and an army of cops were filling the streets. Overhead, the helicopters sounded as if they were about to land on the house. Sneaking through the adjoining neighbor's yard would now be impossible. Dennis turned back to the television. Six patrol cars filled the cul-de-sac, washed in brilliant white light from the helicopter, as many as a dozen cops moving behind them.

Dennis went to Walter Smith, and inspected his wound. The bruising had followed his eye socket under the eye to his right cheek, and moved across most of his forehead above the eye. The eye had swollen closed. Dennis wished now that he hadn't hit the sonofabitch. He turned away and went to the door.

'I'm going to check the windows again, okay? I gotta make sure Kevin isn't falling asleep. Mars, you keep an eye on the TV. If anything happens, yell.'

Mars, leaning against the wall with his face to the shutters, didn't respond. Dennis wasn't sure if Mars heard him or not, but he didn't care. He trotted back to the family room to find Kevin.

'What's going on? Aren't we leaving?'

'The goddamned Sheriffs are here. They're crawling all over the goddamned neighborhood. They got *snipers* out there!'

Dennis was consumed with the sudden notion that he would be assassinated. These cops would want to pay back the bastard who had wounded one of their own, and that was him. If he passed a window or showed himself in the goddamned French doors, those sniper bastards would bust a cap and put one right through his head.

Kevin, of course, made it worse by putting on the pussy face.

'What are we going to do?'

'I don't know, Kevin! They got so many lights out there I can't see a goddamned thing. Maybe I can see better on those televisions back there in the safety room.'

Kevin suddenly turned toward the rear of the house.

'Did you hear that?'

Dennis listened, scared shitless that SWAT killers were even now slipping into the house like a tapeworm up a cat's ass.

'Hear what?'

'I thought I heard a bump from back there.'

Dennis held his breath to listen more closely, but there was nothing.

'Asshole. Just let me know if Mars is coming. I might be with the money.'

Dennis left Kevin at the mouth of the hall, then trotted back to the master bedroom, and into the safety room.

He hadn't checked the monitors since the sky was rimmed with red. Now he saw Mars standing by the shutters; the front entry with bullet holes in the door; and the girl tied to a chair in her upstairs room. He couldn't see the boy, but didn't think twice about it; Dennis searched the monitors for angles outside the house, but those views were shadowed and unreadable.

'Shit!'

He spun away from the monitors, frustrated and pissed. He jerked an armful of hangered jackets from the clothes rack and threw them at the far wall. If there was any way to get fucked, he could find it!

Dennis turned back to the monitors. He considered the buttons and switches beneath the monitors. Nothing was labeled, but he didn't have anything to lose. If it was up, he pushed it down; if it was out, he pushed it in. Suddenly a monitor that had shown nothing but shadows on the dark side of the house filled with a lighted view. He pushed a second button, and the pool area filled with light. A third, and the side of the house by the garage was lit. He saw the cops at the front of the house pointing at the lights that suddenly blazed at them.

Dennis pushed more buttons, and the wall at the rear of the property beyond the pool was bathed in light. Two SWAT cops with rifles were climbing over the wall.

'SHIT!!!'

Dennis sprinted back through the house, shouting.

'THEY'RE COMING!!! KEV, MARS!!! THEY'RE COMING!'

Dennis raced to the French doors in the dark beyond the kitchen. He couldn't see the cops past the blinding outside lights, but he knew they were there, and he knew they were coming.

Dennis fired two shots into the darkness, not even thinking about it, just pulling the trigger, *bam bam*. Two glass panes in the French doors shattered.

'The fuckin' cops are comin'! Talley, that fuck! That lying fuck!'

Dennis thought his world was about to explode: They would fire tear gas, then crash through the doors. They were probably rushing the house right now with battering rams.

'Mars! Kev, we gotta get those kids!'

Dennis ran for the stairs, Kevin shouting behind him.

'What're we gonna do with the kids?'

Dennis didn't answer. He hit the stairs three at a time, going up.

Thomas

Three minutes before Dennis Rooney saw the SWAT officers and fired two rounds, Thomas lowered himself through the ceiling into the laundry room. It was so dark that he cupped his hand over the flashlight and risked turning on the light, using the dim red glow through his fingers to pick his footing. He let himself down onto the top of the hot-water heater, felt with his toe to find the washing machine, then slid to the floor.

He held still, listening to Kevin and Dennis. The laundry room turned a corner where it opened onto the kitchen; the pantry was off that little hall. He could hear them talking, though he couldn't understand what they were saying, and then the voices stopped.

Thomas crept through the laundry room to his father's tiny hobby room at the end opposite the kitchen. Both rooms were at the rear of the garage, though you could only get to the garage through the laundry. That's how everyone came into the house from their cars: through the laundry room and into the kitchen.

When Thomas reached the hobby room, he eased the door closed, then once more turned on his flashlight. His father's hobby was building plastic models of rocket ships from the early days of the space program. He bought the kits off eBay, built and painted them at a little workbench, then put them on shelves above the bench. His father also had a Sig Sauer 9mm pistol in a metal box on the top shelf. He had heard his mom and dad fighting about it: His dad used to keep it under the front seat of the Jaguar, but his mom raised such a stink that his father had taken it out of the car and put it in the box.

On the top shelf.

A long way up.

His hand cupped over the bell of the flashlight, Thomas spread his fingers enough to let out a shaft of light. He figured that he could use the stool to climb onto the bench, and, from there, he could probably reach the box.

He climbed. It was so quiet that every creak from the bench sounded like an earthquake. He turned on the flashlight again for a moment to fix the box in his mind's eye, then reached for it, but the box was too high. He stretched up onto his toes. His fingers grazed the box just enough for him to work it toward the edge of the shelf.

That's when he heard Dennis.

'THEY'RE COMING!!! KEV, MARS!!! THEY'RE COMING!'

Thomas didn't waste a moment thinking about the gun; he had come so close, but now he didn't have time. His only thought was to get back to his room before they discovered him. He jumped down from the bench and ran to the laundry as two fast gunshots exploded in the house, so loud that they made his ears ring.

He wasn't thinking about Jennifer's purse. It was on the folding table by the door to the garage, that convenient place where everyone in the family dropped their stuff when they came in from the garage. Jennifer's purse was there, a Kate Spade like every other girl in her high school owned. Thomas grabbed it.

He scrambled up onto the washing machine, from there to the top of the hot-water heater, then through the access hatch into the crawl space. The last thing that he heard before closing the hatch was Dennis shouting that they had to get the kids.

Talley

Handing off the role of primary negotiator was never easy. Talley had already forged a bond with Rooney, and now would pull away, replacing himself with Maddox. Rooney might resist, but the subject was never given a choice. Having a choice was having power, and the subject was never given power.

Talley brought Maddox and Ellison into the cul-de-sac where they hunkered behind their car. Talley wanted to go over his earlier conversations with Rooney in greater detail so that Maddox would have something with which to work, but they didn't have time. The gunshots from the house cracked through the summer air like a car backfiring in a distant canyon: *poppop*.

Almost instantly, a storm of transmissions crackled over their radios:

'Shots fired! Shots fired! We are under fire from the house, west rear at the wall! Advise on response!'

All three of them knew what had happened the instant they heard the calls.

'Damnit, she moved in too close! Rooney thinks he's being breached!'

Ellison said, 'We're fucked.'

Talley felt sick; this is the way it went bad, this is how people got dead, just this fast.

Maddox clawed for his radio as other voices checked off positions and status. The tinny voice of Carl Hicks, the tactical supervisor, came back, calm over the strained voices of his men.

'Will advise, stand by while we assess.'

Talley didn't wait; he dialed the tactical team's frequency into his own transceiver.

'Pull back, pull back, pull back! Do NOT return fire!'

Martin's voice cut over his, short and clipped.

'Who is this?'

'Talley. I told you to respect that perimeter!'

'Talley, get off the freq.'

Maddox finally had his radio, cursing as he keyed the mike.

'One, Maddox. *Listen* to him, Captain. Do not breach that house. Pull back or we're going to have a mess!'

'Clear the frequency! Those people are in danger.'

'Do not breach that house! I can talk to him!'

Talley had his cell phone out. He punched redial to call the house, praying that Rooney would answer, then ran to Jorgenson's car, still there in the street, and turned on the public address system.

Thomas

Thomas scrambled across the joists like a spider. He slammed his head into the low-hanging rafters so hard that his teeth snapped together, but he didn't stop or even think about the noise he was making. He scurried through the long straight tunnel of the crawl space past Jennifer's room, under her window, past her bathroom, past his, and then to the access hatch in his closet. He didn't pause to see if they were in his room, but scrambled through the hatch and ran to his bed. He wanted to retie himself; to pretend that he hadn't moved. He pulled the ropes back over his ankles, working frantically, his hands slick with sweat, as shouts and footsteps pounded toward him through the hall.

He looped the ropes and slipped his hands through, realized in a flash of fear that he had forgotten the tape that had covered his mouth, but then it was too late.

Dennis

Dennis threw open the door. He saw that the boy had damn near untied himself, but he didn't care.

'C'mon, fat boy!'

'Get away from me!'

Dennis jammed his pistol into his waist, then pinned the fat boy with a knee to untie him. Outside, Talley's voice echoed over his P.A., but Dennis couldn't make out the words. He pulled the fat boy from his bed, hooked an arm around his neck, and dragged him back toward the stairs. If the cops crashed through the front door, he would hold his gun to the kid's head and threaten to kill him. He would hide behind the kid and make the cops back down. He had a chance. He had hope.

'Hurry up, Kevin! Jesus! Bring the girl!'

Dennis dragged the fat boy down the stairs and into the office where Mars was waiting by the window. Mars looked totally calm, as if he was killing time in a bar before going to work. He tipped his head when he saw Dennis, that stupid tiny smile on his calm face.

'They're not doing anything. They're just sitting there.'

Dennis dragged the kid to the shutters. Mars opened the shutters enough for Dennis to see. The cops weren't storming the house. They were hunkered behind their cars.

Dennis realized that the phone was ringing just as Talley's voice came over the P.A. again.

'Answer the phone, Dennis. It's me, Talley. Answer the phone so I can tell you what happened.'

Dennis scooped up the phone.

Talley

Martin and Hicks ran into the cul-de-sac without waiting for a cover vehicle, Martin hitting the ground beside Talley so hard that she almost bowled him over, shouting, 'What in hell do you think you're doing, interfering with my deployment?'

'He's shooting at your people because he thinks they're assaulting the house, Martin. You're violating my agreement with him.'

'This scene now belongs to me. You handed off control.'

'Pull back your people, Martin. Just relax. Nothing is going on in there.'

Talley keyed the P.A. mike again.

'Dennis, take it easy in there. Please. Just pick up the phone.'

'Hicks!'

Hicks leaned into the car past Talley and jerked the mike plug from its jack.

Talley's head was throbbing. He felt caught in a vise.

'Let me talk to him, Captain. Order your people to stand down, and let me talk to him. If it's too far gone you can breach, but right now let me try. Tell her, Maddox.'

Martin glared at Maddox, who nodded at her. He looked embarrassed.

'He's right, Captain. Let's not get too aggressive here. If Talley made a deal, we have to honor it or this guy isn't going to trust me any further than a cat can shit a walnut.'

Martin glared at him so hard that she seemed to be trying to cook him with her eyes. She glanced at Hicks, then bit out the words.

'Pull back.'

Hicks, looking uncomfortable, plugged the P.A. mike back into its jack, then mumbled orders into his tactical mike.

Talley turned back to the house.

'Pick up the phone, Dennis. We made a screwup out here, but we are not coming into that house. Check it out. The perimeter is pulling back. Check it out and talk to me.'

Talley held the cell phone to his ear, counting the rings. It rang fourteen times, fifteen . . .

Finally, Rooney answered, screaming.

'You fuck! You fuckin' lied to me! I've got a fuckin' gun to this kid's head right here! We've got these people! We'll fuckin' kill'm, you fuck!'

Talley spoke over him, his voice loud and forceful so that Rooney would hear him, but not strident. It was important to appear in control even when you weren't.

'They're pulling back. They are pulling back, Dennis. Look. You see the officers pulling back?'

The sounds of movement came over the phone. Talley guessed that Rooney had a cordless and was watching the tactical team at the rear of the property.

'Yeah. I guess. They're going back over the wall.'

'I didn't lie to you, Dennis. It's over now, okay? Don't hurt anyone.'

'We'll burn this fuckin' place down, you try to come in here. We've got gasoline all good to go, Talley. You try to come in and this place is going to burn.'

Talley locked eyes with Maddox. Rooney booby-trapping the house with gasoline was a bad turn; if he was creating a situation dangerous to the hostages, it could justify a preemptive breach of the house.

'Don't do anything to endanger yourself or those children, Dennis. For your own sake and for the sake of the innocents in there. This kind of thing can create problems.'

'Then stay on the other side of that wall. You assholes try to come get us and this place is gonna burn.'

Talley muted the phone while Dennis answered to warn Maddox about the gasoline. Maddox relayed the information to the tactical team. If Rooney was telling the truth about the gasoline, firing tear gas or flash-bang grenades into the house could ignite an inferno.

'No one is coming in. We screwed up, is all. Some new guys came out and we got our wires crossed, but I didn't lie to you. I wouldn't do that.'

'You fuckin' well *did* screw up, dude! Jesus!'

The tension lessened in Rooney's voice, and, with it, Talley felt the vise ease its grip. If Rooney was talking, he wouldn't shoot.

'What's the status in there, Dennis? You didn't hurt anyone, did you?'

'Not yet.'

'Those shots you fired, they were out of the house?'

'I'm not saying I fired anything. You're saying that, not me. I know you're recording this.'

'No one needs a doctor?'

'*You're* gonna need a doctor, you try this shit again.'

Talley took a deep breath. It was done; they were past the crisis. Talley glanced at Martin. She looked irritated, but attentive.

Talley muted the receiver again.

'He's calming down. I think now would be a good time for the handoff.'

Martin glanced at Maddox.

'You ready?'

'I'm ready.'

Martin nodded at Talley.

'Go.'

Talley uncovered his phone.

'Dennis, have you been thinking about what we talked about earlier?'

'I got a lot on my mind.'

'I'm sure. It was good advice, what I said.'

'Whatever.'

Talley lowered his voice, trying to sound like what he was about to say was just between them, guy to guy.

'Can I tell you something of a personal nature?'

'What?'

'I gotta piss real bad.'

Rooney laughed. Just like that, and Talley knew that the handoff would work. He made his voice relaxed, putting a friendly spin on it, indicating that everything that was about to happen was the most natural thing in the world and beyond all objection. Rooney was just as relieved to be past this hump as Talley.

'Dennis, I'm going to take a break out here. You see all the new people we have?'

'You got a thousand guys out there. Of course, I see'm.'

'I'm going to put an officer named Will Maddox on the line. You scared me so bad that I've gotta go clean my shorts, you know? So Maddox will be here on the line if you want to talk or if you need anything.'

'You're a funny guy, Talley.'

'Here he is, Dennis. You stay cool in there.'

'I'm cool.'

Talley handed the phone to Maddox, who introduced himself with a warm, mellow voice.

'Hey, Dennis. You should've seen ol' Jeff out here. I think he crapped his pants.'

Talley didn't listen to any more. The rest of it would be up to Maddox.

He slumped down onto the street and leaned against the car, feeling drained.

He glanced at Martin, and found her watching him. She duck-walked over, and hunkered on the pavement beside him, then searched his eyes for a moment as if she were trying to find the right words. Her face softened.

'You were right. I got in a hurry and screwed up.'

Talley admired her for saying it.

'We survived.'

'So far.'

Thomas

After the screaming, after those frantic moments when Thomas thought that Dennis would shoot him in the head as he was threatening, Jennifer glared at him and said one word.

'Don't.'

No one heard but Thomas; Dennis was pacing and talking to himself, Kevin following Dennis with his eyes the way a nervous dog will watch its master. They were in the office, the TV on, just now reporting that shots had been fired in the house. Dennis stopped to watch, suddenly laughing.

'Jesus, but that was close. Jesus Christ.'

Kevin crossed his arms, rocking nervously.

'What are we going to do? We can't get away now. They're all around the house. They're even in the neighbor's yard.'

Dennis's face darkened, and he snapped.

'I don't know, Kevin. I don't know. We'll figure out something.'

'We should give up.'

'Shut up!'

Thomas rubbed his neck, thinking he might yak. Dennis had carried him down to the office by the neck, an arm hooked around his throat in a headlock, squeezing so hard that Thomas couldn't breathe. Jennifer came over and knelt by him, making as if to help him, but pinching his arm, instead, her whisper angry and frightened.

'You see? You see? You almost got caught!'

She went to their father.

Mars returned from elsewhere in the house, his arms filled with big white candles. Without saying a word, he lit one, dripped wax on the television, seated the base in the wax. He moved to the bookcase, did it again. Dennis and Kevin were coming apart, but Thomas thought that Mars looked content.

Dennis finally noticed.

'What the fuck are you doing?'

Mars answered as he lit another candle.

'They might cut the power. Here, take this.'

He stopped with the candles long enough to toss a flashlight to Dennis. It was the one from the kitchen utility drawer. He tossed a second to Kevin, who dropped it.

Dennis turned on the light, then turned it off.

'Those candles are a good idea.'

Soon, the office looked like an altar.

Thomas watched Dennis. Dennis seemed inside himself, following Mars with a kind of watchful wariness, as if Mars held something over him that he was trying to figure out. Thomas hated them all, thinking that if he only had the gun he could kill them, Mars with the candles, Dennis with his eyes on Mars, Kevin staring at Dennis, none of them looking at him, pull out the gun and shoot every one of them, bangbangbang.

Dennis suddenly said, 'We should stack pots and pans under the windows in case they try to sneak in, things that will fall, so we'll hear.'

Mars grunted.

'Mars, when you're back there, do that, okay? Set up some booby traps.'

Jennifer said, 'What about my father?'

'Jesus, not that again. Christ.'

Her voice rose.

'He needs a doctor, you asshole!'

'Kevin, take'm back upstairs. *Please.*'

Thomas didn't care. That was what he wanted.

'Do you want me to tie them again?'

Dennis started to answer, then squinched his face, thinking.

'It took too long to cut all that shit off, you and Mars tying them like a couple of fuckin' mummies. Just make sure they're locked in real good, not just with the nails.'

Mars finished with the candles.

'I can take care of that. Bring them up.'

Kevin brought them, holding Jennifer's arm, almost having to drag her, but Thomas walking in front, anxious to get back to his room though he tried to hide it. They waited at the top of the stairs until Mars rejoined them, now with a hammer and screwdriver. He trudged up the steps, thump thump thump, with the slow inevitability of a rising freight elevator, dark and dirty. Mars led them to Thomas's room first, the end of the hall. It was spooky without light.

'Get in there, fat boy. Pull your covers over your head.'

Mars pushed him inside hard, then knelt by the knob, the one Thomas would use to get out. He hammered the screwdriver under the base, popped it off, unfastened three screws, then pulled the knob free, leaving only a square hole. He looked at Jennifer then, no one else, Jennifer.

'You see? That's how you keep a child in its room.'

They left Thomas like that, pulling the door, then hammering the door closed. Thomas listened until he heard the crash of Jennifer's knob coming free and her door being nailed, and then he scrambled for his closet. He was thinking only of the gun, but as soon as he turned on his flashlight he saw Jennifer's purse. He had dropped it just inside the hatch when he scrambled back into the room. He clawed it open and upended it.

Out fell her cell phone.

10
Palm Springs, California
Friday, 8:32 p.m.

Sonny Benza

The three of them had Glen Howell on the speaker, Benza, Tuzee, and Salvetti, the TVs muted so they could hear. Benza, on his third pack of Gaviscom, nursed an upset stomach, his acid reflux acting up.

Howell, his voice crackling with the shitty cell connection, sitting in his car somewhere in the dark, said, 'He's got a wife and kid, a daughter. They're divorced or separated or something. The wife and kid live down in LA, but he sees the kid every two weeks or something.'

Tuzee, his face pasty beneath the tan, looking like a corpse from the strain, rubbed irritably at his face and interrupted.

'Stop it.'

'What?'

'Stop with the "or something." Don't end every sentence with "or something." It's pissing me off. You've got a college education.'

Benza reached out, patted Tuzee's leg, but didn't say anything.

Tuzee had his face in his hands, the flesh folded around his fingers like a man twice his age.

'He either sees them every two weeks or he doesn't; it's either a fact or it isn't. Find out the fucking facts before you call us.'

The connection popped and hissed, a background roar.

'Sorry.'

'Keep going.'

'He's seeing them this weekend. The wife is bringing up the daughter.'

Benza cleared his throat, phlegm from the Gaviscom.

'And you know this to be a fact?'

'Book it. We got that from his office, an older woman there who likes to talk, you know, how sad it is and all because the Chief's such a nice man.'

'Where are they now, the family I mean?'

'That, I don't know. I got people on that. They're due up tonight, though. That part I know for sure.'

Benza nodded.

'We've gotta think about this.'

Salvetti had already made up his mind. He leaned back, crossed his arms, his legs splayed and open.

'That shit just happened, that was too close. We've gotta move.'

'You mean the Sheriffs?'

'Yeah.'

'Yeah, that was close.'

They were silent for a time, each man lost in his own thoughts. Benza had dialed up Howell as soon as he saw the Sheriffs rolling into the neighborhood. Then, when the TV reported that shots were fired, he damn near tossed his soup, thinking this was it, SWAT was going in and they were cooked.

Howell said, 'There's more.'

'Okay.'

'They're looking into the building permits.'

'Why the fuck?'

'Something like this happens, some asshole barricades himself in a building, they want the floor plans. So now they're trying to find the people who built the house so they can get the plans.'

'Shit.'

Benza sighed and leaned back. Tuzee glanced at him, shaking his head. Benza owned the construction companies that built the house and installed the security systems. He didn't like where this was going. He stood.

'I'm going to walk, so if you can't hear me just say, okay?'

'Sure, Sonny.'

'First thing first. Our records. I'm looking at this house on the TV right now. There's a ring of cops around it like they're about to hit the beach at Normandy, but let me ask you something.'

'Okay.'

'Could we get our people in there?'

'In the house?'

'Yeah, in the house. Right now, right in front of the cops, the TV cameras, everything; get a couple guys inside the house?'

'No. I've got good people, Sonny, the best, but we can't get in right now. Not the way it stands now. We'd have to own the cops to do that. You give me a day, two days, I could probably do it.'

Benza, irritated, glowered at the televisions, two pictures, one showing the house with a bunch of SWAT cops out front, the other some blond dyke being interviewed, short hair slicked back, dressed like a man.

'Could we get close? Now. Not owning the cops, but now.'

Howell thought about it.

'Okay, look, I don't have a TV. I'm not seeing what you're seeing right now, okay? But I know Smith's house and I'm familiar with the neighborhood, so I'm going to say yeah. We could probably get close.'

Benza looked at Tuzee and Salvetti.

'How about we burn it down? Right now, tonight. Get some guys in there with some accelerant, everybody's gonna know it's arson so who gives a shit what, torch the place, burn it to the ground.'

He spread his hands, looking at them, hopeful.

Salvetti shrugged, unimpressed.

'No way to know the disks would be destroyed. Not for sure. I promise you this, if Smith has any of that stuff in his security room, it isn't gonna burn. Then we're fucked.'

Benza stared at the floor, ashamed of himself, thinking what a stupid idea, burn the place.

Tuzee leaned back now, crossing his arms, stared at the ceiling.

'Okay, look. Here it is the way I see it: If these kids were going to give up, they would've given up. Something's keeping them in that house, I don't know what, but they're sticking. The more cops pile up around that place, the more likely we are to have a breached entry.'

Salvetti sat forward, raising a hand like he was in class, interrupting.

'Wait. Call me crazy, but how about this? Why don't we just call'm? Talk to these dicks ourselves, cut a deal.'

Howell's voice hissed from the speaker.

'The lines are blocked. The cops did that.'

'Smith's regular lines, maybe, but not our lines. We pay extra for those lines.'

Tuzee was saying, 'What do you mean, cut a deal?'

'We lay it out for these assholes who they're dealing with, say they think they're in trouble with the cops, they haven't seen the kinda trouble we can bring down. We cut a deal, pay'm something like fifty K to give up, we'll provide the lawyers, all of that.'

'No fuckin' way. Uh-uh.'

'Why?'

'You want to tell three punk assholes our business? Jesus, Sally.'

Salvetti fell silent, embarrassed.

Benza caught Tuzee looking at him, resigned.

'What, Phil?'

Tuzee slumped in his chair, more tired now than ever.

'Talley's family.'

'We've got a lot to think about with that.'

'I know. I'm thinking about it. Once we go down that road, no turning back.'

'You know where that ends, don't you?'

'You're the guy just suggested we burn the fucking house down, six people inside, the whole world watching.'

'I know.'

'We can't just sit. We came damned close with what happened tonight, and now they're looking at the building permits and God knows what else.'

That's bad enough, but I'm worried about New York. I'm thinking, how long can we keep the lid on this?'

'We've got the lid on. I trust the guys we have on the scene.'

'I trust our guys, too, but old man Castellano is going to find out sooner or later. It's bound to happen.'

'It's only been a few hours.'

'However long it's been, we need to get a handle on things before they find out. By the time that old man hears, we've gotta be able to tell him that we're no longer a threat to him. We've gotta laugh about this over schnapps and cigars, else he'll hand us our asses.'

Benza felt tired in his heart, but relieved, too. Comfort came with the decision.

'Glen?'

'I'm here, Sonny.'

'If we move on Talley like this, you got a man there who can handle it?'

'Yes, Sonny.'

'He can do whatever needs to be done? All the way?'

'Yes, Sonny. Can and will. I can handle the rest.'

Benza glanced at Phil Tuzee, Tuzee nodding, then Salvetti, Salvetti ducking his head one time.

'Okay, Glen. Get it done.'

11

Eastern time
Friday, 11:40 p.m.

Pacific time, New York City
8:40 p.m.

Vic Castellano

His wife was a light sleeper, so Vittorio 'Vic' Castellano left their bedroom to take the call. He put on the thick terry-cloth bathrobe, the birthday present from his kids with *Don't Bug Me* embroidered on the back, and gimped alongside Jamie Beldone to the kitchen. Beldone held a cell phone. On the other end of it was a man they employed to keep an eye on things in California.

Vic, seventy-eight years old and two weeks away from a hip replacement, poured a small glass of orange juice, but couldn't bring himself to drink it. His stomach was already sour.

'You sure it's this bad?'

'The police have the house locked down with all Benza's records inside, including the books that link to us.'

'That sonofabitch. What's in his records?'

'They show how much he kicks to us. I don't know if it'll show business by business, but it's going to show something like that so he can keep track of where his money goes. If the Feds recover this, it will help them build an IRS case against you.'

Vic poured out the orange juice, then ran water in the glass. He sipped. Warm.

'It's been how long this is going on?'

'About five hours now.'

Castellano checked the time.

'Does Benza know that we know?'

'No, sir.'

704

'That chickenshit sonofabitch. Heaven forbid he call to warn me like a real man. He'd rather let me get caught cold than have time to fuckin' prepare.'

'He's a piece of shit, skipper. That's all there is to it.'

'What's he doing about it?'

'He sent in a team. You know Glen Howell?'

'No.'

'Benza's fixer. He's good.'

'Do we have our own guy there?'

Beldone tipped the phone, nodding.

'He's on the line now. I have to tell him what to do.'

Vic drank more of the warm water, then sighed. It was going to be a long night. He was already thinking of what he would say to his lawyers.

'Should we maybe get our own team in there?'

Beldone pursed his lips, then shook his head.

'We'd have to get the guys together, plus the five-hour plane flight; not enough time, Vic. It's Sonny's show. Sonny and Glen Howell.'

'I can't believe that chickenshit hasn't called me. What's he thinkin', back there?'

'He's thinking that if it goes south, he's going to run. He's probably more afraid of you than the Feds.'

'He should be.'

Vic sighed again, then went to the door. Forty years as the boss of the most powerful crime family on the East Coast had taught him to worry about the things he could control, and let other people worry about the things he couldn't.

He stopped in the door and turned back to Jamie Beldone.

'Sonny Benza is an incompetent asshole, and so was his fuckin' father.'

'The Mickey Mouse mob, Vic. Brain damage from all the tan.'

'If it goes south, Sonny Benza isn't goin' anywhere. You understand?'

'Yes, sir.'

'If they fuck this up, they gotta pay.'

'They'll pay for it, skipper.'

'I'm goin' to bed. You let me know if anything happens.'

'Yes, sir.'

Vic Castellano shuffled back to his bed, but could not sleep.

12
Friday, 8:43 p.m.

Talley

Talley was in Mrs. Peña's home with the Sheriffs, sipping her coffee, rich and heavy with brown sugar and cream though none of them had asked for it that way; she told them it was the Brazilian way. They were watching the security tape.

Talley pointed at the television with his cup.

'The first one inside is Rooney, this next guy is Krupchek. Kevin comes in last.'

Martin watched with the flat, uninvolved expression of an experienced officer. Talley found himself watching her instead of the tape, curious about her background and how she'd become a SWAT captain.

Martin nodded at the screen.

'What's that on his head, a tattoo? There, on the big one.'

'That's Krupchek.'

'Right, Krupchek.'

'It says "burn it." We're running it through the computer.'

Talley told them what he had learned from Brad Dill about Krupchek and the Rooney brothers, then filled them in on having dispatched Mikkelson and Dreyer to locate landlords and neighbors.

Ellison said, 'These guys have any family we can bring out? We had a guy once, he backed us off for twelve hours until his mama gets there. She gets on the phone, tells him to get his ass out of that house, the guy comes out crying like a baby.'

Talley had worked with subjects like that, too.

'Rooney might have an aunt in Bakersfield, but Dill didn't know about Krupchek. If we can find their landlords or friends, we might get a line on the families. You want, I'll have Larry Anders, he's my senior officer here, put your Intelligence Officer in touch with whoever we find.'

Maddox nodded, his face creased with attention.

· 'I might want to talk to Dill and those people myself. You okay with that?'

'I know the job. Whatever you want. Tell Anders, and he'll arrange to bring them here.'

As the new primary negotiator, Maddox had the responsibility to form his own opinions on the behavior characteristics of a subject. Talley would have done the same thing.

Martin stepped closer to the television. They had reached the part of the tape where Krupchek leaned over the counter.

'What's he doing?'

'Watch.'

Maddox joined Martin at the TV. He crossed his arms in a way that Talley thought was protective.

'Jesus, he's watching that man die.'

Talley nodded.

'That's what I thought.'

'The sonofabitch is smiling.'

Talley finished his coffee and put down the cup. He didn't need to see it again.

'We told the Sheriff's investigators up at Kim's about the hand. See there on the counter? They should have a pretty good palm print from that, but I haven't heard.'

Martin glanced at Ellison.

'Run the prints for wants and warrants.'

'Yes, ma'am.'

Metzger came up behind Talley and touched his arm.

'Chief, see you a second?'

Talley excused himself from the Sheriffs and followed Metzger into the adjoining room. Metzger glanced back at the Sheriffs, then lowered her voice.

'Sarah wants you to call her right away. She's says it's important. She says I should knock you down and drag you to a phone, it's so important.'

'Why are you whispering?'

'She says it's *important*. You're supposed to call on your office line, not use a radio.'

'Why not the radio?'

'Because other people can *hear* on the radio. She says use the phone.'

Talley felt a hot burn of concern that something had happened to Jane and Amanda. He took out his cell phone, hitting the autodial for his office. Out by the television, Maddox was looking at him, concerned.

Sarah answered on the first ring.

'It's me, Sarah. What's up?'

'Oh, thank God. There's a little boy on the phone. He says that his name is Thomas Smith, and that he's calling from inside the house.'

'It's a crank. Forget it.'

Warren Kenner, who was Talley's personnel supervisor and one of only two Bristo sergeants, came on the line.

'Chief, I think we got something here. I checked the phone number the boy says he's calling from with the cell company. It's registered to the Smiths, all right.'

'Did you talk with the boy, or just Sarah?'

'No, I talked to him. He sounds real, saying things about the three guys in that house, and his sister and father. He says his dad's hurt in there, that he got knocked out.'

Talley worried his lip, thinking, getting just a little excited.

'Is he still on the phone?'

'Yes, sir. Sarah's talking to him right now on another line. They locked him in his room. He says he's on his sister's cell phone.'

'Stand by.'

Talley went to the door; several officers and Highway Patrolmen were milling near Mrs. Peña's kitchen, drinking coffee and eating cheese enchiladas. He called Martin, Maddox, and Ellison into the room, then led them as far from the others as possible.

'I think we've got something here. Kid on the phone, saying he's Thomas Smith from inside the house.'

Martin's face tightened, coming together in a kind of expectant question.

'Is this bogus or real?'

Talley went back to the phone.

'Warren? Who else knows about this?'

'Just us, Chief. Me and Sarah, and now you.'

'If this turns out to be real, I don't want the press finding out about this, you understand? Tell Sarah. That means you don't talk about this with anyone, not even the other police, not even off the record.'

Talley looked at Martin as he spoke. She nodded, agreeing.

'If Rooney and those other guys see the press talking about someone in the house calling out, I don't know what they might do.'

'I understand, Chief. I'll tell Sarah.'

'Put him on.'

A boy came on the line, his voice low and careful, but not frightened.

'Hello? Is this the Chief?'

'This is Chief Talley. Tell me your name, son.'

'Thomas Smith. I'm in the house that's on TV. Dennis hit my dad and now he won't wake up. You gotta come get him.'

An edge of fear crept into the boy's voice when he mentioned his father, but Talley couldn't yet be sure the call wasn't a hoax.

'I have a couple of questions for you first, Thomas. Who's in the house with you?'

'These three guys, Dennis, Kevin, and Mars. Mars said he was going to eat my heart.'

'Besides them.'

'My father and sister. You gotta make Dennis send my dad to a doctor.'

The boy could have gotten all of this information off the news, but so far as Talley knew, no one had as yet reported, or knew, the whereabouts of the mother. They were still trying to locate her.

'What about your mother?'

The boy answered without hesitating.

'She's in Florida with my Aunt Kate.'

Talley felt a blossom of heat in his chest. This might be real. He made a scribbling gesture with his hand, telling Martin to get ready to write. She glanced at Ellison, who fumbled out his spiral notepad and a pen.

'What's your aunt's name, bud?'

'Kate Toepfer. She has blond hair.'

Talley repeated it, watching Ellison write.

'Where does she live?'

'West Palm Beach.'

Talley didn't bother to cover the phone.

'We got the boy. Get a number for this woman, Kate Toepfer in West Palm Beach, that's where the mother is.'

Maddox and Ellison exchanged words, Talley not hearing because he had already gone back to the boy. Martin stepped close, pulling at his arm to tip the phone so that she could hear.

'Where you are now, son, are you okay? Could they catch you talking to me?'

'They locked me in my room. I'm on my sister's cell phone.'

'Where's that, your room?'

'Upstairs.'

'Okay. Where's your dad and sister?'

'My dad's down in the office. They got him on the couch. He needs a doctor.'

'Was he shot?'

'Dennis hit him, and now he won't wake up. My sister says he needs a doctor, but Dennis won't listen.'

'Is he bleeding?'

'Not anymore. He just won't wake up. I'm really scared.'

'How about your sister? Is she okay?'

Maddox said, 'Ask him does he know the subject locations.'

Talley raised a hand, the boy still talking, saying something about his sister.

'What was that, Thomas? I missed that. Is she okay?'

'I said she won't leave. I tried to get her to leave, but she won't without our dad.'

Martin plucked at him.

'Can he get out? Ask him if he can get out.'

Talley nodded.

'Okay, Thomas, we're going to get you out of there as fast as we can, but I want to ask something. You're alone in your room on the second floor, right?'

'Yeah.'

'Could you let yourself out your window if we were down below to catch you?'

'They've got the windows nailed shut. But even if they didn't, they could see me.'

'They could see you climbing out the window even though you're alone?'

'We have security cameras. They could see on the monitors in my folks' room if they were looking. They would see you sneaking up to the house, too.'

'Okay, son, one more thing. Dennis told me that he had set up the house to burn with gasoline. Is that true?'

'They've got a bucket of gas in the entry hall. I saw it when they brought me downstairs. It really stinks.'

Talley heard brushing sounds on the phone, and the boy's voice dropped.

'They're coming.'

'Thomas? Thomas, are you all right?'

The boy was gone.

Martin said, 'What's happening?'

Talley listened, straining now, but the line was dead.

'He said they were coming, then he hung up.'

Martin took a deep breath, let it hiss out.

'You think they caught him?'

Talley closed the phone and put it away.

'I don't think so. He didn't sound panicked when he shut the phone, so I don't think he was discovered; he just had to end the call.'

'Was Rooney telling the truth about the gasoline?'

'Yes.'

'Shit. That's a problem. That's a fucking big problem. All we need is a goddamned barbecue.'

'He also said that there's a video security system. That's how he saw your people approaching the house.'

Martin turned to Ellison.

'Have the I.O. check the phone lines to see if there's a security feed. We might be able to back-trace it to the provider and find out what we're dealing with.'

Talley started to say that his people had already come up empty with that, but he let it go. If it was him, he'd double-check, too.

'He says the father is injured. That's why he called out, to say his father needs a doctor.'

Martin's expression turned grim. She hadn't heard that part.

'First the goddamned gas, and now this. If the man is in imminent danger, we might have to risk a breach.'

Maddox shifted, uncomfortable.

'How're we gonna breach knowing this guy can see it coming, him with gasoline ready to go? We'll get people killed.'

'If we have someone dying in there, we can't ignore it.'

Talley held up his hands like he was pushing them apart.

'The boy didn't say anyone is dying, he just said the man is hurt.'

He repeated Thomas's description of Walter Smith's condition. Martin listened, head down, but glancing at Maddox and Ellison from time to time as if to gauge their reactions. When Talley finished, she nodded.

'Well, that's not a lot of information.'

'No.'

'All right, at least we know we're not talking about a gunshot victim here. Smith's not in there bleeding to death.'

'Sounds like head trauma.'

'So we've got a possible concussion, but we can't be sure about that. We can't very well call Rooney back to ask about the father. He might get it in his head that one of those kids is calling out.'

Talley had to agree.

'We have to protect the boy. If he gets the chance to call again, I'm pretty sure he will.'

Maddox nodded.

'When I talk with Rooney again I'll push him to find out how everyone's doing. Maybe I can kick free some information about the father.'

They agreed that for now the best plan was to let Rooney and the others in the house calm down. Martin looked back at Talley.

'If the boy calls again, he'll call through your office.'

'I would guess so. He must've gotten the department's number from information.'

Talley knew what she wanted.

'I'll have someone in my office around the clock. If the boy calls, they'll page me and I'll bring you in.'

Martin checked her watch, then looked at Maddox.

'We've got to get to it. I want you and Ellison set up in front of that house so we can start breaking these assholes down.'

Talley knew what that meant: They would maintain a high noise level profile, phoning Rooney periodically throughout the night to keep him awake. They would try to wear him down by depriving him of sleep. Sometimes, if you got them tired enough, they gave up.

Martin turned back to Talley, and now her face softened. She put out her hand, and Talley took it. Her grip wasn't as hard as before.

'I appreciate your help, Chief. You've done a good job keeping this situation under control.'

'Thanks, Captain.'

Martin squeezed his hand, then let go.

'You want to relieve your people now, that's fine. I'd like four of your officers to liaison with the locals, but past that, we've got it. I know you have a slim department up here.'

'It's yours, Captain. You have my numbers. If you need me, call. Otherwise, I'll grab a few hours' sleep and see you in the morning.'

'We're good.'

Martin gave him an uncertain smile that almost looked pretty, then walked away. Talley thought that she probably had a hard time smiling, but people often did, and for reasons that surprised you. Maddox and Ellison followed her.

Talley brought his cup to the kitchen, thanked Mrs. Peña for her help, then went to his car. He brought Larry Anders up to speed, then checked the time, wondering if Jane and Amanda were still at dinner or were waiting at home.

He wondered why Martin had squeezed his hand.

Ken Seymore

The television crews wouldn't share their food, cheap pricks, big urns of Starbucks coffee that someone had brought, Krispy Kreme donuts, and pizza. Just as well, or Ken Seymore would have missed seeing Talley leave.

Rather than eating, Seymore was seated in his car, a Ford Explorer, near the gate. He told the two cops there, who had asked him what he was doing, that he was waiting for a pool photographer to arrive from Los Angeles. Going to snap some shots of the guys guarding the development, he had said. That had been enough. They'd left him alone.

When Seymore saw Talley drive out, he picked up his phone.

'He's leaving.'

That was all he needed to say.

13

Friday, 8:46 p.m.

Jane

Her heart pounding, her lips tingling from the kiss, his voice a whisper in her ear there in the dark, parked outside her house.

'We would be good together. I've thought that for weeks, the two of us, fitting together like pieces of a puzzle.'

He was a doctor at her hospital, newly divorced, two boys in high school, one a year older than Mandy, the other a year younger.

'You know it would be good.'

'It would.'

She loved the warm hardness of him, something that had been missing so long; this large male body, holding her, hers to hold. And a nice man. A nice man. They had the same sense of humor, wacky and sarcastic.

'Come home with me tonight. For a little while.'

Her first date with another man since Jeff moved out, almost a year; Jeff up there in Bristo, Jeff who had simply shut down on her, stopped feeling, pulled back, withdrawn, disappeared, whatever the hell. It felt like cheating.

'I don't know.'

'I don't want the night to end. We don't have to do anything. Not for at least five minutes.'

She laughed. Couldn't help herself.

He kissed her, and she kissed back, the sensuous play of lips and tongues. She felt drunk with it, and so SO alive.

'I told Amanda I would be in by now.'

'I'll cry. Worse, I'll sulk. It's terrible when I sulk.'

Laughing, she put her hand over his face and pushed him away. Gently. He sighed, and now they were serious.

'Okay. I had fun.'

'Me, too.'

'I'll see you at work tomorrow. I'll drop around the floor, find you.'

'I'm off tomorrow and the day after.'

'Thursday, then. That would be Thursday. I'll see you then.'

She kissed him a final time, a quick peck, though he wanted more, then hurried into the empty house. Amanda was sleeping over at her friend Connie's. She hadn't told Amanda that she was going out, let alone that she would be in by now. That had been a lie.

The next day, Jane changed her hair color, going with the dark red, the red that's almost black, wondering if it made her look younger, wondering what Jeff would think.

Everything that night, it had felt like cheating.

'Earth to Mom?'

Jane Talley focused on her daughter.

'Sorry.'

'What were you thinking?'

'If your father likes my hair.'

Amanda's face darkened.

'Like you should care. Please.'

'All right. I was wondering if that mess is going to blow up in his face. Is that better?'

They had stopped at *Le Chine,* a Vietnamese-Thai place in a mall near the freeway, ordering *pho ga,* which was a rice noodle soup, and crispy shrimp, which was, well, crispy shrimp. They ate there often, sometimes with Jeff. Jane had toyed with the plain white rice, but that was it. She put down her fork.

'Let me tell you something.'

'Can't we just go home? I don't want to be here, anyway. I told him that.'

'Don't say "him." He's your father.'

'Whatever.'

'He's having a hard time.'

'A year ago it was a hard time, now it's just boring.'

Jane was so tired of keeping all the balls in the air, of being the supportive nurturing mother, of waiting for Jeff to come to his senses, that she wanted to scream. Some days, she did; she would press her face into the pillow and scream as hard as she could. A flash of anger shook her so deeply that if Mandy rolled her eyes one more time she would snatch up the fork and stab her.

'Let me tell you something. This has been hard on everybody; on you, on me, on him. He's not like this. It was that goddamned job.'

'Here we go with the job.'

Jane called for the check, so livid that she didn't trust herself to look at her daughter. As always, the owner, a woman named Po who knew they were Talley's family, insisted that there was no charge. As always, Jane paid, this time quickly, in cash, not waiting for change.

'Let's go.'

Jane walked out to the parking lot, still not looking at Amanda, her heels snapping like gunshots on the pavement. She got behind the wheel but did not start the car. Amanda slid in beside her, pulling the door. The night air smelled of sage and dust and garlic from the restaurant.

'Why aren't we moving?'

'I'm trying not to kill you.'

When Jane figured out what she needed to say, she said it.

'I am scared to death that your father is finally going to give up and call it quits. I could see it in him tonight. Your father, he knows what this is doing to us, he's not stupid. We talk, Amanda; he says he's empty, I don't know how to fill him; he says he's dead, I don't know how to bring him to life. You think I don't try? Here we are, split apart, time passing, him wallowing in his goddamned depression; your father will end it just to spare us. Well, little miss, let me tell you something: I don't want to be spared. I *choose* not to be spared. Your father used to be filled with life and strength, and I fell in love with that special man more deeply than you can know. You don't want to hear about the job, fine, but only a man as good as your father could be hurt the way that job hurt him. If that's me making excuses for him, fine. If you think I'm a loser by waiting for him, tough. I could have other men; I don't want them. I don't even know if he still loves me, but let me tell you something: I love him, I want this marriage, and I goddamned fucking well care whether or not he likes my hair.'

Jane, crying, saw that Amanda was crying, too, great honey drops inflating her eyes. She slumped back in the seat, bouncing her head on the headrest.

'Shit.'

Sharp rapping on the window startled her.

'Ma'am? Are you all right?'

Jane rolled down the window, just an inch, two. The man seemed embarrassed, leaning forward, one hand on the roof, the other on her door, his expression asking if there was anything he could do.

'I'm sorry, I know it's not my business. I heard crying.'

'That's all right. We're fine. Thank you.'

'Well, if you're sure.'

'Thank you.'

She was reaching for the key when he jerked open the door, pushing her sideways into Amanda, the smell of donuts suddenly strong in the car.

Later, she would know that his name was Marion Clewes.

14
Friday, 9:12 p.m.

Talley

The sky was strange without red and green helicopter stars. Talley turned off his command radio and rolled down the windows, letting the silky air rush over him, still warm from the earth and smelling of yucca. It wasn't his show anymore, so he didn't need the radio. He needed to think.

Stretched out ahead and curving between the mountains, the street was bright with headlights rushing toward him. The past six hours had flicked past, one moment overtaking the next like a chain of car crashes, piling one atop the next with an intensity of experience that Talley hadn't known in a long time; part fear, part elation. Talley found himself working through the events of the day, and realized after a time that he was enjoying himself. That he would, or could, surprised him. It was as if some dormant part of himself was waking.

The hot night air brought a memory of Jane.

They had come to the desert for their honeymoon. Not when they first married; they didn't have enough money for that. But later, when his six-month probation was over, they had each taken two vacation days to make a long weekend, thinking they would drive to Las Vegas. The idea, the great plan, was to beat the summer heat by making the drive after sundown, but Vegas was a long way, four hours. They stopped at the halfway point for something to eat, a nothing little town at the edge of the California desert, and went no farther. The honeymoon cottage that night was a twenty-dollar motel off the highway; dinner was a cheap steak at the Sizzler, after which they explored the town. Driving now, Talley remembered the desert heat of that night; Jane had scared him, Talley the tough young SWAT cop, by climbing out the car's window and sitting on the door as they raced along the back desert roads.

Talley hadn't recalled those memories in years, and now felt uneasy with their absence, as if they had been lost within himself. He wondered what else might be lost within himself.

Talley turned onto the condominium grounds. He found Jane's car parked in the first of the two spaces that were his, and pulled in beside it.

He stared up the walk toward his condo, uneasy about the conversation they were about to have. She had finally called him out on their future, and now he had to deal with it. No more running, no more denial, no more excuses; he could keep her, or he could lose her. Tonight it was going to be as simple as that.

As Talley stepped from his car, he noticed that the parking lot was darker than usual; both security lights were out. Talley was locking his car as a woman stepped from the walk that led to his building.

'Chief Talley? Could I have a word with you?'

Talley thought she might be one of his neighbors. Most of the people in the complex knew he was the chief of police, often coming to him with complaints and problems.

'It's pretty late. Could this keep until tomorrow?'

She was attractive, but not pretty, with a clean, businesslike expression, and hair that cupped her face. He did not recognize her.

'I wish it could, Chief, but we have to discuss this tonight.'

Talley heard a single footstep behind him, the *shush* of shoe on grit, then an arm hooked his throat from behind, lifting him backward and off his feet. Someone held a gun before his face.

'Do you see it? See the gun? Look at it.'

Talley clawed at the arm that was choking him, but only until he saw the pistol. Then he stopped struggling.

'That's better. We're only going to talk, that's all, but I will kill you if I have to.'

They lowered him, gave him his feet again. Someone opened his car again as someone else felt beneath his jacket and around his waist.

'Where's your gun?'

'I don't carry it.'

'Bullshit. Where is it?'

The hands went to his ankles.

'I don't carry it. I'm the Chief. I don't have to.'

They pushed him behind the wheel. Talley saw shapes; he wasn't sure how many; maybe three, could have been five. Someone in the backseat directly behind him smashed the ceiling light with the gun, then pushed the gun hard to his neck.

'Start the car. Back up. We're just going to talk to you.'

'Who are you?'

Talley tried to turn, but strong hands shoved his face forward. Two men wearing black knit ski masks and gloves were in the backseat.

'The car. Back up.'

Talley did as he was told, his headlights swinging across the walk. The woman was gone. Red taillights waited at the far end of the parking lot.

'See that car? Follow it. We won't go far.'

Talley pulled in tight on the car. It was a late-model Ford Mustang, dark green with a hard top and California plates. Talley worked at remembering the tag number, 2KLX561, then glanced in the rearview mirror as a second car tucked in tight behind his.

'Who are you?'

'Drive.'

'Is this about what's happening?'

'Just drive. Don't worry about it.'

The Mustang drove carefully, leading him back to the street, then out along Flanders Road to a minimall less than a mile away. All the shops were closed, the parking lot empty. Talley followed the Mustang into the alley behind the shops, where it stopped beside a Dumpster.

'Pull up closer. Closer. Bumper to bumper.'

He bumped the Mustang.

'Turn off the ignition. Give me the key.'

Talley had known a kind of fear when he had worked the tactical teams on SWAT before he was a negotiator; but that was an impersonal fear, a going-into-combat fear leavened by the armor you wore, the weapon you carried, and the support of your teammates. This was different, up close and personal. Men were assassinated like this, their bodies left in Dumpsters.

He turned off the ignition, but didn't take out the key. The second car came up so close that it was inches from his own, blocking him in. Talley told himself this was a good sign; they didn't want him to try to run. They wouldn't worry about it if they simply wanted to shoot him.

'Give me the damned key.'

He held it up; the hand snatched it away.

The passenger door opened. A third man slipped inside, also wearing a mask and gloves. He was wearing a black sport coat over a gray T-shirt and jeans. When his left sleeve hiked up, a gold Rolex flashed. He wasn't large, about Talley's size, maybe one-eighty, trim. The skin around his mouth and eyes was tan. He held a cell phone.

'Okay, Chief, I know you're scared, but trust me, unless you do something stupid, we're not here to hurt you. So you control that, okay? Do you understand?'

Talley tried to recall the Mustang's tag number. Was it KLX or KLS?

'Don't just stare at me, Chief. We've got to make some headway here.'

'What do you want?'

The third man gestured to the backseat with the phone, giving Talley another glimpse of the watch. Talley thought of the third man as the Watchman.

'The man behind you is going to reach around and get hold of you. Don't freak out. That's for your own good. Okay? He's just going to hold you.'

The arm looped around his neck again; a hand took his left wrist, twisted it behind his back; another took his right; the second man in the back was helping. Talley could barely breathe.

'What is this?'

'Listen.'

The Watchman put the phone to Talley's ear.

'Say hello.'

Talley couldn't imagine what they wanted or who they were. His mouth felt stuffed with cotton batting. The phone was cold against his ear.

'Who is this?'

Jane's voice, shaky and frightened.

'Jeff? Is that you?'

Talley tried to buck away from the arm crossing his throat; he strained to pull his arms free, but couldn't. Seconds passed before Talley realized the Watchman was talking to him.

'Take it easy, Chief; I know, I know. But just listen, okay? She's all right. Your kid, she's all right, too. Now just relax, breathe deep, listen. You ready to listen? Remember: Right now, from this point on, you're in control. You. You control what happens to them. You want to hear her again? You want to talk to her, see that she's okay?'

Talley nodded against the pressure of the arm, finally managed to croak.

'You sonofabitch.'

'Bad start, Chief, but I understand. I'm married myself. Me, I *wish* somebody would take my old lady, but that's just me. Anyway, here.'

The Watchman held the phone to Talley's ear again.

'Jane?'

'What's going on, Jeff? Who are these people?'

'I don't know. Are you all right? Is Mandy?'

'Jeff, I'm scared.'

Jane was crying.

The Watchman took back the phone.

'That's enough.'

'Who the hell are you?'

'Can we let you go? You past your shock and all that, we can turn you loose and you won't do something stupid?'

'You can let go.'

The Watchman glanced at the backseat, and Talley was released. The Watchman leaned toward Talley, going eye to eye and doing it with purpose.

'Walter Smith has two computer disks in his house that belong to us. Don't worry about why we want those disks. More important, don't care. But we want them, and you're going to see that we get them.'

Talley didn't know what the Watchman was talking about; he shook his head.

'What does that mean? What?'

'You're going to control the scene.'

'The Sheriffs control the scene.'

'Not anymore. It's your scene. You'll take it back or whatever it is you have to do, because no one – let me repeat that – *no one* is going into that house until *my* people go in that house.'

'You don't know what you're talking about. I can't control that.'

The Watchman raised his finger, as if he was offering a lesson.

'I know exactly what I'm talking about. You have a coordinated mixed scene now with your people – the Bristo Police Department – and the Sheriffs. In a couple of hours, a group of my people are going to arrive at York Estates. You will tell everyone involved that they are an FBI tactical team. They'll look the part, and they know how to act the part. You see where I'm going with this?'

'I don't have any idea what you're talking about. I can't control any of this. I can't control what happens in that house.'

'You better get up to speed fast, then. Your wife and kid are counting on you.'

Talley didn't know what to say. He worked his fingers under his thighs, trying to think.

'What do you want me to do?'

'You get my people set up, then you stand by and wait to hear from me.'

The Watchman handed Talley the cell phone.

'When this phone rings, you answer. It'll be me. I'll tell you what to do.'

Talley stared at the phone.

'When it comes time to go in the house, my people will be the first in. Nothing, and I mean *nothing*, will be removed from that house except by my people. Do you get that?'

'I can't control what those kids do. They could be giving up right now. They could start shooting. The Sheriffs might be going inside right now.'

The Watchman slapped him, a hard straight push hitting him square in the forehead with his open palm. Talley's head rocked back.

'Don't panic, Talley. You should *know*. SWAT guys *know*. Panic kills.'

Talley gripped the phone with both hands.

'Okay. All right.'

'You're going to be thinking, What can I do? Here you are, a policeman, you're going to think about calling the FBI or bringing the Sheriffs in, about getting me before something happens to your wife and child, but, Chief, think about this: I have people right there in York Estates, right under your nose, reporting everything that happens. If you bring anyone in, if you do *anything* other than what I am telling you to do, you'll get your wife and kid back in the mail. Are we clear on that?'

'Yes.'

'When I have what I want, your wife and daughter will be released. We're cool with that. They don't know who has them just like you don't know who we are. Ignorance is bliss.'

'What is it you want? Disks? Like computer disks? Where are they, where in the house?'

'Two disks, bigger than normal disks. They're called Zip disks, labeled

Disk One and Disk Two. We won't know where they are until we find them, but Smith will know.'

The Watchman opened the door, paused before leaving, his glance flicking to the phone.

'Answer when it rings, Chief.'

The keys were dropped into Talley's lap. Doors opened, closed, and Talley was alone there in the alley behind the minimall in the middle of nowhere. The Mustang pulled away. The second car roared away, backwards. Talley sat behind the wheel, breathing, unable to move, feeling apart from his own body as if this had just happened to someone else.

He clawed for the keys, started his car, and spun the wheel hard, flooring it, fishtailing gravel. He hit his lights and siren, rolling code three, blasting straight back to his condo, never bothered to pull into a spot, just left the car like that in the parking lot, lights popping, and ran inside, almost as if they might be sitting there, all of this some hallucination.

The condo was empty, the silence of it outrageously loud. He called them anyway, not knowing what else to do.

'Jane! Amanda!'

Their only sign was the keys to Jane's car, sitting plainly on the dining room table, small and hard, left there as a threat.

Talley put Jane's keys in his pocket. He went upstairs to the little desk in his bedroom where he stared at the photographs. Jane and Amanda, much younger then, stared back in a picture taken at Disneyland, Jane sitting at one of those outdoor restaurants in Adventureland, her arms wrapped around Amanda, both of them showing more white teeth than a piano. They had eaten tostadas or tacos, one, with some salsa that was so mild that they'd laughed about it, the three native Angelenos, salsa with all the kick of Campbell's tomato soup, something that only people from Minnesota or Wisconsin would find spicy. Talley choked a sob in his chest. He took the picture from the frame, put it in his pocket with the keys. He went to his closet for the blue nylon gym bag on the top shelf, and brought the bag to his bed. He took out the pistol that he had carried during his SWAT days, a Colt .45 Model 1911 that had been tuned by the SWAT armorer for accuracy and reliability. It was big, ugly, and supremely dangerous. It held only seven bullets, but SWAT used the .45 as their combat pistol because just one of those big heavy bullets could knock a large man off his feet. A .38 or a 9mm couldn't promise that, but the .45 could. It was a killer.

Talley ejected the empty magazine, filled it with seven bullets, then reseated it. He dug through the gym bag for the black ballistic nylon holster. He took off his uniform, then put on blue jeans and tennis shoes. He fitted the holster onto his belt at his side, then covered it with a black sweatshirt. He clipped his badge to his belt.

The cell phone that the Watchman gave him was sitting on his desk.

Talley stared at it. What if it rang? What if the Watchman ordered him into Walter Smith's house right now and the people inside that house were killed? What if he answered that phone to hear Jane and Amanda screaming as they were murdered?

Talley sat on the edge of the bed thinking that he was a fool. He should go directly to both the Sheriff's Detective Bureau and the FBI; even the Watchman knew it. That would be the smart way to play this mess, and that was what he would have done except that he believed that the Watchman was telling the truth about having someone at York Estates, and would kill his family. Talley was scared; it's easy to say what someone should do when they're not you; when it's you, it's a nightmare. He told himself to be careful. The Watchman was right about something else, too: Panic kills. That same message had hung on the wall at the Special Weapons and Tactics School: Panic kills. The instructors had hammered it into them. It didn't matter how urgent the situation, you had to think; act quickly but efficiently. A mind is a terrible thing to waste, and nothing wastes your mind faster than getting your ass shot off. Think.

Talley put the Watchman's phone in his pocket and drove to his office.

The Bristo Camino Police Department was a two-story space in the mall that used to be a toy store. Talley's officers jokingly called it 'the crib.' This time of night, the mall parking lot was empty; only one radio car was out front, along with the personal cars belonging to his officers. Talley left his car at the curb. The second floor contained a single holding cell, a ready room for briefings, a bathroom, and a locker room. The most serious criminals it had held were two sixteen-year-old car thieves who had driven a stolen Porsche up from Santa Monica only to wrap it around a palm tree; mostly, the cell was used to let drunk drivers sleep off their buzz. Office space for Sarah filled most of the ground floor, with the front desk being designated for the duty officer of the watch, though Sarah, herself not a sworn officer, served that post whenever she wasn't ensconced in the communications bay. Talley's office sat in the rear, but his own computer wasn't tied into the National Law Enforcement Telecommunication System; only one computer in the office could access the NLETS, and that was up front by Sarah.

Kenner, sitting at the front desk, raised his eyebrows in surprise when Talley entered.

'Hey, Chief. I thought you went seven.'

Seven was the code for taking a meal break, but it was also slang for going off duty. Talley let himself through the gate that separated the public space from the desks without making eye contact. He didn't want conversation.

'I've got more to do.'

'What's happening out at the house?'

'The Sheriffs have it.'

Sarah waved from the communications bay. She was a retired public school teacher with bright red hair who worked the job because she enjoyed it. Talley nodded at her, but didn't stop to chat the way he ordinarily would. He went straight to the NLETS computer.

Sarah called, 'I thought you went home?'

'More to do.'

'Isn't that sad about that little boy? What happened with that?'

'I just stopped by to look up something. I've got to get back to the house.'

He made his manner brusque to discourage her.

Talley typed in the Mustang's license number, 2KLX561, and requested a California Department of Motor Vehicles search.

'Ah, Chief, I'd like to get some time out there. You know, at the house.'

Kenner had come up behind him, looking hopeful. Talley leaned forward to block the computer's screen.

'Call Anders. Tell him I said to rotate you out there at the shift change.'

Talley turned back to the computer.

'Ah, Chief? You think I could work the perimeter?'

Talley blocked the screen again, letting his annoyance show.

'You want some trigger time? That it, Kenner?'

Kenner shrugged.

'Well, yes, sir.'

'See Anders.'

Talley stared at Kenner until he returned to the front desk. The DMV search came back, showing that license plate 2KLX561 was currently an unregistered listing. Next, he typed in the name *Walter Smith* and ran it through the National Crime Information Center, limiting the search to white males in the Southwest within a ten-year time frame. The NCIC search kicked back one hundred twenty-eight hits. That was too many. Talley could have limited the search if he had Smith's middle name, but he didn't. He cut the frame to five years, tried again, and this time got thirty-one hits. He skimmed the results. Twenty-one of the thirty-two arrestees were currently incarcerated, and the remaining ten were too young. As far as the law enforcement computer network knew, the Walter Smith who lived in York Estates was just another upstanding American with something in his house that men were willing to kill for.

Talley deleted the screen, then tried to recall as many details as possible about the three men and the woman who kidnapped him. The woman: short dark hair that cupped her face, five-five, slender, light-colored blouse and skirt; it had been too dark to see any more. The three men had worn nicely tailored sport coats, gloves, and masks; he had noticed no identifying characteristics. He tried to remember background noise from when he spoke with Jane, some telling sound that could identify her location, but there had been none.

Talley took out the Watchman's phone, wondering if a print could be lifted. It was a new black Nokia. The phone's battery indicator showed a full charge. Talley felt a sudden fear that the battery would fail, and he would never hear from Jane and Amanda again. He trembled as the panic grew, then forced those thoughts down. *Think*. The cell phone was his link to the people who had Jane and Amanda, a link that might lead back to them. If the Watchman had called Jane's location, that number would be in the memory. Talley's heart pounded. He pressed redial. No number came up. Talley checked the phone's stored memory, but no numbers were listed. *Think!!!* If the people holding Jane had phoned the Watchman, Talley might be able to reverse-dial the number with the star 69 feature. He pressed star 69. Nothing happened. Talley's heart pounded harder; he wanted to smash the fucking phone. He wanted to throw it against the wall, then stomp it to splinters. *Goddamnit, THINK!!!* Someone had paid for the phone and was paying for its service. Talley turned off the phone, then turned it back on. As the view screen lit, the phone's number appeared. 555–1367. Talley wanted to jump up and pump his fist. He copied the number, his only lead.

Then Talley realized he had another lead: Walter Smith. Smith could identify these people, Smith had what they wanted, and Smith might even be able to tell him where they had taken Jane and Amanda. Smith had answers. All Talley had to do was reach him.

And get him out of that house.

Talley called Larry Anders when he was five minutes from the development, saying to meet him inside the south entrance, and to wait there alone. The traffic passing the development was less than it had been earlier, but a long line of gawkers still made the going slow once Talley turned off Flanders Road. He burped his siren to make them pull to the side, then waved himself through the blockade.

Anders was parked on the side of the road. Talley pulled up behind him and flicked his lights. Anders walked back to Talley's window, looking nervous.

'What's up, Chief?'

'Where's Metzger?'

'Up with the Sheriffs in case they need something. Did I do something?'

'Get in.'

Talley waited as Anders walked around the front of the car and climbed in. Anders wasn't the oldest person on his department, but he was the senior officer in years served, and Talley respected him. He thought again that the man in the ski mask had someone here, and wondered if that person was Larry Anders. Talley recalled a photograph that had appeared in the *Los Angeles Times*, one taken at the day-care center that showed Spencer Morgan, the man who had held the children hostage, holding a gun to Talley's head. Talley thought of the trust it had taken for him to stand there while his friend Neal Craimont lined up the crosshairs.

Anders squirmed.

'Jesus, Chief, why are you staring at me like that?'

'I have something for you to do. You're not to tell anyone else what you're doing, not Metzger, not the other guys, not the Sheriffs, no one; just tell them that I want you to run down some background info, but don't tell them what. You understand me, Larry?'

Anders replied slowly.

'I guess so.'

'I can't have you guessing. Either you can keep your mouth shut or you can't. This is important.'

'This isn't something illegal, is it, Chief? I really like being a cop. I couldn't do something illegal.'

'It's police work, the real thing. I want you to find out as much as you can about Walter Smith.'

'The guy in the house?'

'I believe he's involved in illegal activity or associates with people who are. I need to find out what that is. Talk to the neighbors, but don't be obvious about it. Don't tell anyone what you're doing or what you suspect. Try to find out whatever you can about him, where he's from, stuff like that; his business, his clients, anything that will give us a handle on him. It will help if you can learn his middle name. When you've finished here, go back to the office and run him through the FBI and the NLETS database. I went back five years, but you go back twenty.'

Anders cleared his throat. He was uncomfortable with all this.

'What's the problem with telling our guys? I mean, why not?'

'Because that's the way I want it, Larry. I have a good reason, I just can't tell you right now, but I'm trusting that you'll keep your word.'

'I will, Chief. Yes, sir, I will.'

Talley gave him the Nokia's cell phone number.

'Before you do any of that, I want you to trace this cell phone number. You can do this by phone from here. Find out who it's billed to. If you need a court order, call the Palmdale District Court. They have a judge on page for night work. Sarah has the number.'

Anders looked at the slip of paper.

'The judge, he'll want to know why, won't he?'

'Tell him we believe this number will provide life-or-death information about one of the men in the house.'

Anders nodded dully, knowing it was a lie.

'All right.'

Talley thought, trying to remember if there was something else, something that might give him a line to find out who he was dealing with.

'When you get back to the office, run a DMV stolen-vehicle search for a green Mustang, this year's model. It would be a recent theft, maybe even today.'

Anders took out his pad to make notes.

'Ah, you got a tag?'

'It's running a dead plate. If you get a hit, note where it was stolen. Who was checking into the building permits?'

'Ah, that was Cooper.'

'I want you to stay on that.'

'It's midnight.'

'If you have to get the city supervisors out of bed, do it. Tell them the Sheriffs are desperate for the house plans, it's life or death, whatever you have to say, but find out who built that house.'

'Yes, sir.'

'You're going to have to work all night, Larry. It's important.'

'That's okay.'

'Update me with everything you find out, whatever time it is. Don't use the radio. Call my cell. You got the number?'

'Yes, sir.'

'Get to it.'

Talley watched Anders drive away. He told himself that Anders could be trusted; he had just placed the lives of his family in Larry Anders's hands.

Talley parked outside Mrs. Peña's house and went to the Sheriff's command van. The back gate was open, glowing crimson from the soft red lights within. Martin, Hicks, and the I.O. supervisor were clumped around the coffee machine.

Talley rapped on the side of the van as he climbed inside. When Martin glanced over, she smiled with a warmth that surprised him.

'I thought you left.'

'I'm taking back command of the scene.'

It took a moment for his statement to register, then Martin's brow furrowed. The warmth was gone.

'I don't understand. *You* requested our help. You couldn't wait to hand off to me.'

Talley had readied the lie.

'I know I did, Captain, but it's a liability issue. The city supervisors want a representative of Bristo to be in charge. I'm sorry, but that's the way it has to be. As of now, I'm resuming command of the scene.'

Hicks put his fists on his hips.

'What kind of half-assed hicktown crap is this?'

Talley pointedly looked at Hicks.

'No tactical action is to be taken without my approval. Is that clear?'

Martin stalked across the van, stopping only inches away. She was almost as tall as Talley.

'Outside. I want to talk about this.'

Talley didn't move. He knew that the Sheriffs regularly worked under local restraints when they functioned in advisory and support roles; Martin would still be in direct control of her people, though Talley would command the operation. Martin would go along.

'There's nothing to talk about, Captain. I'm not going to tell you how to do your job; I need you, and I appreciate your being here. But I have to sign off on any action we take, and right now I'm saying that there will be no tactical action.'

Martin started to say something, then stopped. She seemed to search his eyes. Talley met her gaze and did not look away, though he felt embarrassed and frightened. He wondered if she could see that he was lying.

'What if those assholes lose it in there, Chief? You want me to track you down and waste time asking your permission to save those kids?'

Talley could barely answer.

'It won't come to that.'

'You don't know that. That house could go to hell in a second.'

Talley stepped back. He wanted to get out of the van.

'I want to talk to Maddox. Is he still at the house?'

Martin continued to search his eyes, and now she lowered her voice.

'What's wrong, Chief? You look like something's bothering you.'

Talley looked away.

'It has to be this way, that's all. I have this city council.'

Martin considered him again, then lowered her voice still more as if she didn't want Hicks and the Intelligence Officer to hear.

'Maddox told me a little about you. You were pretty hot stuff down there in Los Angeles.'

'That was a long time ago.'

Martin shrugged, then smiled, though not so warmly as before.

'Not so long.'

'I want to see Maddox.'

'He's in the cul-de-sac. I'll tell him you're on the way.'

'Thanks, Martin. For not making this worse.'

She stared at him, but turned away without answering.

Talley found Maddox and Ellison waiting at their car in the mouth of the cul-de-sac.

Ellison looked curious.

'Can't get too much of a good thing, huh, Chief?'

'Guess not. Has he made any more demands?'

Maddox shook his head.

'Nothing. We've been phoning every fifteen or twenty minutes to keep him awake, but other than that, there's nothing.'

'All right. I want to move up by the house.'

Maddox opened his driver's-side door.

'You taking back the phone?'

'That's it. Let's go.'

Talley checked the Watchman's cell phone, making sure it was on. They eased the car into the cul-de-sac and returned to the house.

Jennifer

Jennifer nodded in and out of a light drowse, never quite sleeping, listening to the helicopters and the squawk of police voices that she could not understand. She thought they might be dreams. Jennifer couldn't get comfortable with her wrists taped, lying in her bed, on top of the covers, the room so hot it left her sweaty and gross. Every time she felt herself falling asleep, the phone rang, distant from downstairs, and left her head filled with thoughts she could not stop: Her father; her brother, thinking that he might be creeping through the walls to do something stupid.

Jennifer jerked upright when the door opened. She saw Mars framed in dim light. Her skin crawled, being on the bed with him there, him and his toad eyes. She scrambled to her feet.

Mars said, 'We can't make the microwave work.'

'What?'

'We're hungry. You're going to cook.'

'I'm not going to cook for you. You're out of your mind.'

'You'll cook.'

'Fuck yourself!'

The words came before she could stop them.

Mars stepped close, then searched her eyes the way he had when she was tied to the chair, first one eye, then the other. She tried to step back, but he laced his fingers in her hair, holding her close. He spoke so softly that she could barely hear.

'I told you, that's a bad thing.'

'Leave go of me.'

He bunched his fist, pulling her hair.

'Stop.'

He twisted his fist, pulling tighter. His face held no expression except for a mild curiosity. The pain was enormous. Jennifer's entire body was rigid and clammy.

'I can do anything I want to you, bad girl. Remember that. Think about it.'

Mars pushed her through the door, then roughly along the hall and down the stairs. The kitchen lights were on, bright and blinding after so long in the black of her room. Mars cut the tape at her wrists, then peeled it away. She had not seen his knife before. It was curved and wicked. When he turned to the refrigerator, she glanced at the French doors, and fought the urge to run even though Thomas had given her that chance. Two frozen pizzas were sitting on the counter and the microwave oven was open.

'Heat the pizza.'

Mars turned away from her and went to the refrigerator, his back wide and threatening. Jennifer remembered the paring knife, pushed behind the food processor when they first invaded her home. She glanced toward the food processor, looking for it. When she looked back at Mars, he was watching her, holding a carton of eggs. It was like he could see inside her.

'I want scrambled eggs and hot dogs on mine.'

'On the pizza?'

'I like it with hot sauce and butter.'

As Jennifer got a frying pan and a bowl and the other things she would need, Dennis appeared from the entry. His eyes were dark and hollow.

'Is she cooking?'

'She's making eggs.'

Dennis grunted listlessly, then turned away without another word. She found herself wishing that he would die.

'When are you going to let us go?'

'Shut up. All you have to do is make the pizza.'

She broke all nine eggs into a glass bowl, then put the frying pan on to heat. She didn't bother with salt and pepper. She wanted the eggs to taste nasty.

Mars stood in the family room, staring at her.

'Stop watching me. I'm going to burn the eggs.'

Mars went to the French doors.

Him walking away was like a weight being lifted. She could breathe again. Jennifer beat the eggs, sprayed the pan with PAM, then poured in the eggs. She got hot sauce from the refrigerator, then glanced at Mars. He was standing by the French doors, staring at nothing, with his right hand on the glass. She shook hot sauce into the eggs until the eggs were orange, hoping it would poison them, then she thought that she might be able to poison them for real. Her mother had sleeping pills, there was probably rat poison or weedkiller in the garage, there was Drāno. She thought that Thomas might be able to get the sleeping pills. Then, if they made her cook again, she could put it in the food.

She glanced over at Mars again, expecting that he had read her mind again and would be watching her, but he had moved deeper into the family room. She looked at the paring knife. The handle was sticking out from behind the food processor, directly beneath the cabinet with the plates. She glanced at Mars again. She couldn't see his face, only the shadow of his bulk. He might have been looking at her, but she couldn't tell. She walked directly to the cabinets, took down some plates, and picked up the knife. She fought the urge to glance at Mars, knowing that if their eyes locked he would know, he could tell. She pushed the knife under her shirt into the waist of her shorts and into the bottom of her bathing suit, horizontally so that it lay against the flat of her belly.

'What are you doing?'

'Getting plates.'

'You're burning the eggs. I can smell'm.'

She brought the plates to the stove, feeling the hard shape of the knife low on her belly, thinking that now if they turned their backs, she could kill them.

Across the house in the office, the telephone rang.

15

Friday, 11:02 p.m.

Talley

The Sheriffs had set up a dedicated phone for Maddox and Ellison. It was looped by a cell link from Maddox's radio car to the command van, where it was hardwired into the Smith's phone line beneath the street. It provided the negotiators with a cell phone's freedom of movement while allowing all conversations to be recorded in the van. Martin, Hicks, and everyone else in the van would be listening to every word. Talley didn't want that.

Talley took out his cell phone, but he had forgotten Smith's number and had to ask for it.

Maddox, watching him, said, 'We've got the hard line.'

Talley ignored him.

'I'm more comfortable with this. You got the number?'

Unless the Sheriffs had changed the phone block, the Smiths' phone should still accept Talley's calls. Ellison read off the number as Maddox watched Talley. Talley knew they thought this was odd, but he didn't care.

'Why are you doing this?'

'What?'

'Out of the blue, you're back, you're calling the house. Every call has to have a point. Why?'

Talley stopped dialing the number and tried to order his thoughts. He had developed a certain amount of respect for Maddox and wanted to tell him the truth, but his fear wouldn't allow it. He wanted Smith. That's all he knew. Smith was his link to the people who had his wife and daughter. He considered the house and what might be on the other side of its door, then looked back at Maddox. He needed to say something that would bring Maddox onto his side.

'I'm scared that Smith is dead. I think I can push Rooney into telling us without tipping him off that the boy called.'

'If he's dead, Rooney isn't going to say shit and the boy would've told us.'

'So what do we do, Maddox? You want to breach the house?'

Maddox held his gaze, then looked back at the house and nodded.

'All right, then.'

Talley redialed the number, then waited for the ring. The front and sides of the house glowed from the banks of white lights that the Sheriffs had erected, the glare so hot that the house seemed washed out and pale. Exaggerated black shadows stretched across the lawn like grave markers. The phone rang four long times before Rooney picked up.

'That you, Talley? I saw you come back.'

For the space of three heartbeats, Talley said nothing. That had never happened before, but it took that time for Talley to push aside the anxiety that he knew would be in his voice. He could have nothing weak in his voice. Nothing that might warn Rooney or put him on guard.

'Talley?'

'Hello, Dennis. You there in the office, watching us?'

The shutters flicked open, then closed.

'I guess you are. Did you miss me?'

'I don't like that new guy, Maddox. He thinks I'm stupid, calling every fifteen minutes, pretending he wants to make sure we're all right, but it's to keep us awake. I'm not stupid.'

Talley felt himself grow calm now that he was back on the phone. He had hated it earlier today, but now the familiarity of it strengthened him, just him and the phone and the subject, a small self-contained world where he played a game against the voice on the other end. It surprised him that he felt a confidence that he hadn't known in years, a deep sense that he could control this world if not the larger one. He glanced up at the helicopters. Red and green angels.

'I came back tonight because we've got a big problem out here.'

Rooney hesitated as Talley knew he would; thinking. Talley knew that what he was about to say would surprise Maddox and Ellison, so he glanced at them and touched his lips. Then he filled the silence that Rooney left, firming his voice to show that he was serious and concerned.

'I need you to let me talk to Mr. Smith.'

'We been through that, Talley. Forget it.'

'I can't forget it this time, Dennis. These people out here, the Sheriffs, they think you won't let me talk to Mr. Smith or his children because they're dead. They think you've murdered them.'

'That's bullshit!'

Maddox and Ellison shifted next to him, staring. Talley felt the weight of their eyes but ignored them.

'If you don't let me speak with Mr. Smith, they are going to assume that he is in fact dead, and they are going to breach the house.'

Rooney started cursing and shouting that everyone was going to die and that the house would burn. Talley expected his reaction and let him vent.

Maddox gripped Talley's arm.

'What the hell are you saying? You can't say somethin' like that!'

Talley held up a hand, telling him to back off. He waited for a break in Dennis's rant.

'Dennis? Dennis, I'm telling you right now that I believe you, but they don't. This isn't up to me, son. I believe you. But unless you give me something to convince them, they're going in. Let me speak to him, Dennis.'

Talley was taking a big chance. If Smith was conscious and able to speak, Rooney might very well put him on the phone. If that happened, Talley would still try to get the information about the men in the car, but he knew the odds of that would be slim. Talley's only hope was that Smith was still unconscious. If Rooney would admit his condition, Talley had a shot at getting Smith released.

Rooney said, 'Fuck you and fuck them! If you try to come in here, these kids are gonna die!'

'Let me speak to him, Dennis. Please. They think he's dead, and they are going to come in.'

Rooney screamed, 'SHIT!'

Talley could hear the frustration in Rooney's voice. He waited. Rooney was silent and that meant he was thinking; he couldn't put Smith on the phone, but he was scared to admit that Smith was injured. Talley felt a surge of excitement, but hid it. He softened his voice, made it understanding and sympathetic. *We're both in this together, pal.*

'Is something wrong in there, Dennis? Is there a reason you can't put Smith on the phone?'

Rooney didn't answer.

'Talk to me, Dennis.'

Rooney took almost a full minute before he finally answered.

'He got knocked out. He won't wake up.'

Talley knew better than to ask how; it would put Rooney on the defensive, and Talley didn't want to do that. He had Smith's situation out in the open, so now he could try to get Smith. Maddox, still watching, raised his eyebrows in a question. Talley nodded, getting there; he repeated the admission for Maddox.

'So you're saying that Mr. Smith is unconscious. Okay, okay, I'm glad you're telling me this, Dennis. That explains things. Now we can deal with it.'

'They better not try to come in here.'

They, not *you.*

'I think we can work with this, Dennis. Are we talking about a head injury here? I'm not asking how this happened, but is that what's wrong with him?'

'It was an accident.'

'Is he breathing?'

'Yeah, but he's out cold. He can't talk.'

Now Talley had to move it to the next level. Now he had to get in the house, or get Smith out.

'Dennis, now I understand why you couldn't put him on, but you've got a guy in there who needs to be in the hospital. Let me come get him.'

'Fuck that! I know what you bastards will do, you'll rush the house.'

Rooney was scared. He was flat-out terrified.

'No. No, we wouldn't do that.'

'Fuck yourself, Talley. You ain't comin' in!'

Talley pressed harder. He knew that he could have suggested sending in a paramedic or a doctor, but he didn't want anyone going in; he wanted Walter Smith coming out.

'If you won't let us come in, then all you have to do is put him outside, right outside the front door.'

'I'm not stupid! I'm not gonna walk out the door with all the snipers you have out there!'

Talley saw movement to his side, Maddox and Ellison. He heard Maddox key his radio, telling someone to have the ambulance brought up.

'No one is going to shoot you. Just put him outside and we'll come get him. If you save his life, Dennis, it will help you when you get to court.'

'No!'

'That's all it takes, Dennis. Put him outside.'

Rooney's voice rose.

'No!'

'Save him.'

Rooney shouted again.

'No!'

'Help me help you.'

Rooney slammed down the phone.

'Dennis?'

Nothing. Rooney was gone.

'DENNIS?!'

Maddox and Ellison stared at him, motionless, waiting.

'What?'

Talley had been so close, but he had wanted it too much. He had pressed too hard. He had lost.

Dennis

Dennis slammed down the phone, then picked it up and smashed it on Smith's desk.

'That fuck! That fuck wants me dead!'

He was so angry that his head felt swollen and thick. Kevin paced in front of the television with his arms crossed, a nervous wreck. Kevin went to the couch and stared down at Walter Smith.

'We should let them have him. He's a lot worse.'

'*Fuck* them! They didn't give us a helicopter, did they?'

'What does that matter? Look at him, Dennis! I think he's having seizures.'

Smith would be still as a corpse, then he would suddenly jerk, his whole body twitching. Dennis couldn't look at him.

'You wouldn't know a seizure if it bit you on the ass.'

'*Look* at him. Maybe it's brain damage.'

Dennis went to the shutters. Nothing had changed since he'd looked the time before, or from the time before that: The cul-de-sac was filled with cops and cop cars, and more seemed to be coming. Dennis wouldn't admit it to Kevin, but he was scared. He was hungry and tired, and the smell of the gasoline in the entry was making him sick. His pockets bulged with the money he had stuffed in them.

Kevin came over to him.

'Dennis, he's dying. It's bad enough we got the Chinaman and that cop, this guy dies they'll add another murder charge.'

'Shut up, Kevin. Jesus.'

'We should talk to a lawyer like that cop said. We need a lawyer to cut us a deal. We can blame Mars.'

'Don't let him hear you!'

'I don't care if he hears!'

'Just calm down, Kevin. I'm working on it. I just need some food, is all. Some food and some time. We'll think of something. The girl is in there cooking.'

'How can you even think about eating? I'm about to puke.'

'I saw some Gaviscom in the bathroom. Eat that.'

'I want to sleep.'

'Would you shut the fuck up?! The cops will put you in jail, where you can sleep every night for the rest of your life!'

Dennis knew Kevin was right, but he tried not to think about it. Every plan he hatched had holes big enough to hide a house, and now the cops were threatening to break down the doors. Walter Smith twitched and trembled again. It looked like he was freezing to death, the way you'd shiver if you were sleeping on a block of ice. Dennis felt tears well in his eyes because he was so scared. Here he was, sitting on a million bucks, and he didn't know what to do.

Mars and the girl came in with the pizzas, Dennis thinking that maybe the food would help, but when the girl saw her father, she dropped the pizza and ran straight to her father.

'What's wrong with him? *Daddy?!*'

Dennis thought his head would burst.

She dropped down to her knees, leaning over her father but not touching him.

'Look at the way he's shaking. Why is he shaking like this? Aren't you going to do something?'

Kevin put on the pussy face.

'Dennis, he needs a doctor.'

Dennis wanted to smash him.

'No.'

The girl glared at him, screaming.

'He's ice-cold! Can't you see this? Don't you know he's dying?!'

Kevin stepped closer, in Dennis's face now, pleading.

'*Please*, Dennis. If he dies, we got another murder charge. We're fucked up bad enough.'

Dennis was scared. He didn't want the sonofabitch to die. He didn't want another murder charge.

Kevin picked up the phone.

'Call them. Let them have him.'

'No.'

'They'll like it that you're trying to help. They might even cut us some slack. Think about it, Dennis. *Think*.'

Kevin stepped closer, his whisper more than a plea.

'If those SWAT guys come in here, you'll never keep the money.'

Dennis glanced at Mars, who sat on the floor with a plate of eggs and pizza, eating. Mars met Dennis's eyes, then made a little smile like he knew it all along, like Dennis didn't have the balls to play it hard.

Fuck Mars.

Dennis wanted the money.

He took the phone and punched in Talley's number.

Talley

Talley was charging his phone off the cigarette lighter in Maddox's car when the phone rang. He tensed, a jag of fear jolting him because he thought it was the Watchman's Nokia.

Maddox said, 'That's your phone.'

Talley opened his phone.

'Talley.'

It was Rooney.

'Okay, Talley. If you want him, come get him. But just you.'

Talley had thought it was over, thought he had completely blown any chance at getting to Smith, but here was Rooney delivering him. Talley was dead, but now he lived again. He had a chance at Jane and Amanda!

Talley rolled to his knees and peered over the car's hood. He muted the phone to hiss at Maddox.

'Ambulance. He's coming out.'

Ellison said, 'Sonofabitch.'

Maddox went back on the hard line as Talley un-muted his phone.

'Okay, Dennis. I'm here. I'm with you. Let's figure this out.'

'There's nothing to figure out, goddamnit. Come get him. But you better keep SWAT outta here. That's the deal.'

'I can't carry him by myself. I'll have to bring someone else.'

'Fuckin' liar! You're going to try to kill me!'

'That won't happen, Dennis. You can trust me. Me and one other person and a stretcher. That's it.'

'Fuck you, Talley, *fuck you!* All right! You and one other guy, but that's it! You gotta strip down! I want you stripped! I gotta know you aren't carrying guns!'

Talley looked at Maddox and twirled his finger, telling Maddox to have the ambulance get here fast.

'Okay, Dennis. If that's what you want, that's what we'll do.'

'You'll keep'm outta here. That's the deal, right? We have a deal?'

'That's the deal.'

'I swear to Christ if those bastards try something these kids are gonna die! Everybody's gonna die.'

'Just take it easy. Work with me and no one has to die.'

'Fuck you!'

The connection popped in Talley's ear. Rooney was gone.

Talley stared at the house. Several moments passed before he lowered the phone; his hand was okay, but his ear hurt from the pressure. His sweatshirt was soaked, and the Colt cut into his belly. He felt numb.

Maddox stared at him, and Ellison smiled.

'Sonofa*bitch*. You kicked one free. That was great work, man. That was a *clinic.*'

Talley left them without a word. He climbed into the backseat, stripped off his clothes except for his underwear and shoes, and waited for the ambulance. In an earlier life Talley would have felt proud, but now he wasn't. He hadn't done it for Walter Smith. He was risking Smith's life, his own, and likely the children's in the house. He had done it for himself, and for Amanda and Jane.

16
Friday, 11:19 p.m.

Talley

Martin buzzed around him like an angry wasp. She had ridden up in the ambulance with an ER doctor named Klaus from Canyon Country Emergency.

'Wear a vest. Just strap it over your chest, he'll be able to see you're not armed.'

'The deal was that we would be stripped. I don't want to spook him.'

Klaus was a young, thin man in black-framed glasses. He introduced himself as he shook Talley's hand.

'I was told that we have a head trauma and possible gunshot wounds.'

'Let's hope not, Doctor.'

Klaus smiled awkwardly, embarrassed.

'I guess they sent me because I did two years at Martin Luther King down in South Central. You see everything down there.'

One of the paramedics, an overweight man named Bigelow, volunteered to go with Talley. Here was Bigelow, walking over from the ambulance in the dim light behind the front line, wearing only striped boxers with his clunky paramedic shoes and black socks up to his knees. Bigelow's partner, a woman named Colby, brought the stretcher.

Talley said, 'You ready?'

'Yes, sir. Good to go.'

Martin seemed irritated.

'You know it's stupid to agree to something like this. You were SWAT. You know you never expose yourself without protection. We could end up with two bodies out there.'

'I know.'

Talley didn't mention the day-care center. He folded his Colt into his sweatshirt, left it on Maddox's backseat with his clothes, then joined Bigelow. He wanted this thing to happen before Rooney changed his mind.

Talley called the house on his cell phone. Rooney answered on the first ring.

'Okay, Dennis. Put him outside. We're stripped, so you can see we're

737

unarmed. We'll wait in the drive. We won't approach the house until after you've closed the door.'

Rooney hung up without answering.

Martin said, 'I don't like this. Tactical people should recover this man.'

Talley ignored her, and glanced at Bigelow.

'Here we go. I'll walk in front of you going up to the door. Once we have him on the stretcher, I'll take the rear position coming out. Okay?'

'You don't have to do that.'

'It'll be fine.'

Talley and Bigelow went around the car and stepped in front of the lights. It was like passing into a world of glare. Stick-figure shadows moved into the mouth of the drive, then stopped, waiting. Talley could tell that Bigelow was frightened; he was probably worried because of what Martin had said.

'It's going to be all right.'

'Oh, sure. I know.'

'We'd look pretty silly if they put our picture in the paper.'

Bigelow smiled nervously.

Talley watched the house. First, the shutters opened like a narrowed eye. That would be Rooney, looking them over for weapons. Smith's front door opened, a crack at first, then wider. Talley sensed the difference in the line of officers behind him; their shuffling stopped, no one cleared their throat or coughed. The sound from one of the helicopters changed in pitch and a light swept to the door, offering nothing against the glare of the floodlights. It wasn't Dennis Rooney. Kevin and Mars Krupchek waddled out with Smith between them, put him on the front entry about six feet from the door, then returned to the house.

'Okay, let's do it.'

Talley went directly to Walter Smith. Here was this middle-aged man wearing a Polo shirt, stonewashed jeans, and sneakers, and men were willing to murder Jane and Amanda for something in his house. The contusion on the side of his head was visible even from the mouth of the drive.

Bigelow said, 'Let me set down by his head.'

Talley stepped away, letting the paramedic open the stretcher and lock out the frame. Talley kept his eyes averted from the shutters and did not try to look into the house. He watched Smith. He wanted to see some sign that Smith was waking, but the depth of Smith's sleep scared him. Smith trembled from the center of his body, and Talley grew frightened that the man might be in a coma.

'How's he look?'

Bigelow peeled back an eyelid, flashed a penlight in Smith's eye, and grunted.

'Pretty bad concussion for sure.'

Bigelow fingered Smith's neck, probing for a cervical injury, and seemed satisfied by what he found.

'Okay. We're good. We don't need a brace. I'll support his head and shoulders. You lift beneath his hips and knees. He's going to be heavier than you think, so be ready. On three. Three.'

They slid Smith onto the stretcher. Bigelow started fastening a strap across Smith's chest, but Talley stopped him.

'Don't bother with it. Let's get him out of here while we can.'

They moved straight down the sidewalk to the street and into the lights, where they were immediately surrounded by Hicks's tactical team. Klaus ran up alongside the stretcher, snapping at Bigelow.

'Why isn't this man's neck braced?'

'I didn't see any sign of cervical injury.'

'Goddamnit, he should've been braced anyway.'

Colby took over from Talley to help Bigelow. Ellison brought over Talley's clothes, and Talley pulled on his pants while they loaded Smith into the ambulance. Talley followed Klaus inside.

'I have to talk to him.'

'Hang on.'

If Klaus was shy and awkward before, now he was focused and intense. He peeled back Smith's eyelid and flashed a penlight in his eye just as Bigelow had done. Then he did the same with the other eye.

'We've got unequal pupilation. At best it's a severe concussion, but it could mean brain damage. We'll have to do plates and a CT scan at the hospital to know for sure.'

'Wake him. I need to talk to him.'

Klaus kept working. He checked Smith's pulse.

'I'm not going to wake this man.'

'I just need him for a few minutes. That's why I got him.'

Klaus pressed his stethoscope to Smith's neck.

'He's going to the hospital. He could have an intra-cranial hematoma or a fracture, or both. You get a pressure buildup in the brain, it can be bad.'

Talley leaned past Klaus. He took Smith by the face and shook him.

'Smith! Wake up!'

Klaus grabbed Talley's hand, trying to pull it away.

'What the fuck are you doing? Get away from him!'

Talley shook Smith harder.

'Wake up, goddamnit!'

Smith's eyes fluttered, one open more than the other. He didn't seem to be looking at Talley, so Talley leaned closer. The eyes seemed to focus.

Talley said, 'Who are you?'

Klaus pushed at him now.

'Let go of him. I'll have you brought up on charges, you sonofabitch.'

Smith's eyes lost their focus and closed. Talley took Klaus by the arm, trying to make him see.

'Use smelling salts, give him a shot, whatever. I just need a minute.'

Colby cranked the engine, and Talley slapped at the wall, shouting. '*Don't move this van!*'

Klaus and Bigelow both stared at him. Klaus slowly looked at Talley's hand gripping his arm.

'I'm not going to wake him. I don't even know that I can. Now let go of me.'

'We're talking about lives here. Innocent lives. I just need to ask him a few questions.'

'Let go of me.'

Talley stared into the hard, angry eyes. Tension knotted his face and neck. He held tight to Klaus's arm and thought about the Colt folded in his sweatshirt.

'Just one question. Please.'

The hard little eyes showed no mercy.

'*He can't answer you.*'

Talley stared at Smith's still form. So close. So close.

Klaus looked down at his arm again, Talley still squeezing tight.

'Let go of me, goddamnit. We're taking this man to the hospital.'

Martin was watching him from the door, Ellison and Metzger behind her. Talley released the doctor's arm.

'When is he going to wake up?'

'I don't know if he'll ever wake up. You get bleeding between the skull and brain, the pressure can build to such a degree that brain death can result. I don't know. Now stay in or get out, but just let us go.'

Talley looked at Smith again, feeling helpless. He climbed out of the ambulance and pulled Metzger aside.

'Who's still here? Which of our guys is still here?'

'Jorgy. I think Campbell is still –'

'Then Jorgenson stays here. I want you waiting in this guy's lap. I want to know the *second*, and I mean the second, that he wakes up.'

Metzger turned away, keying her shoulder mike for Jorgenson.

Talley walked back to Maddox's car for the rest of his gear. His chest heaved. He felt angry and closed. He had put everyone at risk, and Smith was beyond him. Smith couldn't talk. He stared at the house, wanting to do something, but there was nothing to do.

Talley felt himself hating Dennis Rooney, and wanted to kill him.

He turned away and saw Martin watching him. He didn't care.

Dennis

None of it looked real: Talley and the other guy in their underwear, carrying Smith away; Smith being loaded into the ambulance; the search-lights from the helicopters crisscrossing each other over the ground like light sabers. The pools of light were so bright that all the color was washed from the picture; the cops were gray shadows, the ambulance pink, the street blue. Dennis watched the ambulance work its way from the cul-de-sac, thinking only then that the ambulance could have been his ride out, that he could have made it a part of the deal, grab the suitcase with the money, tape his hand to a gun and the gun to Smith, then take over the ambulance and make them drive him south to the border. Why did all the best ideas come when it was too late?

Mars stepped up beside him with the same look he had for the Mexicans at work: I can see inside you; I know what you're thinking; you have no secrets from me.

'They would have killed you as soon as you got into the ambulance. Better to stay in here.'

Dennis glanced at Mars, then walked away, pissed that Mars found him so obvious. Mars was getting to be a pain in the ass. Dennis sat at Smith's desk and put up his feet.

'Staying here sucks, Mars. You might like it, but I want to get the hell out. I bought us some time, now we've got to figure this out. Any ideas?'

He looked from Mars to Kevin, but neither of them answered.

'Great. That's just fucking great. If anyone decides to help, just speak up.'

Dennis turned to the girl and spread his hands.

'All right. Your old man's out. You happy now?'

'Thank you.'

'I'm fuckin' starving. Go back in the kitchen and fix something else. This time don't throw it on the floor. And make some coffee. Make it strong. We're gonna be up all night.'

Mars took the girl back to the kitchen.

When they were gone, Dennis noticed that Kevin was staring at him.

'What?'

'We're not going to get out of here.'

'For chrissake! *Please!*'

'Mars and I don't care about the money. You won't let go of it and that's why we're still here. There's no way to get away with it, Dennis. We're surrounded. We're on fucking television. We're *fucked.*'

Dennis pushed out of the chair so quickly that Kevin jumped back. He was sick of dealing with their negativity.

'We're fucked until we think of a way out, asshole. Then we're not fucked, we're rich.'

Dennis stalked around the desk and went to the den. The smell of gasoline was strong there, drifting in from the hall, but he wanted a drink, and he wanted to be in the den. The den was his favorite room. The dark wood paneling and plush leather furniture made Dennis feel rich, like he was in the lobby of a fine hotel. And the bar itself was beautiful: beaten copper that looked bright and shiny and a thousand years old, bar cabinets

741

inlaid with frosted glass, and stainless steel fixtures gleaming with the overhead light. Dennis selected a bottle of Stolichnaya vodka, then found ice in a small refrigerator and glasses on a smoked glass shelf. He poured a short one, then went back around the bar to sit on a stool. Dennis peeled a hundred-dollar bill from the roll in his pocket and tossed it on the bar.

'Keep the change, m'man.'

Dennis drank most of the vodka, loving the way it raked his throat, a stiff belt that pushed its way into his head. He refilled his glass. The clean cold vodka burned his nose and made his eyes water. He rubbed his eyes, but couldn't make the water stop.

They lived in a one-bedroom apartment above an Exxon station, Dennis, age eleven, Kevin, two years younger, and their mother, Flo Rooney. Dennis didn't know her age then or now; their father was long gone, a pothead named Frank Rooney who fixed transmissions and didn't pay child support. Well, fuckit, they weren't married anyway; common-law.

Dennis shoved Kevin toward the bedroom, Kevin with big bug eyes like they were gonna pop from his head, scrambling backwards because he was scared. They were supposed to be sleeping; the world was dark.

'*They're doing it.*'

'*Nuh-uh. Stop saying that.*'

'*Can't ya hear'm? They're doin' the nasty. Let's go see.*'

They had lived in more apartments than Dennis could remember, some for just a week or two, once for almost a year; dingy places with stained ceilings and toilets that ran. Flo Rooney usually worked a job, once she worked two, and more than once she had none. There was never enough money. Flo was a short woman with a body like a bowling ball, Q-Tip legs, and bad skin. She liked her gin and smelled of Noxzema. When she got in her mopes and had too much gin, she would bitch to the boys that she didn't have enough money to keep them, that she would have to put them in a home. Kevin would cry, but Dennis would pray: Please, please, put me in the fuckin' home. *It was always about money.*

Dennis shoved Kevin toward their mother's bedroom door. Both boys were trying to be quiet because she was with a man she had brought home from the bar. This month she was working as a barmaid, next month it would be something else, but there was always a man. She called them her 'little pleasures.' Dennis called them drunks.

'*Don't ya want to see'm doin' it?*'

'*No!*'

'*You said you did! Listen to what he's doin' to her!*'

'*Dennis, stop! I'm scared!*'

The scent of sweat and sex hung sharp in the air, and Dennis hated her for it. He was jealous of the time she gave them, and humiliated by what she let them do, and by what she did to them. He was ashamed, but at the same time excited. Her gasping, grunting curses drew him.

He pushed Kevin again, this time more gently.

'*Go on. Then you'll know.*'

This time Kevin went, creeping to the door. Dennis stayed on their sleeper couch, watching. He wasn't sure why he was pushing Kevin so hard to see; maybe he wanted Kevin to hate her as much as he did. With their father on the bum and Flo working, Dennis usually had to see after his younger brother, making their breakfast and getting them to school, seeing that Kevin got home okay and making dinner. If Dennis had to be Kevin's father and mother, there wasn't room for another. Maybe that was it, or maybe he just wanted to punish her.

Kevin reached the door and peeked inside. Dennis knew that something nasty was going on because he could hear the man telling her what to do. She hadn't even bothered to close the door.

Kevin watched for the longest time, and then he stepped into the door, right out in the open where their mother could see.

Dennis whispered loudly.

'*Kev!*'

Kevin sobbed, then began to cry.

Inside the room, the man yelled, '*Sonofabitch! Get the hell outta here!*'

Kevin stumbled backward as the man came lurching through the door, naked and with a huge glistening erection. He was carrying his jeans.

'*I'll teach you to watch, you little shit!*'

He was a big man, his body white and arms dark, coarse and hairy with tattoos on his shoulders and a loose flabby gut. His eyes glowed bright red from booze and pot. He stripped a thick leather belt from the jeans, then chased after Kevin, swinging the belt. Its buckle was a great brass oval inlaid with turquoise. The belt came down, cracking across Kevin's back, and Kevin screamed.

Dennis drove into the man as hard as he could, flinging punches that had no effect, and now the belt was his, snapping across him over and over and over until all his tears were gone.

She never came out, and after a while the man went back into the room. Her little pleasure.

'Dennis?'

Dennis cleared his eyes, then slid off the bar stool.

'Be quiet, Kevin. I'm not leaving here until I can take that cash.'

Dennis went back to the office and unplugged the phone. There was no point in talking to the cops until he knew what to say. He wanted the money.

Ken Seymore

The Channel Eight news van was parked at the edge of the empty lot. The reporter was a pretty boy, couldn't have been more than twenty-five, twenty-six, something like that, who got off telling everyone he went to

USC. Trojan this, Trojan that, God's a Trojan. A Trojan was a fuckin' rubber, but Seymore didn't say that. The reporter pool complained all evening because there were no toilets; the local cops promised that a honeywagon was coming out, but so far, zip.

Seymore asked the guy if it would be all right to step behind their van, take the lizard for a walk.

The pretty boy laughed, sure, but watch where you step, they got a regular lizard trail back there. Dick. Seymore thought he was the kind of guy who ordered chocolate martinis.

Seymore stepped behind the van where no one could see him and did two spoons of crank. It hit the top of his head like a blast of cold air and made his eyes burn, but it kept him awake. It was after two and all of them were fighting the hours. Seymore noted that the Asian chick with the hot ass kept ducking into her SUV and had a fine set of the sniffles to show for it. A regular one-woman Hoover convention.

Coming out from behind the van, Seymore saw the Channel Eight reporter conferring with his producer and cameraperson, a man with hugely muscled arms. They looked excited.

Seymore said, 'Thanks, buddy.'

'No problem. You hear? They're getting one out of the house.'

Seymore stopped.

'They are?'

'I think it's the father. He's hurt.'

A siren spooled up, and they all knew it was the ambulance. Every camera crew in the lot hustled to the street in hopes of a shot, but the ambulance left from a different exit; the siren grew louder, peaked, then faded.

Seymore's phone rang as the siren dopplered away. He answered as he walked away, lowering his voice but unable to hide his irritation. He knew who it was; he started right in.

'Why the fuck I gotta hear this from a reporter? Fuckin' Smith comes out, forchrissake, and I gotta learn about it *last*?'

'Do you think I can get to a phone any time I want? I'm right out front in this; I have to be careful.'

'All right, all right. So tell me, was he talking? The guy here says he was hurt.'

'I don't know. I couldn't get close enough.'

'Did he have the disks? Maybe he had the disks.'

'I don't know.'

Seymore felt himself losing it. Fuckups like this could cost him his ass.

'If anyone should know, it's you, goddamnit. What the fuck are we paying you for?'

'They're taking him to Canyon Country Hospital. Go fuck yourself.'

The line went dead.

Seymore didn't have time to get pissed about it. He called Glen Howell.

Part Three

The Head

17

Pearblossom, California

Friday, 11:36 p.m.

Mikkelson and Dreyer

It was late when Mikkelson and Dreyer found Krupchek's trailer, a thirty-foot Caravan split at the seams, waiting for them at the end of a paved road in Pearblossom, a farm community of fruit orchards and day workers in the low foothills at the base of the Antelope Valley. That was Mikkelson's notion when they finally found the damned place, that it was waiting, wide, flat, and dusty, the way a desert toad waits for a bug.

Dreyer swiveled the passenger-side floodlight and lit up the place. Somewhere under the dust, it was pale blue going to rust.

Dreyer, more cautious by nature, said, 'You think we should wait for Palmdale?'

Mikkelson, anxious to get inside, said, 'Why'd we go to the trouble of getting the warrant, if we're gonna wait? We don't have to wait. Leave the light.'

Krupchek's road ran the gut of a shallow canyon between two low ridges. No streetlights, no cable TV, no nothing out here; they had phone service and power, but that was about it; the sun went down, it was *black*.

Mikkelson, tall and athletic, behind the wheel because she got carsick when Dreyer drove, got out first. Dreyer, short and square, came up beside her, the rocky soil crunching. Both had their Maglites. They stood there, staring at the trailer, both a little bit nervous.

'You think anyone is home?'

'We'll find out.'

'You think that's his car?'

'We'll run the tag when we finish inside.'

An eighties-era Toyota Camry, itself dusty and speckled with rust, sat outside the darkened trailer.

They were late getting here, having gone to the Rooneys' apartment first, where they'd had to dick around with his landlord and the goofy woman who lived above them, the stupid cow asking over and over if she was

747

going to be on the news. Mikkelson had wanted to slap her. When they had finally come up to Pearblossom, finding the trailer had been a bitch because it was dark and these little roads weren't marked, most of them, so they'd had to stop to ask directions three times. The last stop, a Mexican up from Zacatecas who worked for rich women as a stable groom, turned out to live next door. Here's the Mexican, a small man with his small wife and six or seven small children, saying that Krupchek kept to himself, never any sounds, never any trouble, had only spoken with Krupchek the one time someone had left a heart carved of bone on their step, the Mexican walking over that evening to ask if it was Krupchek, Krupchek saying no, then closing the door. No help there.

Mikkelson said, 'Let's go.'

They approached the trailer, then walked from end to end, just looking. It was like they didn't want to touch it, these creepy feelings you get.

Dreyer said, 'How do we get in? We look for a key or something?'

'I don't know.'

Here they had the warrant, but how did they get in? They hadn't thought of that.

Mikkelson rapped on the door with her Maglite, calling, 'Anyone in there? This is the police.'

She did that twice, getting no answer, then tried the door, one of those flimsy knobs that was tougher than it looked. It was locked.

'We could jimmy it, I guess.'

'Maybe we should try to find the landlord, have him open it.'

The Mexican had told them that all the land along the road was owned by a man named Brennert, who rented out the properties, mostly to migrant farmworkers.

'Shit, that'll take forever. We'll just pop the damned thing.'

Dreyer made a dogged face, unhappy.

'I don't want to pay for breaking it.'

'We've got the warrant, we're not going to have to pay.'

'You know the bastard might sue, not Krupchek but Brennert. You know how people are.'

'Oh, hell.'

Dreyer could be like that. He was terrified of getting sued. They talked about it all the time, how police officers were sued right and left these days just for doing their jobs, Dreyer hatching plans to put everything in his wife's name to protect it from the lawyers.

Mikkelson got the tire iron from their trunk, wedged it in the jamb by the knob, and popped the door. She put her back into it because these damned things were always stronger than they looked.

A smell like simmering mustard greens rolled out at them.

'Jesus, does this guy ever wash?'

Mikkelson leaned inside, feeling full of herself because this was the first time she had ever broken into a property with the full force of the law behind her and it felt pretty damned cool.

'Anyone home? Knock, knock, knock, it's your friendly neighborhood police.'

'Cut the crap.'

'Relax. There's no one in here.'

Mikkelson found the light switch and stepped inside. The interior of the trailer was dingy and cramped with tattered furniture in listless colors, stifling with accumulated heat.

Dreyer said, 'Well, okay, now what?'

But it was Dreyer who saw them first, having turned to the kitchen, Dreyer saying, 'Jesus, look at *that*.'

It would have been funny except there were so many of them; five or six boxes, maybe, or even ten or twelve, and Mikkelson would have laughed, making a joke, but the overwhelming sight of so many screamed insanity in a way that made her cringe. Later, the Sheriff's forensics people would count: seven hundred sixteen Count Chocula boxes, empty, flattened, and folded, all neatly bound with cord, stacked against the walls and on the kitchen counters and in the cupboards in great teetering towers, each box mutilated in exactly the same way, a single cigarette burn, charred and black, on the point of Count Chocula's nose. They would understand the burns later, too.

Dreyer, not getting the same creepy read as Mikkelson, went for the joke.

'You think he got something good for all these box tops?'

'Put on your gloves.'

'What?'

'The gloves. Let's be careful here.'

'It's cereal, for chrissake.'

'Just put on the gloves.'

'You think he ate it?'

'What?'

'All this cereal. You think he eats it? Maybe he just scrounges for the boxes. There must be a giveaway, you know, a contest.'

The Caravan was cut into three sections, the kitchen to their right, the living room where they entered, the bedroom to their left, all of it cramped and claustrophobic, littered with free newspapers, Jack-in-the-Box wrappers, soiled clothes, and beer cans; the little kitchen with a tiny sink, an electric range, a half-size refrigerator.

Mikkelson, ignoring Dreyer's speculations, moved left to the bedroom, pulling on the vinyl disposable gloves, wondering about the smell. At the door, she lit up the bed with her Maglite, saw stained sheets in a rumpled mess, paper and clothes on the floor, and the jars.

'Dreyer. I think we should call.'

Dreyer stepped up behind, his own light beam dancing into the room.

'Shit. What is that?' Dreyer's voice was hushed.

Mikkelson stepped in, holding out her light. Gallon-sized glass jars lined the walls, jars that you get when you buy the big pickles in one of those discount stores, lining the walls, stacked to windows that were latched tight to hold out the air. Shapes floated in the jars, suspended in yellow fluid. Some of the jars were so jammed with fleshy shapes there was almost no fluid.

'Goddamn. I think it's rats.'

'Jesus.'

Mikkelson squatted for a better look, wanting to cover her mouth, maybe put on a gas mask or something so she wouldn't have to breathe the fetid air.

'Shit, it's squirrels. He's got squirrels in here.'

'Fuck this. I'm calling.'

Dreyer left, keying his radio as he fled to the safer night air.

Mikkelson backed out of the room, stood in the door, thinking what to do. She knew she should go through Krupchek's things, look for identifying information, family phone numbers, things like that which might help Talley at the scene. She went back to the kitchen, looking for the phone, figuring to find what she needed there.

Mikkelson, thoroughly creeped out, stood by the phone but stared at the oven. She had this creepy feeling, she would later say, that's all there was to it; the smell, the squirrels, all those mutilated boxes. She took a deep breath as if she were about to plunge into cold water and jerked open the oven.

More Count Chocula.

Mikkelson laughed at herself. Ha ha, like what else did she expect to find?

Tension now gone, she opened the cupboards, one after the other, all with Count Chocula, bound and burned. She returned to the phone, but hesitated again, then found herself standing at the refrigerator.

Outside, Dreyer called, 'You coming out?'

'I'm okay.'

'Wait out here. The Sheriffs are sending detectives.'

'Dreyer?'

'What?'

'You ever notice, a refrigerator is like a white coffin standing on end?'

'Jesus, would you just come out?'

The refrigerator came open without effort, empty and strangely clean against the squalor of the trailer, no soda, no beer, no leftovers, just white enamel that had been lovingly polished. This refrigerator, Mikkelson would later testify, was the cleanest thing in the trailer.

A thin metal door was set in the top of the box; the freezer. Her hand had a mind of its own, reaching out, pulling the door. Her first thought was that it was a cabbage, wrapped in foil and Saran Wrap. She stared at it, stared hard, then closed the doors, never once, not once, tempted to touch that thing in the freezer.

Mikkelson left the trailer to wait with Dreyer in the hot night air, the two of them saying nothing, waiting for the Sheriffs, Mikkelson thinking, *Let them touch it.*

18
Santa Clarita, California
Friday, 11:40 p.m.

Glen Howell

Howell took three rooms in the Comfort Inn, all at the rear of the motel with outside entrances. Marion Clewes had the woman and the girl bound hand and foot in one room, tape over their eyes and mouths. Howell had checked to make sure they were secure, then went back to his own room even though the place smelled of cleaning products and new carpets. He didn't like being around Clewes.

Howell was sitting on his bed when he received the call from Ken Seymore, his heart trying to jump out of his nose as he heard that Walter Smith had been removed from the house.

'Did the cops go in? What the fuck is happenin' out there?'

'No one went in, it was just Smith coming out.'

'He just walked out?'

'They carried him. He's fucked up. One of the pricks in there must've beaten him. They took him out in an ambulance.'

Howell sat silent for a moment, thinking. Smith out while his kids were still inside was a problem. Smith in the hospital where they'd pop him full of dope, get him high, that was a problem, too.

'Did anything else come out of that house?'

'Nothing they're telling the news pool.'

Howell hung up and immediately phoned information for the Canyon Country Hospital's phone number and address, then called the hospital for directions off the freeway. He found the location in his *Thomas Guide* to double-check the directions, then he used his cell phone to call Palm Springs.

Phil Tuzee answered. Howell filled him in, then waited as Tuzee talked it over with the others. It was Sonny Benza who came back on the line.

'This is fuckin' bad, Glen.'

'I know.'

'He have the disks on him?'

'I don't know, Sonny. I just heard about this two minutes ago. It just happened. I'm going to send someone over.'

'Find out if he has the disks and see if he's been talking to anyone. That won't be good if he's talking. His kids are still in that house?'

'Yeah.'

'Sonofabitch.'

Howell knew they were all thinking the same thing; a man desperate to save his kids might say anything. Howell tried to sound hopeful.

'They say he's fucked up pretty bad. I don't know that for sure, Sonny, but if he's unconscious he can't be talking. The press pool out there is talking a concussion with possible brain injury. They make it sound like the guy's in a coma.'

'Listen, don't tell me anything you don't know for sure. I wipe my ass with rumors. You just hold your shit tight out there and take care of this.'

'It's tight.'

'That's why those pricks let him out, he's hurt? Maybe we'll get lucky and the fucker will die.'

'Talley talked them into letting him out.'

'You know something, Glen? That doesn't sound like your shit is tight. That sounds like the fuckin' wheels are comin' off. Do I have to come out there myself?'

'No way, Sonny. I got it.'

'I want those goddamned disks.'

'Yes, sir.'

'I don't want Smith talking, not to anyone, you understand?'

'I understand.'

'You know what I'm saying?'

'I know.'

'Okay.'

Benza hung up. It was their call; they had made it. Howell picked up the hotel phone and called two rooms down.

'Come over here. I got something for you to do.'

19

Friday, 11:52 p.m.

Talley

Talley checked the time, then took out the Watchman's Nokia and checked its charge. Crazy thoughts of holding a gun to the doctor's head flashed like pinwheels through his mind. Smith knew who was behind this. Smith knew who had his family. Talley paced the mouth of the cul-de-sac, his thoughts kaleidoscoping between Amanda and Jane, and Dennis Rooney. Maddox and Ellison had the phone again, but Dennis refused to answer their calls and had taken his own phone off the hook. Talley sensed that Dennis was working through something, but Talley didn't know what.

When the phone rang Talley again thought it was the Nokia, but it was his private line.

Larry Anders said, 'Chief? Can you talk?'

Anders's voice was low, as if he were trying to keep his words private. Talley lowered his own voice even though no one was near.

'Go, Larry.'

'I'm with Cooper here in the city planner's office. Man, that guy was pissed. He didn't want to get up.'

Talley took out his notepad.

'First tell me about the cell number. You run that yet?'

'I had to get a telephone for that. It's unlisted, so the cell company didn't want to release.'

'Telephone' meant that Anders had to get a telephonic search warrant.

'Okay.'

'The number is registered to Rohiprani Bakmanifelsu and Associates. It's a jewelry company in Beverly Hills. You want me to try to contact them?'

'Forget it. It's a dead end.'

Talley knew without hearing more that the cell number had been cloned and stolen. Since Bakmanifelsu hadn't yet deactivated it, he hadn't yet discovered the pirated activity on his account; the number had probably been cloned within his past billing period.

'What about the Mustang?'

'There's nothing, Chief. I ran wants for the past two model years. We got sixteen hits for cars that were still unrecovered, but nothing green came up.'

'Were any of them stolen today?'

'No, sir. Not even in the past month.'

Talley let it go.

'Okay. What about the building permits?'

'We can't find any of that, but we might not need'm. The planner knew the developer who opened York Estates, a man named Clive Briggs. It used to be nothing but avocado orchards out there.'

'Okay.'

'I just got off the phone with him. He says that the contractor who built the Smiths' house is probably at Terminal Island.'

Terminal Island was the federal prison in San Pedro.

'What do you mean, probably?'

'Briggs didn't know for sure, but he remembered the contractor. The guy's name was Lloyd Cunz. Briggs remembers because he liked the guy's work so much that he tried to hire him for another development he had goin', but Cunz turned him down. He was based in Palm Springs, he said, and they didn't want to take any more long-range jobs.'

'The contractor came all the way from Palm Springs?'

'Not just the contractor. He brought his crew: the carpenters, the cement people, plumbers, electricians, everybody. He didn't hire anyone locally. He said it was to keep up the quality of the work. Three or four years later, Briggs tried to hire Cunz again and learned that he'd been indicted on racketeering and hijacking charges. He was out of business.'

Talley knew that a builder wouldn't bring an entire construction crew that far unless he was building something he didn't want the locals to know about. Talley already had a sense of where this was going. Organized crime.

'Did you run Cunz through the computer yet?'

'Well, I'm still here at the planner.'

'When you get back to the office, run him and see what you get.'

'You're thinking these guys are in organized crime, aren't you?'

'Yeah, Larry. That's what I'm thinking. Let me know what you find.'

'I won't tell anyone.'

'No. Don't.'

Talley closed his phone and stared at the cul-de-sac. Walter Smith was almost certainly a member of organized crime. The Watchman was probably his partner, and the disks probably contained evidence that could put them away. The pressure he felt was like an inflating balloon in his head and chest. Talley knew that he was losing control of the scene, and of the events that would soon happen. When the Watchman's phony FBI agents arrived, he would have even less control, and that would put the people in the house in even greater jeopardy. The Watchman didn't care who died; he just wanted the disks.

Talley wanted the disks, too. He wanted to know what was on them.

These people would never have taken Talley's family if the disks in Smith's house didn't pose a terrible threat to them. They feared those disks being discovered more than they feared the investigation that would come from having kidnapped Talley's family. They figured they could survive the investigation, but they knew the disks would make them fall. That meant the disks named names.

Talley believed that he and his family would not survive the night. The men in the car, they could not afford to trust that the police couldn't build a case against them for what was happening here. They would not take that chance. Talley was absolutely certain that as soon as the Watchman had the disks, he would murder all three of them. Talley wanted the disks first. He thought he knew how to get them.

Talley trotted into the cul-de-sac to join Maddox and Ellison at their car.

'He answer your calls yet?'

Ellison sipped black coffee from a Styrofoam cup.

'Negative. Phone company says he's still got it unplugged.'

'You guys have a P.A. in this car?'

'No. What're you thinking?'

Talley duck-walked to the lone Bristo car that remained in the street. He grabbed the mike, then flipped on the public address system. Maddox had followed him over, curious.

'What are you doing?'

'Sending a message.'

Talley keyed the mike.

'This is Talley. I need you to call me.'

His voice echoed over the neighborhood. The officers around the perimeter glanced at him.

'If it's safe, call me.'

Talley didn't expect Rooney to call. He wasn't talking to Rooney.

Rooney's voice answered from the house.

'Fuck you!'

Ellison laughed.

'It was a good try.'

Maddox said, 'What was that about being safe?'

Talley didn't answer. He tossed the microphone into the car, then crept to the far side of the cul-de-sac, where he sat on the curb behind the patrol cars. He wanted the boy. He hoped that Thomas would understand that Talley had been asking him to call.

His phone rang almost at once.

'Talley.'

It was Sarah, sounding excited.

'Chief, it's the little boy again.'

Talley's heart raced. If Smith couldn't tell him who had his family, maybe the disks could.

'Thomas? You okay, son?'

The boy sounded calm.

'I wasn't sure you were talking to me. Is my daddy okay?'

This time Thomas sounded even more hushed than before, his voice a whisper. Talley turned up the volume on his phone, but still could barely hear him.

'He's in the hospital over in Canyon Country. What about you and your sister? Are you all right?'

'Yeah. She's not in her room anymore. They took her downstairs. I thought they were doing something bad to her, but they didn't know how to use the microwave.'

'Are you in any danger right now?'

'Uh-uh.'

Talley stared out of the cul-de-sac. The Sheriff's tactical units were in their positions behind the radio cars. Hicks and Martin would be in the command van, waiting for something to happen. Talley remembered his first day with SWAT, how a sergeant-supervisor told him that SWAT stood for Sit, Wait, and Talk. Talley's eyes welled as he fought to control his fear. He put his thoughts on the children in the house. If Talley thought either Thomas or Jennifer was in immediate mortal danger, he would launch the breach. He would launch without hesitation. He believed that they were not.

'How's your battery on that cell phone?'

'Ah, it's showing half a charge, maybe a little less. I turn it off when I'm not using it.'

'Good. Can you plug it into a charger when you're not using it?'

'Uh-uh. All the chargers are downstairs. My mom does that 'cause everyone else forgets.'

Talley worried that if the boy's battery failed, they would lose communication, but all he could do was press ahead and move fast.

'Okay, Thomas, turn it off when we're not talking and conserve as much power as possible, okay?'

'Okay.'

'Your dad has business partners. Do you know who they are?'

'Uh-uh.'

'He ever mention names?'

'I don't remember.'

'Was he working in his office today?'

'Uh-huh. He was trying to finish something because a client was coming to pick it up.'

Talley had trouble taking it to the next level, but he knew that this boy was his wife's and daughter's only chance.

'Thomas, I need your help with something. It might be easy or it might be dangerous. If you think those guys in there could find out and hurt you, then I don't want you to do it, okay?'

'Sure!'

The boy was excited. He was a boy. He didn't understand risk.

'Your dad has a couple of computer disks. I'm not sure, but they're probably on his desk or in his briefcase. He was probably working with them today. They're called Zip disks. You know what that is?'

Thomas made a derisive snort.

'I've had a Zip drive for years, Chief. Jeez. Zip disks are big and thick. They hold more information than regular disks.'

'These disks are labeled disk one and disk two. When you're downstairs in the office again, could you get to your dad's desk? Could you find those disks and try to see whose files they are?'

'No, they wouldn't let me go to the desk. Dennis makes me sit on the floor.'

The slim hope that Talley had felt only moments before withered. Then Thomas went on.

'But I might be able to sneak into the office if they're not around. Then I could just swipe the disks and open them on my computer up here in my room.'

'I thought they locked you in your room.'

'They do, but I can get out.'

'You can?'

Talley listened as Thomas described being able to move through the crawl space in the eaves and attic, and how he was able to emerge in different parts of the house through access hatches.

'Thomas, could you get to his office that way, through the crawl space?'

'Not into his office, but I can get into the den. There's a service door in the wine cellar behind the bar. It's right across from my dad's office. My mom says she can always tell when he sneaks across one time too many.'

Talley's hope surfaced again, but it was dampened by the knowledge that he could not allow this child to risk his life.

'That sounds too dangerous.'

'It won't be if they don't see me. Mars spends most of his time in the office, but Kevin is back by the French doors. Dennis walks around a lot. He stays in the safety room sometimes, the one where all the monitors are. But once I'm in the den, all I have to do is sneak across the entry and go to my dad's desk. That wouldn't take any time at all.'

Talley thought it through, trying not to let the need he felt cloud his judgment. He would have to get all three subjects away from that area of the house. He would have to blind the cameras in case one or all of the subjects were in the safety room with the monitors.

'If I could get Rooney and the others away from the office, do you think you could get the disks without being caught?'

'No problemo.'

'Could you do it in the dark?'

'I do stuff like that almost every night.'

Thomas laughed when he said it. Talley didn't laugh. He was supposed to help this child; now he wanted this child to help him. He felt as much a hostage as Thomas or Jane, and hoped that he could forgive himself for what he was about to do.

'All right, son. Let's figure this out.'

The night air was so clear that the houses and cars and cops in the street all seemed etched in glass. House lights, street lamps, and the red flares of cigarettes were hard sharp points of glare; overhead, the helicopters floated against the star field like nighthawks balanced on the sky, waiting for something to die. Talley checked his watch and knew the Watchman would call again soon. Thomas was still up in his room and the sister was still cooking, but that could change at any moment. Talley didn't have much time.

Talley found Jorgenson and brought him to the Department of Water and Power truck. The DWP technician, a young guy with a shaved head and a braided chin beard, was stretched across the bench seat of his truck, sleeping. Talley shook his foot.

'Can you cut the power to the house?'

The service tech rubbed at his face, blotchy with sleep.

'I could do that, yeah. Good to go.'

'Not now. You turn it off, that means all the power in the house goes off, not just in part of the house?'

Talley couldn't afford a mistake, and neither could Thomas.

The tech slid out of his truck. The manhole was open. A short aluminum fence circled it as a warning.

'Not just the one house, the entire cul-de-sac. I control the branch line from here. I cut the juice, it's all going dead. If I set up there in the cul-de-sac I could cut it just to a single house, but they told me out here.'

'Out here is fine. How long does that take, to cut the power?'

'On-off, like flipping a switch.'

'The phones won't be affected?'

'I got nothin' to do with that.'

Talley left Jorgenson with the technician, then radioed Martin to have Hicks and Maddox meet him at the command van. Martin answered stiffly.

'Listen, I appreciate that you talked Rooney into releasing Mr. Smith, but then you walked away without a word. You want command, you have to stay available. We might have needed to clear an action, but you weren't here.'

Talley felt defensive, but also resentful that she was calling him on this and wasting time.

'I didn't walk away. I was with Maddox and Ellison, and then I made some calls.'

He didn't tell her that he had spoken with Thomas.

'You have command of this action, but please don't try any more stunts without including me in the loop. If you want my cooperation, then you have to keep me informed.'

'What are you talking about?'

'I heard you on the public address, ordering Rooney to call you. That's why we have negotiators.'

'Maddox was right beside me.'

'He claims you did that without consulting him.'

'Can we talk about this later, Captain? Right now I want to deal with Rooney.'

Martin agreed to have Hicks and Maddox meet him in the command van. When Talley arrived, he still did not tell them that he had spoken with Thomas again, nor the true reasons for everything he was about to do.

'We know that Rooney is sensitive to the perimeter. I want to cut the power to the house, then shake him up with a Starflash to make him start talking.'

A Starflash was a shotgun-fired grenade built of seven to twelve submunitions that exploded like a string of powerful firecrackers. It was used to disorient armed subjects during a breach.

Hicks crossed his arms.

'You're going to fire into the house with the gas in there?'

'No, outside. We need to get his attention. The last time I pushed the perimeter, we didn't have to call him because he called us.'

Martin glanced at Maddox. Maddox nodded. So did Hicks.

Martin shrugged, then looked back at Talley.

'I guess you're in command.'

They were on.

Thomas

Thomas listened at his door. The hall was quiet. He edged back along the walls to his closet, and then into the crawl space. He stopped to listen at each vent. Jennifer was still in the kitchen, but he couldn't hear anyone else. All he needed was a laugh or cough or sneeze to fix their locations, but he heard nothing.

Thomas's house was shaped like a short, wide U with the wide base of it facing the cul-de-sac and the stubby arms reaching toward the pool. Most of the crawl space followed the inside of the U except for a branch into a dead space above the wine cellar. Thomas had always thought it weird that they called it a cellar when it was just a little room behind the bar in the den.

It wasn't easy to reach. The wine cellar had its own air-conditioning system, a single compressor that hung in the dead space, suspended from the rafters by four chains and filling the crawl space with its width. Thomas had to wiggle under the compressor to reach the hatch on the far side; there was no way around. Thomas had squeezed under it before, but not often, and he was smaller then. He lay on his back and inched under. Flat like that, his nose still scraped the compressor's smooth flat bottom. It smelled damp.

When he reached the hatch side óf the compressor he was wet with sweat. The dust that covered him turned to slick mud. It had taken a lot longer to get under it than he thought.

Thomas listened at the access hatch. After a few seconds, he slowly lifted the hatch. The wine cellar was empty and dark. It was a long narrow room lined with floor-to-ceiling wine racks, kept at a chilly fifty-two degrees. Thomas clicked on his flashlight, wedged it in the rack against one of the bottles, then turned himself around to dangle his feet and feel for footing. In a few moments he had reached the floor.

He eased open the door. The den beyond was bright with light. He could hear the TV in his father's office across the hall and Jennifer in the kitchen. He heard a male voice, but he couldn't tell if it was Dennis or Mars; he was pretty sure it wasn't Kevin.

The den was a cozy, wood-paneled room that his father used for business meetings and smoking cigars. Two dark leather couches faced each other across a coffee table, and the shelves were filled with books that his dad liked to read for fun, old books about hunting in Africa and science fiction novels that his father told him were worth a lot of money to collectors. A bar lined by four leather stools filled one side of the room. It was the one room in the house where Thomas's mom let his father smoke, though she made him close the doors when he had the stogies fired up. Thomas's father liked calling them 'stogies.' It made him smile.

All Thomas had to do to reach the office was cross the den to the double doors, then run across the hall. To his right would be the front door; to his left, the entry hall that led to the kitchen and back of the house.

Thomas took out his cell phone and turned it on.

He called Chief Talley.

Talley

Talley checked his radio.

'Jorgenson?'

'Here, Chief.'

'Stand by.'

Talley was at the rear of Smith's property with a Sheriff's tac officer named Hobbs. Hobbs had a Remington Model 700 sniper rifle fitted with a night-vision scope. The chamber was clear and the magazine empty. Talley carried a shotgun fixed with the Starflash grenade.

'Let me see.'

Talley took the rifle from Hobbs and focused the scope on the French doors. He had been peering over the top of the wall for almost six minutes, waiting for Thomas to call. Jennifer and Krupchek were in the kitchen. He thought Kevin was in the family room, but he wasn't sure. Dennis passed through the kitchen twice. He had exited toward the master bedroom three minutes earlier and had not returned. Talley thought he was probably in the safety room, watching the perimeter on the monitors.

Talley's phone rang. He was expecting it, but he wasn't ready for it. He jumped, startled.

Hobbs whispered, 'Easy.'

Talley handed the rifle back to Hobbs, then answered, his voice low. 'Talley.'

Thomas whispered back at him.

'Hi, Chief. I'm in the den.'

Talley watched the shadows play on the French doors.

'Okay, bud. You ready? Just like we said?'

'Yeah. I won't get caught.'

'If there's any chance – any! – you get back up to your room.'

Talley felt like a liar even saying it. The whole thing was a chance.

'Here we go.'

Talley keyed his shoulder mike.

'Kill the lights.'

The house plunged into darkness.

Dennis

Dennis sat at Walter Smith's desk, watching television. Kevin was back by the French doors, and Mars had the girl in the kitchen. All but two of the local stations had resumed regular programming, breaking in every few minutes with an aerial shot of York Estates, but the national cable channels didn't bother. Dennis felt slighted. He watched MTV with the sound low, black guys with blond hair pretending to be gangsters. He pointed his pistol at them, try this, motherfuckers.

Dennis had progressed from vodka on the rocks to vodka from the bottle, racking his brain for a way he could escape with the money. He was pissed off and frustrated, and grew scared that Kevin was right: that he wouldn't be able to get away with the cash, and that he would go back to being just another shitbag in a cell. Dennis took another hit of the vodka, thinking that he'd rather be dead. Maybe he should just run. Stuff his pockets with as much cash as possible, torch the friggin' house like Mars said, then duck through the little window into the oleander and run like a bat out of hell. They would probably machine-gun him before he got ten feet, but what the hell, it was better than being a turd.

'Shit.'

Dennis left the office, went back to the bedroom, and put the suitcase on the bed. He stared at the cash. He touched the worn bills, silky smooth and soft. He wanted it so badly that his body trembled. Cars, women, clothes, dope, copper bars, Rolex watches, fine food, boats, homes, freedom, happiness. Everybody wanted to be rich. Didn't matter who you were or where you came from or how much money you had; everyone wanted more. It was the American Dream. Money.

The notion came to Dennis like a rush of Ecstasy as he stared at the money: Cops are poor. Cops wanted to be rich like everyone else. Maybe he could split the loot with Talley, trade cash for safe passage to Mexico, work out a scam so that the other cops wouldn't know, something like pretending to swap the hostages for Talley so that the two of them could drive down to TJ together, laughing all the way because the other cops wouldn't dare try to assassinate him if they thought Talley's life hung in the balance. He would even toss in Kevin and Mars; let'm have someone to swing for the Chinaman. Dennis grew excited as he spun through the possibilities. Everyone knew that cops didn't make shit for a living. How far would Talley go for a hundred thousand dollars? Two hundred thousand? A half a million?

Dennis decided to call Talley right away. He was halfway back to the office, thinking how best to persuade Talley that he could be a wealthy man, when the house died. The lights went out, the TV stopped, the background hum that fills all living homes vanished.

Kevin shouted from the other side of the house.

'Dennis? What happened?'

'It's the cops! Get those fuckin' kids!'

Blind in the darkness, Dennis rushed forward, following the wall. He expected to hear the doors crashing open at any second, and knew his only chance was to reach the girl or her fat brother.

'Kevin! Mars! Get those kids!'

Milky light from the French doors filled the family room. Kevin was behind the sofa; Mars was in the kitchen, holding the girl by her hair. Mars was smiling, the crazy bastard. Like this was fun.

'Told you they'd cut the power.'

Talley's amplified voice echoed through the house, not from the street this time, but from the backyard.

'Dennis? Dennis Rooney?'

Dennis wondered why Talley was behind the house.

'Dennis, it's time to talk.'

Then the backyard erupted: Explosions jumped and careened over the surface of the water like automatic gunfire. Star-bright flashes lit the backyard like a Chinese New Year parade. The world was going to hell.

Dennis threw himself behind the kitchen counter, waiting for it to end.

Thomas

Thomas pushed out of the wine cellar as soon as the lights went off, slipped around the end of the bar, and scurried to the double doors. Dennis and Kevin were shouting, their voices coming from the family room. He knew he wouldn't have much time.

Thomas got down on his hands and knees, and peeked through the doorway. Across the hall, his father's office flickered with light from the candles. Thomas leaned farther out into the entry to see if anyone was coming. The hall was empty.

No guts, no glory.

Thomas ran across the hall into his father's office just as Chief Talley's voice boomed through the house. He knew that something loud was going to go off, so he tried to ignore all that. He concentrated on listening for footsteps.

Thomas went directly to the computer on his father's desk. He had brought his flashlight, but the candles gave enough light so that he didn't need it. The desk was scattered with papers, but he didn't see any disks. He checked the computer's Zip drive. It was empty. He lifted the papers around the computer and keyboard, but he didn't see any disks there, either.

A series of explosions cut through the house like a giant string of firecrackers. Thomas thought Dennis was shooting. Kevin shouted something, but Thomas didn't understand him. He was scared that they were on their way. He ran to the door to go back into the den, but stopped at the hall, listening. His heart pounded so loud he could barely hear, but he didn't think they were coming.

Chief Talley had told him not to spend more than a minute or two. He didn't have much time. He had used too much already.

Thomas looked across the entry hall to the safety of the den, then glanced back at the desk. A picture flashed in Thomas's memory: Earlier that day, after all the shooting, his father had tried to talk Dennis into getting a lawyer and giving up; he had gone to his desk, placed the disks in a black case, and put the case into the drawer. The disks were in the drawer!

Thomas went back to the desk.

Dennis

The back of the house exploded with noise and light as if the Marines were hitting the beach. Dennis saw cops at the wall, lit by the glare from their lights, but they didn't rush the house.

Dennis thought, *What the fuck?*

Talley's voice echoed from the backyard.

'It's time to talk, Dennis. Me and you. Face-to-face. I want you to come out, just you, I'll meet you and we'll talk.'

Kevin scrambled into the kitchen on all fours, fast, like a cartoon.

'What are they doing? What's going on?'

Dennis didn't know. He was confused and suspicious, and then suddenly very afraid.

'Mars! Those fuckers are trying to blindside us! See what they're doing in front!'

Dennis grabbed the girl from Mars, who lurched to his feet and went down the hall.

Thomas

The black leather case was a soft black leather folder about the size of a compact disk. The candlelight behind the desk was too dim to see into the drawer, so Thomas turned on his flashlight, cupping the lens to hide most of the light.

The case was in the top drawer.

It opened like a book. Each side had pockets to hold disks. Two disks were in the right pockets, labeled just as Chief Talley had described, disk one and disk two. Thomas was closing the drawer when he heard footsteps coming fast down the hall.

Thomas wanted to run, but it was too late.

The footsteps came *fast!*

They were coming to the office!

They were at the door!

Thomas turned off his flashlight and ducked under the desk. He pulled himself into a tight ball, hugging his knees, and he tried not to breathe.

Someone was in the room.

His father's desk was a great oak monster, heavy and ancient and as big as a boat (his dad jokingly called it the *Lexington,* after the aircraft carrier). It sat on curvy legs that left a small gap between the desk and the floor. Thomas saw feet. He thought it was Mars, but he couldn't be sure.

The feet went to the window.

Thomas heard the shutters snap open. Light from outside poured into the room. The shutters snapped closed.

The feet stayed at the shutters. Thomas imagined he must be peeking through the cracks.

Dennis shouted from the back of the house.

'What in hell's going on out there?'

It was Mars in the room. He stood at the shutters without moving.

'Goddamnit, Mars!'

The feet stepped away from the window, but Mars didn't leave. The feet turned toward the desk. Thomas tried to squeeze himself smaller. He hugged his legs so tight that his arms hurt.

The feet took a step toward the desk.

'Mars! What the fuck are they doin'?'

The feet walked to the end of the desk. Thomas tried to close his eyes; he tried to look away, but he couldn't. He watched the feet as if they were snakes.

'*Mars!*'

The feet turned and left. Thomas followed them with his ears, down the hall, away, gone.

Thomas scrambled from under the desk and went to the door. He peeked down the hall, then ran across to the den. He heard Chief Talley talking over the public address system as he pushed into the wine cellar, climbed the racks, and found the safety of the crawl space.

Talley

Talley knew that Rooney and the others would be panicked. They would believe that Talley had launched a breach and Dennis or one of the others would probably run to the front of the house to see what the Sheriffs were doing. Talley had to keep their attention focused here at the back of the house. On him.

'Is he still in the kitchen?'

Hobbs was peering through the night-vision scope.

'Yeah, him and the girl. He's trying to see us, but he can't see past the lights. The big one went down the hall. I don't see the brother.'

Talley keyed the portable P.A.

'We are *not* breaching the house, Dennis. We need to talk. Me and you. Face-to-face. I'm coming out to the pool.'

Martin and Hicks hustled toward him through the shadows. Martin wasn't happy.

'What face-to-face? We didn't discuss that.'

'I'm going out.'

Talley dropped the P.A. and heaved himself over the wall before she could say anything more. He wanted to draw Rooney's attention away from the front of the house even if it meant offering himself up to do it.

Martin's voice followed him over the wall.

'Damnit, Talley, all you'll do is make yourself a target.'

Talley walked to the edge of the pool and raised his voice.

'I'm unarmed. I'm not going to strip for you this time, so take my word for it. I'm unarmed, and I'm coming alone.'

Talley held his hands out from his sides, open palms forward, and walked toward the house along the side of the pool. A dark raft floated effortlessly on the water. A towel was spread on the deck, the radio that had played earlier silent, its batteries dead.

He reached the end of the pool nearest the house and stopped. A flashlight lay on the kitchen floor, its beam cutting a white slash that bounced off the counters. Talley raised his hands higher. Again, the bright lights behind him cast his shadow toward the house. It looked like a crucifix.

'Come out, Dennis. Talk to me.'

Dennis shouted from the house, his voice muffled through the closed French doors.

'You're fucking crazy!'

'No, Dennis. I'm tired.'

Talley walked closer.

'No one's going to hurt you. Not unless you hurt those kids.'

Talley stopped outside the French doors. He could see Dennis and Jennifer plainly now. Dennis held the girl with one hand, a pistol with the other. A shadow moved to Talley's left, deep in the family room, and Talley saw a slender figure. Kevin. He looked like a child. On the other side of the kitchen, opposite the family room, a hall disappeared into the house. Talley saw a flickering glow from a door. A large shape blocked the light, growing in the shadows. That would be Krupchek. Talley felt a well of relief; wherever the boy was, they didn't have him. He had to keep them focused. He spread his hands wider. He went closer.

'I'm standing here, Dennis. I'm looking at you. Come out and let's talk.'

Talley heard them talking, Dennis calling Kevin into the kitchen. Krupchek stood at the mouth of the hall now, floating in the darkness. He held something in his hands, a flashlight, a gun, Talley couldn't tell.

Dennis got to his feet and came to the French doors. He looked out past Talley, then tried to see the sides of the house, probably thinking he would be rushed if he opened the doors. Talley spoke calmly.

'No one here but me, Dennis. You have my word.'

Dennis placed his gun on the floor, then pushed open the door and stepped out. Talley knew that people always looked heavier in pictures, but Rooney was shorter and thinner than Talley would have guessed from the videotape, and younger.

Talley smiled, but Rooney didn't smile back.

'How ya doin', Dennis?'

'Had better days.'

'This has been a long one, I'll hand you that.'

Dennis tipped his head toward the far wall.

'You got a sniper out there, gonna shoot me?'

'If you tried to grab me, they probably would. Otherwise, no. We could have shot you from the wall if we wanted to do that.'

Dennis seemed to accept that.

'Can I come out there, closer to you?'

'Sure. It's all right.'

Dennis stepped away from the door and joined Talley out by the foot of the pool. Dennis took a deep breath, looking up at the stars as he let it out.

'Good to be outside.'

'I guess.'

Talley said, 'I'm going to lower my arms, okay?'

'Sure.'

Talley could see Kevin still with the girl in the kitchen and Krupchek still in the hall. The boy was inside somewhere, getting the disks. Talley hoped it wouldn't take long.

Talley said, 'We've been at this a long time now. What are you waiting for?'

'Would you be in a hurry to go to prison for the rest of your life?'

'I'd be doing everything I can to get the best deal possible. I'd let these people go, I'd cooperate, I'd let a lawyer do my talking. I'd be smart enough to realize that I'm surrounded by police officers and I'm not getting out of here except through their good graces.'

'I want that helicopter.'

Talley shook his head.

'It's what I said before, where's it going to land? I can't give you a helicopter. That's not going to happen.'

'Then a car. I want a car to take me to Mexico, a car and an escort and a free pass south of the border.'

'We've been through that.'

Rooney seemed to be working himself up to something. He waved his arm in a flash of anger.

'Then what fuckin' good are you?'

'I'm trying to save your life.'

Dennis glanced back into the house. Talley watched him, thinking that Rooney showed the day's strain. Finally, Rooney faced him again and lowered his voice still more.

'Are you a rich man?'

Talley didn't answer. He didn't know where Rooney was taking this. He had learned to let them get wherever they were going on their own.

Rooney patted his pocket.

'Can I reach in here, show you something?'

Talley nodded.

Rooney stepped closer. Talley couldn't make out what Rooney took from his pocket at first, but then he saw that it was money. Rooney seemed to be trying to shield it so that only Talley could see.

'That's fifty one-hundred-dollar bills, Chief. Five thousand dollars. I got a whole suitcase of this stuff in the house.'

Rooney pushed the bills back into his pocket.

'How much would it be worth to you, getting me out of here? A hundred thousand dollars? You could drive me down to Mexico, just me and you, no one the wiser, just tell the others that was the deal we made without mentioning any money. I wouldn't tell. They got money in this house, Chief. More money than you've ever seen in your life. We could carve it up.'

Talley shook his head.

'You picked a bad house to hole up in, Dennis.'

'Two hundred thousand, cash, hundred-dollar bills, right in your pocket, no one needs to know.'

Talley didn't answer. He wondered about Smith, what he did here in the middle of nowhere, here in the safe, anonymous community of Bristo Camino, with so much cash and information in his house that this kid was willing to die for it and the men in the car were willing to kill for it. Do you ever really know your neighbors?

'Give up, Dennis.'

Rooney wet his lips. His eyes flicked past Talley again, then back.

'You tryin' to drive up the price? Okay, three hundred. Three hundred thousand dollars. Could you ever earn that much? You can have Mars and Kevin. Fuckin' bust *them*. Make that part of the deal.'

'You don't know what you're dealing with. You can't buy your way out of this.'

'Everybody wants money! Everybody! I'm not giving this up!'

Talley stared at him, wondering how far to go. If Rooney quit now, Amanda and Jane might pay for it. But if Rooney quit now, walked out right now, Talley would have the disks. Once the Watchman's people arrived, Talley might not have the chance.

'This house isn't what you think it is. You believe some guy has this kind of cash just laying around in his house?'

'There's a million bucks in there, maybe *two* million! I'll give you half!'

'The man you sent to the hospital, Walter Smith, he's a criminal. That money belongs to him.'

Rooney laughed.

'You're lying. What a crock of shit.'

'He has partners, Dennis. This is their house, and they want it. The way I'm offering is the only way out for you.'

Rooney stared at him, then rubbed at his face.

'Fuck you, Talley. Just fuck you. You think I'm an idiot.'

'I'm telling you the truth. Give up. Work with me here, and at least you'll have your life.'

Rooney sighed, and Talley could see the sadness settle over him like a cloak.

'And what's that worth?'

'Whatever you make of it.'

'I'll go back in now. I'll think about it and give you my answer tomorrow.'

Talley knew that Dennis was lying. Talley had a sense for when they would give up and when they wouldn't, and Rooney had hold of something he couldn't turn loose.

'Please, Dennis.'

'Fuck off.'

Rooney backed to the door, then stepped inside and pulled it closed. The darkness inside swallowed him like dirty water.

Talley turned back to the officers lining the wall and walked away, praying that Thomas had the disks and was safe. Rooney wasn't the only one holding onto something he couldn't turn loose.

20
Saturday, 12:04 a.m.

Thomas

Thomas dripped with sweat. His knees were cut from the rafters, and, where streaks of sweat washed the cuts, they burned. Thomas didn't care. He was excited and happy – dude, he was *pumped!*; this was the best sneak ever, better than any he'd made with Duane Fergus!

With the power off, Thomas didn't have to worry about being seen on the monitors. He pushed through the hatch into his closet, and crossed the room to his computer. He took the computer apart and lugged it to the floor at the foot of his bed so that he wouldn't be seen by the camera when the power returned. His hands were so sweaty that he almost dropped the screen and caught it on his knee.

The lights came on without warning. Thomas worried that the turds would probably come upstairs to check on him, so he hurried to load the first disk.

The file icon that appeared was unnamed. He double-clicked on the icon to open it. A list of corporate names appeared that Thomas didn't know anything about. He opened a random file, but saw only tables and numbers. Thomas felt a stab of fear that he had snatched the wrong disks even though these were the *only* disks. Nothing that he saw made sense to him, but these were the disks Chief Talley wanted, so maybe the Chief would understand.

Thomas stopped in his work to listen for squeaks. The hall was quiet.

Thomas turned on his phone again, but this time the power indicator showed that less than half the power remained. He was down to almost a quarter of a charge.

Thomas pushed his redial button to call Chief Talley.

Talley

Talley climbed back over the wall where Martin and Hicks were waiting for him. Martin was angry.

'That was really dumb. What do you think you accomplished?'

Talley hurried away without answering her. He didn't want her around when Thomas called. He radioed Maddox to recount his conversation with Rooney as he walked around the side of the neighbor's house, and kept it short. He left out that Rooney had told him about the enormous store of cash in the house, as that would raise too many questions, and felt terrible about it. Talley was a negotiator. Another negotiator was depending on him, and Talley was lying by omission. Maybe that was why he kept the call short; he couldn't stand himself for doing it.

His phone rang as he reached the cul-de-sac. He hurried into a neighboring drive, out of sight of the house, and stood by himself.

'I got'm!'

Talley forced himself to stay calm. He didn't have anything yet.

'Good work, son. You're back in your room now, right? You're safe?'

'That big guy, Mars, he almost caught me, but I hid. What was that thing you blew up in the backyard? That was so *cool!*'

'Thomas, when we're done with this, I'll let you blow up one of those things yourself, you want. But not now, okay? I need to know what's on those disks.'

'Numbers. I think it's somebody's taxes.'

'You've opened them?'

'I told you I could.'

Martin and Hicks came out of the neighboring drive and joined the other officers behind the police vehicles that filled the cul-de-sac, Martin working her way to Maddox. Talley moved farther away.

'You sure did, Thomas. Are those disks labeled?'

'Uh-huh. Just like you said, disk one and disk two.'

'Tell me what you got when you opened them.'

'I got one open right now.'

'Okay, tell me what you see.'

Talley patted himself down for his pad and pen in case he had to write.

Thomas described a list of files named for companies that Talley didn't recognize, anonymous names like Southgate Holdings and Desert Entertainment. Then Thomas mentioned two more companies: Palm Springs Ventures and The Springs Winery. There was the Palm Springs connection: Smith's home had been built by a Palm Springs contractor. Talley had Thomas open the Palm Springs Ventures file, but from Thomas's descriptions it sounded like a balance sheet or some kind of profit-and-loss statement without identifying the individuals involved. Talley scratched down the names on his pad.

'Open the files and see if there are any names.'

After a second, Thomas said, 'All I see is numbers. It's money.'

'Okay. Open the other disk. Tell me what that one says.'

Even the few seconds that it took Thomas to change the disks seemed to take forever, Talley sweating every moment of it that the boy would be discovered. But then Thomas read off file names and Talley knew that this was the one: Black, White, Up Money, Down Money, Transfers, Source, Cash Receipts, and others. Thomas was still reading file names when Talley stopped him.

'That's enough. The file named Black. Open that one.'

'It's more files.'

'Named what?'

'I think it's states. CA, AZ, NV, FL. Is NV Nevada?'

'Yeah, that's Nevada. Open California.'

Thomas described a long table that went on for pages listing names that Talley didn't recognize, along with dates and payments received. Talley grew antsy. This was taking too much time.

'Read off more of the file names.'

Thomas read off six or seven more names when Talley stopped him again.

'Open that one. Corporate Taxes.'

'Now there's more numbers, but I think they're years. Ninety-two, ninety-three, ninety-four, like that.'

'Open this year.'

'It's a tax form that my dad makes up to send to the government.'

'Up at the top of the page, does it say whose tax it is, maybe a company name?'

The boy didn't answer.

'Thomas?'

'I'm looking.'

Talley glanced toward the cul-de-sac. Martin was watching him. She held his eye for a moment, then said something to Hicks and came toward him, hunched over to stay under cover of the cars.

'It says Family Enterprises.'

'But there's no one's name?'

'Uh-uh.'

Talley wanted to look at the disks himself; if he could see them he knew he could find what he needed instead of depending on a ten-year-old boy.

'Look for something like Officers or Executive Compensation, something like that.'

Martin had cleared the line of police vehicles and was out of the line of fire from the house. She straightened and came toward him. He held up his hand to warn her off, but she frowned and kept coming.

Martin said, 'I want to talk to you.'

'In a minute.'

'It's important.'

Talley moved away from her, annoyed.

'*When I'm off the phone.*'

His tone stopped her. Martin's eyes hardened angrily, but she kept her distance.

Thomas said, 'Here it is.'

'You found the name?'

'Yeah, there's a place called Compensation to Officers, but there's only one guy listed.'

'Who?'

'Charles G. Benza.'

Talley stared at the ground. The cool night air suddenly felt close. Talley looked at the house, then glanced at Martin. Talley had been wrong. Walter Smith wasn't a mobster with something valuable in his house. The boy's father kept Sonny Benza's books. That's what it had to be: Smith was Benza's accountant, and he had Benza's financial records. It was all right there in Smith's house, enough to put Benza away and his organization out of business. Right here in Bristo Camino.

Talley sighed deeply, the breath venting from his core in a way that seemed to carry his strength with it. This was why people were willing to kidnap and murder. Smith could put them out of business. Smith knew their secrets and could put them away. The mob. The men in the car were the mob. The head of the largest crime family on the West Coast had Jane and Amanda.

Thomas's voice suddenly came fast and thin.

'Someone's coming. I gotta go.'

The line went dead.

Martin put her hands on her hips.

'Are you going to talk to me now?'

'No.'

Talley ran for his car. If the disks could put Benza away, so could Walter Smith. He radioed Metzger at the hospital as he ran.

Thomas

Thomas heard the nail being pried from his door. He jerked the computer's plug from the wall, then vaulted onto his bed, shoving the cell phone under the covers as the door opened. Kevin stepped inside, carrying a paper plate with two slices of pizza and a Diet Coke.

'I brought you something to eat.'

Thomas pushed his hands between his crossed legs, trying to hide the fact that he wasn't tied, but the tape he'd stripped from his wrists was in plain sight on the floor. Kevin stopped when he saw it, then glared.

'You little shit. I oughta kick your ass.'

'It hurt my wrists.'

'Fuckit, I don't guess it matters anyway.'

Thomas was relieved that he didn't seem too upset. Kevin handed over the pizza and soda, then checked the nails that held the windows closed.

Thomas worried that he would notice that the computer was in a different spot, but Kevin seemed inside himself.

Kevin made sure that the windows were secure, then leaned against the wall as if he needed the support to keep his feet. His eyes seemed to find everything in the room, every toy and book, every piece of furniture, the clothes strewn in the corner, the posters on the walls, the smashed phone thrown on the floor, the TV, the CD player, even the computer against the wall, all with an expression that seemed empty.

Kevin's gaze finally settled on Thomas.

'You're fucking lucky.'

Kevin pushed off the wall and went to the door.

Thomas said, 'When are you leaving my house?'

'Never.'

Kevin left without looking back and pulled the door closed.

Thomas waited.

The nail was hammered back into the doorjamb. The floor squeaked as Kevin moved away.

Thomas tried to count to one hundred, but stopped at fifty and once more made his way to the closet. He wanted to know what they were planning. He also wanted the gun.

21
Canyon Country, California
Saturday, 12:02 a.m.

Marion Clewes

The Canyon Country Hospital sat between two mountain ridges in a pool of blue light. It was modern and low, not more than three stories at its tallest, and sprawled across the parking lot. Marion thought it looked like one of those overnight dot-com think tanks you see in the middle of nowhere, sprung up overnight at a freeway off-ramp, all earth-colored stone and mirrored glass.

Marion cruised around the hospital, finding the emergency room entrance at the rear. Friday night, a little after midnight, and the place was virtually deserted. Marion knew hospitals that saw so much action on Friday nights they ran double ER staffs and you could hear screams from a block away. The Santa Clarita Valley must be a very nice place to live, he thought. He was liking everything he found about it.

The small parking area outside the ER showed only three cars and a couple of ambulances, but four news vehicles were parked off to the side. Marion expected this, so he wasn't put off. He parked close to the entrance with the nose of his car facing the drive, then went into the hospital.

The newspeople were clumped together at the admitting desk, talking to a harried woman in a white coat. Marion listened enough to gather that she was the senior emergency room physician, Dr. Reese, and that tests were currently being run on Walter Smith. Two young nurses, both pretty with dark Toltec eyes, stood behind the admitting counter, watching with interest. Marion thought that this was probably very exciting for them, having the newspeople here.

Marion went to a coffee machine in the small waiting area and bought a cup of black coffee. A female police officer sat watching the interview. A young Latino man sat across from her, rocking a small baby while an older child slept half in his lap, half on the seat next to him. The man looked frightened in a way that let Marion think that his wife was probably the reason they were here. Marion's heart went out to him.

'It's like they've forgotten you, isn't it?'

The man glanced up without comprehension. Marion smiled, thinking he probably didn't speak English.

'That's so sad,' he said.

Marion turned away and went back to the admitting area. A gate opened to a short hall, beyond which was a kind of communal room with several beds partitioned by blue curtains, and another hall with swinging doors at the end. Marion waited at the gate until an orderly appeared, then he smiled shyly.

'Excuse me. Dr. Reese said someone would help me.'

The orderly glanced at Reese, who was still busy with the reporters across the room.

'I'm Walter Smith's next-door neighbor. They told me to pick up his clothes and personal effects.'

'That the guy who was the hostage?'

'Oh, yes. Isn't that terrible?'

'Man, the stuff that happens, huh?'

'You never know. We're worried sick. Those children are still in there.'

'Man.'

'I'm supposed to bring his things home.'

'Okay, let me see what I can do.'

'How's he doing?'

'The doctor's checking the CT results now. They should know soon.'

Marion watched as the orderly disappeared into one of the doors farther up the hall, then he stepped through the gate and walked up the hall just far enough so that the nurses at the admitting desk could no longer see him. He waited there until the orderly returned with a green paper bag.

'Here you go. They had to cut his clothes off, but there isn't anything we can do about that.'

Marion took the bag. He could feel shoes in the bottom.

'Do I have to sign?'

'No, that's all right. We're not that formal around here. I used to work for County-USC; man, you had to sign for everything. Here, it's not like that. These small towns are great.'

'Listen, thank you. Is there another way out of here? I don't want to leave past the reporters. They were asking so many questions before.'

The orderly pointed to the swinging doors at the far end of the hall.

'Through there, then take a left. You'll see a red exit sign at the end. That'll bring you out the front.'

'Thanks again.'

Marion put the bag on the floor to go through Smith's things. He did it right there. The bag contained jeans, a belt, a black leather wallet, white Calvin Klein briefs, a Polo shirt, gray socks, black Reebok tennis shoes, and a Seiko wristwatch. The clothes had all been split along the centerline.

Marion felt the pants pockets, but found only a white handkerchief. There were no computer disks. Mr. Howell would be disappointed.

Marion tucked the bag under his arm and walked down the hall past the beds in the communal room. The beds were empty. Marion wondered about the Latino man's wife, but stopped thinking about it when he found Smith in a room at the end of the hall. Smith's left temple was covered in a fresh white bandage, and an oxygen cannula was clipped to his nose. Two nurses, one red-haired and one dark, were setting up monitor machines that Marion took to be an EEG and an EKG. That the nurses were only now setting up the monitors told Marion that the tests had just finished but the doctors were still waiting for results. That gave him time. When the doctors knew Smith's true condition, they would either proceed with some additional intervention or move Smith into the main body of the hospital. A room there would make things easier, but surgery would make Marion's job impossible. He decided not to take the chance.

Marion found a quiet spot farther down the hall where a gurney was resting against the wall. He put the bag on the gurney, then put a syringe pack and a glass vial of a drug called lidocaine into the bag. Both the syringe and the lidocaine were Marion's, brought in from the car.

A tall young man pushed an empty wheelchair around a corner. He looked sleepy.

Marion smiled pleasantly.

'I used to tell myself I would get used to these hours, but you never do.'

The man smiled back, sharing the tragedy of late hours.

'You're telling me.'

When the man was gone, Marion worked inside the bag so no one could see. He tore open the syringe pack, twisted off the needle guard, and pierced the top of the vial. He drew deep at the lidocaine, filling the syringe. Lidocaine was one of his favorite drugs. When injected into a person with a normal healthy heart, it induced heart failure. Marion placed the syringe on top of Smith's torn clothes so that it would be easy to reach, then closed the bag and waited.

After a few minutes, the dark-haired nurse left Smith's room. Shortly after that, the second nurse left.

Marion let himself into the room. He knew that he didn't have much time, but he didn't need much. He put the bag on the bed. Smith's eyes fluttered, opening partway, then closing, as if he was struggling to wake. Marion slapped him.

'Wake up.'

Marion slapped him again.

'Walter?'

Smith's eyes opened, not quite making it all the way. Marion wasn't sure if Smith could see him or not. Marion slapped him a third time, leaving a bright red mark on his cheek.

'Are the disks still in your house?'

Smith made a murmuring sound that Marion could not understand. Marion gripped his face again and shook it violently.

'Speak to me, Walter. Have you told anyone who you are?'

Smith's eyes fluttered again, then focused. The eyes tracked to Marion.

'Walter?'

The eyes dulled and once more closed.

'Okay, Walter. If that's the way you want it.'

Marion decided it was time. He felt confident that he could report that the disks were still in the house and that Smith hadn't been able to speak since his release from the house. The people in Palm Springs would be pleased. They would also be pleased that Walter Smith was dead.

'This won't hurt, Walter. I promise.'

Marion smiled, and suppressed a laugh.

'Well, that's not exactly true. Heart attacks hurt like a motherfucker.'

Marion opened the bag and reached in for the syringe.

'What are you doing?'

The red-haired nurse stood in the door. She stared at Marion, clearly suspicious, then came directly to the bed.

'You're not supposed to be in here.'

Marion smiled at her. She was a small woman with a thin neck. His hands still in the bag, Marion let go of the syringe and lifted the clothes so that the syringe would fall to the bottom. He never took his eyes from the nurse or stopped smiling. Marion had a fine smile. Sweet, his mother always said.

'I know. I came for his belongings, but I got the idea of leaving something from home, you know, like a good-luck piece, and there was no one to ask.'

Marion took out the wallet and opened it. He took out a worn picture of Walter with his wife and children. He showed it to the nurse.

'Could I leave it? Please? I'm sure it will help him.'

'It might get lost.'

Marion looked past her. No one was in the hall. He glanced at the far side of the room. Another door; maybe to a bathroom, maybe a closet or a hall. He could cover her mouth, lift her, it would only take seconds.

'I know, but . . .'

'Well, just tuck it under the pillow, then. You're not supposed to be here.'

The dark-haired nurse stepped through the door and went to one of the monitors. Marion closed the bag.

The red-haired nurse said, 'Is it okay if he leaves this picture? It belongs to Mr. Smith.'

'No. It'll get lost and someone will bitch. That always happens.'

Marion put the picture into his pocket and smiled at the red-haired nurse.

'Well, thanks anyway.'

Marion was patient. He was content to wait until Smith was once more alone, but he heard sirens as he walked back to the admitting room where he saw the female police officer outside the entrance. Marion thought that she was talking to herself, but then realized she was talking into her radio. The sirens grew closer. The reporters trickled outside, joining her, asking questions, but she suddenly broke away from them and ran back into the hospital. Marion decided not to wait.

Marion went out to his car, feeling dispirited by the way things had worked out. Palm Springs was not going to like his report after all, but there was nothing to be done about it. Not yet.

Then two police cars arrived. Marion watched the officers run through the shouting reporters into the hospital, and then he phoned Glen Howell.

Talley

Running for his car, Talley radioed Metzger at the hospital. He told her that there had been a threat to Smith's life, and to put her ass outside Smith's door. He grabbed Jorgenson and Campbell from Mrs. Peña's home and told them to follow him.

Talley rolled code three, full lights and siren. He knew that Benza's people would learn what he was doing, and that this might jeopardize himself and his family, but he couldn't let them simply kill the man. He didn't know what else to do.

When they reached the hospital, Talley saw the knot of reporters coming toward him from the entrance. Talley hurried out of his car to meet Jorgenson and Campbell.

'Don't say a word. Everything is no comment. You got that?'

Their eyes were confused and overwhelmed as the reporters surrounded them.

'Let's get in there.'

As they entered the hospital, Talley glanced from face to face, from hands to bodies, hoping for a glimpse of a deep tan, a heavy Rolex watch, and for clothes similar to those worn by the men and woman he had seen in his parking lot. Everyone was a suspect. Everyone was a potential killer. Anyone could lead him back to his Amanda and Jane.

The hospital security chief, an overweight man named Jobs, met them at the admitting desk with Klaus and the ER supervisor, an older woman who introduced herself as Dr. Reese. Talley asked that they speak somewhere more private, and followed them past the admitting desk through a gate and around a corner into a hall. Talley saw Metzger standing outside a door not far away. Talley went directly to her, telling Reese and the others to wait.

'Is everything okay?'

'Yeah. It's fine. What's going on?'

Talley stood in the door. Smith was alone in the room. His head lolled to the side, then righted. Talley glanced back at Metzger.

'I'll be right back.'

Talley told Jorgenson and Campbell to wait with Metzger, then explained to the doctors.

'We have reason to believe that there could be an attempt made on Mr. Smith's life. I'm going to post a guard outside his room and have police here on the premises.'

Klaus made his face into a pinched, sulky frown.

'An attempt on his life? Like what you did in the ambulance?'

Reese ignored him.

'We work at an ER pace here, Sheriff. Things move quickly. I can't have that disrupted.'

'I'm the chief of police in Bristo. I'm not a sheriff.'

'I understand. Are my staff in danger?'

'Not with my officers here, no, ma'am.'

Klaus said, 'This is bullshit. Who would want to kill this guy?'

Talley didn't want to lie. He was tired of lying. He shrugged.

'We have to take the threat seriously.'

Jobs, the security chief, nodded.

'The world is filled with nuts.'

Talley worked it out that his officers would remain the primary guard outside Smith's room with Jobs's security personnel as supplement; if Smith was moved to another part of the hospital, the Bristo police would accompany him. They were still talking about it when Metzger called from her post.

'Hey. He's waking up.'

Klaus pushed past them and hurried into the room, Talley following. Smith's eyes were open and focused, though still vague. He mumbled something, then spoke again, more clearly.

'Where am I?'

The words were slurred, but Talley understood them.

Klaus drew out the penlight, peeled open Smith's eyes, then passed the light, first over one, then the other.

'My name is Klaus. I'm a doctor at Canyon Country Hospital. That's where you are. Do you know your name?'

It took Smith a few moments to answer, as if it took him a while to understand the question, then figure out the answer. He wet his lips.

'Smith. Walter Smith. What's wrong?'

Klaus glanced at the monitors.

'Don't you know?'

Smith seemed to think again, but then his eyes widened and he tried to sit up. Klaus pushed him down.

'Easy. Stay down or you'll faint.'

'Where are my children?'

Klaus glanced at Talley.

Talley said, 'They're still in the house.'

Smith's eyes tracked vaguely over. Talley lifted his sweatshirt so that Smith could see his badge.

'I'm Jeff Talley, the Bristo chief of police. Do you know what happened to you?'

'People came into my house. Three men. What about my children?'

'They're still in the house. So far as we know, they're okay. We're trying to get them out.'

Klaus grudged a nod.

'Chief Talley is the one who got you out.'

Smith looked up at him.

'Thank you.'

His voice was soft and fading. Smith settled back, his eyes closed. Talley thought they were losing him again.

Klaus didn't like what he saw on the monitors. His face pulled into the pinched frown again.

'I don't want him to overdo it.'

Talley brought Klaus aside and lowered his voice.

'I should have a word with him now. About what we talked about.'

'I don't see as it would do any good. It will only upset him.'

Talley stared at Smith, knowing he could punch the right button because he could read Klaus as easily as he read a subject behind a barricade.

'He has a right to know, Doctor. You know he does. I'll only be a moment. Now, please.'

Klaus scowled some more, but he left.

'Smith.'

Smith opened his eyes, not quite as wide as before. Talley watched as they flagged closed. He bent close.

'I know who you are.'

The eyes opened again.

'Sonny Benza has my wife and daughter.'

Smith stared up at him, as blank as a plate, showing no surprise or shock, revealing nothing. But Talley knew. He could sense it.

'He wants his financial records. He's taken my wife and daughter to make sure I cooperate. I need your help, Smith. I need to know where he has them. I need to know how to get to him.'

Something wet dripped on Smith's shoulder. Talley's eyes blurred, and he realized that he was crying.

'Help me.'

Smith wet his lips. He shook his head.

'I don't know what you're talking about.'

The eyes closed.

Talley leaned closer, his voice raspy.

'He's going to kill you, you sonofabitch.'

Klaus came back into the room.

'That's enough.'

'Let me speak to him a few more minutes.'

'I said, *That's enough.*'

Talley posted the guards, then left. He drove again with the windows down, frustrated and angry. He punched at the steering wheel and shouted. He wanted to race back to the house; he didn't want to go back to the house. He wanted to crash through doors and keep crashing until he found Amanda and Jane. It was impotent rage. He pulled the Nokia from his pocket and set it on the seat. He knew it would ring. He knew the Watchman would call. He had no other choice.

It rang.

Talley swerved to the shoulder of the road. He was in the middle of nowhere, on the stretch of highway between Canyon Country and Bristo, nothing but rocks and road and truckers trying to make it to Palmdale before dawn. Talley skidded to a stop and answered the call, the Watchman shouting before Talley spoke.

'You fucked up, you dumb fucking cop, you fucked up bad!'

Talley was shouting back, shouting over the Watchman's words.

'*No, YOU fucked up, you sonofabitch!* Do you think I'm going to let you just murder someone?!'

'*You wanna hear them scream?* That it? You want a blowtorch on your daughter's pretty face?!'

Talley punched the dash over and over, never felt the blows.

'I got YOU, you motherfucker! *I got YOU!* You touch them, you harm one fucking hair, and I'll go in that house right fucking now, I'll get those disks, and I'll see what's on them. You want them in the newspaper? You want the *real* FBI to have'm? I don't think you want that, you COCKSUCKINGMOTHERFUCKER! And I've got *Smith!* Don't you fucking forget that! *I've got Smith!*'

Talley's hands shook with rage. It was the way he felt in the minutes after a SWAT entry when shots had been fired, his blood running so hot that only more blood could cool it.

When the Watchman spoke again, his voice was measured.

'I guess we each have something the other wants.'

Talley forced himself to be calm. He had bought himself time.

'Remember that. You fucking remember that.'

'All right. You have a guard on Smith. Fair enough. We'll deal with Smith when we deal with Smith. Right now we want our property.'

'Not one fucking hair. One hair and you bastards are mine.'

'We're off that, Talley. Move on. You still have to make sure that I get those disks. If I don't, more than hair will be harmed.'

'So what's next?'

'My people are good to go. You know who I mean?'

'The FBI.'

'Six in two vans. If there's any fuckup, if you do anything other than what I tell you to do, you'll get your family back in the mail.'

'I'm doing what I can, goddamnit. Tell me what you want.'

'Whatever they say they need, you give it to them. Whatever they want you to do, you do it. Remember, Talley, I get those disks, you get your family.'

'Jesus, man, we can't have an assassination squad out here. The neighborhood is full of professional police officers. They're not stupid.'

'I'm not stupid, either, Talley. My guys know how to walk the walk and talk the talk. They will behave in a professional manner. Use the Sheriffs for your perimeter, but have their tactical team stand down. My guy, the team leader, he'll cover that with the Sheriffs. They were in the area on a joint training mission with the Customs Service and the U.S. Marshals. They called you, offered their assistance, and you accepted.'

Talley knew that Martin would never buy that. He saw the whole thing blowing up in his face.

'No one will believe that. Why would I accept with the Sheriffs already here?'

'Because the Feds told you that Walter Smith is part of their witness protection program.'

'Is he?'

'Don't be stupid, Talley. My man will cover it with the Sheriffs when he gets there. He knows what to say so they'll go along. Do you want to hear your wife again?'

'Yes.'

The line was empty for a time, then Talley heard voices, and then Jane screamed.

'Jane??'

Talley clutched the phone with both hands. He shouted, forgetting where he was, what he was doing.

'*JANE!*'

The Watchman came back on the line.

'You heard her, Talley. Now take care of my people and get them set up.'

The line went dead. Talley was left shaking and sweating. He pressed star 69, trying to call back, but nothing happened. Jane was gone. The Watchman was gone. Talley shook so badly he felt drunk. He got himself together. He put away the phone. He drove back to the house.

22

Saturday, 12:03 a.m.

Dennis

When Dennis went back into the house, Mars didn't say anything, but Kevin started on him right away.

'What did he say? Did he offer a deal?'

Dennis felt dull; not desperate anymore, or even very frightened. He was confused. He didn't understand how Talley could turn down so much money unless Talley didn't believe him. Maybe Talley thought he was lying about how much money was in the house just as Talley had lied to him about the house belonging to mobsters.

'What *happened*, Dennis? Did he give us an ultimatum?'

The girl was on her hands and knees on the kitchen floor, staring at him.

'Is your old man in the mob?'

'What are you talking about?'

He could tell that the girl didn't know a goddamned thing. It was all stupid. He was stupid just for asking.

'Mars. Get her out of here. Take her back to her room.'

Dennis went to the office for the vodka, then brought it to the den, drinking on the way. The lights came on as he dropped onto the thick leather couch.

Kevin stopped in the door.

'Are you going to tell me what happened?'

'I shouldn't have told him about the money. Now he's gonna keep it all for himself.'

'He said that?'

'I tried to cut him in. What the fuck, it's a lot of cash, I thought we could buy our way out. See, that was my mistake. Once I told him how much money we had, he probably started thinking he could keep it for himself. Fuck that. If we don't escape, I'm telling everybody. All three of us will tell them about the cash, so if Talley tries to keep it they'll nail his ass.'

Dennis pulled deeper at the bottle, his mouth numb to it, angry at that bastard, Talley, for stealing his money.

'He's gonna kill us, Kev. We're fucked.'

'That's crazy. He's not going to kill us.'

Kevin was so fuckin' stupid.

'He's got to kill us, you idiot. He can't let us tell people about the money. The only way he can keep it is if nobody knows about it. He's probably gonna cap all three of us before they even read our rights. He's probably plannin' how to do it right now.'

Kevin came over and stood by the couch, crowding him.

'It's over, Dennis. We have to give up.'

'Fuck it's over! That money is *mine!*'

Dennis felt his anger building, and drank more of the vodka. That had always been Kevin's role in life, to hold him back, dragging behind him like an anchor, keeping him down.

Kevin stepped closer.

'You're going to get us all killed for that money. Talley's not playing games. The cops are going to get tired of waiting for us to give up, then we'll all be fuckin' killed!'

Dennis raised the bottle, and shrugged.

'Then we might as well die rich.'

'No!'

Kevin slapped the bottle from his hand, and then Dennis was off the couch. Dennis felt out of himself, his head a red blur of rage and frustration. He shoved Kevin over the coffee table and followed him down. Kevin grunted with the impact and tried to cover his face, but Dennis held him with his left hand and punched with his right, hitting his brother again and again.

'Dennis, stop!'

He hit Kevin as hard as he could.

'Stop crying, goddamnit!'

He hit Kevin harder.

'*Stop crying!*'

Kevin rolled into a ball, his face blotched red, sobbing. Dennis hated him. He hated their father and their mother, hated all the rathole apartments and the brutal assholes their mother had brought home, hated his shitty job and the Ant Farm and every day of their failed lives, but most of all he hated Kevin for reminding him of these things every time he looked at him.

'You're fuckin' pathetic.'

Dennis climbed to his feet, breathless and spent.

'That money is mine. I'm not leaving without it, Kevin. Get that in your head. *We're not giving up.*'

Kevin crawled away, whimpering like a beaten dog.

Dennis picked up the bottle, and saw Mars standing in the door, watching without expression. Dennis wanted to hit Mars, too, the sonofabitch.

'What? You got something to say?'

Mars did not respond, the shadows in the dim light masking his eyes.

'*What?*'

Mars responded somberly.

'I like it here, Dennis. We're not going to leave.'

'Fuckin' A we're not.'

The vague smile flickered at Mars's lips, the only part of him that Dennis could see.

'We're going to be fine, Dennis. I'll take care of everything.'

Dennis turned away and sucked down another belt of the vodka.

'You do that, Mars.'

Mars melted into the darkness and disappeared.

Dennis burped.

Creepy bastard.

Talley

Quiet settled over York Estates. The traffic on Flanders Road had thinned; the line of cars filled with the morbid gawkers who wanted a brush with crime was gone, leaving the California Highway Patrol motor officers who were manning the barricades with nothing to do. Inside the development, the Sheriffs sat in their cars or at their posts. No one talked. Everyone waited.

Talley pulled his car to the curb outside Mrs. Peña's home and cut the engine. He looked at the command van. With nothing going on at the house, Maddox and Ellison would have pulled back to the van to alternate shifts on the phone, the off negotiator catching a catnap in the van's bunk or the backseat of a car. Talley was tired. The center of his back between his shoulder blades was knotted with a pronounced pain that cut into his spine. His head felt cloudy from more than fatigue, leaving him to mistrust his thinking. He wasn't a kid anymore.

Talley went inside for a cup of black coffee, but returned to his car. Three of the CHiPs and two Sheriffs were in Mrs. Peña's kitchen, but he didn't want to talk. He sat on the curb with the Nokia and his own phone beside him. He sipped the coffee, thinking about Amanda and Jane, seeing them seated together on a couch in the anonymous room where they were held, seeing them alive, seeing them unharmed, seeing them safe. Imagining them that way helped.

Talley's radio popped at his waist.

'Chief, Cooper.'

'Go, Coop.'

'Ah, I'm here at the south gate. We got some FBI guys asking for you.'

Talley didn't answer. He worked at breathing. He stared at the Sheriff's command van and the line of police cars lining the street and the officers moving among them, feeling frightened and unsure. He was about to lie to them. It would be like letting the enemy into the camp. It would be lying to these people who were here to help him and help the people in that house.

'Chief? They say you're expecting them.'

'Let them in.'

Talley walked up the street to the corner. He didn't know what to expect and wanted to meet them alone, away from everyone else. He stood beneath a street lamp so they would stop in its light. He wanted to see them.

Two gray Econoline vans eased to the corner, four men in the lead van, two in the rear. Talley raised his hand, stopping them. Both vans pulled to the curb and cut their engines. The men inside had short haircuts and were wearing black tactical fatigues, standard issue for FBI tactical units. One of the men in the back wore a ball cap that read FBI.

The driver said, 'You Talley?'

'Yes.'

The man on the passenger side of the lead van got out and came around the nose of the van. He was taller than Talley and muscular. He looked the part: black tac fatigues, jump boots, buzzed hair. A black pistol hung beneath his left arm in a ballistic holster.

He stopped in front of Talley, glanced up the street at the Sheriffs, then turned back to Talley.

'Okay, Chief, let me see some ID. I want to be sure who I'm talking to.'

Talley lifted his sweatshirt enough to show his badge.

'I don't give a shit about that. Show me a picture.'

Talley took out his wallet and showed the photo ID. When he was satisfied, he took out his own badge case and opened it for Talley to see.

'Okay, here's mine. My name is Special Agent Jones.'

Talley inspected an FBI credential that identified the man as William F. Jones, Special Agent of the Federal Bureau of Investigation. It showed a photograph of Jones. It looked real.

'Don't sweat anyone asking for our papers. Every man in my group has the ID.'

'Are you all named Jones?'

Jones snapped the case closed and put it away.

'Don't be funny, Chief. You can't afford it.'

He slapped the nose of the lead van, nodding at the driver. The doors of both vans opened. The remaining five men stepped out, moving to the rear of the second van. Like Jones, they looked the part down to the haircuts. They strapped into armored vests with FBI emblazoned on the back.

Jones said, 'In a few minutes your phone is going to ring. You know the phone I mean. So let's get some stuff straight before that. Are you paying attention?'

Talley was watching the men. They strapped on the vests, then snapped on new thigh guards with practiced efficiency. Someone at the rear of the second van passed out black knit masks, flash-bang grenades, and helmets. Each man folded the mask twice and tucked it under his left shoulder strap where he could reach it easily later. They clipped the grenades to their harnesses without fumbling and tossed their helmets into the seats or balanced them atop the van. Talley knew the moves, because he had practiced them himself when he worked SWAT Tactical. These men had done this before.

'I'm paying attention. You used to be a cop.'

'Don't worry about what I used to be. You've got other stuff to worry about.'

Talley looked at him.

'How can you people expect this to work? The Sheriffs have a full crisis response team here. They're going to be pissed off and they're going to have questions.'

'I can handle the Sheriffs and anything else that comes up. What's my name?'

Talley didn't know what in hell he wanted.

'What?'

'I asked you my name. You just saw my commission slip. What's my fucking name?'

'Jones.'

'All right. I'm Special Agent Jones. Think of me that way and you won't fuck up. I can lift my end, you got a wife and kid praying you can lift yours.'

Talley's head throbbed. His neck was so tight that it burned, but he managed a nod.

Jones turned so that they both faced the line of vehicles.

'Who's in charge there?'

'Martin. She's a captain.'

'You told her about us yet?'

'No. I didn't know what to say.'

'Good, that's better for us. The less time she has to ask questions, the better. Now, the man on the phone, you know who I mean, did he tell you how we're going to cover this?'

'Smith is in witness protection.'

'Right, Smith is in the program so we have a proprietary interest. What's my name again?'

Talley flashed with anger and fought to control it. Everything seemed out of control and surreal, standing there in the purple street light, moths ticking and snapping into the glass, with these cops who weren't cops.

'Jones. Your name is Jones. I wish I knew your fucking real name.'

'Keep it tight, Chief. We gotta work together here. I'm in charge of a special operations unit that was working training exercises on the border with the Customs Service when Washington learned what was happening here. The D.C. office called you, explained the situation, and asked for your cooperation. We owe Smith, we're obligated to protect him and his cover, so you agreed. I'm going to explain all this to Captain Martin, and all you're going to do is sit there and nod. You got that?'

'I've got it.'

'Martin won't like it, having us here, but she'll go along because what we're telling her makes sense.'

'What if she checks? What if she knows people in the LA office?'

'It's after midnight on a Friday night. She phones LA, all she'll get is a duty agent, and he'll have to check with someone else, which he won't want to do. Even if she calls the agent in charge in Los Angeles and wakes him, he'll wait until tomorrow to call D.C., because none of these people, not one, will have any reason to doubt us. We're not gonna be here that long.'

Jones handed Talley a white business card with the FBI seal pressed into the left corner and a phone number with a Washington, D.C., area code.

'If she gets it into her head to call someone, tell her that this is the guy back there who called you. She can talk to him until she's blue.'

Talley put the card in his pocket, wondering if the name on the card was a real agent, and thought that he probably was. Thinking that scared him. It was like a warning, this is how much power we have.

Talley glanced at the men. They were geared up now. A man in the second van was passing out MP5s, CAR-15s, and loaded magazines.

'What are you people going to do?'

'You and I are going to straighten this out with the Sheriffs. Two of my people are going to reconnoiter the house, see what we have. After that, we'll deploy in a secure position and wait for the man to call. You've got your phone, I have mine. When he gives the word, we move. If something happens in the house that provokes a launch beforehand, we'll do it. But we will control the scene until we've recovered our target. After that, the house is yours.'

Talley thought about the man's words, thought he might have done this in the military, for the Rangers or Special Forces.

'I won't be able to keep the others out. You know that. The Sheriffs will come in, and I'm going, too.'

Jones met Talley's eyes and shook his head.

'Listen, man, if it helps you get through this, we don't want to kill anyone, not even the three dicks who started this mess. We just want the stuff in the house. But we know what's required when we breach that house. We'll have to secure the scene before we can recover what we want. We'll do that, Talley. We're professionals.'

The phone in Talley's pocket chirped. He had a phone in his left pocket and a phone in his right, and didn't remember which was which. Talley pulled out the phone in his left pocket. It was the Nokia. It chirped again.

'Answer it, Chief.'

Talley pressed the button to answer the call.

'Talley.'

'Is Mr. Jones with you?'

'Yes, he's here.'

'Put him on.'

Talley passed the Nokia to Jones without a word. Jones put it to his ear, saying his name to let the caller know he was on. Talley watched Jones. His eyes were pale blue or gray, Talley couldn't tell which in the dim light. A man in his mid-forties, maybe, who kept himself in good shape and could be hard when he had to be. As Jones spoke, his eyes flicked nervously to the Sheriffs in the distance. Talley thought that he was probably scared. Any sane man would be scared, doing what he was doing. Talley wondered what the Watchman had on this man, or if Jones was doing it for money.

Jones ended the call and passed the phone back to Talley.

'Let's go, Chief. Time to get it done.'

'What does he have on you?'

Jones stared at him, then looked away without answering.

'I know why I'm doing this. What does he have on you?'

Jones cinched down his vest, tighter than necessary, so tight the straps cut.

'You don't know shit.'

Jones started up the street.

Talley followed him.

Kevin

The stink of gasoline was so thick in the closed space of the entry hall that it burned Kevin's eyes and filled his throat with the taste of metal. He gagged, acid washing the back of his throat, then he couldn't hold back and vomited, puke splashing the wall. Dennis, in the den with his vodka, was too far gone to have heard.

They were going to die.

Kevin remembered a story from elementary school that explained how coastal Africans caught the tiny monkeys that lived at the edge of the water. The Africans would bore a hole in a coconut just big enough so that the monkey could squeeze its hand inside. They would put a peanut touched with honey into the coconut. The monkey would reach inside to grab the peanut, only with the peanut in its hand and its hand balled into a fist, the monkey's hand would no longer fit through the hole. As long as it held onto the peanut, the monkey couldn't take its hand out of the coconut. These monkeys wanted the honey-coated peanuts so badly that they would not let go even as the monkey-hunters walked up to cover them with nets. Dennis was the monkey in this house, surrounded by police but unwilling to let go of his peanut.

Kevin stumbled into the little bathroom off the entry and splashed his face with water. His lip and eye were swelling from the beating Dennis had given him. He washed out his mouth, then washed his face, rubbing the water through his hair and around his neck. After the shootings, the fear, the running, the nightmare terror of the day, he finally knew what he had to do, and why: He was not willing to die with his brother; no matter their childhood, no matter Dennis taking the old man's belt for him, no matter the horrors they had endured. Dennis was willing to die for money he couldn't have, and Kevin refused to die with him. He would take the girl and her brother, and the three of them would get the hell out of here. Let Dennis and Mars do what they want.

Kevin dried his face, then went back to the den to see if Dennis was still there. Kevin expected that Dennis and Mars would try to stop him from leaving. He knew that they could, so he wanted to get the kids out of the house without being seen. Dennis's feet sprouted up over the end of the couch, still flat on his back. Kevin peeked into the office, checking for Mars, but Mars wasn't there. Kevin thought that he might be back in the family room by the French doors, but suddenly he had the prickly feeling that Mars was watching him on the monitors. Kevin slipped past the den back along the hall to the master bedroom. If Mars was in the security room, he was going to tell Mars that Dennis wanted him to watch the front of the house again, but the master bedroom was empty and so were the closets and security room. Kevin stared at the monitors, seeing the police outside, seeing his brother in the den and the girl in her room, but he didn't see Mars. He thought maybe he should break the monitors or figure out a way to turn off the security system, but if he moved quickly enough it wouldn't matter; once he had the kids, they would be out of the house in seconds or they wouldn't be out at all.

Kevin hurried back through the house to the entry, and then up the stairs. He knocked twice softly on the girl's door, pulled the nail from the door, and let himself inside. The girl was curled into a ball on her bed, her eyes open, the lights full on. She swung her feet out and stood as the door opened.

'What do you want?'

'Shh. Keep your voice down.'

Kevin was scared. Here he was a grown man, and he felt like a child whenever he crossed wills with his brother. Sometimes he felt such a strong mix of fear and a desperate need to please Dennis that he couldn't move.

'We're going to get out of here.'

She seemed confused, her eyes flicking to the door, then back to him.

'Where are you taking me?'

'Not with them. I don't mean with Dennis and Mars. I'm taking you and your brother. We're going to leave them here.'

The marks on his face registered with her for the first time, and Kevin felt himself flush.

'What happened to you?'

'Don't worry about it. Dennis isn't going to give up. He's going to stay here no matter what, but we're not.'

'They're letting us leave?'

'Mars and Dennis don't know I'm doing this. They would stop us, so we have to be careful, but we're getting out of here and they can do what they want.'

Uncertainty played across her face. She glanced at the door again.

Kevin said, 'Do you want to go or not? I'm offering you a way out of here.'

'I can't go without Thomas.'

'I know that. All three of us will go, but we have to be careful and move fast. Now do you want to go or not?'

'I want to go!'

'Stay here and pretend like nothing's happening. I'll get Thomas and come back for you. When the three of us are together, we'll go straight downstairs and out the front door. Do you have a white pillowcase?'

'We're going to walk out the door? Just like that?'

'Yes! We need a white flag or something so the cops don't shoot us.'

He could tell she was scared, but excited, too, anxious to get out of the house.

'All right, okay. I have a pillowcase.'

'Get it while I'm getting your brother. When I get back, don't say a word. Just follow me and try to be quiet, but be ready to *move*. We're going to walk fast.'

She nodded, her head bouncing.

'I will.'

Kevin eased the door open and peered into the hall. Dim light glowed at the stairwell, coming from below. The hall seemed darker than before, masked in a blackness that made him wish for a flashlight. He heard voices and grew even more worried. If Mars and Kevin were in the office, they would see the three of them coming down the stairs.

Kevin pulled the door shut behind him and crept back along the hall to the stairwell, listening. Twice the hall creaked, making Kevin cringe. When he reached the top of the stairs, he listened harder, then felt a well of relief. The voices were coming from the television.

He turned back toward the boy's room, telling himself to hurry, to do this quickly without noise, to do it *now* or else the moment would pass and he would never do it; he would be trapped in this house with Dennis and Mars, and he would die. Kevin was so frightened that it was difficult to think. The boy, the girl, out. He repeated it to himself like a chant.

Something moved in the darkness ahead of him.

Kevin froze, his senses straining, his heart pounding. The girl must have come out of her room. He whispered.

'Stay in your room.'

A black shadow drifted against the darkness outside her door, but the shadow did not answer. Kevin strained to see into the bottomless grave of the hall, but saw nothing.

The floor creaked behind him. Kevin spun around.

Mars stood inches away, backlit by the light from the stairs. Kevin jerked backwards. They were screwed unless he could keep Mars away from the front door. He thought of the security room, as far from the front door as it was possible to get in this house.

'Jesus, Mars, you scared the shit out of me. I was looking for you. Dennis wants you to watch those monitors back in the bedroom.'

Mars stepped closer, his pale face empty.

'I heard you with the girl, Kevin. You're going to leave.'

Kevin stepped back. Mars followed him, staying uncomfortably close. 'That's bullshit, Mars. I don't know what you're talking about.'

'Don't ruin a good thing, Kevin. You'll regret it later.'

Kevin felt a stab of anger that shook him. Fuck it. Mars had heard; let him hear it all. Kevin stopped backing up.

'Then you can stay! I've had enough of this, Mars. We're trapped. It's over! If we stay, the cops will kill us. Don't you get that?'

Mars stared down at him, his pasty face thoughtful. Then he stepped aside. 'I get it, Kevin. If you want to go, go.'

Kevin waited for more, thinking that Mars was upset or angry, or would drag him downstairs to Dennis, but Mars only raised his hand, offering the way to the stairs. His voice was soft and encouraging.

'Go.'

Kevin glanced toward Thomas's room.

'I'm going to take these kids.'

Mars nodded.

'That's okay. Go.'

Kevin stared up at Mars, then turned and stepped into darkness.

Talley

After Talley and Jones had spoken with Martin, Jones moved his two vans to the mouth of the cul-de-sac. Talley returned to his car, where he sat by himself, watching the two vans. Jones and one of his men, a blond guy with a crew cut and wire-rimmed glasses, left the vans to scout the perimeter.

Talley felt like a traitor and a coward. He had returned to his car so that he could avoid the Sheriffs and his own men. When he and Jones were in the command van with Martin, he couldn't bring himself to look at her. He let Jones do the talking.

When Jones and his man disappeared into the cul-de-sac, the street was still.

Martin climbed down from the command van, saw Talley in his car, and walked over. She had taken off the flak vest and all the crap SWAT cops clip to themselves, and was wearing only the black fatigues and a cap. The cap read BOSS. Talley watched her approach, hoping that she would continue into Mrs. Peña's, but she came to his side of the car.

Martin stopped a few feet away, took out a pack of cigarettes, and offered one to Talley.

'Don't smoke.'

Martin lit up without a word. She drew the smoke in deep, then blew a plume that gassed into the night air like a shroud of fog. Talley didn't know many SWAT cops who smoked. Bad for the wind.

When she spoke, her voice was calm and reasonable.

'You gonna tell me what's going on?'

Talley watched the smoke.

'What do you mean?'

'I'm not stupid.'

Talley didn't answer.

'All the phone calls. That scene in the ambulance between you and the doctor, wanting him to wake Smith; I thought you were going to shoot the guy. Whatever you were talking about with that kid, then charging off to the hospital. I had my I.O. call over there, Talley; if someone phoned in a death threat, it's news to everybody else out here, including the people back at your office.'

She drew more smoke, then appraised him.

'Now we got the FBI with this bullshit about Smith being in witness protection. What's going on, Chief? Who is Walter Smith?'

Talley glanced over. Her eyes were steady and cool, meeting his without guile. He liked her measured attitude, and her direct manner. He thought he would probably like her, given the time for it; she was probably a pretty good cop. The weight of the day suddenly pressed down on him with an intensity that left him numb. There were too many things to control and too many lies to tell. It was all too complicated, and he couldn't afford to mess this up. Like a juggler with a hundred balls in the air, he was going to drop one sooner or later. A ball would hit the ground and someone would die. He couldn't let that happen. He couldn't fail Amanda and Jane or the kids in that house or even Walter Smith.

'I need help.'

'That's why we rolled out, Chief.'

'Do you know the name Sonny Benza?'

She searched his face, Talley thinking that she couldn't place the name, but then she did.

'That's the mob guy, right?'

'Smith works for him. Smith has something in that house that can put Benza away, and Benza wants it.'

'Jesus.'

Talley looked at her, and felt his eyes go wet.

'He has my wife and daughter.'

Martin looked away.

Talley told her about the disks, the Watchman, and Jones. He told her how he had played it, and how he intended to play it. She listened without question or comment until he was finished, then she crushed her cigarette beneath her heel and stared at the two vans where Jones's people waited.

'You have to bring this to the Bureau.'

'I can't do that.'

'Turn it over to Organized Crime. With what you have they could move on Benza right now, pull him straight out of bed and hang him by his thumbs. We breach into that house, get these disks he wants, and that's all she wrote. That's how you save your family.'

'It's not your family.'

She considered the dead cigarette, and sighed.

'No, I guess not.'

'All I have is a voice on a phone, Martin. I don't know where they are, I don't know who has them. Benza has people out here; he knows what we're doing. He could make Jane and Amanda vanish even before we read him his rights, and what do I have? Three men I can't identify in cars I can't identify, and Jones over there. I don't give a shit about making a case. I just want my family.'

Martin stared at the two vans, and sighed again. It was getting to be a long night for all of them.

'I am not going to let murder happen out here, Talley. I can't do that.'

'Me neither. Jesus.'

'Then what are you going to do?'

'I can't let those disks go into evidence. They're the only leverage I have.'

'What do you want from me?'

'Help me. Keep it between us, but help me get those disks. I can't let Jones go into that house alone.'

Talley watched her, hoping that she would go along. He couldn't stop her from going upstairs. All he could do was trust her. She looked back at him, and nodded.

'I'll do what I can. You keep me informed, Talley. I don't want to get shot in the back. I can't let my people get hurt, either.'

Talley felt better, the load lessened because now she helped bear it.

'All I need are those damned disks. I get those disks, and then I'll have something to trade.'

She considered him, then put her cigarettes back into her jumpsuit. Talley knew what she was going to say before she said it.

'You need more than that. You know too much for Benza to leave you alive. You realize that, don't you? You, your family, Smith; he can't leave any of you alive. What are you going to do about that?'

'I'll deal with it when I have the disks.'

Talley's cell phone rang, loud in the silence of the night. Martin jumped. 'Shit.'

Talley thought it might be Thomas, but it was Mikkelson, sounding far away and strange.

'Chief, Dreyer and I are still out here at Krupchek's trailer with detectives from the Sheriff's Bureau. We got some stuff to report.'

Talley had forgotten about Mikkelson and Dreyer. It took a moment for him to gather his thoughts.

'Go, Mikkelson.'

'Krupchek isn't Krupchek. His real name is Alvin Marshall Bonnier. His mother's head is in the freezer.'

Part Four

Tactics

23

Saturday, 12:52 a.m.

Talley

Alvin Marshall Bonnier, age twenty-seven, also known as Mars Krupchek, was wanted in connection with four counts of homicide in Tigard, Oregon. The local authorities theorized the following chain of events based on witness interviews and forensic evidence: Bonnier, who lived alone with his mother at the time of the murders, abducted and raped his next-door neighbor, Helene Getty, age seventeen, and disposed of her body in a wooded streambed near their homes. She had been strangled and repeatedly stabbed in the chest, abdomen, and vaginal area. Mrs. Bonnier, an invalid suffering from crippling arthritis, subsequently discovered Getty's bloodstained panties and left Reebok tennis shoe, also splattered with blood, in her son's bedroom. She confronted her son, at which time Alvin stabbed his mother to death in the living room, then carried her body to the bathroom, where he dismembered it. Bonnier wrapped the limbs and torso in newspapers and plastic trash bags, then buried these remains in Mrs. Bonnier's rosebed. Neighbors stated that when the boy was young, Mrs. Bonnier made switches from the thorny rose branches with which she beat the boy. Bonnier kept his mother's head in the refrigerator, but transferred the head to the trunk of the family car several days later. With his mother's head along for company, he befriended sixteen-year-old Stephen Stilwell at a local shopping mall and enticed the boy to take a drive, probably offering cigarettes and beer. Instead, Bonnier drove Stilwell to a nearby abandoned drive-in movie theater, where he sodomized the boy, then stabbed him repeatedly. He placed Stilwell in the trunk with his mother's head, then drove to the same area where he had disposed of Helene Getty's body. Upon arrival at that location, he discovered that Stilwell was still alive, whereupon he cut the young man's throat, mutilated his genitals, and abandoned the body without attempting to conceal it. Witnesses at the shopping mall were able to provide a description of Bonnier and his automobile. Twelve days later, an eighteen-year-old high school senior named Anita Brooks hitched a ride with Bonnier after missing her bus. Instead of bringing her to school, Bonnier drove to a nearby lake, where he strangled her before branding the victim's breasts and vagina with her own cigarettes. Evidence gathered at the scene indicated that he had placed his mother's head on a nearby picnic table, probably so that she could watch the mutilation. Bonnier immediately returned home, parked his car in its usual spot, then, so far as the police know, departed the area. Authorities discovered Anita Brooks's body first. Alvin Marshall Bonnier was not identified as the suspect until two days later when neighbors investigated the foul smell coming from the Bonnier residence and summoned the police, who located his mother's body between the roses. Stilwell and Getty were found within the following week.

Talley listened to Mikkelson's recitation of the facts with a growing sense of urgency that Martin read in his expression.

'What in hell is happening?'

Talley raised his hand, telling her to wait.

'Mikki, they're positive that Bonnier and Krupchek are the same person?'

'That's affirm, Chief. The palm print he left in Kim's matched dead on, and the Bureau guys brought a copy of the warrants fax from Oregon. I saw the photo. It's Krupchek.'

'What's happening out there now?'

'The VICAP hit automatically notified the FBI. The detectives here have locked down the scene to wait for a team from the LA field office.'

Talley checked his watch.

'What's their ETA?'

'I dunno. You want me to check?'

'Yeah.'

Talley filled in Martin while he waited for Mikkelson. As Martin listened, her face grew closed and uncertain, but Mikkelson was back on the line before she could respond.

'Chief?'

'Go, Mikki.'

'The Feds should be here within a couple of hours. You want us to wait for them or come back to York?'

Talley told her to come back, then snapped the phone shut. He ran his hand across his head and stared toward the cul-de-sac.

'This is fucking great. I've got the mafia outside and fucking Freddy Krueger in the house.'

Martin watched him calmly.

'This changes things.'

'I *know* it changes things, Captain! I'm trying to save my wife and daughter, but I have to get those kids out of that house.'

'Because of Krupchek? They've been in there all day with him, Talley. Another few hours won't matter.'

'It matters. All of this matters.'

Talley left Martin at the command van and found Jones briefing his people at their vans. Jones saw Talley approaching, and separated from the others. Talley noted that Jones appeared apprehensive, resting a hand on the MP5 slung from his shoulder.

'What's up, Chief?'

'We have a problem. One of the three subjects in the house isn't who we thought. Krupchek. His true name is Alvin Marshall Bonnier. He's wanted for multiple homicides in Oregon.'

Jones smiled tightly, like Talley was making an unfunny joke.

'You're shittin' me.'

'You're going to be swimmin' in shit when you hear this: The real FBI are on their way. This isn't bullshit, Jones or whatever your name is. The Sheriffs pulled a palm print from the minimart these assholes robbed. They got a VICAP hit. You know what that is?'

Jones wasn't smiling anymore, but he didn't look concerned, either.

'I know.'

Talley explained that detectives from the Sheriff's Homicide Bureau were presently at Krupchek's home awaiting the arrival of FBI agents from the LA field office.

'They'll visit that house, then they'll come here, and they won't leave. By morning, this place is going to be covered with FBI, including a *real* FBI SWAT team.'

'We'll be gone by then. We're breaching the house as soon as I hear back from the man.'

'I want to go in now.'

Jones shook his head.

'Not until I get the call.'

Talley couldn't tell if Jones was suspicious or simply didn't understand.

'Listen to me. It's different now. This isn't just three turds holding a family hostage anymore. Those kids are in there with a lunatic.'

'It'll be fine, Talley.'

'We're talking about a man wanted for multiple homicide, Jones. He cut off his own mother's head and keeps it in the freezer.'

'I don't give a shit.'

'He's psychotic. Psychotics decompensate in stressful situations, and this guy has been in a pressure cooker all day. If that happens, he might do anything.'

Jones was unmoved.

'We'll breach when I get the call. It won't be long.'

'Fuck you.'

'After the call.'

Talley walked away. He saw Martin watching from the command van, but didn't know what to say to her. He recalled his conversations with

Rooney, and decided that Rooney did not know that Krupchek was really Alvin Marshall Bonnier. If Rooney was knowingly associating with a serial killer, it would mean he derived a vicarious pleasure from Bonnier's company. Rooney's need to be seen as special would have forced him to drop hints of Bonnier's identity in hopes of impressing Talley, but Rooney had not done that. Rooney didn't know, which meant that Rooney might as easily end up Bonnier's victim as the rest of them.

Talley glanced back at Jones. He and his men were waiting together at the rear of their van. Waiting for the call.

Talley decided that he couldn't wait any longer. He had to warn Rooney and Thomas, and he had to get those kids out of there.

Then he heard screaming from the house.

Dennis

Dennis reached for the Stoli bottle and fell off the couch, landing on his face and knees in a pool of vodka. His ass was in the air, pointing toward the front of the house, toward the cops who filled the cul-de-sac.

Dennis patted his ass, and giggled.

'Too bad you cops can't see this! You can kiss my skinny white ass right here.'

Dennis collected the bottle and pushed to his feet. He caught himself on the sofa arm to keep from tipping over, then took his pistol from his waist. Holding it made him feel better. The television showed a woman on her knees, pushing a rolling platform back and forth on the floor. Her abdominal muscles were so beautifully defined that she looked like an anatomy chart. Dennis watched her with a sense of profound loss, then raised the pistol to his own head.

'Bang.'

He lowered the gun.

'Shit.'

Dennis dropped his gun onto the couch, then considered the money. Stacks of hundred-dollar bills lined the coffee table. He fished the remaining packs of cash from his pockets and fanned the bills like a deck of cards. He had tried every way he could think of to keep the money, but failed. He had tried to get a car and a helicopter, and he had tried to buy Talley, and all of that had failed. He had tried to find a route out of the house, but the cops had him locked down. Dennis Rooney had run out of ideas, and now he was thinking that maybe his parents and teachers had been right all along: He was stupid. He was a small-time loser, who would always be a loser, living on dreams. A panicked urge to run with a bag of cash, sprinting through the shadows in a final lame attempt to get away swept over him, but he believed in his heart that the cops would kill him and he did not want to die. He didn't have the balls for it. As much as he wanted this money, Dennis Rooney admitted to himself that he was a chickenshit. His eyes filled with tears of regret and shame. Kevin was right. It was time to quit.

Dennis wiped the snot from his nose, and pulled himself together.

'I guess that's it, then.'

He tossed the money into the air, watched the fluttering green bills fall around him, then called Kevin.

'Kev!'

Kevin didn't answer.

'Mars!'

Nothing.

'Shit!'

Dennis lurched to the hall and made his way to the kitchen. It was still wrapped in shadows, lit only by the glare from the police lights shining in through the French doors. He wanted a glass of water, and then he would call Talley. He thought he might be able to trade one of the kids for a conversation with an attorney, then see what kind of deal he could cut for himself before surrendering.

'Kevin, goddamnit, where are you?!'

Here the sonofabitch had begged to surrender, and now that Dennis was ready, the wimpy puss wasn't around.

'*Mars!*'

The voice from the other side of the kitchen startled him.

'What are you doing, Dennis?'

Dennis wheeled around like a tall ship under sail, squinting into the shadows.

'Where's Kevin?'

'He's not here.'

'Where is he? I need to see him.'

Dennis wanted to get things straight with Kevin before telling Mars. Part of him was afraid that Mars might try to stop him.

Mars took shape in the light. Dennis thought he must have been in the pantry, or maybe the garage.

'Kevin left.'

Dennis grew irritated, not understanding.

'That doesn't help me, Mars. Is he in the security room, the office, what? I've got to talk to him.'

'He didn't want to stay here anymore. He left.'

Dennis stared at Mars, understanding, but not believing it, telling himself that Kevin could not have deserted him.

'Waitaminute. Are you telling me that he *left*, as in went out the door and surrendered to the cops?'

'I overheard him talking to the girl.'

'SHIT! That *FUCK*!'

'I'm sorry, Dennis. I came down to find you.'

Dennis felt sick. If Kevin had surrendered and taken the kids with him, he had taken Dennis's last chance to cut a deal with Talley.

'Did he take those kids with him?'

'I don't know.'

'Jesus, Mars! Get upstairs and see! If he took those kids, we're fucked!'

Mars went for the stairs without another word, and Dennis raged at the top of his lungs.

'KEVIN!! You ASSHOLE!'

Dennis threw the vodka bottle at the Sub-Zero so hard that his shoulder flashed with pain. He stalked back to the den for a fresh bottle. Even when he wanted to surrender, things got fucked up.

Thomas

Thomas heard Dennis and Kevin fighting through the air-conditioning vent. Kevin wanted them to give up, but Dennis wouldn't. Thomas knew what that meant: If Dennis wouldn't give up, the three turds might stay here for days, and one of them might try to do something to his sister. Thomas had seen the way Mars watched her.

The shouting died quickly. Thomas waited for someone to come upstairs, but the hall remained silent. He decided that they were trying to sleep.

Thomas slipped back into his closet and returned to the crawl space. He thought about stopping in Jennifer's room to tell her what he was doing, but he knew she didn't want him to mess with the gun. He worked his way across the house, stopping at the air vents to listen, but all he heard was the television playing in the den. The rest of the house was silent.

Thomas let himself down through the ceiling hatch into the laundry room, climbing down from the hot-water heater to the washer to the floor. It was dark, lit only by some slight dim light filtering from the kitchen through the pantry. He had to use his flashlight.

Just as he reached the floor he heard Dennis shouting for Kevin and Mars. Dennis was close, just on the other side of the kitchen or maybe in the family room. Thomas panicked. He started climbing back to the ceiling, but then Mars answered Dennis, and Thomas stopped. They were talking. Thomas was still scared, but he was so close to the gun that he didn't want to once more leave without it. He strained to listen. Dennis was cursing Kevin; they weren't coming this way, they weren't looking for him.

Thomas hurried into the utility room. He cupped his hand over the flashlight and flicked it on again, just long enough to mark the spot in his mind where the gun box waited on the highest shelf. He rested the flashlight on the bench, then climbed onto the bench.

He went up onto his toes, stretching as tall as he could, but the box was still out of reach. He flicked on the light again, and spotted a gallon metal paint can at the edge of the bench. He pulled it into position, put one foot on it, and stepped up. The paint can creaked, but held. He stretched high again, and this time his hands found the gun box. He had it! Thomas pulled the box from the shelf, then lowered himself from the can and climbed down from the bench. His heart pounded with excitement. The box was a lot heavier than he had imagined! It felt as if a cannon were inside!

Thomas opened the box and lifted out the gun. It felt as heavy as a brick, way too big for his hand. Thomas didn't know its caliber or anything about it, even though his father had let him fire it once when they had gone to the pistol range. It had kicked so hard that his hand stung!

Thomas would need his hands free to climb, so he pushed it into his pants. The gun made him feel powerful, but scared at the same time; he was buoyant with confidence that he could protect himself and Jennifer, and that now they could get out, but he didn't want to hurt anyone. He hoped he wouldn't have to use it.

Thomas was on his way back to the laundry room when his foot slipped from under him. He almost fell, catching himself on the bench just in time. He explored the floor with his foot, and found something slippery and wet. He lifted his foot. His shoe came free with a tacky sound. Thomas turned on his light. A dark liquid like oil was spreading on the floor. He followed it with his light. It was coming from the broom closet. Thomas opened his fingers to let out more light. The oil was red.

The closet door zoomed close in Thomas's mind's eye as if he had telephoto vision. The cramped space in the utility room shrank as the door grew larger. The gun was forgotten, leaving only the door and the viscous red liquid seeping out from beneath.

Thomas stared at the door. He wanted to open it. He wanted to run.

He stepped across the red pool, reached for the knob, but couldn't touch it. His fingers hovered an inch away.

Open it!

Thomas gripped the knob carefully, terrified that whatever was on the other side of the door might try to hold it closed. He slowly pulled open the door.

Kevin fell out, collapsing in a lifeless heap at Thomas's feet, his dead arms thrown around Thomas's legs.

His throat was slashed, his head lolling on white bone; the horrible second smile was locked in silent laughter.

His eyes were open.

Thomas screamed.

Jennifer

Jennifer listened at her door, pressing her ear to the cold wood, hoping to hear Kevin return. He only had to go down the hall to reach Thomas, but he was taking so long that she feared Mars or Dennis had interfered. Her stomach knotted and she pressed her fists into her belly in a useless attempt to make it stop. The knife hidden in the waist of her pants pricked her skin, making her gasp. She rearranged the blade to make it more comfortable.

The hall outside her door creaked.

Kevin!

She heard the nail being pulled from the doorjamb. She was excited and happy and ready to run. She wanted to see her father again! She wanted to hug Thomas so tight that he squirmed! She wanted her Mommy!

The door swung open, and Mars stepped inside, tall, wide, and massive as a bear. She jumped back so fast that she almost fell.

His smile made her think of bad boys burning ants.

He said, 'Were you expecting someone else?'

She backed away from the door, wishing that Kevin would come back right now because Mars was so awful and gross.

She forced herself to meet his eyes without looking away.

'I'm not expecting anyone except the police.'

Mars nodded agreeably.

'They'll be here soon. You probably don't have long to wait.'

She cursed her smart mouth; she didn't like anything he said or how he said it or his expressions. She just wanted him to leave.

Mars stepped into the room and pushed the door shut. He held the big nail that they used to wedge the door. He tapped it absently on his leg, tap-tap, tap-tap. Jennifer didn't like that he closed the door. She didn't like that he tapped the nail. She crossed her arms protectively over her breasts.

'What do you *want?*'

Mars watched her with bright nervous eyes that didn't match with his slack-jawed expression. It was as if he wasn't in the room with her, but was on the other side of a glass wall, here but not here, outside looking in, in his own horrible world.

'What do you want?'

'Kevin left without you.'

She felt herself flush. Her arms tightened so fiercely that her nails dug into her flesh, and she wanted to scream.

'He wanted me to tell you. He thought about it and decided it was just too risky to sneak past Dennis with you and your brother, so he went by himself. He said to tell you he was sorry.'

Jennifer shook her head, not knowing what was real and what wasn't, what he knew or what he didn't, or if her only hope of getting out of here had slipped out the door without her.

'I don't know what you're talking about.'

Mars came closer.

'No? Well, it doesn't matter. All the lights are almost off.'

'What are you talking about?'

Mars seemed to grow as he got closer, filling the room. Jennifer backed away.

'Good boys turn off the lights so that no one can see them doing bad things in the dark. My mother told me that.'

Jennifer's rear end bumped into her desk. She had gone as far as she could and now Mars was very close. He touched the nail to her chest, tap-tap.

'Don't touch me.'

Tap-tap.

'Stop it.'

Tap.

'Kevin's gone. Dennis is gone. Your father is gone. The little fat boy, he's gone, too. Now we can have fun.'

He pressed the nail onto her chest, a steady pressure that hurt but did not break her skin. Jennifer tried to lean away, but there was nowhere to go. Mars raked the nail slowly down between her breasts. Jennifer stared into his eyes, watching him watch her, her vision blurred with tears. His eyes were black pools, their surface rippled by secret winds. He knew he was doing something bad; he knew he was being naughty. He didn't watch the nail; she sensed that his pleasure came in seeing her fear. Jennifer slid her hand down along her belly. She worked her fingers beneath the waist of her pants, searching for the knife. He pushed the nail harder. He was breathing harder. She wanted to scream.

'Do you like this?'

Jennifer jerked the knife free and stabbed, striking out blindly, trying to force him away. The stiff short blade struck something hard. Mars grunted in surprised pain, like a dog coughing, as they both looked down. The knife was buried high on his chest in his left shoulder.

Mars whimpered, a pathetic moan, his face knotted with pain.

Jennifer pushed at him, screaming, trying to get away, but he didn't move. He grabbed her throat, squeezing hard, pressing his hips into hers to pin her to the desk.

He grabbed the knife with his free hand, whimpered again, then pulled out the blade. A crimson flower blossomed from the wound.

He looked back into her eyes, then brought the knife to her face. He squeezed harder, cutting off her breath.

'You're going to enjoy this.'

Jennifer felt herself fainting.

*

Dennis

The scream from the rear of the house cut through the alcohol, surprising Dennis more than startling him. It was high-pitched like a girl shrieking, followed by bumping, slamming noises that came from the far side of the kitchen near the garage. Dennis pulled out his gun, shouting.

'What the fuck was that? Who is that?'

It couldn't be Mars, who had just left, or the two kids, who were both upstairs unless that chickenshit Kevin had taken them. Maybe Kevin had returned.

'Kev? Is that you, you asshole?'

Dennis turned on his flashlight and swept the light beam across the kitchen. No one answered and nothing moved.

'Goddamnit, who's there?'

No one answered.

Dennis flashed the light toward the French doors, paranoid with the notion that the police were tricking him.

'Talley?'

Nothing.

Dennis pushed the gun ahead of him and eased through the kitchen toward the garage.

'Is that you, fat boy?'

Nothing.

'Kevin, if that's you, say something, goddamnit. Mars said you left.'

Nothing.

Dennis stepped into the pantry, shining the light through into the laundry room beyond. The floor was covered with a growing red stain that oozed toward him. Dennis frowned, not understanding. He took a step closer, then another. He saw his brother on the floor. Dennis lowered the gun, and straightened.

'Kevin, what the fuck? Get up.'

A deep trembling started at his center, filling him, growing until his entire body shook and the light beam danced mindlessly around the small room.

'Kevin, get up.'

Dennis walked on mile-long legs without feeling. It was hard to keep his balance. He stopped at the edge of the pool of blood and shined the light on his brother. He saw the open neck, the grotesque white bone within the flesh, the wide, staring eyes. Dennis turned off the light.

The fat boy and the girl could not have done this.

Mars.

Mars lied.

Mars killed Kevin.

Dennis backed out of the pantry into the kitchen, then ran for the stairs.

'Mars!'

He took the stairs two at a time, intent only on finding Mars, killing him. Halfway up, he heard the girl scream.

'MARS!'

Dennis slammed into the girl's door, shoving it open so hard that it crashed against the wall. Mars had the girl by her throat, pinned against her desk. Dennis aimed his gun.

'You're dead, you fuck.'

Mars calmly pulled the girl in front of him, blocking Dennis's aim. Dennis saw the knife and the growing bloodstain on Mars's left shoulder.

Mars smiled at Dennis with wide-eyed innocence.

'What's wrong, dude? What are you so pissed off about?'

Dennis could see the terror on the girl's face, her eyes swollen and red. She managed a word.

'Please.'

Dennis raised his gun. He didn't want to shoot past her, but he wanted that fucker Mars square between the eyes. He wanted to make Mars scream.

'This fuck killed Kevin. He cut his damned throat. There's blood everywhere.'

Like he needed her absolution.

The girl closed her eyes and cried harder.

Dennis should have been ready, but he wasn't. He should have pulled the trigger, but he didn't.

And then it was too late.

Mars lifted the girl by the neck and rushed forward, charging Dennis, crossing the short space in no time at all. Dennis hesitated only a heartbeat because he didn't want to shoot the girl, but that was too long. The girl crashed into him, the full force of Mars's weight behind her, knocking Dennis backwards into the hall. Then the girl was cast aside, Mars was on top of him, and Dennis saw a glint off the knife as it came down.

Thomas

Rational thought was beyond him; he was filled with a suffocating fear that drove him to run, to get out, to *move*. Thomas did not know that he screamed. He slipped in the blood, falling hard into the red pool, then slipped again as he climbed onto the washer. He clambered up into the crawl space, cutting his hands and knees as he scrambled across the rafters. He couldn't move fast enough, once banging his head so hard that he saw bright flashes. He had the gun now. He could save himself. His only thought was to reach Jennifer. The two of them would run downstairs and out the door, and neither Mars nor Dennis could stop them. *He had the gun!*

Thomas heard Jennifer's door crash open as he squeezed through the hatch into her closet. He froze, listening, and heard voices. Dennis was shouting at Mars. Mars was holding Jennifer as Dennis faced him, shouting that Mars had cut Kevin's throat. Thomas drew the gun from his pants, big and heavy and awkward, but he didn't know what to do. Dennis had a gun, too!

Then Mars pushed Jennifer into Dennis, and all three of them sprawled into the hall. Thomas crept into the room. Mars grunted like a pig when it eats, drool streaming from his mouth as he stabbed Dennis over and over. Jennifer was crawling away, splattered with blood.

'Jen! C'mon!'

Thomas darted past Mars into the hall, and grabbed Jennifer's arm. He pulled her toward the stair.

'Run!'

The two of them stumbled away as Mars heaved to his feet. His eyes were wild and darting. He was bigger, stronger, faster; Thomas knew that he would catch them.

Thomas whirled around and jerked up the pistol with both hands.

'I'll shoot you!'

Mars stopped. He was streaked with blood, and breathing hard. Blood dripped from his face. Even more blood painted the walls and floor. Dennis bubbled like a fountain and moaned.

The pistol was heavy and hard to hold. It wobbled, even though Thomas held it with both hands. Jennifer pulled at his shoulder, her voice a frightened whisper.

'Keep going. Let's get out of here.'

They backed away, Thomas trying to hold the gun steady.

Mars walked after them, matching them step for step.

Thomas pushed the gun at him.

'Stay away! I'll shoot you!'

Mars spread his arms as if to embrace them. He continued walking.

'Remember what I told you when I tied you to your bed?'

Thomas remembered: *I'm going to eat your heart.*

They reached the landing. Jennifer started down the stairs.

Mars walked faster.

'I'm going to cut out your heart. But I'm going to cut out your sister's heart first, so you can watch.'

'Stay away!'

Fear amped through Thomas like electric current. His body shook with it, and his bladder let go. He didn't want to shoot; he was scared to shoot, scared that it would be wrong even though he feared for his life, scared that he would be punished for it and would burn in hell and branded a bad person who had made a terrible awful mistake, but Mars came on and he was too scared not to shoot, too scared of that awful knife and the blood that dripped and ran over everything and that Mars really would do it, would cut out his heart, and Jennifer's, and eat them both.

Thomas pulled the trigger.

Click!

Mars stopped, frozen at the sharp sound.

Click!

The gun didn't fire.

All the things that his father had showed him at the pistol range came flooding back. He gripped the slide hard and pulled back to load a bullet into the chamber, but the slide locked open and did not close. Thomas glanced down into the open action. The magazine was empty. The pistol was unloaded. There were no bullets. *There were no bullets!*

When Thomas looked up again, Mars smiled.

'Welcome to my nightmare.'

Jennifer screamed, 'Run!'

Thomas threw the gun at Mars and ran, following Jennifer down the stairs. The air was thick with the smell of gasoline and vomit. Jennifer reached the front door first, and clawed at the handle, but the door would not open.

'Open it!'

'The deadbolt is locked! Where's the key?'

The key wasn't in the lock. Thomas knew with certain dread that it was probably upstairs in Dennis's bloody pocket.

Mars pounded down the stairs, closing the ground between them. He would be on them in seconds. They would never reach the French doors or garage before he caught them.

Jennifer grabbed his arm and pulled.

'This way! *Run!*'

She pulled him toward their parents' room. Thomas realized that she was taking him to the safest place in the house, but Mars was getting closer, off the stairs now and out of the entry and right behind them.

Thomas raced after his sister down the hall, through their parents' bedroom, and into the security room. They slammed the steel door and threw the bolt in the same moment that Mars crashed into the other side of the door.

The world was silent.

Thomas and Jennifer held each other, shaking and scared. All that Thomas could hear was his own heavying breath.

Then Mars pounded on the door; slow, rhythmic thuds that echoed through the tiny room ... boom ... boom ... boom.

Jennifer squeezed Thomas, whispering.

'Don't move. He can't reach us in here.'

'I know.'

'We're safe.'

'Shut up!'

His father had told him that the door could stop *anything*.

The pounding stopped.

Mars cupped his hands to the door and shouted to make himself heard. His muffled voice came through the steel.

'You're bad. You're bad. You're bad. Now I'm going to punish you.'

Mars hit the door once more, then walked out of the room.

Thomas remembered the cell phone.

He clawed it out of his pocket, and turned it on.

The cell phone chimed as it came to life.

'Thomas! Look!'

Jennifer was watching Mars on the monitors. He was in the entry by the front door. He picked up the two containers of gasoline, then walked through the house splashing gasoline on the walls. He smiled as he worked.

Jennifer said, 'Ohmigod, he's going to burn us.'

The cell phone chimed again, and Thomas glanced at the display. The battery indicator flickered.

The cell phone was going dead.

24

Saturday, 2:16 a.m.

Mars

Mars turned off the remaining lights as he passed them. The entry hall turned black. The office followed, then the den. Mars knew that the police would see the rooms fail like closing eyes, and wonder why the house was dying.

Mars went to the kitchen first. He found matches in a jar by the range, then blew out the pilot lights. He splashed gasoline over the range top and gas line, then moved back toward the master bedroom, carefully pouring an unbroken trail of gas along the walls. He loved moving through the house. Shadows gave him the power of invisibility; darkness was his friend. Mars regretted that he would never see his mother again, but only because he enjoyed torturing the rotten bitch. He heard her voice even now, alive in his head:

I hate to see a boy do bad things! I hate to see a bad boy, Marshall! Why do you make me punish you this way?

I don't know, Mama.

This will make you a better man.

She didn't like to see a boy do bad things, so now he made her watch *all* the bad things, and sometimes even made her participate. He regretted that she wasn't with him now; he would have enjoyed introducing her to Kevin and Dennis.

Mars emptied the first bucket of gasoline, then used the second, continuing the trail of gas into the bedroom. He splashed the bed and the walls and the security door.

Then he took out the matches.

Thomas

Thomas dialed Talley's number and pressed the button to send the call.

The phone died.

'Thomas!'

'The battery's low! You never charge it!'

Jennifer snatched the phone from him and pressed the power button. The phone chirped as it came to life, but once more failed.

Jennifer angrily shook the phone.

'Piece of *shit!*'

'Do you think he's really gonna do it?'

'I don't know!'

'Maybe we should run!'

'We would never get past him!'

Thomas watched as Jennifer pried off the cell phone's battery. She rubbed the copper contacts hard on her shirt sleeve, then licked them before snapping the battery back onto the phone.

'What are you doing?'

'Thomas, I *live* on this phone. I know every trick in the book for making it work.'

Mars grinned at the monitors, then lit a match. He held it up to make sure that they saw it. The tiny flame was a glob of flickering white on the monitor screen. He let the flame grow, then brought it close to the door.

Thomas grabbed Jennifer's arm.

'He's going to do it!'

Jennifer pushed the power button. The phone chirped again as it came to life, and this time it stayed on. She jammed the phone into his hands.

'Here! It's working!'

Thomas punched in Talley's number, then glanced up at the monitors. Mars was staring into the camera as if he saw directly into their eyes and hearts. Then Thomas saw his lips move.

'What's he saying?'

Jennifer grabbed Thomas and pulled him away from the door.

'He's saying good-bye.'

Mars tossed the match.

The room erupted in flame.

Talley

When Talley heard the first scream from the house, he took a position behind a Highway Patrol car. The CHiPs in the cul-de-sac shifted uncomfortably because they heard it, too. Talley couldn't tell if the voice was male or female, but there had only been the one scream. Now the house was still.

Talley moved to the nearest Highway Patrol officer.

'You on the command frequency?'

'Yes, sir. You heard that in the house? I think something's going on.'

'Give me your radio.'

Talley radioed Martin, who acknowledged his call without comment.

Talley moved down the line of patrol cars, listening hard for something more from the house, but it was silent.

Then, room by room, the lights went off.

Talley saw Martin approaching, and moved out to meet her. The scream had scared him, but the silence now scared him more. Jones was too far away to have heard.

Martin huffed up, excited.

'What's going on? Why is the house so dark?'

Talley was starting to explain when they saw a dull orange glow move inside the house at the edges of the window shades. He thought it was a flashlight.

His phone rang.

'Talley.'

It was Thomas, incoherent from shouting and from a weak connection.

'I can't understand you! Slow down, Thomas; *I can't understand you!*'

'Mars killed Kevin and Dennis, and now he's burning the house! We're in the security room, me and Jennifer! We're trapped!'

The cell connection faltered again. Talley knew that the boy must be getting low on power.

'Okay, son. Okay. I'm coming to get you! How much power do you have?'

'It's dying.'

Talley checked his watch.

'Turn it off, son. Turn it off, but turn it on again in two minutes. I'm on my way in!'

Talley felt strangely distant from himself, as if his feelings were bound in cotton. He had no choice now; he would act to save these children. It didn't matter what the Watchman wanted, or Jones, or even if it put Jane and Amanda at risk. He pulled Martin by the arm, taking her with him as he ran back along the street toward Jones, shouting instructions as they ran.

'Krupchek's torching the house! Get the fire truck up here!'

'What about Jones?'

'I'm getting him now. We're going in!'

'What about your wife?'

'Get the fire truck, and tell your people to stand by; if Jones won't move, we'll go in without him!'

Martin fell behind to use her radio. Talley ran toward Jones.

'Krupchek's torching the house. We have to go in.'

Jones glanced toward the house without expression. Talley could see that Jones didn't believe him.

'We're waiting to hear from the man.'

Talley grabbed Jones's arm, and felt him stiffen. Behind them, the fire engine rumbled to life and swung around the corner.

'The house is burning, goddamnit. Krupchek has those kids trapped in the security room. We can't wait.'

'That's bullshit.'

'Look at it!'

Talley shoved Jones toward the house.

Flames were visible in the den window. Police radios crackled as the perimeter guards reported the fire, and the officers in the cul-de-sac openly milled behind their cars, waiting for someone to do something. Hicks and the Sheriff's tactical team trotted toward Martin.

Jones seemed frozen in place, anchored by his expectation of the Watchman's call.

Talley jerked his arm again, pulling him around.

'I'm breaching that house, Jones. Are you coming or not?'

'We go when the man says. Not before.'

'We can't wait for the man!'

'They'll fuckin' kill your family.'

'*Those kids are trapped!*'

Jones gripped his MP5. Talley slipped his hand under his sweatshirt and touched the .45.

'What? You want to shoot it out with the chief of police here in the street? You think you'll get the disks that way?'

Jones glanced at the house again, then grimaced. None of this was in the game plan. Everything had suddenly grown beyond their control, and Jones, like Talley, was being swept forward by the storm.

Jones decided.

'All right, goddamnit, but it's just us going into that house. We'll secure the structure, then retrieve the disks.'

'If you don't get your people on the hump, the firemen will get there first.'

They made their assault plan as they ran to the house.

Mars

The flames built slowly, growing up the doors and the walls like flowers on a trellis. Mars followed the flames as they crept along the trail of gas he had made through the house. He thought that the fire would spread with a whoosh, but it moved with surprising lethargy. The air clouded with smoke that smelled of tar.

Mars wanted music.

He went to the den, where he remembered a nice Denon sound system. He tuned to a local hip-hop station, and cranked the speakers to distortion. He helped himself to a bottle of scotch, then returned to the bedroom.

The bed was a raging inferno. Fire covered the doors and walls, and a layer of smoke roiled at the ceiling. The heat made him squint. A layer of smoke roiled at the ceiling. Mars took off his shirt and drank. He checked the Chinaman's gun, saw that there were still plenty of bullets, then took out his knife.

Mars crouched at the far side of the room, far from the flames and below the smoke. He watched the door. He hoped that if the security room grew hot enough, and the children grew frightened enough, the kids would open the door to escape.

Then he would have his way.

Talley

Two men would breach the front door, two the French doors; Talley and Jones would breach through a window to enter a guest bedroom located next to the master. Once inside, Jones would radio the sixth man, who would shatter the sliding doors in the master bedroom to distract Krupchek from the bedroom door, which would be the point of egress for the assault. All of them would carry fire extinguishers to suppress the flames.

Talley didn't have time to get his own vest from his car. He borrowed a vest from one of the CHiPs, strapping it over his sweatshirt, then slung a fire extinguisher over his shoulder. The firemen ran out their hoses, remaining under cover until word would come down that the hostiles had been neutralized.

When they agreed on the assault plan, Talley phoned Thomas. The connection was even weaker than before, and this time Talley told him to keep the phone on. Powering up the system probably cost more power than it saved. If Jones thought anything of Talley and the boy talking, he did not comment.

Martin edged close to Talley as Jones deployed his men.

'What do you want me to do?'

'I don't know.'

'You just going to let them leave with the disks?'

'I don't know what I'm going to do, Martin. I don't know. I just gotta get those kids.'

Talley finished strapping on the vest and adjusted his radio. Everything moved quickly and efficiently, without wasted moves or words. When he was set, he looked over at Jones.

'You ready?'

Jones seated his helmet, then shook himself a last time to settle his equipment.

'Remember, Talley.'

'Let's just do this damned thing.'

Jones set off for the house. Talley let him get a step ahead, then turned back to Martin.

'If I don't get out, don't let him leave. Bring in the detectives and try to save my family.'

'Just make it your business to get out.'

She turned away before he could answer and shouted at her SWAT team to remain in place.

Talley caught up to Jones at the corner of the house outside the guest bedroom window. They heard music, loud and throbbing within the burning house. Talley was thankful for it, because the noise of the music and the fire would cover their entrance. They pulled away the screen, then Jones used a crowbar to wedge open the window. He pushed aside the shade, then gave Talley a thumbs-up, saying the room was clear. They lifted the fire extinguishers into the room, then they waited. They would not enter the house until the others were in position. Talley took the phone from his pocket and checked in with Thomas.

'Thomas?'

'I'm here, Chief.'

The boy's voice broke up, salty with static.

'We're almost there. Three minutes, maybe four. As soon as we get Krupchek, the firemen will come in.'

'It's getting hot.'

'I know. Is Krupchek still in the bedroom?'

Talley wanted to keep the boy talking. If he was talking, he wouldn't have time to think about how scared he was. Neither would Talley.

'He's sitting on the floor by the –'

The cell line went dead.

'Thomas? *Thomas?*'

Nothing.

The boy's phone had finally failed.

Jones glanced over his shoulder at Talley, and twirled his finger. They were spooling up, getting ready to launch.

'Let's go, goddamnit.'

Jones jabbed his finger at the window.

'Go!'

Jones went first, Talley giving him a boost up, then scrambling inside after him. The room was lit only by the low wall of flame that barred the door to the hall. The master bedroom door was only ten feet away. Jones shot the bolt on his MP5; Talley popped the slide on his pistol. They turned on their flashlights, then met each other's eyes. Talley nodded. Jones keyed his mike.

'Now.'

Talley heard the sliding glass doors in the master bedroom shatter at the same time that the front door blew inward off its hinges.

Two fast shots came from the master bedroom. Talley and Jones charged down the hall as a third shot cracked in the bedroom, then they were through the door.

The bedroom was an inferno. The man who had shattered the glass doors was down, writhing in agony. Talley glimpsed a flash of movement from his right and saw Krupchek heave up from behind a Morris chair, chest bare and glistening, an angry, strictured smile on his face. Krupchek screamed, a high-pitched screech, as he swung his pistol, pumping out shots even as Talley and Jones fired. Krupchek stumbled backwards, arms windmilling as he fell into the flames, thrashing and still screaming. Jones fired two short bursts into him and he was still.

They unstrapped their fire extinguishers as Jones's other men cleared through the door, covering the room with their weapons.

Talley shouted, 'We're clear!'

Jones pointed at the first two, then the fallen man.

'You and you, him, out to the van.'

Talley blasted gouts of CO_2 at the burning security door, and shouted for Jones to help.

'Jones! The kids are in here.'

Jones shoved the next man toward the door.

'The office is at the front of the house. Make sure the hall is clear.'

'Help me get these kids!'

Jones and the last man joined Talley at the wall. Their CO_2 extinguishers hissed like dragons. The red walls turned black as the flames engulfing them died. Talley banged at the door with his fire extinguisher.

'Thomas! It's me!'

The fire on the walls licked to life again, eating away the paint.

'Thomas!'

Talley fogged the door as it opened. The boy and his sister stood back, wary of the heat. Jones grabbed Talley's arm.

'They're yours, Talley. We're getting the disks.'

Talley let them go. He blasted the walls around the door again to beat back the flames, then stepped through and took the boy's hand.

'We're going to move fast. Stay behind me.'

Jennifer crowded next to him, nervously peering around him into the room.

'Is he dead?'

Talley ached when he saw her. Jennifer and Amanda were close to the same age. They wore their hair in the same cut. He wondered where Amanda was now. He wondered if she was looking for her own monster.

'He's dead, Jennifer. Come on. You guys did great.'

Talley hurried them along the hall, using the fire extinguisher whenever the flames crowded too close. He paused only long enough to switch his radio to the Bristo frequency, and called Mikkelson.

'Mikki!'

'Go, Chief!'

'The kids are coming out the front. Take care of them.'

When they reached the entry, Talley could see into the office. Jones and his men were searching Smith's desk. Talley pulled Thomas aside out of their view, knowing that these were his last few moments to save his own family. The Watchman would know that they had entered the house. He would be calling Jones for a report, and he would be expecting the disks.

Talley bent close to the boy.

'Are the disks still up in your room?'

'Yeah. With my computer.'

Talley pointed at Mikkelson waiting in the cul-de-sac, and pushed the kids through the door.

'Go to her. Go!'

Talley waited to see that both kids ran toward the cars, then he slipped up the stairs. The air on the second floor was dense with smoke so thick that it choked the beam from his flashlight to a dull glow. He couldn't see more than a few feet. He worked his way along the wall and found Rooney lying outside the first door. Red bubbles clustered on Rooney's chest and mouth like glass mushrooms. Talley couldn't tell if he was dead or alive, and didn't take the time to check. He kicked Rooney's pistol away, then looked in the first room long enough to realize that it belonged to Jennifer. He moved down the hall. The second room belonged to the boy. Talley found his computer on the floor at the far side of the bed. One disk sat on the floor, the other in a disk drive beside the keyboard. Talley held the light close to read their labels, his heart pounding, and saw that he had them – disk one and disk two; the only leverage he had that could save his family!

'Talley!'

Talley jerked at the voice, then saw that Martin was standing in the door. Her helmet was cinched tight and her pistol was at her side.

'Did you find them?'

He joined her. The smoke was heavier now. Talley saw flames at the end of the hall.

'Where's Jones?'

'They're tearing up the office. They haven't found the disks.'

'The boy had them in his room.'

Talley showed her the disks. He wanted to find a way out without seeing Jones and started for the stairs. Martin grabbed his arm. She brought up her gun.

'Give them to me.'

He was startled by her tone. He glanced at the gun, then saw that Martin was watching him with anxious eyes.

'What are you talking about?'

'Give me the disks.'

He glanced at the gun again, and knew with certainty that Benza owned her.

Talley shook his head.

'When did they get to you?'

She thumbed off the safety lever.

'Give me the disks, Talley. You'll get your family.'

He knew that he wouldn't. He knew that once Benza was safe, anyone who knew anything about Smith's relationship to Sonny Benza would die.

Talley stepped back, holding the disks at his side. Once she had the disks she would kill him. It would be easier that way.

'Where's Jones?'

'Still downstairs. He doesn't even know.'

'What are you going to do, Martin? Tell them I was shot in the confusion? You going to blame Krupchek and Rooney?'

'If I have to.'

'How much are they paying you?'

'More than you'll ever know.'

She raised the gun higher.

'Now give me the disks.'

The flames crept up the stairwell at the end of the hall. Talley saw their twisting red glow through the smoke, and something moving in the glow.

'Give me the disks, Talley. It's the only way to get out of this alive.'

A shadow lifted itself from the floor.

'Rooney's alive.'

Her eyes flicked once to the side, then came back to him. She didn't believe him.

'*Give me the disks!*'

Dennis Rooney lurched into the light, eyes glassy and dripping with blood. He had found his gun.

'*Martin!*'

She turned, but not in time. Rooney fired before she could swing her gun to him. Something hard slapped Talley in the chest. The next bullet caught Martin in the thigh, and the third in the cheek beneath her right eye.

Martin spun slowly into the smoke as Talley drew his weapon and fired.

25

Saturday, 2:41 a.m.

Talley

The heavy bullet from Talley's combat pistol bounced Dennis Rooney off the wall, leaving a gory smear of blood. Talley planted a knee in Rooney's chest and knocked away his gun, but this time Rooney was dead. Talley listened for the sound of Jones's team coming up the stairs, but he couldn't hear anything over the crackling, snapping sound of the fire.

He radioed Mikkelson.

'You got the kids?'

'We heard shots!'

'*Do you have the kids?*'

'Yes, sir. They're safe.'

'The FBI agents took out a wounded man. Three of them went to their van.'

'Ah, roger. We saw that.'

Talley's mind raced. He had taken the offensive, and now he had to finish the assault. Time was his enemy. He had to take the fight to the Watchman and press his advantage.

'Get Jorgenson and Cooper. If Larry's back, get him, too. Arrest them. Strip their radios and cell phones, cuff them, and don't let them communicate with anyone.'

'Ah, arrest the FBI?'

'They're not FBI. Arrest them, Mikki. They are armed and dangerous, so you watch your ass. Have someone bring them to the jail, but do not – I repeat, do *not* – let them talk to anyone: no phone calls, no press, no lawyers, nothing. Don't tell anyone about this. Do you understand?'

'Ah, sure, Chief.'

'Stand by.'

Everything now depended on speed. The Watchman might learn that his people were being arrested, but his information would be spotty and incomplete; he wouldn't know what had happened or why, so he wouldn't act against Jane and Amanda until he knew the details. Talley was counting on that. He was betting his family on it. If Talley had any hope of saving his family, he had to do it before the Watchman knew what he was doing.

Talley pushed the disks under his vest and ran to the stairwell. The fire in the entry had jumped to the stairs and was climbing the walls. The smoke was a twisting orange haze. Talley crept down the stairs with his eyes on the office, then crossed to the door just as one of Jones's men stepped out. Talley aimed at his face, touching his own lips to motion the man quiet, then stripped his pistol and MP5. Talley handcuffed him and pushed him into the office.

Jones was frantically searching the floor around the desk, his flashlight beam dim in the haze; the drawers had been pulled, their contents scattered. The second man was stripping books from the shelves. They both looked up when Talley pushed the first man to the floor.

Talley trained his gun on them. He no longer felt the fire's heat; he was so amped on adrenaline and fear that he was totally focused on the two men in front of him.

'Hands on your heads, lace your fingers, turn around with your backs to me.'

Jones said, 'What the fuck are you doing?'

The second man swung his MP5, but Talley squared him with a round, the heavy .45 punching through his vest. Talley had fired ten thousand practice rounds a year every year on the LAPD's combat training range when he was with SWAT. He didn't have to think about it.

Talley brought his gun back to Jones.

'Lace your fingers. *Now!*'

Jones raised his hands, then slowly turned. He laced his fingers over the top of his head.

'You're fucking up, Talley. They've got your family.'

Talley stripped the second man of his weapons, never taking his gun from Jones. He tossed the weapons to the side, checked the pulse in the man's neck, then went to Jones. He took his pistol and MP5, tossed them with the others, then ripped the power cord from Smith's computer. He forced Jones onto his belly, then pulled his hands behind his back. He pressed the gun to Jones's neck.

'Move, I'll fucking kill you.'

Talley planted his knee in the small of Jones's back, then tied his wrists. He wanted to get Jones out of the house, but he didn't want to do it on television. He keyed his radio.

'Mikki?'

'Jesus, Chief, are you all right? We heard more shots.'

'Have the firemen move in, then roll your car to the back of the house on Flanders Road. Meet me there.'

Talley knew that the television cameras would be trained on the firefighters. He wanted everyone's attention on the front of the house, not the rear. He didn't want the Watchman seeing this on television.

'What's going on?'

'*Do it!*'

Talley pushed Jones and the surviving man to the rear of the house. The fire was consuming the house; wallpaper was peeling off the walls and chunks of drywall fell from the hall ceiling. When they reached the French doors, Talley changed his radio to the Sheriff's command frequency and told the officers on the back wall to kill their lights. The backyard plunged into darkness. Talley pushed the two men outside and hustled them straight to the wall. When the Sheriff's sergeant-supervisor saw that Talley had two FBI agents bound, he said, 'What the fuck's going on?'

'Help me get these guys over.'

Mikkelson and Dreyer were climbing out of their car by the time Talley jumped to the ground.

The SWAT officers stared at Jones and the other man. Here they were, the backs of their vests blazoned with a huge white FBI, cuffed and dragged over the wall. The sergeant again asked Talley what was happening, but Talley ignored him.

'Martin's inside. The second floor. She's been shot.'

Talley got the response he wanted. The SWAT cops poured over the wall and rushed toward the house.

Talley shoved his prisoners toward Mikkelson's car.

Jones said, 'You're finished, Talley.'

'I'm not the guy with his hands tied.'

'You know what he's going to do, don't you? You understand that?'

'I've got the disks, you motherfucker. We'll see how much your boss wants them now.'

When Mikkelson saw the two FBI agents, she pooched out her lips in confusion.

'Jesus. Did I miss something here?'

'These people aren't FBI.'

Talley pushed the first man into the backseat of their car, then shoved Jones against the fender.

'Where are they?'

'I don't know. I'm not part of that.'

'Then where is *he?*'

'I don't know.'

'What's his name?'

'It doesn't work like that, Talley. He's a voice on the phone.'

Talley searched Jones's pockets as he spoke, and found Jones's cell phone. He pressed star 69, but nothing happened.

'Shit!'

He pushed the cell phone in Jones's face.

'What's his number?'

'I don't know any more than you.'

Talley kneed him in the stomach.

Dreyer said, 'Holy shit.'

Talley slammed Jones into the car.

'You fucking well know his number!'

'I want to talk to an attorney.'

Talley kneed him again, doubling Jones over. Mikkelson and Dreyer squirmed uneasily.

'Ah, Chief...'

'These bastards have my family.'

Talley cocked the .45 and pressed it into Jones's cheek.

'We're talking about my wife and daughter, you sonofabitch. You think I won't kill you?'

Talley wasn't on Flanders Road anymore; he had stepped into the Zone. It was a place of white noise where emotions reigned and reason was meager. Anger and rage were nonstop tickets; panic was an express. He had been all day coming to this, and here he was: The SWAT guys used to talk about it. You went to the Zone, you lost your edge. You'd lose your career; you'd get yourself killed, or, worse, somebody else.

Talley bent Jones backwards across the trunk of the car. He had to reach the Watchman, and this man knew how. He didn't have time to wait for the Watchman to call. He needed the Watchman off guard. Time was his enemy.

'He calls me. Just like with you.'

Talley's head throbbed. He told himself to shoot the sonofabitch, put one in his shoulder joint and make him scream. Mikkelson's voice came from far away.

'Chief?'

The white noise cleared and Talley stepped back from the Zone. He lowered his gun. He wasn't like them.

Jones glanced away. Talley thought he seemed embarrassed.

'I don't call him. He calls me, just like with you. That's how they stay safe. Just hang on to the phone. He'll call.'

Talley stared at Jones's phone, then dropped it to the street and crushed it. He had the Nokia, but if it rang, he would not answer it. If the Watchman placed the call, the Watchman would expect him to answer. Talley didn't want to do what the Watchman expected.

'Put him in a cell with the others.'

Everything seemed like it was ending even before it began. He couldn't stop now. Once you breached the structure, you pressed on until the end. If you stopped, you died.

Smith would know. They trusted Smith with their closest secrets. It had all come back to Smith again.

'Where are the kids?'

'Cooper has them with the paramedics. They're okay. We finally got the mother, Chief. She's flying back from Florida.'

'Tell Cooper to meet me at the hospital. Tell him to bring the children.'

Talley wiped the smoke from his eyes as he looked back at the house. The fire was eating its way through the roof. Tongues of flame lapped beneath the eaves even as silver rainbows of water arced over the house. Talley could smell the fire on his skin and in his clothes. He smelled like a funeral pyre.

Ken Seymore

Seymore was trading Adderall for cold dim sum with a news crew from Los Angeles when a string of dull pops snapped from the direction of the house. The Los Angeles remote producer, a skinny kid with a goatee and no life experience, stopped his discourse on news selection as a political vehicle.

'What was that?'

Ken Seymore recognized the sound right away: gunfire.

Seymore knew that Howell hadn't launched the breach, because Howell would have told him. He trotted to the nearest news van to find out what was happening. The tech there monitored a police scanner tuned to the Sheriff's tactical frequency.

'You guys get anything on that?'

The tech waved him silent. He listened to the scanner with a bug in his ear, because their news director didn't want anyone else to hear.

'They called up the fire company. The goddamned house is on fire.'

'What was the shooting?'

'That was gunfire?'

'Hell, yes.'

The tech waved Seymore quiet again and tuned his receiver, working through the frequencies.

'The SWAT team went in. Shit, they got casualties. It sounds like they got the kids. Yeah, the kids are coming out.'

The technician pulled the plug from his ear and shouted for his producer.

A heavy column of smoke rose into the light from the helicopters, and then another string of pops echoed over the neighborhood.

Seymore took out his phone.

Glen Howell

The local stations resumed live coverage because of the fire. Flames lapped from the windows on the left side of the house, but the fire at the rear, back by the pool, was going pretty good. Fire crews hosed the roof and shadows ran along the perimeter, but the aerial shot was so murky that

Howell couldn't tell who was who or what was happening, just that everything was going to hell.

'You sure Jones's people got hit?'

'They said it was FBI, so it hadda be Jones's guys. We're getting this shit off the scanner.'

'They get the disks?'

'I don't know. It's happening right now; no one's talking to us.'

'Why the fuck did they go in?'

'I thought you gave'm the green light.'

'It wasn't me.'

'Hang on a sec; there's more traffic on the scanner. Okay, they're saying two FBI agents came out and both kids. The kids are out.'

Howell tried to stay calm.

'Who's in the fuckin' house?'

'I don't know.'

'Is Jones still in the goddamned house?'

'I don't know.'

'Where's Talley?'

'I don't know.'

'You're paid to know, goddamnit. That's why you're there.'

Howell broke the connection, then punched in Jones's number. The phone rang once, then a computer voice came on telling him that the user had left the service area or turned off his phone. Howell called Martin. He let her phone ring fifteen times, and finally hung up.

'Fuck!'

He dialed Talley's number and listened to the Nokia ring. He let it ring twenty times, and then he snapped his phone shut so hard he thought he might have broken it.

Talley

Talley rolled code three all the way to the hospital. He beat Cooper, arriving a few minutes after three A.M. The parking lot was almost deserted; the remaining press camped by the emergency room entrance. Talley parked at the side of the hospital to avoid them, but got out of the car because sitting was difficult. He leaned against the door with his arms crossed, watching the street, then realized he was still wearing the bullet-resistant vest and the radio. He took them off and tossed them into the backseat. He found the Nokia, and dropped it onto the front seat.

The Nokia rang.

Talley hesitated in the door of the car, thinking the Watchman had finally heard about the house. He stared at the ringing phone as if he was hiding from it, as if any movement might draw the Watchman's eye and the Watchman would somehow know that Talley was there. Talley should have turned the goddamned thing off. He wanted the Watchman to wonder.

Talley felt his chest tighten, and realized that he had stopped breathing. The phone stopped ringing as Cooper turned into the parking lot. Talley took a breath, then raised his hand, but Cooper was already turning toward him.

Talley watched carefully as Thomas and Jennifer got out of Cooper's car. They looked pale and tired, and their eyes were anxious with apprehension. Talley knew that they might seem fine now in the initial elation of being released, but later there could be nightmares, flashbacks, and other symptoms of post-traumatic stress disorder. Jennifer reminded him of Amanda all over again. Talley felt himself lifted by such a swell of feeling that he wanted to both cry and hug them, but he only let himself smile.

Jennifer said, 'Are we going to see our father?'

'That's right. Did Officer Cooper tell you about your mother? We spoke with her in Florida. She's flying back now.'

They beamed. Jennifer actually said, 'Yay.'

Talley put out his hand.

'We didn't really meet before. My name is Jeff Talley.'

'I'm Jennifer Smith. Thank you for what you did.'

She shook his hand firmly, her smile blinding. Thomas shook his hand as if it were serious business. They stood so close together that their arms touched, and both children stood very close to him. He knew that this was normal. He was the man who had saved them.

'It's good to finally meet you, Thomas. You were a big help. You were very brave. You both were.'

'Thank you, Chief. You're really dirty.'

Jennifer rolled her eyes, and Cooper laughed.

Talley glanced at his hands. They were streaked with soot and sweat, as was his face.

'I guess I am. I haven't had time to clean up.'

Jennifer said, 'He can be so rude. You should look at yourself, Thomas. You've got ash on your nose.'

Thomas rubbed at his nose, but his eyes never left Talley.

'Is our daddy okay?'

'He's doing better. Let's go see him.'

Talley brought them through the side entrance. He held their hands, letting go only to badge an orderly who led them through the hospital to the emergency room. Everyone they passed stared at them. Talley knew that it was only a matter of time before word spread to the press that the chief of police had brought the hostage children to their father. When the press knew, the Watchman would know.

Talley refused to bring the children through the ER admitting area. The orderly led them past the hospital laboratory along a hall that the ER personnel used to bring samples to the lab. Klaus and Reese were no longer present, but a nurse that Talley recognized from before stopped them.

'You're the Chief, aren't you? May I help you?'

'I'm bringing the Smith children to see their father.'

'I'd better get Dr. Reese.'

'Fine, you go get her. We'll be in the room.'

Talley found Smith's room without waiting. He thought that Smith would be sleeping, but Smith was staring at the ceiling, his eyes blinking. He was still wired to the monitors.

Jennifer said, 'Daddy?'

Smith lifted his head enough to see, and then his face registered surprise and elation.

The kids ran to him, both to the side of the bed without wires, and hugged their father. Talley waited in the door, giving them a moment, then entered and stood at the end of the bed. Jennifer cried, her face buried in her father's chest. The little boy wiped at his eyes and asked if it hurt.

Talley watched. Smith wrapped his arm around Jennifer and held Thomas's arm. He looked up past them, met Talley's eyes, then hugged his children tighter.

'Thank God you're all right. You're all right, aren't you? You're okay?'

'Mommy's coming home.'

Talley stepped up behind Jennifer.

'We reached your wife. She's in the air now.'

Smith met Talley's eyes again, then looked away.

Talley said, 'Your family is safe.'

Smith nodded, still not looking at him.

'What happened to the three men?'

'They're dead.'

Thomas pulled at his father's arm.

'Daddy, our *house* is on fire. We almost *burned.*'

Thomas jerked his father's arm again, then coughed a great shuddering sob and buried his face in his father's stomach. It was all coming out now, all of Thomas's tension and fear. Smith stroked his son's hair.

'It's okay, partner. It's okay. You're safe. That's all that's important.'

Talley waited until the boy had calmed, then squeezed Jennifer's shoulder.

'Could you guys wait in the hall for a second? I need to talk to your dad.'

Smith glanced up, then nodded to send his children to the hall. Jennifer took Thomas's hand and led him outside. Smith took a deep breath, let it out, then looked up.

'Thank you.'

Talley took out the two disks.

Smith stared at them, then looked away again.

'Did you tell my kids?'

'No. They'll have questions. Thomas helped me get them. He opened them on his computer.'

'It wouldn't mean anything to him.'

'He'll wonder. He's going to ask sooner or later.'

Smith sighed again.

'Shit.'

'Those are good kids you got there. That little boy, Thomas, he's something else.'

Smith closed his eyes.

Talley watched Smith, wondering if there was anything he could say to get this man to help him. He had negotiated with hundreds of subjects, and that was the game: Figure out what they needed to hear and say it; find their buttons and push them. All of that seemed beyond Talley now. He didn't know what to say. He glanced over at Thomas and Jennifer standing in the hall, and felt a pain so deep and pure that he thought it might break him. If he could just get Jane and Amanda back, he would never let them go.

He patted Smith's arm.

'I don't know where you come from or what you've done in your life, but you'd better do right by those kids. You've got your family now, Smith. They're safe. Help me get mine.'

Smith blinked hard at the ceiling. He shook his head, then closed his eyes tight. He took another deep breath, then looked past Talley to his own children.

'Shit.'

'Yeah. Shit.'

Smith looked at him. Smith's eyes were wet.

'If you've got the disks, you've got everything. You can put them all away.'

'Who has my family?'

'That would be Glen Howell. He was coming to the house today. He's Benza's man on the scene.'

Talley touched his wrist.

'Gold Rolex here? Dark tan?'

Smith nodded.

Talley was getting excited. He had something now. He was close by the door and ready to breach.

'Okay, Smith. Okay. Glen Howell. He's been calling me, but now I need to call him. How do I reach him?'

Smith gave him Howell's phone number.

26

Saturday, 3:09 a.m.

Talley

Talley doubled the guards on Smith and his children, then hurried back to his car. He closed his eyes and tried to find focus. He was a crisis negotiator; Howell was a subject; Amanda and Jane were hostages. He had done this before; he could do it again. It was just him and the phone.

I'm going to kill this dog!

The overhead lights made the world purple. Talley looked up at the sky, but could see only a few stars past the bright lights. A few stars were enough; Jane and Amanda were under these same stars. So was Howell.

When his breathing was even and his shoulders relaxed, Talley got into the car. His task was to sound confident and controlled. His task was to assume control.

Talley punched Howell's number into the Nokia. His body began to shake with tension, but he fought it. He closed his eyes again. He breathed.

The Watchman answered on the second ring, sounding abrupt and irritated.

'What?'

Talley made his voice soft.

'Guess who.'

Howell recognized his voice. Talley heard it in the quality of the silence even before Howell answered.

'How'd you get this number?'

'Here are two words for you: Glen Howell.'

'Fuck yourself.'

'I think Sonny Benza is going to fuck *you*. I have his financial records. I have your SWAT team. I have Captain Martin. I have you. And I have Walter Smith.'

Howell's voice rose.

'I have your fucking family. Don't forget that.'

Talley kept his voice even. He knew that if he remained calm, Howell would grow more frightened. Howell would suspect that Talley was up to something, and, by suspecting it, he would believe that it was true.

Howell's only way out now was through Talley. Talley had to make him see this.

'You know where you screwed up? If you had sat tight and let this thing play out, if you hadn't brought me into it or sent in your fucking animals, I would never have known. The disks would have slipped through the cracks, and Benza would be safe. Now you have to deal with me.'

'You're drowning in deep water, Talley. You're just some fuckin' cop who doesn't have a clue. You're killing your family. You're committing suicide.'

'I'll give you five minutes. Call Benza. Ask him if he wants to spend the rest of his life in prison.'

'I'll ask him how many times he wants me to fuck your daughter.'

'Ask him if I can keep the money.'

All Talley heard was the hiss of the cell connection.

'I have something else that belongs to you. I found some money in the house. Looks like almost a million dollars.'

Talley had learned from a hundred negotiations that all liars think everyone lies, all thieves think everyone steals, crooked people think everyone is crooked. The strain in the silence was the sound of Howell trying to read Talley just as Talley was reading Howell. He would be scared and suspicious, but he would also want to believe. His belief was everything.

Howell answered slowly.

'What do you want, Talley?'

'How much money did I find?'

'One-point-two million.'

'I'll sell you a pass. My wife and daughter, and the money, for the disks. If you hurt them, the disks go straight to the FBI and I'll keep the money anyway.'

Talley knew that Howell would never consider a straight-up trade, his family for the disks, because there was no reason for Talley to keep his word. But the money changed things. Howell would understand greed. He would see himself in Talley and believe that a cop might think he could get away with that.

Talley didn't wait for Howell to answer.

'I'll tell you how this is going to work. I'll bring the disks to the north entrance of the mall by the freeway. You bring my family. If they're okay, we'll trade. If I don't make it home tonight, my officers will still have Smith and your phony FBI SWAT team.'

'You make it home, you'll cut them loose?'

'I'll cut them loose.'

'Okay, Talley, I think we can do this.'

'I thought we might.'

'But not at the mall. We'll do this where I want to do this.'

'As long as it's not in the middle of nowhere.'

'The Comfort Inn west of Bristo.'

'I know it.'

'Be there in ten minutes. Someone will be waiting in the parking lot. One minute late, there won't be anyone there to find.'

Talley ended the call. He placed the Nokia carefully on the seat, then closed his eyes. The Comfort Inn was less than a mile away. He got out of the car, stripped off his sweatshirt, then strapped on the vest. He pulled the sweatshirt over it. He checked his pistol; one in the chamber, safety on. He left his radio on, but turned the speaker volume down to zero. He got back into the car.

He still had much to do.

Glen Howell

Howell was shaking when he put down the phone. Talley had caught him off guard and jammed him into making a deal that might be a setup, but he didn't see what other choice he'd had. His job was to recover the disks.

Howell picked up the house phone. Duane Manelli was sitting in a room two doors down with LJ Ruiz.

'I need you and LJ outside. Talley's coming here.'

'What the fuck!'

'I don't know if he's coming alone. Get your ass outside and set up to watch the area.'

'What happened to Jones?'

'Jones is down.'

Howell hung up. He checked his watch. He didn't want to make his next call, but he didn't have a choice about that, either. Making the next call scared him more than waiting for Talley.

He dialed Sonny Benza.

Palm Springs

'Sonny? Sonny, wake up.'

Benza opened his eyes, and saw Phil Tuzee. Charles Salvetti was pacing by the desk, looking upset. Benza was stretched out on the couch, the three of them still in his office at four in the morning. Benza's back ached like a sonofabitch. Another fuckin' trip to the chiropractor.

'What?'

'Glen Howell's on the phone. We got a friggin' mess here. Look.'

Benza sat up and squinted at the television. Smith's house was in flames.

'Jesus Christ. What happened?'

'It's a fuckin' bloodbath. Howell's team went in, and everything went to hell. Now they're pulling bodies out of the place.'

'Did we get the disks?'

Benza knew the answer from Tuzee's expression. Acid flooded his stomach.

'No, skipper. Talley has the disks.'

Salvetti called from the desk.

'C'mon. Howell's on the speaker. He says we don't have much time.'

Benza went to the phone, trying to control his anger.

'What the fuck are you doing down there?'

Howell cleared his throat, leaving Benza to conclude that the man was rattled. Benza didn't like that. Glen Howell wasn't a man to rattle.

'It isn't working out the way we planned.'

'I guess it fuckin' well isn't.'

Howell explained the situation. Talley not only had the disks; he had Smith, Jones, and Jones's team. Benza saw himself killing Glen Howell. He saw himself driving Howell to the desert and chopping him into sausage with a machete.

'Sonny?'

Benza's rage cleared, and he saw Salvetti and Tuzee watching him. Howell was still talking. Sonny Benza was more frightened now than he had ever been in his life. He interrupted.

'Glen? Listen to me, Glen.'

He spoke softly, trying to keep his voice from shaking. Salvetti and Tuzee watched him.

'I want to tell you something here, Glen, before you go any further. I trusted you to handle this, and you've fucked it up. You're letting me down here, Glen.'

'Sonny, Talley has the disks, but we can still get this settled.'

Howell's voice shook.

'It's good you've got a plan for that.'

'He wants the money that Smith was holding for us, the one-point-two. He gets his family and the money, he says he'll give us the disks and cut loose our guys.'

Salvetti said, 'Waitaminute. Are you saying that this asshole wants to be paid off? He's *extorting* us?'

'One-point-two is a lot of money.'

Tuzee shook his head, looking at Benza but speaking to Howell.

'It's a setup. He's baiting you to get the wife.'

'What other choice do we have?'

Benza answered, softly again, without waiting for Tuzee's or Salvetti's opinion.

'You don't have any other choice.'

Howell didn't answer for several seconds.

'I understand.'

'Hang on.'

Benza muted the phone. He stretched his back, trying to lessen the ache, but it only hurt worse. He tried to figure out which way to jump; either Talley was really trying to scam the cash or he wasn't. If Talley was setting up Howell, the next few hours would be a shit storm. Federal agents might already be pouring over the disks and petitioning for warrants. Benza knew that he should warn New York, but the thought of it made his bowels clench.

'Phil, call the airport and have the jet prepped. Just in case.'

Tuzee went to the other phone.

Benza took the speakerphone off mute. He didn't want to accept defeat yet; there might still be a way out.

'Okay, Glen, listen: I don't care about the money. If I gotta lose the cash to buy some time, so be it.'

'That's what I figured.'

'If Talley is setting you up, we're fucked anyway.'

'I'll give you fair warning.'

'Fuck you and your fair warning. Get the disks, then get rid of him. If you don't get the disks, you're gonna have a problem, Glen. You understand that?'

'Our guys will still be in custody. He's not going to cut them free until after he has his family.'

Benza glanced at Tuzee again. He didn't like the idea of killing his own employees, but he had done it before. He had to get rid of Smith, Talley, Jones and his crew, and anyone else who was vulnerable after tonight. That was the only way he would be safe.

'After Talley is dead, we'll take care of Smith and Jones and his people. That's the best way to do this. Everyone has to die.'

'I understand.'

Benza pressed the button to end the call, then went back to the couch. Salvetti came over and sat next to him.

'This thing is goin' south, Sonny. We gotta think about that. We should warn New York. We let'm know what's comin', old man Castellano might cut us some slack.'

Benza considered that, then shook his head.

'Fuck New York. I'm not that anxious to die.'

'You sure about that, Sonny? We still got a few minutes here.'

'We lose those disks, the last thing I want is a conversation with that old man. Even prison looks good by comparison.'

Salvetti frowned.

'That old man has long arms. He'll reach us even in prison.'

Benza looked at him.

'Jesus, Sally, always the cheery word.'

Tuzee crossed his arms, and shrugged.

'What the fuck, we get those disks, we'll beat the Feds and Castellano will never know this happened. Things could still work out.'

Benza decided to pack. In case things didn't.

27
Santa Clarita, California
Saturday, 3:37 a.m.

Talley

Talley drove without lights, swerving far onto the shoulder whenever he passed an oncoming vehicle. He pulled off the road a hundred yards before the motel and left his car in the weeds, thankful for the black sweatshirt he had pulled on earlier. He tied a roll of duct tape to a belt loop, then shoved a handful of plastic restraints into his pocket. He rubbed dirt on his face and hands to kill their shine, then drew his pistol and trotted toward the motel. The moon was up, bright like a blue pearl, giving him light.

Talley guessed that Howell would post observers to warn him if the police were approaching. He worked his way to the edge of the motel property and froze beside a spiky-leafed manzanita bush, searching the shadows at the edge of the light for some bit of movement or blackness that did not fit. Talley had approached a thousand armed houses when he was on SWAT; this time was no different. The motel was a long two-story barn surrounded by a parking lot. A smattering of cars were sleeping outside the ground-floor rooms. Two huge tractor-trailer trucks sat at the rear; a third was parked near the street. Talley worked his way around the perimeter of the grounds, moving outside the field of light, pausing every two paces to look and listen.

He spotted one observer on the east side parking lot, sitting between the wheels of an eighteen-wheeler that had been docked for the night. A few minutes later, he found the second man hunkered beneath a pepper tree across the street on the west side. Talley looked carefully for others, but only two men were posted.

Duane Manelli

Manelli lay belly-down in the hard dirt at the base of a pepper tree, watching LJ Ruiz move between the wheels of the eighteen-wheeler. They were hooked up by cell phone. If either saw an oncoming vehicle or anything suspicious, they could alert the other, and then Glen Howell. Manelli didn't like it that he could see movement. This meant that LJ was bored, and bored men made mistakes.

He whispered into his phone.

'LJ, you in position?'

'Yeah, I'm here.'

'Settle in and stop moving around.'

'Fuck yourself. I'm not moving.'

Manelli didn't respond. LJ had stopped moving, so Manelli let it go. Duane Manelli had spent enough time on night recon training exercises when he was in the army to respect radio silence.

Manelli settled into the dirt.

Ruiz said something, but Manelli didn't understand.

'Say again.'

Ruiz didn't answer.

'I didn't hear you, LJ. What'd you say?'

Nothing came back.

'LJ?'

Manelli heard the rocks crunch behind him, then his head exploded with rainbow light.

Talley

Talley bound Manelli's wrists behind the man's back with the plastic restraints, pulling the leads tight. He secured Manelli's ankles the same way, then rolled the man over.

Talley slapped Manelli's face.

'Wake up.'

Talley slapped harder.

'Wake up, goddamnit. You're under arrest.'

Manelli's eyes fluttered. Talley waited until the eyes focused, then pressed the gun into Manelli's neck.

'You know who I am?'

'Talley.'

'Which room are they in?'

'They're not. Howell sent them away.'

Talley cursed under his breath. He didn't expect that Howell would have kept them with him, but he had hoped.

'All right. Where are they?'

'I don't know. Clewes took them.'

Talley had not heard that name before, Clewes, but it didn't matter. He had not heard of any of these people.

'Where did Clewes take them?'

'I don't know. In the car. Howell is gonna call him. I don't know what they're gonna do. That was between Clewes and Howell.'

Talley glanced at the motel, fighting down his panic. The passing seconds loaded onto his back like bags of sand. He was wasting time, and he needed a plan. He told himself to think. He chanted the SWAT mantra: Panic kills. If Jane and Amanda were being held somewhere else, he would have to force Howell to bring them back.

He looked back at Manelli.

'How many people does Howell have?'

'Five here at the motel, plus Clewes.'

'You and the asshole at the truck, leaves three inside?'

'That's right, plus Clewes. He has more people, but I don't know where they are. They could show up here anytime.'

Talley thought it through. Three in the room. Three against one, with more on the way. None of it mattered. He had no other choice.

'Which room?'

Manelli hesitated.

Talley pushed the .45 harder into Manelli's throat. The sweat and dirt from his face dripped onto Manelli like muddy rain.

'Which room?'

Manelli sighed.

'One twenty-four. Let me ask you a question, Talley?'

Talley hesitated. He didn't have time for questions.

'What?'

'You're not just some hick cop?'

'No. No, I'm not.'

Talley covered Manelli's mouth with duct tape, then slipped across the road and returned to the parking lot, searching for room 124. He found the green Mustang on the far side of the motel, parked one parking place down from 124. A man in a blue knit shirt was standing by it, smoking. This man outside left two more men in the room. Talley saw a silver wristwatch on his left arm; this man wasn't Glen Howell.

Talley worked his way as close to the Mustang as possible. The man finished his cigarette, then leaned against the car. He was less than fifteen yards away. Forty-five feet. Talley told himself that it wasn't very far.

The door to room 124 opened, and a man with a dark tan stepped out.

'Keep your eyes open. He should've been here.'

Talley saw a gold Rolex on his wrist, and recognized the voice. Howell.

Talley released the safety on his pistol, and readied himself to move.

The Mustang man complained to Howell.

'This is bullshit. That chickenfuck ain't gonna come. We should get outta this shithole while we still can.'

'He'll come. There's nothing else he can do.'

Howell went back into the room, closing the door.

The Mustang man lit a fresh cigarette. When he turned away, Talley rushed forward.

The Mustang man startled at the sound, but he was too late. Talley hit him hard on the side of the head, using the .45 as a club. The Mustang man staggered sideways. Talley grabbed him around the neck from behind in a choke hold, and pushed him toward the room. He didn't want the Mustang man unconscious; he wanted him as a shield.

Talley moved fast now; he kicked the door next to the knob, busting the jamb, and shoved the Mustang man through, screaming his identification.

'Police! You're under arrest!'

Talley didn't think they would shoot him until they had the disks. He was counting on that.

Glen Howell brought up a pistol as he dropped into a crouch, shouting at a man with a big head seated by the window. The man rolled out of his chair and also came up with a gun, aiming from the floor in a two-handed grip as Howell shouted not to fire.

'Don't shoot him! Don't shoot!'

Talley shifted his aim between the two men, making himself as small as possible behind the Mustang man. Insects spiraled in from the night, hungry for the light.

Talley shouted, 'Where's my family?'

They sucked air like freight engines. No one was shooting, but if one person fired, everyone would fire. They each had something the other wanted. Talley knew it. He knew that Howell knew it. It was the only thing holding them back.

Howell abruptly released his gun, letting it swing free on his finger.

'Just take it easy. Take it easy. We're here to do business.'

'Where are they?'

'Do you have the disks?'

Talley shifted his aim to the man with the big head. He felt as if he was at the day-care center again, held hostage by men with guns.

'You know I have the disks, you sonofabitch. Where's my family?'

Howell slowly stood, hands out, letting his gun hang.

'Let's just take it easy. They're all right. Can I take a phone from my pocket?'

'They were supposed to be here.'

'Let me get the phone. You can talk to them, see they're okay.'

Talley shifted his aim from the big-headed man to Howell, then back again. Howell took out a cell phone and pressed in a number. Someone on the other end answered, and Howell told them to put the woman on. He held out the phone.

'Here. Talk to her. She's all right.'

Talley jammed his gun under the Mustang man's jaw, and warned him not to move. Howell brought the phone over, holding it with two fingers like a teacup. Talley took it with his free hand, and Howell stepped back.

'Jane?'

'Jeff! We're −'

The line went dead.

'SHIT!'

Howell shrugged, reasonably.

'You see? They're alive. Whether they stay that way depends on you.'

Talley tossed the phone back to Howell, then took out a single disk. This was where everything could go bad. This was where he took his biggest chance, and risked everything.

'One disk. You'll get the other when I have my girls. Not talk to them on the phone, but *have* them. I get my girls, you get the disks. You don't like it, tough. You kill me, everyone still goes to jail.'

He tossed the disk onto the bed.

Talley could read that Howell wasn't happy with just the one disk, but Talley was counting on that. He wanted Howell off-balance and worried. It was a negotiation. Talley knew that Howell would be weighing his options just as Talley weighed his; Howell would be wondering if Talley had the second disk with him, thinking that if Talley had both disks, Howell could simply shoot him and take the disks and this would be over. But Howell couldn't be sure. If he killed Talley, and Talley didn't have both disks, then Howell would be fucked. So Howell wouldn't shoot him. Not yet. And that gave Talley a chance to jam him into revealing Amanda and Jane.

Talley watched the tension play over Howell's face. Talley offered nothing.

Howell picked up the disk.

'I have to see if it's real.'

'It's real.'

'I have to make sure.'

An IBM ThinkPad with a Zip drive attached was set up on the nightstand. Howell sat on the edge of the bed as he opened the disk, then grunted at the contents.

'All right. This is one of them. Where's the other?'

'First my girls. I see my girls, you get the disks. That's the way it works.'

Sweat leaked from Talley's hair and ran down his neck. It felt like crawling ants. Howell would either take the chance or he wouldn't. Neither of them had any other choice. It had all come down to which one would break first.

It was a face-off.

Talley waited as Howell considered his options. Talley already knew what he would decide. Talley had left Howell no other choice.

Howell picked up his phone.

Glen Howell

Talley wasn't acting like a has-been cop who had been broken by the job and come to nowhereland to hide; he was carrying on like a full-blown SWAT tactical streetmonster. But Talley was also scared. Howell knew that he had to use that fear; he had to make Talley so frightened of losing his wife and daughter that he stopped thinking. Howell figured that Talley had the second disk on him, but the only way he could find out was to kill him. If he killed Talley, and Talley didn't have the disk, Howell would be fucked. Sonny Benza's message was clear; Benza would kill him.

The phone at the other end rang once before Marion Clewes answered. 'Yes?'

Howell spoke clearly, never taking his eyes from Talley. He wanted Talley to know that Glen Howell held the lives of his wife and child in his hands.

'Bring them. Stop the car outside the room, but don't get out. I want to show him that they're all right.'

'Okey-doke.'

Howell watched Talley closely, and noticed that Talley tensed when Howell told Clewes to stay in the car. Talley didn't like that, but tried not to show it. Howell felt encouraged. He felt as if he had played a winning card.

'Don't hang up. It's very important that you stay on the line. I'll want to talk to you again.'

'All right.'

Howell lowered the phone. Clewes was parked behind a Mobil station down the street. He would be here in seconds.

'Okay, Talley, they're on the way.'

'I want more than just seeing them. I won't give you the disk until I have them.'

'I understand.'

Howell heard the car before he saw it. Clewes wheeled to a stop in the empty space next to the Mustang, the nose of his car framed dead-center in the open door. The woman, Jane, was in the passenger seat. The daughter was in the rear. They were both tied, their mouths taped.

Howell saw Talley move slightly toward the door and his wife, then catch himself before looking back at Howell.

'Tell him to get out of the car.'

Howell raised the phone.

'Marion?'

Outside, Clewes lifted his own phone. They could see each other clearly through the open door.

'Yes, sir?'

'Aim your gun at the woman's head.'

Marion Clewes

The world was comfortable here within Marion's car, which still held that yummy new-car smell; with the windows up, the engine idling, and the air-conditioning blowing softly, Marion could hear only the two women crying and the voice in his ear. He took no pleasure in their tears.

'Yes, sir.'

Marion had his orders. Just as Glen Howell's job was to recover the disks, Marion knew exactly what he was supposed to do and when he was supposed to do it. It was all about doing your job, being rewarded if you succeeded, being punished if you failed. Success or failure were defined by the disks.

Marion raised his gun to the mother's head. She trembled, and clenched her eyes. Behind her, in the backseat, the daughter moaned loudly.

Marion smiled warmly, trying to lend comfort, even as he watched the events within the motel.

'Don't worry, ladies. You'll be fine.'

His gun did not waver from its mark.

Talley

The world collapsed to an automobile only ten steps away. Talley saw everything happening inside the car with a clarity so great it seemed unreal: The man behind the wheel touched a small black pistol to Jane's temple. Glistening tears spilled from Jane's eyes. In the backseat, Amanda rocked from side to side, also crying.

Talley screamed, 'NO!'

Howell kept the phone to his mouth, speaking to Talley but also the man in the car.

'Give me the second disk or he'll kill your wife.'

'NO!'

Talley jerked his gun to the man in the car but was scared that the angle of the windshield would deflect his shot. This wasn't like when Neil Craimont had killed the man holding a gun to Talley's head at the day-care center; the man in the car was surrounded by glass. An accurate shot could not be guaranteed. Talley jerked his aim back at Howell. Everything was suddenly wrong; everything that he was trying to do had gone to hell.

Howell was winning.

'I'll kill you, Howell! You'll never get the disk!'

'He'll kill your wife, but your daughter will still be alive. Are you listening to this, Marion?'

Talley saw the man behind the wheel nod. Talley shifted his aim again, back to the man in the car.

'I'll fucking kill you! Can you hear *that*, you sonofabitch?!'

The man in the car smiled.

Howell spoke reasonably.

'I'll still have your daughter. Your wife will be dead, but your daughter will be alive. Do you see her there in the car, Talley? But if you shoot me, then he'll kill your daughter, too. Do you want to lose both of them?'

Talley aimed at the man in the car again. His breath was coming so hard that his gun shook. If he shot low, the bullet would deflect high, but he didn't know how much; anything short of a perfect shot would cost Jane's life. If Talley shot at the man in the car, Howell or the man with the big head would shoot him, and then all of them would be dead.

Howell said, 'The negotiation is over, Talley. I won.'

Talley glanced at Howell. He measured the shots; first the man in the car, then Howell, lastly the man on the floor. He would have to make all three to save his family. He didn't think that he could make them.

Howell said, 'Drop your gun, and give me the second disk. Give me the disk or he'll put her brain on the window.'

Talley's eyes filled because he thought they would all die anyway, but he still had one chance left. One small chance, because Howell and Benza still wanted the disks.

Talley dropped his gun.

The Mustang man jumped out of the way. Howell and the big-headed man charged forward. They scooped up Talley's gun and shoved him against the wall, pinning him like an insect to a board. Howell searched him even as Talley told him about the second disk.

'It's in my left front pocket.'

Talley felt numb. Defeated. Outside, the man behind the wheel climbed out of the car and came to the door. Talley watched Amanda and Jane in the car. Jane met his eye, and in that moment he felt buoyed by a tide of love that felt as if it could carry him away.

Howell loaded the disk into the ThinkPad.

Talley watched him open the disk, and took a grim pleasure in watching Howell's face darken and grow fierce.

'You sonofabitch. This isn't the disk. This isn't the second disk! It's a goddamned blank!'

Talley felt strangely removed from this room and these people. He glanced at Jane again. He smiled at her, the same small smile they had often shared at night when they were alone in bed, and then he turned back to Howell.

'I don't have the second disk anymore. I gave it to the Sheriffs, and they're giving it to the FBI. Benza's over. You're over. There's nothing either of us can do.'

Talley watched the disbelief float to the surface of Howell's face like a great slow bubble.

'You're lying.'

'I'm not lying. We're done here, Howell. Let us go. Let us go and save yourself the murder charge.'

Howell stood stiffly, like a mechanical man. He lumbered around the bed as if he was in shock, picked up his gun from the floor, and aimed it at Talley.

'Are you out of your mind?'

'I just want to take my family home.'

Howell shook his head as if he still couldn't believe that this was happening, and then he blinked numbly at the man in the door, the man who had been in the car.

'Kill every one of these people.'

Marion Clewes

Marion watched as Glen Howell opened the second disk. He was disappointed to see that Talley had tried to fake them out with a false disk, but he had expected as much. Talley was a policeman, after all; Marion had never expected that he would let a man like Sonny Benza walk away, not even with his family being held. In the end, turning over the disk to the proper authorities had been the right thing to do.

'Kill every one of these people.'

It was all about doing your job, being rewarded if you succeeded, being punished if you failed. Success or failure was defined by the disks, and Glen Howell had not recovered the disks.

Marion felt sad about that; he had always liked Glen Howell even though Mr. Howell hadn't liked him.

Marion had his orders.

Marion lifted his gun.

Talley

The man in the door whom Howell had called Marion raised his gun and aimed it squarely at Talley's face. Marion was a small man, ordinary in appearance, the type of anonymous man who would be invisible in a mall and impossible for witnesses to describe. An Everyman; average height, average weight, brown, brown.

Talley stared into the black hole of the muzzle and braced for the bullet.

'I'm sorry, Jane.'

Marion shifted his gun hard to the side and fired. He adjusted his aim, and fired again, then again. The first bullet took Howell above the right eye, the second the Mustang man dead-center in the left eye, and the third caught the man with the big head in the temple.

Marion lowered his gun.

Talley stood motionless against the wall, watching Marion the way a bird watches a snake.

Marion shrugged.

'Life is unforgiving.'

Marion crossed the room to retrieve the one good disk, pocketed it, then went to the car. He helped Jane out, then opened the back door and helped Amanda. He walked around the car, climbed in behind the wheel, and drove away without another word. Talley saw him using his cell phone even before he was out of the parking lot.

The motel was quiet.

A dark wind had blown through Bristo Camino, something beyond Talley's control, beyond his pain and his loss, and now it was gone. Now, only the three of them were left.

'Jane?'

Talley stumbled out of the room and ran to his wife. He hugged her with frantic desperation, then pulled his daughter close, squeezing them to him as the tears spilled down his face. He held them and knew then that he would never let them go, that he had lost them once and now had almost lost them this second time, lost them forever, and that he could and would never allow that to happen again.

It was over.

28
Palm Springs
Saturday, 4:36 a.m.

Sonny Benza

Sonny Benza didn't try to sleep again after they got off the phone with Glen Howell. He popped twenty milligrams of Adderall and snorted two lines of crank to prop himself up, then the three of them sat down to wait.

The first time the phone rang, he damn near jumped off the couch.

Tuzee looked at him, asking if Sonny wanted him to answer the phone. Benza nodded, saying, Yeah, answer it.

Tuzee answered.

'It's the airport. They wanna know where you want to go. They gotta file a flight plan.'

'Tell them Rio. We'll change it in the air.'

As Tuzee hung up, Salvetti said, 'They're still gonna know where we go. These jets fly so high that air-traffic control watches them all the way.'

'Don't worry about it, Sally. We'll take care of it.'

'I'm just saying.'

'Don't worry about it.'

The second time the phone rang, Tuzee answered without asking. Benza could tell from Tuzee's expression that this was the word.

Salvetti said, 'Shit.'

Tuzee punched on the speaker, saying, 'It's Ken Seymore. Ken, Sonny and Charlie are here. What do you have down there?'

'It's gone to shit. All of it's gone to shit. I'm still here at the development, but – '

Benza shouted over him. The fear in Seymore's voice infuriated him.

'I don't give a shit where you are. Do we have the goddamned disks or not?'

'No! They got the disks. Glen Howell and two more of our guys are dead. They got Manelli and Ruiz and I don't know who else. It's a goddamned clusterfuck down here. I don't know what happened.'

'Who killed Howell? Talley?'

'I don't know! Yeah, I think it was Talley. I don't know. Man, I'm hearing all kinds of things.'

Sonny Benza closed his eyes. Just like that it was gone, everything was gone, three low-class assholes break into a house and everything that he had worked for his entire life was about to end.

Tuzee said, 'You *sure* they got the disks?'

'Talley gave the disks to the Sheriffs. That much I know for sure. Then I don't know what happened. Glen got jammed up at the motel, they had a big fuckin' firefight or somethin', and now the FBI just rolled up, the *real* FBI. What do you want me to do?'

Benza shook his head; there wasn't anything Ken Seymore or anyone else could do.

Tuzee said, 'Vanish. Anyone who isn't in custody, take off. You're done.'

The line went dead without another word. Ken Seymore was gone.

Benza stood without a word and went to the great glass windows overlooking Palm Springs. He was going to miss the view.

Salvetti came up behind him.

'What do you want us to do, Boss?'

'How long do you figure we have before the Feds get here?'

He had a pretty good idea, but he wanted to hear it.

Salvetti and Tuzee traded a shrug.

Tuzee said, 'Talley will tell them what's on the disks, then they'll probably talk to Smith. I don't know if he'll corroborate or not.'

'He'll talk.'

'Okay, they'll want to detain you as a flight risk to give themselves time to write the true counts, so they'll get a warrant based on our alleged involvement with the killings and kidnaps in Bristo. Say they get a telephonic warrant and coordinate with the state cops out here through the substation . . . I'd say two hours.'

'Two hours.'

'Yeah, I don't think they can get here before that.'

Benza sighed.

'Okay, guys. I want to be in the air in an hour.'

'You got it, Sonny.'

Salvetti said, 'You gonna tell New York?'

Benza wouldn't tell New York. He was more frightened of their reaction than he was of battling the Feds.

'Fuck'm. Go get your families. Don't bother packing, we'll buy new when we get there. Meet me at the airport as soon as you can. Forty-five minutes tops.'

The three of them stood mute for a time. They were in deep shit, and all three of them knew it. Benza shook each man's hand. They were good and dear friends. Sonny Benza loved them both.

'We had a good thing here, guys.'

Charlie Salvetti started to cry. He turned away and hurried from the office without another word.

Tuzee stared at the floor until Salvetti was gone, then offered his hand again. Benza took it.

'All this will blow over, Sonny. You'll see. We'll get this straight with New York, and we'll be fine.'

Benza knew that was bullshit, but he appreciated Tuzee trying to cheer him. He even found it within himself to smile.

'Philly, we're gonna be looking over our shoulders the rest of our lives. Fuck it. It's all part of the game.'

Tuzee smiled tiredly.

'Yeah, I guess so. See you at the airport.'

'You bet.'

Tuzee hurried away.

Sonny Benza turned back to the window. He admired the lights in the desert below, glittering like fallen dreams, and remembered how proud his father had been, how much the old man had bragged, *Only in America, Sonny, only in America; right down the fuckin' street from Francis Albert!*

Frank Sinatra had been dead for years.

Benza went to wake his wife.

New York City
Saturday, 7:49 a.m., Eastern time
Vic Castellano

Vic Castellano sat on his terrace overlooking the Upper West Side of Manhattan. It was a beautiful morning, clear and pleasant, though it would be hotter than a sonofabitch before noon. He still wore the white terry-cloth bathrobe with *Don't Bug Me* on the back. He liked that sonofabitch so much he'd probably wear it until it was threads. He put down his coffee.

'I can tell by your expression it ain't good.'

Jamie Beldone had just come out to see him.

'It's not. The police have the disks. They have Benza's accountant, and several of his people. Once the Feds develop the information, we're going to have a fight on our hands.'

'But we'll survive it.'

Jamie nodded.

'We'll take a few shots, but we'll survive. Benza, that's something else.'

'That sonofabitch still hasn't had the decency to call. You imagine that?'

'It shows a lack of class.'

Castellano settled back in his chair, thinking out loud. He and Jamie had gone over this a hundred times last night, but it never hurt to go over such things again.

'We'll survive, but because of this Mickey Mouse West Coast asshole we're exposed to serious heat from the federal prosecutor. This means we've got just cause to seek redress.'

'The other families will see it that way.'

'And since the Feds are going to put Benza out of business, no one can beef if we take care of it for them.'

'It's a fair trade.'

Castellano nodded.

'All in all, it's probably good for everyone that all this happened. We can send somebody out west, take over Benza's end of things, and cut ourselves a bigger piece of the pie.'

'The silver lining that everyone will enjoy. What are you going to do, skipper?'

Castellano had known what he was going do for the past six hours. He took no pleasure in it, but he had it all arranged.

'Make the call.'

Beldone started back into the house.

'Jamie!'

'Yes, sir?'

'I want to be sure about this. That guy Clewes, Marion Clewes, he's kinda flaky. I don't want to just take his word that Benza fucked up. I want to know for sure.'

'I'm sure, Vic. I double-checked. I just hung up with Phil Tuzee.'

Castellano felt better. He knew that Phil Tuzee wouldn't steer him wrong.

'That's good enough. Make the call and finish this.'

Palm Springs, California

Saturday, 4:53 a.m., Pacific time

Sonny Benza

Benza's wife moved so slowly that he wanted to stuff a cattle prod up her ass. The kids were even worse.

'Would ya hurry it up, for chrissakes? We gotta get outta here.'

'I can't leave my things!'

'I'll buy you new things!'

'We can't leave our pictures! What about our wedding album? How can you buy a new wedding album?'

'Five minutes, you got *five minutes!* Get the kids and meet me out front or I'll leave your ass here.'

Benza trotted back through the house to the garage. All he carried was a blue nylon gym bag with one hundred thousand in cash, his blood pressure meds, and his .357. Anything else he needed he could buy when they landed; Benza had over thirty million dollars stashed in foreign accounts.

Benza hit the button to open the garage door. He tossed the nylon bag into the backseat of his Mercedes, then slid behind the wheel. He started the car, threw it into reverse, then hit the gas hard, backing in a wide arc toward the front door. He was moving so fast that he almost broadsided the nondescript sedan that blocked his path.

Flashes of light speckled the air around the sedan, exploding Benza's rear window. The bullets knocked him into the steering wheel, then sideways onto the seat. Sonny Benza tried to get the .357 out of his bag, but he didn't have time. Someone pulled open the driver's-side door and shot Sonny Benza in the head.

Part Five
The Avocado Orchard

29

Sunday, 2:16 p.m.
Two weeks later

Talley

The fantasy was always the same: On the days that Jeff Talley visited the avocado orchard, he imagined Brendan Malik playing in the trees. He saw the boy laughing, kicking up dust as he ran, then climbing into the branches where he swung by his knees. Brendan was always happy and laughing in these daydreams, even with his skin mottled in death and blood pulsing from his neck. Talley had never been able to imagine the boy any other way.

Jane said, 'What are you thinking?'

The two of them were slouched down in the front seat of his patrol car, watching red-tailed hawks float above the trees. Amanda had stayed in Los Angeles, but Jane had come up for the weekend.

'Brendan Malik. Remember? That boy.'

'I don't remember.'

Talley realized that he had never told her. He had not mentioned Brendan Malik to anyone after that night he left the boy's house, not even the police psychologist.

'I guess I never told you.'

'Who was he?'

'A victim in one of the negotiations. It's not important anymore.'

Jane took his hand. She turned sideways so that she faced him.

'It's important if you're thinking about it.'

Talley considered that.

'He was a little boy, nine, ten, something like that. About Thomas's age. I think about him sometimes.'

'You've never mentioned him.'

'I guess not.'

Talley found himself telling her about the night with Brendan Malik, of holding the boy's hand, of staring into his eyes as the little boy died, of the overwhelming feelings of failure and shame.

Listening, she cried, and he cried, too.

'I was trying to see his face right now, but I can't. I don't know whether to feel happy or sad about that. You think that's bad?'

Jane squeezed his hand.

'I think it's good we're talking about these things. It's a sign that you're healing.'

Talley shrugged, then smiled at her.

'About goddamned time.'

Jane smiled in that way she had, the smile that was encouraging and pleased.

'Did you find out about Thomas?'

'I tried, but they won't tell me anything. I guess it's best this way.'

Walter Smith and his family had entered the U.S. Marshals' witness protection program. They had simply vanished; one day here, the next gone, hidden by the system. Talley hoped that Thomas would one day contact him, but he didn't think it likely. It was safer that way.

Jane said, 'How much time before you have to get back?'

'I've got time. I'm the Chief.'

Jane smiled wider.

'Let's walk.'

They walked from sunlight to shade to sun, bees swirling sluggishly around them, lazy in the midday heat. It was good to walk. It was peaceful. Talley had been away for a very long time, hiding inside himself, but now he was back. He was on the way back.

The orchard, as always, was as still as a church.

'I'm glad you're here, Jane.'

Jane squeezed his hand. Talley knew, then, that though a church was a place to bury the dead, it was also a place to celebrate the living. Their lives could begin again.